THE ADVENTURES OF PINOCCHIO

THE ADVENTURES OF PINOCCHIO

CARLO COLLODI

Armada

First published in this edition in Armada in 1977
by Fontana Paperbacks, 14 St. James's Place,
London SW1A 1PS

This impression 1978

Printed in Great Britain by
Love & Malcomson Ltd., Brighton Road,
Redhill, Surrey

CHAPTER ONE

*How it Happened that Mr. Cherry, the Carpenter,
Found a Piece of Wood that Laughed and Cried
like a Baby*

ONCE upon a time there was . . .

"A king!" my small readers will exclaim. No, children,
you are mistaken. Once upon a time there was a piece of
wood.

It was not the best wood, but just a common piece,
such as we use in stoves and fireplaces to kindle a fire
and warm our rooms in winter.

I can't say how it happened, but the fact is that one
fine day this piece of wood happened to be in the shop
of an old carpenter whose name was Mr. Antonio, but
everyone called him Mr. Cherry, because the end of his
nose was always red and shiny like a ripe cherry.

As soon as Mr. Cherry saw this piece of wood, he was
very pleased: he rubbed his hands together joyfully, and
said to himself:

"This has come in the nick of time; it is just what I
want to make a leg for my little table."

Without losing a moment he took his sharp hatchet,
and was going to strip off the bark and trim it into shape.
But just as he raised the hatchet to strike the first blow,
he paused with his hand in the air, for he heard a tiny,
tiny voice which said warningly:

"Don't strike me too hard!"

Imagine Mr. Cherry's surprise!

He glanced around the shop in a fright to see where that little voice could have come from, but he saw no one. He looked under his bench. No one. He looked in a cupboard which he always kept locked; but there was no one. He looked in his basket of chips and sawdust. No one. He opened the shop door and looked out into the street, and no one! What then?

"I see," he said at last, laughing and scratching his wig, "I must have imagined that little voice. Let us get to work."

He took up his hatchet again, and down it came on the piece of wood.

"Oh, you hurt me!" whimpered that same little voice.

This time Mr. Cherry was thunderstruck. His eyes stood out of his head with fear; his mouth was wide open, and his tongue hung down over his chin like a mask at a fountain.

As soon as he could speak he said, trembling and stammering with fright:

"But where did that little voice come from that cried 'Oh'? There's not a living soul here. Can it be that this piece of wood has learned to cry and complain like a baby? I can't believe it. This piece of wood—look at it! It's just a piece of firewood, like all the others; when you put it on the fire it will help to boil a kettle. Well, then? Is someone hidden inside it? If there is, so much the worse for him. I'll attend to his case!"

With these words he grasped that poor piece of wood with both hands, and began to beat it against the wall without mercy.

Then he stopped and listened to see if any little voice was complaining this time. He waited two minutes—

nothing; five minutes—nothing; ten minutes—and still nothing!

"Now I understand," he exclaimed, laughing and rumpling his wig. "I must have imagined that little voice that said 'Oh!' Let us get to work."

And because he felt very much afraid, he began to sing to give himself courage.

Meanwhile he put the hatchet down and taking up his plane he began to plane and shape the piece of wood. But while the plane went back and forth, he heard again that little voice which said, laughing:

"Stop! You're tickling me!"

This time poor Mr. Cherry dropped as if struck by lightning. When he opened his eyes he was sitting on the floor.

He was so changed you would hardly have recognised him. Even the end of his nose, which was always crimson, had turned blue with fright.

CHAPTER TWO

Mr. Cherry Gives the Piece of Wood to his Friend Geppetto, who Plans a Marvellous Marionette that can Dance, and Fence, and Turn Somersaults in the Air

At that moment someone rapped on the door.

"Come in," said the carpenter, but he did not have strength enough to get up.

A little, lively old man walked into the shop. His name was Geppetto, but when the boys in the neighbourhood

7

wanted to tease him, they called him by his nickname of Polendina, on account of his yellow wig which looked very much like a dish of *polenta*, which is like porridge.

Geppetto was very quick-tempered. Woe to him who called him Polendina! He simply went wild, and no one could do anything with him.

"Good morning, Mr. Antonio," said Geppetto, "what are you doing down there?"

"I am teaching the ants their letters."

"Much good may it do you!"

"What brought you here, Mr. Geppetto?"

"My legs. Do you know, Mr. Antonio, I have come to ask a favour of you."

"Here I am, ready to serve you," replied the carpenter, getting to his knees.

"I had an idea this morning."

"Let us hear it."

"I thought I would make a fine wooden marionette, a really wonderful one, that could dance, and fence, and turn somersaults in the air. Then, with this marionette, I would travel round the world, and earn my bit of bread and my glass of wine. What do you think of that?"

"Bravo, Polendina!" cried that same little, mysterious voice.

When he heard himself called Polendina, Mr. Geppetto became so angry that he turned as red as a ripe pepper-pod. He whirled on the carpenter, and said in a rage:

"Why do you offend me?"

"Who is offending you?"

"You called me Polendina!"

"No, indeed I didn't!"

"Oh! perhaps *I* said it! But I say that it was you."

"No!"

"Yes!"

"No!"

"Yes!"

And getting more and more excited, from words they came to blows. They snatched at one another's wigs, and even slapped and bit and scratched each other.

At the end of the combat Mr. Antonio found Geppetto's yellow wig in his hands, and Geppetto had the carpenter's grey wig between his teeth.

"Give me my wig," said Mr. Antonio.

"And you give me mine, and let us make a treaty of peace."

So the two little old men, after each had put on his own wig, shook hands, and vowed to be good friends as long as they both should live.

"Now, neighbour Geppetto," said the carpenter, to show that they were friends again, "what is it that I can do for you?"

"I would like a little piece of wood to make my marionette."

Mr. Antonio, well pleased, went quickly to his bench, and took the piece of wood which had given him such a fright. But just as he was giving it to his friend it shook so hard that it slipped out of his hands, and struck poor Geppetto violently on the shin.

"Ah! this is a fine way to make me a present, Mr. Antonio! You have almost lamed me."

"Upon my honour, I didn't do it!"

"Oh! so *I* did it then!"

"It's all the fault of this piece of wood . . ."

"Yes, I know the wood struck me, but you threw it at my legs!"

"I did not throw it at you!"

"That's a falsehood!"

9

"Geppetto, don't insult me; if you do I will call you Polendina!"

"Blockhead!"

"Polendina!"

"Donkey!"

"Polendina!"

"Ugly monkey!"

"Polendina!"

When he heard himself called Polendina for the third time, Geppetto, blind with rage, rushed at the carpenter, and the second battle was worse than the first.

When it was over, Mr. Antonio had two more scratches on his nose, and the other two buttons less on his jacket. The accounts thus being even, they shook hands again, and vowed to be good friends as long as they both should live. Then Geppetto took his piece of wood, and after thanking Mr. Antonio, went limping home.

CHAPTER THREE

Geppetto Goes Home and Makes his Marionette: he Calls him Pinocchio: the Marionette Gets into Mischief

GEPPETTO lived in a little room on the ground floor that was lighted by a window under the stairs. His furniture could not have been simpler. A rickety chair, a shaky bed, and a broken-down table. At the back of the room a fireplace could be seen, with the fire lighted; but the fire was painted, and over the fire was a painted kettle which was boiling merrily, and sending forth a cloud of steam that was just like real steam.

As soon as he came home, Geppetto took his tools and began to carve his marionette.

"What shall I call him?" he said to himself. "I think I will call him Pinocchio. This name will bring him good luck. I once knew a whole family of Pinocchios: there was Pinocchio the father, and Pinocchia the mother, and Pinocchii the children, and they all got along splendidly. The richest of them was a beggar."

When he had thought of a name for his marionette, he set to work with a will. He made his hair, and his forehead, and his eyes in a very short time.

As soon as the eyes were finished, imagine his amazement when he saw them move, and look at him intently.

When Geppetto saw those two wooden eyes watching him, he didn't like it at all, and he said crossly:

"Naughty wooden eyes, why are you looking at me?"

But no one answered.

After the eyes he made the nose; but as soon as it was finished it began to grow. It grew, and it grew, until in a few minutes it was so long that it seemed as if there was no end to it.

Poor Geppetto worked fast to shorten it, but the more he pared it down and cut it off, the longer that impertinent nose became.

After the nose he made the mouth; but before he had finished with it, it began to laugh and make fun of him.

"Stop laughing!" said Geppetto irritably, but he might as well have spoken to the wall.

"Stop laughing, I say!" he shouted in a menacing voice.

The mouth stopped laughing, and stuck out its tongue. However since Geppetto did not want to spoil the

11

marionette, he pretended not to see it, and went on with his work.

After the mouth he made the chin, then the neck, the shoulders, the stomach, the arms, and the hands.

The moment the hands were finished, Geppetto's wig was snatched from his head. He glanced upwards, and what did he see? There was his yellow wig in the marionette's hands.

"Pinocchio! Give me back my wig this moment!"

But Pinocchio, instead of returning the wig, put it on his own head, and was almost hidden under it.

This insolent, mocking behaviour made Geppetto feel sadder than ever before in all his life. He turned to Pinocchio and said:

"You rogue of a son! You are not yet finished, and you begin to disobey your father! That's bad, my boy, very bad!"

And he wiped away a tear.

There were still the legs and feet to make.

When Geppetto had finished the feet, a kick landed on his nose.

"It serves me right," he said to himself. "I should have thought of that before! Now it is too late."

He took the marionette in his hands and placed him on the floor to see if he could walk; but Pinocchio's legs were stiff, and he didn't know how to move them. So Geppetto took him by the hand, and showed him how to put one foot before the other.

When the stiffness was out of his legs, Pinocchio began to walk alone, and run around the room; and finally he slipped out of the door into the street and ran away.

Poor old Geppetto ran after him as fast as he could, but he could not catch him, for the little scamp jumped like a rabbit, and his wooden feet clattered on the pavement, making as much noise as twenty pairs of wooden shoes.

"Catch him! Catch him!" cried Geppetto; but when the people saw that wooden marionette running as fast as a racehorse, they stared at him in amazement, and then laughed, and laughed, until their sides were sore.

At last, by some lucky chance, a policeman appeared. When he heard such a clatter he thought somebody's horse had got away from its master; so he courageously planted himself in the middle of the street with his legs wide apart, determined to stop it and prevent any further trouble.

While Pinocchio was still a long way off he saw the policeman barricading the street, and he decided to run between his legs before he realised what he meant to do; but he failed dismally.

The policeman, without moving from his position, picked him up neatly by the nose (that ridiculous, long nose, that seemed made on purpose to be seized by policemen) and returned him to Geppetto, who meant to pull his ears well to punish him for his naughtiness. Imagine, therefore, how he felt when he couldn't find any ears: and do you know why? Because he had made him in such a hurry that he had forgotten his ears.

So he took him by the nape of his neck, and as they walked away he said, shaking his head threateningly:

"Come along home. I will settle accounts with you when we get there!"

At this ominous remark Pinocchio threw himself down on the ground and refused to walk any farther. A crowd of idlers and inquisitive people gathered around him.

Some said one thing, some another.

"The poor marionette!" some of them exclaimed, "he

is right in not wanting to go home! Who knows how dreadfully that bad Geppetto might beat him!"

And others added maliciously:

"Geppetto *seems* like a good man, but he is a perfect tyrant with children. If we leave that poor marionette in his hands, he is capable of tearing him to pieces!"

In short, so much was said and done that the policeman let Pinocchio go, and decided to take poor Geppetto to prison. He was not able for the moment to say anything in his own defence, but cried like a calf, and as they walked towards the prison he sobbed:

"Wretched son! And to think that I worked so hard to make a fine marionette! But I deserve it. I ought to have known what would happen!"

What happened afterwards is almost too much to believe and I will tell you about it in the following chapters.

CHAPTER FOUR

The Story of Pinocchio and the Talking Cricket in which it is Shown that Children Do Not Like to be Corrected by Those Who Are Wiser than They Are

Now I must tell you, children, that while poor Geppetto was taken to prison for no fault of his own, that scamp Pinocchio, left to himself, ran away across the fields in order to get home as quickly as possible. In his haste he jumped over high banks and thorn hedges, like a little goat, or a hare running from the hunters.

When he got home, he found the door ajar. Pushing it

open, he went in, and locked it securely after him. Then he threw himself down on the floor with a great sigh of relief.

But the relief did not last long, for he heard something in the room saying:

"Cri-cri-cri!"

"Who is calling me?" said Pinocchio in a fright.

"It is I."

Pinocchio turned and saw a large cricket crawling slowly up the wall.

"Speak to me, Cricket. Who are you?"

"I am the Talking Cricket, and I have lived in this room for more than a hundred years."

"But today this is my room, and you will oblige me by going away immediately, without even looking behind you."

"I shall not leave this place," replied the Cricket, "until I have told you a very unpleasant truth."

"Well, then, tell me, and be quick about it!"

"Woe to those children who rebel against their parents, and who run away from their homes. They will never be happy in this world, and sooner or later they will repent it bitterly."

"Sing away, Cricket, just as you please; but tomorrow, at sunrise, I am going to leave for if I stay here it will happen to me just as it happens to other children: I shall be sent to school and, by love or by force, I shall be made to study. Now I will tell you in confidence that I don't intend to study at all; I should be far happier chasing butterflies, and climbing trees to rob birds' nests."

"You poor simpleton! Don't you know that, if you spend your time in that way, you will grow up to be a great donkey, and everyone will laugh at you?"

"Be still, you croaking Cricket!" cried Pinocchio.

15

But the Cricket, who was patient, and also a philosopher, instead of being offended by such impertinence, proceeded in the same tone as before:

"And if you don't like to go to school, why don't you learn a trade? Then you could, at least, earn your bread honestly."

"Do you want me to tell you something?" retorted Pinocchio, who was beginning to lose his patience. "Among all the trades in the world there is only one which really suits me."

"And what might that be?"

"To eat, drink, sleep, and amuse myself, and to lead a vagabond life from morning to night."

"Let me say for your information," said the Talking Cricket, calm and patient as usual, "that those who follow that trade finish, almost always, in a hospital or a prison."

"Be careful, you Cricket of bad omen! If you make me angry, the worse for you!"

"Poor Pinocchio! I am really sorry for you!"

"Why are you sorry for me?"

"Because you are a marionette, and what is worst of all you have a wooden head."

At these last words Pinocchio lost his temper entirely. He seized a mallet from the bench, and threw it at the Cricket.

Perhaps he did not intend to hit him but unluckily the mallet struck him right on the head. The poor Cricket had only time to cry "Cri-cri-cri," and there he was stretched out stiff, but still clinging to the wall.

CHAPTER FIVE

Pinocchio is Hungry, and he Looks for an Egg to Make an Omelette: but just as he Breaks it in the Pan the Omelette Flies out of the Window

IT began to grow dark, and Pinocchio remembered that he had had nothing to eat. There was an uncomfortable feeling in his stomach that closely resembled appetite.

With children appetite grows fast. In fact, after a few minutes it became hunger, and in no time at all he was as hungry as a wolf, so hungry he could have eaten nails.

Poor Pinocchio ran to the fireplace where the kettle was boiling and put out his hand to lift the cover and see what was in it but the kettle was painted on the wall. What a disappointment! His nose, which was already too long, grew several inches longer.

He ran about the room and searched in every dish and cupboard for a little bread—even dry bread—yes, he would have been thankful for a crust, or a bone left by a dog, or a fishbone or cherry stone, in short, anything he could chew on; but he found nothing, just nothing, absolutely nothing.

Meanwhile he grew hungrier every moment, and there was nothing left to do but yawn. He yawned such enormous yawns that his mouth reached away back to his ears; and after he yawned, he spat, and it seemed as if he hadn't any stomach left.

17

At last, in despair, he began to weep, saying:

"The Talking Cricket was right. I did wrong to rebel against my father and run away. If my father were here now, I shouldn't be yawning myself to death. Oh, hunger is a dreadful disease!"

Suddenly in a pile of rubbish he saw something white and round that looked like an egg. Instantly he pounced upon it. It really was an egg.

It would be impossible to describe his joy; you must imagine it. He feared he might be dreaming. He rolled the egg from one hand to the other, he patted it and kissed it as he said:

"Now shall I cook it? Shall I make an omelette? No, it would be better to poach it. But perhaps it would be more tasty if I fried it; or shall I cook it in the shell? No, the quickest way would be to poach it. I cannot wait to eat it."

No sooner said than done. He set a little stewpan over a brazier of lighted charcoal, put some water in it, instead of oil or butter, and when the water began to boil, tac! he broke the eggshell and held it over the pan.

But instead of the yolk and white of an egg, a little chicken flew out gaily, and making a polite bow, said cheerfully:

"A thousand thanks, Mr. Pinocchio, for having spared me the trouble of breaking the shell! Good-bye, take care of yourself, and give my love to the folks!"

With that the chicken spread its wings and, flying through the open window, was soon lost to sight.

The poor marionette stood there as if hypnotised, with his eyes fixed in his head, his mouth open, and the pieces of eggshell in his hands. When he recovered a little from his first fright, he began to cry, and scream, and stamp on the floor in despair; and as he wept he said:

"Yes, the Talking Cricket was right! If I hadn't run away from home, and if my father were only here, I should not now be dying of hunger. Oh, hunger is a dreadful disease!"

His stomach felt emptier than ever, and since he could find nothing to put into it he thought he would go out again into the village, in the hope of meeting some charitable person who would give him a little bread.

CHAPTER SIX

Pinocchio Goes to Sleep with his Feet on the Brazier, and when he Wakes Up in the Morning they are Burned Off

IT was a bitterly cold night. The thunder rolled, and the lightning flashed as though the heavens were afire. A fierce wind whistled angrily, raising clouds of dust, and making all the trees writhe and groan as if in torment.

Pinocchio was dreadfully afraid of thunder and lightning, but his hunger was greater than his fear, so he opened the door and hurried as fast as he could to the village, arriving there with his tongue hanging out like a hunting dog's.

But all was dark and silent. The shops were closed, the doors of the houses were closed, the windows were closed, and there was not even a dog to be seen in the street. It seemed a village of the dead.

However, Pinocchio, conquered by hunger and despair, gave a long, long ring at the door of one of the houses, saying to himself:

19

"Someone will certainly look out!"

And in fact a lively old man with a nightcap on his head looked out of a window and shouted crossly:

"What do you want at this hour?"

"Will you be so good as to give me a piece of bread?"

"Wait! I'll be right back!" replied the old man, believing that he had to do with one of those scapegraces who amuse themselves at night by ringing doorbells, and annoying good people who want to sleep in peace.

In half a minute the window was opened again, and the same voice called to Pinocchio:

"Stand under the window, and hold your cap!"

Pinocchio had never yet had a cap, but he stood under the window, and a great kettleful of water rained down on him, drenching him from head to foot, as if he had been a wilted geranium.

He went home wet as a drowned rat, and almost dead with fatigue and hunger. He could not stand up any longer, and so he sat down, and put his wet, muddy feet on the warm brazier.

In this position he fell asleep, and while he was asleep his feet, which were of wood, caught fire and slowly burned away to ashes.

Pinocchio slept and snored as if his feet belonged to someone else. At last, at daybreak, he was roused by someone rapping on the door.

"Who is it?" he called, yawning and rubbing his eyes.

"It is I!" replied a voice.

That voice was the voice of Geppetto.

CHAPTER SEVEN

Geppetto Comes Home, and Gives the Marionette the Breakfast that the Poor Man had Bought for himself

POOR Pinocchio's eyes were still half-shut, and he had not noticed that his feet were burned away; so when he heard his father's voice he jumped down from his stool to run and draw the bolt, but after staggering a little he fell his full length on the floor, making a noise as if a whole bag of wooden spoons had fallen from the fifth storey.

"Open the door!" cried Geppetto.

"I can't, Daddy," replied the marionette, bursting into tears and rolling over and over on the floor.

"Why not?"

"Because someone has eaten my feet!"

"And who has eaten them?"

"The cat," said Pinocchio, seeing the cat who was just then playing with some shavings.

"Open the door, I tell you!" cried Geppetto again; "if you don't I'll give you the cat-o'-nine-tails when I get in!"

"Truly, I can't stand up. Oh, poor me! poor me! I shall have to walk on my knees all the rest of my life!"

Geppetto, thinking that all this lamenting was just another of the marionette's tricks, decided to end it once and for all. He climbed up on the wall, and went in at the window.

At first he was furious; but when he saw his own Pinocchio lying on the floor, and actually without any feet, his anger melted away. He took him up in his arms, kissed and caressed him, and with tears running down his cheeks, he said, as well as he could for sobbing:

"My dear little Pinocchio, how did your feet get burned away?"

"I don't know, Daddy, but believe me it has been a dreadful night. I shall never forget it as long as I live. It thundered and lightened, and I was so hungry, and the Talking Cricket said: 'It serves you right; you have been naughty and you deserve it!' and I said: 'Be careful, Cricket!' and he said: 'You are a marionette with a wooden head!' and I threw the mallet at him, and he died, but it was his fault, for I didn't want to kill him and the proof of that is that I put the stewpan on the brazier, but the chicken flew away and said: 'Good-bye, give my love to the folks!' and I got hungrier every moment, and that's the reason that little old man with the nightcap on put his head out of the window, and said: 'Stand under the window and hold up your cap,' and there I was with a whole kettleful of water on my head, and it isn't a disgrace to ask for a bit of bread, is it? I ran back home as fast as I could, and because I was so dreadfully hungry I put my feet on the brazier to dry them, and then you came home, and my feet were burned off, and I'm still so hungry, and I haven't any feet! Boo-hoo-hoo!"

And poor Pinocchio began to cry and scream so loudly that he could have been heard for miles around.

Geppetto had only understood one thing in all this jumble of words; and that was that the marionette was dying of hunger. He took three pears out of his pocket, and said as he gave them to him:

"These three pears were for my breakfast; but I gladly give them to you. Eat them, and may they do you good."

"If you want me to eat them, you must pare them for me."

"Pare them for you?" cried Geppetto in astonishment. "I would never have believed, my son, that you were so finicky and full of odd notions. That's too bad! We should accustom ourselves from childhood to eat whatever is set before us, and be thankful to get it because one never knows what might happen. This is a curious world."

"That's all very well," retorted Pinocchio, "but I shall never eat any fruit that isn't pared. I can't abide parings."

So that patient, kind Geppetto took out his pocketknife and pared the three pears, putting all the parings on the corner of the table.

When Pinocchio had made two mouthfuls of the first pear, he was about to throw away the core, but Geppetto stopped him.

"Don't throw it away, there might be some use for it."

"Do you imagine I would eat the core?" cried Pinocchio, turning on him in a rage.

"Who knows! This is a curious world," replied Geppetto calmly.

So the three cores, instead of being thrown out of the window were put on the corner of the table to keep the parings company.

When he had eaten or rather devoured the three pears, Pinocchio stretched himself, yawned, and then began to whine:

"I'm hungry again!"

"But, my son, I have nothing more to give you."

"Nothing, nothing at all?"

"These parings and cores are all I have."

"Patience!" said Pinocchio, "if there's really nothing else, I might eat a bit of paring."

And he began forthwith. At first he grimaced over it, but one after another all the parings quickly disappeared; and after them the cores and when he had eaten everything, he patted his stomach and said cheerfully:

"Now I feel better!"

"You see," said Geppetto, "that I was right when I said you should not be so dainty and particular about your food. My dear boy, one never knows what may happen. This is a curious world."

CHAPTER EIGHT

Geppetto Makes Pinocchio some New Feet, and Sells his own Coat to Buy him a Primer

JUST as soon as the marionette had satisfied his hunger, he began to whimper and grumble because he wanted some new feet.

But Geppetto, in order to punish him for all his naughtiness, let him cry and complain a whole half-day. At last he said:

"Why should I make you new feet? So that you can run away from home again?"

"I promise," said the sobbing marionette, "that from this day forth I will be good."

24

"That's just what all children say when they want something," replied Geppetto.

"I promise to go to school, and study, and make you proud of me . . ."

"All children say that very thing when they want something."

"But I'm not like other children! I am better than any of them, and I always tell the truth. I promise you, Daddy, that I will learn a trade, and become the staff and consolation of your old age."

Although Geppetto tried to look very fierce, his eyes were full of tears, and his heart was very sad when he saw his poor Pinocchio in that dreadful state. He did not say another word, but he took up his tools and two little pieces of seasoned wood and began to work as hard as he could.

In less than half an hour the feet were done; two slender, nimble, swift little feet that might have been carved by a real artist.

Then Geppetto said:

"Shut your eyes and go to sleep. I want to surprise you."

Pinocchio shut his eyes, and pretended to go to sleep; and while he was pretending Geppetto melted some glue in an eggshell, and fastened the feet in place; and he did it so neatly that you could not even see where they were joined to his legs.

As soon as the marionette felt that he had feet again, he jumped down from the table where he was lying and began to caper and dance around, fairly crazy with joy.

"Now to show you how grateful I am," said Pinocchio to his father, "I want to go right to school."

"What a good boy!"

"But if I'm going to school I need some clothes."

Geppetto was a poor man: he hadn't a penny in his pocket: so he made Pinocchio a suit out of flowered paper, a pair of shoes out of bark, and a cap out of a soft piece of bread.

Pinocchio ran to look at himself in a basin full of water, and he was so pleased that he said as he strutted about:

"I look just like a gentleman!"

"Yes, indeed," replied Geppetto, "but remember, it is not fine clothes that make a gentleman, but rather, clean clothes."

"Speaking of school," continued Pinocchio, "there's still something lacking, and it's the most important and necessary of all."

"And that is . . ?"

"I have no primer."

"That's right; but how shall we get one?"

"That is easy! Go to the bookshop and buy one."

"And the money?"

"I haven't any."

"Neither have I," added the good old man sadly.

Pinocchio became sad, too, although he was usually very cheerful; for poverty, when it is real poverty, destroys all joy, even in children.

"Patience!" cried Geppetto suddenly, and jumping up he put on his old fustian coat, all holes and patches, and ran out of the house.

In a little while he was back again with a primer in his hand for his son; but the poor man was in his shirt-sleeves, and it was snowing outside.

"Where is your coat, Daddy?"

"I have sold it."

"Why did you sell it?"

"It made me too warm."

26

Pinocchio understood instantly, and he was so overcome that he threw his arms around Geppetto's neck and
kissed him all over his face.

CHAPTER NINE

*Pinocchio Sells his Primer in order to See the
Marionettes*

WHEN it stopped snowing, Pinocchio took his fine new
primer under his arm, and started for school. On the way
he made all sorts of fine plans, and built a thousand air
castles, each one more beautiful than the other.

He began saying to himself:

"At school today I will learn to read immediately;
tomorrow I will learn to write, and day after tomorrow
I will learn arithmetic. Then I shall be so well educated
that I can earn heaps of money; and with the very first
pennies I earn I will buy my father a nice new cloth coat.
But why do I say cloth? It shall be all of gold and silver,
with diamond buttons. That poor man really deserves it,
for in order that I may get an education he stripped off
his coat to buy me a book—in this cold weather! Only
a father would make such a sacrifice!"

While he was saying this, and becoming more and more
excited, he heard the music of fife and drum in the distance: fi-fi-fi . . . zum, zum, zum, zum.

He stopped and listened. The sounds came from the
end of a long street that crossed the one which led to
school. At the end of it there was a little village close
to the sea.

"What can that music be? What a shame that I have to go to school! If it weren't for that . . ."

He hesitated. At any rate, he must decide either to go to school or to listen to the fifes.

"Today I will listen to the fifes, and tomorrow I will go to school. There's always time to go to school," said that bad boy, shrugging his shoulders.

No sooner said than done. He ran down the cross-street as fast as he could go. The farther he ran the more distinctly he heard the tune the fifes were playing, and the beating of the big drum: fi-fi-fi, fi-fi-fi, fi-fi-fi . . . zum, zum, zum, zum.

All at once he found himself in a little square full of people who were crowding around a great, gaily-painted building of boards and cloth.

"What is that big building?" inquired Pinocchio, turning to a boy who seemed to live there.

"Read the poster if you want to know."

"I would gladly read it, but I don't know how to read today."

"Bravo, simpleton! Then I'll read it for you. Know then that on that big poster with the letters red as fire it is written:

"GREAT MARIONETTE THEATRE"

"Is it long since the play began?"

"It's just beginning."

"How much does it cost to go in?"

"Twopence."

Pinocchio was so consumed with curiosity that he lost his wits, and without any shame he said to the boy:

"Will you give me twopence until tomorrow?"

"I would just love to," said the boy, laughing at him, "but I can't do it today."

28

"I will sell you my jacket for twopence," said the marionette.

"What would I do with a jacket of flowered paper? If it should rain, I couldn't take it off."

"Will you buy my shoes?"

"They're only good for firewood."

"What will you give me for my cap?"

"That would be a fine bargain! A cap made of bread! The rats might eat it right off my head!"

Pinocchio was on pins and needles. He was almost ready to make one more offer, but he lacked the courage. He hesitated, and stammered, and at last he said:

"Will you give me twopence for this new primer?"

"I am only a boy, and I do not buy things from other boys," said the other, who had much more sense than Pinocchio.

"I'll give you twopence for the primer," cried an old clothes man who had overheard the conversation.

The book was sold instantly. And only to think that poor Geppetto was at home shivering in his shirt-sleeves, because he had sold his coat to buy that primer for his son!

Chapter Ten

The Marionettes Recognise Pinocchio as One of their Family and are Delighted to See him, but Fire-Eater, the Showman, Appears in the Midst of their Joy, and Pinocchio almost Comes to a Dreadful End

WHEN Pinocchio entered the marionette theatre he nearly caused a riot.

You see, the curtain was up and the play had begun.

Harlequin and Punchinello were on the stage and quarrelling as usual, threatening every moment to come to blows.

The audience were paying the closest attention. They laughed until their sides were sore to see those two marionettes quarrel, and gesticulate, and call each other names. It was just as if they were really two reasoning animals, two real human beings.

But all at once Harlequin stopped playing his part, and, turning towards the public and pointing to the back of the theatre, he shouted in his best dramatic manner:

"Heavens above! Am I awake, or am I dreaming? That is certainly Pinocchio back there!"

"Yes, it's really Pinocchio!" cried Punchinello.

" 'Tis he, indeed!" exclaimed Signora Rosaura, putting her head out at the back of the stage.

"Here's Pinocchio! Here's Pinocchio!" shouted all the marionettes in chorus, running out of the wings. "Here's Pinocchio! Here's our brother Pinocchio! Hurray for Pinocchio!"

"Come up here to me, Pinocchio," cried Harlequin, "come and throw yourself into the arms of your wooden brother!"

At this affectionate invitation Pinocchio made one jump from the back of the theatre to the front seats; another jump, and he landed on the head of the orchestra leader, and from there he made a flying leap to the stage.

It is impossible to describe the hubbub which followed: the hugging and kissing, the friendly pinches, the brotherly thumps which Pinocchio received from the actors and actresses of that puppet company.

I can only say that it was a thrilling spectacle. But the audience, when they saw that the play was not going forward, became impatient and began to shout:

"The play! The play! Go on with the play!"

However, their breath was wasted, for the marionettes, instead of getting on with it, redoubled their tumultuous cries of joy and, placing Pinocchio on their shoulders, they carried him in triumph down to the footlights.

Suddenly the puppet Showman appeared. He was very tall, and so ugly that it frightened one only to look at him. His beard was like a smear of black ink, and it was so long that it came down to the ground, so that he stepped on it when he walked. His mouth was as large as an oven; his eyes were like two red lanterns, and he was cracking a great whip made of serpents and foxes' tails, twisted together.

When the Showman appeared so unexpectedly no one breathed. You could have heard a pin drop. All those poor marionettes trembled like so many leaves.

"Why have you come here to disturb my theatre?" he asked Pinocchio, in a voice like that of an ogre with a bad cold.

"Believe me, your Honour, it was not my fault."

31

"Not another word! We will settle our accounts tonight."

As soon as the play was over, the Showman went into the kitchen, where a whole sheep which he was roasting for his supper was slowly turning on the spit. When he saw that there was not enough wood to finish cooking it, he called Harlequin and Punchinello and said:

"Bring me the marionette which you will find hanging on a nail. He is made of nice, dry wood, and will make a fine fire for my roast."

At first Harlequin and Punchinello hesitated; but the Showman glared at them menacingly, and they obeyed. In a few moments they returned to the kitchen carrying poor Pinocchio, who was squirming like an eel out of water, and shrieking desperately: "O Daddy, save me! I don't want to die! I don't want to die!"

CHAPTER ELEVEN

Fire-Eater Sneezes and Forgives Pinocchio and Pinocchio later Saves the Life of his Friend Harlequin

FIRE-EATER (this was the Showman's name) appeared to be a frightful man, there's no doubt about it, with that black beard hanging down like an apron, quite covering his chest and legs, but at heart he was really not so bad. When he saw poor Pinocchio struggling and screaming, "I don't want to die! I don't want to die!" he began to feel sorry for him, and although he tried to prevent it, at last he could resist no longer, but sneezed with all his might.

Harlequin had been looking as dejected and sorrowful as a weeping willow, but when he heard that sneeze his face grew brighter, and bending towards Pinocchio he whispered:

"Good news, brother. The Showman has sneezed. That's a sign that he is sorry for you. You are saved."

For you must know that while other men weep, or at least wipe their eyes when they are sorry for someone, whenever Fire-Eater really pitied anyone, he had the habit of sneezing. Perhaps it's as good a way as any other to show one's kindness of heart.

After the Showman had sneezed, he continued to speak gruffly, and shouted at Pinocchio:

"Stop that crying! It gives me an uncomfortable feeling in the pit of my stomach . . . I feel such a pain that . . . that . . . a-tchoo! a-tchoo!"—and this time he sneezed twice.

"Long life to you!" said Pinocchio.

"Thank you. And your father and mother, are they still alive?" asked Fire-Eater.

"My father is, but I never knew my mother."

"How sorry your old father would be if I should throw you on the fire! Poor old man! I pity him! A-tchoo! a-tchoo! a-tchoo!"—and he sneezed three times.

"Long life to you!" cried Pinocchio to Fire-Eater.

"Thank you. On the other hand you should be sorry for me, because, as you see, I haven't wood enough to finish roasting my supper; and take my word for it, you certainly would have been very handy. But now I have spared you, and I must make the best of it. I will put some marionette of my Company under the spit in your stead. Olà, police!"

33

Two wooden policemen appeared immediately in response to this command. They were very tall, and very thin. They wore policemen's helmets, and carried drawn swords in their hands.

The showman said in a hoarse voice:

"Take that Harlequin, bind him tightly and throw him on the fire. My mutton must be well roasted!"

Imagine poor Harlequin! He was so terrified that his legs doubled up under him, and he fell forward on his face.

At that melancholy sight Pinocchio threw himself at the Showman's feet and, weeping such quantities of tears that the whole length of his long beard was drenched, he cried in an imploring voice:

"Have mercy, Signor Fire-Eater!"

"There are no signori here!" replied the Showman sternly.

"Have mercy, Cavalier!"

"There are no Cavaliers here!"

"Have mercy, Commander!"

"There are no Commanders here!"

"Have mercy, Your Excellency!"

When he heard himself called "Your Excellency," the Showman pursed up his lips, and, suddenly becoming more human and tractable, he said to Pinocchio:

"Well, what can I do for you?"

"I implore you to spare poor Harlequin!"

"It is useless to ask for that. If I spare you, I must put him on the fire, for my mutton must be well roasted."

"In that case," cried Pinocchio, rising to his feet, and throwing away his cap of bread, "in that case I know my duty. Forward, police! Bind me and throw me in the fire. It is not just that poor Harlequin, my own true friend, should die for me!"

These words, uttered in a loud, heroic voice, caused all the marionettes who were present to weep. Even the policemen, although made of wood, cried like babies.

At first Fire-Eater remained as hard and cold as a piece of ice; then, little by little, he began to melt, and to sneeze. When he had sneezed four or five times, he opened his arms affectionately to Pinocchio, saying:

"You are a fine, brave boy! Come here, and give me a kiss."

Pinocchio ran quickly, and, climbing up the Showman's beard like a squirrel, gave him a resounding smack on the end of his nose.

"And is my life spared?" asked poor Harlequin, in a trembling voice that could hardly be heard.

"Your life is spared," replied Fire-Eater; then he added, as he shook his head: "Patience! This evening I must resign myself to eat my mutton half done; but another time woe to him who must help roast it!"

When they knew that their brothers were safe, all the marionettes ran back to the stage, lit all the lights as for a grand performance, and began to skip and dance. They were still dancing at sunrise.

Chapter Twelve

Fire-Eater Gives Pinocchio Five Gold Pieces to Take to his Father, Geppetto: but Pinocchio is Deceived By the Fox and the Cat and Goes Away with them

The next day Fire-Eater called Pinocchio aside and asked him:

"What is your father's name?"

"Geppetto."

"And what trade does he follow?"

"That of a poor man."

"Does he earn very much?"

"He earns as much as is necessary in order never to have a farthing in his pocket. Just think of it! In order to buy my primer so that I could go to school, he had to sell the coat off his back: a coat that was full of holes and patches!"

"Poor fellow! I am almost sorry for him. Here are five gold pieces. Go quickly and give them to him with my compliments."

As one can easily imagine, Pinocchio thanked the Showman a thousand times. One by one he embraced all the marionettes of the Company, and even the policemen; then, almost beside himself with joy, he set out for home.

But before he had travelled half a mile he met a Fox who was lame in one foot, and a Cat who was blind in both eyes, hobbling along as well as they could, like good companions in misfortune. The Fox, who was lame, was leaning on the Cat: and the Cat, who was blind, was guided by the Fox.

"Good morning, Pinocchio," said the Fox politely.

"How is it that you know my name?" asked the marionette.

"I know your father well."

"Where did you see him?"

"I saw him yesterday in the doorway of his house."

"And what was he doing?"

"He was in his shirt-sleeves, and trembling with cold."

"Poor Daddy! But, thank Heaven, from this day forth he shall tremble no more."

"Why not?"

"Because I have become a rich man."

"You? A rich man?" said the Fox, and he began to laugh scornfully. The Cat laughed, too, but he stroked his whiskers with his fore paws in order to conceal it.

"There's nothing to laugh at," cried Pinocchio irritably. "I'm really sorry to tantalise you, but these, if you understand such things, are five beautiful gold pieces."

And he took the money Fire-Eater had given him from his pocket. At the fascinating jingle of gold the Fox made an involuntary movement of the leg that seemed lame, and the Cat opened wide both his blind eyes; but he shut them again so quickly that Pinocchio never noticed it.

"And now," inquired the Fox, "what are you going to do with this money?"

"First of all," answered the marionette, "I am going to buy a fine new coat for my father; a coat made of gold and silver, with diamond buttons; then I will buy myself a primer."

"For yourself?"

"Certainly: for I mean to go to school and study hard."

"Look at me," said the Fox; "because of my foolish passion for study, I lost the use of my leg."

"And look at me," said the Cat; "because of *my* foolish passion for study, I lost the sight of both my eyes."

Just then a white blackbird that was sitting on a hedge by the side of the road sang its usual song, and said:

"Pinocchio, don't heed the advice of evil companions: if you do, you'll be sorry."

Poor blackbird, if only he hadn't said it! The Cat made a great leap right upon him, and, without giving him time to say *ouch*, swallowed him at a mouthful, feathers and all.

When he had devoured him and wiped his mouth, he shut his eyes and became blind as at first.

"Poor blackbird," said Pinocchio; "why did you treat him so?"

"I did it to teach him a lesson. He will learn not to interfere again when other people are talking."

They had gone more than half-way towards Pinocchio's home, when the Fox stopped suddenly and said:

"Would you like to double your gold pieces? Would you like to turn those five miserable gold pieces into a hundred, a thousand, two thousand?"

"*Would* I ? But how can it be done?"

"It's the easiest thing in the world. Instead of going home, you must come with us."

"And where are you going?"

"We are going to Dupeland."

Pinocchio thought a moment, and then said resolutely:

"No, I don't want to go. I am almost home, and I want to go to my father, who is waiting for me. Who knows how he must have worried when I didn't come home! I know only too well that I have been a very bad boy. The Talking Cricket was right when he said: 'Disobedient children will never be happy in this world.' I have proved it to my cost, for I have suffered all sorts of misfortunes; and last night, in Fire-Eater's house, I was in danger of . . . Brrr! It gives me goose-flesh to think of it."

"Well, then," said the Fox, "so you really want to go home? Run along then, and so much the worse for you!"

"So much the worse for you!" repeated the Cat.

"Think well, Pinocchio, because you're turning your back on a fortune!"

"On a fortune!" repeated the Cat.

"Your five gold pieces might become two thousand in one day!"

"Two thousand in one day!" repeated the Cat.

"But how could they possibly become so many?"

demanded Pinocchio, with his mouth wide open in astonishment.

"I will explain immediately," said the Fox.

"You must know that in Dupeland there is a sacred field called 'the Field of Miracles'. You dig a hole in this field, and you put in it, for example, a gold sequin. Then you cover it up with earth, water it with two buckets of spring water, sprinkle a pinch of salt over it, and go peacefully to bed. During the night the sequin sprouts and blossoms and the next morning you get up, go back to the field, and what do you find? You find a lovely tree, loaded with as many gold sequins as an ear of corn has kernels."

"Then," said Pinocchio, more bewildered than ever, "if I should bury my five gold pieces in that field how many should I find the next morning?"

"That's an easy problem," replied the Fox, "a problem that can be done on one's fingers. Suppose that every gold piece becomes a cluster of five hundred gold pieces; multiply five hundred by five, and the next morning you will find in your pocket two thousand five hundred shining, clinking gold pieces."

"Oh, how splendid!" cried Pinocchio, dancing for joy. "As soon as I have harvested these gold pieces, I will take two thousand for myself, and I will make you two a present of the other five hundred."

"A present—to us?" exclaimed the Fox disdainfully. "You offend us! God forbid!"

"God forbid!" repeated the Cat.

"What good people!" thought Pinocchio; and straightway forgetting his father, the new coat, the primer, and all his good resolutions, he said to the Fox and the Cat:

"Well, lead on, I will go with you."

Chapter Thirteen

The Red Crab Inn

THEY walked, and walked, and walked, and finally towards evening, tired almost to death, they arrived at the Red Crab Inn.

"Let us stop here a little while," said the Fox, "at least long enough to eat a bite, and rest a few hours. At midnight we must go on again, so that we can arrive at the Field of Miracles by sunrise."

They entered the Inn and sat down at a table, but none of them had any appetite.

The poor Cat had a bad stomach-ache, and could only eat thirty-five mullet in tomato sauce, and four helpings of tripe with Parmesan cheese; and because he thought the tripe was not well seasoned, he asked three times for more butter and grated cheese.

The Fox, too, would gladly have nibbled something, but since the doctor had put him on a diet he had to be content with a hare in sweet-sour sauce, with a light border of fat spring chickens. After the hare, in order to stimulate his appetite, he asked for a dish of pheasants, partridges, rabbits, frogs, lizards, and paradise grapes. After this he would not touch anything more. He said he was so sick of the sight of food that he could not eat another mouthful.

The one who ate least of all was Pinocchio. He asked for a quarter of a nut, and the small end of a loaf of bread, but he left it all on his plate. The poor child's thoughts were fixed on the Field of Miracles, and he was suffering from a prospective indigestion of gold pieces.

When they had supped, the Fox said to their host:

"Give us two nice rooms: one for Signor Pinocchio, and the other for me and my companion. We will take a little nap before we leave. Do not forget to call us at midnight, for we must continue our journey."

"Yes, sir," replied the host, winking at the Fox and the Cat as if to say: "I understand what you are up to."

As soon as he was in bed, Pinocchio fell soundly asleep, and began to dream. He thought that he was in the middle of a field, and the field was full of little trees whose branches were loaded with gold pieces swinging gently in the breeze, and clinking as if to say: "Whoever wants us, come and get us." But just at the most interesting point, that is, when Pinocchio stretched out his hand to gather them and put them in his pocket, he was suddenly awakened by three violent blows on the door of his room.

It was the host, come to tell him it was midnight.

"Are my companions ready?" asked the marionette.

"Ready! They left two hours ago."

"Why were they in such a hurry?"

"Because the Cat received a message that his eldest son, who has chilblains, is not expected to live."

"Did they pay for their supper?"

"What an idea! They were far too polite to offer such an insult to a gentleman like you."

"That's too bad! Such an insult would have been most welcome!" said Pinocchio, scratching his head. Then he inquired:

"And where did these good friends of mine say they would wait for me?"

"In the Field of Miracles, tomorrow morning, at sunrise."

Pinocchio parted with a gold piece for his supper, and that of his fellow travellers, and left the Inn.

He had to feel his way, for it was so dark it was impossible to see one's hand before one's face. In the country round him not a leaf could be heard stirring. Only a few night birds, flying across the path from one hedge to the other, brushed Pinocchio's nose with their wings, making him start backwards in a fright, crying: "Who goes there?" an echo answered from the far-off hills: "Who goes there? Who goes there? Who goes there?"

As he trudged along he saw a little animal on the trunk of a tree, which shone with a pale, faint light, like a night lamp with a porcelain shade.

"Who are you?" asked Pinocchio.

"I am the ghost of the Talking Cricket," was the reply in a faint, faint voice, that seemed to come from another world.

"What do you want of me?" said the marionette.

"I want to give you some advice. Go back home, and carry the four gold pieces you have left to your poor father, who is weeping and longing for you."

"My father will be a rich gentleman tomorrow, for these four gold pieces will have become two thousand."

"My boy, never put your faith in people who promise to make you rich in a day. They are generally swindlers, or crazy. Listen to me, and go back home."

"No, I am going forward."

"It is very late."

"I am going forward."

"It is a dark night."

"I am going forward."

42

"And it's a dangerous way . . ."

"I am going forward."

"Remember that children who do as they please are sorry for it sooner or later."

"That's an old story. Good night, Cricket!"

"Good night, Pinocchio; may Heaven preserve you from fogs and assassins!"

With these words the Talking Cricket's light went out, as when one blows out a candle, and the path was darker than before.

CHAPTER FOURTEEN

Pinocchio does not Heed the Good Advice of the Talking Cricket, and Meets the Assassins

"REALLY," said the marionette to himself, as he continued his journey, "how unfortunate we poor children are! Everybody scolds us, everybody warns us, everybody advises us. To hear them talk you would think they were all our fathers, or our schoolmasters—every one of them: even the Talking Crickets. The ideas! Just because I would not listen to that tiresome Talking Cricket, who knows, according to him, how many disasters will befall me! I shall even encounter assassins! It's a good thing I don't believe, and never have believed, in assassins. I am perfectly certain that assassins have been invented by our fathers on purpose to frighten us, so that we shall be afraid to go out at night. And even supposing I should meet them, would I be afraid of them? Not for a moment! I should walk right up to them and say: 'Mr. Assassins, what do you want of me? Just bear in mind that there's no joking with me. Now be quiet, and go about your business!' If those poor assassins should hear me talking like that, I can just see them running off like the wind. If it should happen, though, that they didn't run away, I should, and that would be the end of it.''

Pinocchio was going to say something more, but at that moment he thought he heard a rustling of leaves behind him.

Turning quickly he saw two horrid black figures wrapped in coal sacks leaping towards him on their toes, like two spectres.

"There they are, for sure!" he said to himself, and not knowing where to hide his four gold pieces he put them in his mouth, under his tongue.

Then he started to run; but before he had taken the first step he felt himself seized by his arms, and heard two horrible, cavernous voices behind him.

"Your money, or your life!" the terrible voices cried.

Pinocchio couldn't speak, for his money was in his mouth. He made a thousand bows and gestures to show those masked robbers, of whom he could only see their eyes through the holes in the sacks, that he was a poor man, and hadn't even a counterfeit penny in his pocket.

"Come, come, less nonsense, and hand over your money!" the two brigands cried menacingly.

But the marionette made signs with his head and hands as if to say: "I have not a penny!"

"Hand over your money, or you are a dead man," said the tall assassin.

"A dead man!" repeated the other.

"And after we have killed you, we will kill your father too!"

"Your father, too!" repeated the other.

44

"No, no, no, my poor father, no!" cried Pinocchio in despair; but at this the gold pieces clinked in his mouth.

"Ah, ha, you rascal, so you hid your money under your tongue! Spit it out, immediately!"

Pinocchio paid no attention.

"Oh! so you don't understand? Wait a moment, we'll make you spit it out!"

In fact one of them seized the marionette by the end of his nose, and the other grasped his chin, and they pulled without mercy, one this way, and the other that way, in order to make him open his mouth, but it was no use; the marionette's mouth was as tightly shut as if it had been nailed and riveted.

Then the smaller assassin drew a knife, and tried to force it between his lips, but Pinocchio, quick as lightning, bit off his hand. Imagine his astonishment when he saw that it was a cat's paw!

Encouraged by this first victory, he freed himself from the assassins' clutches and, jumping over the hedge, fled across the country with the assassins after him, like dogs after a hare. The smaller one, who had lost a paw, ran on one leg, though how he managed it was never known.

After they had run about nine miles, Pinocchio was completely exhausted. Seeing himself lost, he climbed a tall pine tree, and seated himself on a branch at the very top. The assassins tried to climb up after him, but halfway up the trunk they slipped and fell to the ground, skinning their hands and feet.

In spite of this they did not give up, but, gathering a heap of dry sticks at the foot of the tree, they set fire to it. In less than no time the pine caught fire, and blazed like a candle in the wind. Pinocchio, seeing that the flames were climbing fast, and not wanting to be roasted like a pigeon, leaped down from his perch and took to his legs again across the fields and vineyards. The assassins followed after, running close behind him, never seeming to be tired at all.

It was nearly daybreak and they were still running, when suddenly Pinocchio found the way barred by a wide, deep ditch full of dirty water, the colour of coffee and milk. What should he do? "One, two, three!" cried the marionette, and dashing forward like the wind he jumped clean over it. The assassins jumped too, but they had not gauged the distance properly and swash, spatter! they fell right in the middle of the ditch.

Pinocchio heard the splash, and as he ran he laughed, and shouted:

"Take a good bath, Mr. Assassins!"

He was just thinking that they must be drowned when, turning to look, he saw them both running after him, still wrapped in their sacks, and dripping like two leaky baskets.

CHAPTER FIFTEEN

The Assassins Follow Pinocchio, and having Caught him they Hang him on the Big Oak Tree

THIS time the marionette felt that his case was hopeless. He was ready to throw himself to the ground and surrender when his eyes fell upon a little house, as white as snow, far off among the dark green trees.

"If only I have breath enough to get to that house, perhaps I should be safe," he said to himself.

Without losing a moment he ran towards the grove at his best speed, with the assassins hot on his track.

After a desperate run, which lasted nearly two hours, he arrived at last, completely worn out, at the door of the little house.

He rapped; but no one answered.

He rapped again, louder than before, for he heard the footsteps and the panting breath of his persecutors; but all was silent as before.

Seeing that it was useless to rap, he began to kick the door, and beat his head against it. At that a lovely child came to the window. Her hair was blue, and her face as white as wax; her eyes were closed, and her hands were crossed on her breast. Without moving her lips in the least she said in a low voice that seemed to come from another world:

"There is no one in this house. They are all dead."

"But at least you will let me in," cried Pinocchio, weeping and entreating her.

"I am dead, too."

"Dead? Then what are you doing at the window?"

"I am waiting for the hearse to come, and take me away."

As she said this the child disappeared, and the window closed of itself, silently.

"Oh, lovely blue-haired child," implored Pinocchio, "open the door, for pity's sake. Have mercy on a poor boy who is pursued by assass . . ."

But before he could finish the word he felt himself seized by the neck, and heard those cruel voices snarling:

"This time you won't escape us!"

The marionette felt that his end was near, and he began

to tremble. He shook so violently that the joints of his wooden legs creaked, and the four gold pieces under his tongue clinked together.

"Now, then," demanded the assassins, "will you, or will you not open your mouth? You won't answer, eh? Well, leave it to us: we'll see that you open it this time!"

And drawing two great knives as sharp as razors, *zaff* . . . they struck at him savagely. Luckily for him the marionette was made of the hardest kind of wood; and the knife blades were splintered into a thousand pieces. Only the handles remained in the assassins' hands, who stood staring at each other in amazement.

"I see," said one, "he must be hung. Let us hang him!"

"Let us hang him!" repeated the other.

No sooner said than done. They bound his hands behind his back, and, putting a running noose around his neck, they tied him to a branch of a big oak tree.

Then they sat on the grass, and waited for him to stop kicking; but after three hours the marionette's eyes were wide open, and he was kicking harder than ever.

At last, tired of waiting, they turned to Pinocchio and said with a sneer:

"Good-bye, until tomorrow. We will come back then, and we hope you will be so obliging as to see that we find you good and dead, and with your mouth wide open."

Then they went away.

Meanwhile a fierce north wind had begun to blow; it raged, and whistled, and blew poor Pinocchio back and forth as fast as a bell-clapper on a holiday. It hurt him dreadfully, and the noose tightened around his neck so that he could not breathe.

Little by little his eyes grew dim, and although he felt that death was near, still he hoped that some kind soul might come that way and release him. He waited and waited, but no one came, no one at all. Then he remembered his poor father, and he stammered, half dead as he was:

"O Daddy! If you were only here!"

He could say no more. He closed his eyes, opened his mouth, stretched out his legs, shuddered all over, and became as stiff as if he were frozen.

Chapter Sixteen

The Lovely Blue-Haired Child Saves the Marionette: she Puts him in Bed and Calls Three Doctors to See whether he is Alive or Dead

WHILE poor Pinocchio, hung by assassins on the big oak tree, seemed more dead than alive, the lovely child with blue hair looked out of the window again. She felt very sorry for the unlucky marionette who, hanging by his neck, was dancing to the tune played by the cold north wind. She clapped her hands three times, making a faint sound.

At this signal there was a rustling as of hurrying wings, and a large Falcon appeared and perched on the window-sill.

"What are your commands, beautiful Fairy?" said the Falcon, lowering his beak in homage (for you must know that the child with blue hair was no other than a kind fairy, who had lived in the neighbourhood of that grove for more than a thousand years).

"Do you see that marionette hanging on the big oak?"

"I see him."

"Very well; fly there quickly; break the knot that holds him with your strong beak, and lay him gently on the ground at the foot of the oak."

The Falcon flew away, and in two minutes he returned, saying:

"Your commands have been obeyed."

"How did you find him? Alive or dead?"

"To look at him he seems dead, but he cannot be quite dead, for as soon as I loosened the noose around his neck, he sighed and murmured: 'Now I feel better!' "

The Fairy clapped her hands twice, and a magnificent poodle appeared, walking upright on his hind legs, as if he were a man. The Poodle was dressed like a coachman on a holiday. He had a little three-cornered hat trimmed with gold braid, a white curly wig, a chocolate-coloured doublet with diamond buttons and two big pockets for the bones which his mistress gave him at dinner, short trousers of crimson velvet, silk stockings, low shoes, and a sort of umbrella case behind, made of blue satin, to put his tail in when it rained.

"Be quick, Medora!" said the Fairy; "get out my finest carriage and drive to the grove. When you come to the big oak you will find a poor, half-dead marionette lying on the ground. Take him up carefully, put him gently on the cushions, and bring him to me. Do you understand?"

The Poodle wagged the blue satin case he carried behind him three or four times to show that he understood, and was off like a shot.

In a few moments a handsome carriage was driven out of the stable. It was the colour of air, and was padded with canary feathers and lined with whipped cream and custard, with sweet cakes. It was drawn by a hundred pairs of white mice, and the Poodle on the box cracked his whip over their heads like a cab-driver afraid of being late.

In less than a quarter of an hour he was back again. The Fairy, who was waiting at the door, took the poor marionette in her arms, carried him to a little chamber with mother-of-pearl walls, and sent instantly for the most famous doctors in the neighbourhood.

The doctors came hurrying, one after another: they were a Crow, an Owl, and a Talking Cricket.

"I would like these gentlemen to tell me," said the Fairy, as they stood around Pinocchio's bed, "I would like these gentlemen to tell me if this unfortunate marionette is dead or alive."

The Crow came forward first, and felt Pinocchio's pulse; then he felt his nose, and lastly his little toe. When he had examined them carefully he said with great solemnity:

"It is my opinion that this marionette is quite dead; but if, unluckily, he is not dead, that would be a sure sign that he is still alive."

"I am sorry," said the Owl, "to contradict the Crow, my illustrious friend and colleague, but it is my opinion that this marionette is still alive; but if, unluckily, he is not alive, that would be a sign that he is actually dead."

"And have you nothing to say?" inquired the Fairy, turning to the Talking Cricket.

"I think that when a prudent physician does not know what to say, the best thing he can do is to be silent. As for that, this marionette's features are not new to me; I have seen him before."

Pinocchio, who until that instant had seemed as lifeless as a genuine piece of wood, gave a convulsive shudder that shook the whole bed.

"That marionette there," continued the Talking Cricket, "is an accomplished rogue . . ."

Pinocchio opened his eyes, but closed them quickly.

"He is a scamp, a shirker, a vagabond . . ."

Pinocchio hid his face under the sheet.

"That marionette is a disobedient son, who will cause his poor old father to die of a broken heart!"

Just then a smothered sobbing and weeping could be heard in the room. Imagine how surprised every one was when they lifted up the sheet a little, and saw that Pinocchio was the cause of it.

"When a bad boy weeps, it's a sign that he is on the way to recovery," said the Crow solemnly.

"I am sorry to contradict my illustrious friend and colleague," said the Owl, "but it's my opinion that in such a case it is a sign that he does not want to die."

CHAPTER SEVENTEEN

Pinocchio Eats the Sugar, but is not Willing to Take the Medicine: however, when he Sees the Grave-Diggers Coming to Carry him away he Swallows it: then he Tells a Lie and his Nose Grows Longer by way of Punishment

As soon as the three doctors had left the room, the Fairy came to his bedside. She put her hand on Pinocchio's forehead, and saw that he had a burning fever.

So she dissolved a white powder in half a glass of water, and holding it to his lips said affectionately:

"Drink this, and in a few days you will be well."

Pinocchio looked at the glass, pursed up his lips, and said in a whining voice:

"Is it sweet, or bitter?"

"It is bitter, but it will do you good."

"If it's bitter I don't want it."

"Listen to me, and drink it."

"But I don't like anything bitter."

"Drink it, and afterwards I will give you a lump of sugar, to take the taste out of your mouth."

"Where is the lump of sugar?"

"Here it is," said the Fairy, taking one out of a golden sugar bowl.

"First I want the lump of sugar, and then I'll drink that bitter water."

"Will you promise to drink it?"

"Yes."

The Fairy gave him the sugar, and Pinocchio crunched and swallowed it in an instant, saying as he picked his fingers:

"It would be pretty fine if sugar were medicine. I would be sick every day."

"'Now keep your promise, and drink these few drops of water; they will make you well."

Pinocchio took the glass in his hand most unwillingly. He sniffed at it, and held it to his lips; then he sniffed again, and at last he said:

"It's too bitter! It's too bitter! I can't drink it!"

"How can you say so, when you haven't even tasted it!"

"Oh, I know it is! I can smell it. Give me another lump of sugar, and then I'll drink it."

So the Fairy, with all the patience of a kind mother, put another lump of sugar in his mouth: then she offered him the glass.

"I can't drink it this way," said the marionette, making all sorts of grimaces.

"Why not?"

"Because that pillow on my feet makes me so uncomfortable."

The Fairy removed the pillow.

"It's no use, I can't drink it this way, either."

"Whatever is the matter now?"

"The door bothers me, it's half open."

The Fairy shut the door.

"In fact," cried Pinocchio, bursting into tears, "I don't want to drink that bitter water, no, no, no . . ."

"My child, you will be sorry."

"I don't care."

"You are very ill."

"I don't care."

"This fever will send you to the other world in a few hours."

"I don't care."

"Are you not afraid to die?"

"Not a bit! I had rather die than drink that dreadful medicine!"

At that very moment the door of the room was thrown open, and four rabbits black as ink came in, carrying a little black coffin.

"What do you want of me?" screamed Pinocchio, sitting up in terror.

"We have come for you," said the largest rabbit.

"For me! But I'm not dead yet!"

"Not quite yet, but you have only a few minutes to live, because you refused to drink the medicine that would have cured you."

"O Fairy, kind Fairy," cried Pinocchio, "give me the

glass quickly . . . hurry, for mercy's sake, for I don't want to die, no, I don't want to die!"

He took the glass in both hands, and emptied it at one gulp.

"Patience!" said the rabbits. "This time we have made a trip for nothing."

And replacing the little coffin on their shoulders they went out of the room, muttering and grumbling through their teeth.

In a few minutes Pinocchio jumped out of bed perfectly well; for you must know that wooden marionettes have the privilege of being ill very seldom, and of getting well very quickly.

When the Fairy saw him running and playing around the room as gay as a young rooster, she said:

"So my medicine really did you good?"

"More than that! It brought me back to the world."

"Then why was it so much trouble to make you drink it?"

"Well, we children are all like that. We are more afraid of the medicine than of the disease."

"For shame! Children should know that the right medicine taken in time may save them from a serious illness, perhaps even from death."

"Oh, another time I will not make so much trouble. I will remember those black rabbits with the coffin on their shoulders and I'll take the glass in my hand instantly, and down it will go!"

"Now come here to me, and tell me how it happened that you fell into the hands of assassins."

"It was like this: Fire-Eater, the Showman, gave me some gold pieces and said: 'Here, take these to your father.' But on the way I met the Fox and Cat, two very nice persons, and they said: 'Would you like to change these pieces into a thousand, yes, two thousand? Come with us, and we will take you to the Field of Miracles.' So I said: 'Let us go'; and they said: 'Let's stop at the Red Crab Inn, and set out again after midnight.' And when I woke up they were not there, because they had gone away. Then I started after them in the night. It seemed impossible that it could be so dark, and I met two assassins in coal sacks, who said: 'Hand over your money!' And I said, 'I haven't any,' because I had hid the four gold pieces in my mouth. One of the assassins tried to put his hand in my mouth, and I bit it off, but when I spat it out it wasn't a hand, but a cat's paw. And the assassins ran after me, and I ran and ran as fast as I could go until they caught up with me, and hung me by the neck to a tree in the grove saying: 'We will come back tomorrow, and then you will be dead, and your mouth will be open, and we can get the money which is under your tongue.' "

"Where are the four gold pieces now?" asked the Fairy.

"I have lost them," replied Pinocchio, but he told a lie, for he had them in his pocket.

As soon as he had told this lie his nose, which was already very long, became two inches longer.

"Where did you lose them?"

"In the grove nearby."

At this second lie, his nose became still longer.

"If you lost them there," said the Fairy, "we can go and find them; for everything that is lost in that grove can be found."

"Oh! Now that I remember," replied the marionette in great confusion, "I didn't lose the money, I swallowed it when I was taking your medicine."

At this third lie his nose lengthened to such an extraordinary degree that poor Pinocchio could not move in any direction. If he turned one way, his nose hit the bed or the window-panes; if he turned the other, it struck the walls or the door; if he raised it a little more, there was danger of putting out the Fairy's eye.

The Fairy watched him, and laughed.

"What are you laughing at?" asked the marionette, much embarrassed and worried about that nose, which was growing while he looked at it.

"I am laughing at the lies you have told, little Pinocchio."

"However did you know that I told lies?"

"Lies, my child, can be easily recognised. There are two sorts of them: those with short legs, and those with long noses. The sort you tell have long noses."

Pinocchio would have hidden his face for shame. He tried to run out of the room, but he could not do it; his nose was so long that he could not reach the door.

CHAPTER EIGHTEEN

Pinocchio Finds the Fox and the Cat and Goes with them to Sow the Four Gold Pieces in the Field of Miracles

As you may, perhaps, imagine, the Fairy let the marionette scream and cry a good half-hour because he could not get to the door on account of his long nose. She did this to teach him a good lesson, and to cure him of the bad habit of lying, which is one of the worst habits

57

a boy can have. But when she saw his face swollen with crying, and his eyes starting out of his head in his despair, she was moved to pity and clapped her hands. At that signal a thousand big wood-peckers flew in at the window, and perching on Pinocchio's nose pecked away at it so industriously that in a few minutes his enormous, ridiculous nose was reduced to its natural size again.

"How kind you are, dear Fairy," said the marionette, wiping his eyes. "I love you so much!"

"I love you too," replied the Fairy, "and if you will stay with me you shall be my little brother, and I will be your loving sister."

"I would love to stay with you . . . but what about my poor father?"

"I have thought of everything. Your father knows all about you, and he will be here before night."

"Really?" exclaimed Pinocchio, jumping for joy. "Then, dear Fairy, if you are willing, I would like to go to meet him. I can't wait to see that poor old man, who has suffered so much for me!"

"Go, by all means, but don't get lost. Take the path through the grove, and you will be sure to meet him."

Pinocchio departed; and as soon as he entered the grove he began to run like a deer. At a certain point just in front of the old oak he stopped, because he thought he heard something moving in the bushes. In fact, there appeared all at once in the path—can you guess?—the Fox and the Cat, his two travelling companions with whom he had supped at the Red Crab Inn.

"Here is our dear Pinocchio," exclaimed the Fox, hugging and kissing him. "How do you happen to be here?"

"How do you happen to be here?" repeated the Cat.

"It's a long story," said the marionette. "I will tell it

58

when I have time, although you should know that the other night when you left me alone in the Inn, I encountered assassins on the way."

"Assassins? Oh, my poor friend! And what did they want?"

"They wanted to rob me of my money."

"Infamous!" said the Fox.

"Most infamous!" added the Cat.

"But I began to run," continued the marionette, "and they ran after me until they caught me, and hung me to a branch of that oak."

And Pinocchio pointed to the big oak nearby.

"Did you ever hear of anything worse than that!" said the Fox. "What a world this is, in which we are condemned to live! Where can honest men like us find a refuge?"

While they were talking Pinocchio noticed that the Cat was lame in his right foreleg, because the whole paw was missing. He therefore said to him:

"What has become of your paw?"

The Cat started to say something, but he began to stammer—and the Fox said quickly:

"My friend is too modest; that is why he doesn't answer. I will reply for him. You know, about an hour ago we met an old wolf, who was almost dying of hunger. He begged us for a crust of bread, but we hadn't even a fishbone to give him; so what do you suppose my friend here did, he who has the heart of a Caesar? He bit off his own paw and gave it to that poor beast, so that he could break his fast."

As he said this, the Fox wiped away a tear.

Pinocchio's heart was so touched by this story that he went close to the Cat, and whispered in his ear: "If all cats were like you, the rats would be fortunate!"

"And what are you doing here?" asked the Fox.

"I'm waiting for my father; he may be here any moment."

"And your gold pieces?"

"They are all in my pocket, except the one I spent at the Red Crab Inn."

"Just to think that instead of four gold pieces they might be a thousand, or two thousand by tomorrow! Why not take my advice? Why not plant them in the Field of Miracles?"

"Impossible, today; I will go some other time."

"Another time will be too late," said the Fox.

"Why?"

"Because a rich man has bought the field, and after tomorrow no one will be allowed to plant his money there."

"How far is it to the Field of Miracles?"

"Only a little over a mile. Will you come with us? You will be there in half an hour; you can sow your four gold pieces immediately, and after a few minutes you can gather two thousand and come home in the evening with your pockets full. Will you come?"

Pinocchio hesitated; he remembered the good Fairy, old Geppetto, and the warnings of the Talking Cricket; but he finished by doing as all children do who have no judgment, and no heart: that is to say, he tossed his head and said to the Fox and the Cat:

"Come on: I'll go with you."

And off they went.

They had walked about half a day when they came to a place called Zanytrap. As soon as they entered the city, Pinocchio saw that the streets were full of dogs whose hair had fallen off, and whose mouths were wide open with hunger; there were shorn sheep, trembling with cold;

chickens without their crests and wattles, who were begging for a grain of corn; big butterflies who could not fly, because they had sold their beautiful wings; peacocks without their tails, who were ashamed to be seen; and pheasants who were slinking along, mourning for their lovely gold and silver feathers, which were lost for ever.

In the midst of this throng of beggars and shamefaced beasts, elegant carriages rolled by now and then, with a Fox, or a thievish magpie, or some bird of prey inside.

"But where is the Field of Miracles?" inquired Pinocchio.

"Just a few steps farther on."

They traversed the city, and, going beyond the walls, stopped in a lonely field which, by the way, was just like any other field.

"Here we are," said the Fox. "Now get down and dig a little hole with your hands, to put your gold pieces in."

Pinocchio obeyed. He dug the hole, put in the four gold pieces he had left, and covered them up.

"Now, then," said the Fox, "go to the mill-dam close by, get a bucket of water, and water the ground where you have sown your seed."

Pinocchio went to the mill-dam, and, since he did not have a bucket, he took off one of his shoes, filled it with water, and watered the earth which covered his money.

"What else must I do?"

"Nothing more," replied the Fox. "Now you can go away. Come back in about twenty minutes, and you will find a little tree already growing, with its branches covered with money."

The poor marionette was almost beside himself with joy. He thanked the Fox and the Cat a thousand times, and promised them a fine present.

"We don't want presents," replied those two miserable

wretches; "it is enough for us to have shown you how to get rich without work. That makes us perfectly happy."

With these words they wished Pinocchio a splendid harvest, bade him farewell, and went about their business.

Chapter Nineteen

Pinocchio Loses his Gold Pieces and Spends Four Months in Prison

The marionette went back to the city, and began to count the minutes, one by one. When he thought he had waited twenty minutes, he hurried back to the Field of Miracles.

He went as fast as he could, while his heart beat like a clock, tick, tock, tick, tock, and he said to himself:

"What if, instead of a thousand gold pieces, I should find two thousand on the branches of the tree? Or instead of two thousand, I should find five thousand? Or instead of five thousand, one hundred thousand? Oh, what a grand gentleman I should be then! I should have a splendid palace, and a thousand wooden horses and a thousand stables to play with, and a cellar full of toffee, and lemonade, and a library just full of candied fruit, and tarts, and sweet rolls, and almond paste, and lollipops, and cream puffs!"

While he was indulging in these fancies, he came within sight of the field. He stopped to see if he could catch a glimpse of a tree, with its branches laden with money, but he saw nothing. He went a little farther, still nothing. He entered the field, went up to the place where he had buried his gold pieces, and there was nothing at all. He stood there thinking; and, forgetting the rules of etiquette, he took one hand out of his pocket, and scratched his head vigorously.

At that moment a loud laugh rang in his ears. Looking up he saw a large parrot on the branch of a tree, picking the lice off the few feathers he had left.

"Why are you laughing?" said Pinocchio peevishly.

"I am laughing because, in cleaning my feathers, I tickled myself under my wings."

The marionette did not reply. He went to the mill-dam, filled his shoe with water again, and poured it on the earth which covered his money.

But lo, another laugh, more impertinent than before, rang out over the lonely field.

"See here," shouted Pinocchio angrily, "might one ask what you are laughing at, you ill-mannered parrot?"

"I am laughing at those simpletons who believe all the nonsense they are told, and who are always cheated by those who are more cunning than themselves."

"Are you, perhaps, speaking of me?"

"Yes, poor Pinocchio, I am speaking of you, of you who are so simple as to believe that you can sow and reap money, like beans and pumpkins. There was a time when I believed that, too, and today I am suffering for it. Today alas! Too late! I have learned that to get a little money together honestly, you must know how to earn it by the labour of your hands or your head."

"I don't understand," said the marionette, beginning to tremble with fear.

"Patience! I will try to speak plainer," replied the Parrot. "While you were in the city the Fox and the Cat came back here; they dug up your money and ran away like the wind. It will take a swift runner to catch them."

Pinocchio stood there with his mouth wide open. He

could not believe what the Parrot said, and he began wildly to dig up the earth he had watered. He dug, and dug, and dug, until he had a hole big enough for a haystack, but the money was not there.

Then in desperation he ran back to the city, and went straight to the Court House, to denounce the villains who had robbed him.

The Judge was an old Gorilla. He was very old, and presented a most respectable appearance, with his long white beard, and his gold spectacles without any glass in them, which he was obliged to wear all the time on account of a disease of the eyes which he had had for many years.

In the Judge's presence Pinocchio related all the circumstances of the iniquitous fraud, of which he had been the victim. He gave the names, surnames, and all the particulars concerning the rascals, and finished by demanding justice.

The Judge listened benevolently, for he was greatly interested in his story, and very sorry for him. When the marionette had no more to say, he put out his hand and rang a bell.

At the sound two mastiffs appeared, dressed like policemen.

The Judge pointed to Pinocchio and said:

"This poor fellow has been robbed of four gold pieces. Take him to prison immediately."

Pinocchio was thunderstruck. Such a sentence as this was like a flash of lightning out of a clear sky. He was about to protest, but the policemen didn't want to waste any time, so they clapped their paws over his mouth, and took him to gaol.

And there he stayed for four months; four long months, and it would have been longer if it had not happened, luckily, that the young Emperor of Zanytrap, having won a glorious victory over his enemies, commanded a great public rejoicing. There were illuminations, fireworks, horse and bicycle races, and, best of all, he ordered the prisons to be thrown open, and all the rascals to be set free.

"If the others leave the prison, I want to go too," said Pinocchio to the gaoler.

"Oh, no, you can't leave," replied the gaoler, "for you are not in that class."

"I beg your pardon," said Pinocchio, "I am a rascal too."

"In that case, you are perfectly right," said the gaoler, and lifting his cap respectfully he made a low bow, opened the prison door, and let him pass.

CHAPTER TWENTY

When Pinocchio is Liberated from Prison he Starts for the Fairy's House, but on the Way he Meets with a Horrible Serpent, and afterwards is Caught in a Trap

IMAGINE Pinocchio's joy when he was free once more! Without losing a moment he hurried out of the city, and took the street that led to the Fairy's little house.

It had been raining, and the mud was so deep that it came half-way up his legs; but he paid no attention to it. He was so anxious to see his father, and his little blue-haired sister, that he ran and jumped like a greyhound,

65

C

and the mud spattered as high as his head. As he ran he said to himself:

"What dreadful misfortunes have befallen me! . . . and I deserve them, too. I always want my own way, and never listen to those who love me, and who have a thousand times more judgment that I have! But from this time forward I will lead a different life, and become a sensible, obedient boy; for I have seen by this time that disobedient children always get the worst of it, and never gain anything by having their own way. I wonder if my father is waiting for me? Shall I find him at the Fairy's house? It's so long since I have seen him that I cannot wait to throw my arms around his neck and kiss him. Will the Fairy forgive me for disobeying her? What good care she took of me. and how kind she was! If I'm alive today it's all owing to her! Was there ever a boy more ungrateful and heartless than I am?"

As he said this he stopped suddenly in fright, and stepped backwards quickly.

What had he seen?

He saw a great Serpent stretched across the way. His skin was green, his eyes were like fire, and smoke was coming from his pointed tail as if from a chimney.

Words fail me to express Pinocchio's terror. He went back a quarter of a mile, and sat down on a little heap of stones to wait until the Serpent should go about his business, and leave the road free for him to pass.

He waited an hour; two hours; three hours; but the Serpent was still there, and even from where he sat he could see his fiery eyes, and the column of smoke coming out of his tail.

At last Pinocchio summoned all his courage, and coming near the Serpent he said, in a very small, sweet, insinuating voice:

"Excuse me, Mr. Serpent, but would you be so kind as to move just a little, barely enough to let me pass?"

He might just have well have spoken to a wall. There was no reply.

He began again, with that same small voice:

"You must know, Mr. Serpent, that I am going home, where my father is waiting for me, and it's so long since I have seen him! Would you be willing for me to go on my way?"

He waited for some sign in reply to his request, but no sign came. Instead, the Serpent, who had until then seemed full of life, became perfectly quiet and rigid. He closed his eyes, and his tail stopped smoking.

"Perhaps he is really dead," said Pinocchio, rubbing his hands together for joy, and without waiting another second he was about to step over him. But just as he was lifting one leg the Serpent rose up suddenly like a watch spring, and the marionette in his fright leaped backwards so quickly that he stumbled and fell.

It was truly a bad fall, for he came down with his head sticking in the mud, and his legs up in the air.

At the sight of the marionette standing on his head in the mud, and kicking faster than any marionette had ever kicked before, the Serpent was seized with a fit of laughter. He laughed, and he laughed, and he laughed, until he burst a blood vessel, and this time he was dead for good.

And now Pinocchio began to run again as fast as he could, in order to reach the Fairy's house before dark. But he became so dreadfully hungry that he jumped over a hedge to pick a few bunches of grapes. If only he had not done so!

He had barely reached the vines, when—*crack!* he felt his legs gripped by two sharp irons: the pain was so terrible that he saw all the stars there were in the sky.

The poor marionette was caught in a trap put there to catch some large polecats that had been terrorising all the henhouses in the neighbourhood.

Chapter Twenty-One

Pinocchio is Captured by a Farmer who Makes him Act as a Watchdog for his Henhouse

As you can easily imagine, Pinocchio began to scream and cry and call for help; but it was perfectly useless, for there were no houses to be seen, and not a living soul passed by.

Meanwhile night came on.

Pinocchio was almost fainting: partly on account of the pain caused by the irons which cut into his shins, and partly because he was afraid, there all alone in the dark, in the midst of the fields. Seeing a firefly above his head, he called to him:

"O, little Firefly, won't you be so merciful as to deliver me from this torment?"

"Poor boy!" replied the Firefly, gazing at him compassionately. "How did you ever get caught in the grip of those sharp irons?"

"I came into the field to pick a few bunches of grapes and . . ."

"But are they your grapes?"

"No . . ."

68

"And who ever taught you to take things that do not belong to you?"

"I was hungry . . ."

"Hunger, my child, is not a good excuse for taking what does not belong to you."

"That's true, that's true," wailed Pinocchio, "I won't do it again."

This dialogue was interrupted by the sound of footsteps drawing near. It was the owner of the field, who was coming on tiptoe to see if he had caught one of those polecats that were eating his chickens at night.

When he drew his lantern from under his coat he was amazed to see that, instead of a polecat, he had caught a boy.

"Ah, you thief!" the farmer said angrily, "so it's you who are stealing my chickens!"

"It isn't me, it isn't me," sobbed Pinocchio; "I only came into the field to pick a few bunches of grapes!"

"Anyone who will steal grapes will steal chickens. Leave it to me! I'll teach you a lesson you'll remember for a while!"

He opened the trap, seized the marionette by the collar, and lugged him off under his arm as he would have carried a lamb.

When he reached the yard in front of his house, he threw Pinocchio on the ground, and putting one foot on his neck he said:

"It's late, and I want to go to bed. I will settle with you tomorrow. Meanwhile, since my watchdog died today, you may take his place. You shall be my watchdog."

So saying he put a heavy collar covered with sharp brass studs around his neck, and fastened it so tightly that it was impossible to slip his head through it. A long iron chain was attached to the collar, and fixed firmly to the wall.

"If it should rain tonight," said the farmer, "you may crawl into that little wooden kennel. The straw there has served for four years as a bed for my poor dog. Remember to keep your ears pricked up and, if, unluckily, thieves should come, don't forget to bark."

With this last caution the farmer went into the house and locked the door, leaving poor Pinocchio crouching in the yard, more dead than alive with hunger and fright. From time to time he thrust his fingers under the collar which pinched his throat, and exclaimed, weeping:

"It serves me right! It serves me perfectly right! I wanted to be a loafer and a vagabond. . . . I listened to evil companions, and as a consequence I always have bad luck. If I had only been a good boy, like so many others, if I had been willing to work and study, if I had stayed at home with my poor father, I would not be now away out here in this lonely place, acting as a watchdog for a farmer. Oh, if I could only be born again! But it's too late, now, I must have patience!"

This sorrowful plaint, which came from the bottom of his heart, relieved him a little. He crawled into the kennel, and went to sleep.

CHAPTER TWENTY-TWO

Pinocchio Discovers the Thieves and is Set Free as a Reward for his Fidelity

HE had been sleeping soundly for more than two hours, when about midnight he was awakened by a whispering and muttering of strange voices that seemed to come from the yard. He put the point of his nose out of his kennel and saw four animals with dark fur, talking together. They looked like cats, but they were not cats. They were polecats, carnivorous animals that are especially fond of eggs and young chickens. One of them left his companions, and coming to the door of the kennel said in a low tone:

"Good evening, Melampo."

"My name is not Melampo," said the marionette.

"Who are you, then?"

"I am Pinocchio."

"And what are you doing there?"

"I am a watchdog."

"But where is Melampo? Where is the old dog that lived in this kennel?"

"He died this morning."

"Died? Poor beast! He was so kind! However, judging by your countenance, you seem to be a good-natured dog."

"Excuse me, I am not a dog!"

"Ah! What are you, then?"

"I am a marionette."

"And you act as a watchdog?"

"Alas, yes: it's for a punishment!"

"Well, I'll make the same bargain with you that I made with old Melampo; I'm sure you will be satisfied."

"And what might that be?"

"We will come to the henhouse one night a week, as in the past, and carry off eight hens. We will eat seven, and give you one, on condition, you understand, that you pretend to sleep when we come, and never bark and wake up the farmer."

"Is that what Melampo did?"

"Yes, indeed, and we always got on splendidly together. Now sleep in peace, and be sure that before we leave we will bring you a chicken, already picked, for tomorrow. Do you understand?"

"I understand only too well," replied Pinocchio, shaking his head menacingly, as if he would have preferred to say: "We'll see about that pretty soon!"

When the four polecats felt sure of their safety, they went straight to the henhouse, which was close to the kennel. They tore open the little wooden door with their teeth and claws, and slipped inside, one after the other. But no sooner were they all inside when the little door closed with a loud bang.

It was Pinocchio who had closed it, and not content with this, he put a big stone against it for greater security.

Then he began to bark, and he barked just like a watchdog: "Bow-wow-wow-wow!"

When the farmer heard him barking, he jumped out of his bed, seized his gun, and raising the window, he called out:

"What's the matter?"

"The thieves are here!" cried Pinocchio.

"Where are they?"

"In the henhouse!" replied Pinocchio.

"I am coming immediately."

In less time than you can say "Jack Robinson" the farmer appeared. He ran to the henhouse, and after catching the four polecats and popping them into a sack he exclaimed in high glee:

"At last you have fallen into my hands! I might chastise you, but I am not so cruel. I will therefore satisfy myself by taking you to the landlord in the village, who will skin you and cook you in a sweet-sour sauce, and serve you for rabbit. It is an honour you do not deserve, but generous people like me do not mind doing such good turns."

Then he went to Pinocchio, caressed and praised him, and asked him among other questions:

"How did you discover the plot of these thieves? To think that Melampo, my faithful Melampo, never suspected anything!"

The marionette could have revealed the truth; that is he could have told the farmer of the shameful bargain between the dog and the polecats; but he remembered that the dog was dead, and he said to himself: "What good will it do to accuse the dead? Since they are dead and gone, the best way is so leave them in peace."

"Were you awake, or asleep, when the polecats first appeared?" inquired the farmer.

"I was asleep," replied Pinocchio, "but they woke me by talking together, and one of them even came to my kennel, and said: 'If you will promise not to bark and wake up the farmer, we will give you a chicken, already picked.' What do you think of that? The impudence of making such a proposal to me! I am a marionette, and

I know I am full of faults, but I would never plot with thieves, nor receive stolen goods!"

"Good for you, my boy," said the farmer, patting him on the back. "Such sentiments do you honour; and to show how pleased I am with you I will set you free, and you may go home."

And he took off the dog collar.

CHAPTER TWENTY-THREE

Pinocchio Weeps for the Death of the Lovely Blue-Haired Child: then he Finds a Dove who Carries him to the Seashore where he Throws himself into the Water to Save his Father

WHEN Pinocchio no longer felt the weight of that heavy, humiliating collar on his neck, he began to run across the fields, never stopping for a moment, until he reached the highway which led to the Fairy's house.

When he reached it he paused to look down on the surrounding country. He could see plainly, with the naked eye, the site of his unlucky encounter with the Fox and the Cat: he could see the grove with the big oak on which he had been hanged, rising high above the other trees: but although he looked in all directions, he could not discover the little white house where he had found the lovely blue-haired child.

Fearing he knew not what, he took to his heels, and ran with all his might and main. In a few minutes he found himself in the field where the little white house once stood. But the little house was no longer there. Instead there was a little slab of white marble on which these sad words were inscribed:

HERE LIES
THE BLUE-HAIRED CHILD
WHO DIED OF GRIEF
ON BEING ABANDONED BY HER
LITTLE BROTHER
PINOCCHIO

I leave you to imagine the marionette's feelings when he had spelled out these words. He fell to the ground, and kissing the cold marble a thousand times, he burst into a flood of tears. He wept all that night, and at daybreak he was still weeping, although his tears were all spent. His groans and lamentations were so loud and piercing that they were echoed from all the hills around him.

As he wept he said:

"O dear Fairy, why are you dead? Why am I not dead, who am so naughty, instead of you, who were so good? And my father, where is he? O dear Fairy, tell me where I can find him, for I want to stay with him always, and never, never, never leave him. Dear Fairy, tell me it is not true; that you are not dead! If you really love me, if you love your little brother, live once more, come back as you were before! Are you not sorry to see me here alone, abandoned by everyone? If the assassins come, they will hang me again, and then I should be dead for good. What will become of me, alone in the world? Now that I have lost you and my father, who will give me something to eat? Where will I sleep? Who will make me a new jacket? Oh, better a hundred times better, that I should die too! Yes, I want to die! Boo-hoo-hoo!"

While he was in this desperate state he tried to tear out his hair, but since it was of wood he couldn't even run his fingers through it.

At this moment a very large dove, that was flying high in the air above him, stopped short with outstretched wings, and cried:

"Tell me, child, what are you doing down there?"

"Don't you see? I'm crying!" said Pinocchio, turning up his face towards the voice, and rubbing his eyes with the sleeve of his jacket.

"Tell me," continued the dove, "do you happen to know among your playmates a marionette called Pinocchio?"

"Pinocchio? Did you say Pinocchio?" cried the marionette, jumping to his feet. "I'm Pinocchio!"

At this reply the dove dropped swiftly to the ground. He was larger than a turkey.

"Do you know Geppetto?" he asked of the marionette.

"Do I know him? He is my poor father! Has he spoken to you of me? Will you take me to him? Is he still alive?"

"I left him three days ago on the sea coast."

"What was he doing?" Pinocchio asked the large dove.

"He was making a little boat in which to cross the ocean. That poor man! It is more than four months that he has been wandering around the world looking for you. Not having found you he has taken it into his head to search for you in far-off countries across the sea."

"How far is it from here to the sea coast?" Pinocchio inquired anxiously.

"More than five hundred miles."

"More than five hundred miles? O dear Dove, what a fine thing it would be if I had your wings!"

"If you want to go I will carry you."

"How?"

"Astride my back. Are you very heavy?"

"Heavy? No, indeed! I'm as light as a feather."

Without another word Pinocchio jumped on the Dove's back, with a leg on each side of him like a real horseman, and cried joyfully: "Gallop, gallop, little horse, for I'm in such a hurry!"

The dove took flight, and in a few minutes he was so high up that he almost touched the clouds. Arrived at that great height the marionette was seized with curiosity, and he looked down at the world below him; but it frightened him, and made him so dizzy that he wound his arms tight around the neck of his feathered steed to keep from falling off.

They flew all day. Towards evening the Dove said:

"I am so thirsty."

"And I am so hungry!" added Pinocchio.

"Let us stop a few minutes at this dovecote; then we will continue our journey, and by sunrise we shall be at the sea coast."

They entered a deserted dovecote where they saw only a basin of water, and a basket full of lettuce.

The marionette had never in his life been able to eat lettuce. He always said it turned his stomach; but that evening he simply devoured it, and when it was all gone he said to the Dove:

"I never would have believed that lettuce could taste so good!"

"You will learn, my boy," replied the Dove, "that when you are actually hungry, and there is nothing else to eat, even lettuce seems delicious. Hunger is never particular or finicky."

After this little snack they did not wait to rest themselves, but hurried on their way, and the next morning they were at the seashore.

The Dove stopped just long enough for Pinocchio to dismount, and then flew away immediately, to avoid being thanked for having performed a kindness.

The beach was covered with people who were shouting and gesticulating as they looked out over the ocean.

"What is the matter?" Pinocchio inquired of a little old woman.

"A poor father has lost his son, and he was going to cross the sea in a little boat to look for him, but the waves are so high that the boat will be capsized."

"Where is the boat?"

"Right there, in front of my finger," said the old woman, pointing to a little boat which at that distance looked like a nutshell with a tiny man in it.

Pinocchio looked closely, and uttered a piercing shriek:

"It's my father! It's my father!"

Meanwhile the little boat, beaten by the angry waves, now disappeared entirely, and again could be seen on the crest of a wave. Pinocchio, standing on a high rock, called his father's name over and over, making signs with his hands, and waving his cap and handkerchief.

Although Geppetto was so far away, it seemed as if he recognised his son, for he took off his cap and waved it: he also made signs as if he would gladly return to land, but the sea was so furious that he could not use his oars.

Suddenly there came a mighty wave, and the little boat disappeared. They waited to see it afloat once more, but they never saw it again.

"The poor man!" said the fishermen who were gathered on the beach; and murmuring a prayer they turned to go to their homes.

Suddenly there was a desperate shout, and turning to

look they saw a boy throw himself into the sea from the top of a high rock, crying:

"I will save my father!"

Pinocchio, being made of wood, floated easily and swam like a fish. They saw him disappear under the water, and reappear to be beaten about by the waves. Now a leg appeared, now an arm at a great distance from land, and at last they lost sight of him altogether.

"Poor boy!" said the fishermen who were gathered on the beach; and murmuring a prayer went back to their homes.

Chapter Twenty-Four

Pinocchio Arrives at Busy-Bee Island and Finds the Fairy

INSPIRED by the hope of arriving in time to save his poor father, Pinocchio swam all that night.

And what a terrible night it was! Floods of rain, hailstones, fearful thunderclaps, and flashes of lightning that made the world as bright as day.

Towards morning he saw not far off a long strip of land. It was an island in the midst of the ocean.

He put forth every effort to reach the shore, but all in vain. The tumbling waves tossed him back and forth as if he were straw or chaff. At last, luckily for him, there came a monstrous wave which picked him up and threw him violently on the beach.

He struck the earth so hard that all his ribs and joints rattled; but he comforted himself by saying:

"That was another narrow escape!"

Little by little the clouds disappeared, the sun shone forth in all his splendour, and the sea became as smooth as oil.

The marionette spread his clothes to dry in the sun, and began to look in every direction over that immense waste of waters to see if there was anywhere a tiny boat with a little man in it. But although he looked and looked he saw only the sky and the sea, and the sails of some ships, so far away that they looked like flies.

"If I only knew the name of this island!" he said. "If I only knew whether it is inhabited by well-bred people, who are not in the habit of hanging boys on trees! Is there no one of whom I could inquire?"

The idea of being alone, all alone in an uninhabited country made him so melancholy that he was just going to cry when he saw a large fish close to the shore, swimming along about his business, with his head out of the water.

Since he did not know his name, he cried as loud as he could:

"Hallo, Mr. Fish, may I say a word to you?"

"Two of them," replied the fish, who was such a very polite dolphin that there were few like him in all the seas of the world.

"Will you be so kind as to tell me if there are places in this island where one may eat, without danger of being eaten?"

"Certainly there are," replied the Dolphin; "there is one only a short distance from here."

"Which way shall I take to go there?"

"Take that little path on your left, and follow your nose. You can't make a mistake."

"Tell me something more. You swim in the sea all day

and all night: have you, perchance, seen a little boat with my father in it?"

"Who is your father?"

"He is the best father in the world; and I am the worst possible son."

"Considering the storm we had last night," said the Dolphin, "his boat was probably sunk."

"And my father?"

"By this time he must have been eaten by the terrible shark that has been spreading death and destruction in these waters for a long time."

"Is he very big, this shark?" inquired Pinocchio, trembling with fright.

"*Is* he!" exclaimed the Dolphin. "Well, just to give you an idea, I will say that he is larger than a five-storey house, and his mouth is so wide and deep that it would easily hold a railway train, engine and all."

"Heavens above!" cried the terrified marionette and, hurrying into his clothes, he turned to the Dolphin saying: "Good-bye, Mr. Fish, pardon the trouble I have caused you, and a thousand thanks."

With these words he almost ran down the little path. At the least sound he turned quickly to look behind him, fearing to see that horrible shark as large as a five-storey house, and with a railway train in his mouth, coming after him.

He had travelled about half an hour when he came to Busy-Beeville. The streets were full of people hurrying back and forth on business, everybody had something to attend to; everybody was working; you could not have found an idler or a vagrant if you had searched with a lantern.

"I see," said that lazybones of a Pinocchio to himself, "this place will never do for me. I was not born to work."

By this time he was suffering dreadfully from hunger, for he had had nothing to eat for more than twenty-four hours, not even a dish of lettuce.

What could he do?

There were only two ways of getting something to eat: to ask for work, or to beg for a few pennies or a bit of bread.

He was ashamed to beg. His father had always taught him that only the aged and helpless have a right to beg. The poor in this world, those who really deserve to be helped and pitied, are those who by reason of old age or sickness are no longer able to earn their bread by their own labour. It is the duty of all others to work; and if they refuse to do so, and suffer hunger, so much the worse for them.

While Pinocchio hesitated, a man passed by, perspiring and panting, who was pulling alone, and with great difficulty, two carts loaded with coal.

Pinocchio judged by his countenance that he was a kind man; so he went up to him, and, casting his eyes downwards in shame, he said in a low tone:

"Will you please give me a penny, for I am dying of hunger."

"Not only one penny," replied the coal dealer, "but I will give you four, if you will help me to draw these loads of coal home."

"'I wonder at you!'" exclaimed the marionette indignantly. "Allow me to inform you that I am not a donkey!'"

"The better for you!" replied the coal dealer. "Then, my boy, if you are really dying of hunger, eat a couple of slices of your pride, and be careful not to have indigestion."

After a few minutes a bricklayer passed by, carrying a hod of cement on his shoulder.

"Kind sir, would you be so generous as to give me a penny to a poor boy who is starving?"

"Willingly: come with me and carry cement," replied the bricklayer, "and instead of one penny, I will give you five."

"But cement is so heavy," objected Pinocchio, "and I don't want to work."

"If you don't want to work, my boy, amuse yourself by being hungry, and much good may it do you."

In less than half an hour twenty people passed by, and Pinocchio begged of every one of them, but they all replied:

"Aren't you ashamed! Instead of begging on the street, go to work, and earn your bread!"

At last a kind little woman appeared carrying two pitchers of water.

"Kind lady, will you let me have a sip of water from your pitcher?" asked Pinocchio, who was burning with thirst.

"Yes, drink, my child," said the little woman, putting the pitchers on the ground.

When Pinocchio was as full as a sponge, he wiped his mouth and grumbled:

"Now I'm no longer thirsty! If I were only no longer hungry!"

When the good little woman heard these words she said quickly:

"If you will carry one of these pitchers home for me, I will give you a large slice of bread."

Pinocchio looked at the pitcher, and said neither yes nor no.

"And with the bread I will give you a fine dish of

cauliflower, seasoned with oil and vinegar," the good woman added.

Pinocchio looked at the pitcher again, but he did not say yes or no.

"And after the cauliflower I will give you some delicious pastry."

At this last temptation Pinocchio could resist no longer; he drew a long breath and said resolutely:

"Patience! I will carry the pitcher home for you."

The pitcher was very heavy, and the marionette's hands not being strong enough to hold it, he had to set it on his head.

When they arrived at her home the good woman placed Pinocchio at a little table already set, and put the bread, the cauliflower, and the pastry before him.

Pinocchio did not eat like a human being, but rather like a pig. His stomach was like a house that has been empty and tenantless for months.

Little by little the worst pangs of his hunger were appeased, and he raised his head to thank his benefactress. No sooner had he looked at her than he uttered a long "O-o-o-oh!" of astonishment, and sat as if turned to stone, with his eyes starting from his head, his fork in the air, and his mouth full of bread and cauliflower.

"Whatever is the matter with you?" said the good woman, laughing.

"It's because . . ." stammered Pinocchio, "it's because . . . because . . . you are like . . . you remind me of . . . yes, yes, the same voice . . . the same eyes . . . the same hair . . . you have blue hair, too, just like her! O dear Fairy, O dear Fairy, tell me, is it you? Is it really you? Don't make me cry any more! If only you knew! I have cried so much, I have suffered so much!"

As he said this, Pinocchio wept floods of tears and, falling on his knees before her, he threw his arms about that mysterious little woman.

CHAPTER TWENTY-FIVE

Pinocchio Promises the Fairy that he will be Good and Study, because he is Tired of being a Marionette and Wants to Become a Real Boy

AT first the little woman would not admit that she was the Fairy with the blue hair; but seeing that she had been recognised, and not wishing to continue the comedy any longer, she revealed herself, saying to Pinocchio:

"You rogue of a marionette, how did you recognise me?"

"It's because I love you so much that I knew you."

"Do you remember? I was a little girl when you left me, and now I am a woman. I could almost be your mother."

"I should like that so much; then instead of calling you my little sister, I could call you mamma. I have always wished that I had a mother like other boys! But how did you manage to grow so quickly?"

"That's a secret."

"Teach it to me: I would like to be a little bigger. Just look at me! I have never been more than knee-high."

"But you can't grow," replied the Fairy.

"Why not?"

"Because marionettes never grow. They are born

marionettes, they live marionettes, and they die marionettes."

"I am sick to death of always being a marionette!" cried Pinocchio, striking his wooden head. "It's about time I became a man, like other men!"

"If only you deserved it, you could become one."

"Truly? And what can I do to be worthy of becoming a man?"

"It's very easy: you begin by being a good boy."

"Oh! do you mean to say that I am not a good boy?"

"You are anything but a good boy! Good boys are obedient, and you . . ."

"I am never obedient," Pinocchio said to the Fairy.

"Good boys like to work and study, and you . . ."

"And I am a blockhead and a vagrant all the year round."

"Good boys always tell the truth . . ."

"And I always tell lies."

"Good boys like to go to school . . ."

"And school gives me a pain. But from this day forward I will lead a different life."

"Will you promise to do so?"

"Yes, I promise. I want to become a good boy, too, and be the consolation of my father. Where can my poor father be now?"

"I don't know."

"Will I ever be so fortunate as to see him again?"

"I hope so; yes, I am sure of it."

Pinocchio was so happy when he heard this that he grasped the Fairy's hands and kissed them, almost crazy with joy. Then looking up at her affectionately, he said:

"Tell me, Mamma, it wasn't true, then, that you were dead?"

"It seems not," replied the Fairy with a smile.

"If you only knew how sad I felt and how my heart ached when I read, HERE LIES . . ."

"I know, and that is why I forgave you. You were truly sorry, and then I knew that you had a good heart; and if a child has a good heart, even if he is mischievous and brought up badly, one can always hope that he will mend his ways. That is why I came here to look for you. I will be your mamma . . ."

"Oh, how splendid!" cried Pinocchio, jumping for joy.

"You will always obey me, and do as you are told."

"Oh, yes, yes, yes!"

"Tomorrow," added the Fairy, "you will begin by going to school."

Pinocchio became a little less joyful.

"Then you will choose some profession or trade, whichever you would like . . ."

Pinocchio looked straight at the Fairy and made a wry face.

"What are you muttering between your teeth?" inquired the Fairy indignantly.

"I was saying," grumbled Pinocchio, "that it seems to me it's too late now for me to go to school."

"No, indeed! Bear this well in mind: that it's never too late to study and get an education."

"But I don't want to learn any profession or trade . . ."

"Why not?"

"Because I don't like work."

"My child," said the Fairy, "those who talk in that way generally finish in a hospital, or in a prison. Remember this: that whether a man is born rich or poor, it is his duty to find something to do in this world; to busy himself about something. Woe to those who idle their time away! Idleness is a dreadful disease, of which one should be cured while still a child; if not, one never gets over it."

These words touched Pinocchio's heart. He lifted his head quickly and said to the Fairy:

"I will study, I will work. I will do everything you want me to, for I am sick of leading the life of a marionette. I want to become a real boy, cost what it may. You promised that I could, didn't you?"

"Yes, I promised, and now it depends on you."

CHAPTER TWENTY-SIX

Pinocchio Goes to the Seashore with his Schoolmates to See the Terrible Shark

THE very next day Pinocchio went to school. Imagine what those mischievous children did when they saw a marionette coming to school! They laughed as if they would never stop. First one and then another played some trick on him. They snatched his cap out of his hand, and pulled his jacket from behind. They tried to make a big moustache under his nose with ink, and finally they tried to tie strings to his hands and feet to make him dance.

Pinocchio pretended not to notice them at first, and attended to his own business; but at last he lost his patience, and turning on the worst of his tormentors he exclaimed menacingly:

"Be careful, boys! I didn't come here to play the clown for you. I respect others, and I want to be respected."

"Good for you, scallywag! You talk just like a book!" shouted the rogues, doubling up with laughter; and one of them, more impertinent than the rest, put out his hand to seize the marionette by the nose.

But he was not quick enough, for Pinocchio kicked his shins under the table.

"Oh, oh! what hard feet!" cried the boy, rubbing his aching shins.

"And what elbows! They're harder than his feet!" exclaimed another who had received a blow in the pit of his stomach in return for his unkind jokes.

After a few of these proofs of his ability to defend himself, Pinocchio won the esteem and goodwill of the whole school, and they became very fond of him.

Even the Master praised him, because he was attentive, studious, and intelligent. He was always the first at school, and the last to rise from his desk when school was out.

His only fault was that he made too many friends, and some of them were only too well known as scapegraces, who were unwilling to study. The Master warned him daily, and the kind Fairy never failed to say over and over:

"Be careful, Pinocchio, those bad schoolmates of yours will end by making you cease to love your books; they may even get you into trouble."

"Oh, there's no danger!" replied the marionette, shrugging his shoulders and touching his forehead with his finger as if to say: "There's so much good sense inside!"

Now it happened one day as he was on his way to school that he met some of these companions of his, who said:

"Have you heard the great news?"

"No."

"They say there's a shark in the sea as big as a mountain."

"Is it possible! What if it should be the same shark that I heard of the night my poor father was drowned?"

"We're going to the beach to see it. Won't you come too?"

"Not I! I want to go to school."

"What do you care for school? We can go to school tomorrow. What's one lesson more or less? We shall still be the same blockheads."

"But what will the Master say?"

"Let him say what he likes. That's what he is paid for, to find fault all the time."

"And my mamma?"

"Oh, she'll never find out!" replied those wicked boys.

"I know what I'll do," said Pinocchio; "I have certain reasons for wanting to see the shark, but I'll go to see him after school."

"You poor simpleton!" retorted one of the boys, "do you suppose a fish of that size will wait until you are ready to call on him? When he's tired of being in one place, he whisks away to another, and good night!"

"How long will it take to go to the beach?" asked the marionette.

"We can go and come back in an hour."

"Well, come on then, he who runs fastest is the best fellow!" cried Pinocchio.

At this declaration all those scamps ran off across the fields with their books and slates under their arms. Pinocchio was at their head; he ran as if he had wings on his feet.

From time to time he turned to tease his companions, who were a long way behind him; and when he saw them panting, exhausted, covered with dust, and with their tongues hanging out, he laughed heartily. The unhappy boy little knew at that moment what terrors and what dreadful disasters awaited him.

CHAPTER TWENTY-SEVEN

There is a Great Battle between Pinocchio and his Companions during which One of them is Wounded and Pinocchio is Arrested

WHEN he arrived at the seashore, Pinocchio looked quickly around, but he saw no shark. The sea was as smooth as a great mirror.

"Well, where's the shark?" he inquired, turning to his companions.

"Perhaps he has gone to breakfast," said one of them, laughing.

"Or perhaps he has gone to bed to take a nap," said another, laughing still louder.

Their silly answers and stupid laughter showed Pinocchio that it was all a practical joke, and that they had told him something that was not true. He was very angry, and he said indignantly:

"And now? Did you have any object in telling me that story about the shark?"

"Indeed we did!" the rogues replied in chorus.

"Well, what was it?"

"We wanted you to run away from school, and come with us. Aren't you ashamed to be so punctual and studious every day? Aren't you ashamed to study so hard?"

"And what business is it of yours how hard I study?"

"It certainly is our business, for you make us cut a sorry figure before the Master."

"Why?"

"Because boys who study always make those who don't, like us, cut a poor figure; and we don't like to cut a poor figure. We have some pride, too."

"What can I do to satisfy you?"

"You must do as we do, and hate the school, and the lessons, and the Master: our three greatest enemies."

"And suppose I choose to keep on studying at school?"

"Then we will have nothing more to do with you, and at the very first chance we'll get even with you!"

"Really, you make me laugh," said the marionette, shaking his head.

"Be careful, Pinocchio," said one of the largest boys, walking towards him. "Don't think you can bully us; don't think you can crow over us. If you aren't afraid of us, we're not afraid of you. Remember that you are alone, and there's seven of us!"

"Seven, like the mortal sins," exclaimed Pinocchio, laughing boldly.

"Did you hear that? He has insulted all of us. He has called us the seven mortal sins!"

"Pinocchio, beg our pardon, or it will be the worse for you!"

"Coo-coo!" said the marionette, tapping his nose with his forefinger, derisively.

"Pinocchio, you'll be sorry!"

"Coo-coo!"

"We'll beat you like a dog!"

"Coo-coo!"

92

"You'll go home with a broken nose!"

"Coo-coo!"

"I'll give you 'Coo-coo!'" cried the most daring of those bullies; "take this on account, and keep it for supper."

With this, he gave him a blow on the head.

But it was, as we say, charge and counter-charge, for the marionette, as was to be expected, replied with another blow, and in a moment the combat became general and furious.

Although Pinocchio was alone, he defended himself like a hero. His hard wooden feet worked so fast that his enemies were kept at a respectful distance. Wherever those feet touched they left a black-and-blue mark that would not be soon forgotten.

Then these bad boys, angry because they could not get near Pinocchio, began to throw things at him. They unstrapped their schoolbooks, and began to throw their primers and grammars and other schoolbooks. But the marionette's sharp eyes kept such a good look-out, and he dodged so quickly, that the books all flew over his head into the sea.

What do you suppose the fishes did? They thought those books were something to eat, and they came to the surface in shoals; but no sooner had they tasted a page or two, or a frontispiece, than they spat it out again with a grimace which seemed to say: "We are accustomed to much better food than this!"

The battle was growing more furious when suddenly a large crab that had crawled out of the water up on to the beach croaked loudly in voice like that of a trombone with a cold:

"Stop it, you rascals! These schoolboys' battles always end badly. Someone is sure to be injured!"

Poor old Crab! He might as well have preached to the wind. Indeed that imp of a Pinocchio scowled back at him, and said rudely: "Shut up, you detestable Crab! You had much better be taking some lozenges to cure the cold in your throat. Go to bed, now, and take a sweat!"

Just then the boys, who had thrown away all their own, saw the marionette's books lying on the ground, and in less time than it takes to tell it they took possession of them.

Among these books there was a large one bound in paper, with sheepskin back and corners. It was a "Treatise on Arithmetic". I leave you to imagine how heavy it must have been!

One of those rogues seized this volume, and aiming at Pinocchio's head, he let it fly with all the force he could muster: but instead of hitting the marionette it struck one of his companions on the head. The child turned as white as a sheet, and crying out, "Oh, Mamma, help me, I am dying!" he fell his full length on the sandy beach.

At that, the frightened boys took to their legs, and in a few moments they were out of sight.

But Pinocchio remained there, and although he was more dead than alive himself from sorrow and fright, he soaked a handkerchief in the sea, and put it on the poor boy's temples, while he wept bitterly, calling him by name, and saying:

"Eugene, poor Eugene! Open your eyes and look at me! Why don't you answer me? It was not I who hurt you so! Believe me, it was not I! Open your eyes, Eugene. If you keep them closed, I shall die too. Alas! alas! how can I go back home? How can I have the courage to go back to my mother? What will become of me? Where shall I fly? Where can I hide myself? Oh, better, a thou-

94

sand times better, if I had gone to school! Why did I listen to evil companions? They will be my ruin! The Master told me so, and my mother said the same thing: 'Beware of evil companions!' But I am headstrong . . . and obstinate . . . I listen to all they say . . . and then do as I please! And afterwards I have to pay for it. It has been like that ever since I was born. I was never good for a quarter of an hour at a time. Oh, dear, oh, dear, what will become of me?"

Pinocchio was still crying, and moaning, striking himself on the head, and calling Eugene, when suddenly he heard footsteps approaching.

He turned. There were two policemen.

"What are you doing there on the ground?" they demanded.

"I was helping my schoolmate."

"Is anything the matter with him?"

"I think so."

"I should think so, indeed!" said one of the policemen, bending over Eugene and looking at him closely. "This boy is wounded on the temple; who has done this?"

"Not I," stammered Pinocchio, who was so frightened he could hardly breathe.

"If it was not you, who was it, then?"

"Not I," repeated Pinocchio.

"With what was he wounded?"

"With this book."

The marionette picked up the "Treatise on Arithmetic" bound in paper and sheepskin, and showed it to the policeman.

"Whose book is this?"

"Mine."

"That's enough. I don't need to know anything more. Get up quickly, and come with us."

"But I . . ."

"Come along!"

"But I am innocent . . ."

"Come along!"

Before leaving the spot the policemen called some fishermen who were rowing by close to the shore, and said to them:

"We will leave this wounded boy with you. Take him home and care for him. We will come back tomorrow."

Then they turned to Pinocchio, and placing him between them they said in military accents: "Forward! and step lively! If you don't so much the worse for you!"

Without waiting for them to repeat it, the marionette started down the path that led to the village. The poor fellow did not know wether he was awake or dreaming; however, he thought he must be dreaming a dreadful dream. He was almost beside himself with shame and despair. His eyes saw double, his legs trembled under him, his tongue stuck to the roof of his mouth, so that he could not say a word. Yet in the midst of his stupefacation and bewilderment one thought pierced his heart like a sword: the thought that he would have to pass under the kind Fairy's window between two policemen. He would rather have died.

They were just entering the village when a gust of wind blew off Pinocchio's cap, and carried it some ten paces away.

"Will you permit me to go and get my cap?" asked Pinocchio of the policemen.

"Yes, go, but be quick about it."

The marionette picked up his cap, but instead of placing it on his head, he put it between his teeth, and then began to run with all his might towards the sea. He went as if he had been shot out of a gun.

Seeing that it would be difficult to catch him, the policemen sent a great mastiff after him, that had won the first prize in all the dog races. Pinocchio ran, but the mastiff ran faster. The people all came to the window, or rushed into the street to see the end of that wild race. But they never saw it, for Pinocchio and the mastiff raised such a dust that in a few moments it was not possible to see anything.

Chapter Twenty-Eight

Pinocchio is in Danger of being Fried like a Fish

DURING this desperate race there came a terrible moment when Pinocchio felt himself lost, for you must know that Alidoro (that was the mastiff's name) had almost come up to him.

The marionette could hear the dreadful beast panting close behind him, and he even felt his hot breath.

Luckily, he was by this time, close to the beach, and it was only a few steps to the sea.

As soon as he reached the shore the marionette gave a great leap, just like a frog, and fell far out in the water. Alidoro would have stopped, but he was going so fast that he shot out into the water, too. Unfortunately he did not know how to swim, and he began to paw wildly, trying to keep his nose above water; but the harder he tried, the more he went under.

When he came to the surface his eyes were almost starting out of his head. He barked and yelped:

97

D

"I'm drowning! ! I'm drowning!"

"Drown then," replied Pinocchio, who was now far away and out of all danger.

"Help me, Pinocchio, save my life!"

At that cry of despair the marionette, who at the bottom had a very kind heart, had pity on him, and turning to the dog, he said:

"If I save your life, will you promise not to bother me or run after me any more?"

"I promise! I promise! Be quick, for pity's sake! Another half-minute and I shall be drowned."

Pinocchio hesitated an instant, but, remembering that his father had told him many times, that one never loses by doing a good deed, he swam to Alidoro, and taking him by the tail with both hands, he pulled him safe and sound to dry land.

The poor dog could not stand on his feet. He had drunk, in spite of himself, so much salt water that he had swelled up like a balloon. However, the marionette did not dare to trust him too far, so he thought it might be better to throw himself into the sea again. As he swam away he called to the friend he had rescued:

"Good-bye, Alidoro, a good journey to you, and give my love to the folks at home."

"Good-bye, Pinocchio," replied the dog, " a thousand thanks for saving me from death. You have done me a great kindness, and in this world one good turn deserves another. If you should ever need me, I will not fail you."

Pinocchio continued to swim, but he kept near the shore until at last he thought he had reached a safe place. Looking at the beach he saw a sort of grotto in the rock, from which issued a long column of smoke.

"There must be a fire in that grotto," he said to himself. "So much the better! I can warm and dry myself . . . and then? And then we shall see what next."

Having made this decision he drew near the rocky shore. But just as he was climbing out, he felt something under the water rising, rising, rising, until it lifted him out on the beach. He tried to run away, but it was too late, for, to his great astonishment, he found himself inside a big net, and in the midst of a multitude of fish of every shape and size, that were flapping and jumping as if they were crazy.

And at the same time he saw, coming out of the grotto, a frightful fisherman, who was so ugly that he looked like some marine monster. Instead of hair, a bush thickly covered with green leaves grew on his head. His skin was green, his eyes were green, and his long beard that almost touched the ground was green. He looked like a great green lizard standing on his hind legs.

When the fisherman had drawn the net out of the sea, he cried joyfully:

"Thank providence! I shall have a finer dinner of fish today!"

"It's lucky for me that I'm not a fish," said Pinocchio to himself, plucking up a little courage.

The net full of fish was carried into the grotto. It was a dark, smoky grotto, and in the middle of it there was a big frying-pan full of hot oil, which smelled like a stuffed-out candle, and nearly took one's breath away.

"Now, let's see what sort of fish we've caught!" said the green fisherman, and, putting one of his big, misshapen hands, which looked like shovels, into the net, he drew out a handful of mullet.

"These mullet will be good!" he said, looking at them, and smelling them contentedly; then he threw them into a tub without any water in it.

He repeated this operation many times; and as he drew

out the fish his mouth began to water, and he jumped for joy, saying:

"These haddock will be good!"

"These whiting will be exquisite!"

"These sole will be delicious!"

"These sea spiders will be excellent!"

"These anchovies will be fine, head and all!"

As you may imagine the haddock, the whiting, the sole, the sea spiders, and the anchovies all went together into the tub, to keep the mullet company.

The last one to come out of the net was Pinocchio.

When the fisherman pulled him out, he opened his green eyes wide in astonishment, and cried, almost in a fright:

"What sort of fish is this? I have never eaten a fish like this!"

After turning him over and over, and examining him carefully, he finished by saying:

"I see· this must be a sea crab."

"What do you mean by calling me a crab? This is a nice way to treat me! Let me tell you, for your information, that I am a marionette!"

"A marionette?" said the fisherman. "To tell you the truth, a marionette fish is a new one for me. All the better! I shall eat you with the greatest of pleasure!"

"Eat me? Can't you understand that I am not a fish? Don't you see that I can talk and reason as you do?"

"That's very true," replied the fisherman, "and since I see that you are a fish that can speak and reason like me, I will treat you with great consideration."

"And what may that mean?"

"As a token of friendship and particular esteem, I will let you decide how you shall be cooked. Would you like to be fried in oil, or would you prefer to be cooked in the stewpan with tomato sauce?"

"To tell the truth," replied Pinocchio, "if I must choose, I would prefer to be set free, so that I can go home."

"You're joking! Do you think that I will lose this chance to taste such a rare fish? It doesn't happen every day that one catches a marionette fish. Leave it to me: I will fry you in the pan with all the other fish, and you will be quite content. To be fried in company is always a consolation."

On hearing this, the unhappy Pinocchio cried and screamed, and begged for mercy, sobbing: "How much better it would have been if I had gone to school! Oh! Oh! Oh!" And because he squirmed like an eel, and put forth all his strength trying to escape from his claws, the green fisherman took a big bulrush, and after binding him hand and foot like a sausage, he threw him into the tub with the others.

Then he got a wooden keg full of flour, and began to roll all the fish in it; and as fast as he had floured them well he threw them into the frying-pan.

The first to dance in the boiling oil were the poor haddock: then came the spider crabs, the whiting, the sole, and the anchovies; and then it was Pinocchio's turn, who, when he saw himself so near death, and such a terrible death, trembled so much, and was so dreadfully afraid that he could no longer find breath to beg for mercy.

The poor boy could only implore with his eyes; but the green fisherman, without even looking at him, rolled him over five or six times in the flour, covering him so completely that he looked like a plaster marionette.

Then he took him by the head and . . .

CHAPTER TWENTY-NINE

Pinocchio Returns to the Fairy's House: she Promises him that the Next Day he Will no longer Be a Marionette, but a Real Boy: Grand Breakfast of Coffee and Cream to Celebrate the Coming Event

JUST as the fisherman was about to drop Pinocchio into the frying-pan, a large dog came into the grotto, drawn there by the delicious, penetrating odour of the frying fish.

"Get out!" cried the fisherman, menacing him, and still holding the floury marionette in his hand.

But the poor dog was almost starved. He howled, and wagged his tail as if to say:

"Just give me one mouthful, and I'll go away."

"Get out, I tell you!" repeated the fisherman, drawing back his foot to kick him.

But the dog was so hungry that he was determined not to be kicked out, and he growled at the fisherman, showing his sharp teeth.

Just then a faint little voice was heard saying:

"Save me, Alidoro, if you don't save me I shall be fried!"

The dog instantly recognised Pinocchio's voice, and he was amazed to see that it came from that floury bundle that the fisherman held in his hand.

What did he do then? He jumped high in the air,

seized the bundle, and holding it carefully between his teeth ran out of the grotto and away like the wind.

The fisherman was frightfully angry to see the fish that he was so eager to taste snatched away from him, and he ran after the dog; but he had run only a little way when he had a violent fit of coughing, and had to go back home.

When Alidoro came to the path that led to the village, he stopped and put Pinocchio down gently on the ground.

"How can I ever thank you?" said the marionette.

"You need not thank me," replied the dog; "you saved my life, and one good turn deserves another. You know we must all help each other in this world."

"How did you happen to come to the grotto?"

"I was lying on the beach more dead than alive, when the wind brought me the odour of frying fish. If it had been a moment later . . ."

"Don't speak of it!" exclaimed Pinocchio, who was still trembling with fear. "Don't speak of it! If you had come a moment later, I should be, at this very instant, fried, and eaten, and digested. Br-r-r-r! It makes me shiver to think of it!"

Alidoro laughed and held out his right paw to the marionette, who grasped it and pressed it hard, as a sign of friendship, and then they parted.

The dog went home; but when Pinocchio was alone he went to a little cabin nearby where an old man was sunning himself at the door, and said:

"Tell me, kind sir, do you know anything about a poor boy named Eugene who was wounded on the head?"

"Some fishermen brought him here to this cabin, but now . . ."

"Now he is dead!" Pinocchio interrupted sadly.

103

"No, he is alive, and has gone back home."

"Truly? Truly?" cried the marionette, jumping for joy. "So then his wound wasn't serious?"

"It might have been serious; it might even have killed him," replied the old man, "for they threw a large bound book at his head."

"Who threw it?"

"One of his schoolmates, a certain Pinocchio."

"Who is this Pinocchio?" inquired the marionette, as if he had never heard of him.

"They say he's a very bad boy, a vagabond, and a perfect scallywag."

"Slanders! All slanders!"

"Do you know this Pinocchio?"

"I know him by sight," replied the little marionette.

"And what do you think of him?" asked the old man.

"I think he is a very good boy who loves to study, who is obedient, and who loves his father and his family."

While the marionette was telling all these bold-faced lies, he happened to touch his nose, and seeing that it had grown several inches, he cried in fright:

"No, kind sir, don't believe what I have told you! I know Pinocchio very well, and I assure you that he really is a very bad boy. He is a laggard, and disobedient, and instead of going to school he spends his time with evil companions."

As soon as he had said this, his nose grew shorter, and became as it was at first.

"Why are you so white?" asked the old man suddenly.

"I'll tell you. Without noticing it I rubbed against a wall that had just been whitewashed," replied the marionette, for he was ashamed to confess that he had been rolled in flour like a fish, in order to be fried.

"But what has become of your jacket, and your trousers, and your cap? What have you done with them?"

"I met thieves, and they robbed me of my clothes. Tell me, kind sir, do you happen to have some old clothes you could give me, so that I can go home?"

"My child, I have nothing but a little bag in which I keep beans; if you want that, take it: there it is."

Pinocchio didn't think twice, but he took the little bean bag, which was empty, and after cutting a hole in the bottom with scissors, and one on each side for his arms, he put it on like a little shirt. And in that excuse for clothes he started home.

But as he went along he began to feel very uneasy. He took one step forward, and then one backwards, as he said to himself:

"How can I show myself to that kind Fairy? What will she say when she sees me? Will she forgive this second offence? I don't believe she will; oh, I'm sure she will not. And it will serve me right, for I am a bad boy, always promising to do better, and never keeping my word."

He arrived in the village after dark, and because it was a stormy night, and the rain was coming down in bucketfuls, he went straight to the Fairy's house, resolved to knock at the door and ask for shelter.

But when he came to the door he was afraid to knock, and ran back a little way; he came up to the door a second time, but he could not bring himself to knock; a third time, it was just the same: the fourth time he took hold of the iron knocker and let it fall very lightly, trembling as he did so.

He waited and waited, and at last, after half an hour, a window on the top floor was opened (the house had four floors) and a big snail with a tiny light on her head looked out, and said:

"Who is it, at this hour?"

"Is the Fairy at home?" asked Pinocchio.

"The Fairy is asleep and does not want to be disturbed! But who are you?"

"I am I."

"I? Who is I?"

"Pinocchio."

"Who is Pinocchio?"

' "The marionette who lives with the Fairy."

"Ah! I see," said the Snail; "wait for me. I will come down at once and open the door."

"Hurry, for pity's sake, I am dying of cold!"

"My son, I am a Snail, and Snails are never in a hurry."

An hour passed, two hours, and the door was not opened; so Pinocchio, who was shaking with cold and fright and dampness, plucked up his courage and knocked once more, a little louder.

At this a window opened on the third floor. and the same Snail looked out.

"Kind Snail," cried Pinocchio from the street, "I have been waiting two hours! And two hours in this horrid weather are longer than two years. Hurry up, for mercy's sake!!"

"My son," said that sluggish, peaceful Snail, "my son, I am a Snail, and Snails are never in a hurry."

And the window on the third floor was closed.

Not long after the village clock struck midnight; then one o'clock, two o'clock, and the door was still closed.

Finally Pinocchio lost his patience. He seized the knocker in a rage, and was about to strike a blow that would shake the whole house, when suddenly the iron knocker turned into a live eel, slipped out of his hands, and disappeared in the rivulets of water that were running in the street.

"Oh, ho!" shouted Pinocchio, boiling over with rage, "if the knocker has run away, I will kick the door down!"

And drawing back, he let fly a furious kick against the door. He kicked so hard that half his foot went through the door, and when he tried to pull it back, it was impossible. His foot was stuck in the door as firmly as a nail that has been driven in and clinched.

Imagine poor Pinocchio now! He had to pass all the rest of the night with one foot on the ground, and the other in the door.

Finally, at daybreak, the door was opened. That obliging Snail had spent only nine hours coming down from the fourth story to the street door. She must have been all of a lather!

"What are you doing there, with your foot sticking in the door?" she inquired, laughing.

"It was an accident. Won't you please see, kind Snail, if you can free me from this torment?"

"My son, this is a case for a carpenter, and I have never been a carpenter."

"Beg the Fairy to help me."

"The Fairy is sleeping, and does not want to be disturbed."

"But what am I going to do all day, riveted to this door?"

"You can amuse yourself by counting the ants that crawl by."

"At least bring me something to eat, for I am faint with hunger."

"Immediately!" said the Snail.

In fact three hours and a half later Pinocchio saw her coming back with a tray on her head. There was bread, a roast chicken, and four ripe apricots.

"Here is the breakfast the Fairy sends you," said the Snail.

At the sight of all those good things the marionette was quite consoled. But how great was his disappointment, when he began to eat, to discover that the bread was plaster, the chicken was made of paper, and the four apricots of alabaster, coloured to look like fruit.

He wanted to weep, to resign himself to despair, to throw away the tray and all that was on it; instead, whether because of his grief, or the great weakness he felt in his stomach, the fact is that he fainted away.

When he came to himself he was lying on a sofa, and the Fairy was bending over him.

"I will forgive you just once more," said the Fairy, "but woe betide you if you do wrong again."

Pinocchio promised and vowed that he would study, and always be good; and he kept his word all the rest of the year. He stood first in the examinations, and was called the best scholar in the school. His conduct in general was so satisfactory and praiseworthy, that the Fairy was greatly pleased, and said:

"Tomorrow your desires shall finally be granted."

"Do you mean . . . ?"

"Tomorrow you shall cease to be a wooden marionette, and become a real boy."

No one who did not see Pinocchio at the moment when he received this longed-for announcement can imagine his joy. All his friends and classmates were invited to the Fairy's house the next day, for a grand breakfast to celebrate the wonderful event. The Fairy prepared two hundred cups of coffee with cream, and four hundred rolls, buttered on both sides. The day promised to be a most happy and joyful one, but . . .

Most unfortunately, in the lives of marionettes there is always a *but* that spoils everything.

CHAPTER THIRTY

Pinocchio Listens to his Friend Lampwick, who is Going to Toyland...

As was to be expected, Pinocchio asked the Fairy's permission to go around the village and invite his friends for the next day. The Fairy said:

"Yes, indeed, go and invite all your friends for breakfast, but remember to come home before dark. Do you understand?"

"I promise to be back in an hour," said the marionette.

"Be careful, Pinocchio; it's very easy for children to promise, but not so easy for them to keep their promises."

"But I am not like other children; when I say a thing, I do it."

"We shall see. If you disobey me, the worse for you."

"Why?"

"Because children who do not listen to those who are wiser than they are always come to grief."

"And I have proved it!" said Pinocchio; "but I shall never be naughty again."

"We shall see if that is true."

The marionette said no more, but kissed the kind

Fairy, who was a sort of a mother to him, and ran out of the house singing and dancing.

In less than an hour all his friends had been invited. Some of them accepted immediately with great pleasure; others, on principle waited to be urged; but when they learned that the rolls which were to be dipped in the coffee and cream would be buttered on both sides, they all said: "Yes, we'll come too, just to please you."

Now I must tell you that Pinocchio had among his schoolmates one of whom he was especially fond. His name was Romeo, but everybody called him by his nickname of "Lampwick", because he was so thin, and long, and flabby just like a new lampwick.

Lampwick was the laziest and most mischievous boy in the school, but Pinocchio was very fond of him. In fact, he went to his home first of all, but he was not there. He went back again, but no Lampwick; a third time, but in vain.

Wherever could he be? He searched high and low, and finally found him hiding under the porch of a farmer's house.

"What in the world are you doing there?" inquired Pinocchio, crawling under the porch.

"I'm waiting for midnight, when I'm going away."

"Where are you going?"

"Far, far away."

"I went to your house three times looking for you."

"What do you want of me?"

"Haven't you heard the great news? Don't you know of the good fortune that's coming to me?"

"What?"

"Tomorrow I shall stop being a marionette, and become a boy like you, and like all the others."

"Much good may it do you!"

"And tomorrow morning I shall expect you at my house for breakfast."

"But didn't I tell you that I am going away tonight?"

"At what time?"

"At midnight."

"Where are you going?"

"I'm going to live in a place—the most beautiful place in the world—a perfect paradise!"

"What is the name of it?"

"It's called Toyland. Why don't you come too?"

"I? No, indeed!"

"You're making a mistake, Pinocchio! Believe me, if you don't come you will regret it. Where could you find a place better suited to us boys? There's no school there, and no masters, and no books. In that blessed place no one ever studies. There's no school on Saturday; and every week is composed of six Saturdays, and one Sunday. Just imagine! The autumn holidays begin in January, and last until the thirty-first of December. Now that's a place where I would really like to live! That's how all the civilised countries should be!"

"But how do they pass the time in Toyland?"

"They play and amuse themselves from morning till night. Then they go to bed, and begin over again in the morning. What do you think of that?"

"Ummm!" said Pinocchio, and he wagged his head as if to say: "That sort of life would suit me too."

"Now then, will you come with me? Yes, or no, make up your mind!"

"No, no, no, and no. I have promised the kind Fairy that I would be a good boy and I must keep my promise. In fact, I see it's nearly sunset, so I must leave you and hurry away. Good-bye, and a pleasant journey."

"Where are you going in such a hurry?"

"I'm going home. The kind Fairy wants me to come home before dark."

"Wait a little bit."

"I shall be too late."

"Just two minutes."

"And if the Fairy should scold me?"

"Let her scold. When she's done scolding, she'll stop," said that scamp of a Lampwick.

"How are you going? Alone, or is someone going with you?"

"Alone? There will be more than a hundred of us!"

"Are you going on foot?"

"A stagecoach is coming at midnight to take us to that glorious country."

"What wouldn't I give if it were midnight now!"

"And why?"

"So that I could see you all go off together."

"Stay a little longer, and you can see us."

"No, no, I must go home."

"Just wait only two more minutes." Lampwick pleaded.

"I have waited too long now. The Fairy will be worrying about me."

"Poor Fairy! Is she afraid the bats will eat you?"

"And so," continued Pinocchio, "are you perfectly certain there are no schools in that country?"

"Not a sign of one!"

"And no masters?"

"Not one."

"And no one has to study?"

"Never, never, never!"

"What a wonderful country!" sighed Pinocchio. His mouth watered just to think of it. "What a wonderful country! Of course I've never been there, but I can imagine what it must be like."

"Why don't you come too?"

"It's useless to tempt me. I have promised my kind Fairy that I would be a sensible boy, and I don't propose to break my word."

"Well, good-bye then, and give my love to all the grammar schools, and to all the high schools, too, if you meet them on the way."

"Good-bye, Lampwick; a pleasant journey to you. Have a fine time, and remember your friends once in a while."

Saying this, the marionette took a few steps as if to leave him; then stopped and turning to his friend he inquired:

"Are you perfectly certain that all the weeks are composed of six Saturdays and one Sunday in that country?"

"Absolutely."

"Are you perfectly certain that holidays begin on the first of January, and last until the thirty-first of December?"

"Perfectly certain."

"What a wonderful country!" said Pinocchio again, smacking his lips in a transport of delight.

Then summoning all his resolution, he added hastily:

"Well, good-bye for the last time, and a good journey to you!"

"Good-bye for the last time to you, Pinocchio."

"How long before you leave?"

"About two hours."

"Too bad! If it were only one hour, I might, perhaps, wait to see you off."

"And the Fairy?"

"I have waited so long already, that an hour more or less wouldn't matter."

"Poor Pinocchio! And what if the Fairy should scold you?"

"Never mind! I would let her scold; when she's done scolding she'll stop."

By this time it was very dark. Suddenly, far away, they saw a little light moving, and heard bells tinkling and the tooting of a tiny horn very faint and low, like the hum of a bee.

"There it is!" exclaimed Lampwick, jumping to his feet.

"What is it?" said Pinocchio in a low tone.

"It's the stagecoach coming to get me. Do you want to go too? Yes, or no?"

"But is it actually true," demanded the marionette, "that children never have to study in that country?"

"Never, never, never!"

"What a wonderful country! What a wonderful country! What a wonderful country!"

CHAPTER THIRTY-ONE

Instead of Becoming a Real Boy, Pinocchio Steals Away to Toyland where he Spends Five Months of Paradise

AT last the stagecoach arrived; and it drove up without making the least noise, for the wheels were wound with rags and tow.

It was drawn by twelve pairs of donkeys, all of the same size, but different colours.

Some were grey, some white, some spotted, and some were yellow and blue in broad stripes.

But the strangest thing about them was that these twelve pairs, or twenty-four donkeys, instead of being shod like most other animals, wore men's boots of white calfskin.

And the driver?

Imagine a little man broader than he is long, soft and oily as a butterball, with a little face like a red apple, a little mouth that is always laughing, and a soft, caressing voice like that of a cat that is mewing for cream.

All the boys fell in love with him as soon as they saw him; and they all scrambled to get in first, and go with him to that delightful country which is known on the map by the enticing name of Toyland.

Indeed the stagecoach was already full of boys between eight and twelve years of age, huddled together like so many sardines. They were so crowded and uncomfortable that they could hardly breathe, but no one said *ouch!* no one complained. The consolation of knowing that in a few hours they would be in a country where there were no books, or schools, or masters, made them feel resigned to anything. They were so happy that they were neither uncomfortable, nor weary, nor hungry, nor thirsty, nor sleepy.

As soon as the stagecoach stopped, the little man turned to Lampwick, and with a thousand bows and grimaces, said with the sweetest of smiles:

"Tell me, my fine boy, would you like to go to that happy country?"

"Certainly, I want to go."

"But you see, my dear, there is no more room, the coach is full."

"Never mind," replied Lampwick, "if there's no more room inside, I can ride on the swingle-tree."

And he jumped up astride of the swingle-tree.

"And you, my love," said the little man, looking admiringly at Pinocchio, "what are you going to do? Are you coming with us, or staying behind?"

"I remain here," replied Pinocchio, "I am going home. I want to study and be a good scholar, like all well-brought-up boys."

"Much good it may do you!"

"Pinocchio," cried Lampwick, "listen to me: come with us, we will be so happy."

"No, no, no!"

"Come away with us, we will all be so happy!" cried a few voices inside the stagecoach.

"Come with us, we will all be so happy," shouted a hundred voices together.

"If I should come with you, what would my good Fairy say?"

"Don't worry yourself about that. Only remember that we are going to a country where we shall do nothing but frolic from morning till night."

Pinocchio did not reply: he only sighed; he sighed a second time; a third. At last he said:

"Make a little room for me: I will come too."

"Everything is full," replied the little man, "but to show you how glad I am that you are coming with me, I will give you my place."

"What will you do?"

"I will walk."

"No, really, I can't let you do that. I would rather ride on one of the donkeys!" cried Pinocchio.

So saying he went up to the right wheeler, and made as if to jump on his back, but the beast whirled and kicked him in the stomach, sending him flying with his legs in the air.

Imagine, if you can, how all those impertinent boys nearly burst themselves laughing.

But the little man did not laugh. He just went up to that donkey, and pretending to give him a kiss, he bit off half of his right ear.

While he was doing this, Pinocchio, who was very angry at the treatment he had received, jumped up from the ground, and with one leap was on the donkey's back. It was such a splendid jump that all the boys stopped laughing, and shouted, "Hurray for Pinocchio!" and clapped their hands as if they would never stop.

But all of a sudden the donkey kicked so high with both of his hind legs that he threw the poor marionette off on to a pile of stones.

The boys began to laugh at him again; but the little man, instead of laughing, went to the other side of that fractious animal, and bit half of his left ear clean off. Then he said to the marionette:

"Now get on his back, and don't be afraid. That donkey is as obstinate as a mule; but I've put a flea in his ear, and I think he'll behave himself now."

Pinocchio mounted again, and the stagecoach began to move; but while the donkeys galloped along, and the coach rolled over the paving-stones, he thought he heard a voice which was so low that he could barely make out the words, saying:

"You poor simpleton! You are determined to do as you please, but you will be sorry for it!"

Pinocchio was frightened, and he looked around him to see where these words came from, but there was nothing to be seen. The donkeys galloped along, the stagecoach rolled over the stones, and the boys inside slept. Lampwick snored like a trooper, and the little man sang through his teeth:

"Everyone sleeps all through the night,
While I, never sleep . . ."

They had gone only a little way farther when Pinocchio heard the low voice again saying:

"Remember this, you little blockhead, boys who will not study, and who turn their backs on their school, and their books, and their masters, always come to a bad end. I have tried it, and I know what I am talking about. The day will come when you will weep as I do now, but then it will be too late! "

When he heard these whispered words, the marionette was more frightened than ever. He jumped down from the donkey's back, and took him by the bridle.

Imagine his surprise when he saw that the donkey was crying, and crying just like a child!

"Hallo, little man," Pinocchio called to the driver. "do you know what's happening? This donkey is crying."

" Let him cry! He can laugh on the thirty-first of June."

"Did you teach him to speak?"

"No, he taught himself to mumble a few words; he was in a company of trained dogs for three years."

"Poor beast!"

"Come, come," said the little man, "don't waste time watching a donkey cry. Get on his back again, and let us go. The night is chilly, and the way is long."

Pinocchio did as he was told, without another word. The stagecoach rolled along once more, and at daybreak the next morning they reached Toyland, safe and sound.

Toyland was like no other country in the world. The entire population consisted of children. The eldest were fourteen, and the youngest barely eight years old. The clamour and shouting and hullabaloo in the streets were enough to drive one crazy.

There were swarms of children everywhere. Some were playing skittles; others were playing quoits, or rounders; some were riding bicycles or wooden horses; others were playing blind-man's buff, or tig; some of them, dressed as clowns, were eating burning tow; some were playing comedies, or singing, or turning somersaults in the air; others were walking on their hands, while still others were rolling hoops, or, dressed like generals, were marching along with paper helmets on their heads, and squadrons of toy soldiers. They were hallooing and laughing, and shouting; some were clapping their hands; some were whistling; some were cackling like a hen that has laid an egg; in short, there was such a chattering, such a pandemonium, such a wild tumult, that it would have made you deaf, unless you had put cotton wool in your ears. There were little theatres in every open space which were crowded all the day long; and on all the walls of the houses refined remarks like the following had been scrawled with coal; "Hurrah for Toiland!" (instead of Toyland). "We want no more scools!" (instead of schools). "Down with Arit Metick!" (instead of arithmetic); and many more fine sayings like these.

As soon as they set foot inside the city, Lampwick and all the other boys who had come with the little man hurried to join these children, and in a few minutes, as you may well suppose, they had made friends with them all. Who could be more happy and contented than they were?

In the midst of continual amusement and all sorts of pastimes, the hours and days and weeks passed like lightning.

119

"Oh, what a glorious life!" exclaimed Pinocchio, every time he happened to run across Lampwick.

"Do you see now that I was right?" replied Lampwick. "And to think that you didn't want to come! To think that you were going to go back home to your Fairy, and waste your time in study! If you are free today from bothersome books and schools, you owe it to me, to my advice, to my anxiety for your welfare. Isn't that so? It's only a true friend who would do you such a kindness."

"Yes, that's so, Lampwick! If I am today a perfectly contented boy it's all owing to you. And do you know what the Master used to say to me about you? He always said: 'Don't have anything to do with that good-for-nothing Lampwick; he is a bad boy, and he will get you into trouble.'"

"Poor old Master!" replied the other, shaking his head. "I know only too well that he didn't like me, and enjoyed speaking ill of me; but I am generous, and I forgive him!"

"You noble boy!" said Pinocchio, embracing his friend affectionately, and kissing him on the bridge of his nose.

Five months had passed away in this paradise of playthings and amusements which occupied the whole of the day, without even looking a book in the face, or seeing so much as the outside of a school, when Pinocchio, on waking up one morning, had a most unpleasant surprise and quite lost his good spirits.

CHAPTER THIRTY-TWO

Pinocchio Grows Donkey's Ears and then Becomes a Real Donkey and Begins to Bray

AND what was this surprise?

I will tell you, my dear readers: The surprise was that Pinocchio when he woke up began, naturally, to scratch his head; and while he was doing this he . . .

Can you guess what he noticed?

He noticed, to his great astonishment, that his ears had grown several inches longer.

You know, marionettes, from their birth, have very, very small ears; so small that they are not visible to the naked eye. You can imagine, therefore, how startled he was when he became aware that his ears had grown so long during the night that they resembled two sweeping brushes.

He hurried in search of a mirror in order to see himself, but he could not find one: so he filled the hand-basin with water and looking into it saw what he would never in the world have wanted to see, he saw himself decorated with a magnificent pair of asses' ears.

I will leave you to imagine poor Pinocchio's sorrow, and shame and despair.

He began to cry, and scream, and beat his head against the wall, but the more he wept, the longer his ears grew, and they became hairy at the top.

A pretty little squirrel that lived on the floor above

him heard his piercing cries, and came down to see what the matter was; and seeing the marionette in such a state, she inquired anxiously:

"What is the matter, my dear neighbour?"

"I am sick. Oh, Squirrel, I am very sick, and of such a frightful disease. Do you know how to count one's pulse?"

"Yes, I believe so."

"Then, Squirrel, will you please see if I have a fever?"

The Squirrel put her right front paw on Pinocchio's wrist, and then said with a sigh:

"My friend, I am sorry, but I must give you bad news."

"What is it?"

"You have a raging fever."

"What kind of fever is it?"

"Donkey fever."

"I never heard of any such fever!" retorted the marionette, although he knew only too well what she meant.

"Then I will tell you about it," replied the Squirrel, "for you should know that in two or three hours you will no longer be a marionette, or a boy . . ."

"What will I be?"

"In two or three hours you will be a perfect donkey, like those that draw carts, and carry cabbages and herbs to market."

"Oh! Poor me! Poor me!" cried Pinocchio, seizing his ears with both hands, and twitching and jerking them angrily, as if they belonged to someone else.

"My dear," said the Squirrel by way of consolation, "what would you have? It is your destiny. For it is written in the decrees of Providence that all those lazy children who can't endure books, and schools, and amusements must finish, sooner or later, by becoming so many little donkeys."

"Is that really true?" sobbed the marionette.

"It's only too true! It's useless to weep now. You should have thought of that before it was too late."

"But it's not my fault: believe me, little Squirrel, it's all Lampwick's fault!"

"Who is this Lampwick?"

"One of my schoolmates. I wanted to go home; I wanted to be obedient; I wanted to study and do myself credit . . . but Lampwick said: 'Why do you bother about studying? Why in the world do you want to go to school? Instead, come with me to Toyland: there we will never study any more; we will play from morning to night, and always be happy!' "

"Why did you take the advice of that false friend? Of that bad companion?"

"Because . . . because, dear little Squirrel, I am a heartless marionette, without any sense. Oh, if I had the least bit of heart, I should never have abandoned that kind Fairy who loved me like a mother, and who had done so much for me! . . . and at this hour I should no longer be a marionette, but a fine boy, like the others! Oh! If I meet Lampwick, he'd better look out for himself! I'll fix him!"

He started to go out of the room, but in the doorway he remembered that he had asses' ears, and he was ashamed to be seen. So then what did he do? He took a large cotton cap, and pulled it down over his head, right down to his nose.

Then he went out, and began to look for Lampwick. He searched the streets, the squares, the theatres, everywhere, but he could not find him. He inquired of everyone he met, but no one had seen him.

At last he went to his house and knocked on the door.

"Who is it?" said Lampwick, who was inside.

"Pinocchio," said the marionette.

"Wait a minute, and I'll let you in."

After half an hour the door was opened. Imagine Pinocchio's surprise, when he went in, to find that his friend Lampwick wore a great cotton cap that came down over the end of his nose.

At that sight Pinocchio was somewhat consoled, and he said to himself:

"Perhaps he is sick the same as I am. Can it be that he, too, has the donkey fever?"

But he pretended not to notice anything, and said with a smile:

"How are you, my dear Lampwick?"

"Very well, indeed, like a mouse in a Parmesan cheese."

"Do you really mean it?"

"And why should I tell you a lie?"

"Pardon me, my friend, but why then do you wear that cap that covers your ears?"

"The doctor prescribed it, because I have hurt my knee. And you, dear marionette, why do you wear that cap that comes down over your nose?"

"The doctor prescribed it, because I bruised my shin."

"Oh! Poor Pinocchio!"

"Oh! Poor Lampwick!"

A long silence followed, during which the two friends gazed at each other ironically.

At last the marionette said in a sweet, insinuating voice:

"Just to satisfy my curiosity, dear Lampwick, won't you tell me if you ever had any disease in your ears?"

"Never! And you?"

"Never! Although I have had the earache in one ear this morning."

"Yes, so have I."

"You too? Which ear is it that aches?"

"Both of them. And you?"

"Both of them. Do you suppose it's the same disease?"

"I'm afraid it is."

"Will you do me a favour, Lampwick?"

"Yes indeed, with all my heart."

"Will you let me see your ears?"

"Why not? But first I want to see yours, dear Pinocchio."

"No, you first."

"No, my dear, you first, and then I'll show mine."

"Well," said the marionette, "let us make a bargain, like good friends."

"Let us hear the bargain."

"We'll take off our caps at the same time. Agreed?"

"Agreed."

"Now, ready!"

And Pinocchio began to count in a loud voice:

"One! Two! Three!"

At "Three!" they took off their caps, and threw them in the air.

And then something unbelievable happened. When Pinocchio and Lampwick saw that the same misfortune had befallen them both, instead of feeling ashamed and sorry, they began to wag their long ears and laugh at each other.

They laughed and laughed, until they had to hold their sides; but suddenly Lampwick became silent; he staggered and turned pale as he exclaimed:

"Help, help, Pinocchio!"

"What is the matter?"

"Alas! I can't stand up straight."

"Neither can I," cried Pinocchio, stumbling and weeping.

While they were speaking they went down on all fours,

125

and began to run around the room on their hands and feet. As they ran their arms became legs, their faces grew longer, and became muzzles, and their backs were covered with light grey hair, spotted with black.

But the most terrible moment for those two miserable boys—the most humiliating moment—was when they felt their tails sprouting. Overcome then by shame and sorrow, they began to weep and lament over their unhappy fate.

Oh, if they had only been silent! Instead of groans and lamentations, they brayed like donkeys. Yes, both together, in chorus they brayed loud and clear: "Hee-haw! Hee-haw! Hee-haw!"

Meanwhile there was a knock at the door, and a voice cried:

"Open the door! I am the little man, the driver of the stagecoach which brought you here. Open quickly, or it will be the worse for you!"

CHAPTER THIRTY-THREE

Having Become a Real Donkey, Pinocchio is Sold to the Ringmaster of a Show who Teaches him to Dance and Jump through a Hoop: but he is Lamed One Evening and then is Bought by a Man who Wishes to Make a Drum out of his Skin

SEEING that they did not open the door, the little man kicked it open and said, with his usual chuckle:

"Hurrah for you! You brayed very well; I recognised you at once. And now here I am."

Hearing these words the two donkeys stood very still,

126

with their heads hanging down, and their tails between their legs.

At first the little man stroked and caressed and patted them; then drawing forth a curry comb, he curried them well. When they shone so that you could see your face in them, he bridled them, and took them to market, hoping to sell them for a round sum. In fact, buyers were not lacking.

Lampwick was bought by a farmer whose donkey had died the day before: and Pinocchio was sold to the Ringmaster of a company of clowns and rope-walkers, who intended to teach him to jump and dance with the other animals belonging to the company.

Do you understand now, my readers, the fine business which the little man carried on? This cruel little monster, who seemed all milk and honey, went about the world with his coach from time to time. By means of promises and caresses he collected all the children who did not like their books, and did not want to go to school, and after packing them into his coach he carried them off to Toyland, so that they could spend all their time playing and amusing themselves. When these poor children, by reason of always playing and never studying, became so many donkeys, he was very happy, and he took them to market and sold them. In a few years, by this means, he had become a millionaire.

I do not know what happened to Lampwick, but I know that Pinocchio, from the beginning, led a life of drudgery and abuse.

When he was led into the stable his new master filled his manger with straw, but Pinocchio spat it out after he had tasted it.

Then his master, grumbling, filled the manger with hay, but Pinocchio did not like that either.

"Ah! You don't even like hay?" cried his master angrily. "Leave it to me, my fine donkey, if you are going to be particular, I know how to cure you!"

And as a beginning he struck his legs with his whip.

The pain made Pinocchio cry, and bray: "Hee-haw! I can't digest straw!"

"Then eat hay," replied his master, who understood donkey dialect perfectly.

"Hee-haw! Hay gives me the stomach-ache!"

"Do you think that I am going to feed a donkey like you on chicken breasts and capon cutlets?" said his master still more angrily, and he gave him another cut with the whip.

After this second slash Pinocchio thought it would be wiser to keep quiet, and he said no more. The stable door was shut, and Pinocchio was left alone. It was so long since he had eaten anything that hunger made him yawn; and as he yawned he opened a great mouth as large as an oven.

At last, since there was nothing else in his manger, he resigned himself to eat a little hay, and after chewing it a long time, he shut his eyes and swallowed it.

"This hay isn't bad," he said to himself, "but how much better it would have been if I had kept on with my studies! By this time, instead of hay, I might be eating the crusty end of a fresh loaf, with a fine slice of sausage! Patience!"

As soon as he was awake in the morning, he looked for a little more hay; but he found none, for he had eaten it all during the night.

Then he tried a mouthful of chopped straw, but as he chewed away at it he thought what a difference there was between the taste of chopped straw, and rice, as it is served in Milan, or macaroni, as they cook it in Naples.

"Patience!" he said again, as he continued to chew. "At least my misfortune may serve as a lesson to disobedient children who hate to study. Patience! Patience!"

"Patience, my hat!" shouted his master, who came into the stable at that moment. "Do you imagine, my fine donkey, that I bought you just to feed you? I bought you to work, and help me make money. Come on, now, and do your best! Come into the Circus, and I'll teach you to jump through a hoop and break a paper ring with your head, and to waltz and polka on your hind legs."

So poor Pinocchio, for love or by force, had to learn all these fine tricks; but it took him three months, with many sharp cuts of the whip.

At last the day came when his master announced a really wonderful show. Gaily-coloured posters were pasted up at all the street corners, which read thus:

GRAND GALA SPECTACLE

This evening
THE USUAL DARING LEAPS
AND ASTOUNDING FEATS
BY ALL THE ARTISTES
And by all the horses of the company
EXTRA!
*There will appear for the first time
the famous*
LITTLE DONKEY PINOCCHIO
called
THE STAR OF THE DANCE
The theatre will be brilliantly illuminated

129

You may take my word for it that the theatre was full an hour before the performance.

Not another seat could have been purchased even for its weight in gold. All the seats around the ring were filled with girls and boys who were wild to see the famous donkey Pinocchio dancing.

When the first part of the show was over, the Ringmaster came before the audience. He wore a black coat, white tights, and boots that reached above his knees. After making a very low bow, he delivered the following ridiculous speech:

"Honourable public, ladies and gentleman!

"The humble undersigned, who is stopping in your city for a time, wishes to have the honour and pleasure of presenting to this intelligent and noble audience a celebrated little donkey, who has had the honour of dancing before the Emperors of all the principal courts of Europe.

"I thank you for your attention, and beg that you will assist us by your inspiring presence, and excuse our shortcomings."

This discourse was received with much laughter and applause; but the applause was redoubled and became a veritable tempest at the appearance of the Little Donkey Pinocchio in the middle of the ring. He was magnificently dressed up! He had a new bridle of shiny leather, with buckles and studs of brass, and a white camellia behind each ear. His mane was divided into tiny curls, each one decorated with a white silk tassel; a broad band of gold and silver ran round his body, and his tail was braided with red and blue velvet ribbons. In short, he was a darling little donkey.

In presenting him to the public the manager added these words:

"Honourable audience! I am not here to deceive you

130

as to the immense difficulties I had to overcome in order to capture and subjugate this mammal as he was feeding, wild and free, from mountain to mountain in the plains of the torrid zone. Observe I implore you, the ferocity which gleams in his eyes, so that when every other means of domesticating him failed, I was forced to resort to the lash. But in spite of all my kindness, which should have aroused his love for me, he has grown fiercer day by day. However, following the system of Galles, I found in his cranium a bump, which the Faculty of Medicine in Paris declare to be the regenerator of the hair and of the Pyrrhic dance. On account of this, I have taught him to dance, and also to jump through a hoop, and casks lined with paper. Admire him, and judge him! But before I take my leave of you, permit me to invite you to the daily spectacle tomorrow evening. But if bad weather threatens to rain, then the show, instead of tomorrow evening, will be set back to tomorrow morning, at eleven o'clock in the afternoon."

Here the Ringmaster made another low bow, and then, turning to Pinocchio, he exclaimed:

"Come, Pinocchio, before beginning your performance, salute this honourable audience: the ladies and the gentleman, and the children!"

Pinocchio obediently bent his forelegs, and remained kneeling until the Ringmaster cracked his whip and cried:

"Walk!"

Then the little donkey got up and went round the ring, walking all the time.

After a bit the Ringmaster cried:

"Trot!" Pinocchio obeyed the command, and began to trot.

"Gallop!"—and Pinocchio broke into a gallop.

"Run!"—and Pinocchio ran with all his might. Suddenly the Ringmaster raised his arm in the air and fired off a pistol.

At that the donkey pretended to be wounded, and fell down in the ring as if he were dead.

He rose up amid shouts of applause and a clapping of hands that could have been heard for a mile away. Naturally he lifted his head to look up at the people, and there he saw, in one of the boxes, a lovely lady wearing a heavy gold chain round her neck, from which hung a medallion. On the medallion was the portrait of a marionette.

"That is my portrait! ... That lady is the Fairy!" said Pinocchio to himself, recognising her immediately; and he was so overcome with joy that he tried to cry out:

"Oh, my dear Fairy! Oh, my dear Fairy!"

But instead of these words there issued forth from his throat a "Hee-haw!" so long and loud that all the spectators laughed, and especially all the children who were present.

Then the Ringmaster, in order to teach him that it was not good manners to bray like that before the public, struck him lightly on the nose with his whip handle.

The poor little donkey put out his long tongue, and licked his nose at least five minutes, to comfort himself for the pain he felt.

But what was his despair when, turning to look at the box a second time, he saw that it was empty—the Fairy had disappeared!

He thought he was going to die; his eyes filled with tears and he began to weep bitterly. However, no one noticed it, least of all the Ringmaster, who cracked his whip and cried:

"Bravo, Pinocchio! Now show these ladies and gentlemen how gracefully you can jump through the hoop."

Pinocchio tried two or three times: but every time he came up to the hoop he found it easier to run under it. At last he leapt through it, but his hind legs caught in the hoop, and he fell heavily to the ground.

When he got up he was lame, and could hardly walk back to the stable.

"Bring out Pinocchio! We want the little donkey! Bring out the little donkey!" shouted the children, who were all very sorry for his accident.

But the little donkey was seen no more that evening.

When the veterinary surgeon—that is, the animal doctor—saw him the next morning, he declared that he would be lame for the rest of his life.

Then the Ringmaster said to his stable boy:

"What do I do with a lame donkey? I would have to feed him for nothing. Take him to market and sell him."

As soon as they arrived at the market they found a purchaser who inquired:

"How much do you want for this lame donkey?"

"Five pounds."

"I will give you fivepence. Don't imagine that he will be of any use to me. I am only buying him for his skin. I see he has a very hard skin, and I want to make a drum for the town band."

Only think how Pinocchio must have felt when he knew that he was destined to be a drum!

As soon as the fivepence was paid, his new owner led the little donkey to a rock by the sea, tied a stone around his neck, and a long rope to one leg. Then he suddenly gave him a push and he fell into the water.

Pinocchio, with that stone around his neck, went straight to the bottom; and his owner holding tight to the rope, sat down on the rock to wait until he was drowned, so that he could skin him.

CHAPTER THIRTY-FOUR

*Pinocchio, Thrown into the Sea and Eaten by the Fishes,
Becomes a Marionette again: but while he is Swimming
for the Shore he is Swallowed by a Terrible Shark*

WHEN the little donkey had been under water nearly an hour, his new owner said to himself:

"That poor little lame donkey must be surely drowned by this time! Let us pull him up, and make a fine drum out of his skin."

He began to pull up the rope, which he had tied to one of his legs: he pulled and pulled, and pulled, and at last there appeared on the surface . . . can you guess? Instead of a dead donkey, there was a live marionette, wiggling like an eel.

When he saw that wooden marionette, the poor man thought he must be dreaming. He was struck dumb, and stood there with his mouth wide open and his eyes starting from his head.

When he had come to himself a little he said, crying, and stammering:

"Where . . . where is the little donkey I threw into the water?"

"I'm the little donkey!" replied the marionette, laughing.

"You!"

"Me!"

"Ah, you rogue, don't try to play tricks on me!"

134

"Play tricks on you? No, indeed, my dear master; I am perfectly serious."

"But how can it be that you, who were a little donkey a few minutes ago, have now become a wooden marionette?"

"It must be the effect of the sea water. It works that way sometimes."

"Be careful, marionette, be careful! Don't try to play any jokes on me! It will go hard with you if I lose my patience!"

"Well master, do you want to hear my true story? If you will take this rope off my leg, I will tell it to you."

The good man was very curious to hear his story, so he quickly untied the rope on his leg. Then Pinocchio, free as a bird once more, began to speak as follows:

"You must know that I was once a wooden marionette, just as I am now; and I was on the point of becoming a real boy, like so many others. But I didn't like to study, and I listened to evil companions, and so I ran away; and one fine day I woke up to find myself a donkey with long ears, and a long tail. Oh, I was so ashamed of myself! Oh, my dear master, may the good Saint Antonio keep you from ever feeling so ashamed! I was taken to market with the other donkeys and sold to the Ringmaster of a circus. He made me learn to dance, and jump through a hoop, but one evening during the show I fell and lamed myself. The Ringmaster had no use for a lame donkey, and so he sent me to market, and you bought me."

"I know that only too well! And I paid fivepence for you. And now who will give me back my five poor pennies?"

"And why did you buy me? To make a drum out of my skin! A drum!"

"That's only too true! And now where will I find another skin?"

"Don't despair master, there are so many donkeys in this world!"

"Well, you impertinent monkey, is that the end of your story?"

"No," replied the marionette, "just two words more, and I am done. After having bought me, you brought me here to kill me; and then because you were sorry for me, you preferred to tie a stone to my neck, and throw me into the sea. This delicate sentiment does you great honour, and I shall be eternally grateful to you. But this time, my dear master, you reckoned without the Fairy."

"And who is this Fairy?"

"She is my mother, and she is like all other mothers who love their children dearly, and never lose sight of them, and help them in all their troubles, even when, because of their escapades and their naughty ways, they deserve to be left to themselves. So, as I was saying, as soon as the kind Fairy saw that I was in danger of drowning, she sent an immense shoal of fishes who thought I was a dead donkey, and began to eat me. And what big bites they took! I never would have believed that fishes could be more ravenous than boys! Some ate my ears, others my muzzle, others my neck and mane, my hoofs, and even the skin off my back. And there was one of them that was so polite that he even condescended to eat my tail."

"From this day forward," said his horrified listener, "I vow never to eat another fish. It would be a pretty how-de-do to open a mullet, or a whiting, and find a donkey's tail inside it!"

"I agree with you," said the marionette, laughing; "as for that, you must know that when the fishes had eaten

136

away all the donkey disguise that covered me from head to foot, they came, naturally, to the bones, or to be exact, to the wood, because, as you see, I am made of very hard wood. But after the first bite they saw that I was no longer meat for them, and disgusted by such indigestible food, they swam off in all directions, without even saying thank you. That is why when you pulled up the rope you found a live marionette, instead of a dead donkey."

"A fig for your story!" cried the man in a rage. "I have paid fivepence for you, and I want my money back! I know what I'll do! I will take you back to the market and sell you for firewood."

"Sell me if you want to; I wouldn't mind," said Pinocchio.

But as he spoke he jumped as far as he could, and came down with a splash in the sea; and as he swam gaily away he cried to the poor man who had bought him:

"Good-bye, master! When you want a little nice dry drum, remember me."

He continued to laugh as he swam farther away: after a little he turned again, and shouted louder than before:

"Good-bye master! When you want a little nice dry firewood remember me."

In the wink of an eye he was so far off that he could hardly be seen; in fact, there was only a black dot on the surface of the water that now and then lifted an arm, or a leg, or jumped out of the water like a good-humoured dolphin.

Pinocchio was swimming without any idea as to where he was going when he saw in the midst of the sea a rock which looked like white marble. On the top of the rock a little goat was bleating and beckoning to him.

The strangest thing about it all was this: the goat's fleece, instead of being black or white, or a mixture of these two colours like that of other goats, was blue, a bright blue, that reminded him of the hair of that lovely child of long ago.

Oh, how Pinocchio's heart began to beat! Redoubling his energy, he swam towards the rock. He was already half-way there, when what should he see, rushing towards him on the surface of the water, but a sea monster, with a horrible head, and with its mouth, which was like an abyss, wide open, showing three rows of teeth that would have frightened anyone, even in a picture.

Do you know what this monster was?

It was no other than that gigantic Shark, which has been mentioned more than once in this history, and which, on account of its dreadful destruction of life and its insatiable voracity, was called "The Attila of the Fish and Fishermen."

Poor Pinocchio was terribly frightened at the sight of such a monster. He tried to dodge him, to go some other way, or to swim faster than this terror, but that immense wide-open mouth came right after him, as swift as an arrow.

"Hurry, Pinocchio, for mercy's sake!" bleated the pretty little goat.

Pinocchio swam desperately, putting forth every ounce of his strength.

"Hasten, Pinocchio, the monster is close behind you!"

And then Pinocchio swam very much faster than before.

"Beware, Pinocchio, the monster is catching up with you! Here he comes! Here he comes! Hurry, for pity's sake, or you will be lost!"

And Pinocchio swam faster than ever, on, on, on, like a ball out of a gun. He was close to the rock, and the little goat was leaning out over the sea, and holding out her front hoofs to help him out of the water . . .

But it was too late! The monster had reached him, and drawing in his breath he swallowed him as one swallows an egg. He swallowed him so violently and voraciously, and Pinocchio struck so hard against the monster's inside, that he was stunned for a quarter of an hour.

When he came to himself he could not have told where he was. All around him there was a great darkness; a darkness so thick and profound that he felt as if he had dived head first into a bottle of ink. He listened, but he heard nothing; only, from time to time, a great blast of wind struck him in the face. At first he did not know where the wind came from, but he soon saw that it came from the monster's lungs. For you should know that the Shark was a great sufferer from asthma, and when he breathed it was like the north wind blowing.

At first Pinocchio tried to pluck up a little courage; but when he was perfectly sure that he was imprisoned in the Shark's body he began to weep and wail, saying:

"Help! Help! Oh, poor me! Will no one come and save me?"

"Who could save you, miserable wretch?" said a voice in the darkness, like a guitar out of tune.

"Who is speaking here?" asked Pinocchio, turning cold with fear.

"It's me. I'm a poor Tunny, who was swallowed with you. What kind of fish are you?"

"I have nothing to do with fishes. I am a marionette."

139

"If you are not a fish, why did you come here inside this monster?"

"I didn't *come* here: he swallowcd me. What are we going to do now, in this dark place?"

"We must resign ourselves, and wait for the Shark to digest us."

"But I don't want to be digested!" screamed Pinocchio, beginning to cry again.

"Neither do I want to be digested!" continued the Tunny, "but I am enough of a philosopher to be able to console myself by thinking that when one is born a Tunny, it is more dignified to die under water than under oil."

"Foolishness!" cried Pinocchio.

"That is my opinion," replied the Tunny, "and opinions, as the Tunny politicians say, should be respected."

"However that may be, I want to get out of this, I want to escape . . ."

"Escape then if you can!"

"Is he very big, this Shark that has swallowed us?"

"His body is more than half a mile long, without counting his tail."

While they were talking in the darkness, it seemed to Pinocchio that he saw a gleam of light, very far off.

"Whatever can that little light be that is so far away?" asked Pinocchio.

"It's probably one of my companions in distress who, like us, is waiting to be digested."

"I'm going to find him. Mightn't it be some old fish who could tell me how to escape from this place?"

"I hope it may be, dear marionette."

"Good-bye, Tunny."

"Good-bye, marionette, good luck to you."

"Where shall we meet again?"

"Who knows? It's better not to think about it!"

CHAPTER THIRTY-FIVE

Pinocchio Finds in the Body of the Shark . . . whom does he Find? Read this Chapter and you will See

AS soon as Pinocchio had said good-bye to the Tunny, he began to feel his way in the darkness inside the Shark's body, working his way along, step by step, towards that tiny, flickering light, so far away.

As he walked along, his feet slipped in puddles of fat, greasy water, and there was such a strong smell of fried fish that he felt as if he were in the middle of Lent.

The farther he went the more distinctly he could see that little light. He walked and walked, and at last, when he reached it, what did he find? I will give you a thousand guesses. He found a little table all set, with a lighted candle stuck in a green glass bottle, and sitting at the table was an old man, as white as if he were made of snow, or whipped cream. He was eating some live fish, that were so very much alive that sometimes they hopped out of his mouth while he was eating them.

At the sight poor Pinocchio felt such a sudden rush of joy that he came within an inch of fainting away. He wanted to laugh, to cry, to say a hundred things, and instead he only stammered broken words, without any sense. At last he managed to utter a cry of joy, and opening his arms wide, he threw them around the old man's neck, shouting:

"Oh, Daddy! my Daddy! Have I found you at last? I will never leave you again, never, never, never!"

"So my eyes do not deceive me?" said the old man, rubbing them vigorously. "Are you really my dear Pinocchio?"

"Yes, yes, it's really, truly me! You haven't forgotten me, have you? Oh, my dear Daddy, how good you are! And to think that I . . . Oh! but when you know how many disasters have befallen me, and how many things have gone wrong? You know, poor Daddy, that the very day that you sold your coat to buy me a primer so that I could go to school, I ran away to see the marionettes, and the Showman was going to put me in the fire, so his sheep would be well roasted: it was he who gave me five gold pieces to carry home to you, but I met the Fox and the Cat, and they took me to the Red Crab Inn, where they ate like hungry wolves, and I went away alone in the night, and I met assassins who ran after me, and I ran until they hung me to a branch of the big oak, where the beautiful child with blue hair sent a carriage for me, and the doctors when they saw me said right away, 'If he isn't dead it's a sign that he's alive,' and then I told a lie, and my nose began to grow so I couldn't get out of the room; and so I went with the Fox and the Cat to bury the four gold pieces, for I spent one at the Inn, and the parrot laughed at me, and instead of two thousand gold pieces I didn't find anything, and when the Judge heard that he put me in prison right away, to please the thieves, and when I got out I saw a bunch of grapes in a field and I was caught in a trap, and the farmer was perfectly right to put a dog collar on me, and make me guard the henhouse, but he found

I was innocent and let me go, and the serpent with the tail that smoked began to laugh, and burst a blood vessel, and so I came back to the home of the lovely child, but she was dead, and the Dove saw me crying and said, 'I saw your father building a boat to go and look for you,' and I said, 'Oh, if only I had wings too!' and he said, 'Do you want to go to your father?' and I said, '*Do I*? But who will take me?' and he said, 'I will take you,' and I said, 'How?' and he said 'Get on my back,' and so we flew all night long, and in the morning we saw the fishermen looking out over the sea, and they said, 'There's a poor man in a little boat, who is going to be drowned,' and I knew you at once, for although you were so far away, my heart told me it was you, and I made signs to you to come back . . ."

"I knew you, too," said Geppetto, "and I should have been glad to come back, but how could I? The waves ran so high and an enormous one upset my boat. A horrible Shark that was nearby swam quickly towards me as soon as he saw me in the water, and sticking out his tongue he lapped me up as if I had been a tart."

"How long have you been shut up in here?" asked Pinocchio.

"It is two years since that day: two years, my Pinocchio, that have seemed like two centuries!"

"How have you managed to live here? And where did you find the candle? And the matches to light it? Who gave them to you?"

"I will tell you the whole story. In that same tempest which overturned my boat, a merchant ship was also sunk. The sailors were all saved, but the ship was wrecked. The Shark had an excellent appetite that day, and after he had swallowed me, he swallowed the ship, too."

"What! Did he swallow it in one mouthful?" cried Pinocchio in amazement.

"All in one mouthful, only he spat out the mainmast, because it got between his teeth, like a fish bone. Luckily for me the ship was laden with cans of preserved meat, and biscuits or toasted bread, and bottles of wine, and dried grapes, and cheese, and coffee, and sugar, and candles, and matches. With all these supplies I have been able to live for two years, but now I am at the end of everything. There is nothing more in the pantry, and this candle that you see is the very last one."

"And then?"

"And then, my dear, we shall be left in the dark."

"Then, Daddy," said Pinocchio, "there is no time to be lost. Let us try to find a way to escape immediately."

"To escape . . . but how?"

"We can escape by way of the Shark's mouth; throw ourselves into the sea, and swim for the shore."

"That sounds very fine, dear Pinocchio, but I can't swim."

"That doesn't matter, I am a good swimmer. You can get on my back, and I will carry you safe and sound to the shore."

"It is useless, my boy," replied Gepetto, shaking his head and smiling sadly. "Do you think it possible that a marionette like you, only three feet tall, would be strong enough to swim with me on his back?"

"Try me, and you will see! At any rate, if it is written that we must die, we shall have the consolation of dying in each other's arms."

Without any more words Pinocchio took the candle, and going ahead to show the way he said to his father:

"Follow me, and don't be afraid."

They travelled like this for some time, all through the

144

body and the stomach of the Shark. When they came to his great throat they stopped to look around, and seize the right moment for their flight.

Now the Shark was very old, and since he was a great sufferer from asthma and palpitation of the heart, he had to sleep with his mouth open: so when Pinocchio came to his throat and looked upwards, he could see a broad band of starry sky and a large bright moon.

"This is just the right moment to escape," he whispered, turning to his father. "The Shark is sleeping like a dormouse. The sea is smooth, and it's as light as day. Come, Daddy, follow me, and in a few moments we shall be free."

No sooner said than done. They climbed up the monster's throat, and when they were in that immense mouth they walked along his tongue on the tips of their toes. His tongue was so long and large that it looked like a broad garden path. They were just ready to jump down into the sea when the Shark sneezed, shaking them so violently that they fell back into his stomach.

The candle was extinguished by their fall and father and son were left in the dark.

"Now what shall we do?" said Pinocchio anxiously.

"Now my son, we are surely lost!"

"Why are we lost? Give me your hand, Daddy, and be careful not to slip."

"Where are you going?"

"We must try again. Come with me, and don't be afraid."

With these words Pinocchio took his father by the hand, and always walking on tiptoe, they went again up the monster's throat, walked along his tongue, and climbed over the three rows of teeth. Before jumping into the sea the marionette said to his father:

145

"Now get on my back, and hang on tight. I will do the rest."

As soon as Geppetto was settled on his back, Pinocchio jumped into the water and began to swim. The sea was as smooth as oil; the moon shone brightly, and the Shark continued to sleep so soundly that he would not have been disturbed by the firing of a cannon.

CHAPTER THIRTY-SIX

At Last Pinocchio Ceases to be a Marionette and Becomes a Real Boy

WHILE Pinocchio was swimming for the shore as fast as he could, he noticed that his father, who was sitting on his back with his legs in the water, was shivering violently, as if he had the ague.

Was he shivering with cold, or fear? Who knows? Perhaps a little of both. But Pinocchio thought he was afraid, and he said by way of comforting him:

"Courage, Daddy, in a few minutes we shall reach the shore and be safe."

"But where is the blessed shore?" inquired the old man, becoming more uneasy every moment, and squinting like a sailor when he threads a needle. "Here I am looking in every direction, and I see nothing but sea and sky."

"But I see the shore too," said the marionette. "You know I am like a cat; I can see better at night than in the daytime."

Poor Pinocchio pretended to be cheerful, but he was beginning to feel discouraged. He was growing weaker, and he breathed with difficulty; in short, his strength was almost gone, and the shore was still far away.

He swam until his breath filled him: and he turned to his father and said brokenly:

"Daddy, help me . . . I am dying! "

Father and son were about to drown together, when a voice like a guitar out of tune said:

"Who is it that's dying?"

"It's me and my poor father! "

"I recognise that voice! You are Pinocchio! "

"Precisely: and you?"

"I am the Tunny, your companion in the Shark's body."

"How did you escape?"

"I followed your example. You showed the way; I followed you, and I, too, escaped."

"Dear Tunny, you have come just in time! I beg you, for the love you bear your children, the little Tunnies, to help us, or we are lost."

"Willingly! With all my heart. Take hold of my tail, and let me tow you. You will be on the beach in four minutes."

You may be sure that Geppetto and Pinocchio accepted the invitation instantly; but instead of taking hold of the Tunny's tail, they found it more convenient to sit on his back.

"Are we too heavy?" asked Pinocchio.

"Heavy! Why you are as light as a feather! It's as if I had two empty sea shells on my back," replied the Tunny, who was as large and robust as a two-year-old calf.

Arrived at the beach, Pinocchio jumped down first, and then helped his father do the same. Then he turned to the Tunny and said in a trembling voice:

"My friend, you have saved my father's life! I have no words with which to thank you. Will you permit me to give you a kiss, as a token of my everlasting gratitude?"

The Tunny put his nose out of the water, and Pinocchio, kneeling on the ground, imprinted an affectionate kiss on his mouth. At this sign of real, spontaneous affection the Tunny, who was not accustomed to anything of the sort, was so moved that, ashamed to be seen crying like a baby, he dived under the water, and disappeared.

Meanwhile the sun had risen.

Pinocchio gave his arm to Geppetto, who was so weak that he could scarcely stand, and said:

"Lean on me, dear Daddy, and let us go. We will walk very slowly, like snails, and when we are tired we will stop and rest."

"And where shall we go?" inquired Geppetto.

"We will look for a house, or a cabin where we can ask for a bit of bread, and a little straw for a bed."

They had not taken a hundred steps when they saw by the roadside two ugly faces, waiting to beg of the passers-by.

They were the Fox and the Cat, but so changed you would hardly have known them. The Cat had pretended to be blind until he had actually become so; the Fox grown old, and his fur was so moth-eaten that it had entirely disappeared on one side, and he had even lost his tail. That's the way it goes. That sorry thief had fallen into such depths of poverty that he had been forced, one day, to sell his beautiful tail to a travelling pedlar who wanted it to drive away the flies.

148

"Oh, Pinocchio," whined the Fox, "give something to two poor invalids."

"Invalids," repeated the Cat.

"Good-bye, imposters," replied the marionette; "you fooled me once, but you never will again."

"Believe me, Pinocchio, we are truly poor and unfortunate!"

"Poor and unfortunate!" repeated the Cat.

"If you are poor, you deserve to be. Remember the proverb: 'Stolen money bears no fruit!' Good-bye, imposters!"

"Have pity on us!"

"On us!"

"Good-bye, imposters, remember the proverb: 'The devil's flour is all bran.'"

"Do not abandon us!"

"Us!" repeated the Cat.

"Good-bye, imposters! Remember the proverb: 'He who steals his neighbour's cloak, usually dies without a shirt.'"

So saying, Pinocchio and Geppetto went peacefully on their way, but they had gone only another hundred steps when they saw at the end of a little path in a meadow a pretty little cottage made of straw, with a roof of bricks and tiles.

"Someone must live in that cottage," said Pinocchio. "Let us rap on the door."

"Who is it?" said a tiny voice inside.

"A poor father and his son, without bread and without a home," replied the marionette.

"Turn the key and the door will open," said the little voice.

Pinocchio turned the key and the door flew open. They went in and looked all around, but they saw no one.

"Where can the man of the house be?" said Pinocchio in astonishment.

"Here I am up here."

Father and son looked up at the ceiling, and there on a little cross-beam was the Talking Cricket.

"Oh, my dear Cricket," said Pinocchio, with a polite bow.

"So I am your 'dear Cricket' now, am I? Do you remember when you drove me from your house by throwing a mallet at me?"

"You are right, Cricket; drive me away, too, throw a mallet at me, too, but have pity on my poor father."

"I will have pity on father and son; but I wanted to remind you of the cruel treatment I received, in order to teach you that in this world we should treat everyone kindly when it is possible, so that we may be treated kindly in the day of our need."

"You are right, Cricket, you are perfectly right, and I will remember your lesson. But tell me, how did you manage to buy this pretty cottage?"

"This cottage was given to me yesterday, by a fine goat with beautiful blue hair."

"What has become of the goat?"

"I don't know."

"When will she return?"

"She will never return. She went away yesterday, very sad, and bleating as if to say: 'Poor Pinocchio, now I shall never see him again! The Shark must have devoured him by this time!' "

"Did she say that? It must have been the Fairy, it was surely the Fairy, my dear little Fairy!" shouted Pinocchio, sobbing bitterly and shedding floods of tears.

When he had had a good cry, he wiped his eyes and

made up a comfortable bed of straw for old Geppetto. Then he said to the Talking Cricket:

"Tell me, Cricket, where can I get a cup of milk for my poor father?"

"Giangio, the gardener, lives three fields from here. He keeps cows. If you go there you can get some milk."

Pinocchio ran all the way to Giangio's house; but the gardener said:

"How much milk do you want?"

"I want a cupful."

"A cup of milk costs a penny. First give me the penny."

"I haven't even a farthing," replied Pinocchio, very sadly and shame-facedly.

"That's too bad," replied the gardener. "If you haven't even a farthing, neither have I a drop of milk."

"Patience!" said Pinocchio, and he turned to go away.

"Wait a minute," said Giangio, "perhaps we can make a bargain. Will you turn the windlass for me?"

"What is the windlass?"

"It's that machine that brings up water from the cistern to water the orchard."

"I will try."

"Well, if you will draw a hundred buckets of water, I will give you a cup of milk."

"All right."

Giangio took the marionette into the orchard and showed him how to turn the windlass. Pinocchio set to work at once, but before he had drawn the hundred buckets of water he was dripping with sweat from head to foot. He had never worked like that before.

"My donkey has done this work until now," said the gardener, "but the poor beast is dying today."

"May I go and see him?" asked Pinocchio.

"Certainly."

When Pinocchio entered the stable, he saw a fine donkey lying on the straw. He was dying of hunger and hard work. He looked closely at him and said to himself in great agitation:

"I believe I know that donkey; his features are not new to me." And bending over him he said in donkey dialect:

"Who are you?"

At this question the dying donkey opened his eyes and stammered in the same dialect:

"I . . . am . . . Lamp . . . wick . . ." after which he closed his eyes and expired.

"Oh, poor Lampwick!" murmured Pinocchio, and taking a handful of straw he wiped away a tear that was running down his cheek.

"Are you sorry for a donkey that doesn't cost you anything?" said the gardener. "What shall I do, who bought him for cash down?"

"I'll tell you . . . he was my friend."

"Your friend?"

"A schoolmate of mine."

"What!" shouted Giangio, bursting out laughing. "What! you had a donkey for a schoolmate! Fine lessons you must have learned!"

The marionette was so shamed by these words that he made no reply, but took his cup of milk and went back to the cottage.

From that day onward, for more than five months, he rose before daybreak every morning and turned the windlass, in order to earn the cup of milk that was so good for his father. And not content with this, he learned in his spare time to weave panniers and baskets of reeds. These he sold for enough to pay all their expenses. Among other things he made a fine little cart in which to take his father out for a ride and a breath of fresh air when the weather was good.

Every evening he practised reading and writing. For a few pennies he had purchased a large book in the town nearby. The index and the frontispiece were missing, but it served its purpose very well. He whittled a pen out of a little twig, and having neither ink nor inkwell, he used a little bottle of cherry and blackberry juice.

In fact, by reason of his ingenuity and his willingness to work, his father, whose health was still very poor, was able to live quite comfortably. He was even able to save two shillings to buy himself a new suit.

One morning he said to his father:

"Im going to market today, to buy myself a new jacket and a cap and a pair of shoes. When I return," he added, laughing, "I shall be so fine that you will mistake me for a grand gentleman."

He felt perfectly happy and contented as he ran along. Suddenly he heard someone calling him; he turned and saw a fine snail crawling out of the hedge.

"Don't you recognise me?" said the snail.

"Perhaps, but I'm not sure . . ."

"Don't you remember that Snail who was the blue-haired Fairy's chambermaid? Don't you remember that time I came downstairs to let you in, and found you with your foot sticking in the door?"

"I remember everything!" cried Pinocchio. "Tell me quickly, kind Snail, where did you leave my good Fairy? What is she doing? Has she forgiven me? Does she still remember me? Does she love me still? Is she very far from here? Can I go and find her?"

Pinocchio asked all these questions as fast as he could,

without stopping to breathe; but the Snail replied with her usual deliberation:

"My dear Pinocchio, the poor Fairy lies in bed in a hospital!"

"In a hospital!"

"It's only too true. Overcome by a thousand disasters, she is very, very ill, and she has no money with which to buy even a crust of bread."

"Is it possible? Oh, what dreadful news! Oh, the poor Fairy! the poor Fairy! If I had a million pounds, I would run and give them to her; but I have only two shillings . . . here they are; I was just going to buy myself a new suit. Take them, Snail and carry them quickly to the kind Fairy."

"But your new suit?-"

"What do I care for a new suit! I would even sell these rags I wear if it would help her. Go, Snail, hurry. If you will come back in two days, I can give you a little more. I have worked until now to maintain my father; henceforth I will work five hours longer every day to maintain my kind mother, also. Good-bye, Snail, I will expect you in two days."

The Snail, contrary to her custom, began to run like a lizard in summer.

When Pinocchio returned his father inquired:

"Where is your new suit?"

"I couldn't find one that fitted me. Patience! I will buy it another time."

That evening instead of working until ten o'clock, Pinocchio worked until the clock struck twelve; and instead of making eight baskets, he made sixteen.

Then he went to bed and fell asleep. As he slept he dreamed that he saw the Fairy, lovely and smiling, who gave him a kiss, saying:

"Bravo, Pinocchio! In return for your generosity, I forgive you all your past escapades. Children who love their parents, and help them when they are sick and poor, are worthy of praise and affection, even if they cannot be called models of obedience and good conduct. Be wise in the future, and you will be happy."

Then the dream ended, and Pinocchio awoke full of wonder.

You can easily imagine how astonished he was when he saw that he was no longer a marionette, but a real boy like other boys. He looked around, but instead of the straw walls of the cottage, he saw a pretty little room simply but beautifully furnished and decorated. He jumped out of bed, and found a lovely new suit, a new cap, and a pair of boots as pretty as a picture.

As soon as he was dressed, he naturally put his hands in his pockets, and what did he find there but a little ivory purse on which these words were written:

"The blue-haired Fairy returns Pinocchio's two shillings, and thanks him for his generosity." He opened the purse, and instead of two silver shillings, there were twenty gold pieces, fresh from the mint.

Then he went to look in the mirror, but he did not recognise himself. He no longer saw the usual image of a wooden marionette, but the expressive, intelligent features of a fine boy, with brown hair and blue eyes, who looked as happy and joyful as an Easter Sunday.

In the midst of all these wonders coming one after the other, Pinocchio no longer knew whether he was really awake or asleep with his eyes open.

"And my father, where is he?" he cried suddenly. He went into the next room where he saw old Geppetto, well and lively, and good-natured, just as he was before. He had taken up his old art of wood-carving, and at that moment he was designing a beautiful cornice, richly ornamented with leaves and flowers, and heads of animals.

"Daddy, explain this to me: what is the meaning of this sudden change?" asked Pinocchio, throwing his arms around his neck and kissing him.

"This sudden change in our circumstances is all owing to you," replied Geppetto.

"Why is it owing to me?"

"Because when children who were naughty become good, it gives a new and smiling appearance to the whole family."

"And the old wooden Pinocchio, where is he?"

"There he is," replied Geppetto, pointing to a large marionette that was leaning against a chair with his head on one side, his arms dangling, and his legs doubled up and crossed, so that it was a miracle that he stood there at all.

Pinocchio turned and looked at him for a little while, and then he said to himself contentedly:

"How ridiculous I was when I was a marionette! And how glad I am that I have become a real boy!"

Armada has a wonderful range of Famous Stories for children. How many have you read?

Kidnapped *Robert Louis Stevenson*
Treasure Island *Robert Louis Stevenson*
What Katy Did *Susan M. Coolidge*
What Kay Did At School *Susan M. Coolidge*
What Katy Did Next *Susan M. Coolidge*
The Children of the New Forest *Captain Marryat*
Heidi *Johanna Spyri*
Heidi Grows Up *Charles Tritten*
Heidi's Children *Charles Tritten*
The Railway Children *E. Nesbit*
Little Women *Louisa M. Alcott*
Good Wives *Louisa M. Alcott*
Black Beauty *Anna Sewell*
The Wizard of Oz *L. Frank Baum*
The Marvellous Land of Oz *L. Frank Baum*
Glinda of Oz *L. Frank Baum*
Ozma of Oz *L. Frank Baum*

Armada

The Hardy Boys Adventure Stories

by Franklin W. Dixon

The escapades of Frank and Joe Hardy, sons of a famous detective, and their staunch friend, Chet Morton, lead to breathtaking dangers and adventures. If you can't resist a gripping plot, daring heroes, death-dealing villains, hair's-breadth escapes and plenty of action, the Hardy Boys are for you!

1. **The Mystery of the Aztec Warrior**
2. **The Arctic Patrol Mystery**
3. **The Haunted Fort**
4. **The Mystery of the Whale Tattoo**
5. **The Mystery of the Disappearing Floor**
6. **The Mystery of the Desert Giant**
7. **The Mystery of the Melted Coins**
8. **The Mystery of the Spiral Bridge**
9. **The Clue of the Screeching Owl**
10. **While the Clock Ticked**
11. **The Twisted Claw**
12. **The Wailing Siren Mystery**
13. **The Secret of the Caves**
19. **The Sign of the Crooked Arrow**
20. **The Clue in the Embers**
21. **What Happened at Midnight**
22. **The Sinister Signpost**
23. **Footprints Under the Window**
24. **The Crisscross Shadow**
25. **Hunting For Hidden Gold**
26. **The Mystery of Cabin Island**
27. **The Mark on the Door**
28. **The Yellow Feather Mystery**

Armada

From Alfred Hitchcock,

Master of Mystery and Suspense—

A thrilling series of detection and adventure. Meet The Three Investigators – Jupiter Jones, Peter Crenshaw and Bob Andrews. Their motto, "We Investigate Anything", leads the boys into some extraordinary situations – even Jupiter's formidable brain-power is sometimes stumped by the bizarre crimes and weird villains they encounter. But with the occasional piece of advice from The Master himself The Three Investigators solve a whole lot of sensational mysteries.

Armada

CAPTAIN ARMADA

has a whole shipload of exciting books for you

Here are just some of the best-selling titles that Armada has to offer:

- ☒ **Little Women** Louisa M. Alcott 50p
- ☒ **Good Wives** Louisa M. Alcott 50p
- ☒ **The Railway Children** E. Nesbit 50p
- ☒ **The Children of the New Forest** Captain Marryat 45p
- ☒ **Black Beauty** Anna Sewell 50p
- ☒ **The Water Babies** Michael Robson 60p
- ☒ **Heidi Grows Up** Charles Tritten 45p
- ☒ **Alice in Wonderland** Lewis Carroll 40p
- ☒ **The Wizard of Oz** L. Frank Baum 50p
- ☒ **Glinda of Oz** L. Frank Baum 50p
- ☒ **Kidnapped** Robert Louis Stevenson 50p
- ☒ **Treasure Island** Robert Louis Stevenson 40p

Armadas are available in bookshops and newsagents, but can also be ordered by post.

HOW TO ORDER

ARMADA BOOKS, Cash Sales Dept., GPO Box 29, Douglas, Isle of Man, British Isles. Please send purchase price of book plus postage, as follows:—

    1—4 Books .... 8p per copy
    5 Books or more .... no further charge
    25 Books sent post free within U.K.

Overseas Customers

    1 Book: 10p. Additional books 5p per copy.

NAME (Block letters)

ADDRESS

While every effort is made to keep prices low, it is sometimes necessary to increase prices on short notice. Armada Books reserve the right to show new retail prices on covers which may differ from those previously advertised in the text or elsewhere.

Fluid Therapy
for the
Surgical Patient

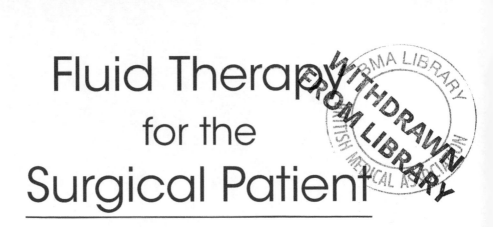

Fluid Therapy for the Surgical Patient

Edited by

Christer H. Svensen
Professor and Director for Doctoral Education
Karolinska Institutet, Department of Clinical Science and Education
Unit of Anesthesiology and Intensive Care, Stockholm South General Hospital
Stockholm, Sweden

Donald S. Prough
Professor and Chair, Department of Anesthesiology
Rebecca Terry White Distinguished Chair of Anesthesiology
The University of Texas Medical Branch
Galveston, TX, USA

Liane S. Feldman
Professor of Surgery and Chief of the Division of General Surgery
McGill University, Montreal, QC, Canada

Tong J. Gan
Professor and Chairman, Department of Anesthesiology
Stony Brook University, NY, USA

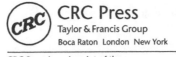

CRC Press
Taylor & Francis Group
Boca Raton London New York

CRC Press is an imprint of the
Taylor & Francis Group, an **Informa** business

CRC Press
Taylor & Francis Group
6000 Broken Sound Parkway NW, Suite 300
Boca Raton, FL 33487-2742

© 2018 by Taylor & Francis Group, LLC
CRC Press is an imprint of Taylor & Francis Group, an Informa business

No claim to original U.S. Government works

Printed on acid-free paper by Ashford Colour Press Ltd.

International Standard Book Number-13: 978-1-4987-3543-8 (Paperback)
978-0-8153-9311-5 (Hardback)

Visit the Taylor & Francis Web site at
http://www.taylorandfrancis.com

and the CRC Press Web site at
http://www.crcpress.com

Contents

Preface

Fluid therapy for surgical and critically ill patients is considered a ubiquitous part of treatment. Since all interventions for our patients should be based on evidence and proven experience, you would expect fluid therapy to be based on firm and robust evidence. Unfortunately, fluid therapy is a complex intervention and it can be difficult to test single elements.

The overall aim of perioperative fluid management is to stabilize an unstable patient and prevent further harm. The target of all treatment is to provide a range of therapeutic interventions to heal the patient. It can be very difficult to attribute single interventions to be responsible for one major outcome. By providing fluids, one must maintain effective intravascular volume, compensate for intraoperative volume losses, and prevent intraoperative and postoperative complications of inadequate tissue perfusion. All surgical patients, ranging from those having minimally invasive outpatient procedures to those having major intra-abdominal or intrathoracic surgery, receive some quantity of fluid intraoperatively and postoperatively. Historically, both the composition and quantity of perioperative fluid management have generated controversy, for example, crystalloids versus colloids, liberal versus restricted regimens, and goal-directed versus more empirical approaches. Consequently, although perioperative fluid therapy is generally considered necessary, specific characteristics remain controversial. It is also important to not forget the basics in physiology and pathophysiology.

Admittedly, there are many textbooks covering the topic of fluid therapy. However, this book tries to cover the most recent evidence and practical guidelines to date and is edited by experienced clinicians and researchers who are experts in their respective fields. Recently, there have been several randomized studies covering the topic of sepsis and septic shock. These studies have challenged the commonly used bundles of interventions used for the last decade for this severe disease.

Furthermore, there are new and innovative methods of monitoring the microcirculation by noninvasive methods, which should have great impact for the future. We truly hope this book will be of help for the clinician and researcher interested in this area.

Christer H. Svensen
Karolinska Institutet

Donald S. Prough
University of Texas Medical Branch

Liane S. Feldman
McGill University

Tong J. Gan
Stony Brook University

Editors

Dr. Christer H. Svensen is professor in the Department of Clinical Science and Education, Unit of Anesthesiology and Intensive Care, at Karolinska Institutet, Stockholm South General Hospital, Stockholm, Sweden, and a board member of the Royal Swedish Society of Naval Sciences.

He is a diplomate of the European Board of Anesthesiology. Dr. Svensen is United States educated and licensed in the states of Texas and New York. Earlier, he worked as an associate professor at University of Texas Medical Branch (UTMB) Health in Galveston, TX. Originally a naval officer, Dr. Svensen also holds a master of business administration degree from the Stockholm School of Economics.

Dr. Svensen is currently the director for Doctoral Education at Karolinska Institutet, Stockholm South General Hospital. He has published more than 120 papers, book chapters, and books. His research focus includes fluid kinetics, fluid therapy, and hemodynamic management particularly related to sepsis.

Dr. Donald S. Prough is professor of anesthesiology, neurology, pathology, and allied health sciences (respiratory care) and Rebecca Terry White Distinguished Chair of Anesthesiology at UTMB Health, Galveston, TX, USA. He received his MD degree from the Milton S. Hershey Medical Center of the Pennsylvania State University. Donald Prough has published more than 250 scientific papers and 100 book chapters. Dr. Prough's research has been funded by the National Institutes of Health, the Department of Defense, the Moody Foundation, and other sources. His most recent research projects involve the development of optoacoustic technology, which he coinvented, to provide continuous, noninvasive measure of blood oxygenation in traumatic brain injury victims, patients at risk for shock, and intrapartum fetuses and newborns. Dr. Prough currently serves as co-principal investigator of the Moody Project for Translational Traumatic Brain Injury Research. His main research focuses on noninvasive monitoring, traumatic brain injury, cerebrovascular blood flow, and fluid management therapy. He has received, among others, the Distinguished Investigator Award (ACCM) in 1999 and

Lifetime Achievement Award from the American Society of Critical Care Anesthesiologists in 2001.

Dr. Liane S. Feldman is professor of surgery and chief of the Division of General Surgery at McGill University, Montreal, Canada. She holds the Steinberg-Bernstein Chair in Minimally Invasive Surgery and Innovation at the McGill University Health Centre, where her clinical focus is advanced laparoscopic gastrointestinal surgery. She is also the program director for the Minimally Invasive Surgery Fellowship.

Dr. Feldman's clinical and research interests center on the measurement and improvement of recovery and other outcomes of gastrointestinal surgery.

Dr. Feldman is author of more than 200 articles, book chapters, and videos and is editor of two books, including *The SAGES/ERAS Society Manual on Enhanced Recovery for Gastrointestinal Surgery*.

Dr. Tong J. Gan is professor and chairman of the Department of Anesthesiology at Stony Brook Medicine in Stony Brook, New York. He is a diplomate of the American Board of Anesthesiology and is both a fellow of the American Society of Anesthesiologists and the Royal College of Anaesthetists of England and is trained in acupuncture. Dr. Gan holds a master's degree in clinical research and a master's degree in business administration.

Dr. Gan is a founding president of the American Society for Enhanced Recovery (ASER) and a past president of the Society for Ambulatory Anesthesia (SAMBA) and the International Society for Anaesthetic Pharmacology (ISAP). He is the executive section editor of *Ambulatory Anesthesia and Perioperative Medicine of Anesthesia and Analgesia*. Dr. Gan has published more than 250 manuscripts in peer-reviewed journals and numerous books and book chapters. His research focus includes enhanced recovery, postoperative nausea and vomiting, as well as pain, fluid, hemodynamic management, and anesthetic pharmacology.

Contributors

Ramon Abola, MD
Department of Anesthesiology
Stony Brook University
Stony Brook, NY

**Andreas Andersson, MD,
PhD, DEAA**
Department of Paediatric
    Anaesthesia, Intensive Care and
    ECMO Services
Astrid Lindgren Children's
    Hospital
Karolinska University Hospital
Stockholm, Sweden
and
Unit of Anaesthesiology and
    Intensive Care
Department of Physiology and
    Pharmacology
Karolinska Institutet
Stockholm, Sweden

Gabriele Baldini, MD, MSc
Department of Anaesthesia
McGill University
Montreal, QC, Canada

Fredrick J. Bohanon
Department of Surgery
Shriners Hospitals for
    Children®—Galveston
University of Texas Medical Branch
Galveston, TX

Cecilia Canales, MPH
Department of Anesthesiology
    and Perioperative Care
UC Irvine Health
UC Irvine School of Medicine
University of California
Irvine, CA

Maxime Cannesson, MD, PhD
Department of Anesthesiology
    and Perioperative Care
UC Irvine Health
University of California
Irvine, CA

Ronald Chang, MD
Center for Translational Injury
    Research
University of Texas Health Science
    Center at Houston
Houston, TX
and
Division of Acute Care Surgery
Department of Surgery
University of Texas Health Science
    Center at Houston
Houston, TX

Diego Orbegozo, MD
Department of Intensive Care
Erasme Hospital
Université Libre de Bruxelles
Brussels, Belgium

Liane S. Feldman, MD
Department of Surgery
McGill University
Montreal, QC, Canada
and
Steinberg-Bernstein Centre for
    Minimally Invasive Surgery and
    Innovation
McGill University
Montreal, QC, Canada

Stefanie Fischer, MD
Department of Anesthesiology
University of Texas Medical
    Branch at Galveston
Galveston, TX

**Tong J. Gan, MD, MBA,
MHS, FRCA**
Department of Anesthesiology
Stony Brook University
Stony Brook, NY

Juan C. Gómez-Izquierdo, MD
Department of Anaesthesia
McGill University
Montreal, QC, Canada

David N. Herndon
Department of Surgery
Shriners Hospitals for
    Children®—Galveston
University of Texas Medical
    Branch
Galveston, TX

Thuan M. Ho, MD
Department of Anesthesiology,
    Perioperative and Pain
    Medicine
Stanford University School of
    Medicine
Stanford, CA

John B. Holcomb, MD
Center for Translational Injury
    Research
University of Texas Health Science
    Center at Houston
Houston, TX
and
Division of Acute Care Surgery
Department of Surgery
University of Texas Health Science
    Center at Houston
Houston, TX

Pedro Ibarra, MD
Department of Trauma Anesthesia
    and Critical Care
Clinicas Colsanitas
Anesthesia and Perioperative
    Medicine Residency Program
Unisanitas
Bogota, Colombia

Can Ince, PhD
Department of Intensive Care
Erasmus Medical Center
Rotterdam, the Netherlands

**Michael G. Irwin, MD, MB,
FRCA, FANZA, FHKAM**
Department of Anaesthesiology
University of Hong Kong
Pokfulam, Hong Kong

George Kramer
Department of Anesthesiology
University of Texas Medical Branch
Galveston, TX

Husong Li, MD, PhD
Department of Anesthesiology
University of Texas Medical
    Branch at Galveston
Galveston, TX

Sophie E. Liu, MBBS, FRCA
Department of Anaesthesiology
University of Hong Kong
Pokfulam, Hong Kong

Per-Arne Lönnqvist, MD, PhD, DEAA, FRCA
Department of Physiology and
    Pharmacology
Karolinska Institutet
Stockholm, Sweden
and
Department of Paediatric
    Anaesthesia
Intensive Care and ECMO Services
Astrid Lindgren Children's Hospital
Karolinska University Hospital
Stockholm, Sweden

Kirstie McPherson, MD
Department of Anaesthesia and
    Perioperative Medicine
University College London
    Hospital, UK
Surgical Outcomes Research
    Centre (SOuRCe)
London, UK

Charles Mitchell
Department of Anesthesiology
University of Texas Medical Branch
Galveston, TX

Monty Mythen, MD
Department of Anaesthesia and
    Perioperative Medicine
University College London, UK
University College London
    Hospital, UK
Surgical Outcomes Research
    Centre (SOuRCe)
National Institute of Health Research
Biomedical Research Centre
London, UK

Ronald G. Pearl, MD, PhD
Department of Anesthesiology,
    Perioperative and Pain
    Medicine
Stanford University School of
    Medicine
Stanford, CA

Donald S. Prough, MD
Department of Anesthesiology
University of Texas Medical
    Branch at Galveston
Galveston, TX

Mats Rundgren, PhD
Department of Physiology and
    Pharmacology
Karolinska Institutet
Stockholm, Sweden

Mustafa Suker, MD
Department of Surgery
Erasmus Medical Center
Rotterdam, the Netherlands

Christer H. Svensen, MD, PhD
Department of Clinical Science
    and Education
Unit of Anesthesiology and
    Intensive Care
Karolinska Institutet
Stockholm South General Hospital
Stockholm, Sweden
and
Department of Anesthesiology
University of Texas Medical
    Branch
Galveston, TX

Andy Trang, BS
UC Irvine School of Medicine
University of California
Irvine, CA

Jean-Louis Vincent
Department of Intensive Care
Erasme Hospital
Université Libre de Bruxelles
Brussels, Belgium

Patrick A. Ward, MB ChB, BSc, FRCA
Department of Anaesthesiology
University of Hong Kong
Pokfulam, Hong Kong

Paul Wurzer
Department of Surgery
Shriners Hospitals for
   Children®—Galveston
University of Texas Medical
   Branch
Galveston, TX

chapter one

Fluid balance, regulatory mechanisms, and electrolytes

Mats Rundgren
Karolinska Institutet
Stockholm, Sweden

Christer H. Svensen
Karolinska Institutet, Stockholm South General Hospital
Stockholm, Sweden

Contents

Key points:

- Total body water (TBW) is divided into the following compartments (spaces):
  - *Intracellular fluid space* (ICF)—about two-thirds of TBW.
  - *Extracellular fluid space* (ECF)—about one-third of TBW, which in turn is divided into the following:
    - Interstitial fluid space (ISF)—about three-quarters of the ECF.
    - Intravascular fluid space (IVS)—about one-quarter of the ECF.
- The quantitatively most important electrolytes are sodium (Na^+), potassium (K^+), calcium (Ca^{2+}), magnesium (Mg^{2+}), phosphate, sulfate, and chloride (Cl^-).
- The amount of Na^+ in the body determines the ECF volume. The distribution of fluid between the intravascular and extravascular compartments is decisive for the plasma volume.
- The approach taken by Starling to describe the movement of fluids across the endothelial wall is now known to be too simplistic. The endothelium consists of a thin layer of cells with an inner fragile layer, the endothelial glycocalyx, which contains glucose aminoglycans amongst other components. This layer, easily destroyed, is decisive for vascular barrier persistence.
- Hormonal compensatory mechanisms take great part in fluid distribution.

1.1 Water

Fluid balance in a general sense involves the metabolism of water and electrolytes. The well-being of all cells places demands on the surrounding (*extracellular*) as well as the interior (*intracellular*) environment. It is important that there is a stable body fluid osmolality, or rather tonicity, regulating cell volume, which in turn appears to affect many cellular functions. The ECF is determined by the amount of body sodium (Na^+), while the body fluid osmolality mainly reflects water metabolism. This chapter focuses on the turnover of water and Na^+, the regulation of body fluid osmolality and ECF volume, and factors influencing the interchange of water between fluid compartments.

1.1.1   Distribution

The body water is distributed between different fluid compartments, or rather *spaces*. Water transport is mainly governed by tonicity gradients (from lower to higher) but also via hydrostatic pressure gradients (from higher to lower). The two major fluid spaces, the intracellular (ICF) and extracellular (ECF) fluid spaces, are separated by the cell membrane.

Somewhat surprisingly, the effect of cell volume on cellular function has rarely been investigated. The ability of many kinds of cells to change their intracellular tonicity in anisotonic environments, and thereby actively regulate their own volume, reflects the functional importance of cell volume. Most importantly, it is a phenomenon that should be considered in the treatment of both hyper- and hypo-osmolar conditions. The cell membranes are generally sufficiently water permeable for slow passage of water needed for leveling out osmotic gradients between ICF and ECF. Higher water exchange volume is facilitated by specific water channels (aquaporins). These channels are ubiquitously distributed but are mainly expressed in epithelia (kidneys, gastrointestinal tract, airways, and exocrine glands) and in capillary endothelial cells. The epithelia of collecting ducts in the kidneys constitute a unique part where the water permeability is hormonally controlled by antidiuretic hormone (vasopressin) [1].

The other barrier separates the intra- and extravascular (interstitial fluid, ISF) parts of the ECF space and is made up of the wall of the exchange blood vessels (capillaries and postcapillary venules). The fluid exchange across this barrier is dependent on both osmotic and hydrostatic forces. It is appropriate to consider the characteristics of the barrier, that is, the walls of the exchange vessels, which may vary in different parts of the body, as well as in different pathological states such as inflammation. In principal, this may also be true for the cell membrane in general but less apparent than in different parts of the cardiovascular system [2].

The total body water (TBW) is divided into the following spaces:

- ICF—about two-thirds of TBW
- ECF—about one-third of TBW

The ECF is divided into

- ISF—about three-quarters of the ECF
- Intravascular fluid (IVS), where plasma water is the water component of plasma volume (PV)—about one-quarter of the ECF

An additional part of the ECF, not included above, is the *transcellular fluid*, which is separated from the ISF by epithelia. These are fluid spaces (approximately 1 L in adults) that contain cerebrospinal fluid, joint fluid, and eye chamber fluid. Being surrounded by epithelia with different transport capacities and permeability characteristics, transcellular fluid usually has a quite different composition than the rest of the ECF. The transcellular fluid is not included in fluid balance calculations.

Large variations of water content of different tissues are obvious. The main reason for the variability in the TBW percentage of the body weight is the amount of fat tissue. The variability of TBW related to body weight is about 45%–70%. This raises the question whether fluid therapy calculations ought to be based on lean body mass, rather than total body weight. Women have somewhat lower TBW in relation to body weight due to more subcutaneous fat. With increasing age TBW decreases, mainly reflecting tissue atrophy (cell mass reduction). Infants have a much higher TBW percentage of b.w. (80%), mainly due to a higher ECF volume. Towards puberty, TBW gradually decreases towards adult conditions, with by far the greatest change occurring during the first year of life.

1.1.2   Turnover

The daily water turnover is about 40 mL/kg body weight in a healthy adult. This corresponds to more than 2.5 L in an individual weighing 70 kg. Variations are usually quite extensive without obvious reasons like body and environmental temperature and physical activity. Intake of water is usually more governed by food and drinking habits, rather than "physiological" need due to dehydration. Most people drink in advance, and the kidneys normally maintain the water balance via a controlled excretion of water [3]. The urine production is determined by the appropriate quantity of water, electrolytes, and metabolites needed to balance intake/production and the renal concentrating capacity. Water is lost from the body via several different routes like the skin, airways, gastrointestinal tract, and kidneys. The urine is normally the major route for excretion of water and electrolytes and many of the regulatory mechanisms target renal function. A common cause for increased water loss is elevated body temperature during fever or hyperthermia. Usually, a 10% increase in water loss per degree C elevation of body temperature is considered. The change is highly dependent on environmental factors such as ambient temperature, humidity, and dressing and therefore is a rather uncertain parameter. During hyperthermia and profuse sweating, the correlation between body temperature and water loss is even more unreliable.

In infants, the daily water turnover is much higher compared to adults (about 100–150 mL/kg body weight/day). Contributing factors are a larger skin area for evaporation in relation to body mass, a higher metabolic rate, and a reduced urinary concentrating ability. This should normalize to adult conditions around puberty.

1.2   Electrolytes

The quantitatively most important electrolytes are sodium (Na^+), potassium (K^+), calcium (Ca^{2+}), magnesium (Mg^{2+}), phosphate (several forms), sulfate (several forms), and chloride (Cl^-). These ions constitute slightly more than 80% of the inorganic material in the body. A characteristic feature, as the term implies, is their electric charge. In many contexts, among them fluid balance, it is therefore more relevant to talk about positively (cations) and negatively (anions) charged ions and additionally include some organic substances. The physiologically most important cations are Na^+, K^+, Ca^{2+}, Mg^{2+}, and H^+ (strictly speaking H_3O^+). Correspondingly, important anions are Cl^-, HCO_3^- och phosphate (mostly as HPO_4^{2-}). It is also important to recall that proteins have many negative charges at the pH levels present in body fluids.

The electrolyte composition of the body fluid spaces is commonly depicted in a Gamble diagram, where the concentrations are expressed as mEq/L, to make clear that the number of positive and negative charges is the same within a fluid space (electroneutrality). A somewhat more lucid illustration of the electrolyte composition of the fluid spaces is given in Figure 1.1.

Electrolytes have structural (e.g., calcium and phosphate in bone tissue) as well as biochemical (almost all electrolytes) cellular functions. The metabolism of each electrolyte is effectively controlled, usually with involvement of hormones. Regulatory mechanisms are mainly involved in control of urinary excretion. So far no precise control of intake of any electrolyte has been observed in humans, although increased appetite for salt (NaCl) may appear in sodium deficiency. It is anyway far less accurate than that observed in many mammals, mainly herbivores. For calcium, and to some extent phosphate, the degree of intestinal absorption is under regulatory control. Another principal aspect is that the extracellular concentration of certain electrolytes (mainly Ca^{2+} and K^+) influences cell excitability. This may have acute serious effects on nerves, heart, and skeletal muscle. The influence on excretion or intake would be too slow, and therefore mechanisms are available to influence distribution between body fluid compartments, like insulin- or epinephrine-induced cellular uptake of K^+ in acute hyperkalemia. A basic problem is that the extracellular (plasma) electrolyte concentration will not give information about the total balance. Appropriate conclusions must be drawn together with the clinical situation and prevailing acid base status.

		mEqv/L	
Na⁺	150	144	10
K⁺	4	4	160
Ca²⁺	5	2,5	2
Mg²⁺	3	1,5	26
Total	**162**	**152**	**198**
Cl⁻	110	114	3
HCO₃⁻	27	30	10
HPO₄³⁻	2	2	100
SO₄²⁻	1	1	20
Organic acids	5	5	–
Protein	17	–	65
Total	**162**	**152**	**198**

Figure 1.1 Electrolyte composition of body fluid spaces.

1.3   Sodium (Na⁺)

1.3.1   Distribution

More than 95% of the osmoles (particles in solution) in ECF are sodium and chloride ions. Since Na⁺ is mainly allocated in the ECF, the total amount of this ion determines the ECF volume. Some 20%–25% of total body sodium resides in the mineral part of bone tissue. It is usually stated that up to about 70% of the body Na⁺ content is exchangeable. This would mean that a substantial part of the sodium content in bone is available in sodium deficiency states. Clinically relevant demineralization of bone tissue is commonly not observed, even in chronic severe Na⁺ deficiency, although recent experimental findings in animals indicate that bone tissue density may decrease in such situations. Normal Na⁺ concentration in the different fluid compartments is shown in Figure 1.1.

1.3.2 Normal intake

Recommended daily intake of sodium is 80–100 mmol (corresponding to 5–6 g NaCl). The average intake in the Western diet is twice as much. Intake above 300 mmol/day as part of a daily diet is uncommon. The minimum need should be about 25–30 mmol/day (~2 g NaCl). Still, several populations, among them the Yanomami Indians in the Amazon, eat clearly less (<10 mmol/day).

1.3.3 Excretion

The urine is the major route for excretion (80%–90%). As already stated, the regulatory mechanisms are focused on renal function. Losses via sweat are highly variable but amount to 10%–20% of the daily excretion at moderate sweating. Large amounts of sodium and other electrolytes may be lost via the gastrointestinal tract (vomiting and diarrhea), which normally excrete only a few percent of the daily losses. Profound sweating in hot, humid climates and/or strenuous exercise may justify extra intake of NaCl, partly because the control of sodium intake in humans is rather unreliable. It is also worth noting that sweat is always hypotonic, meaning that more water than osmoles (Na^+ and Cl^-) is lost. Since the kidneys filtrate about six times the total body Na^+ content per day, any reduced ability to reabsorb sodium in the tubules may cause profound renal losses.

1.4 Potassium (K^+)

1.4.1 Distribution

Potassium is the dominating cation in the ICF, which contains 98% of total body amounts. The concentration of K^+ in the different fluid spaces is shown in Figure 1.1. It is apparent that the total content of potassium in blood plasma is only 15 mmol. The intracellular K^+ concentration varies between different cell types but is commonly between 140 and 160 mmol. The plasma concentration of K^+ in most cases reflects the total body potassium, despite uneven distribution between ECF and ICF. Typical situations where plasma K^+ is a less reliable indicator of total body potassium are in acid–base disturbances and changes in insulin effects on tissues. Insulin stimulates cellular uptake of potassium, as does epinephrine and aldosterone.

Normal daily potassium intake is 40–90 mmol. The variation is rather large, depending on eating habits. A Western diet is usually stated to contain 70 mmol/day. The minimum requirement for an adult is calculated to be 20–40 mmol/day.

1.4.2   Excretion

Normally about 90% of daily intake is excreted via the urine and the remaining part via feces and only a small amount via sweat. Gastrointestinal secretions contain rather high concentrations of potassium and are a potential route for major losses in vomiting and diarrhea. The renal handling of potassium is rather complex and is not yet fully understood. The major part of urinary potassium is via tubular secretion in the distal parts of the nephron, and osmotic diuresis tends to increase urinary K^+ excretion.

1.5   Fluid exchange across the cell membrane (between ECF and ICF)

For practical purposes, only osmotic forces are considered when explaining fluid transfer across the cell membrane. The osmotic pressure (π) may be described by the general gas law in accordance with van't Hoff's equation:

$$\pi = C \times R \times T$$

    C = concentration expressed as molality (mol/kg solvent, i.e., in the
          body mol/kg H_2O)
    R = general gas constant $(8,214 \times 10^{-3}$ J/K/mmol)
    T = temperature in degrees Kelvin (K)

For an osmotic force (expressed as osmotic pressure) to be exerted, a barrier that is not freely permeable for the solutes needs to be present, that is, the force is only generated by the solutes that are not freely permeable. However, there are two circumstances to consider. Van't Hoff's equation is valid for "ideal" solutions (i.e., there is no interaction between the solutes among themselves or between the solutes and the solvent molecules). Since this is usually not the case under physiological conditions, the concentration needs to be corrected by an "activity" factor (f), ("osmotic coefficient"), which can vary between 1 (ideal solution) and 0 (increasing deviation from ideal conditions). The activity factor is not only dependent on the properties of the solutes but also on their concentration. The interactions between solutes and solvent increase with increasing concentration and therefore a lower value for f. The activity factor for, for example, Na^+ (respectively Cl^-) in the relatively dilute body fluids is about 0.93. In Box 1.1, the consequences of this fact for calculation of "effective" osmolality of an isotonic NaCl solution are shown. In daily clinical practice the activity factor is commonly not used for different calculations, but knowledge of the concept facilitates

BOX 1.1 CALCULATION OF OSMOLALITY FOR ISOTONIC SALINE

A 0.9% NaCl solution (isotonic NaCl) contains 9 g/L.

The molar mass for NaCl is 58.5 g/mol, which gives (9 ÷ 58.5) a molar concentration of Na^+ (respectively Cl^-) = 0.154 mol/L (154 mmol/L). Thus, the solution has an osmolarity (moles/liter solution) of $154 \times 2 = 308$ mOsm/L.

Correction with the "activity" factor 0.93 gives a concentration of 143 for Na^+ and Cl^- and the osmolarity of 286 mOsml/L. This corresponds to normal extracellular $[Na^+]$, but a notably higher $[Cl^-]$ than in plasma.

Crystalloid (electrolyte) solutions at physiological concentrations have almost identical numerical values expressed either as osmolarity (osmol/L solution) or osmolality (osmol/kg solvent).

the understanding of why commonly used solutions for infusion have a theoretically higher osmolality than expected.

As mentioned above it is sometimes also important to consider possible variations in membrane permeability between different cells and during different conditions. Water follows an osmotic pressure gradient ($\Delta\pi$), which is determined by the concentration difference (rather than difference in "activity"—see previous paragraph) for the solutes that cannot pass the barrier. The degree of permeability for each solute can be expressed by a reflection coefficient (σ) that can vary between 0 (freely permeable solute, i.e., passes equally easy as the solvent [water] molecules) and 1 (totally impermeable solute). Due to its composition, the cell membrane is hydrophilic at its surfaces but hydrophobic in its middle layer. Small lipophilic substances pass with great ease (e.g., oxygen, carbon dioxide, and in most instances urea) and create no osmotic gradients between ICF and ISF. Most low molecular hydrophilic substances, like glucose and amino acids, have varying reflection coefficients, whereas larger molecules (proteins) have a very low permeability. To further complicate matters, not only passive permeability characteristics but also different transport mechanisms in the cell membrane play a role. Administration into the ECF of glucose in a concentration higher than normal may induce osmosis across the cell membrane, depending on the capacity for cellular glucose uptake.

In common clinical practice, it is usually not necessary to consider variations in different cell membrane permeability characteristics. The basis for classification of clinically used solutions as iso-, hyper-, or hypotonic is their effect on water passage over the erythrocyte cell membrane.

A striking example of changes in water permeability over time is the regulatory effect of vasopressin on the collecting tubule chief cells in the kidneys (see the section "Hormonal Compensatory Mechanisms").

1.6   Exchange across blood vessels (between plasma and ISF)

The amount of Na^+ in the body determines the ECF volume. The distribution of fluid between the intravascular and extravascular (ISF) compartments is decisive for the PV. The PV in turn is the most important factor for the blood volume and thereby of crucial importance for effective perfusion of the tissues and organs. Increased displacement of fluid from the plasma compartment to the interstitial fluid is commonly called *edema*, whereas cellular accumulation of fluid is usually specified as *cellular edema*. The increased interstitial fluid volume may be equally hazardous with increased diffusion distance for oxygen and nutrients to the cells and impaired diffusion of metabolites in the other direction. There is no obvious direct control of the ISV volume, and known mechanisms for regulation of the ECF volume are directly or indirectly related to the blood volume or the degree of intravascular filling (see the section "Disturbances and Compensatory Mechanisms"). Control mechanisms relate to effects on the amount of Na^+, that is, the total ECF volume.

Blood vessels for exchange of fluids consist of capillaries and postcapillary venules. For simplicity, the following is restricted to the capillaries. Several structural components, of varying amount and functional characteristics, make up the barrier. There are three main categories of capillaries—continuous, fenestrated, and discontinuous (sinusoids). There are intercellular clefts between the endothelial cells, which to a varying extent contain constitute *adhesion lines* made up of several protein-rich *tight junctions*. They are of crucial importance for the permeability of low molecular hydrophilic substances. The intercellular clefts are tortuous and commonly have a length exceeding the thickness of the endothelial cell. In fenestrated capillaries, transcellular "pores" are observed covered by a very thin membrane. Outside all epithelial and endothelial cells a basal membrane is found, which is composed of several different macromolecules, among them collagen (type IV), supplying support and mechanical strength to the very thin vessel. Discontinuous capillaries (sinusoids) have large openings between the cells and the surrounding basal membrane may also be discontinuous.

The capillary wall consists of a single layer of endothelial cells (1–3 µm to cover the vessel circumference of 4–8 µm). The surface facing the inside of the wall is covered by a layer of proteoglycans and other macromolecules and is called the *glycocalyx* [2].

1.6.1   Glycocalyx—revised version of the Starling principles

Fluid movement across the cell membrane is controlled mainly by osmotic forces, and the forces governing fluid movement across the endothelial (capillary) wall were first described by Ernest Starling in 1896. Originally, this concept described an outward movement of fluid due to the hydrostatic pressure on the arterial side of the capillary, while there is a slight inward movement on the venous side. This was due to the lower hydrostatic and the increased colloid osmotic pressure within the vessels produced by the protein content of the plasma. Plasma hydrostatic and colloid osmotic pressures are supposedly counteracted by weak interstitial hydrostatic and colloid osmotic pressures. The vascular wall is permeable to water and small molecules but less so to protein or other large molecules. If isotonic solutions are given, there are no movements of fluid across the cell membrane and fluids remain in the extracellular space. Under normal conditions with an intact vascular barrier, there is a flow of fluid and albumin across the barrier with fluid and albumin returning via the lymph vessels.

The approach taken by Starling to describe the movement of fluids across the endothelial wall is now known to be too simplistic. The endothelium consists of a thin layer of cells with an inner fragile layer, the endothelial glycocalyx (EG), which contains glucose aminoglycans. The glycocalyx binds plasma proteins to form the endothelial surface layer, which has a high internal oncotic pressure. The low net flux passing through the EG has low concentrations of proteins, and the oncotic pressure beneath this layer is low. Thus, there is a zone where almost no circulation occurs and noncirculating protein-rich plasma predominates. The intravascular volume can, therefore, be considered to consist of circulating red cells and PV as well as a noncirculating PV. The function of the glycocalyx appears to be the maintenance of an effective colloid osmotic pressure close to 70% of the luminal osmotic pressure while keeping the colloid concentration outside the endothelium equal to that inside the lumen of the microvessel. Thus, transcapillary fluid exchange seems to depend not on the difference between the hydrostatic and oncotic pressure between blood and tissue but rather between the blood and the small space underneath the EG but still within the lumen of the capillary (see Figure 1.2a and b).

Destruction of the glycocalyx, which can occur during surgery, trauma, and septicemia, will eventually cause a change in the global difference between hydrostatic and oncotic pressures. If the interstitial colloid osmotic pressure then equals that of the plasma, interstitial edema will occur. Reduction or destruction of the EG leads to platelet aggregation, leukocyte adhesion, and increased permeability, all of which are hallmarks of interstitial edema. Factors that can cause destruction of the EG are proteases, ischemia/reperfusion, tumor necrosis factors, oxidized low density lipoproteins, and atrial natriuretic peptide triggered by hypervolemia.

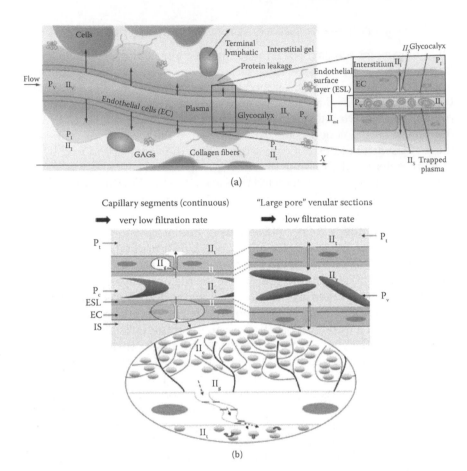

(a)

(b)

Figure 1.2 (a) A capillary vessel with surrounding tissue. Endothelial cells permit leakage of water, small solutes, and proteins. Abbreviations refer to the Starling formula, here modified by the existence of the glycocalyx. P_A, arterial vascular hydrostatic pressure; P_v, venous vascular hydrostatic pressure; Π_A, arterial vascular oncotic pressure; Π_v, venous vascular oncotic pressure; P_i, interstitial hydrostatic pressure; and Π_i, interstitial oncotic pressure. (b) In the capillaries, there is a relatively high hydrostatic pressure gradient, but this is opposed by a large oncotic pressure gradient established between the endothelial surface layer and the underside of the glycocalyx. In addition, there is a high resistance to flow through the narrow inter-endothelial clefts. In the venular sections, the hydrostatic pressure gradient is small and owing to the easy egress of colloids, there is hardly any oncotic pressure gradient. The enlargement of the inter-endothelial cleft illustrates the ability of the endothelial glycocalyx to establish an oncotic gradient and the maintenance of the protein-poor zone under the glycocalyx by the low flow of ultrafiltrate through the narrow cleft. This convection prevents interstitial proteins from diffusing up to the luminal side of the endothelial cells. P, hydrostatic pressure; Π, oncotic pressure; c, capillary lumen; e, endothelial surface layer (ESL); g, underside of the glycocalyx; t, tissue; IS, interstitial space; and v, venular lumen.

Factors that have been shown experimentally to protect the endothelium are hydrocortisone, antithrombin, and the anesthetic gas sevoflurane.

These structures (glycocalyx, endothelial cells, intercellular clefts with "tight junctions," fenestrations, and basal membranes) constitute the barrier for fluid and solute exchanges between the plasma and interstitial compartments. Apart from the sinusoids, the most apparent property of the barrier is that it has a low permeability for proteins. Still, some proteins do pass the barrier, but there are uncertainties about the detailed mechanisms. Slow passage via vesicles, possibly through successive fusion of several vesicles after initial invagination of the cell membrane, has been suggested and partly supported by electron microscopy. Others have suggested the presence of transcellular "pores," where some are sufficiently large to permit transit of proteins, whereas another population of smaller pores probably consists of the intercellular clefts. Regardless of the structural basis for these functional pores, calculations show that they make up a very small part of the total capillary wall surface.

As indicated previously, the permeability characteristics of the barrier are not static and may vary in different situations. For example, the permeability of the intercellular clefts increases in response to factors enhancing the intracellular concentration of cyclic guanine monophosphate, cGMP, (e.g., nitric oxide NO, atrial natriuretic peptide [ANP], etc.). The opposite effect is regularly seen when intracellular cyclic adenosine monophosphate, cAMP, increases. The most dramatic change in permeability is seen during inflammation, when all capillaries increase their permeability in general, which together with hemodynamic changes of the microcirculation causes a classic interstitial edema.

Through active control of the balance between pre- and postcapillary resistance, the hemodynamic conditions in the exchange vessels can be changed to allow a net absorption of fluid as in hemorrhage (transcapillary refill). Finally, increased knowledge about the extent of possible active control of permeability and exchange area (filtration coefficient) would be of great importance for the understanding of the distribution of administered fluids in clinical practice. So far, traditional pharmacokinetic principles (volume kinetics) are extremely difficult to apply in the clinical field to understand the fate of administered fluids.

1.7   Disturbances and compensatory mechanisms

If the concept of fluid balance is restricted to include the turnover of water and salt only, its main task is to maintain a constant body fluid osmolality and preserve an optimal ECF volume. The osmolality is one of the most actively and accurately controlled variables in the body. A deviation by 1% from normal (in either direction) is sufficient to activate relevant compensatory mechanisms. Control of the ECF volume, however, has a large degree of tolerance.

Here, no obvious counter-regulatory mechanisms are observed until it has changed by 5%–10%. Body fluid osmolality is mainly controlled via the water turnover, whereas the ECF volume is governed by the Na$^+$-balance. From a practical point of view, it is therefore relevant to consider any large deviation from normal osmolality as a sign of a primary disturbance in water turnover. Correspondingly, a primary disturbance in Na$^+$ turnover is reflected as a change in ECF volume [4]. Direct measurements of the PV or the total ECF by indicator dilution methods are time- and labor-consuming and have errors of about 10%. It is therefore not generally available in the clinical setting.

Another important issue in investigating and interpreting fluid balance disturbances is that they are commonly a combination of perturbations in water and Na$^+$ turnover. In addition, some regulatory mechanisms (e.g., the renin–angiotensin system) are involved in the control of water as well as Na$^+$ balance, although with somewhat different priority, and this may contribute to some confusion in understanding pathophysiological mechanisms.

In Figure 1.3, effects on body fluid osmolality (usually reflected by the plasma/serum Na$^+$ concentration) and volume of the two

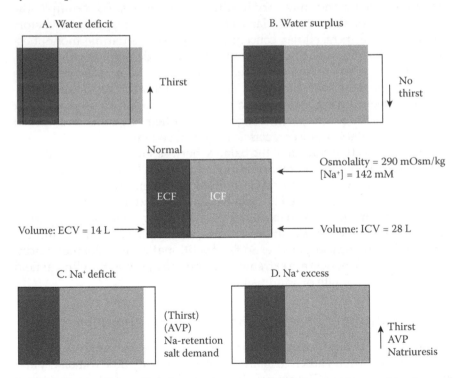

Figure 1.3 Disturbances and compensatory mechanisms at excess/shortage of water (A and B) (respectively Na$^+$; C and D). Changes in osmolality along the y-axis and changes in volume along the x-axis. Na$^+$ = Na$^+$ concentration. See comments in text on possible changes in osmolality/Na$^+$ concentration in Na$^+$-deficit and -excess.

major fluid compartments plus major compensatory mechanisms are summarized for four typical "pure" disturbances in water (respectively Na⁺) homeostasis. The aim is to form the basis and facilitate understanding of the pathophysiology of more complex disturbances in fluid balance. The terminology for the four typical situations in the figure is commonly used in physiology. In clinical practice the disturbances are classified as isotonic, hypotonic, or hypertonic dehydration (respectively hyperhydration). The first three indicate if the "effective" osmolality (i.e., tonicity) over the cell membrane is normal, decreased, or increased. Dehydration (respectively hyperhydration) only indicates whether the total amount of body water is lower or higher than normal. This terminology does not distinguish the distribution of existing body water between the ICF and ECF.

A. Water deficit, which produces the so-called absolute dehydration (example of hypertonic dehydration) with decreased ECF and ICF volumes and increased body fluid osmolality/elevated Na⁺ in plasma (*hypernatremia*). One-third of the deficit falls upon the ECF and the remaining two-thirds on the ICF. Clinically the degree of dehydration is graded in relation to the reduction in body weight. Moderate dehydration corresponds to a 2%–3% reduction in body weight, marked dehydration to 5%, and 5%–10% reduction in body weight is classified as severe dehydration. In severe dehydration, obvious signs of impaired peripheral circulation are seen and the patient is in hypovolemic pre- or manifest shock. With increasing degree of dehydration, the reduced ECF volume gradually reinforces the stimulation of AVP release and thirst. The former only reduces further urinary water loss, whereas drinking water replenishes the water deficit and eventually normalizes the fluid balance.

B. Surplus of water (hyperhydration) results in increased ECF and ICF volume, with the same distribution pattern between the spaces as mentioned above for the water deficit. The dilution of body fluids leads to lowered osmolality and plasma Na⁺ (*hyponatremia*). The adequate compensation is decreased water intake and an increased urinary excretion of water (via decreased release of AVP), which eliminates the excess.

C. Na⁺ deficit is associated with decreased ECF volume (*hypovolemia*) and an expansion of the ICF volume, that is, a transfer of fluid from the ECF to the ICF. At moderate degrees of Na⁺ deficit the osmolality and the Na⁺ are unchanged, or at least within the reference interval, and only primary salt-retaining mechanisms are activated. When the degree of hypovolemia begins to interfere with efficient tissue perfusion, increasing stimulation of AVP release and thirst (shown within brackets in the figure) ensues. In this situation, lowered osmolality and Na^+ may appear. If the amount of water is lower than normal (i.e., a combined water and Na^+ deficit) an isotonic or hypotonic dehydration may be at hand. The latter is commonly seen when Na^+ and water losses (as in copious sweating) are replenished with electrolyte-free solutions (water) only. The delayed water-retaining response illustrates that maintenance of osmolality has a higher priority than preservation of ECF volume, until hypovolemia reaches a stage where vital circulatory functions are threatened. In humans, the control of salt intake appears to be less pronounced (see the section "Nonhormonal Compensatory Mechanisms"), despite observation of obvious salt hunger in situations of severe Na^+ deficit.

Hyponatremia is one of many difficult diagnoses to make and it is also difficult to treat. The different causes of hyponatremia are dealt within other chapters (see Chapter 11, "Pediatric Fluid Therapy"), but Table 1.1 could enhance the understanding of hyponatremia and its different causes.

D. Excess of Na^+ causes relative dehydration (or cellular dehydration) with redistribution of water from the ICF to the ECF (*hypervolemia*). The associated effects on osmolality are highly dependent on how the surplus of Na^+ has been achieved, or rather to what extent there is also a concurrent retention of water. In a slowly developing excess, like in primary hyperaldosteronism, when the excretion of Na^+ is low in relation to intake, and there is also a certain degree of water retention, the osmolality and plasma Na^+ are principally unchanged (usually in the upper range of the reference interval). On the contrary, acute intake of salt-rich food

Table 1.1 Hyponatremia

Hyponatremia–$Na^+ < 135$ mmol/L			
Hypovolemia		**Euvolemia**	**Hypervolemia**
Extrarenal salt loss ($Fe_{Na} < 1\%$)	Renal salt loss ($Fe_{Na} < 2\%$)		Edematous
Dehydration	Diuretics	SIADH	CHF
Diarrhea	Nefropathia	Hypothyroidism	Liver disease
Vomiting	Mineralcorticoid	Psycogen	Nefrotic syndrome
CSW	deficiency	polydipsia	
		Beer potomania	

Note: Fe, Fractional excretion of sodium; CSW, Central Salt Wasting Syndrome; SIADH, Syndrome of Inappropriate Secretion of ADH; CHF, Cardiac Heart Failure.

or administration of concentrated NaCl solutions raises the osmolality and plasma Na+. In this situation, thirst and AVP release are stimulated, which if anything aggravates the hypervolemia but simultaneously lowers the osmolality towards normal. Again, this illustrates the higher priority of osmolality maintenance over ECF volume. Increased renal Na+ excretion is the most adequate compensatory response for the underlying disturbance, and it takes place regardless of how the excess has been obtained. In fact, the natriuretic mechanisms (see the section "Hormonal Compensatory Mechanisms") are improved by the aggravated hypervolemia caused by the water addition in acute NaCl excess. There are also contributory mechanisms elicited by gastrointestinal factors involved, since oral salt loading elicits faster and larger increase in Na+ excretion than corresponding intravenous administration. It has also been shown in humans and animals that elevated plasma Na+ *per se* may increase the renal Na+ excretion, although much less than that induced by an increase in ECF volume.

1.8 Hormonal compensatory mechanisms

1.8.1 Vasopressin

Vasopressin (AVP, antidiuretic hormone) is a 9-amino acid peptide synthesized in hypothalamic neurons. Long axons from these neurons terminate in the neurohypophysis, from which the peptide is released into the blood in response to appropriate incoming neuronal signals to the hypothalamic neurons.

1.8.1.1 Effects

The most important physiological effect of AVP is its urinary concentrating effect, that is, reduction of water excretion. This is caused by increasing the water permeability in the apical membrane of the epithelial cells renal collecting ducts via so-called V_2 receptors [5].

The net result is an accentuated reabsorption of water to the hyperosmotic medullary interstitium and concentration of the urine (antidiuresis). Small amounts of AVP are released from the neurohypophysis which leads to a urine osmolality clearly above that in body fluids and consequently a reduced demand on water turnover. When plasma levels decrease below normal large amounts of dilute urine (water diuresis) are excreted and may amount to 15–25 L per day. Recently AVP has also been observed to affect different transporters involved in Na+ reabsorption in different parts of the nephron. Based on animal experiments in preferentially rodent species, AVP has also been suggested to influence (increase) renal Na+ excretion, whereas no such effect on net excretion of Na+ has been confirmed in humans.

As the name implies, AVP also exerts effects on blood vessels. AVP is a potent vasoconstrictor in some vascular beds, preferentially in the skin, mucous membranes, and in splanchnic organs. Vasoconstriction is exerted via V_1-receptors in the vascular smooth muscle. Hypertensive effects of AVP in conscious individuals are seen only at very high plasma levels, partly due to a potentiating effect of AVP on the arterial baroreflex, which counteracts the increase in blood pressure caused by the elevated total vascular resistance. Other V_1-receptor-mediated effects include stimulation of prostaglandin synthesis, inhibition of renal renin release, stimulation of pituitary adrenocorticotropic hormone (ACTH) release (V_{1b}-receptor), and increased glycogenolysis in the liver. Via the other main receptor (V_2) synthesis of coagulation factors (Factor VIII and the von Willebrand factor) are stimulated. The physiological importance of all these effects in the healthy human is not fully elucidated. The same seems to apply for the central nervous effects (e.g., memory function) exerted by other nonhypothalamic AVP-containing neurons (probably also AVP-releasing).

The possible role of AVP in several clinical conditions may be clarified and enlarged by the increasing use of a more easily handled but reliable "surrogate" method of monitoring the AVP release. Similarly, the relationship between insulin and C-peptide, a biologically inactive peptide (*copeptin*), is co-released with AVP in equimolar amounts. Due to its longer half-life and stability in plasma, copeptin is more suitable to analyze in clinical settings than AVP, which demands careful pre-analysis sample handlings and is time-consuming [6].

1.8.1.2   Regulation

There are basically two types of stimuli that exert the physiological control of AVP release. Of foremost importance is the osmolality/tonicity of the ECF ("osmotic control"), but the release is also influenced by factors related to the ECF volume ("volumetric control") [7]. The osmotic control is mediated via sensory cells in the hypothalamus (osmosensors, commonly called *osmoreceptors*), which sense the surrounding tonicity. There is some evidence that the ECF Na+ exert a particularly important influence, rather than tonicity as such [8]. Increased tonicity activates the sensors, whereas hypotonicity has the opposite effect. In turn, the sensors control the activity of the AVP-producing cells in another part of the hypothalamus. A corresponding, but separate, type of sensors influence thirst mechanisms (see the section "Nonhormonal Compensatory Mechanisms"). Most individuals appear to have a threshold level of 280 mOsm/kg where the AVP begins to be released. The corresponding "osmotic threshold" for thirst is somewhat higher [4].

A doubling of the low basal plasma AVP levels causes a maximum antidiuretic effect. Still, AVP levels continue to rise linearly when the plasma osmolality increases beyond that, giving rise to maximal antidiuretic response. In the opposite direction, AVP levels diminish to undetectable levels at about 10% lowering of plasma osmolality. The volumetric control of AVP release consists of two components, a *humoral* and a *reflex (neuronal)* part. The humoral component is represented by angiotensin II (ANG II) (see below), whose formation is increased during hypovolemic conditions. A clear stimulatory effect by ANG II on AVP release is not seen until rather high levels in humans. This may partly be due to the concurrent hypertensive effect of ANG II, which is a potent vasoconstrictor agent. Basal ANG II levels under normovolemic conditions have a rather small effect on AVP release. The influence of ANG II on AVP release, and on water intake, is clearly reinforced by concurrent elevation of the [Na^+] (hypernatremia). The reflex mediated influences of the ECF volume on AVP release consist of active inhibitory signals from arterial baroreceptors and distension sensors in the cardiac atria and pulmonary veins. The possible importance of mechanistic sensors in the left ventricle in this regard is still unclear.

Increased ECF volume and/or elevated blood pressure increase the activity of these sensors, which accentuates the inhibition, and the AVP release decreases. In hypovolemia and/or hypotension, the tonic inhibition is released and AVP levels increase. About 5%–10% deviation from normal blood pressure (or ECF volume) is needed before AVP release is affected. Then, an exponential increase in AVP levels is seen in response to further lowering of the blood pressure. A corresponding degree of changes of AVP levels (in the other direction) in response to hypertension/hypervolemia is not seen. Plasma AVP levels far above those needed for maximal urinary concentration are reached after distinct blood pressure falls, while the hormone contributes to the compensatory elevated peripheral resistance. The osmotic and volumetric influences act jointly in the control of AVP release. The osmotic threshold and the slope of the relationship between plasma osmolality and plasma AVP are both influenced by the concurrent ECF volume. A practical consequence of this phenomenon is that in chronic hypovolemic conditions the AVP release is regulated around a lower osmotic level, like a reset of a hypothetical "osmostat." Principally, the opposite changes occur in hypervolemia, but they are not as evident as in hypovolemia.

There are several other factors that may influence the AVP release. Among stimulatory factors or situations, nausea (strong effect), hypoglycemia, nicotine, and different kinds of stress (particularly painful stimuli) ought to be kept in mind. Inhibitory influences are exerted by cortisol, ethanol (usually at relatively low concentrations only), and hypothermia, for instance. A range of pharmaceutical drugs have effects (in either direction) on plasma AVP levels, but that is outside the scope of this chapter.

1.8.1.3 Pathophysiology

1.8.1.3.1 Diabetes insipidus In diabetes insipidus (DI), there is a decreased or total lack of AVP effect. There are two main forms of DI:

- Central DI (sometimes called *cranial DI*), where there is an insufficient or total lack of synthesis and/or release of biologically active AVP.
- Nephrogenic DI, when the target organ (kidney) does not respond normally to AVP.

In both forms, the patient has a deficient capacity to concentrate the urine, consequently associated with excretion of large volumes of dilute urine and secondary polydipsia (increased water intake) [9]. There are several different underlying causes for both forms of DI. Both have hereditary forms. Central DI may be caused by brain tissue injury (inflammation, trauma, etc.) or due to different mutations in the AVP gene. Mild forms of central DI may pass undiagnosed, whereas severe lack of AVP is strikingly obvious. Complete forms of nephrogenic DI (usually caused by mutation[s] in the AVP V_2-receptor or water channel protein AQP2) are difficult to manage and if untreated commonly cause larger water turnover than central DI—up to 20–25 L/day. Importantly, some electrolyte disturbances (hypokalemia and hypercalcemia) and pharmacological treatment (lithium chloride in bipolar disease) may cause nephrogenic DI. These forms are usually corrected by normalizing electrolyte balance or adjustment of therapy.

The polydipsia is usually capable of maintaining largely normal amounts of body water, but naturally the patients tend to be "on the dehydrated side," that is, serum Na^+ and plasma osmolality are in the upper range of the reference interval.

1.8.1.3.2 Syndrome of inappropriate antidiuretic hormone secretion The condition is caused by inadequately high AVP release for the prevailing fluid balance. It is characterized by low plasma osmolality and [Na^+] due to water retention. The urine osmolality is not necessarily high, which could be misleading. In fact, from a water balance perspective, any condition with low plasma osmolality should be accompanied by maximally diluted urine. An important part of the diagnosis is normal renal and adrenal function and absence of concurrent hypovolemia.

Several clinical conditions may be associated with syndrome of inappropriate antidiuretic hormone secretion (SIADH). The relationship between plasma osmolality and AVP levels is altered. Four different types of disturbances in this relationship have been identified. High (in absolute terms) AVP levels in plasma are found in only 20% of SIADH cases (usually ectopic hormone production). In most cases, the water retention is slow, due to a marginal imbalance in intake and output, and it takes days to weeks to develop clinically significant hyponatremia. The symptoms are related to signs of water intoxication and are critically dependent on both degree and rate of water retention.

1.8.2 Renin–angiotensin system

Renin is a proteolytic enzyme that is synthesized in and released from juxtaglomerular cells in the kidney. In plasma, renin splits a globulin (angiotensinogen) from the liver, forming the decapeptide angiotensin I. Two further amino acids are split off from this peptide by angiotensin I converting enzyme (ACE) and the octapeptide ANG II is formed. Textbooks usually emphasize that ACE is preferentially produced by the endothelium in pulmonary vessels, but the enzyme is present in all parts of the peripheral circulation. The pulmonary vessels have a high concentration of ACE, but even higher concentrations are found in choroid plexus in the brain ventricles. All mentioned components of the renin–angiotensin system (RAS), summarized in Figure 1.4, are present in

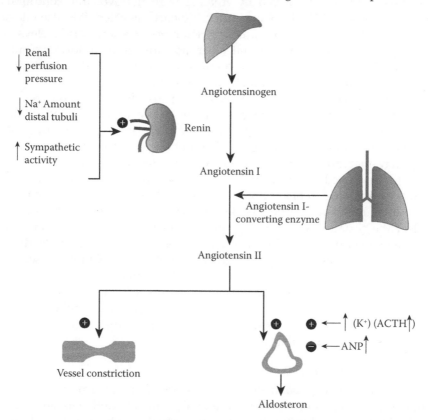

Figure 1.4 The renin-angiotensin-aldosterone system (RAS).

blood plasma and are governed almost exclusively by renin released from the kidneys (Figure 1.4).

There are, however, several tissue-bound paracrine forms of the RAS, for example, in the brain, blood vessels, heart, and other parts of the kidneys than the juxtaglomerular apparatus. Much less is known about the functions and control of these "local" RAS. The schematic illustration in Figure 1.4 is a simplification, since there are more biologically active forms of angiotensin (ATs), as well as several isoforms of involved enzymes. ANG II acts via two main classes of receptors, AT1 and AT2. Almost all established classical effects of ANG II are mediated via AT1 receptors. Pharmacological interference with RAS activity is common, and renin, ACE, and AT receptor inhibitors are available.

1.8.2.1 Effects

In experimental situations, an abundance of effects can be demonstrated for ANG II and AT1 receptors are widely expressed in the body. Probably the most evident role played by ANG II is in hypovolemic conditions when the plasma ANG II concentration is clearly elevated. It is also one of the most potent endogenous vasoconstrictor agents known and it elevates the blood pressure above normal when administered to normovolemic individuals. The peptide also acts on the brain to increase the blood pressure via stimulation of sympathetic nerve activity.

In fluid balance control, the most obvious role for ANG II is to reduce renal Na^+ excretion. It is achieved by a direct effect on proximal tubular Na^+ reabsorption but more importantly as the primary stimulating factor for adrenal aldosterone release (see below). The fact that Na^+ excretion may increase if ANG II levels are elevated in normovolemia has sometimes caused some confusion about the true effect on Na^+ balance. The acute increase in blood pressure seen in those situations is the main natriuretic mechanism (the so-called pressure natriuresis) and does not reflect the situation when endogenous ANG II formation is stimulated (i.e., hypovolemia). ANG II may also stimulate intake of sodium (sodium appetite) in species who express a distinct control of NaCl intake (see the section "Sodium Intake"). It is commonly stated that ANG II is involved in the control of water intake and AVP release, which is true but more so in pathophysiological situations. In humans, somewhat higher ANG II levels are needed to stimulate thirst and AVP release than those needed to clearly affect sodium balance.

1.8.2.2 Regulation

RAS activity is mainly controlled via regulation of renal renin release. It is only in certain situations that substrate availability (angiotensinogen) and/ or ACE activity are limiting factors. There are three classical stimuli that control renin release. All of them are related to the ECF volume, which in turn is directly related to the amount of sodium in the body. The stimuli are (1) low renal perfusion pressure; (2) increased renal sympathetic nerve activity; and (3) low Na+ and Cl⁻ uptake in the tubular "macula densa" epithelial cells (last portion of the loop of Henle). In hypervolemia, these variables change in the opposite direction and inhibit renin release. Other factors of less certain relative importance in the control of renin release are prostaglandins/prostacyclins, nitric oxide (NO) (stimulatory) and AVP and natriuretic hormones (inhibitory).

1.8.2.3   Pathophysiology

Renal hypoperfusion may appear without systemic hypovolemia. Different renal injuries and renal artery stenosis activate the RAS and cause hypertension, aggravated by the secondary hyperaldosteronism that ensues. The latter is typical for all forms of chronic hypovolemia, where, in contrast, hypertension is absent.

1.8.3   Aldosterone

The steroid hormone aldosterone is synthesized in the outermost layer (*zona glomerulosa*) of the adrenal cortex. Aldosterone is a vital so-called *mineralocorticoid*, whose main effect is to increase reabsorption of Na+ in the distal parts of the nephrons. About 500 of the fully 24,000 mmol Na+ filtered each day in the kidneys has been estimated to be under control by aldosterone. In the aldosterone-controlled reabsorption of Na+, water follows in "normal" proportions, since it takes place in parts of the nephron where water permeability is sufficiently high, regardless of AVP levels. This means that aldosterone mediates reabsorption of a largely isotonic NaCl solution, which explains why ECF volume increases as in primary hyperaldosteronism, without concomitant major effects on [Na+] in plasma.

Aldosterone has the opposite effect on urinary excretion of K+ and protons (H+), which consequently increases. The cellular mechanisms for the renal effects of aldosterone are only partly understood. As usual for steroid hormones, effects are mainly mediated via regulation at the transcriptional level. Aldosterone-stimulated synthesis and incorporation in the luminal (apical) cell membrane of epithelial Na+ channels and K+ channels occur in the distal tubules and cortical collecting ducts. In addition, the Na+–K+ pump (Na+–K+–ATPase) in the basolateral membrane and an ATP-driven proton pump (in the apical cell membrane of intercalated cells) are stimulated by aldosterone.

1.8.3.1   Regulation

The most important factor regulating aldosterone synthesis and release is the plasma ANG II concentration (see above), but the plasma K+ should also be regarded as a physiologically relevant component. Hyperkalemia stimulates aldosterone release, whereas low plasma K^+ has a smaller effect in the opposite direction. There is no obvious direct acute control of aldosterone release via ACTH in the traditional hypothalamus–hypophysis–adrenal axis. However, ACTH has important trophic effects on the adrenal cortex and is of importance for maximal synthetic capacity of aldosterone, since the pituitary hormone stimulates early steps in the adrenal hormone synthesis. Fever has been suggested to involve a relatively stronger influence of ACTH on aldosterone release than under normal conditions. Often, hyponatremia as such is suggested to stimulate aldosterone release, but evident effects are not seen until at very low plasma Na^+. Atrial natriuretic peptides (see below) have a relatively strong inhibitory effect on aldosterone release in experimental situations. Still, the relative importance in physiological control of hormone release is unclear.

1.8.3.2   Pathophysiology

Primary hyperaldosteronism is seen with overproducing adrenal tumors (Conn's syndrome) or more commonly in general adrenal cortical hyperplasia. The cardinal effects are hypervolemia, hypertension, hypokalemia, and metabolic alkalosis (usually a rather mild form). Plasma Na^+ is commonly within, but in the upper part of, the reference interval for healthy individuals. The degree of hypervolemia is to some extent self-limiting, since the low urinary Na^+ excretion increases again at a certain degree of volume expansion, despite persistent high levels of aldosterone ("aldosterone escape"). Counteracting effects of natriuretic peptides, whose release is increased in hypervolemia, are probably a major contributory factor for the escape phenomenon. Hypervolemia is important for the development of hypertension but the increased aldosterone effects also, via largely unknown mechanisms, contribute to increased peripheral resistance, which maintains the high blood pressure. Apparently, both cerebrally mediated effects on the cardiovascular system and changes in vascular smooth muscle cell ionic composition with altered sensitivity to vasoconstrictor stimuli play a role. Over the last decade the prevalence of hyperaldosteronism (expressed as the aldosterone/renin ratio) in hypertension has been observed to be more common than previously appreciated. It is particularly obvious in more severe forms of hypertension and a relationship between aldosterone levels and different negative cardiac and vascular effects has been noticed. This has led to increased use of aldosterone antagonists as a supplement in the pharmacological treatment of hypertension [10].

In *secondary hyperaldosteronism,* the hormone release is stimulated via increased activation of RAS (see above). Most commonly, it is a physiological response to hypovolemia. In this situation (chronic hypovolemia), the ECF volume is of course decreased and hypertension is absent, whereas the other effects mentioned above are present (hypokalemia, metabolic alkalosis). The RAS activation in this situation aims at restoring ECF volume toward normal and counteracting hypotension. In contrast, when RAS activity is increased during normovolemia (e.g., renin-producing tumor, renal artery stenosis, etc.), there are similar effects as seen in primary hyperaldosteronism, but plasma renin and angiotensin levels are high.

Isolated aldosterone deficiency is a rare occasion, but could be seen when general destruction of the adrenal cortex occurs (*Addison's disease*). Fluid balance-related symptoms and signs include hypovolemia, hypotension (orthostatism), hyperkalemia, and metabolic acidosis. Plasma osmolality and Na$^+$ are often lowered; however, they are not primarily due to increased urinary Na$^+$ losses but mainly due to the reflecting secondary stimulated AVP release (hypovolemia and low cortisol levels).

1.8.4   Natriuretic peptides

Natriuretic peptides constitute a family of closely related peptides. Traditionally, the most well-known member is ANP, which was the first to be isolated. Today, brain natriuretic peptide (BNP) is equally well known and has exceeded ANP as a diagnostic tool.

The peptides are named after the tissue where they were first isolated, but both ANP and BNP are primarily synthesized in and released from the heart. ANP can mainly be found in the atrial myocytes (in adults) and BNP in the ventricular myocardium. Increased release of the peptides occurs in response to increased filling of the atria and the ventricles (increased wall tension) as in general hypervolemia. During "isolated" increased filling of central parts of the circulation, as in heart failure or certain forms of arrhythmias, stimulation of natriuretic peptide occurs. Other stimulatory, but probably less important, factors are cardiac sympathetic activity, ANG II, and endothelin.

1.8.4.1   Effects

As evident from their names these peptides increase the urinary excretion of Na$^+$. The effect is achieved via several different mechanisms, among others by inhibition of RAS and aldosterone at different sites of action. Direct inhibitory effects on renal renin release and on adrenal cortex aldosterone are well documented. The peptides are also general vasodilators, with particularly strong effects on renal circulation. Consequently, the glomerular filtration rate is increased, which facilitates renal excretion of Na$^+$. Not surprisingly, direct effects on tubular reabsorption of Na$^+$ also contribute to the natriuretic effect.

There are receptors for natriuretic peptides in the brain, and inhibition of sodium intake (sodium appetite) has been observed in several species that express a specific regulation of salt intake. At very high doses central inhibitory effects on water intake (thirst) and AVP release have also been observed. The physiological importance of natriuretic peptides is still unclear, but several of their effects have been shown to counteract the development of hypervolemia in experimental situations. There may also be a specific effect in protection against intravascular overfilling, by affecting the distribution of fluid between the intra- and extravascular (interstitial fluid) compartments. Regulation of natriuretic peptide release and their main effects are summarized in Figure 1.5.

1.8.4.2   Pathophysiology

The highest plasma levels of ANP and BNP are seen in chronic congestive heart failure (CHF). Plasma levels of pre-proBNP are used clinically as an indicator to follow the degree of heart failure. CHF is characterized by severe sodium retention from ineffectively circulating blood volume, which activates sodium-retaining mechanisms (mainly RAS and aldosterone). In animal experiments the natriuretic peptides have been shown to have a certain counteracting effect on the sodium retention in CHF.

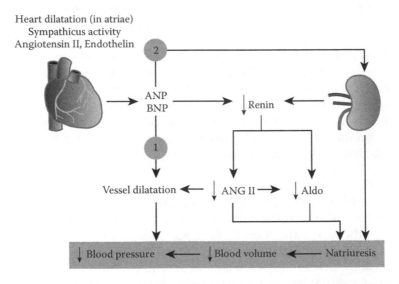

Figure 1.5 The regulation of ANP and BNP release and their effects. ANP, atrial natriuretic peptide; BNP, brain natriuretic peptide; ANG II, angiotensin II; and Aldo, aldosterone.

1.9   Nonhormonal compensatory mechanisms

1.9.1   Water intake

The feeling of thirst is aroused in dehydration and we usually associate it with mouth dryness. However, the actual sensory function to identify water deficit is mediated via hypothalamic osmosensors, but probably separated from those involved in the control of AVP release (see above). Information from the mouth cavity (and probably several other places in the body) obviously contributes to the sensation of thirst but is not of primary regulatory importance, which used to be a longstanding belief. The control of AVP release water intake is also influenced by signals related to the ECF volume (volumetric control), although not of any obvious importance for the normal daily water intake. The thirst mechanism appears to be even less influenced by the volumetric control than the AVP release, contrary to several reports of severe thirst in acute hypovolemic conditions, like hemorrhage.

Genuine thirst is commonly not experienced during normal sedentary life, and we usually drink in advance of physiological need in association with feeding and other social activities [7]. Quite often, fluid intake is driven by needs other than that for water, like coffee, tea, beer, etc. Therefore, it is the kidneys that, via regulated water excretion, normally maintain body water content. The idea that healthy adult individuals generally have an inadequately low water intake, and therefore are continuously slightly dehydrated, seems to have contributed to the apparent change in water drinking habits in the Western world over the last 20 years. Small water bottles for frequent sipping have become common accessories for many. There is no evident support for this idea, but at the same time knowledge is lacking about the more precise hydration status in the general population as well as possible health risks or general well-being during mild dehydration. It is also to be noted that humans, in contrast to many animal species, are slow in voluntary rehydration, which commonly occurs in several steps in response to acute dehydration. Further, replenishment of water deficit by spontaneous drinking during hard physical exercise, particularly in competitive situations, tends to be on the short side of needs. The strong thirst most of us occasionally experience may be suppressed by different distracting stimuli. Still, the thirst mechanism is considered one of our strongest autonomic drives, which is fully corroborated in more severe forms of dehydration as witnessed by individuals "caught" in hot, dry environments without access to water and patients with severe water losses (i.e., diabetes insipidus).

Regardless of the precision of rehydration in humans mentioned above, there is reflex inhibition of thirst as well as AVP release in association with water drinking. It is mediated by a plethora of signals (triggered by temperature, osmolality, etc., of the beverage) from several levels of the upper gastrointestinal tract. They aim at giving information about the intake of fluid before it has been absorbed and normalized the dehydration-induced elevation of the osmolality. Without this mechanism, rehydration would lead to a transient overcompensation and the osmolality would not be as tightly regulated as most cells appear to demand.

1.9.2   Sodium intake

Specific control of sodium intake is most evident in herbivores, which commonly have a rather Na+-deficient diet. Mechanisms for regulated sodium intake have probably been of less evolutionary importance in humans, who to a greater or smaller extent have had a mixed diet of vegetarian and animal products. The commonly used phrase "salt appetite" rather expresses that NaCl (table salt) is found tasty and is associated with positive palatable experiences.

Ingestion of salt in amounts above bodily needs is common in humans as well as animals. Human use of NaCl as a spice and for conservation of food is not very old from an evolutionary perspective. There may of course be an underlying biological mechanism for salt appetite related to our physiological need for NaCl. In animal species expressing an evident regulation of sodium intake, cerebral Na+-sensitive sensory mechanisms are involved, as are ANG II and sex hormones. Intense salt craving has been reported in humans with marked sodium deficiency. However, the degree of salt hunger is not as strongly correlated to the degree of sodium deficiency as strength of thirst is in relation to degree of dehydration.

References

1. Li Y, Wang W, Jiang T, Yang B. Aquaporins in Urinary System. *Advances in experimental medicine and biology*. 2017; 969: 131–148.
2. Gizowski C, Bourque CW. The neural basis of homeostatic and anticipatory thirst. *Nature reviews Nephrology*. 2017.
3. Bourque CW. Central mechanisms of osmosensation and systemic osmoregulation. *Nature reviews Neuroscience*. 2008; 9(7): 519–531.
4. Knepper MA, Kwon TH, Nielsen S. Molecular Physiology of Water Balance. *N Engl J Med*. 2015; 373(2): 196.
5. Morgenthaler NG, Struck J, Jochberger S, Dunser MW. CopeptIn: clinical use of a new biomarker. *Trends in endocrinology and metabolism: TEM*. 2008; 19(2): 43–49.
6. Danziger J, Zeidel ML. Osmotic homeostasis. *Clin J Am Soc Nephrol*. 2015; 10(5): 852–862.
7. McKinley MJ, Yao ST, Uschakov A, McAllen RM, Rundgren M, Martelli D. The median preoptic nucleus: front and centre for the regulation of body fluid, sodium, temperature, sleep and cardiovascular homeostasis. *Acta physiologica (Oxford, England)*. 2015; 214(1): 8–32.

8. Harring TR, Deal NS, Kuo DC. Disorders of sodium and water balance. *Emergency medicine clinics of North America.* 2014; 32(2): 379–401.
9. McKinley MJ, Johnson AK. The physiological regulation of thirst and fluid intake. *News in physiological sciences : an international journal of physiology produced jointly by the International Union of Physiological Sciences and the American Physiological Society.* 2004; 19: 1–6.
10. Lu HA. Diabetes Insipidus. *Advances in experimental medicine and biology.* 2017; 969: 213–225.

chapter two

Infusion fluids

Christer H. Svensen
Karolinska Institutet, Stockholm South General Hospital
Stockholm, Sweden

Pedro Ibarra
Clinicas Colsanitas, Unisanitas
Bogota, Colombia

Contents

Key point:

- This chapter describes properties of the common infusion fluids used in clinical practice.

2.1   Introduction

The terms "crystalloid" and "colloid" were coined by Thomas Graham
in the early nineteenth century. He discovered that some substances diffused quickly through parchment paper and tissue membrane from animals and that they also formed crystals after drying. He named these
small molecular substances *crystalloids* to differ them from larger molecular substances. Administration of saline solutions during the cholera out-
break in the nineteenth century was described by O'Shaughnessy and
later published in *The Lancet* by Thomas Latta in 1832. Sydney Ringer
(1834–1910) studied the effects of various inorganic salts on the functions
of the heart and smooth musculature. He discovered that very precise
concentrations of Na^+, K^+, Ca^{++}, and Cl^- were required in irrigation solutions to optimize protoplasmatic activity. These studies culminated in
the creation of a primary form of a solution that today bears his name.
Crystalloids can be described as solutions containing small molecules less
than 30 kilodaltons (kDa), mainly consisting of salt or sugar. To compile
a solution that contains all crystalloid plasma components at physiological concentrations and at the same time is protein free, has a neutral pH,
and is isotonic is not possible. Current crystalloids have varying levels of
electrolyte content and may also have lactate or acetate; they are used for
bolus, resuscitation, and maintenance infusions. In the past, much was
focused on isotonicity and less on the physiological electrolyte pattern.

Colloids can be described as macromolecular substances of different
sizes that are microscopically dispersed and remain afloat in carrier solutions. Colloids can either be artificial (dextran, hydroxyethyl starch, gelatin) or natural (albumin, plasma). Colloids are supposed to expand plasma
volume more consistently and remain in the vascular space, although it
appears that during critical illness, the volume effects of infused crystalloids and colloids are almost equal. Regardless of whether crystalloids or
colloids are used, a majority of commercially available solutions are isotonic, which means they are iso-osmolar with plasma, with an osmolarity
of approximately 280–300 mOsmol/kg water. On the contrary, *hypertonic*
salt solutions (3%–7.5% sodium chloride) are available and have a very
high level of osmolality. These solutions sometimes contain a colloid in
addition (dextran or hydroxyethyl starch).

2.2   Crystalloids

2.2.1   *Solutions providing basic fluid requirements/rehydration*

The basic fluid requirement consists of replacement for evaporation, loss
of water and electrolytes through sweat (perspiratio sensibilis), urine, and
the small amount that is passed through defecation. Sodium has a crucial
impact on the extracellular fluid volume. Potassium is the predominant

cation in the intracellular compartment, electrophysiologically active and important to renal function (see Chapter 1). Calcium is required for neuronal excitability and electromechanical coupling of muscle cells. During anesthesia and surgery, the level of antidiuretic hormone is increased, which reduces the elimination of free water. If the patient is administered hypotonic solutions, S-Na will decrease, with potentially dangerous hyponatremia. This could have deleterious effects on brain cells, particularly in small children [1].

Pure glucose solutions distribute to all fluid spaces. Glucose solutions supply a basic number of calories, which in many situations may help to prevent hypoglycemia. The glucose content can vary (2.5% or 5%, i.e., 25 or 50 mg/mL) depending on the nutritional status of the patient. A certain amount of water is released during the metabolism of glucose and acetate, which makes a positive contribution to the total water balance.

2.2.2   Isotonic sodium chloride

Isotonic sodium chloride (9 mg/mL, 0.9% w/v of NaCl) is usually described as "normal" or "physiological," reflecting that it has an osmolality similar to plasma and the interstitial space (see Table 2.1). It is made from common salt that has been dissolved in sterile water. The solution provides a chloride content that is higher compared to plasma. Consequently, isotonic sodium chloride will result in an excess of chloride ions and can lead to the development of hyperchloremic acidosis, explained by the fact from Stewart's concept that the strong ion difference (SID—the sum total of sodium, potassium, and magnesium minus the sum total of chlorides and lactate) determines pH in extracellular fluid (ECF) [2]. The SID is usually +40 in the ECF, but the equivalent total figure in isotonic sodium chloride is 0. Supplying sodium chloride will therefore decrease the SID and cause acidosis. In animals and healthy volunteers, it has been demonstrated that chloride induces vasoconstriction and decreases glomerular filtration rate. It also prevents the release of renin and lowers systemic blood pressure [3].

Despite this, isotonic saline is still one of the most commonly used crystalloid solutions in the world. It is cheap and compatible with blood, which in the early days was an important issue. This has partly been overcome with multilumen infusion catheters.

2.2.3   Balanced solutions

To replace the inevitably absent negative charges after as exact replication of the concentrations of strong ions as possible, metabolizable anions are used. Anions could be either acetate (acetic acid), lactate (lactic acid), gluconate (gluconic acid), malate (malic acid), or citrate (citric acid).

Table 2.1 Different types of crystalloid solutions

Crystalloid	Na+ (mEq/L)	K+ (mEq/L)	Ca++ (mEq/L)	Mg++ (mEq/L)	Cl-	HCO$_3^-$	Dextrose	Osmolality (mOsmol/kg)
Plasma	140	3.6–5.1	–	–	100	30	–	295
Rehydrex with glucose 25 mg/mL	70	2	1,15	–	45	25	2.5%	280
5% dextrose in water D$_5$W	–	–	–	–	–	–	5%	253
0.9% saline (9 mg/L)	154	–	–	–	154	–	–	308
Acetated Ringer	130	4	2	1	110	30	–	270
Lactated Ringer	130	4	2	1	110	30	–	270
Ringerfundin	145	4	2,5	1	127	24	Malate 5 (mEq/L)	309
Plasma-Lyte, Normosol	140	5		1,5	98	27	Gluconate 23 (mEq/L)	295
3% saline	513	513	–	–	513	0	0	1026
7.5% saline	1250				1250			2400

Note: All solutions are isotonic except the 3% and 7.5% saline solutions.

Consuming H^+ ions and oxygen, these anions are metabolized in the liver (mainly lactate) or in muscle (mainly acetate and malate) to replace HCO_3^-. Replacing Cl^- with lactate decreases the total Cl^- load, and when lactate is metabolized in the liver Na^+ is released, which could react with other anions. Ringer solutions usually have a Cl^- level of 110 mmol/L in contrast to 154 mmol/L as in isotonic saline.

The chemical equation for the oxidative breakdown of lactate to bicarbonate is

$$CH_3-CHOH-COONa + 3\ O_2 = 2\ CO_2 + 2\ H_2O + NaHCO_3$$

Ringer's lactate (in the United Kingdom labeled as *Hartmann's solution*) is used almost everywhere in the world. In Scandinavia researchers found that the decomposition of lactate is first and foremost dependent on the liver but also to a certain degree on the kidneys. When lactate is supplied exogenously, the gluconeogenesis is the principal pathway for lactate. This could have implications for perioperative care. A report published by the National Academy of Sciences in the United States in the late 1990s suggested that lactated Ringer should be modified because the D-lactate moiety available in most preparations had adverse effects in critically ill patients.

Acetate, on the other hand, can be metabolized by most cells in the body, which implies they should be more suitable for critically ill patients. The chemical equation for the reaction of sodium acetate with oxygen is

$$CH_3-COONa + 2\ O_2 = CO_2 + H_2O + NaHCO_3$$

Compared to lactate, acetate produces HCO_3^- more quickly, creates moderate O_2 consumption, has lower effect on the respiratory quotient, is unchanged in patients with diabetes, and can be used as a hypoxia marker. Like Ringer's lactate, the sodium level in Ringer's acetate is considerably lower compared to plasma. This has been regarded as a disadvantage, and therefore the sodium level was increased in Ringerfundin to resolve this shortcoming. However, this solution also contains a higher concentration of chloride (127 mmol/L) compared to Ringer's acetate (110 mmol/L).

2.2.4 Plasma-Lyte

Plasma-Lyte is a solution with an osmolality and electrolyte content more similar to plasma. The buffering capacity consists of gluconate, which is a slow-acting weak buffer. The solution has mainly been used in the United Kingdom and South Africa but is now registered in other countries. Many think it is the "ideal" crystalloid. However, a large clinical trial in Australia and New Zealand has shown no differences in acute kidney injuries or death in critically ill patients when comparing buffered crystalloid such as Plasma-Lyte to isotonic saline [4].

2.2.5   Pure buffer solutions

Sodium bicarbonate, 50 mg/mL (Na^+ 600 mmol/L, HCO_3^- 600 mmol/L with an osmolality of approximately 1,000 mOsmol/kg H_2O, pH 8), is a hypertonic infusion solution used to treat metabolic acidosis. Bicarbonate essentially has an extracellular buffering effect that eliminates CO_2. That is why respiratory insufficiency with P_aCO_2 > 6.5–7 kPa (~50 mmHg) is a relative contraindication for administering sodium bicarbonate, since it will require enhanced ventilation work to eliminate exogenously administered CO_2.

To facilitate extra- as well as intracellular acidosis treatment, a combination buffer based on trometamol, bicarbonate, and acetate has been developed (Tribonat®). The solution has the following composition: Na^+ 195 mmol/L, HCO_3^- 155 mmol/L, phosphate 20 mmol/L, acetate 200 mmol/L, trometamol (tris-hydroxymethyl-aminomethane) 300 mmol/L; osmolality 800 mOsmol/kg. Infusion of this solution produces both extracellular (HCO_3^-) and intracellular (metamol) buffering, as well as a slower buffering effect when the acetate metabolizes. The phosphate content reduces the risk of hypophosphatemia development during the correction of acidosis.

2.2.6   Mannitol

Mannitol is an osmotic carbohydrate (contains 150 mg/mL with approximately 930 mOsmol/kg H_2O) that is excreted in the kidneys but not reabsorbed in the tubules. The high osmolality attracts fluid from the intracellular to the extracellular space. Mannitol is used when kidney failure is imminent and to treat brain edema due to traumatic injuries.

2.2.7   Hypertonic saline with or without colloid

In the 1930s, it was discovered that it was possible to prevent tissue preparations from swelling by storing them in a hypertonic solution. In 1980, studies showed that the addition of small volumes (4–6 mL/kg body weight) of hypertonic salt (7.5% NaCl; 2,400 mOsmol/kg H_2O) provided treatment for hypovolemic shock and improved survival in animal models. Hypertonic solution mobilizes extravascular fluid from the interstitial and intracellular spaces into the bloodstream. Together with hemodilution and vasodilation there is also a de-swelling of endothelial cells, which improves microcirculation. This was considered an ideal solution for prehospital and military use (approximately 250 mL hypertonic NaCl was equivalent to 3 L Ringer's acetate).

The effects of hypertonic infusion solution are summarized in Table 2.2.

Table 2.2 Physiological effects of hypertonic solutions

Fluid redistribution

Mobilization of fluid from extra- and intracellular spaces into the bloodstream results in:
- increased intravascular volume
- hemodilution
- decreased blood viscosity
- increased venous return
- increased preload for the heart
- increased cardiac output

Vascular dilatation

The vasodilating effects of hypertonic solutions result in:
- decreased afterload
- improved regional blood flow
- decreased cardiac workload

Cellular decongestion

The edema-reducing effects of hypertonic solutions result in:
- improved capillary blood flow
- decreased tissue enema
- increased diuresis

The hypertonic effect is, however, short lived. Adding a colloid will substantially prolong the effect of retaining fluid in the vascular space. Examples of these solutions are as follows: NaCl 7.5%, NaCl 7.5%/6% dextran 70 (Rescueflow®), both with osmolality 2,462 mOsmol/kg H_2O and in NaCl 7.2% 6% hydroxyethyl starch (HES) 200/0.4–0.65 HyperHAES® (osmolality of 2,464 mOsmol/L).

Clinical experiences of fluid therapy using hypertonic crystalloid–colloid mostly come from prehospital and military settings. Randomized studies in Australia and North America have, however, shown that despite promising laboratory findings there is no clinical benefit in neurological or mortality outcomes [5–7].

In Latin America, hypertonic saline at 3% is commonly used as a "bridge," to transiently maintain mean blood pressures above 45 mmHg of mean arterial pressure in bleeding patients, until bleeding is controlled and blood products are available. Some studies have shown similar effects of the use of 3% versus 7.5% of hypertonic saline [8].

2.3 Colloids

Thomas Graham used the name "colloids" (from the Greek *collodion*, meaning "a gluey substance" or "glue") since they diffused very slowly through parchment or membrane and did not form crystals such as albumin and gel-like compounds. The large molecules found in colloid solutions expand the plasma volume, resulting in a colloid osmotic pressure that is the equivalent of the natural pressure of the plasma. Colloid solutions are retained longer in the intravascular fluid compared to crystalloid solutions, which means that presumably smaller quantities are needed. A positive effect is achieved more quickly than when the same volume of crystalloid is administered. In addition, there is considerably less expansion of the interstitial fluid space, which in turn decreases the amount of edema, improves microcirculation, and therefore also provides better conditions for an adequate oxygen supply to the tissues. This applies to patients whose glycocalyxes are intact (see Chapter 1). Due to side effects and lacking volume effects, there is little evidence to justify the use of colloids in critically ill patients. In elective surgery, the evidence is less clear. This will be further explained in other chapters in this book [9].

Colloids are categorized either as natural or as artificial colloids. There has been debate ongoing for many years about which colloid, if any, to use and discussion of the merits of colloid solutions versus crystalloid solutions. The results of studies carried out do not indicate any general advantages of one solution over the other.

2.3.1   Natural colloids

2.3.1.1   Plasma

Plasma infusion expands the intravascular fluid space slightly less than the volume of fluid supplied. Plasma is less effective as a volume expander compared to an infusion of equivalent volumes of dextran, starch, or albumin solutions. This is because plasma contains elements that increase capillary permeability. Infusion of plasma causes activation of inflammatory responses and cascade systems may be activated. As such, plasma should only be administered if there is justification to do so, mainly to provide coagulation factors or coagulation inhibitors.

2.3.1.2   Albumin

Plasma protein levels and the physiological significance of albumin are summarized in Box 2.1.

Albumin is a natural colloid and the predominant protein in human plasma. Albumin accounts for 60%–80% of the colloid osmotic pressure in the bloodstream. Normal transcapillary leakage is 5%–10% per hour. The albumin is returned to the bloodstream via the lymphatic system. Leakage may increase in the event of trauma or septic conditions, which leads to redistribution of the albumin so that a much larger proportion ends up in the interstitial fluid space ("albumin trapping"). Extravascular edema may be formed from the albumin binding the fluid, which impedes microcirculation and impairs oxygenation of the tissues.

> ## BOX 2.1 PLASMA PROTEIN LEVELS AND THE PHYSIOLOGICAL SIGNIFICANCE OF ALBUMIN
>
> **Plasma protein levels g/L**
>
> *Approximately 70 g/L in total (adults 65–80 g/L, children 45–75 g/L):*
> - Albumin: 45 g/L
> - Globulins: 25 g/L
> - Fibrinogen: 3 g/L
>
> *Physiological significance of albumin:*
> - Regulates transvascular fluid flow
> - Binds anions and cations reversibly
> - Transports free fatty acids, hormones, enzymes, trace elements, drugs, etc.
> - Has detoxifying effects
> - Catches free radicals
> - Has an inhibiting effect on platelet aggregation
>
> *Source:* Hahn, R.G., et al., *Acta. Anaesthesiol. Scand.*, 60(5), 569–578, 2016.

2.3.2   Artificial colloids

2.3.2.1   Dextran

Dextran consists of polysaccharides made of glucose. It is excreted to a certain degree through kidneys, the remaining part being broken down in the plasma into carbon dioxide and water.

The most common preparations are 6% dextran 70; 3%, 4%, and 6% dextran 60; and 3.5% and 10% dextran 40. Its ability to expand plasma volume varies from between slightly less than infused volume (3% 60) to more than the infused volume (10% 40), while 6% dextran 70 has the longest duration. Dextrans improve rheology and are also used for prophylaxis of thrombosis (Table 2.3). Dextran inhibits platelet aggregation, lowers factor VIII/von Willebrand factor levels, reduces leukocyte adhesion, and can also be used in thromboprophylaxis. Intravascular accumulation may increase in the event of kidney disease.

The maximum dose recommended is 1.5 g/kg body weight in a 24-hour period. To reduce the risk of allergic reaction, low molecular dextran-1 (Promit®, 20 mL 15% dextran 1) is administered to bind the reactive points on any antibodies directed towards dextran. Antibodies may have been created because of administration of dextran earlier in life or may occur naturally in the gastrointestinal system. Dextrans can also interfere with blood group tests and crossmatch.

Table 2.3 Different types of colloid solutions

Colloid	Na$^+$	K$^+$	Ca^{++}	Mg$^+$	Cl$^-$	Acetate$^-$	Bicarbonate	Osmolality
Dextran-60, 3%	130	4	2	1	110	30		270
Dextran-70, 6% (Macrodex)	154	–	–	–	154	–		300
Dextran-40, 10% (Rheomacrodex)	154	–	–	–	154	–		350
HES 130/0.4 (corn starch)	154	–	–	–	154	–		308
HES 130/0.42 (potato starch)	154	–	–	–	154	–		309
Gelatin 4% (succinylated)	154				154			275
Albumin 4–5%	148				128			250
Plasma	135–145	4–5	2.2–2.6	1–2	95–110	0	23–26	291

There is a risk of overhydration if dextran is administered too quickly. This risk applies to patients with latent or manifest heart failure.

2.3.2.2 Gelatin

Gelatin consists of polypeptides made from bovine gelatin. If kidney function is normal, it is excreted quickly through the urine. There is a certain risk of histamine-mediated anaphylaxis, although this risk applied more to older, now deregistered, gelatin solutions. The main gelatin solution used is a succinylated gelatin (modified fluid gelatin) 4% solution in a physiological common salt solution with a molecular weight of approximately 35 kDa. The volume effect of this lasts about 2–3 hours. Thereafter the solution is eliminated in two phases, with a half-life of around 8 hours in the first phase and several days in the second phase. The gelatin is excreted primarily through the urine; only around 1% of the infused dose is metabolized.

2.3.2.3 Starch

The following parameters are usually stated to determine the biochemical properties of hydroxyethyl starch:

* Mass concentration
* Mean molecular mass
* Degree of substitution
* Pattern of substitution

The mass concentration determines the oncotic value. If 6%, the product contains 6 g HES per 100 mL solution, which makes it iso-oncotic with plasma. The mean molecular mass is given in kilodaltons (kDa). The closer the mean molecular mass is to the renal threshold of 40–70 kDa, the more it is eliminated by the kidney. The degree of substitution gives the proportion of hydroxylated glucose units of the total number. That is, a degree of 0.4 means that of 10 glucose units in the original molecule, 4 have a hydroxyethyl group in Positions 2, 3, and 6. HES is differentiated into high (0.7), medium (0.5), and low substituted (0.4) preparations. The pattern of substitution that is the ratio of hydroxylation at Position 2 (strong interference with plasma amylase) and Position 6 (weak interference with plasma amylase) is also an important issue. The higher the C2/C6 ratio, the longer duration in the circulation.

There are several different preparations available that are made from HES. There are several HES solutions differentiated by the molecular weight (MW 70–450 kDa), the substitution ratio (0–1), and the concentration (6% or 10%). Starch molecules with a weight of more than 70 kDa to some extent are broken down by amylase and then secreted via the kidneys. Other parts accumulate in reticulo-endothelial tissues and have

been attributed as a cause of pruritus. Available preparations for perioperative use are HES 130/0.4 (corn starch) and HES 130/0.42 (potato starch).
The potato starch is mixed with a balanced solution (Tetraspan®), and corn
starch solutions are mixed either with a common salt solution (Voluven®)
or a balanced solution (Volulyte®). HES preparations with larger molecular sizes are registered in the United States (Hespan® and Hextend®), but
are not used in Europe.

In the early 2000s, it was suspected that HES with larger molecular
sizes (>200 kDa) caused kidney problems in critically ill patients. Although
this was thought to be attributed to the molecular size per se [10], it has
now been established that nephrotoxic problems also occur with lower
molecular sized preparations in critically ill settings [11,12]. Although
there are conflicting opinions and the perioperative and trauma settings
have shown no evidence of renal problems [13–16], HES has been widely
restricted; as of the time of publication of this book the products have been
black boxed by many regulatory authorities around the world. However, it
has been suggested that there may be an intraoperative safe area to replace
blood loss before the threshold of transfusion. In critically ill patients the
investigational studies were done when patients were already resuscitated and the glycocalyx was more damaged; therefore there still might
be a window for use of HES during an initial stabilization phase.

2.4   Volume kinetics (VK)

Infusion fluids have traditionally been described in relation to their
expected ability to fill anatomical spaces such as the vascular and interstitial spaces. In reality, the pattern is more complex [17,18]. Fluid distribution
is dependent on well- and less-perfused parts of the body. Apparently,
a two-volume model would best suit isotonic solutions during anesthesia and surgery, dehydration and hypovolemia. If the rate of infusion is
known, distribution volumes of central and peripheral volumes can be
calculated together with elimination rate constants and intercompartmental constants. This will elucidate directions and rate of fluid movements between spaces. A simple sketch of a two-volume model is shown
in Figure 2.1.

It would be tempting to resemble the central fluid space (Vc) with the
plasma volume and the peripheral volume (Vt) with the interstitium (see
Figure 2.1). This is not entirely true. The fractional dilution of the plasma
expansion would change the pressure in tissues and thereby merely
reflect distribution of fluid over time. The elimination constant between
spaces (Cld) rather reflects differences in perfusion and changing permeability between body regions. Stated in other words, the estimates derived
from VK are not measurements of anatomical spaces but rather functional
volumes indicating how the body handles fluid.

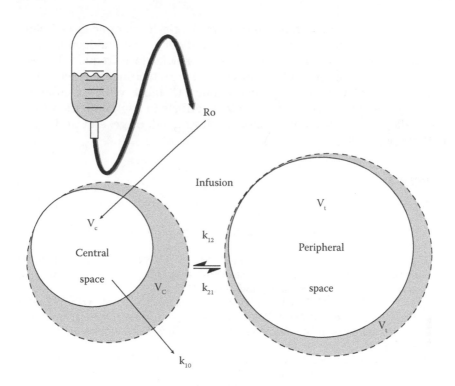

Figure 2.1 Two-volume model for volume kinetics. Infusion rate (Ro) will expand a central space (V_c, difference between expandable v_c and V_c) with an elimination rate constant of k_{10}. The fluid infusion at some points will expand a peripheral space V_t governed by k_{12} and return constant k_{21}. The following equations apply:

$$\frac{dvc}{dt} = Ro - k_{10} \left(v_c - V_c\right) - k_{12} \left(v_c - V_c\right) + k_{21} \left(v_t - V_t\right)$$

(2.1)

$$\frac{dvt}{dt} = k_{12} \left(v_c - V_c\right) - k_{21} \left(v_t - V_t\right)$$

(2.2)

$$\frac{v_c - V_c}{V_c} = \frac{[Hb / hb] - 1}{(1 - Hct)}$$

(2.3)

Equations (2.1) and (2.2) are differential equations that can be solved with nonlinear regression. Equation (2.3) expresses the Hb-derived fractional plasma dilution and indicates the volume expansion of V_c. Hb, hemoglobin; Hct, hematocrit.

Currently, VK has had little clinical impact. The most important contribution from this research field is that it has broadened our understanding of how fluids are handled by the body. It has, however, been hampered by the lack of obvious receptors and the need for plasma dilution as a central key for calculation of parameters. To clarify parameter estimates, the models require stressful infusions and repetitive endogenous dilution markers. The latter is currently an obstacle since frequent invasive observations are not possible in the clinical area. Noninvasive determinations of hemoglobin are not precise enough to allow robust calculations. Recently, there have been commendable efforts to use population kinetics to allow for confounding factors such as gender, age, and underlying pathology [19,20].

References

1. Moritz ML, Ayus JC. Maintenance intravenous fluids in acutely ill patients. *N Engl J Med.* 2016;374(3):290–1.
2. Stewart PA. Modern quantitative acid-base chemistry. *Can J Physiol Pharmacol.* 1983;61(12):1444–61.
3. Raghunathan K, Murray PT, Beattie WS, Lobo DN, Myburgh J, Sladen R, et al. Choice of fluid in acute illness: What should be given? An international consensus. *Br J Anaesth.* 2014;113(5):772–83.
4. Young P, Bailey M, Beasley R, Henderson S, Mackle D, McArthur C, et al. Effect of a buffered crystalloid solution vs saline on acute kidney injury among patients in the intensive care unit: The SPLIT randomized clinical trial. *JAMA.* 2015;314(16):1701–10.
5. Bulger EM, May S, Kerby JD, Emerson S, Stiell IG, Schreiber MA, et al. Out-of-hospital hypertonic resuscitation after traumatic hypovolemic shock: A randomized, placebo controlled trial. *Ann Surg.* 2011;253:431–41.
6. Bulger EM, Jurkovich GJ, Nathens AB, Copass MK, Hanson S, Cooper C, et al. Hypertonic resuscitation of hypovolemic shock after blunt trauma: A randomized controlled trial. *Arch Surg.* 2008;143:139–48.
7. Cooper DJ, Myles PS, McDermott FT, Murray LJ, Laidlaw J, Cooper G, et al. Prehospital hypertonic saline resuscitation of patients with hypotension and severe traumatic brain injury: A randomized controlled trial. *JAMA.* 2004;291(11):1350–7.
8. Han J, Ren HQ, Zhao QB, Wu YL, Qiao ZY. Comparison of 3% and 7.5% hypertonic saline in resuscitation after traumatic hypovolemic shock. *Shock.* 2015;43(3):244–9.
9. Chappell D, Jacob M, Hofmann-Kiefer K, Conzen P, Rehm M. A rational approach to perioperative fluid management. *Anesthesiology.* 2008;109(4): 723–40.
10. Brunkhorst FM, Engel C, Bloos F, Meier-Hellmann A, Ragaller M, Weiler N, et al. Intensive insulin therapy and pentastarch resuscitation in severe sepsis. *N Engl J Med.* 2008;358:125–39.
11. Perner A, Haase N, Guttormsen AB, Tenhunen J, Klemenzson G, Åneman A, et al. Hydroxyethyl starch 130/0.4 versus Ringer's acetate in severe sepsis. *N Eng J Med.* 2012;367:124–34.
12. Myburgh JA, Finfer S, Bellomo R, Billot L, Cass A, Gattas D, et al. Hydroxyethyl starch or saline for fluid resuscitation in intensive care. *N Engl J Med.* 2012;367:1901–11.

13. Annane D, Siami S, Jaber S, Martin C, Elatrous S, Declere AD, et al. Effects of fluid resuscitation with colloids vs crystalloids on mortality in critically ill patients presenting with hypovolemic shock: The CRISTAL randomized trial. *JAMA.* 2013;310(17):1809–17.

14. Kancir ASP, Johansen JK, Ekeloef NP, Pedersen EB. The effect of 6% hydroxyethyl starch 130/0.4 on renal function, arterial blood pressure, and vasoactive hormones during radical prostatectomy: A randomized controlled trial. *Anesth Analg.* 2015;120(3):608–18.

15. Van Der Linden P, James M, Mythen M, Weiskopf RB. Safety of modern starches used during surgery. *Anesth Analg.* 2013;116(1):35–48.

16. James MF, Michell WL, Joubert IA, Nicol AJ, Navsaria PH, Gillespie RS. Resuscitation with hydroxyethyl starch improves renal function and lactate clearance in penetrating trauma in a randomized controlled study: The FIRST trial (Fluids in Resuscitation of Severe Trauma). *Br J Anaesth.* 2011;107(5):693–702.

17. Svensen C, Hahn RG. Volume kinetics of ringer solution, dextran 70, and hypertonic saline in male volunteers. *Anesthesiology.* 1997;87(2):204–12.

18. Hahn RG. Volume kinetics for infusion fluids. *Anesthesiology.* 2009; 113:470–81.

19. Norberg A, Hahn RG, Li H, Olsson J, Prough DS, Borsheim E, et al. Population volume kinetics predicts retention of 0.9% saline infused in awake and isoflurane-anesthetized volunteers. *Anesthesiology.* 2007;107(1):24–32.

20. Hahn RG, Drobin D, Zdolsek J. Distribution of crystalloid fluid changes with the rate of infusion: A population-based study. *Acta Anaesthesiol Scand.* 2016;60(5):569–78.

chapter three

Perioperative fluid therapy
A general overview

Husong Li and Donald S. Prough
University of Texas Medical Branch at Galveston
Galveston, TX

Contents

Key point:
> This chapter provides a general and brief historical overview. It gives a summary of microcirculatory physiology and includes a comparison of crystalloids and colloids. Finally, the chapter contains an evidence-based discussion of perioperative fluid therapy.

3.1   Introduction

Perioperative fluid management must maintain effective intravascular volume, compensate for intraoperative volume losses, and prevent intraoperative and postoperative complications of inadequate tissue perfusion. All surgical patients, ranging from those having minimally invasive outpatient procedures to those having major intraabdominal or intrathoracic surgery, receive some quantity of fluid intraoperatively and postoperatively. Historically, both the composition and quantity of perioperative fluid management have generated controversy, for example, crystalloids versus colloids, liberal versus restricted regimens, and goal-directed versus more empirical approaches. Consequently, although perioperative fluid therapy is generally considered necessary, specific characteristics remain controversial. Much of the controversy is directly related to factors that constrain accurate assessment of patients' status. Key limiting factors include the following:

1. We cannot accurately evaluate blood volume.
2. We cannot quickly identify fluid overload.
3. We cannot accurately recognize hypovolemia.
4. We cannot accurately evaluate tissue perfusion.

Those problems persist despite a long history of perioperative fluid therapy.

Although clinical trials of perioperative fluid strategies over the past two decades have provided valuable insights, the answers to several key questions remain incomplete. Those questions are:

1. How is perioperative fluid management influenced by the type of surgery, by intercurrent treatment, and by underlying diseases?
2. Should perioperative fluid management be based on a prescribed "dose" or should it be given to attain certain physiologic goals?
3. If physiologic goals are preferable, which goals should be used?

3.2   Historical considerations

Some of the critical advances in perioperative fluid therapy occurred in the context of caring for mass military casualties. The bloody casualties of World War II facilitated application of intravenous fluid and transfusion therapy and conclusively established the role of intravenous fluid therapy in medical practice [1]. Shires et al. [2,3] introduced the clinically useful, but subsequently discredited, concept of a "third space," considered to be a third component of the extracellular fluid (ECF) volume, along with interstitial fluid volume and plasma volume (PV). The concept of this sequestered volume of fluid seemed to explain fluid deficits that were not clearly attributable to measured blood loss [4,5]. In part because of Shires' work, perioperative resuscitation with substantial volumes of crystalloid was widely incorporated into management of battle casualties in Vietnam. Based on the theoretical need to replace "third space" losses, infusion of large volumes of crystalloid during surgery became standard clinical practice [3,6–9], especially in patients undergoing abdominal surgery. Interstitial accumulation of fluid in tissues was interpreted as an unavoidable consequence of proper fluid management. Postoperative patients commonly gained 7–10 kg of weight (7–10 L of retained fluid) [10–13], prompting increasing concerns about the influence of excessive fluid accumulation on morbidity and mortality [14,15].

Concurrently, investigators clarified the physiologic basis for perioperative fluid therapy. The volumes and compositions of body fluid compartments were quantified [16–19]. Overnight fasting produces a slight loss of total body water because of obligatory water loss, although sodium loss is minimal [20]. Insensible losses continue as a consequence of ventilation with unhumidified gases and perspiration. Evaporative losses increase substantially with damage to the skin barrier [21]. However, in aggregate, the intravascular deficits attributable to these factors is modest. In terms of the physiologic basis of perioperative fluid therapy, the most important recent advance is the rapidly increasing understanding of the vascular endothelial glycocalyx. The endothelial glycocalyx, consisting of membrane-bound proteoglycans and glycoproteins, coats the endothelium on the luminal side [22–24].

Pharmacologic vasodilation produced by general and neuraxial anesthesia was managed by infusing intravenous fluids. However, preanesthetic fluid loading has little influence on anesthesia-related hypotension [25–28], prompting the concept that mild, intermittent, intraoperative hypotension is more appropriately treated with vasopressors [28]. Widespread application of invasive central venous pressure and pulmonary arterial occlusion pressure measurements offered misleading reassurance, in that large volumes of retained fluid often were associated with apparently safe cardiac filling pressures.

In a seminal and highly controversial publication, Arieff et al. [29] proposed, based on experience in his local hospital, that thousands of surgical patients annually developed pulmonary edema as a consequence of unnecessary fluid administration and that some died, even in the absence of cardiac risk factors. Subsequent research demonstrated fundamental flaws in the methodology that generated the concept of third-space fluid accumulations [30]. Consequently, most clinicians accept the premise that, in the absence of major perioperative hemorrhage, large volumes of intravenous fluid are not necessary perioperatively and may lead to hypervolemia with detrimental pulmonary and systemic interstitial edema [3,31].

During the past 10–15 years, clinical studies have generated compelling evidence that restrictive fluid therapy, best defined as avoidance of fluid administration for which there is no clear need, is associated with improved perioperative outcomes in comparison to unnecessarily aggressive fluid therapy [7,32–41]. However, excessive fluid restriction is also associated with complications, such as increased nausea and vomiting, especially in relatively short outpatient procedures [42].

The ultimate goal of perioperative fluid therapy is individualized patient care, that is, administration of the best volume and best composition of fluids for a specific patient undergoing a specific procedure. Ideally, perioperative fluid therapy will avoid both inadequate and excessive fluid administration, both of which in theory or practice could be associated with complications. Bellamy [43] has conceptually depicted fluid therapy as a *U* shape, with complications associated with either side of the *U* and favorable outcomes associated with the base (Figure 3.1) [43]. Most patients have sufficient physiological reserves that they tolerate either under- or overhydration. More fragile patients require more precise fluid therapy. To some extent, individualized fluid therapy can be approximated by referring to published clinical trials, for example, for patients undergoing colon surgery, a protocol resembling that used by Brandstrup et al. [32] appears to be appropriate. More specific information about the hemodynamic status of an individual patient may be obtained from a variety of invasive and noninvasive monitors. Although considerable controversy surrounds the appropriate use of intraoperative monitors, some clinical investigators argue that fluid therapy that is guided by quantitative monitoring is associated with improved surgical morbidity and mortality [31,44].

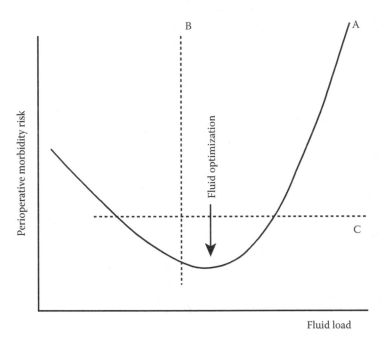

Figure 3.1 Curve A represents the relative risk of perioperative morbidity related to qualitative fluid load. Broken line B represents a hypothetical division between patient groups managed using a dry (limited fluid load) versus a wet (higher fluid load) trial. Broken line C represents a division between patients managed using an optimized (below line C) or non-optimized (above line C). In individual patients, an optimal fluid "dose," that is, one that minimizes perioperative morbidity risk, could be larger or smaller based on the needs of an individual patient. (From Bellamy, M.C., *Br. J. Anaesth.*, 97, 755–757, 2006. With permission.)

In this chapter, we will provide an overview of current practice related to perioperative fluid therapy, including important aspects of microcirculatory physiology, the advantages and disadvantages of crystalloid versus colloid fluids, clinical trials of fluid management strategies in specific types of patients, and the role of monitoring in refining fluid administration.

3.3   Microcirculatory physiology

In theory, intravenous fluids distribute in body fluids based on the relationship between sodium and colloid concentrations in the infused fluid and various body fluid compartments (Figure 3.2). Water, ions, and, to a variable extent, colloids such as albumin pass between plasma, interstitial fluid (ISF), and intracellular fluid (ICF). Total body water constitutes 60% of body weight in lean adults, somewhat more in infants and children, and somewhat less in obese or aged adults. The ICF compartment, which constitutes two-thirds of total body water, contains minimal sodium. The remaining one-third, the ECF compartment, has a sodium

Figure 3.2 Total body water (TBW) constitutes 60% of body weight in lean adults, somewhat more in infants and children and somewhat less in obese or aged adults. The intracellular volume (ICV) compartment, which constitutes two-thirds of total body water, contains minimal sodium. The remaining one-third, the extracellular volume (ECV) compartment, has a sodium concentration ~140 mEq/L. The capillary endothelium separates the ECF compartment into interstitial fluid volume (IFV), which is 75–80% of ECF, and plasma. The sodium concentration in IFV and plasma is equal but plasma contains ~4.0 g/dL of albumin, while the concentration in IFV is much lower.

concentration ~140 mEq/L. The ECF compartment is separated by the capillary endothelium into ISF, which is 75%–80% of ECF [16,17], and plasma. The sodium concentration in ISF and plasma is equal but plasma contains ~4.0 g/dL of albumin, while the concentration in ISF is much lower. The capillary endothelium is freely permeable to water, anions, cations, and other soluble substances such as glucose but is less permeable to protein. The permeability of capillary membranes to specific substances is described by the reflection coefficient (σ), which ranges from 0 for freely permeable substances such as sodium ions in peripheral capillary beds to 1.0 for completely impermeable substances. In peripheral capillaries σ for albumin is ~0.7.

The conventional model of the forces governing fluid shifts between plasma and ISF includes permeability and the hydrostatic and colloid osmotic pressure (COP) gradients across the capillary membrane (Figure 3.3) [45]. In this model, the hydrostatic pressure gradient, which tends to push fluid out of capillaries, is opposed by the inward pull of the COP gradient. Physiological fluid movement occurs continuously through an intact capillary barrier and is returned to the vascular compartment by the lymphatic system, thereby avoiding interstitial edema. Pathological fluid movement occurs when a damaged vascular barrier allows excessive fluid accumulation, leading to interstitial edema [46].

However, the conventional model does not include the endothelial glycocalyx, which, together with bound plasma constituents such as albumin, constitutes a physiologically active endothelial surface layer (ESL)

Conventional starling equilibrium

$$Jv/A = Lp\,[(P_c - P_{is}) - \sigma(\pi_c - \pi_{is})]$$

"Low lymph flow paradox" – Lymph flow is less than calculated.

Figure 3.3 Conventional concept of the Starling principle. Jv/A, volume filtered per unit area; Lp, hydraulic conductance; P_c, capillary hydrostatic pressure; P_{is}, interstitial hydrostatic pressure; σ, osmotic reflection co-efficient; π_c, capillary oncotic pressure; π_{is}, interstitial oncotic pressure. The "low lymph flow paradox," that is, the experimental observation that lymph flow is less than would be predicted from the equation, suggests that the conventional model is incomplete. (From Alphonsus, C.S., and Rodseth, R.N., *Anaesthesia*, 69, 777–784, 2014. With permission.)

with a functional thickness of over 1 mm (Figure 3.4) [45]. Recognition of the importance of the endothelial glycocalyx has substantially modified the concept of the classical Starling equilibrium and redefined the concept of vascular permeability. More recent research has demonstrated the important regulatory contribution of the endothelial glycocalyx to transendothelial fluid movement. The ESL, composed of glycoproteins, proteoglycans, and glycosaminoglycans, contains no erythrocytes and is rich in fluid-binding proteins. Therefore, the intravascular volume, traditionally consisting of the PV and red cell volume, also contains the glycocalyx volume [47], which in adults is noncirculating and approximates 700–800 mL [11,48].

Effectively, the glycocalyx increases the oncotic pressure within the ESL, while a small space between the anatomical vessel wall and the ESL remains nearly protein-free [49]. Therefore, the actual COP gradient that opposes the hydrostatic pressure gradient is higher than is suggested by the calculated gradient between plasma COP and COP in ISF [23]. Physiologically, there is a "double barrier" to fluid movement across capillaries, which consists of both endothelial cells and the ESL [23].

The ESL constitutes the first contact between blood and tissue and contributes to vascular barrier function, inflammation, and coagulation.

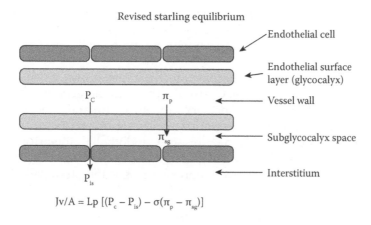

Revised starling equilibrium

Endothelial cell

Endothelial surface layer (glycocalyx)

P_c π_p Vessel wall

π_{sg} Subglycocalyx space

P_{is} Interstitium

$$Jv/A = Lp\,[(P_c - P_{is}) - \sigma(\pi_p - \pi_{sg})]$$

Figure 3.4 The revised Starling equilibrium includes the influence of the endothelial surface layer (glycocalyx) and the colloid osmotic pressure in the subglycocalyx space (π_{sg}). Jv/A, volume filtered per unit area; Lp, hydraulic conductance; P_C, capillary hydrostatic pressure; P_{is}, interstitial hydrostatic pressure; σ, osmotic reflection co-efficient; π_p, oncotic pressure on plasma-side of endothelial surface layer. The osmotic pressure gradient that opposes the hydrostatic pressure gradient is the gradient from π_p to π_{sg}, rather than the gradient from π_p to π_{is} (interstitial oncotic pressure). (From Alphonsus, C.S., and Rodseth, R.N., *Anaesthesia,* 69, 777–784, 2014. With permission.)

Table 3.1 Factors associated with glycocalyx damage and protection

Factors associated with glycocalyx damage
Reperfusion injury
Inflammation and trauma
Atherosclerosis and diabetes
Hypervolemia
Factors associated with glycocalyx protection
Maintain concentration of plasma proteins
Pharmacologic doses of albumin
Glucocorticoids (mast-cell stabilization)
Antithrombin III and protease inhibition
Antioxidants
Normovolemia
Avoid ANP release
Supply raw materials for glycocalyx production

Various drugs and pathologic states impair the glycocalyx scaffolding and reduce the thickness of the ESL. Postischemic reperfusion, both experimental [22] and clinical [50], impairs glycocalyx function, as do systemic inflammatory states such as diabetes, hyperglycemia, surgery, trauma, and sepsis [47]. The systemic inflammatory response syndrome leads to thinning of the ESL, which triggers increased leukocyte adhesion and increased transendothelial permeability [22,49,51,52]. Hypervolemia also impairs the glycocalyx impairment, mediated by liberation of atrial natriuretic peptide [53].

Perioperative protection of the endothelial glycocalyx has the potential to limit interstitial edema. Currently, there are no generally accepted pharmacological strategies to preserve the structure and function of the glycocalyx, although experimental studies suggest that hydrocortisone, antithrombin, and sevoflurane preserve endothelial integrity [54,55]. Avoiding insults that damage the glycocalyx and incorporation of potentially protective agents (Table 3.1) represent reasonable strategies [56].

3.4 Crystalloid and colloid fluids

Intravenous fluids fall into two broad categories: crystalloids and colloids. Crystalloids, which are aqueous solutions of electrolytes, small organic anions, or sugars and are available in varying compositions (Table 3.2) [57], represent the original and the oldest form of intravenous fluid therapy.

In clinical practice, the most commonly used crystalloid, 0.9% saline [58], contains 154 mmol/L each of sodium and chloride. Because the solution contains a higher concentration of chloride than the approximately

Table 3.2 Contents of commonly available crystalloid solutions

Content	Plasma	0.9% Sodium chloride	5% Glucose	Hartmann's[a]	Plasma-Lyte 148
Sodium (mmol/L)	135–145	154	0	131	140
Chloride (mmol/L)	95–105	154	0	111	98
Potassium (mmol/L)	3.5–5.3	0	0	5	5
Bicarbonate (mmol/L)	24–32	0	0	29 (lactate)	50 (27 acetate; 23 gluconate)
Calcium (mmol/L)	2.2–2.6	0	0	2	0
Magnesium (mmol/L)	0.8–1.2	0	0	0	1.5
Glucose (mmol/L)	3.5–5.5	0	278 (40 g)	0	0
pH	7.35–7.45	4.5–7.0	3.5–5.5	5.0–7.0	4.0–6.5
Osmolarity (mOsm/L)	275–295	308	278	278	295

Source: Garrioch, S.S., and Gillies, M.A., *Curr. Opin. Crit. Care*, 21, 358–363, 2015.

[a] Hartmann's solution, Lactated Ringer's solution.

100 mmol/L in plasma, infusions of large volumes of chloride-rich solutions, such as 0.9% saline, result in hyperchloremia metabolic acidosis both in healthy volunteers [59] and surgical patients [60]. The magnitude of the reduction can be readily predicted from the relative volumes of ECF (the distribution volume for chloride and bicarbonate, i.e., 20% of total body weight) and the volume of infused 0.9% saline [61]. Not simply an acid–base issue, hyperchloremia has also been associated with decreased renal blood flow and glomerular filtration rate [62].

Balanced salt solutions, such as lactated Ringer's solution, are crystalloids that more closely resemble plasma constituents in that an anionic component, for example, acetate or lactate, partially replaces chloride. A recent large observational study of over 30,000 adult patients undergoing major abdominal surgery compared morbidity and mortality between those receiving 0.9% saline and 926 patients who only received the balanced crystalloid solution Plasma-Lyte 148 on the day of surgery [63]. The patients receiving Plasma-Lyte 148 had less acidemia, lower mortality (5.6% in the 0.9% saline group vs. 2.9% in the Plasma-Lyte 148 group; $P < 0.001$), fewer postoperative infections, less frequent electrolyte disturbances, less frequent acute kidney injury requiring dialysis, and required fewer blood transfusions. Another large cohort study of over 9,000 patients showed an increased 30-day mortality (odds ratio [OR] 2.05, 95% confidence interval [CI] 1.62–2.59) in hyperchloremic noncardiac surgical patients [64].

Balanced salt solutions that contain potassium have been considered hazardous for patients with renal failure, diabetic ketoacidosis, and those undergoing renal transplantation surgery. However, the low concentration of potassium in balanced salt solutions, ~4.0 mEq/L, is small in comparison to total body potassium stores exceeding 4,200 mEq in a 70-kg adult. A randomized controlled trial comparing 0.9% saline to lactated Ringer's solution in 51 patients undergoing renal transplant surgery demonstrated more frequent clinically significant hyperkalemia (29% vs. 0%; $P < 0.05$) and metabolic acidosis (31% vs. 0%; $P < 0.04$) in patients receiving saline, presumably because the acidemia produced by 0.9% saline caused movement of potassium from intracellular to extracellular fluid [65]. In liver transplantation, a high chloride-based fluid regimen has been associated with acute kidney injury [66]. In ICU patients with sepsis, balanced crystalloid use was associated with reduced hospital mortality (relative risk [RR] 0.86, 95% CI 0.78–0.94) in comparison to 0.9% saline [67]. Because the calcium in Ringer's solution can bind to certain drugs and reduce their effectiveness, aminocaproic acid (Amicar), amphotericin, ampicillin, and thiopental should be infused in another crystalloid. The calcium in Ringer's can also inactivate the citrated anticoagulant in blood products, promoting rouleaux formation in donor blood. These findings suggest that balanced crystalloids are the fluids of choice for fluid resuscitation in the perioperative setting, and the use of 0.9% saline should be reserved for specific conditions such as treatment of hypochloremic metabolic alkalosis.

The term *colloids* refers to aqueous solutions that contain both electrolytes and large organic macromolecules (usually >40 kDa). Because larger molecules cross the endothelium less well, colloids are better retained within the intravascular space than crystalloids. Although the longer plasma half-life of colloids theoretically increases their effectiveness as resuscitation fluids, increased endothelial permeability in critically ill patients may accelerate movement into the interstitial space, thereby reducing the efficacy of volume expansion, increasing tissue edema, and potentially promoting end-organ damage.

The size of colloids is conventionally described in terms of two different expressions of molecular weight: (1) Mw, weight average molecular weight and (2) Mn, number average molecular weight. The Mw determines the viscosity and Mn indicates the oncotic pressure. Albumin is said to be monodispersed because all molecules have the same molecular weight (Mw = Mn). Artificial colloids are all polydispersed with a range of molecular weights [68]. Almost all colloid solutions have an osmolality similar to that of plasma. However, colloid osmotic (oncotic) pressure, which represents a small percentage of osmolality, varies greatly. As colloid osmotic pressure increases, initial volume expansion increases. The sodium content, the primary cationic determinant of osmolality, of commercially available colloid solutions is similar to that of crystalloid solutions, while the potassium, chloride, and calcium concentrations differ. Urea-linked gelatin solutions contain limited concentrations of potassium and calcium.

The plasma half-life of a colloid depends on its molecular weight, elimination route, and function of the metabolizing or excreting organ. Half-lives of colloids vary greatly. The molecular weight mainly determines the degree of volume expansion, whereas intravascular persistence is determined by elimination. When compared to crystalloids, colloids induce greater PV expansion for the same administered volume [68].

Volume expansion produced by colloid administration is context-sensitive. Volume loading with either 6% hydroxyethyl starch (HES) or 5% albumin in normovolemic patients resulted in 68% of the infused volume extravasating from the intravascular space into the ISF within minutes [14,31]. Conversely, when 6% HES or 5% albumin was given to replace withdrawn blood and produce normovolemic hemodilution, the volume remaining in the PV approached 90% [11]. Based on theoretical volumes of distribution (total ECF for crystalloid vs. plasma PV for colloid), at least three to four times more crystalloid than colloid should be necessary to achieve similar hemodynamic effects. The ratio in surgical studies appears to be considerably lower (mean 1.8, SD 0.1) [69], perhaps because vasopermeability to colloid is increased in the clinical setting or because replacement with colloid of shed blood requires a ratio exceeding 1:1.

Though colloids result initially in a greater increase in intravascular volume than colloids, greater intravascular volume expansion does not appear to improve mortality. Two randomized controlled studies, the Saline versus Albumin Fluid Evaluation (SAFE) study and the Fluid Expansion as Supportive Therapy (FEAST) study, addressed that question. In the SAFE study, 6,997 critically ill, ICU-admitted adults were randomized to resuscitation with 4% albumin or 0.9% saline [70]. In the FEAST study, 3,141 febrile, critically ill children were randomly assigned to receive boluses of 5% albumin, 0.9% saline, or no bolus of resuscitation fluid [71]. While neither the FEAST nor the SAFE study detected differences in clinical outcomes between groups receiving 0.9% saline or albumin, a subgroup analysis from the SAFE study showed higher mortality associated with albumin in 460 patients with traumatic brain injury (RR, 1.63; 95% CI 1.17–2.26; $P = 0.003$) [72]. In contrast, another subgroup analysis of the SAFE study indicated a potential decrease in the adjusted risk of death with albumin in severely septic patients

(OR 0.71; 95% CI 0.52–0.97; $P = 0.03$) [73]. Both of these studies assume that all crystalloid solutions are similar. However, several studies now have shown a benefit of balanced crystalloid solutions over 0.9% saline in perioperative mortality and morbidity [63,74]. Therefore a comparison between colloid and crystalloid in which the crystalloid is 0.9% saline might reflect the adverse influence of 0.9% saline rather than the influence of crystalloid fluids *per se*.

Several clinical studies have confirmed that synthetic colloids, like albumin solutions, provide greater volume expansion than crystalloids and therefore greater increases in cardiac index, cardiac output, and stroke volume in cardiac surgery, major vascular surgery, or septic patients [75,76].

Albumin, the first colloid solution used clinically, is harvested from human plasma and is available in several concentrations (4%, 5%, 20%, and 25%). The cost of albumin, which varies widely across the world, has limited its use. Synthetic colloids, in particular HES, gelatins, and dextran, are less expensive but still may not be preferable for clinical use. Gelatins are protein-based products derived from bovine gelatin. HES, large carbohydrate molecules derived from the starch of potatoes or maize, are available in solutions of various molecular weights (130, 200, and 450 kD). Dextrans are carbohydrate-based, polysaccharide molecules made by bacteria during ethanol fermentation. The colloid osmotic (oncotic pressure) of colloid solutions varies depending on molecular weight and concentration. Both hypo-oncotic (gelatins, 4% and 5% albumin) and hyperoncotic solutions (20% or 25% albumin, dextran, and HES 6% and 10%) have been used. The physiological actions, volume expansion properties, and potential morbidities of these solutions are determined by multiple factors, including oncotic pressure, molecular weight, plasma half-life, metabolism, and tissue accumulation [68]. Table 3.3 compares 4% albumin solution to several crystalloid solutions.

In the United States, the only colloid solutions now used commonly are albumin-based. Concerns regarding the toxicity of commonly used synthetic colloid solutions have resulted in a marked decrease in use, especially in critically ill patients, and repeated calls for complete withdrawal from the market. Serious concerns have risen over deleterious effects of semisynthetic colloids on specific systems, such as hemostasis [77] and renal function [78–80]. Significant reductions in factor VIII and von Willebrand factor are observed after infusion of dextrans, gelatins, and HES, with high-molecular weight HES and dextran having the greatest effect on hemostasis [77] Substantial evidence suggests that infusion of semisynthetic colloids is associated with a greater likelihood of renal dysfunction and an increased requirement for renal replacement therapy than albumin or crystalloids. Four well-designed, large, randomized controlled trials, published in 2008, 2012, and 2013, compared the use of HES with

Table 3.3 Comparison of 4% albumin and several commercially available crystalloid fluids

Solute	Plasma	Colloid	Crystalloids			
		4% Albumin	Normal saline	Ringer's lactate	Hartmann's solution	Plasma-Lyte
Na^+ (mmol/L)	135–145	148	154	130	131	140
K^+ (mmol/L)	4.0–5.0	0	0	4.5	5	5
Ca^{2+} (mmol/L)	2.2–2.6	0	0	2.7	4	0
Mg^{2+} (mmol/L)	1.0–2.0	0	0	0	0	1.5
Cl^- (mmol/L)	95–110	128	154	109	111	98
Acetate (mmol/L)	0	0	0	0	0	27
Lactate (mmol/L)	0.8–1.8	0	0	28	29	0
Gluconate (mmol/L)	0	0	0	0	0	23
Bicarbonate (mmol/L)	23–26	0	0	0	0	0
Osmolarity (mOsm/kg)	291	250	308	280	279	294
Colloid osmotic pressure (mmHg)	35–45	20	0	0	0	0

acetated or lactated Ringer's solutions [81,82] or with 0.9% saline [83,84]. The groups receiving HES had an increased risk of death [81] and need for renal replacement therapy [81–84]. Growing concerns about safety, especially of HES colloids, and the lack of conclusive evidence of clinical superiority of colloids suggest that less expensive crystalloids are preferable for routine perioperative use [85]. Defining an optimal perioperative fluid strategy remains an ongoing challenge. Failure to provide adequate intravenous fluid can place a patient at risk of developing hypovolemia, acute kidney injury, and coagulopathy. Although colloid solutions, in comparison to crystalloids, induce greater PV expansion for the same administered volume, growing concerns about safety prompt serious concerns. As noted previously, current evidence suggests that balanced crystalloids and albumin may be safer than 0.9% saline and synthetic colloids, respectively. At the same time, each patient's perioperative fluid therapy should be individualized, based on consideration of intravascular volume status, comorbidities, type of surgery, and goal(s) of fluid resuscitation. These considerations should be considered prone to replacement with others based on results from ongoing clinical trials.

3.5   *Perioperative fluid management*

Planning and delivering an optimal perioperative "dose" of fluid for every patient is currently impossible, although recent clinical studies provide guidance that is sufficient to improve fluid management in comparison to conventional treatment. The factors that theoretically determine an appropriate dose of perioperative fluid constitute the perioperative morbidity risk [43], which is the net effect of the preoperative physical status of a patient, anesthetic administration, the use of positive pressure ventilation, and surgical circumstances, especially the type and duration of the surgery and expected blood loss. Each factor alone can exert a substantial effect on net risk, but precise measurement of the risk associated with any one factor is difficult and measurement of net risk is at this time impossible.

Assume for purposes of discussion that a population of patients could undergo surgery and that all factors but one could be held constant. If all factors but one—preoperative physical status, anesthetic administration, positive pressure ventilation, or surgical circumstances—could be held constant, the optimal dose of fluid for the population of patients would likely be described by a normal distribution curve. Imagine a curve that describes fluid-associated perioperative morbidity for a specific set of surgical circumstances (see Figure 3.1). A few patients should receive very little fluid, a few should receive a substantial quantity of fluid, and the majority of patients would do well with intermediate quantities. Assume then that net perioperative morbidity risk consists of both "minor" complications,

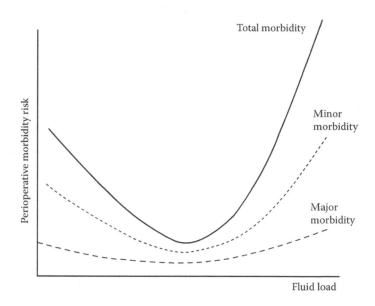

Figure 3.5 Net perioperative morbidity risk consists of both "minor" complications, for example, thirst or postoperative nausea and vomiting, and "major"
complications, for example, organ failure or death. Both may be associated with
inadequate or excessive perioperative fluid therapy.

for example, thirst or postoperative pain severity, and "major" complications, for example, organ failure or death (Figure 3.5). Now assume that
those curves are distinct for different sets of surgical circumstances. If we
convert the horizontal axis to mL/kg of fluid in published clinical studies,
we can visualize the influence of perioperative fluid load on complication
risk for routine outpatient surgery (Figure 3.6) [7], laparoscopic cholecystectomy (Figure 3.7) [38], and colon surgery (Figure 3.8) [32]. Note that the
three studies represented in the figure each studied only two "doses" of
fluid, so the results are represented by two symbols without connecting
curves, because the full curves cannot be predicted based on only two
points each.

Moreover, for any pair of points, it seems likely that the points would
be different if any one factor, such as preoperative physical status or surgical speed and expertise, were variable. From that perspective, consider
the typical randomized clinical trial of fluid administration, in which a
specific surgical procedure is performed by a variety of surgeons, often
in multiple institutions, on a variety of patients with a wide variety of
preoperative medical conditions. For practical reasons, patients in typical
clinical trials are randomized to two strategies of fluid administration,
low and high. Either strategy could be superior—closer to optimal—in a
subset of patients, in which case the overall outcome of the trial could be

Figure 3.6 The data have been abstracted from Maharaj et al., who studied eighty ASA I-III patients undergoing gynecologic laparoscopy. Patients were randomized to receive either a "low-dose" (3 mL/kg total) or a "high-dose" (2 mL/kg per hour fasting) of preoperative sodium lactate solution. Patients in both groups averaged approximately 70 kg. The low dose group had an overall incidence of postoperative nausea and vomiting (PONV) exceeding 80% and the high-dose group had an overall incidence <60%. (Data from Maharaj, C.H., et al., *Anesth. Analg.*, 100, 675–682, 2005.)

determined by the relative numbers of patients in each subset. Therefore, prediction of a proper "dose" of perioperative fluid for a specific patient undergoing surgery is difficult at best, which has prompted a search for effective methods for individualizing fluid therapy.

In any surgical patient, the aim of intraoperative fluid therapy is to maintain an adequate circulating volume to ensure end-organ perfusion and oxygen delivery to the tissues. Traditional fluid therapy was based on four now-controversial pathophysiologic assumptions:

1. Preoperative fasting results in hypovolemia because of ongoing insensible losses.
2. Evaporative losses increase when surgery compromises the dermal barrier.
3. Surgery-induced fluid shifts into a "third space" require generous replacement.
4. Moderate hypervolemia is well tolerated because the kidneys regulate the overload [46].

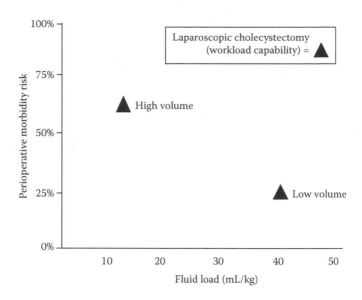

Figure 3.7 The data have been abstracted from Holte et al., who studied 48 ASA I-II patients undergoing laparoscopic cholecystectomy. Patients were randomized to receive either a "low-dose" (15 mL/kg total) or a "high-dose" (40 mL/kg total) of lactated Ringer's solution. Four hours postoperatively, the low dose group had a statistically significantly greater reduction in workload (assessed using tread-mill exercise). (Data from Holte, K., et al., *Ann. Surg.*, 240, 892–899, 2004.)

Recent studies of perioperative fluid management challenge those con-cepts and suggest that significant benefit can be achieved by individual-izing therapy based on patient responses. Perioperative fluid management has long been dictated by a generalized formulaic approach, rather than physiologic and homeostatic needs. However, both under-resuscitation and over-resuscitation can have deleterious effects and lead to increased mor-bidity and mortality [86,87].

Perhaps the greatest influence on current practice was a multicenter study by Brandstrup et al. [32] in 141 patients undergoing major colorectal surgery. A group randomized to perioperative intravenous fluid restric-tion (mean 2,740 vs. 5,388 mL) experienced significantly more major and minor complications, such as anastomotic leakage, pulmonary edema, pneumonia, and wound infection. Despite fluid restriction and a periop-erative decrease in urinary output, acute kidney injury did not occur in any patient. However, the group randomized to restrictive management also received a higher proportion of fluid as colloids. In a similar study, Nisanevic et al. found that restrictive fluid therapy (1.2 vs. 3.7 L) decreased postoperative morbidity and hospital stay in a more heterogeneous group of 152 patients scheduled for abdominal surgery [40]. Protocol-based fluid

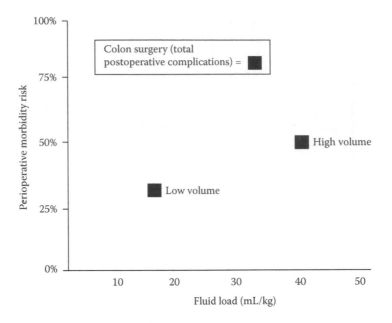

Figure 3.8 The data have been abstracted from Brandstrup et al., who studied 172 ASA I-III patients undergoing elective colorectal resection. Patients were randomized to receive either a fluid restriction or standard perioperative fluid regimen. Total postoperative complications (including minor complications, tissue healing complications and cardiopulmonary complications) were significantly fewer in the fluid restriction group. (Data from Brandstrup, B., et al., *Ann. Surg.*, 238, 641–648, 2003.)

restriction has been associated with a reduced incidence of perioperative complications such as cardiopulmonary events [32,40] and disturbances of bowel motility [5,40], while improving wound and anastomotic healing [32,40] and reducing hospital stay [5,40]. Postoperative fluid restriction was associated with less weight gain, earlier return of bowel function, and shorter hospital stay [5]. If perioperative fluid restriction minimizes weight gain, a surrogate measure of fluid retention, after colon surgery to <1.0 kg (<1.0 L), complications of colon surgery appear to be limited [34].

While restrictive fluid therapy has been associated with fewer complications in intra-abdominal and other major procedures, patients having minor ambulatory surgery may have less postoperative nausea and vomiting (PONV) and postoperative pain if they receive somewhat more fluid. In patients undergoing gynecologic laparoscopy, larger (2 mL/kg per hour of fasting) infusions of sodium lactate solution over 20 minutes preoperatively were associated with less pain and PONV than 3 mL/kg total [7]. Reduced pain resulted in fewer patients receiving morphine (35% vs. 65%), which may partially explain the lower incidence of PONV.

Also, in women undergoing ambulatory gynecologic laparoscopy, Magner et al. [88] reported that intraoperative infusion of 30 mL/kg of sodium lactate solution reduced the incidence of vomiting, nausea, and antiemetic use in comparison to 10 mL/kg. In contrast, McCaul et al. [89] showed that even complete avoidance of perioperative fluid infusion did not increase the risk of PONV in comparison to 1.5 mL/kg of sodium lactate per hour of fasting. In patients undergoing laparoscopic cholecystectomy, intraoperative administration of 40 mL/kg of crystalloid improved postoperative organ function and recovery and reduced vomiting in comparison to 15 mL/kg LR [38]. However, fluid restriction was not associated with clinically important differences in recovery variables after fast-track knee arthroplasty [36].

These data, despite some inconsistencies, suggest that higher volumes of balanced salt solutions might reduce the risk of PONV and improve general well-being after ambulatory surgery or laparoscopic surgery of the gall bladder or female reproductive tract. However, the opposite appears to be true for patients undergoing intra-abdominal surgery, especially colorectal surgery.

Of course, the above studies randomized patients to higher or lower "doses" of perioperative fluids. Goal-directed therapy (GDT) hypothesizes that outcomes may be improved if fluid therapy is individualized, based on quantitative assessment of a patient's individual fluid responsiveness. Assessment could include ability to improve cardiac output, stroke volume, or oxygen delivery in response to fluid administration or a surrogate of fluid administration (e.g., straight-leg raising). However, a variety of goals have been used. In the 1980s, pulmonary artery catheters (PACs) were inserted to measure and maintain tissue oxygen delivery above a target threshold (>600 mL O_2/kg/min/m^2) in high-risk surgical patients; in some surgical series that approach was associated with reduced complications, duration of hospitalization, duration of ICU stay, duration of mechanical ventilation, and costs [90]. Unfortunately, PACs themselves are associated with morbidity.

In recent years, less-invasive methods of monitoring flow-based hemodynamic parameters have been developed. Minimally invasive monitors include esophageal Doppler monitoring and arterial waveform analysis (e.g., stroke volume variation and pulse pressure variation, PPV). Other methods require both arterial and central venous access to measure cardiac output. Both the LiDCO and PiCCO systems use arterial pulse contour analysis to measure stroke volume after initial calibration with either lithium (LiDCO) or thermal indicators (PiCCO). The FloTrac/Vigileo system also analyses pulse contour but does not require calibration, which is based on a computer program after input of biometric data [31].

A recent systematic review and meta-analysis looked at the use of preemptive hemodynamic intervention in moderate- to high-risk patients to improve postoperative outcomes. Twenty-nine studies were identified that used various forms of hemodynamic monitors, including PAC, LiDCO, PiCCO, FloTrac, and PPV. Interventions consisted of fluid therapy with or without inotrope support. Preemptive fluid therapy guided by hemodynamic monitoring appeared to reduce surgical morbidity and mortality [44]. In the intraoperative setting, esophageal Doppler monitor (EDM) has been the most heavily investigated minimally invasive monitoring technique [91,92]. In cardiac surgery, EDM was associated with decreased hospital length of stay, fewer complications, and decreased gastric acidosis [93] Meta-analyses of EDM in major abdominal surgery have shown that it is associated with fewer postoperative complications, reduced ICU admission, reduced hospital length of stay, and faster return of gastrointestinal function [94,95] However, EDM has not been widely adopted in the United States, perhaps in part because of challenges in obtaining proper alignment of the probe and in part because the primary EDM measure of preload, corrected systolic flow time in the descending aorta, is nonintuitive.

In contrast to apparent perioperative value, GDT has been less successful in critically ill patients. Two recent large, multicenter randomized controlled trials, the Australasian Resuscitation in Sepsis Evaluation (ARISE) and Protocolized Care for Early Septic Shock (ProCESS) studies, examined GDT in early septic shock [96,97]. The ARISE study found no reduction in all-cause mortality at 90 days, and the ProCESS study showed no improvement in outcomes including 60-day in-hospital mortality, 90-day mortality, 1-year mortality, or the need for organ support. The OPTIMISE trial [86] was a multicenter, randomized, observer-blinded trial of 734 high-risk patients undergoing major GI surgery in 17 hospitals in the United Kingdom. The aim of the study was to evaluate a GDT algorithm (based on cardiac output measurements using the LiDCO monitor) using intravenous fluid boluses and an inotrope (dopexamine). This multicenter study did not confirm previous data suggesting that GDT improved outcome. There were no significant differences between the groups for infection, length of stay, critical care-free days, morbidity on Day 7, or all-cause mortality at 30 or 180 days.

The clinical value of GDT remains uncertain. Reducing the uncertainty requires answers to several questions. What is the best hemodynamic goal (cardiac output, stroke volume, mixed venous oxygen saturation)? What is the best objective evidence that GDT is necessary—simply falling below the goal or evidence of tissue hypoperfusion? If the latter is necessary, what indicator of tissue hypoperfusion is sufficiently sensitive and specific? What type of fluid should be administered to attain the goal? Does addition of an inotropic agent improve outcome? Most importantly, what algorithm(s) should be used to achieve the goal? Although GDT remains an attractive concept, much more research is necessary to implement successful management, perhaps using monitors that have yet to be introduced.

3.6 Conclusion and suggestions

Intravenous fluid therapy is an important aspect of perioperative care. Evidence suggests that we may be able to modify outcome by our choice of intravenous resuscitation fluid, particularly in high-risk patients. Current clinical evidence favors the use of balanced salt solutions for perioperative fluid therapy and resuscitation. There is no evidence to suggest that synthetic colloids are superior to crystalloids, and because of the possibility of harm they cannot be recommended. In the low-risk patient undergoing low-risk or ambulatory surgery, crystalloid infusions of the order of 20–30 mL/kg (e.g., 2 L over 30 min to the average adult) improves ambulatory anesthesia outcomes such as pain, nausea, and dizziness and increases street readiness. On the other hand, high-risk patients undergoing major intra-abdominal surgery seem to benefit from a restrictive fluid regimen. As less invasive methods of monitoring flow-based hemodynamic parameters have entered clinical practice, the concept of GDT shows promise for improving outcomes. However, further clinical research is necessary to determine if that promise is justified.

References

1. Barsoum N, Kleeman C. Now and then, the history of parenteral fluid administration. *Am J Nephrol* 2002; 22: 284–9.
2. Shires GT, Williams J, Brown F. Acute changes in extracellular fluid associated with major surgical procedures. *Ann Surg* 1961; 154: 803–10.
3. Jacob M, Chappell D, Rehm M. The 'third space'–fact or fiction? *Best Pract Res Clin Anaesthesiol* 2009; 23: 145–57.
4. Haugen O, Farstad M, Kvalheim V, Boe O, Husby P. Elevated flow rate during cardiopulmonary bypass is associated with fluid accumulation. *J Thorac Cardiovasc Surg* 2007; 134: 587–93.
5. Lobo DN, Bostock KA, Neal KR, Perkins AC, Rowlands BJ, Allison SP. Effect of salt and water balance on recovery of gastrointestinal function after elective colonic resection: A randomised controlled trial. *Lancet* 2002; 359: 1812–8.
6. Campbell IT, Baxter JN, Tweedie IE, Taylor GT, Keens SJ. I.V. fluids during surgery. *Br J Anaesth* 1990; 65: 726–9.
7. Maharaj CH, Kallam SR, Malik A, Hassett P, Grady D, Laffey JG. Preoperative intravenous fluid therapy decreases postoperative nausea and pain in high risk patients. *Anesth Analg* 2005; 100: 675–82.
8. Coe AJ, Revanas B. Is crystalloid preloading useful in spinal anaesthesia in the elderly? *Anaesthesia* 1990; 45: 241–3.
9. McCrae AF, Wildsmith JA. Prevention and treatment of hypotension during central neural block. *Br J Anaesth* 1993; 70: 672–80.

10. Rehm M, Orth V, Kreimeier U, Thiel M, Haller M, Brechtelsbauer H, Finsterer U. Changes in intravascular volume during acute normovolemic hemodilution and intraoperative retransfusion in patients with radical hysterectomy. *Anesthesiology* 2000; 92: 657–64.
11. Rehm M, Haller M, Orth V, Kreimeier U, Jacob M, Dressel H, Mayer S, Brechtelsbauer H, Finsterer U. Changes in blood volume and hematocrit during acute preoperative volume loading with 5% albumin or 6% hetastarch solutions in patients before radical hysterectomy. *Anesthesiology* 2001; 95: 849–56.
12. Shackford SR, Fortlage DA, Peters RM, Hollinsworth-Fridlund P, Sise MJ. Serum osmolar and electrolyte changes associated with large infusions of hypertonic sodium lactate for intravascular volume expansion of patients undergoing aortic reconstruction. *Surg Gynecol Obstet* 1987; 164: 127–36.
13. Kudsk KA. Evidence for conservative fluid administration following elective surgery. *Ann Surg* 2003; 238: 649–50.
14. Lowell JA, Schifferdecker C, Driscoll DF, Benotti PN, Bistrian BR. Postoperative fluid overload: Not a benign problem. *Crit Care Med* 1990; 18: 728–33.
15. Holte K, Jensen P, Kehlet H. Physiologic effects of intravenous fluid administration in healthy volunteers. *Anesth Analg* 2003; 96: 1504–9.
16. Haxhe JJ. Body composition and electrolyte studies, in Edited by Belcher EH, Vetter H, *Radioisotopes in medical diagnosis*. London, Butterworths, 1971, pp. 258–97.
17. Altman PL, Dittmer DS. Blood and other body fluids: Analysis and compilation. *Washington: Federation of American Societies for Experimental Biology*, 1961.
18. McMurrey JD, Boling EA, Davis JM, Parker HV, Magnus IC, Ball MR, Moore FD. Body composition: Simultaneous determination of several aspects by the dilution principle. *Metabolism* 1958; 7: 651–67.
19. Renal Physiology. *Physiology of Body Fluids*. pp. 5–17, 2015. http://www.elsevieradvantage.com/samplechapters/9780323034470/9780323034470.pdf Accessed February 12, 2017.
20. Holte K, Kehlet H. Compensatory fluid administration for preoperative dehydration--does it improve outcome? *Acta Anaesthesiol Scand* 2002; 46: 1089–93.
21. Sear JW. Kidney dysfunction in the postoperative period. *Br J Anaesth* 2005; 95: 20–32.
22. Chappell D, Jacob M, Hofmann-Kiefer K, Bruegger D, Rehm M, Conzen P, Welsch U, Becker BF. Hydrocortisone preserves the vascular barrier by protecting the endothelial glycocalyx. *Anesthesiology* 2007; 107: 776–84.
23. Rehm M, Zahler S, Lotsch M, Welsch U, Conzen P, Jacob M, Becker BF. Endothelial glycocalyx as an additional barrier determining extravasation of 6% hydroxyethyl starch or 5% albumin solutions in the coronary vascular bed. *Anesthesiology* 2004; 100: 1211–23.
24. Jacob M, Chappell D. Reappraising Starling: The physiology of the microcirculation. *Curr Opin Crit Care* 2013; 19: 282–9.
25. Jackson R, Reid JA, Thorburn J. Volume preloading is not essential to prevent spinal-induced hypotension at caesaren section. *Br J Anaesth* 1995; 75: 262–5.

26. Norberg A, Hahn RG, Li H, Olsson J, Prough DS, Borsheim E, Wolf S, Minton RK, Svensen CH. Population volume kinetics predicts retention of 0.9% saline infused in awake and isoflurane-anesthetized volunteers. *Anesthesiology* 2007; 107: 24–32.
27. Li H, Koutrouvelis A, Lian Q. Clinical study of the effects of two fluid regimens, restricted and standard, on fetus and mother during cesarean section under spinal anesthesia. *American Society of Anesthesiologists Annual Conference.* San Francisco, CA, October 14, 2013.
28. Jacob M, Chappell D, Conzen P, Finsterer U, Rehm M. Blood volume is normal after pre-operative overnight fasting. *Acta Anaesthesiol Scand* 2008; 52: 522–9.
29. Arieff AI. Fatal postoperative pulmonary edema. Pathogenesis and literature review. *Chest* 1999; 115: 1371–7.
30. Brandstrup B, Svensen C, Engquist A. Hemorrhage and operation cause a contraction of the extracellular space needing replacement–evidence and implications? A systematic review. *Surgery* 2006; 139: 419–32.
31. Doherty M, Buggy DJ. Intraoperative fluids: How much is too much? *Br J Anaesth* 2012; 109: 69–79.
32. Brandstrup B, Tonnesen H, Beier-Holgersen R, Hjortso E, Ording H, Lindorff-Larsen K, Rasmussen MS, Lanng C, Wallin L, Iversen LH, et al. Effects of intravenous fluid restriction on postoperative complications: Comparison of two perioperative fluid regimens-A randomized assessor-blinded multicenter trial. *Ann Surg* 2003; 238: 641–8.
33. Bundgaard-Nielsen M, Secher NH, Kehlet H. 'Liberal' vs. 'restrictive' perioperative fluid therapy–a critical assessment of the evidence. *Acta Anaesthesiol Scand* 2009; 53: 843–51.
34. MacKay G, Fearon K, McConnachie A, Serpell MG, Molloy RG, O'Dwyer PJ. Randomized clinical trial of the effect of postoperative intravenous fluid restriction on recovery after elective colorectal surgery. *Br J Surg* 2006; 93: 1469–74.
35. Holte K, Foss NB, Andersen J, Valentiner L, Lund C, Bie P, Kehlet H. Liberal or restrictive fluid administration in fast-track colonic surgery: A randomized, double-blind study. *Br J Anaesth* 2007; 99: 500–8.
36. Holte K, Kristensen BB, Valentiner L, Foss NB, Husted H, Kehlet H. Liberal versus restrictive fluid management in knee arthroplasty: A randomized, double-blind study. *Anesth Analg* 2007; 105: 465–74.
37. Lambert KG, Wakim JH, Lambert NE. Preoperative fluid bolus and reduction of postoperative nausea and vomiting in patients undergoing laparoscopic gynecologic surgery. *AANA J* 2009; 77: 110–4.
38. Holte K, Klarskov B, Christensen DS, Lund C, Nielsen KG, Bie P, Kehlet H. Liberal versus restrictive fluid administration to improve recovery after laparoscopic cholecystectomy: A randomized, double-blind study. *Ann Surg* 2004; 240: 892–9.
39. Brandstrup B. Fluid therapy for the surgical patient. *Best Pract Res Clin Anaesthesiol* 2006; 20: 265–83.
40. Nisanevich V, Felsenstein I, Almogy G, Weissman C, Einav S, Matot I. Effect of intraoperative fluid management on outcome after intraabdominal surgery. *Anesthesiology* 2005; 103: 25–32.

41. Kabon B, Akca O, Taguchi A, Nagele A, Jebadurai R, Arkilic CF, Sharma N, Ahluwalia A, Galandiuk S, Fleshman J, et al. Supplemental intravenous crystalloid administration does not reduce the risk of surgical wound infection. *Anesth Analg* 2005; 101: 1546–53.
42. Yogendran S, Asokumar B, Cheng DCH, Chung F. A prospective randomized double-blinded study on the effect of intravenous fluid therapy on adverse outcomes on outpatient surgery. *Anesth Analg* 1995; 80: 682–6.
43. Bellamy MC. Wet, dry or something else? *Br J Anaesth* 2006; 97: 755–7.
44. Hamilton MA, Cecconi M, Rhodes A. A systematic review and meta-analysis on the use of preemptive hemodynamic intervention to improve postoperative outcomes in moderate and high-risk surgical patients. *Anesth Analg* 2011; 112: 1392–402.
45. Alphonsus CS, Rodseth RN. The endothelial glycocalyx: A review of the vascular barrier. *Anaesthesia* 2014; 69: 777–84.
46. Chappell D, Jacob M, Hofmann-Kiefer K, Conzen P, Rehm M. A rational approach to perioperative fluid management. *Anesthesiology* 2008; 109: 723–40.
47. Woodcock TE, Woodcock TM. Revised Starling equation and the glycocalyx model of transvascular fluid exchange: An improved paradigm for prescribing intravenous fluid therapy. *Br J Anaesth* 2012; 108: 384–94.
48. Pries AR, Secomb TW, Gaehtgens P. The endothelial surface layer. *Pflugers Archiv Eur J Physiol* 2000; 440: 653–66.
49. Adamson RH, Lenz JF, Zhang X, Adamson GN, Weinbaum S, Curry FE. Oncotic pressures opposing filtration across non-fenestrated rat microvessels. *J Physiol* 2004; 557: 889–907.
50. Rehm M, Bruegger D, Christ F, Conzen P, Thiel M, Jacob M, Chappell D, Stoeckelhuber M, Welsch U, Reichart B, et al. Shedding of the endothelial glycocalyx in patients undergoing major vascular surgery with global and regional ischemia. *Circulation* 2007; 116: 1896–906.
51. Chappell D, Westphal M, Jacob M. The impact of the glycocalyx on microcirculatory oxygen distribution in critical illness. *Curr Opin Anaesthesiol* 2009; 22: 155–62.
52. Bernfield M, Gotte M, Park PW, Reizes O, Fitzgerald ML, Lincecum J, Zako M. Functions of cell surface heparan sulfate proteoglycans. *Annu Rev Biochem* 1999; 68: 729–77.
53. Bruegger D, Jacob M, Rehm M, Loetsch M, Welsch U, Conzen P, Becker BF. Atrial natriuretic peptide induces shedding of endothelial glycocalyx in coronary vascular bed of guinea pig hearts. *Am J Physiol Heart Circ Physiol* 2005; 289: H1993–9.
54. Chappell D, Dorfler N, Jacob M, Rehm M, Welsch U, Conzen P, Becker BF. Glycocalyx protection reduces leukocyte adhesion after ischemia/reperfusion. *Shock* 2010; 34: 133–9.
55. Chappell D, Heindl B, Jacob M, Annecke T, Chen C, Rehm M, Conzen P, Becker BF. Sevoflurane reduces leukocyte and platelet adhesion after ischemia-reperfusion by protecting the endothelial glycocalyx. *Anesthesiology* 2011; 115: 483–91.
56. Becker BF, Chappell D, Bruegger D, Annecke T, Jacob M. Therapeutic strategies targeting the endothelial glycocalyx: Acute deficits, but great potential. *Cardiovasc Res* 2010; 87: 300–10.

57. Garrioch SS, Gillies MA. Which intravenous fluid for the surgical patient? *Curr Opin Crit Care* 2015; 21: 358–63.
58. Stoneham MD, Hill EL. Variability in post-operative fluid and electrolyte prescription. *Br J Clin Pract* 1997; 51: 82–4.
59. McFarlane C, Lee A. A comparison of plasmalyte 148 and 0.9% saline for intra-operative fluid replacement. *Anaesthesia* 1994; 49: 779–81.
60. Scheingraber S, Rehm M, Sehmisch C, Finsterer U. Rapid saline infusion produces hyperchloremic acidosis in patients undergoing gynecologic surgery. *Anesthesiology* 1999; 90: 1265–70.
61. Prough DS, Bidani A. Hyperchloremic metabolic acidosis is a predictable consequence of intraoperative infusion of 0.9% saline. *Anesthesiology* 1999; 90: 1247–9.
62. Williams EL, Hildebrand KL, McCormick SA, Bedel MJ. The effect of intravenous lactated Ringer's solution versus 0.9% sodium chloride solution on serum osmolality in human volunteers. *Anesth Analg* 1999; 88: 999–1003.
63. Shaw AD, Bagshaw SM, Goldstein SL, Scherer LA, Duan M, Schermer CR, Kellum JA. Major complications, mortality, and resource utilization after open abdominal surgery: 0.9% saline compared to plasma-lyte. *Ann Surg* 2012; 255: 821–9.
64. McCluskey SA, Karkouti K, Wijeysundera D, Minkovich L, Tait G, Beattie WS. Hyperchloremia after noncardiac surgery is independently associated with increased morbidity and mortality: A propensity-matched cohort study. *Anesth Analg* 2013; 117: 412–21.
65. O'Malley CM, Frumento RJ, Hardy MA, Benvenisty AI, Brentjens TE, Mercer JS, Bennett-Guerrero E. A randomized, double-blind comparison of lactated Ringer's solution and 0.9% NaCl during renal transplantation. *Anesth Analg* 2005; 100: 1518–24.
66. Nadeem A, Salahuddin N, El HA, Joseph M, Bohlega B, Sallam H, Sheikh Y, Broering D. Chloride-liberal fluids are associated with acute kidney injury after liver transplantation. *Crit Care* 2014; 18: 625.
67. Raghunathan K, Shaw A, Nathanson B, Sturmer T, Brookhart A, Stefan MS, Setoguchi S, Beadles C, Lindenauer PK. Association between the choice of IV crystalloid and in-hospital mortality among critically ill adults with sepsis. *Crit Care Med* 2014; 42: 1585–91.
68. Dubois MJ. *Colloid Fluids, Perioperative Fluid Therapy.* Edited by Hahn RG, Prough DS, Svensen CH. New York, Wiley, 2007, p 153.
69. Hartog CS, Kohl M, Reinhart K. A systematic review of third-generation hydroxyethyl starch (HES 130/0.4) in resuscitation: Safety not adequately addressed. *Anesth Analg* 2011; 112: 635–45
70. Finfer S, Bellomo R, Boyce N, French J, Myburgh J, Norton R. A comparison of albumin and saline for fluid resuscitation in the intensive care unit. *N Engl J Med* 2004; 350: 2247–56.
71. Maitland K, Kiguli S, Opoka RO, Engoru C, Olupot-Olupot P, Akech SO, Nyeko R, Mtove G, Reyburn H, Lang T, et al. Mortality after fluid bolus in African children with severe infection. *N Engl J Med* 2011; 364: 2483–95.
72. Myburgh J, Cooper DJ, Finfer S, Bellomo R, Norton R, Bishop N, Kai LS, Vallance S. Saline or albumin for fluid resuscitation in patients with traumatic brain injury. *N Engl J Med* 2007; 357: 874–84.

73. Finfer S, McEvoy S, Bellomo R, McArthur C, Myburgh J, Norton R. Impact of albumin compared to saline on organ function and mortality of patients with severe sepsis. *Intensive Care Med* 2011; 37: 86–96.
74. Lira A, Pinsky MR. Choices in fluid type and volume during resuscitation: Impact on patient outcomes. *Ann Intensive Care* 2014; 4: 38.
75. Verheij J, van LA, Beishuizen A, Christiaans HM, de Jong JR, Girbes AR, Wisselink W, Rauwerda JA, Huybregts MA, Groeneveld AB. Cardiac response is greater for colloid than saline fluid loading after cardiac or vascular surgery. *Intensive Care Med* 2006; 32: 1030–8.
76. Trof RJ, Sukul SP, Twisk JW, Girbes AR, Groeneveld AB. Greater cardiac response of colloid than saline fluid loading in septic and non-septic critically ill patients with clinical hypovolemia. *Intensive Care Med* 2010; 36: 697–701.
77. de Jonge E, Levi M. Effects of different plasma substitutes on blood coagulation: A comparative review. *Crit Care Med* 2001; 29: 1261–7.
78. Schortgen F, Lacherade JC, Bruneel F, Cattaneo I, Hemery F, Lemaire F, Brochard L. Effects of hydroxyethylstarch and gelatin on renal function in severe sepsis: A multicentre randomised study. *Lancet* 2001; 357: 911–6.
79. Schortgen F, Girou E, Deye N, Brochard L. The risk associated with hyperoncotic colloids in patients with shock. *Intensive Care Med* 2008; 34: 2157–68.
80. Rioux JP, Lessard M, De BB, Roy P, Albert M, Verdant C, Madore F, Troyanov S. Pentastarch 10% (250 kDa/0.45) is an independent risk factor of acute kidney injury following cardiac surgery. *Crit Care Med* 2009; 37: 1293–8.
81. Perner A, Haase N, Guttormsen AB, Tenhunen J, Klemenzson G, Aneman A, Madsen KR, Moller MH, Elkjaer JM, Poulsen LM, Bendtsen A, et al. Hydroxyethyl starch 130/0.42 versus Ringer's acetate in severe sepsis. *N Engl J Med* 2012; 367: 124–34.
82. Brunkhorst FM, Engel C, Bloos F, Meier-Hellmann A, Ragaller M, Weiler N, Moerer O, Gruendling M, Oppert M, Grond S, et al. Intensive insulin therapy and pentastarch resuscitation in severe sepsis. *N Engl J Med* 2008; 358: 125–39.
83. Myburgh JA, Finfer S, Bellomo R, Billot L, Cass A, Gattas D, Glass P, Lipman J, Liu B, McArthur C, et al. Hydroxyethyl starch or saline for fluid resuscitation in intensive care. *N Engl J Med* 2012; 367: 1901–11.
84. Phillips DP, Kaynar AM, Kellum JA, Gomez H. Crystalloids vs. colloids: KO at the twelfth round? *Crit Care* 2013; 17: 319.
85. Severs D, Hoorn EJ, Rookmaaker MB. A critical appraisal of intravenous fluids: From the physiological basis to clinical evidence. *Nephrol Dial Transplant* 2015; 30: 178–87.
86. Pearse RM, Harrison DA, MacDonald N, Gillies MA, Blunt M, Ackland G, Grocott MP, Ahern A, Griggs K, Scott R, et al. Effect of a perioperative, cardiac output-guided hemodynamic therapy algorithm on outcomes following major gastrointestinal surgery: A randomized clinical trial and systematic review. *J Am Med Assoc* 2014; 311: 2181–90.
87. Boyd JH, Forbes J, Nakada TA, Walley KR, Russell JA. Fluid resuscitation in septic shock: A positive fluid balance and elevated central venous pressure are associated with increased mortality. *Crit Care Med* 2011; 39: 259–65.
88. Magner JJ, McCaul C, Carton E, Gardiner J, Buggy D. Effect of intraoperative intravenous crystalloid infusion on postoperative nausea and vomiting after gynaecological laparoscopy: Comparison of 30 and 10 ml kg(–1). *Br J Anaesth* 2004; 93: 381–5.

89. McCaul C, Moran C, O'Cronin D, Naughton F, Geary M, Carton E, Gardiner J. Intravenous fluid loading with or without supplementary dextrose does not prevent nausea, vomiting and pain after laparoscopy. *Can J Anaesth* 2003; 50: 440–4.

90. Fleming A, Bishop M, Shoemaker W, Appel P, Sufficool W, Kuvhenguwha A, Kennedy F. Prospective trial of supranormal values as goals of resuscitation in severe trauma. *Archiv Surg* 1992; 127: 1175–81.

91. Kuper M, Gold SJ, Callow C, Quraishi T, King S, Mulreany A, Bianchi M, Conway DH. Intraoperative fluid management guided by oesophageal Doppler monitoring. *BMJ* 2011; 342: d3016.

92. Bundgaard-Nielsen M, Ruhnau B, Secher NH, Kehlet H. Flow-related techniques for preoperative goal-directed fluid optimization. *Br J Anaesth* 2007; 98: 38–44.

93. Mythen MG, Webb AR. Perioperative plasma volume expansion reduces the incidence of gut mucosal hypoperfusion during cardiac surgery. *Archiv Surg* 1995; 130: 423–9.

94. Abbas SM, Hill AG. Systematic review of the literature for the use of oesophageal Doppler monitor for fluid replacement in major abdominal surgery. *Anaesthesia* 2008; 63: 44–51.

95. Walsh SR, Tang T, Bass S, Gaunt ME. Doppler-guided intra-operative fluid management during major abdominal surgery: Systematic review and meta-analysis. *Int J Clin Pract* 2008; 62: 466–70.

96. Gupta RG, Hartigan SM, Kashiouris MG, Sessler CN, Bearman GM. Early goal-directed resuscitation of patients with septic shock: Current evidence and future directions. *Crit Care* 2015; 19: 286.

97. Yealy DM, Kellum JA, Huang DT, Barnato AE, Weissfeld LA, Pike F, Terndrup T, Wang HE, Hou PC, LoVecchio F, et al. A randomized trial of protocol-based care for early septic shock. *N Engl J Med* 2014; 370: 1683–93.

chapter four

Goal-directed fluid therapy
Use of invasive and semi-invasive devices

Kirstie McPherson and Monty Mythen
University College London
London, UK

Contents

Key points:
There is an abundance of different approaches and protocols used to access physiological responses to bolus fluid administration. Focus has shifted towards the provision of dynamic indices. This chapter mainly deals with semi-invasive devices. Measuring the cardiac output is described. Pros and cons are described for:

- Pulmonary Artery (PA) catheter
- Esophageal Doppler
- Arterial pressure contour analysis
- PiCCO

- LiDCO
- EV1000
- Transesophageal echocardiography

4.1   Introduction

The esophageal Doppler device currently has the strongest evidence.

Today, goal-directed fluid therapy (GDFT) may be defined as the controlled delivery of fluids to patients at a rate and volume such as to optimize end-organ perfusion and function. Typically, a cardiac output monitor is used to individualize fluid therapy and optimize a patient's stroke volume (SV) in the perioperative period.

Fluid is usually delivered as a series of fluid "bolus challenges," the dynamic physiological response to which is monitored. Responsiveness thus indicates the presence of a cardiac "preload reserve," whereby increasing ventricular end-diastolic pressure drives an increase in diastolic myocyte load and thus in subsequent myocyte systolic contractile work. Stroke volume thus rises (in the absence of alterations in afterload).

The literature relating to the use of fluid boluses in both research and clinical arenas reveals marked variation in the type and volume of fluid used and the speed at which it is delivered. Indeed, in a recent meta-analysis, bolus volume varied between 100 and 3,000 mL and rates of infusion from 1 to >60 minutes [1]. Such variation leads to marked differences in the degree of resulting ventricular preload. Studies and practice algorithms also show variation in the provision for augmentation with an inotrope/vasopressor/vasodilator in addition to the fluid challenge given.

Likewise, the physiological response to the fluid challenge in terms of tissue perfusion/oxygen delivery is determined through assessment of a variety of different surrogates. These include measures of cardiac preload (central venous pressure, or left ventricular end-diastolic pressure), simple hemodynamic measures (cardiac output blood pressure, heart rate), or measures of oxygen delivery (e.g., changes in tissue oxygen saturation or mixed venous oxygen saturation). All have benefits and flaws and are discussed in detail below.

In any case, fastidious attention to perioperative fluid management can improve clinical outcome [2,3]. Similarly, inattention to perioperative fluid balance causes harm. Mythen and Webb [4] showed that inadequate perioperative gut perfusion (of which low gastric mucosal pH is an index) is associated with increased morbidity and subsequent healthcare costs. This study showed how the addition of an individualized approach to optimize SV with fluid boluses in patients undergoing cardiac surgery reduced the incidence of gut mucosal hypoperfusion (gastric intramucosal pH <7.32) to 7% (v. 56% in the control group).

Such physiological and clinical benefits of increasing SV with GDFT have since been repeatedly shown to decrease postoperative morbidity, with the greatest benefits accruing in those at greatest risk of occult tissue hypoperfusion and oxygen debt [5]. A systematic review (meta-analysis of 31 studies with 5,292 participants) suggested that GDFT reduced morbidity (renal, respiratory failure, and wound infections) and reduced hospital length of stay [6].

Since then, the Optimisation of Cardiovascular Management to Improve Surgical Outcome (OPTIMISE) trial has been completed [7]. It represents the largest study to date to have examined the effect of goal-directed therapy on outcomes following surgery in 734 high-risk surgical patients, randomized to a goal-directed therapy algorithm using intravenous fluid boluses and an inotrope (dopamine) or usual care. The primary outcome of the study was 30-day moderate or major complications and mortality. This was present in 36.6% of the intervention group as compared to 43.4% in the usual care group with a relative risk (RR) of 0.84 (95% confidence interval [CI] 0.71–1.01; $P = 0.07$). Including this study (and six others) in an updated meta-analysis, the authors demonstrated benefits of goal-directed therapy to reduce complications after surgery [7].

Though most recently published evidence has been less *overtly* favorable, the trend continues to consistently err towards the benefits of GDFT and the use of technology to guide fluid outcomes. Demonstrating meaningful benefits has its challenges, with wide variation in clinical practice, the GDFT protocols and algorithms applied, adherence to their application, and the interpretation of derived data [8].

4.2   Devices used in GDFT

There is a growing abundance of different approaches and protocols used to assess physiological response to bolus fluid administration. Focus has shifted in more recent iterations of technologies towards the provision of *dynamic* indices that guide optimization of volume status by predicting an individual's response to a fluid bolus. Noninvasive approaches will be described in Chapter 5. This chapter will look at invasive and semi-invasive devices used to assess response to a fluid challenge.

4.3   Simple hemodynamic responses

With increased cardiac output, heart rate will tend to fall and blood pressure to rise, if other variables such as afterload and autonomic drive are constant. As such, heart rate, blood pressure, urine output, and central venous pressure have all been used to guide fluid management. However, these variables correlate poorly with end-organ perfusion and are unreliable indicators of volume status. Hamilton-Davies et al. showed that when healthy volunteers were bled to 75% of their baseline blood volume, heart rate and blood pressure did not alter significantly. In contrast, SV (measured by suprasternal Doppler) and gastrointestinal tonometry (a marker of splanchnic perfusion) were markedly changed, providing a more reliable index of hypovolemia [9]. A recent meta-analysis [1] investigating the predictive value of central venous pressure (CVP) measurement as a marker of fluid responsiveness showed that there is no robust data to support the widespread practice of using central venous pressure to guide fluid therapy. The authors as such concluded that CVP should not be used to make clinical decisions regarding fluid management. Urine output in the perioperative setting similarly provides a poor index of volume status. The oliguria (<0.5 mL/kg/hr) typically seen perioperatively usually reflects an appropriate neurohormonal response to "surgical stress" and is an unreliable measure of end-organ perfusion in this setting.

4.4   Measures of cardiac output

4.4.1   Pulmonary artery catheter and thermodilution

The pulmonary artery catheter was for many years the *gold standard* of cardiac output monitoring. Perioperatively, its use has now markedly declined or vanished, due to an increasing number of less invasive devices in the marketplace and a wealth of literature citing risks over benefits in fluid management [10]. A pulmonary artery balloon floatation catheter is typically inserted via an introducer placed in a great vein, for example, the internal jugular. Once the catheter is threaded into the great vein beyond the introducer, then the balloon close to the tip of the Pulmonary Artery (PA) catheter is inflated. The catheter is advanced and the balloon sails the tip following the flow of blood through the right atrium, right ventricle, and into the pulmonary artery. The continuous monitoring of pressure and display of wave form from the most distal lumen of the catheter tracks the passage of the balloon through the various compartments and guides the operator. A chest x-ray is needed to confirm correct placement and lack of knotting. "Wedging" of the inflated balloon at the catheter tip in the pulmonary artery enables measurement of the filling pressures of the left heart—the "wedge pressure." Cardiac output is calculated by thermodilution technique using either an intermittent cold bolus technique or a continuous pulsed hot wire and other variables, such as systemic vascular resistance, are derived. PA catheters can also have continuous measurement of pulmonary artery blood saturation ("mixed venous saturation") by near-infrared oximetry similar to that deployed in a pulse oximeter. Thus the PA catheter offers a wealth of information and was the dominant technology for cardiac output measurement and used exclusively in the early goal-directed therapy trials. However, it is highly invasive and has thus fallen from favor.

4.4.2   Complications

Complications associated with the use of the Pulmonary Artery Catheter (PAC) may be divided into technical problems leading to misinterpretation of data and inappropriate interventions and clinically harmful effects, leading to patient morbidity and mortality (see Table 4.1).

4.4.3   Fall from favor

At its peak of favor, its use in seriously ill hospitalized patients was reported to be 20%–43% [11], considered by many the *gold standard* for cardiac output evaluation. The variables generated by the PAC are however not dynamic, and the risk–benefit profile to patients is increasingly contentious given the morbidity associated with their use.

The use of pulmonary artery catheters has steadily decreased in the last 20 years. Weiner et al. collected data from all US states contributing to the Nationwide Inpatient Sample, part of the Agency for Healthcare Research and Quality's Healthcare Cost and Utilization Project, which contains information on all discharges from a 20% stratified sample of community hospitals in the United States (5–8 million discharges per year). Between 1993 and 2004, pulmonary artery catheterization use in medical and surgical patients decreased by 65% and 63%, respectively, in the United States [11].

Table 4.1 Problems associated with use of pulmonary artery catheters

Technical problems	Clinical problems
Damping of trace	Knotting of the catheter
"Zeroing" errors and obtaining baseline measurements.	Pulmonary artery rupture
Variation of stroke volume throughout respiratory cycle affects accuracy of readings.	Pulmonary hemorrhage
Changing patient position	Pulmonary artery thrombosis
Warming of cold indicator prior to injection.	Arrhythmia
	Endocarditis
	Air embolism

Connors et al. were amongst the first to publish compelling data questioning the benefits of PACs, demonstrating a 24% increased risk of death in ICU patients who received a PAC within 24 hours of admission to an ICU [12]. This observational study appears to have put a break on the widespread use of the PAC, and a raft of studies that followed [13–19] similarly have shown little or no improvement in mortality from the PAC. A Cochrane systematic review and meta-analysis published in 2006 demonstrated no benefit from the use of the PAC in both critical care and high-risk surgery patients [20]. Moreover, exposure to harmful complications and the arrival of more minimally invasive technologies has diminished its use in diverse groups.

The increasing presence of transthoracic and transesophageal echocardiography (TEE) in cardiac surgery now largely supersedes the use of the PAC. Whilst their utility in specific defined groups continues to be efficacious, widespread use is diminishing. A review has suggested that specific and more complex groups of cardiac patients are most likely to benefit from PAC monitoring [21]. These groups include impaired right ventricular systolic function, left ventricular diastolic dysfunction, acute ventricular septal defect, and presence of a left ventricular assist device. Its previously widespread use in cardiac surgery is now very limited, as exampled by a lack of benefit shown for the use of PAC for routine coronary artery bypass grafting surgery [22]. The most compelling use still seems be for perioperative management of patients with severe pulmonary hypertension and acute right ventricular failure, when measurement of pulmonary artery pressures facilitates judicious use of vasopressor and fluids [23].

Prior to the introduction of the PAC, the direct Fick method was the reference standard by which all other methods of determining Cardiac Output (CO) were evaluated. Newer technologies following on from the PAC have nearly always been validated using the PAC as the "gold standard" reference. However, thermodilution is not a sufficiently robust method, with errors arising from its use and a precision error derived by the Bland–Altman method of ±20% being generally accepted [24]. These not-insignificant precision error rates are likely to have affected the quality of the data used for validation of successive technologies. Alternative devices with lower precision error rates (e.g., aortic flow probes) in clinical practice are likely to provide better reference tools.

4.5   Esophageal Doppler

The esophageal Doppler monitor (EDM) is a semi- (or more minimally) invasive device to estimate cardiac output by measuring descending aortic blood velocity. The CardioQ EDM (Deltex Corporation, Chichester, West Sussex, UK) is the only commercially available device of its type on the market. It exploits the Doppler effect—the phenomenon by which the frequency of transmitted sound is altered as it is reflected from a moving object (in this case, aortic red blood cells), represented by the following equation:

$$V = \Delta Fc$$

$$2F_0\cos\theta$$

where V is velocity, ΔF is frequency shift, c is the speed of sound in tissue, F_0 is frequency of emitted sound, cos represents cosine, and θ is the angle between sound and object.

The probe is positioned in the esophagus at the level of T5/6 (a distance of 35–45 cm), and the velocity of blood flow is measured in the adjacent descending thoracic aorta using a transducer at the tip of the probe. Cardiac output measurement is based on the measured flow velocity of blood in the descending aorta. Cross-sectional area of the aorta is estimated using a nomogram [25]. Flow is derived by multiplying this area by velocity. Importantly, the accuracy of measurements is dependent on the angle between the Doppler ultrasound beam and the direction of blood flow in the vessel (known as θ, the angle between sound and object). The EDM is designed to insonate at 45° with the probe shaft lying in the esophagus and parallel to the aorta. As the angle increases, the errors in calculating blood flow velocity due to small errors in angle of measurement become unacceptably high, with the effect of underestimation of Doppler-derived velocity. As such, the manufacturer recommends that this angle should not exceed 60°.

The area under the systolic portion of the waveform is defined as *stroke distance* (SD). The SV is calculated from the measured SD and a calibration constant derived from the nomogram (Figure 4.1 shows the typical waveform seen using the esophageal Doppler). CO is then calculated by multiplying the SV by the heart rate. Hypovolemia is reflected in a reduction in the corrected flow time, abbreviated to FTc (duration of systolic flow divided by the square root of the cardiac cycle time), an increase in stroke volume variation (SVV), and providing useful visual, audible, and quantitative information to the user, prompting assessment of fluid responsiveness. Changes in FTc have been shown to be a more reliable surrogate for preload than other indices, including CVP, left ventricular end-diastolic area index, and the pulmonary artery catheter, using pulmonary capillary wedge pressures in both surgical and critically ill surgical patients [26,27].

Manufacturers and proponents of this technology recommend using an algorithm to guide fluid management with the EDM. Typically, fluid boluses of 200 mL are delivered, and change in SV assessed. If SV increases by 10% or more, a further fluid challenge is indicated to

Figure 4.1 Waveform displaying stroke distance, peak velocity, mean acceleration, and flow time measurements, allowing assessment of preload, contractility, and afterload.

optimize left ventricular end-diastolic volume (see Figure 4.2). When SV does not increase above this threshold or if the FTc has normalized (suggesting normovolemia), further boluses are withheld. In turn, when SV falls by more than 10%, a fluid challenge is repeated and assessment of responsiveness made in the same way.

Using the esophageal Doppler both intraoperatively and in the postoperative critical care setting has been shown to improve outcomes, reduce complications, and shorten postoperative length of stay. More than seven randomized controlled trials have specifically looked at the role of esophageal Doppler for fluid optimization [28–34]. Mean weighted average of these trials (comprising a total group number of 694 subjects) shows a reduction of 3.7 days in hospital length of stay [35]. Additionally, a study matching patients who *did* and *did not* receive GDFT with EDM for major surgery conducted by the United Kingdom's National Health Service Technology Adoption Centre demonstrated a similar reduction in length of stay of 3.6 days [36]. This evidence led to the National Health Service and National Institute for Health and Care Excellence issuing guidance recommending the use of EDM for major surgery in the United Kingdom [37].

Its limitations in the perioperative setting for the surgical patient are that it is principally confined to the operating theatre and the mechanically ventilated patient, though its use may be continued into the postoperative period for patients requiring prolonged mechanical ventilation following surgery. Its use is described in the awake patient [38]. In practice, however, this is poorly tolerated in the absence of sedation and may pose risks of trauma in the coagulopathic patient. Its continuous readings are subject to interference from electrocautery, and the probe may require intermittent repositioning to ensure a high quality signal, though

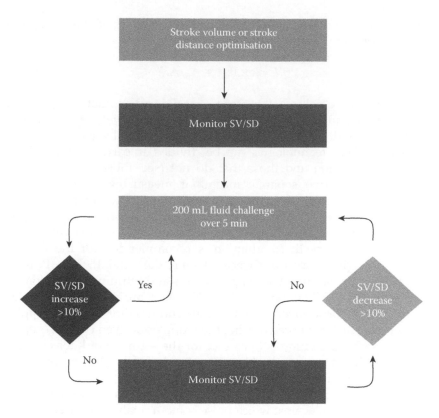

Figure 4.2 Example of a treatment algorithm using the esophageal Doppler monitor. (Suggested by Professor Mervyn Singer, University College London.)

it would appear the learning curve towards competent use is achieved with relative ease [39].

In spite of its limitations, the evidence for GDFT with EDM is compelling. Undoubtedly, the EDM provides a useful tool for trend (if not truly continuous) analysis of cardiac output and fluid responsiveness in the surgical patient [40].

4.6   Arterial pressure pulse contour analysis

Pulse contour analysis relies upon recording the arterial pressure waveform using a catheter placed in a peripheral artery and evaluating an estimate of SV. It is based on the relationship between the area under the arterial waveform, SV, and arterial compliance, as described by the German physiologist Frank in the nineteenth century [41]. Stroke volume may be continuously estimated by analyzing the arterial pressure waveform obtained from an arterial line when the arterial compliance and

systemic vascular resistance are known. These devices operate using the
following equation to appreciate SV.

$$SV = k \times P \left(1 + A_S/A_D\right)$$

where SV is stroke volume, k is a constant, P is an estimate of pressure,
A_S is the area under the systolic portion of the arterial waveform, and
A_D is the area under the diastolic portion of the arterial waveform.

Broadly, these technologies can be divided into two groups: those
that need calibration and those that do not (see Table 4.2). Calibrated
devices integrate two separate means of measuring cardiac output,
using transpulmonary dilution and arterial pressure waveform analysis.
Transpulmonary thermodilution techniques require both a central venous
catheter and a thermistor-tipped arterial catheter. External calibration
with transpulmonary thermodilution is recommended for the EV1000
Volume View (Edwards Lifesciences, Irvine, CA) and PiCCO (Pulsion
Medical Systems, Munich, Germany) systems and lithium dilution for the
LiDCOplus (LiDCO, London, UK). The Doppler Cardio-Q plus integrates
an arterial waveform slaved from the high-end monitor into the Doppler
platform and can be calibrated using the Doppler derived cardiac output.
The purpose of calibration is to correct for the estimate of k for changes
in afterload, and data suggests (though not universally) this improves the
accuracy of measurements [42–45].

Simultaneous transpulmonary thermodilution measurement provides
a calibration factor, *k*, against which pulse contour analysis–derived cardiac
output is measured. In this way, beat-to-beat measurement of cardiac output
is possible and is specifically advantageous in the setting of assessment of
responsiveness to fluid challenges in the surgical patient. Their reliability is

Table 4.2 Pulse pressure contour analysis devices

Calibrated devices (calibrated by transpulmonary thermo- or lithium dilution)	Uncalibrated devices
PiCCO (Pulsion Medical Systems, Munich, Germany)	FloTrac Vigileo (Edwards Lifesciences, Irvine, CA)
LiDCOplus (LiDCO, London, UK)	Pro-AQT (Pulsion Medical Systems, Munich, Germany)
EV1000 Volume View (Edwards Lifesciences, Irvine, CA)	MostCare (Vytech, Vygon, Italy)
Doppler Cardio-Q plus (Deltex, Chichester, UK)	LiDCO Rapid (LiDCO, London, UK)
	Pulsioflex (Pulsion Medical Systems, Munich, Germany)

reduced in episodes of hemodynamic instability [44,46,47]. As such, uncalibrated devices based on assumptions of arterial compliance should be more correctly termed "trending" monitors and their limitations appreciated with sudden changes in loading conditions.

Uncalibrated devices rely on the presence of an arterial catheter alone. Their simplicity of use provides practical advantage over the calibrated devices, in addition to their ability to track changes in cardiac output induced by volume expansion. The FloTrac Vigileo (Edwards Lifesciences) uses an electromechanic transducer, PulsioFlex (Pulsion Medical Systems) a transducer system, and the LiDCO Rapid (LiDCO) requires chip cards to unlock the monitor. The FloTrac Vigileo differs from other devices in its estimation of SV using a proprietary empirically derived algorithm to estimate SV [48].

Dynamic changes in SVV and pulse pressure variation (PPV) provided by these devices in patients undergoing mechanical ventilation have emerged as useful techniques to assess volume responsiveness in mechanically ventilated patients [49–52].

By measuring the area under the curve (or SV) with each heartbeat and evaluating change in values over one respiratory cycle, arterial waveform analyzers are able to measure SVV, an indication of the patient's fluid responsiveness. Importantly, whilst the reliability of some pulse contour analysis devices to measure cardiac output is negatively affected by sudden changes in hemodynamic status, their ability to measure PPV in response to positive pressure ventilation is not compromised in this way. As such, fluid responsiveness may be dynamically assessed in the mechanically ventilated patient.

Advantageous to their design is the ability to use these devices in the awake, unsedated patient. The continuous readings provided by arterial waveform analysis devices make them a favorable choice in the OR. The body of evidence supporting their use perioperatively is not as large as that for EDM and is in part due to their more recent arrival, a decade later to the marketplace. There are, however, a number of studies that have demonstrated improved clinical outcomes and reductions in length of stay for surgical patients [53–57]. The mean weighted average of reduction in length of stay calculated by Thiele et al. in eight intraoperative fluid optimization trials (encompassing 546 patients) was 2.2 days, compared to 3.7 days for EDM [35]. The numbers are too small to draw meaningful inference from these differences, and more trials are needed to demonstrate the benefit (or lack) of one technology over another.

Limitations include their poor reliability in patients with irregular cardiac rhythm and aortic insufficiency. In addition, it is worth noting that much of the data to support the ability of SVV to predict fluid responsiveness (with changes in intrathoracic pressure) is based on large tidal volumes (8–10 mL/kg). Given the trend towards improved outcomes associated with protective ventilation strategies, further validity studies are needed with lower tidal volumes and in spontaneously breathing patients [58]. However, stroke volume estimates are not affected by such changes in intrathoracic pressure and volume.

4.7 Transesophageal echocardiography

TEE is a semi-invasive technique that allows a real-time evaluation of cardiac anatomy, regional and global cardiac function. Its safety profile, less invasive than the PAC, makes it a very attractive device for dynamic assessment of cardiac function. Documented morbidity of 0.2% and 0% mortality has been reported in a large case series of 7,200 patients evaluating the safety of intraoperative TEE [59].

Its role in noncardiac surgery is less well explored, although as TEE skills increasingly become a recognized skill set common to anesthetists, it seems likely that the spread of this modality will continue in critical care and perioperative noncardiac surgery settings. Benefits have been shown to include prompt recognition of ischemia and hemodynamic changes and "rescue" management for determining a cause for perioperative hemodynamic instability [60,61].

Dynamic indices derived using TEE such as vena caval diameters during positive pressure ventilation have shown to be effective for evaluating fluid responsiveness [62]. However, the static parameters that TEE offers are not useful in predicting volume responsiveness [49].

Guidelines have been developed to support clinicians in the perioperative use of TEE, its use endorsed when the nature of the planned surgery or the patient's underlying cardiovascular pathology might result in severe hemodynamic, pulmonary, or neurologic compromise [63]. These guidelines and those produced by the American College of Cardiology/American Heart Association suggest the use of perioperative TEE is reasonable in noncardiac surgery patients with unexplained persistent hypotension, poorly responsive to treatment [64]. Its use is *not* recommended for routine noncardiac surgery in low-risk surgical groups.

4.8 Practical considerations relating to the use of semi-invasive and invasive devices in GDFT

Not all cardiac output monitors are created equally, and central to choice of device must be its purpose and patient-specific information. As such, no single device provides the "best fit" for every eventuality. Bridging the use of a device into the perioperative period (if needed) is advantageous and avoids disposables costs. Avoidance of invasive devices with morbidity associations should also be a priority, specifically in postanesthetic care areas, where nursing ratios and close surveillance of patients may not be as rigorous as in an intensive care unit. As enhanced recovery surgical pathways continue to take traction throughout the world, with focus on minimally invasive surgical techniques, invasive devices will become more redundant, in favor of more minimally invasive approaches that facilitate early mobilization (see Table 4.3 for advantages and limitations of invasive and semi-invasive devices used for GDFT).

A robust understanding of the principles of GDFT and concurrent use of an appropriate algorithm alongside a chosen technology is imperative for good perioperative fluid management. Importantly, hemodynamic monitoring devices will not affect patient outcomes unless they are accompanied and trigger the appropriate clinical response. In high-risk complex surgical patients, the evidence base appears most compelling. As such, it makes sense to extend the use of fluid management technologies beyond the confines of the operating theatre, into the perioperative period. Not unusually, the beneficial effects of good fluid management can be *undone* by less mindful attention to fluid administration postoperatively. In high-dependency care settings, where these technologies can continue to be used beyond the OR, this would seem a sensible continuum of care. Technologies that can evaluate fluid responsiveness in the spontaneously breathing patient are much needed and are missing from the armamentarium of currently available devices. With growing emphasis on enhanced recovery, minimally invasive surgery, and regional anesthesia, this limits clinicians from extending the benefits of GDFT into the perioperative space.

The esophageal Doppler had the strongest evidence base of all technologies currently available, and its minimally invasive profile made it a highly desirable choice. However, in recent years there has been a shift towards arterial waveform analysis, as it is easier to use and thus may have greater clinical utility despite concerns regarding accuracy when uncalibrated. The choice of device used will be influenced by personal preference, cost, and threshold for "invasiveness" that a clinician feels are justified in a given situation.

Ultimately, institutional "buy-in" and acceptance of practice with fluid management technologies will be the greatest challenge to successful implementation of a perioperative strategy with GDFT at its center.

4.9   Adoption of perioperative GDFT

Use of intraoperative fluid management technologies remains patchy and widespread adoption still elusive. This in part may be explained by a "dilutional effect" of the body of evidence, given that GDFT has greatest benefits for high-risk surgical patients, who may not have the physiological

Table 4.3 Advantages and limitations of invasive and semi-invasive devices available for goal-directed fluid therapy

Semi/invasive device	Invasiveness	Advantages	Limitations
Esophageal Doppler	+	Easy to use. Strong evidence base. Less invasive (no requirement for arterial line).	Less well tolerated in conscious patients. Position can shift intraoperatively, requiring repositioning. Subject to signal interference from surgical diathermy. Flow assessment based on assumed proportion of blood flow in descending aorta and that esophagus and descending aorta run parallel.
Transesophageal echo	+	Relatively noninvasive. Useful when cause of hemodynamic instability not known.	Training and skills required. Accreditation time and costs. Less well validated in noncardiac surgery. Subjective assessment may give rise to variation in interpretation of images and "clinical response" to findings. Variable sensitivity and specificity for detection and diagnosis of pathology. Caution in patients with esophageal and gastric disease.

(Continued)

Table 4.3 (Continued) Advantages and limitations of invasive and semi-invasive devices available for goal-directed fluid therapy

Semi/invasive device	Invasiveness	Advantages	Limitations
Arterial pressure pulse contour analysis	++	Continuous monitoring. Can be used in awake patients. Some require no calibration—"plug and play." Used in neonates and pediatric populations.	Need for arterial line. Over- or underdamped trace leads to inaccurate measurement. Less well-validated evidence base. Unreliable in presence of irregular cardiac rhythm/aortic insufficiency. Sudden changes in vascular tone result in inaccuracies (uncalibrated > calibrated). Calibrated devices require recalibrating intermittently.
Pulmonary artery catheter	+++	Gold standard against which other cardiac output monitors have been validated. Useful in complex cardiac cases (assessment of pulmonary artery pressure).	Invasive. Not continuous (original iteration). Complications +++. Training and skills required. Lag time to rapid changes in cardiac output (intermittent measurements). Unreliable with tricuspid regurgitation. Incorrect decisions based on erroneous measurements.

reserves to reverse oxygen debt. The difference seen between intervention and control groups in lower-risk groups is less pronounced, with similar expected outcome metrics anticipated, given the exceptionally low morbidity and mortality that modern-day routine intermediate and low-risk surgery offers. As such these devices are best reserved for the *high-risk* patient, where the benefits are best felt and the margin for error with fluid management is smaller.

In tandem with GDFT and the use of an algorithm should be a routine approach to stratifying risk on surgical patients. The use of predictive risk tools for guiding management in the perioperative period are highly recommended by a number of organizations and bodies, who recommend a preoperative estimate of mortality and classify the "high-risk" population as those with a predicted mortality >5% [65,66]. The highest risk groups have been shown to benefit most from a GDFT approach, and institutions should develop systematic pathways to routinely screen for and identify these patients, allocating resources appropriately [67].

References

1. Marik PE, Cavallazzi R. Does the central venous pressure predict fluid responsiveness? An updated meta-analysis and a plea for some common sense. *Crit Care Med* 2013; 41: 1774–81.
2. Brandstrup B, Tonnesen H, Beier-Holgersen R, et al. Danish Study Group on Perioperative Fluid Therapy. Effects of intravenous fluid restriction on postoperative complications: Comparison of two perioperative fluid regimens: A randomized assessor-blinded multicenter trial. *Ann Surg* 2003; 238: 641–8.
3. Chappell D, Jacob M, Hofmann-Kiefer K, Conzen P, Rehm M. A rational approach to perioperative fluid management. *Anesthesiology* 2008; 109: 723–40.
4. Mythen MG, Webb AR. Perioperative plasma volume expansion reduces the incidence of gut mucosal hypoperfusion during cardiac surgery. *Arch Surg* 1995; 130: 423–9.
5. Hamilton MA, Cecconi M, Rhodes A. A systematic review and meta-analysis on the use of preemptive haemodynamic optimization in high-risk surgical patients. *Anesth Anal* 2011; 112: 1392–402.
6. Grocott MP, Dushianthan A, Hamilton MA, Mythen MG, Harrison D, Rowan K, et al. Perioperative increase in global blood flow to explicit defined goals and outcomes after surgery: A Cochrane systematic review. *Br J Anaesth* 2013; 111(4): 535–48.
7. Pearse RM, Harrison DA, MacDonald N, Gillies MA, Blunt M, Ackland G, et al. Effect of a perioperative, cardiac output-guided hemodynamic therapy algorithm on outcomes following major gastrointestinal surgery: A randomized clinical trial and systematic review. *JAMA* 2014; 311(21): 2181–90.
8. Cannesson M, Pestel G, Ricks C, Hoeft A, Perel A. Hemodynamic monitoring and management in patients undergoing high risk surgery: A survey among North American and European anesthesiologists. *Crit Care* 2011; 15(4): R197.

9. Hamilton-Davies C, Mythen MG, Salmon JB, Jacobson D, Shukla A, Webb AR. Comparison of commonly used clinical indicators of hypovolemia with gastrointestinal tonometry. *Intensive Care Med* 1997; 23(3): 276–81.

10. Koo KK, Sun JC, Zhou Q, et al. Pulmonary artery catheters: Evolving rates and reasons for use. *Crit Care Med* 2011; 39: 1613–18.

11. Weiner RS, Welch HG. Trends in the use of the pulmonary artery catheter in the United States, 1993–2004. *JAMA* 2007; 298(4): 423–9.

12. Connors AF Jr, Speroff T, Dawson NV, et al. The effectiveness of right heart catheterization in the initial care of critically ill patients: SUPPORT investigators. *JAMA* 1996; 276(11): 889–97.

13. Sandham JD, Hull RD, Brant RF, et al. A randomized, controlled trial of the use of pulmonary-artery catheters in high-risk surgical patients. *N Engl J Med* 2003; 348(1): 5–14.

14. Harvey S, Harrison DA, Singer M, et al. Assessment of the clinical effectiveness of pulmonary artery catheters in management of patients in intensive care (PAC-Man): A randomised controlled trial. *Lancet* 2005; 366(9484): 472–7.

15. Rhodes A, Cusack RJ, Newman PJ, et al. A randomised, controlled trial of the pulmonary artery catheter in critically ill patients. *Intensive Care Med* 2002; 28(3): 256–64.

16. Richard C, Warszawski J, Anguel N, et al. Early use of the pulmonary artery catheter and outcomes in patients with shock and acute respiratory distress syndrome: A randomized controlled trial. *JAMA* 2003; 290(20): 2713–20.

17. Wheeler AP, Bernard GR, Thompson BT, et al. Pulmonary-artery versus central venous catheter to guide treatment of acute lung injury. *N Engl J Med* 2006; 354(21): 2213–24.

18. Binanay C, Califf RM, Hasselblad V, et al. ESCAPE investigators and ESCAPE study coordinators. Evaluation study of congestive heart failure and pulmonary artery catheterization effectiveness: The ESCAPE trial. *JAMA* 2005; 294(13): 1625–33.

19. Gore JM, Goldbert RJ, Spodick DH, et al. A community-wide assessment of the use of pulmonary artery catheters in patients with acute myocardial infarction. *Chest* 1987; 92: 721–7.

20. Harvey S, Young D, Brampton W, et al. Pulmonary artery catheters for adult patients in intensive care. *Cochrane Database Syst Rev* 2006;(3): CD003408.

21. Ranucci M. Which cardiac surgical patients can benefit from placement of a pulmonary artery catheter? *Crit Care* 2006; 10(Suppl 3): S6.

22. Tuman KJ, McCarthy RJ, Spiess BD, et al. Effect of pulmonary artery catheterization on outcome in patients undergoing coronary artery surgery. *Anesthesiology* 1989; 70: 199–206.

23. McGlothlin D, Ivascu N, Heerdt PM. Anesthesia and pulmonary hypertension. *Prog Cardiovasc Dis* 2012; 55: 199–217.

24. Critchley LA, Critchley JA. A meta-analysis of studies using bias and precision statistics to compare cardiac output measurement techniques. *J Clin Monit Comput* 1999; 15: 85–91.

25. Lowe GD, Chamberlain BM, Philpot EJ, Willshire RJ. Oesophageal Doppler Monitor (ODM) Guided Individualised Goal Directed Fluid Management (iGDFM) in surgery- A Technical Review. *Deltex Med Tech Rev* 2010. Available at http://www.deltexmedical.com/downloads/TechnicalReview.pdf (accessed September 4, 2015).

26. Lee J-H, Kim J-T, Yoon SZ, Lim Y-J, Jeon Y, Bahk J-H and Kim CS. Evaluation of corrected flow time in oesophageal Doppler as a predictor of fluid responsiveness. *Br J Anaesth* 2007; 99: 343–8.
27. Madan AK, UyBarreta VV, Shaghayegh A, et al. Esophageal Doppler ultrasound monitor versus pulmonary artery catheter in the hemodynamic management of critically ill surgical patients. *J Trauma Injury Infect Crit Care* 1999; 46(4): 807–11.
28. Sinclair S, James S, Singer M. Intraoperative intravascular volume optimisation and length of hospital stay after repair of proximal femoral fracture: Randomized control trial. *BMJ* 1997; 315: 909–12.
29. Gan TJ, Soppitt A, Maroof M, et al. Goal-directed intraoperative fluid administration reduces length of hospital stay after major surgery. *Anesthesiology* 2002; 97: 820–6.
30. Venn R, Steele A, Richardson P, Poloniecki J, Grounds M, Newman P. Randomized controlled trial to investigate influence of the fluid challenge on duration of hospital stay and perioperative morbidity in patients with hip fractures. *Br J Anaesth* 2002; 88: 65–71.
31. Wakeling HG, McFall MR, Jenkins CS, et al. Intraoperative oesophageal Doppler guided fluid management shortens postoperative hospital stay after major bowel surgery. *Br J Anaesth* 2005; 95: 634–42.
32. Noblett SE, Snowden CP, Shenton BK, et al. Randomised clinical trial assessing the effect of Doppler optimized fluid management on outcome after elective colorectal resection. *Br J Surg* 2006; 93: 1069–76.
33. Chytra I, Pradl R, Bosman R, Pelnar P, Kasal E, Zidkova A. Esophageal Doppler-guided fluid management decreases blood lactate levels in multiple-trauma patients: A randomized controlled trial. *Crit Care* 2007; 11: R24.
34. Pillai P, McEleavy I, Gaughan M, et al. A double-blind randomized controlled clinical trial to assess the effect of Doppler optimized intraoperative fluid management on outcome following radical cystectomy. *J Urol* 2011; 186: 2201–6.
35. Thiele R, Bartels K, Gan TJ. Inter-device differences in monitoring for goal-directed fluid therapy. *Can J Anesth* 2015; 62: 169–81.
36. National Institute for Health and Care Excellence. Oesophageal Doppler-Guided Fluid Management During Major Surgery: Reducing Postoperative Complications and Bed Days. Available at http://www.evidence.nhs.uk/ (accessed July 14, 2015).
37. National Institute for Health and Care Excellence. *CardioQ- ODM Oesophageal Doppler Monitor*, 2011. Available at http://www.nice.org.uk/guidance/MTG3 (accessed July 14, 2014).
38. Atlas G, Morr T. Placement of the esophageal Doppler ultrasound probe in awake patients. *Chest* 2001; 119: 319.
39. Lefrant JY, Bruelle P, Aya AG, et al. Training is required to improve the reliability of esophageal Doppler to measure cardiac output in critically ill patients. *Intensive Care Med* 1998; 24: 347–52.
40. Schober P, Loer SA, Schwarte LA. Perioperative haemodynamic monitoring with transesophageal Doppler technology. *Anesth Analg* 2009; 109: 340–53.
41. Frank O. Die Grundform des arteriellen Pulses. *Z Biol* 1899; 37: 483–526.
42. Hadian M, Kim HK, Severyn DA, Pinsky MR. Cross-comparison of cardiac output trending accuracy of LiDCO, PiCCO, FloTrac and pulmonary artery catheters. *Crit Care* 2010; 14: R212.

43. Cecconi M, Dawson D, Casaretti R, Grounds RM, Rhodes A. A prospective study of the accuracy and precision of continuous cardiac output monitoring devices as compared to intermittent thermodilution. *Minerva Anestesiol* 2010; 76: 1010–7.

44. Krejci V, Vannucci A, Abbas A, Chapman W, Kangrga IM. Comparison of calibrated and uncalibrated arterial pressure-based cardiac output monitors during orthotopic liver transplantation. *Liver Transpl* 2010; 16: 773–82.

45. Zollner C, Haller M, Weis M, et al. Beat-to-beat measurement of cardiac output by intravascular pulse contour analysis: A prospective criterion standard study in patients after cardiac surgery. *J Cardiothorac Vasc Anesth* 2000; 14: 125–9.

46. Schuerholz T, Meyer MC, Friedrich L, Przemeck M, Sumpelmann R, Marx G. Reliability of continuous cardiac output determination by pulse-contour analysis in porcine septic shock. *Acta Anaesthesiol Scand* 2006; 50: 407–13.

47. Jeong YB, Kim TH, Roh YJ, Choi IC, Suh JH. Comparison of uncalibrated arterial pressure waveform analysis with continuous thermodilution cardiac output measurements in patients undergoing elective off-pump coronary artery bypass surgery. *J Cardiothorac Vasc Anesth* 2010; 24: 767–71.

48. Pratt B, Roteliuk L, Hatib F, Frazier J, Wallen RD. Calculating arterial pressure-based cardiac output using a novel measurement and analysis method. *Biomed Instrum Technol* 2007; 41: 403–11.

49. Marik PE, Cavallazzi R, Vasu T, et al. Dynamic changes in arterial waveform derived variables and fluid responsiveness in mechanically ventilated patients: A systematic review of the literature. *Crit Care Med* 2009; 37: 2642–7.

50. Biais M, Nouette-Gaulain K, Cottenceau V, et al. Uncalibrated pulse contour-derived stroke volume variation predicts fluid responsiveness in mechanically ventilated patients undergoing liver transplantation. *Br J Anaesth* 2008; 101: 761–8.

51. Berkenstadt H, Margalit N, Hadani M, Friedman Z, Segal E, Villa Y, Perel A. Stroke volume variation as a predictor of fluid responsiveness in patients undergoing brain surgery. *Anesth Analg* 2001; 92: 984–9.

52. Cecconi M, Monti G, Hamilton MA, et al. Efficacy of functional hemodynamic parameters in predicting fluid responsiveness with pulse power analysis in surgical patients. *Minerva Anestesiol* 2012; 78: 527–33.

53. Lopes MR, Oliveira MA, Pereira VO, Lemos IP, Auler JO Jr, Michard F. Goal-directed fluid management based on pulse pressure variation monitoring during high-risk surgery: A pilot randomized controlled trial. *Crit Care* 2007; 11: R100.

54. Benes J, Chytra I, Altmann P, et al. Intraoperative fluid optimization using stroke volume variation in high risk surgical patients: Results of prospective randomized study. *Crit Care* 2010; 14: R118.

55. Jones C, Kelliher L, Dickinson M, et al. Randomized clinical trial on enhanced recovery versus standard care following open liver resection. *Br J Surg* 2013; 100: 1015–24.

56. Ramsingh DS, Sanghvi C, Gamboa J, Cannesson M, Applegate RL 2nd. Outcome impact of goal directed fluid therapy during high risk abdominal surgery in low to moderate risk patients: A randomized controlled trial. *J Clin Monit Comput* 2013; 27: 249–57.

57. Pearse R, Dawson D, Fawcett J, Rhodes A, Grounds RM, Bennett ED. Early goal-directed therapy after major surgery reduces complications and duration of hospital stay. A randomised, controlled trial [ISRCTN38797445]. *Crit Care* 2005; 9: R687–93.
58. Futier E, Constantin JM, Paugam-Burtz C, et al. A trial of intraoperative low-tidal-volume ventilation in abdominal surgery. *N Engl J Med* 2013; 369: 428–37.
59. Kallmeyer IJ, Collard CD, Fox JA, et al. The safety of intraoperative transesophageal echocardiography: A case series of 7200 cardiac surgical patients. *Anesth Analg* 2001; 92: 1126–30.
60. Bilotta F, Tempe DK, Giovannini F, et al. Perioperative transoesophageal echocardiography in non-cardiac surgery. *Ann Card Anaesth* 2006; 9: 108–13.
61. Shillcutt SK, Markin NW, Montzingo CR, et al. Use of rapid "rescue" perioperative echocardiography to improve outcomes after hemodynamic instability in noncardiac surgical patients. *J Cardiothorac Vasc Anesth* 2012; 26: 362–70.
62. Levitov A, Marik PE. Echocardiographic assessment of preload responsiveness in critically ill patients. *Cardiol Res Pract* 2012; 2012: 819696.
63. American Society of Anesthesiologists and Society of Cardiovascular Anesthesiologists Task Force on Transesophageal Echocardiography. Practice guidelines for perioperative transesophageal echocardiography. An updated report by the American Society of Anesthesiologists and Society of Cardiovascular Anesthesiologists Task Force on Transesophageal Echocardiography. *Anesthesiology* 2010; 112: 1084–96.
64. Fleisher LA, Fleischmann KE, Auerbach AD, et al. 2014 ACC/AHA guideline on perioperative cardiovascular evaluation and management of patients undergoing noncardiac surgery: A report of the American College of Cardiology/American Heart Association Task Force on practice guidelines. *J Am Coll Cardiol* 2014; 64: e77.
65. Findlay GP, Goodwin APL, Protopapa A, et al. *Knowing the Risk. A Review of the Perioperative Care of Surgical Patients.* London: NCEPOD, 2011.
66. Royal College of Surgeons and Department of Health. *The Higher Risk Surgical Patient. Towards Improved Care for a Forgotten Group.* London: Royal College of Surgeons and Department of Health, 2011.
67. Cecconi M, Corredor C, Arulkumaran N, et al. Clinical review; Goal directed therapy-What is the evidence in surgical patients? The effect on different risk groups. *Crit Care* 2013; 17: 209.

chapter five

Monitoring the microcirculation

Mustafa Suker and Can Ince
Erasmus Medical Center
Rotterdam, the Netherlands

Contents

Key point:
>   This chapter reviews the possibilities for monitoring the microcirculation. Techniques and parameters are described. Microcirculatory monitoring can be used in the perioperative setting to assess goal-directed fluid therapy. The chapter ends with a case report.

5.1 Introduction

Microcirculation is the main site of oxygen delivery to tissue cells and is essential for the maintenance of cellular life and function. Its function relies on the complex interaction of its component cellular systems including red and white blood cells, endothelial cells, and parenchymal cells. The function of the organs is directly dependent on the function of their respective microcirculation [1].

The aim of resuscitation using fluid therapy is ultimately to promote tissue perfusion to deliver oxygen to sustain the cellular respiration and viability needed to support organ function [2]. This tissue oxygenation can be physiologically divided into three acts. The first act is carried out by the systematic circulation, with the main characters being cardiac output, blood pressure, and oxygen-carrying hemoglobin. The second act is found at locoregional sites and is performed by the microcirculation, with the main task being to distribute flow to each organ. The last act is set at the cellular level, where the mitochondria utilize the oxygen. In other words, there are two main factors that determine oxygen transport to tissue: the convective transport of oxygen by red blood cells and the passive diffusion of oxygen from the red blood cells to the mitochondria to initiate a chain reaction to generate Adenosine Triphosphate (ATP) (Figure 5.1) [3]. The current parameters for fluid management are maintaining cardiac output, blood pressure, and urine excretion [4]. This indicates that almost all fluid therapies are based on the concept that oxygenation is promoted by flow, which is, physiologically speaking, the convective factor for oxygenation. However, an equal contribution, as stated above, comes from the passive diffusion of oxygen to cells. One can imagine that despite optimal flow in the capillaries, the farther away a target cell is from oxygenated red blood cells or the lower the oxygen solubility of the tissue cells is, the more difficult oxygenation of the target cell becomes. This diffusive capacity of the microcirculation is quantified by the capillary density filled with flowing, oxygenated red blood cells. Currently, an optimum perioperative fluid management has not been found [5,6]. However, recent studies have shown that the measurement of microcirculation is considered to be an important adjunct measurement to conventional hemodynamic monitoring [3]. Pranskunas et al. illustrated this in a prospective observational study

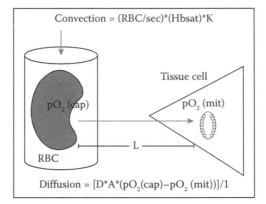

Figure 5.1 The convective and diffusive determinants of oxygen transport from the microcirculation to a tissue cell. Convective flow is defined as the product of the oxygen carrying saturation of the red blood cells, the rate at which red blood cells enter the capillary, and the oxygen-carrying capacity of a red blood cell at 100% saturation (0.0362 pl O_2/red blood cell). The diffusive movement of oxygen from the red blood cells to the mitochondria is defined by Fick's law of diffusion, where the flux of oxygen shown above is the product of the oxygen gradient from red blood cell (RBC) to mitochondria and the diffusion distance times the exchange surface divided by the diffusion distance from the RBC to the mitochondria. (From Ince, C., *Curr. Opin. Crit. Care.*, 20, 301–308, 2014. With permission.)

that examined patients with clinical signs of impaired organ perfusion and their microcirculation. Patients with abnormal microcirculation responded to fluid challenge by an improvement of their microcirculation and more importantly by a reduction of the number of clinical signs of impaired organ perfusion. By contrast, in patients with signs of impaired organ perfusion that had otherwise normal microcirculation, fluid challenge did not improve their microcirculation or their number of signs of impaired organ perfusion. These findings were found to be independent from stroke volume responsiveness after fluid challenge [7].

In this chapter we will review the possibilities for monitoring microcirculation. The known techniques and the current parameters used for microcirculation will be discussed. Furthermore, trials that have examined microcirculatory guided perioperative fluid therapy will be reviewed accompanied by a case report to illustrate the use of microcirculation monitoring. Finally, a recommendation for the perioperative monitoring of microcirculation will be addressed in view of future (randomized) trials.

5.2 Techniques and parameters

There are two ways to examine microcirculation: directly by measuring microcirculatory perfusion or indirectly by measuring tissue oxygenation. Videomicroscopy and laser Doppler are the two techniques for directly visualizing microcirculation. Videomicroscopy at bedside started with nailfold microvideoscopy [8]. The junction between cuticle and nail is investigated by using an ordinary microscope that can be connected to a video recording system, where microvascular blood flow and capillary density can be examined [9]. This has some limitations for clinical use at bedside as the nailfold area is very sensitive to temperature changes [10]. Videomicroscopy was revived, with an increase in use observed at the end of the last century due to the development of orthogonal polarization spectral (OPS) imaging, which allows a clinician to evaluate microcirculation live at bedside and to quantify microcirculation retrospectively [11]. A second generation handheld videomicroscope was introduced using sidestream dark-field (SDF) imaging as the successor of OPS imaging and, more recently, CytoCam incident dark-field (CytoCam-IDF) imaging as the successor of SDF imaging [12,13]. All of these techniques are based on the concept of emitting stroboscopic green light with a wavelength (530 nm) within the absorption spectrum of hemoglobin. These techniques can only be applied to organ surfaces due to the optical penetration depth of around 500 μm. CytoCam-IDF has some technical improvements over its predecessors such as digital signal, lower weight, and higher optical resolution. This optical superiority was recently described in a study that showed that IDF imaging detects more vessels (about 30%) to SDF imaging [14]. Software-assisted analysis is needed to quantify microcirculation. This microcirculation quantification consists of the microvascular flow index (MFI), total vessel density (TVD), and proportion of perfused vessels (PPV) [15]. MFI gives you an idea of the convective transport of oxygen transport in microcirculation as it describes the microcirculatory flow. TVD is a parameter that describes the diffusive factor because it gives you the density of microcirculation and inversely the distance between oxygenated red blood cells and targeted cells. PPV describes the proportion of vessels that have oxygenated red blood cells, thus providing more accurate quantification of the diffusive capacity of microcirculation.

Laser Doppler techniques can also be used for the measurement of microcirculatory blood flow expressed in relative units. This means that this technique can only provide relative changes from baseline. It also measures a surface of 0.5–1 mm^3 without identifying individual vessels. The technique visualizes the tissue of interest, allowing semiquantitative evaluation of the microcirculation.

For indirect evaluation of the microcirculation there are various methods. Clinical evaluation of skin color or temperature such as acrocyanosis or capillary refill time can give an indication of abnormal microcirculation [16]. Unfortunately, these tests are not very sensitive or specific in terms of the functional microcirculatory state [16]. Biological markers can also be used to indirectly assess microcirculation. Blood lactate level is one example that can be useful for this purpose, as it is inversely related to microcirculatory perfusion; however, this test is not that sensitive or specific [17]. Another indirect method for microcirculatory evaluation is tissue oxygenation measurement. These are all based on the concept of measuring tissue oxygen transport and oxygen consumption in that same tissue. Reflectance spectroscopy measures hemoglobin oxygen saturation (SO_2) of tissue using illumination via an optical fiber with different wavelengths sensitive to different parts of the absorption spectrum for hemoglobin. This gives the SO_2 value by measuring the oxy- and deoxyhemoglobin in a certain tissue. The probe used for this technique is very small, which allows a precise measurement of surface tissue but is limited due to a high depth penetration [18]. Near-infrared spectroscopy (NIRS) is another indirect technique that uses near-infrared light to measure different proteins in tissues so that tissue oxygen saturation (StO_2), total tissue hemoglobin, and absolute tissue hemoglobin index can be calculated. In combination with a vascular occlusion test (VOT), where the StO_2 can be measured after a brief period of tissue ischemia, NIRS can give information about microcirculatory reactivity function [19]. As NIRS only measures the difference between oxygen delivery and oxygen consumption, VOT combined with NIRS evaluates the microcirculatory reserve more than the actual perfusion [10]. From CO_2 measurement in tissue, one can obtain the balance between CO_2 production and flow to tissue. This CO_2

Table 5.1 Direct and indirect techniques for monitoring microcirculation

Technique	Parameter	Main limitations
Direct monitoring of microcirculation		
Nailfold videomicroscopy	Microcirculatory flow and density	Restricted to finger Sensitive for temperature and vasoconstriction
OPS, SDF, and IDF	Microcirculatory flow and density	Mostly restricted to retrospective semiquantitative analysis Sensitive for movement and pressure artifacts Limited sites to examine
Laser Doppler	Microcirculatory flow	Semiquantitative relative analysis High sampling volume
Indirect monitoring of microcirculation		
Clinical evaluation	Skin color/temperature Blood lactate levels	Lacks sensitivity and specificity
Reflectance spectroscopy	O_2 saturation	High sampling volume
NIRS	StO_2 of tissue HbT THI	High sampling volume
Electrodes/probes or tonometry	PCO_2 gapof tissue	Interference Difficult interpretation of microcirculatory function

Note: OPS, orthogonal polarization spectral; SDF, sidestream dark-field; IDF, incident dark-field; HbT, total tissue hemoglobin; THI, tissue hemoglobin index; StO_2, tissue oxygen saturation.

in tissue is accumulated by arterial CO_2 as well, so usually one uses the arterial gradient that is calculated (PCO_2 gap). This gap usually provides more information about the adequacy of flow than the presence of tissue hypoxia. Tissue PCO_2 can be measured by electrodes inserted in tissues or probes in contact with the tissue or by means of tonometry [10]. These direct and indirect techniques for monitoring microcirculation and its parameters are summarized in Table 5.1.

5.3   *Perioperative microcirculatory monitoring*

Microcirculatory monitoring can be used in the perioperative setting to assess goal-directed fluid therapy. Many studies have been conducted to evaluate methods of monitoring the microcirculation, especially in cardiac and abdominal surgery [20]. Hoefeijzers et al. published a review on the debate about the use of pulsatile perfusion (PP) during cardiopulmonary bypass [21]. The debate over the use of PP versus nonpulsatile perfusion (NP) is still not settled, and this review evaluated whether microcirculatory monitoring could provide information about the importance of PP. They included five human studies that assessed microcirculation during and after cardiopulmonary bypass. The first study looked with the OPS device at sublingual microcirculation in randomized patients with PP versus NP during cardiopulmonary bypass surgery [22]. This article defined the PPV in the sublingual microcirculation as the primary outcome for the comparison of perfusion. The study showed that PP was significantly better than NP for preserving microcirculation based on PPV. Two other included articles used SDF imaging to monitor the sublingual microcirculation [23,24]. One study was a randomized controlled trial (RCT) for PP versus. NP where sublingual microcirculation assessment was performed measuring the perfused vessel density (PVD) and MFI of small vessels. Both the PVD and the MFI were significantly in favor of PP. The other study investigated PP and NP in a crossover design where sublingual microcirculatory PVD was investigated, and there was no difference between the two perfusion techniques. The fourth article included in the review used NIRS on the forehead in a crossover design between PP and NP to examine cerebral microcirculatory oxygenation, and it did not show a difference between perfusion techniques in this study design [24]. The final study included was an RCT that used laser Doppler flow and tonometry on the gastric wall to monitor microcirculation during NP and PP [25]. The laser Doppler showed a significant reduction of blood flow in the NP arm compared to baseline flow. Tonometry did not show significant differences between the groups. There are three other studies that assessed microcirculation during perioperative cardiac surgery. Two studies used OPS imaging device for this microcirculatory assessment and one study used the SDF imaging. One of the OPS studies looked at changes of microcirculatory PVD during cardiopulmonary bypass in cardiac surgery. This study did not show any significant differences [26]. The other OPS study had a mixed patient group with respect to receiving or not receiving cardiopulmonary bypass during cardiac surgery and compared it to patients who underwent a thyroidectomy, as these patients received the same anesthetics [27]. This study examined TVD and PPV in these three patient groups. In the cardiopulmonary bypass cardiac surgery group and the thyroidectomy group, the PPV of the small vessels significantly decreased, whereas the off-pump cardiac surgery patients did not show a significant alteration in microcirculation. In the SDF study, patients who underwent cardiac surgery with cardiopulmonary bypass were assessed for the MFI of their sublingual microcirculation [28]. The MFI of medium blood vessels significantly decreased after starting the cardiopulmonary bypass. Interestingly, this study showed that decreases in microcirculatory flow occurred irrespective of changes in systematic blood pressure. This last result was reiterated in another observational study where patients who received medication for high blood pressure after undergoing cardiac surgery with cardiopulmonary bypass were assessed for micro- and macrocirculatory parameters [29]. This study used the SDF device to assess sublingual MFI and PVD. As the systolic arterial blood pressure decreased significantly, the mean MFI for small and large vessels did not change. Furthermore, there was a significant increase in mean PVD for large vessels but not for small vessels.

Assessing microcirculation directly and indirectly has been investigated in abdominal surgery as well. One study used serum lactate levels to prevent postoperative complications after major elective surgery for gastrointestinal malignancy [30]. This study randomized between restricted perioperative fluid therapy based on lactate levels versus "normal" restricted fluid therapy. In the restricted perioperative fluid therapy based on lactate levels, serum lactate was routinely monitored, and in the presence of hyperlactatemia an additional fluid bolus was given. This lactate-guided fluid therapy resulted in a significant decrease in systemic complications. Furthermore, the restricted fluid group without routine serum lactate monitoring received significantly more fluids than the serum lactate monitoring group. Moreover, the patients who received supplementary fluids had significantly more complications in the restricted regimen lacking serum lactate monitoring. Another study used NIRS in combination with VOT to assess the microcirculatory response during fluid challenge in patients undergoing abdominal surgery [31]. Fluid challenge was given to patients with evidence of hypovolemia, and they were assessed for fluid responsiveness during surgery. Before and after the fluid challenge, StO_2 values were obtained using NIRS in combination with VOT. There was no significant difference observed in StO_2 between positive and negative fluid challenge. However, hypovolemia was associated with a significant reduction in StO_2 recovery slope, with a significant difference between positive and negative fluid challenge. An RCT was conducted to compare fluid therapy guided by central venous pressure versus stroke volume with and without dopexamine in patients after major gastrointestinal surgery [32]. Sublingual microcirculation was assessed using the SDF device and cutaneous microcirculation was assessed by laser Doppler flow and Clark electrode for PtO_2. The fluid therapy guided by stroke volume with dopexamine showed an improved sublingual and cutaneous microcirculatory flow. Sublingual microcirculation flow remained constant in the stroke volume group but deteriorated in the central venous pressure group. Laser Doppler flow showed a hyperemic response in the stroke volume with dopexamine, whereas this variable remained unchanged in the stroke volume group without dopexamine and deteriorated in the central venous pressure group. Cutaneous PtO_2 initially increased in all three groups after surgery, and this was sustained in the stroke volume combined with dopexamine group but decreased in the other two groups. Another study examined perioperative microcirculatory changes in patients undergoing abdominal surgery [33]. Using the SDF imaging, they assessed PVD and MFI. This study showed that MFI increased in the timeframe from pre- to intra-operative measurement and decreased postoperatively, whereas PVD remained unchanged. Neither the MFI nor PVD was associated with postoperative complications. By contrast, another study evaluated microcirculatory flow and tissue oxygenation after abdominal surgery and found a relation with postoperative complications [34]. In this study, sublingual microcirculation was assessed using the SDF imaging, and cutaneous microcirculation was assessed by laser Doppler flow and Clark electrode for PtO_2. Cutaneous microcirculation assessment did not show a relation with postoperative complications. However, sublingual microcirculation did show a relation with postoperative complications, with the MFI and PVD of the small vessels being significantly lower in the patients who had postoperative complications.

5.4   Case report

A 19-year-old woman was diagnosed with a solid pseudopapillary tumor in the pancreatic tail. She was scheduled to undergo a distal pancreatectomy with splenectomy. To assess her microcirculation, we measured her sublingual microcirculation using a CytoCam-IDF device. The measurement was performed on three different occasions: 1 day before surgery (T0), in the first 24 hours after surgery (T1), and on the fourth day after surgery (T2). At each time point, microcirculation was filmed in three different locations on the sublingual mucosa for a minimum of 10 seconds per sequence. Great care was taken to clear saliva before image acquisition. Film sequences were repeatedly taken until three sequences of good quality were obtained. Flow parameters were analyzed using MFI and TVD and were analyzed offline using a software package associated with the CytoCam-IDF device [35]. Fluid balance was monitored starting from the beginning of the procedure for the first 48 hours as part of the local hospital's protocol. During the surgery, the patient lost 1,230 mL of blood and had 200 mL urine output, while the patient received 2,766 mL of IV fluids. In the first 24 hours after surgery the patient received a total of 984 mL of intravenous fluids and 150 mL of oral intake, while the output consisted of 750 mL of urine output and 70 mL of drain production. Thus, in the first 24 hours the fluid balance, including surgery, was a total of 3,900 mL of fluids in and 2,250 mL out, which gives a positive fluid balance of 1,650 mL. Between the second and third days the fluid balance was positive by 885 mL, and on the third day there was a negative fluid balance of 1,330 mL. On the fourth and fifth days the patient did not receive any fluid therapy as the oral intake was sufficient. On the first and second days the patient had hypotensive blood pressure with a normal heart rate, which can be explained by the epidural analgesia placed during surgery for postoperative pain relief [36]. The preoperative hemoglobin level was 4.8 mmol/L (7.73 g/dL) and decreased to 4.4 mmol/L (7.09 g/dL) on the first postoperative day, and no blood transfusion was given. The patient also had nausea, which quickly resolved after stopping the epidural analgesia, and no serious complaints after surgery. The subsequent postoperative course was uncomplicated, and the patient was discharged after 9 days. The sublingual microcirculation over the three time points is shown in Figure 5.2. Although the MFI was 3.0 at all three time points, the TVD showed a difference over the three time points. At T0 the TVD was 15.20 mm/mm², at T1 the TVD was 12.30 mm/mm², and at T2 the TVD was 17.99 mm/mm² (Table 5.2). This indicated that the flow over the three time points was good. However, the TVD, as indicated earlier, is one of the measures that considers how the diffusive determinant of oxygenation varies over the three time points. At baseline, the TVD was 15.20 mm/mm², which is within the normal hydration situation. After the patient had a very high positive fluid balance of 1,650 mL, the TVD went down to 12.30 mm/mm². Finally, at T2 the patient had a TVD of 17.99 mm/mm², which indicates that the patient was still having a negative balance as it was at Day 3 after surgery, by providing information about the filling status at the level of the microcirculation. This case report indicates therefore that microcirculatory assessment may help goal-directed fluid therapy. As the patient was hypotensive, the fluid balance was positive with normal microcirculatory flow. Nevertheless, the diffusive determinant of oxygenation was decreased. To optimize the fluid therapy, one could have been more restrictive with the resuscitation therapy, assuring that the microcirculatory flow was kept normal, with the TVD close to the baseline measurement [3].

T0   T1   T2

Figure 5.2 The sublingual microcirculation of a patient 1 day before (T0), 1 day after (T1), and 4 days after (T2) undergoing distal pancreatectomy with splenectomy. Images were obtained using the incident dark-field device.

Table 5.2 Sublingual microcirculation of a case report

Time point	T0	T1	T2
Days from surgery	−1	+1	+4
Fluid balance	Normal	+1,650 mL	Negative or normal
MFI	3.0	3.0	3.0
TVD	15.20 mm/mm²	12.30 mm/mm²	17.99 mm/mm²

Note: MFI, microvascular flow index; TVD, total vessel density.

5.5 Conclusion

Fluid therapies are used to promote tissue perfusion to deliver oxygen for sustaining cellular respiration and ultimately promote organ function. This is based on macro- and microcirculatory hemodynamics, which can be divided into convective and diffusive determinants. Blood pressure, cardiac output, and urine output can give an indication of the convective status of the circulation, while microcirculation monitoring can give an indication of the convective and diffusive status. There are different ways to monitor microcirculation in the perioperative setting, and they can be divided into direct and indirect monitoring. Direct monitoring can be performed by videomicroscopy and laser Doppler flow. Indirect monitoring can be performed by clinical evaluation, techniques measuring tissue oxygenation, NIRS, tonometry, and reflectance spectroscopy. As discussed in this chapter, the diffusive determinant for oxygenation is equally as important as the convective determinant. Therefore, we recommend the use of videomicroscopy to monitor microcirculation, as it is the only available technique that gives information concerning the diffusive capacity of microcirculation. However, there are some limitations to this technique that should be addressed first before it impacts clinical decision-making. First, an automated analysis of the microcirculation should be conducted immediately after obtaining the sequence to enhance the decision-making on whether fluid therapy is needed. Furthermore, there is a need for more studies that show the relation between sublingual microcirculation and organ dysfunction. Finally, more (randomized) trials should be conducted that use videomicroscopy for microcirculatory goal-directed fluid therapy.

5.6 Conflicts of interest

Dr. Suker declares no interests. Dr. Ince has received honoraria and independent research grants from Fresenius-Kabi, Bad Homburg, Germany; Baxter Health Care, Deerfield, Illinois, and AM-Pharma, Bunnik, Netherlands. Dr. Ince has developed SDF imaging and is listed as inventor on related patents commercialized by MicroVision Medical (MVM) under a license from the Academic Medical Center. He has been a consultant for MVM in the past but has not been involved with this company for more than 5 years now; however, he still holds shares. Braedius Medical, a company owned by a relative of Dr. Ince, has developed and designed a hand-held microscope called CytoCam-IDF imaging. Dr. Ince has no financial relation with Braedius Medical of any sort, that is, has never owned shares or received consultancy or speaker fees from Braedius Medical.

5.7   Summary

Fluid therapies are used to promote tissue perfusion to deliver oxygen for sustaining cellular respiration and ultimately promote organ function.

This is based on macro- and microcirculatory hemodynamics.

Blood pressure, cardiac output, and urine output can give an indication of the convective status of the circulation, while microcirculation monitoring can give an indication of the convective and diffusive status.

There are different ways to monitor microcirculation in the perioperative setting, and they can be divided into direct and indirect monitoring.

Direct monitoring can be performed by videomicroscopy and laser Doppler flow.

Indirect monitoring can be performed by clinical evaluation, techniques measuring tissue oxygenation, NIRS, tonometry, and reflectance spectroscopy.

Therefore, we recommend the use of videomicroscopy to monitor microcirculation as it is the only available technique that gives information concerning the diffusive capacity of microcirculation.

References

1. Donati A, Tibboel D, Ince C. Towards integrative physiological monitoring of the critically ill: From cardiovascular to microcirculatory and cellular function monitoring at the bedside. *Crit Care*. 2013; 17 Suppl 1: S5.
2. Santry HP, Alam HB. Fluid resuscitation: Past, present, and the future. *Shock*. 2010; 33: 229–41.
3. Ince C. The rationale for microcirculatory guided fluid therapy. *Curr Opin Crit Care*. 2014; 20: 301–8.
4. Chappell D, Jacob M, Hofmann-Kiefer K, Conzen P, Rehm M. A rational approach to perioperative fluid management. *Anesthesiology*. 2008; 109: 723–40.
5. Pro CI, Yealy DM, Kellum JA, Huang DT, Barnato AE, Weissfeld LA, et al. A randomized trial of protocol-based care for early septic shock. *N Engl J Med*. 2014; 370: 1683–93.
6. Pearse RM, Harrison DA, MacDonald N, Gillies MA, Blunt M, Ackland G, et al. Effect of a perioperative, cardiac output-guided hemodynamic therapy algorithm on outcomes following major gastrointestinal surgery: A randomized clinical trial and systematic review. *JAMA*. 2014; 311: 2181–90.

7. Pranskunas A, Koopmans M, Koetsier PM, Pilvinis V, Boerma EC. Microcirculatory blood flow as a tool to select ICU patients eligible for fluid therapy. *Intensive Care Med.* 2013; 39: 612–9.

8. Fagrell B, Fronek A, Intaglietta M. A microscope-television system for studying flow velocity in human skin capillaries. *Am J Physiol.* 1977; 233: H318–21.

9. Shore AC. Capillaroscopy and the measurement of capillary pressure. *Br J Clin Pharmacol.* 2000; 50: 501–13.

10. De Backer D, Ospina-Tascon G, Salgado D, Favory R, Creteur J, Vincent JL. Monitoring the microcirculation in the critically ill patient: Current methods and future approaches. *Intensive Care Med.* 2010; 36: 1813–25.

11. Groner W, Winkelman JW, Harris AG, Ince C, Bouma GJ, Messmer K, et al. Orthogonal polarization spectral imaging: A new method for study of the microcirculation. *Nat Med.* 1999; 5: 1209–12.

12. Goedhart PT, Khalilzada M, Bezemer R, Merza J, Ince C. Sidestream Dark Field (SDF) imaging: A novel stroboscopic LED ring-based imaging modality for clinical assessment of the microcirculation. *Opt Express.* 2007; 15: 15101–14.

13. Aykut G, Veenstra G, Scorcella C, Ince C, Boerma C. CytoCam-IDF (incident dark field illumination) imaging for bedside monitoring of the microcirculation. *Intensive Care Med Exp.* 2015; 3: 4.

14. van Elteren HA, Ince C, Tibboel D, Reiss IK, de Jonge RC. Cutaneous microcirculation in preterm neonates: Comparison between sidestream dark field (SDF) and incident dark field (IDF) imaging. *J Clin Monit Comput.* 2015; 29(5): 543–8.

15. De Backer D, Hollenberg S, Boerma C, Goedhart P, Buchele G, Ospina-Tascon G, et al. How to evaluate the microcirculation: Report of a round table conference. *Crit Care.* 2007; 11: R101.

16. Boerma EC, Kuiper M, Kingma WP, Egbers PH, Gerritsen RT, Ince C. Disparity between skin perfusion and sublingual microcirculatory alterations in severe sepsis and septic shock: A prospective observational study. *Intens Care Med.* 2008; 34: 1294–8.

17. De Backer D, Creteur J, Dubois MJ, Sakr Y, Koch M, Verdant C, et al. The effects of dobutamine on microcirculatory alterations in patients with septic shock are independent of its systemic effects. *Crit Care Med.* 2006; 34: 403–8.

18. Schwarz B, Hofstotter H, Salak N, Pajk W, Knotzer H, Mayr A, et al. Effects of norepinephrine and phenylephrine on intestinal oxygen supply and mucosal tissue oxygen tension. *Intensive Care Med.* 2001; 27: 593–601.

19. Gomez H, Torres A, Polanco P, Kim HK, Zenker S, Puyana JC, et al. Use of non-invasive NIRS during a vascular occlusion test to assess dynamic tissue O-2 saturation response. *Intens Care Med.* 2008; 34: 1600–7.

20. Wilms H, Mittal A, Haydock MD, van den Heever M, Devaud M, Windsor JA. A systematic review of goal directed fluid therapy: Rating of evidence for goals and monitoring methods. *J Crit Care.* 2014; 29: 204–9.

21. Hoefeijzers MP, Ter Horst LH, Koning N, Vonk AB, Boer C, Elbers PW. The pulsatile perfusion debate in cardiac surgery: Answers from the microcirculation? *J Cardiothorac Vasc Anesth.* 2015; 29: 761–7.

22. O'Neil MP, Fleming JC, Badhwar A, Guo LR. Pulsatile versus nonpulsatile flow during cardiopulmonary bypass: Microcirculatory and systemic effects. *Ann Thorac Surg.* 2012; 94: 2046–53.

23. Koning NJ, Vonk AB, van Barneveld LJ, Beishuizen A, Atasever B, van den Brom CE, et al. Pulsatile flow during cardiopulmonary bypass preserves postoperative microcirculatory perfusion irrespective of systemic hemodynamics. *J Appl Physiol (1985)*. 2012; 112: 1727–34.
24. Elbers PW, Wijbenga J, Solinger F, Yilmaz A, van Iterson M, van Dongen EP, et al. Direct observation of the human microcirculation during cardiopulmonary bypass: Effects of pulsatile perfusion. *J Cardiothorac Vasc Anesth*. 2011; 25: 250–5.
25. Ohri SK, Bowles CW, Mathie RT, Lawrence DR, Keogh BE, Taylor KM. Effect of cardiopulmonary bypass perfusion protocols on gut tissue oxygenation and blood flow. *Ann Thorac Surg*. 1997; 64: 163–70.
26. Bauer A, Kofler S, Thiel M, Eifert S, Christ F. Monitoring of the sublingual microcirculation in cardiac surgery using orthogonal polarization spectral imaging: Preliminary results. *Anesthesiology*. 2007; 107: 939–45.
27. De Backer D, Dubois MJ, Schmartz D, Koch M, Ducart A, Barvais L, et al. Microcirculatory alterations in cardiac surgery: Effects of cardiopulmonary bypass and anesthesia. *Ann Thorac Surg*. 2009; 88: 1396–403.
28. den Uil CA, Lagrand WK, Spronk PE, van Domburg RT, Hofland J, Luthen C, et al. Impaired sublingual microvascular perfusion during surgery with cardiopulmonary bypass: A pilot study. *J Thorac Cardiovasc Surg*. 2008; 136: 129–34.
29. Elbers PW, Ozdemir A, van Iterson M, van Dongen EP, Ince C. Microcirculatory imaging in cardiac anesthesia: Ketanserin reduces blood pressure but not perfused capillary density. *J Cardiothorac Vasc Anesth*. 2009; 23: 95–101.
30. Wenkui Y, Ning L, Jianfeng G, Weiqin L, Shaoqiu T, Zhihui T, et al. Restricted peri-operative fluid administration adjusted by serum lactate level improved outcome after major elective surgery for gastrointestinal malignancy. *Surgery*. 2010; 147: 542–52.
31. Futier E, Christophe S, Robin E, Petit A, Pereira B, Desbordes J, et al. Use of near-infrared spectroscopy during a vascular occlusion test to assess the microcirculatory response during fluid challenge. *Crit Care*. 2011; 15: R214.
32. Jhanji S, Vivian-Smith A, Lucena-Amaro S, Watson D, Hinds CJ, Pearse RM. Haemodynamic optimisation improves tissue microvascular flow and oxygenation after major surgery: A randomised controlled trial. *Crit Care*. 2010; 14: R151.
33. Bansch P, Flisberg P, Bentzer P. Changes in the sublingual microcirculation during major abdominal surgery and post-operative morbidity. *Acta Anaesthesiol Scand*. 2014; 58: 89–97.
34. Jhanji S, Lee C, Watson D, Hinds C, Pearse RM. Microvascular flow and tissue oxygenation after major abdominal surgery: Association with post-operative complications. *Intensive Care Med*. 2009; 35: 671–7.
35. Medical B. *CytoCamTools Software*. 2013; Available at http://www.braedius.com/magnoliaPublic/braedius/products/cytocamTools.html. Accessed on May 11, 2017.
36. Wheatley RG, Schug SA, Watson D. Safety and efficacy of postoperative epidural analgesia. *Br J Anaesth*. 2001; 87: 47–61.

chapter six

Noninvasive hemodynamic monitoring

Cecilia Canales, Andy Trang, and Maxime Cannesson
UC Irvine Health, UC Irvine School of Medicine, University of California Irvine, CA

Contents

Key points:
This chapter basically deals with noninvasive devices for the monitoring of fluid therapy.
Arterial blood pressure monitoring physiology is covered.
Several noninvasive cardiac output monitors are described:

- Esophageal Doppler (see also Chapter 4)
- USCOM

- Nexfin
- Bioimpedance and bioreactance monitoring devices
- Continuous noninvasive arterial pressure monitor
- Noninvasive near-infrared spectroscopy (see also Chapter 5)
- Pleth variability index

A goal-directed therapy protocol is described and the chapter ends with an illustrative case report.

6.1   Introduction

The application of goal-directed therapy (GDT) protocols using noninvasive hemodynamic monitoring systems has significantly increased during recent years in the perioperative setting. The availability of noninvasive devices has made it easier to implement GDT protocols, as more and more clinicians are becoming familiarized with the technology. However, confusion still exists about what device to use and whether a noninvasive monitoring system is the right choice. Part of the confusion lies with the misconception that many clinicians believe that the natural progression is to have noninvasive monitors replace more invasive monitoring systems. Each monitor, regardless of level of invasiveness, has value and utility in various patient populations and in different settings. The selection of the monitor should depend on the intended patient population, the clinical setting with available devices, and the ability of the clinician to use and interpret the device (Figure 6.1) [1].

In this chapter, we will outline and discuss potential uses for various noninvasive monitoring systems as they may be useful in applying GDT protocols. This, however, does not mean that we advocate for the use of noninvasive monitors only. Instead, we are providing an outline so that clinicians and health care institutions alike can make informed and appropriate choices regarding acquisition of devices, limitations of each device, and interpretation of the dynamic predictors of fluid responsiveness they employ.

6.2   Device overview

Every patient in the perioperative setting receives hemodynamic monitoring. Whether it is standard monitoring or invasive advanced monitoring, the goal of hemodynamic monitoring is to ensure patients are adequately perfused. Electrocardiogram (ECG), noninvasive blood pressure (NIBP), and pulse oximetry are standard patient monitors in

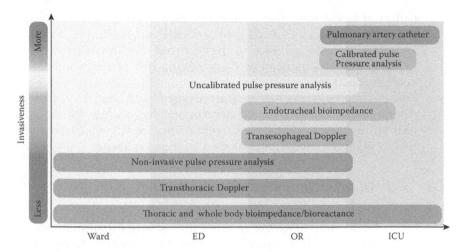

Figure 6.1 Integrative hemodynamic monitoring approach as described by Alhashemi et al. (Reproduced from Alhashemi, J.A., et al., *Crit. Care*, 15, 214, 2011.)

the perioperative area. As needed, because of the level of risk of the surgery, patient comorbidities, or underlying disease processes, more advanced or invasive monitoring such as arterial blood pressure, central venous pressure (CVP), or cardiac output (CO) monitoring is employed. These expanded monitors can be used to detect hemodynamic instability and are used to guide treatment. Until recently, these expanded monitors were reserved for high-risk patients because of the level of invasiveness and risks associated with their use. However, miniature and noninvasive devices that can be used on moderate and low-risk patients also provide dynamic parameters that have been shown to be effective at predicting hemodynamic status and helping guide clinical decisions for GDT.

6.3 Standard monitoring

- ECG is used to monitor the heart rate and rhythm. It is used to identify arrhythmias or myocardial ischemia, which can result in hypoperfusion and indicate the need for clinical intervention.
- NIBP is typically measured intermittently, on an automated basis. The mean arterial pressure (MAP) is routinely used as an indicator of perfusion pressure. Additionally, it is important to note that blood pressure (BP) does not equal blood flow and that these variables are only loosely related. Specifically, because of increased sympathetic tone, or increased systemic vascular resistance, and the dynamic

nature of blood flow and circulation, blood can be shunted, leading to a maintenance of MAP in a normal range, despite low CO and poor perfusion. In fact, studies showed that in patients where hypovolemia was induced by withdrawing 20% of estimated blood volume, the MAP did not change [2].

- Pulse oximetry is used to measure oxygen saturation level (SpO_2). Although the oximeter is used to recognize hypoxemia, the sigmoidal nature of the oxygen desaturation curve, SpO_2 levels can remain relatively high for a period, followed by a rapid descent.

6.4   Advanced hemodynamic monitoring

- Arterial blood pressure (ABP) is an invasive blood pressure measurement, obtained by inserting an arterial line, most often in the radial or femoral artery. It is typically reserved for moderate- to high-risk patients because of the risks associated with vessel cannulation. ABP gives beat-to-beat information on blood pressure, and because of its continuous nature it detects changes in MAP quicker than with NIBP. ABP can be used to measure pulse pressure variation (PPV), which, as we will describe in detail, is a dynamic index of fluid responsiveness that can also be used to apply GDT protocol. Like with NIBP monitoring, MAP may stay high because of shunting, meaning that it may not be an accurate indicator of low CO and low perfusion.

CVP is widely considered to be a poor predictor of fluid status and perfusion. However, it is still widely used in moderate- to high-risk patients, as central lines are routinely placed in this setting primarily for administering drugs, rapid administration of fluid, and as a component of several clinical protocols. However, monitoring CVP has limited value in guiding fluid therapy.

6.5   CO monitors

CO presents the clinician with the opportunity to monitor and optimize the patient's stroke volume and therefore optimize tissue oxygen delivery [3], which is the aim of GDT. Invasive, minimally invasive, and noninvasive monitors exist that either directly or through surrogates monitor CO, providing real-time measurements of the patient's CO status. This is important because hemodynamic optimization, or GDT, has been suggested to improve patient outcomes [4–6], and even short periods of hypoperfusion can affect microcirculation and result in inadequate oxygen delivery to tissues, leading to minor and more severe complications. Table 6.1 summarizes the different CO monitoring systems available. Although the absolute value of CO provides little information about the

Table 6.1 Cardiac output monitoring across various levels of invasiveness

Technology	System	Invasiveness	Mechanism	Dynamic indices
Pulmonary artery catheter	Vigilance	+++	Thermodilution	–
Calibrated pulse contour analysis	PiCCO plus	++	Transpulmonary thermodilution plus contour analysis	–
	VolumeView	++	Transpulmonary thermodilution plus contour analysis	–
	LiDCOplus	+	Continuous cardiac output monitoring	–
Endotracheal bioimpedance	ECOM	+	Bioimpedance plus pulse wave analyses	–
Uncalibrated pulse contour analysis	FloTrac	+	Pulse wave analysis	SVV
	LiDCO Rapid	+	Pulse wave analysis	PPV/SVV
	PulsioFlex	+	Pulse wave analysis	PPV/SVV
	PRAM	+	Pulse wave analysis	PPV/SVV
	Nexfin	0	Noninvasive pulse wave form analysis	PPV/SVV
Ultrasound	CardioQ™	0+	Doppler ultrasound	–
	USCOM	0	Suprasternal ultrasound	–
Bioreactance	NiCOM	0	Bioreactance	SVV
Thoracic bioimp	BioZ	0	Bioimpedance	–

Note: 0, none; 0+, very slight; +, slight; ++, intermediate; +++, high. PiCCO plus, Pulsion Medical Systems, Irving, TX; VolumeView, Edwards, Irvine, CA; LiDCOplus, LiDCO Ltd, London, UK; FloTrac, Edwards, Irvine, CA; LiDCO Rapid, LiDCO Ltd; PulsioFlex, Pulsion Medical Systems; PRAM, multiple suppliers; Nexfin, Edwards; CardioQ, Deltex Medical Limited, Chichester, UK; USCOM, USCOM, Sydney, Australia; NiCOM, Cheetah Medical, Tel Aviv, Israel; ECOM, ConMed, Irvine, CA; BioZ, CardioDynamics, San Diego, CA.

patient's hemodynamic status, changes in CO can be used to guide resuscitation. Likewise, dynamic hemodynamic indices such as stroke volume variation (SVV), PPV, and the pleth variability index (PVI), exploit the Frank–Starling relationship in mechanically ventilated patients, to give us a predictable representation of whether an individual patient would be a responder or nonresponder to fluid expansion to maximize CO. We will focus on noninvasive monitors that can be used together with GDT protocols.

6.6   *Esophageal Doppler*

The esophageal Doppler (ED) uses a flexible ultrasound probe that can measure blood flow velocity and assess changes in blood flow from the descending aorta, allowing for CO to be calculated from the velocity time integral of the Doppler signal and the aortic cross section area. Cardio™ (Deltex Medical Ltd, Sussex, UK) uses nomograms to estimate the diameter of the descending aorta and calculate CO. There are several studies using the ED that confirm that it can rapidly detect changes in CO and improve patient outcomes [6–9]. However, there are limitations in the use of this device, as the Doppler probe needs constant repositioning to obtain a good signal, which means that the measurements are operator dependent [10].

6.7   *USCOM*

USCOM™ (USCOM, Sydney, Australia) is a suprasternal, transthoracic Doppler that calculates CO from aortic or pulmonary arterial flow measurements. The accuracy and precision of USCOM has been verified, when compared to bolus thermodilution [11,12], but its intermittent nature and significant training or high level of experience are required to obtain accurate measurements. To date, this device has not been used for GDT studies in the operating room.

6.8   *Nexfin*

The Nexfin®, or as it is now called, the ClearSight® (Edwards Lifesciences, Irvine, CA), monitor uses a finger cuff to continuously monitor NIBP and uses the arterial pressure curve and pulse wave analyses to compute CO and dynamic variables such as PPV and SVV. In a recent study, Nexfin was used with GDT protocol to discriminate between fluid responders and nonresponders [13]. However, there are limitations on the use of the device, as an accurate determinant of CO and blood pressure such as vasoconstriction and low peripheral perfusion [14].

6.9   Impedance/bioreactance

Bioimpedance (BioZ™, CardioDynamics, San Diego, CA) provides noninvasive CO monitoring by applying a high frequency, low-alternating electrical current across the thorax via skin electrodes.

NICOM™ (Cheetah Medical, Portland, OR), a bioreactance device, measures changes in the frequency of the electrical currents traversing the chest. Although both bioimpedance and bioreactance show promise in healthy volunteers, studies in patients show low precision and agreement, making them unsuitable for clinical practice [15,16].

6.10   Continuous noninvasive arterial pressure

The CNAP 500 (continuous noninvasive arterial pressure; CNSystems, Graz, Austria) system measures continuous pressure, which is obtained by a double finger cuff. The monitor computes CO and PPV, which has been shown to be highly predictive of fluid responsiveness [17,18].

6.11   Other noninvasive hemodynamic monitoring systems

6.11.1   Near-infrared spectroscopy

Near-infrared spectroscopy (NIRS) (see also Chapter 5) uses near-infrared light to measure hemoglobin content in tissues. Since most of the blood in tissues is venous, NIRS can be used to detect decreases in blood flow or in oxygenation. Occlusion tests can be done to detect microvascular changes. Vascular occlusion tests at the forearm use NIRS to measure the tissue oxygenation (StO_2) value at the thenar eminence, which has been purported as a functional evaluation of the microcirculation [19–21]. In a healthy individual as indicated in Figure 6.2a, the vascular occlusion test would induce transient ischemia, with quick recovery indicating intact microcirculation and therefore good perfusion. Patients that have underlying pathology affecting their microcirculation and perfusion pressures are not able to recover as quickly, as shown in Figure 6.2b.

6.11.2   Pleth variability index

The PVI (Masimo Corp, Irvine, CA) is an automated and continuous calculation of respiratory variations in the perfusion index that relies on light absorption through the finger, ear, or forehead. PVI can be used to predict fluid responsiveness in mechanically ventilated patients and has been used in a limited series of GDT studies [22,23]. However, there are

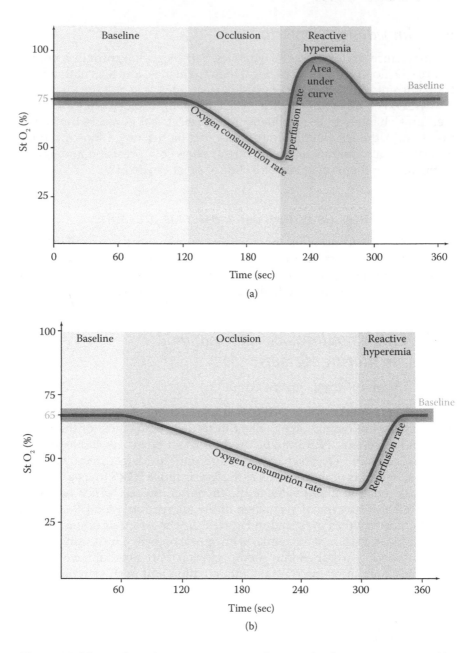

Figure 6.2 Near-infrared spectroscopy recordings at the thenar eminence in (a) a normal volunteer and (b) a pathologic patient with hypoperfusion.

limitations in that vasopressors and vasoconstrictors may interfere with the index [17].

6.11.3 GDT protocol

As we have all learned from basic physiology, the goal of circulation is to provide oxygen and nutrients to tissues and organs. To accomplish this, we need adequate perfusion pressure to force blood to the microvessels of organs and adequate CO to deliver oxygen and substrates, while removing carbon dioxide and other metabolic waste. Monitoring CO and dynamic parameters that focus on the cardiopulmonary interactions, such as PPV, SVV, and PVI, can be used to predict patient preload responsiveness. Specifically, when looking at the Frank–Starling relationship, if a patient is on the steep portion of the curve, large changes in preload (by giving a fluid bolus, for example) will induce large increases in stroke volume (SV), helping to maximize CO and improve perfusion; while if a patient is on the plateau portion of the curve, volume expansions will have little to no effect on the SV, thereby indicating that the patient is already well loaded with fluid, and other clinical measures should be used if the patient is experiencing hemodynamic instability. There is no confirmation, however, that the patient has adequate microvascular perfusion. These parameters can be quantified and applied for the use of GDT together with CO monitoring. Ideally, we would also need to have a perception of venous return, which would be determined by the pressure gradient between the peripheral veins and the right atrium (CVP). The venous system can be divided into two theoretical compartments, the unstressed and the stressed volume. The unstressed volume is that volume that fills the vascular system up to a point where intravascular pressure starts to increase. Above that, filling of the system would be denoted the *stressed volume*. The mean circulatory filling pressure (MCFP) is defined as the pressure when all veins are distended and the heart stopped (no flow). All pressures are equalized. The MCFP is normally in the range of 8–10 mmHg and is the major component of venous return. Organ flow would be determined by the difference between MAP and CVP. Consequently, if we increase CVP, microvascular perfusion will decrease.

6.12 Limitations of current devices for measuring dynamic parameters

Major limitation of dynamic parameters for fluid responsiveness assessment are that patients should fulfill the following criteria:

- Mechanical ventilation
- General anesthesia

- Tidal volume >6 mL/kg
- No arrhythmia
- No right ventricular dysfunction

6.13   Conclusion

Noninvasive advanced technologies offer many options for hemodynamic monitoring and application with GDT. There are limitations we need consider; however, these devices may be useful in the future, applying GDT in patients with a moderate to low risk for perioperative complications and hemodynamic instability.

6.14   Clinical case

The hemodynamic performance of a 49-year-old man, referred for a right nephrectomy under general anesthesia, is shown below. The medical history consists of a history of smoking (one pack a day for 30 years), alcohol use, and IV drug use (now discontinued). The patient's weight is 63 kg and the height is 183 cm. Preoperative EKG is normal, left ventricular ejection fraction is 45%. In addition, the preoperative echocardiography shows mild pulmonary hypertension (systolic pulmonary artery pressure is 40 mmHg) and a moderate right ventricular dysfunction (right ventricle is slightly dilated).

The plan for anesthesia management consists of induction with IV protocol and fentanyl and maintenance using inhaled sevoflurane and fentanyl boluses. Vascular access consists of one peripheral IV (16G), a left subclavian central venous catheter (double lumen) equipped with central venous oxygen saturation ($S_{cv}O_2$) readings, and a left radial arterial line. Hemodynamic monitoring relies on CVP, CO monitoring using ED, and PPV from the arterial line tracing. The goal of the hemodynamic management was to keep PPV below 10%, $S_{cv}O_2$ more than 70%–75%, and to optimize CO.

Baseline crystalloids infusion is 5 mL/kg/hr.

After 1 hour of surgery, the estimated blood loss is 800 mL. The patient's hemodynamic variables (Figure 6.3) are heart rate (HR) 96 bpm, ABP 85/47 (60) mmHg, CVP 13 mmHg, SpO_2 100%, *CO 2.9 L/min, $S_{cv}O_2$ 53%, PPV 18%.*

At this stage, it was decided to administer 500 mL of IV fluids since PPV was high (18%) together with a low CO and a low $S_{cv}O_2$. At this point, we measured hemoglobin and hematocrit.

After IV fluid administration, we observed the following data (Figure 6.4): HR 83 bpm, MAP 94/50 (65) mmHg, CVP 15 mmHg, SpO_2 100%, *CO 3.5 L/min, $S_{cv}O_2$ 59%, PPV 10%.*

Figure 6.3 Data observed after 1 hour of surgery. Estimated blood loss is 800 mL.

Figure 6.4 Data observed after 500 mL of fluid.

Volume expansion thus induced an increase in CO (from 2.9 to 3.5 L/min, i.e., a 21% increase) and a decrease in PPV (from 18% to 10%). At the same time, we observed an increase in $S_{cv}O_2$ and in other hemodynamic parameters. Hemoglobin was 7.9 g/dL and $S_{cv}O_2$ was low. We decided to administer two units of blood (Figure 6.5). PVV was

Figure 6.5 Data observed after two units of blood.

in the "gray zone" (10%): HR 77 bpm, MAP 98/51 (67) mmHg, CVP 17 mmHg, CO 3.7 L/min, $S_{cv}O_2$ 66%, PPV 8%.

At this stage, hemoglobin was measured at 10.7 g/dL and PPV was 8%, thus below the threshold for fluid administration. The only abnormally low parameter was the $S_{cv}O_2$ (66%), indicating that there was a mismatch between oxygen consumption and oxygen delivery. Because Hb and S_aO_2 were normal and because PPV suggested that the patient was now a non-responder to volume expansion, it was decided to introduce a small dose of dobutamine (5 µg/kg/min) (Figure 6.6). Moreover, blood administration increased the $S_{cv}O_2$ but had very little impact on CO (only a 5% increase).

At the end of the surgery the patient was extubated in the operating room. Dobutamine was discontinued 1 hour after surgery. Patient spent the night in the ICU and was transferred to the ward on Day 1. The postoperative course was uneventful.

Fluid management during surgery has a deep impact on postoperative outcome. As seen in this case, fluid management and administration were based on a well-defined strategy aiming at optimizing CO and oxygen delivery. This management allowed better and more rationale fluid administration and helped to tailor hemodynamic optimization based on the patient's specific situation.

In the absence of a simple hemodynamic monitoring system, it is more likely that fluid administration would have been different and would have resulted in a different outcome. Moreover, once CO and PPV were optimized, hemodynamic monitoring helped to us introduce dobutamine to improve $S_{cv}O_2$ (in this case Hb was already normalized).

Figure 6.6 Data observed after introduction of dobutamine (5 µg/kg/min).

Implementing simple protocols for fluid and hemodynamic optimization is easy and can help to improve patients' outcomes. Moreover, this helped to standardize hemodynamic management and to decrease the interindividual variability.

References

1. Alhashemi JA, Cecconi M, Hofer CK. Cardiac output monitoring: An integrative perspective. *Crit Care* 2011; 15: 214.
2. Pizov R, Eden A, Bystritski D, Kalina E, Tamir A, Gelman S. Arterial and plethysmographic waveform analysis in anesthetized patients with hypovolemia. *Anesthesiology* 2010; 113: 83–91.
3. Cannesson M, Pestel G, Ricks C, Hoeft A, Perel A. Hemodynamic monitoring and management in patients undergoing high risk surgery: A survey among North American and European anesthesiologists. *Crit Care* 2011; 15: R197.
4. Pearse R, Dawson D, Fawcett J, Rhodes A, Grounds RM, Bennett ED. Early goal-directed therapy after major surgery reduces complications and duration of hospital stay. A randomised, controlled trial [ISRCTN38797445]. *Crit Care* 2005; 9: R687–93.
5. Hamilton MA, Cecconi M, Rhodes A. A systematic review and meta-analysis on the use of preemptive hemodynamic intervention to improve postoperative outcomes in moderate and high-risk surgical patients. *Anesth Analg* 2011; 112: 1392–402.
6. Gan TJ, Soppitt A, Maroof M, el-Moalem H, Robertson KM, Moretti E, Dwane P, Glass PS. Goal-directed intraoperative fluid administration reduces length of hospital stay after major surgery. *Anesthesiology* 2002; 97: 820–6.

7. Sinclair S, James S, Singer M. Intraoperative intravascular volume optimisation and length of hospital stay after repair of proximal femoral fracture: Randomised controlled trial. *Br Med J* 1997; 315: 909–12.
8. Venn R, Steele A, Richardson P, Poloniecki J, Grounds M, Newman P. Randomized controlled trial to investigate influence of the fluid challenge on duration of hospital stay and perioperative morbidity in patients with hip fractures. *Br J Anaesth* 2002; 88: 65–71.
9. Wakeling HG, McFall MR, Jenkins CS, Woods WG, Miles WF, Barclay GR, Fleming SC. Intraoperative oesophageal Doppler guided fluid management shortens postoperative hospital stay after major bowel surgery. *Br J Anaesth* 2005; 95: 634–42.
10. Lefrant JY, Bruelle P, Aya AG, Saissi G, Dauzat M, de La Coussaye JE, Eledjam JJ. Training is required to improve the reliability of esophageal Doppler to measure cardiac output in critically ill patients. *Intensive Care Med* 1998; 24: 347–52.
11. Tan HL, Pinder M, Parsons R, Roberts B, van Heerden PV. Clinical evaluation of USCOM ultrasonic cardiac output monitor in cardiac surgical patients in intensive care unit. *Br J Anaesth* 2005; 94: 287–91.
12. Chand R, Mehta Y, Trehan N. Cardiac output estimation with a new Doppler device after off-pump coronary artery bypass surgery. *J Cardiothorac Vasc Anesth* 2006; 20: 315–9.
13. Vos J, Poterman M, Salm P, Amsterdam K, Struys M, Scheeren T, Kalmar A. Noninvasive pulse pressure variation and stroke volume variation to predict fluid responsiveness at multiple thresholds: A prospective observational study. *Can J Anesth* 2015; 62: 1153–60.
14. Ameloot K, Palmers PJ, Malbrain ML. The accuracy of noninvasive cardiac output and pressure measurements with finger cuff: A concise review. *Curr Opin Crit Care* 2015; 21: 232–9.
15. de Waal EE, Konings MK, Kalkman CJ, Buhre WF. Assessment of stroke volume index with three different bioimpedance algorithms: Lack of agreement compared to thermodilution. *Intensive Care Med* 2008; 34: 735–9.
16. Conway DH, Hussain OA, Gall I. A comparison of noninvasive bioreactance with oesophageal Doppler estimation of stroke volume during open abdominal surgery: An observational study. *Eur J Anaesthesiol* 2013; 30: 501–8.
17. Biais M, Cottenceau V, Petit L, Masson F, Cochard JF, Sztark F. Impact of norepinephrine on the relationship between pleth variability index and pulse pressure variations in ICU adult patients. *Crit Care* 2011; 15: R168.
18. Monnet X, Dres M, Ferre A, Le Teuff G, Jozwiak M, Bleibtreu A, Le Deley MC, Chemla D, Richard C, Teboul JL. Prediction of fluid responsiveness by a continuous non-invasive assessment of arterial pressure in critically ill patients: Comparison with four other dynamic indices. *Br J Anaesth* 2012; 109: 330–8.
19. Bernet C, Desebbe O, Bordon S, Lacroix C, Rosamel P, Farhat F, Lehot JJ, Cannesson M. The impact of induction of general anesthesia and a vascular occlusion test on tissue oxygen saturation derived parameters in high-risk surgical patients. *J Clin Monit Comput* 2011; 25: 237–44.
20. Pinsky MR, Payen D. Probing the limits of regional tissue oxygenation measures. *Crit Care* 2009; 13 Suppl 5: S1.
21. Gomez H, Torres A, Polanco P, Kim HK, Zenker S, Puyana JC, Pinsky MR. Use of non-invasive NIRS during a vascular occlusion test to assess dynamic tissue O(2) saturation response. *Intensive Care Med* 2008; 34: 1600–7.

22. Cannesson M, Attof Y, Rosamel P, Desebbe O, Joseph P, Metton O, Bastien O, Lehot JJ. Respiratory variations in pulse oximetry plethysmographic waveform amplitude to predict fluid responsiveness in the operating room. *Anesthesiology* 2007; 106: 1105–11.
23. Desebbe O, Cannesson M. Using ventilation induced plethysmographic variations to optimize patient fluid status. *Curr Opin Anaesthesiol* 2008; 21: 772–8.

chapter seven

Fluid therapy for the high-risk patient undergoing surgery

Patrick A. Ward, Sophie E. Liu, and Michael G. Irwin
University of Hong Kong
Hong Kong

Contents

Key points:
   This chapter deals with fluid therapy for

- Patients with cardiac disease
- Patients with respiratory disease
- Patients with renal disease
- Patients with neurological disease
- Patients with liver disease
- Case study: Perioperative fluid therapy in vascular surgery

7.1   Introduction

Perioperative risk can be considered as either procedure-specific or patient-specific. This chapter will concentrate on the latter: patients with preexisting comorbidities and impaired physiological reserve/ functional status.

Each surgical patient should undergo a comprehensive preoperative assessment to identify and optimize comorbidities. The American Society of Anesthesiologists physical status grading system can be used for risk stratification, although it is relatively broad and inconsistent [1]. Since cardiac complications are the commonest cause of nonsurgical perioperative morbidity and mortality, there are a number of scoring systems specifically addressing this [2,3]. An evaluation of functional status is important and aerobic capacity can be estimated from the medical history or directly measured by cardiopulmonary exercise testing. Renal function should be tested in patients with underlying chronic disease such as hypertension and in those taking medications that predispose them to electrolyte disturbance or renal impairment. One must also consider postoperative risk stratification where appropriate, for example POSSUM [4] or APACHE [5] scoring systems.

There is good evidence to suggest that high-risk patients may benefit from manipulation of physiological parameters to improve outcome. Apposite fluid therapy is important in this process. This chapter will consider the target of optimal fluid therapy for each major organ system and the implications of inappropriate or unsuitable fluid regimens for the high-risk patient undergoing surgery.

7.2   Patients with cardiac disease

Cardiac complications are the commonest cause of perioperative morbidity and mortality [6]. Myocardial ischemia, pump failure, or both were found to be most predictive of perioperative decompensation and death [7]. The recent VISION (Vascular Events in Noncardiac Surgery Patients Cohort Evaluation) study [8] found that 8% of patients over 45 years of age suffered myocardial injury after noncardiac surgery, of which 84.2% were asymptomatic. This finding was significant because, amongst these, 1 in 10 died within 30 days.

The main principles of fluid therapy in these patients are to reduce the risk of precipitating myocardial ischemia or cardiac failure and to maintain cardiac output and oxygen delivery to the tissues.

7.2.1   Excess fluid administration

This can increase cardiac workload due to a shift to the right on the Frank–Starling curve and, if excessive, can increase postoperative cardiac morbidity. The Frank–Starling law of the heart (see Figure 7.1) states that up to a certain point along a volume/pressure curve, increased preload (left ventricular end diastolic volume) causes myocardial wall stretch, which contributes to the contractility of the heart, thereby increasing stroke volume and consequently cardiac output. During hypovolemia, the patient is at the responsive end of the curve, where an increase in preload will increase myocardial contractility. In normovolemia, they are on the nonresponsive portion of the curve and have maximized their stretch-related contractility. Whilst a healthy heart can tolerate a certain degree of

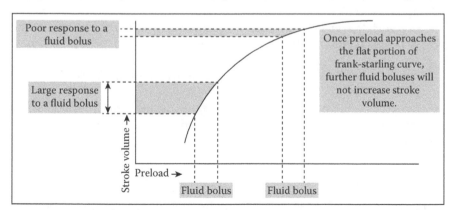

Figure 7.1 The Frank–Starling law of the heart states that up to a certain point along a volume/pressure curve, increased preload (left ventricular end diastolic volume) causes myocardial wall stretch, which contributes to the contractility of the heart, thereby increasing stroke volume and consequently cardiac output.

hypervolemia, any further fluid administration will overstretch the heart, resulting in decreased stroke volume, reduced oxygen delivery, and possible pulmonary edema, which will further compromise oxygenation.

7.2.2   Inadequate fluid administration

With hypovolemia, a decreased venous return results in decreased end diastolic volume and stroke volume (see Chapter 4 on mean capillary filling pressure). Younger, healthier patients can compensate for this by increasing heart rate, but in senescent or diseased myocardium cardiac output and oxygen delivery will fall. A decrease in myocardial perfusion may further exacerbate this problem because of myocardial ischemia and decreased contractility. Hypotension-associated tachycardia leads to shortened diastolic time, increased myocardial workload, and decreased myocardial blood supply. This is a "perfect storm" for myocardial ischemia and infarction. Kherterpal et al. found that there were increased cardiac complications if the mean arterial pressure was less than 50 mmHg or there was a 40% reduction from preoperative baseline. They also found that a heart rate greater than 100 beats per minute increased the likelihood of cardiac events [9].

The perfect balance can be difficult to gauge. Intravascular volume can be estimated using clinical signs such as jugular venous pressure, skin turgor, and urine output. Passive leg raising maneuvers increase cardiac preload and can be used to assess fluid responsiveness. Noninvasive techniques include esophageal Doppler techniques, and invasive techniques include arterial waveform analyses and central venous and pulmonary artery catheters. These methods are described elsewhere in this book (see Chapters 4 and 5).

Oxygen delivery is a product of cardiac output and oxygen content, where oxygen content is being determined by

$$C_aO_2 = (1.34 \times P_aO_2) + (Hemoglobin \times oxygen\ saturation/100)$$

In addition to ensuring optimal cardiac output, care should be taken to correct anemia and to ensure adequate ventilation; however, these areas are beyond the scope of this chapter.

7.2.3   Modifying risk

Hypovolemia is a risk factor for tissue hypoperfusion, leading to adverse effects ranging from delayed wound healing to organ failure [10,11]. On the other hand, excessive fluid administration may compromise cardiac and pulmonary function, cause tissue edema, prolong recovery of gastrointestinal function, and impair tissue oxygenation [12,13] (see Figure 7.2).

Figure 7.2 Hypovolemia is a risk factor for tissue hypoperfusion, leading to adverse effects ranging from delayed wound healing to organ failure. Excessive fluid administration may compromise cardiac and pulmonary function, cause tissue edema, prolong recovery of gastrointestinal function, and impair tissue oxygenation.

There has been ongoing debate about the optimal amount and type of fluid to be administered [14]. Goal-directed fluid therapy (GDFT) uses an individualized flow-related protocol, such as fluid loading and inotropes, to optimize cardiac output and thus increase oxygen delivery. Some studies have shown such strategies to reduce morbidity, mortality, and health care resource consumption in critically ill patients [15,16]. Recently, numerous studies of varying quality have been published investigating the impact of GDFT on complications and length of hospital stay after major surgery [11,17–20].

Concerns regarding cardiac complications from fluid challenges in high-risk patients may prevent clinicians from fully embracing GDFT, but a recent meta-analysis showed no increase in the incidence of pulmonary edema or myocardial ischemia with GDFT, and cardiac complications were actually decreased in high-risk patients compared to conventional management [21].

The role of fluid maintenance rates in the context of GDFT was evaluated in high-risk patients undergoing major surgery. The restrictive group (4 mL/kg/hr) compared to the liberal group (8 mL/kg/hr) showed a significantly reduced rate of major complications, particularly as regards tissue healing and cardiovascular events [22].

7.2.4   Summary

In patients with cardiac comorbidity, cardiac output estimation can help to achieve a balance between adequate volume to maintain myocardial perfusion and oxygen delivery and the risk of overadministration of fluid, resulting in cardiac failure. GDFT using fluid boluses to achieve predefined clinical parameters has been shown to improve outcome and not increase cardiac complications. Current studies tend to favor a more restrictive fluid regime.

7.3   Patients with respiratory disease

The inevitable and unavoidable reduction in pulmonary function post surgery may be compounded by too much fluid as well as too little. Therefore, it is crucial to achieve a balance. Volume overload can lead to tissue and interstitial edema, leading to poor diffusion of gases and metabolites, distortion of lung architecture, and obstruction of capillary blood flow and lymphatic drainage. By contrast, insufficient intravenous fluid administration can lead to poor lung perfusion and impaired gas exchange, reducing global tissue oxygenation and resulting not only in impaired lung function but impaired function of all extrapulmonary organ systems.

7.3.1   "Liberal" perioperative fluid regimens

The adverse effects of volume overload are particularly evident in the lungs, potentially leading to pulmonary edema, atelectasis, pneumonia, compromised gas exchange, and ultimately respiratory failure and failure of oxygenation [12,23]. Following administration of 22 mL/kg saline in six healthy volunteers, pulmonary blood flow was shown to increase by 24%; however, diffusing capacity and functional residual capacity were adversely affected, decreasing by 6% and 10%, respectively, with these deleterious effects still present 40 minutes post-infusion [24]. Similarly, rapid administration of 1 L of 0.9% saline in five healthy subjects was shown to cause small decreases in static and dynamic lung volumes (total lung capacity and forced vital capacity) and an increase in closing volume (with measurements returning to baseline after 1 hour). In the same study, 2 L infusions caused even more marked decreases across all lung volumes (this time with the adverse effects persisting at 1 hour post-infusion but recovering after furosemide administration), and a decrease in static lung compliance was also seen in all subjects during the first 10–15 minutes [25].

An accumulated positive fluid balance over the entire perioperative period and, particularly, overzealous postoperative fluid administration have been shown to cause serious negative respiratory sequelae. A retrospective analysis of 13 postoperative patients who developed fatal pulmonary edema (10 healthy patients and 3 with serious medical comorbidities) demonstrated that net fluid retention had exceeded 67 mL/kg/day in all of the patients [26]. Similarly, a study comparing general versus regional anesthesia for 100 high-risk patients undergoing elective lower limb peripheral vascular reconstructive procedures demonstrated that as many as 10% (three epidural, seven general anesthesia) of patients that received greater than 6 L of crystalloids in the first 24 hours postsurgery had developed respiratory failure [27]. These findings were reinforced by a recent multicenter, prospective cohort study involving 479 patients undergoing high-risk surgery, which found that patients with an intraoperative fluid balance greater than 2 L had a higher rate of respiratory complications (34.3% vs. 11.6%, $P < 0.001$), defined as $P_aO_2/F_iO_2 < 200$, requiring tracheal reintubation or difficulty withdrawing mechanical ventilation postoperatively [23] with no beneficial effect on extrapulmonary organ systems resulting from the positive balance.

Conversely, there is some evidence that higher volume strategies may be beneficial in low-risk patients undergoing minor operations. A double-blinded study comparing intraoperative administration of 40 mL/kg vs. 15 mL/kg of Ringer's lactate solution found improved postoperative pulmonary function (assessed by spirometry) and exercise capacity (submaximal treadmill test) in the liberal fluids group [28].

7.3.2 Restrictive fluid regimens

Relatively restrictive fluid regimens (usually defined as <7 mL/kg/hr) have been adopted in thoracic surgery in order to reduce the risk of postpneumonectomy pulmonary complications, in particular pulmonary edema, which is reported to be as high as 12%–15% [29]. Although multifactorial, a correlation with high volume perioperative fluid administration has been demonstrated in several retrospective studies [30]. Intraoperative crystalloid fluid administration in excess of 6 mL/kg/hr in 139 patients undergoing lung resections was associated with an increased incidence of pulmonary complications including need for tracheal reintubation, atelectasis, and pneumonia [31].

The benefit of restrictive fluid regimens on pulmonary function has also been demonstrated in nonthoracic surgery. When compared to a standard fluid regimen, restrictive perioperative fluid administration was associated with significantly fewer infective complications, including a 50% reduction in pneumonia in 179 patients >65 years with gastrointestinal cancer [32]. In major bowel surgery, pulmonary complications were also shown to be higher in those that received conventional perioperative fluid therapy (30–50 mL/kg/day of crystalloid fluids) when compared to a restrictive protocol (less than 30 mL/kg/day of crystalloid fluids) [33]. Similarly, in a large randomized, observer-blinded, multicenter trial of 172 patients undergoing colorectal resection, the patients allocated to a restrictive perioperative fluid regime (2.7 L average total fluids; no fluid loading pre-epidural and minimal replacement of fasting deficits) had a lower incidence of postoperative pulmonary complications compared with the standard fluid regime (5.4 L average total fluids) [34]. It must be noted, however, that the restrictive group received mainly colloids and the standard group received greater than 5 L crystalloids. Nevertheless, pulmonary benefits of a restrictive regimen (approximately 1.6 L vs. 5 L) have also been demonstrated in patients undergoing fast-track colorectal surgery in terms of improved postoperative lung function and decreased hypoxemia, although they had higher levels of renin, aldosterone, and angiotensin II [35].

Conservative fluid regimens have also been shown to be beneficial in acute lung injury, and similar strategies can be applied to the high-risk surgical patient. A large prospective, randomized trial involving 1,000 patients with acute lung injury compared liberal fluid administration with conservative administration over 7 days and found that the conservative group had significantly improved oxygenation indexes, better lung injury scores, lower plateau pressures, and lower positive end-expiratory pressures together with an increased number of ventilator-free days without negatively affecting extrapulmonary organ function [36].

7.3.3   Summary

There is mounting evidence to support restrictive perioperative fluid strategies in elective abdominal surgery, and this is already accepted practice in thoracic surgery. The concomitant reduction in pulmonary complications (without detrimental effects on other organ systems) supports the wider application of such a conservative approach to perioperative fluid therapy in other surgical patients, especially those who are at high risk of pulmonary complications postoperatively.

7.4   Patients with renal disease

Any patient presenting for major surgery is at risk of renal damage, whether they have preexisting impairment or not. Potential insults include nephrotoxic drugs, hemodynamic instability, hypovolemia, and inflammatory response. The aim is to rectify or lessen any previous damage, maintain adequate flow, diuresis, and oxygenation.

Many patients start with a preexisting fluid deficit, be it due to inadequate fluid resuscitation, excessive fasting, or use of bowel preparation. It should be mentioned that routine bowel preparation has been found to be of limited benefit in colorectal surgery and may complicate intra- and postoperative management of fluid and electrolyte balance [37]; therefore its use is now largely discouraged.

7.4.1   Acute renal failure

In patients presenting with acute renal failure, further deterioration of renal function should be avoided by maintaining renal perfusion, with a mean arterial pressure >70 mmHg (>85 mmHg in hypertension) and a urine output of at least 0.5 mL/kg/hr. It was previously thought that a liberal approach to fluid therapy was optimal for renal protection. Although dehydration is a very well-known cause of acute renal injury, overhydration might be an important predisposing factor in kidney damage. From data extracted from the SOAP (Sepsis Occurrence in Acutely Ill Patients) study, a multicenter, international, observational, cohort study, it was found that in patients with acute renal failure a positive fluid balance was associated with a worse outcome [38].

A randomized, multicenter trial comparing liberal and restrictive fluid regimes in patients undergoing colorectal surgery that has been mentioned previously in this chapter found that the number of patients with postoperative complications was significantly reduced in the restrictive compared to the liberal group (33% vs. 51%, $P = 0.02$). There was no increase in renal complications in the restrictive group [34].

7.4.2   End-stage renal failure

Hemodynamic instability is common in patients with end-stage renal failure, and there is a decreased ability to concentrate urine, regulate sodium, and excrete potassium. In those who are reliant on renal replacement therapy (RRT), current volume status and their ability to regulate their own fluid balance needs to be ascertained. Information such as last dialysis, ability to pass urine, and any daily fluid restriction should be sought. Ideally, dialysis is best performed on the day of or the day before surgery. Any derangement of renal function should be corrected prior to surgery.

Normovolemia is ideal to maintain renal blood flow and avoid hypotension. If large fluid shifts are likely, esophageal Doppler monitoring may be useful. In minor surgery, fluids should be limited to replacement of urine and insensible losses.

7.4.3   Types of fluids

7.4.3.1   Hydroxyethyl starches

Hydroxyethyl starch (HES) is a nonionic starch usually derived from corn or potato and one of the most frequently used volume expanders. HES is a general term and can be subclassified according to an average molecular weight, molar substitution, concentration, and C2/C6 ratio.

Retrospective studies do not offer strong scientific evidence but may assist in designing appropriate randomized, controlled trials. Some small retrospective analyses suggested that critically ill patients receiving HES may be more likely to develop acute kidney injury [39]. Two ICU publications in 2012 have fueled controversy on the safety of these solutions in certain patient populations [40]. The Scandinavian Starch for Severe Sepsis (6S) trial [41] reported significantly increased 90-day mortality and use of RRT in patients with septic shock receiving HES 130/0.42 as compared with Ringer's acetate. Then the Crystalloid versus Hydroxyethyl Starch (CHEST) trial [42], which was nearly nine times larger and was conducted with a different HES (HES 130/0.4), found, *prima facie*, a borderline increase in RRT (significant only in unadjusted analysis) but no significant increase in mortality in mixed ICU patients receiving HES in comparison with 0.9% saline. The exact mechanism of how HES can cause renal dysfunction is not fully understood, but it has been proposed that it may be due to resorption of the macromolecule into the renal tubular cells, leading to osmotic nephrotic lesions or renal plugging due to hyperviscous urine [43]. CHEST and 6S were carried out in different patient groups, using different HES and different crystalloid comparators, and also resulted in very divergent outcomes for HES in both studies. CHEST demonstrated significantly less use of fluid (about 30% less) and a significantly lower incidence of new cardiovascular failure associated with HES, and the incidence of acute renal injury was lower with HES than with 0.9% saline (by RIFLE criteria: 54.0% vs. 57.3; relative risk [RR] 0.94; 95% confidence interval [CI] 0.90–0.98; $p = 0.007$) and no difference in the primary end point of death by 90 days. After the publication of CHEST, five meta-analyses [44–48] on the use of HES were published within about 6 months that suggested harm from HES in critically ill patients. It is well known that high molecular weight colloids may induce hyperoncotic renal failure in susceptible patients, yet these meta-analyses included disparate HES with known chemically different formulae, assuming them all to be a single chemical entity. However, notwithstanding this controversy, a contraindication for patients with sepsis would seem justified, pending further research in this field. In elective surgery, the intraoperative use of 6% HES 130/0.4 appears to be safe.

7.4.3.2   Crystalloids

In animal studies it has been suggested that hyperchloremia is a critical determinant for changes in renal blood flow, mediated by the afferent and intrarenal arterial vessels [49]. As the chloride concentration increases, the renal blood flow decreases. When healthy volunteers were given 0.9% saline or a balanced electrolyte solution (Plasmalyte®), renal cortical tissue perfusion was shown to decrease in the 0.9% saline group [50]. A retrospective study of patients undergoing noncardiac surgery found an association between serum chloride levels greater than 110 mmol/L and an increased mortality risk and RIFLE (risk, injury, failure, loss, end stage) criteria [51]. A meta-analysis of 21 studies involving 6,253 patients found that there was a significantly higher risk of acute kidney injury (RR 1.64, 95% CI 1.27–2.13, $P < 0.001$) when high chloride fluids were used in critically ill or surgical patients [52].

These studies suggest that a balanced electrolyte solution such as Plasmalyte or Hartmann's solution should be used where large volumes of fluid are likely to be required, as in major surgery, rather than 0.9% saline to prevent the risk of hyperchloremia and possible renal impairment.

7.4.4 Summary

All patients undergoing surgery are at risk of renal injury. A modestly restrictive rather than liberal fluid regime appears to improve postsurgical outcome without compromising renal function. Patients with end-stage renal failure need extra attention due to their inability to regulate their own fluid balance and electrolytes. After initial hemodynamic resuscitation, HES 130/0.4 should not be used in critically ill patients, especially those with sepsis or renal impairment. In fact, this may be the case for all colloids. Older-generation high molecular weight colloids, including HES, should be avoided. The continued usage of HES 130/0.4 in the perioperative setting seems fully justified based on available evidence. Balanced solutions are preferable to hyperchloremic solutions such as 0.9% saline, as high chloride concentrations have been shown to reduce renal blood flow, induce acidosis, and increase the risk of kidney injury.

7.5 Patients with neurological disease

Excessive fluid administration or inappropriate choice of fluids may result in cerebral edema and poor neurological outcome. Similarly, insufficient fluid administration may cause hypovolemia and impaired cerebral perfusion.

In the patient with neurological pathology, restrictive fluid regimens have generally been advocated historically in order to avoid exacerbating cerebral edema [53]. However, perioperative fluid restriction (if implemented excessively) may result in equally harmful episodes of hypotension allied with an increase in intracranial pressure, reduced cerebral perfusion pressure, and potentially worse neurological outcome [54,55]; therefore a careful balance must be achieved.

7.5.1 Rate of fluid administration

The rate of fluid administration varies considerably during major surgery. In six healthy adult volunteers who had very rapid administration of Ringer's lactate (25 mL/kg over 15 min), it was found that unpleasant neurological symptoms such as headache and circumoral paresthesia were experienced, which were not observed when the same volume was infused at a slower rate [56].

The rate of fluid administration is important when considering sodium disorders. Whilst covered in greater detail in previous chapters, it must be highlighted that high-risk surgical patients (including patients with brain injury) are particularly prone to electrolyte disturbances that may result in permanent neurological dysfunction if rapid correction with intravenous fluids is undertaken [57].

7.5.2   Volume of fluids

Prevailing evidence appears to support avoidance of excessive or arbitrary administration of perioperative fluids to minimize neurological dysfunction. Perioperative volume administration inevitably results in hemodilution, which is typically accompanied by a compensatory increase in cerebral blood flow (in response to the decrease in arterial oxygen content), although in patients with brain injury the normal responses to hemodilution and hypoxia may be significantly impaired. A hematocrit level of 30%–33% has been shown to be the optimal combination of viscosity and oxygen-carrying capacity and may improve neurological outcome, whereas excessive perioperative fluid administration and marked hemodilution may worsen any neurological injury [55,58].

A large multicenter, prospective cohort study involving 479 high-risk surgical patients demonstrated significantly higher postoperative neurological complications in patients that had an intraoperative fluid balance greater than 2 L (46.2% vs. 13.2%, $P < 0.001$), with greater levels of behavior change, forgetfulness, or psychomotor agitation when compared with those with a less positive fluid balance [23].

Hypovolemia and fluid restriction have also been identified as risk factors for delayed vasospasm (and cerebral ischemia) in patients following surgery for aneurysmal subarachnoid hemorrhage. Prophylactic hypervolemic postoperative fluid regimens have been proposed as a potential therapeutic approach to prevent and treat cerebral vasospasm in this specific cohort of patients, although there is lack of evidence to support this type of fluid regimen at present [59,60].

7.5.3   Types of fluids

High glucose concentrations have been shown to worsen cerebral damage associated with cardiorespiratory arrest [61]; therefore, glucose solutions should generally be avoided in patients having surgery, particularly those with acute stroke and in those undergoing procedures that carry a high risk of perioperative cerebral ischemia, such as cardiopulmonary bypass or carotid endarterectomy [62]. An animal study investigating the effects of rapid infusion of 0.9% saline compared with 5% dextrose following acute head trauma demonstrated an increased mortality and worsened neurological outcome in the 5% dextrose group [63].

Similarly, the use of albumin solutions in patients with head injury has been shown to be potentially deleterious. While the Saline versus Albumin Fluid Evaluation (SAFE) study found no significant difference in outcome in 6,997 critical care patients when albumin 4% was compared with 0.9% saline [64], subgroup analysis of 460 patients with head injury from the same study showed a higher mortality (33% vs. 20%), particularly in those with severe brain injury [65]. It must be noted, however, that an imbalance existed in the trial comparator groups (the albumin group contained a larger number of patients over 55 years of age) and the albumin preparation used in the trial was relatively hypotonic (260 mOsm/L), potentially contributing towards intracranial hypertension. Furthermore, albumin has previously been demonstrated to improve neurological and functional outcomes in animal studies following ischemia and has also shown potentially beneficial effects in patients with ischemic stroke. Therefore, albumin may still be indicated in subarachnoid hemorrhage or vasospasm.

Hyperosmolar crystalloid fluids (hypertonic saline, mannitol) have several physiological and immunological effects [66]. As osmotic agents, they draw interstitial fluid into the intravascular compartment, theoretically restoring circulating volume and tissue perfusion using a smaller volume than would be required with traditional crystalloid fluids [62]. They have also been shown to have positive effects in modifying the inflammatory response associated with tissue injury, including attenuation of neutrophil activation, downregulation of pro-inflammatory cytokines, enhanced production of anti-inflammatory mediators, and enhanced T-cell function. Specifically, hypertonic fluids have been shown to reduce cerebral edema, improve cerebral vasoregulation, reduce vasospasm, reduce intracranial pressure, improve cerebral perfusion, and reduce accumulation of neurotoxic mediators. Therefore, there is a theoretical benefit in resuscitating patients with hypovolemic trauma, traumatic brain injury, and in the attenuation of ischemia and reperfusion injury in vascular procedures, cardiopulmonary bypass, and transplant surgery [67,68]. Unfortunately, clinical studies have been less convincing. A prospective, randomized clinical trial comparing hypertonic saline and Ringer's lactate for resuscitation of 34 patients with head injury failed to demonstrate a significant difference in neurological outcome between the two groups [69]. Similarly, a double-blind, randomized controlled trial of 229 patients comparing a prehospital 250 mL bolus of either hypertonic saline or Ringer's lactate in hypotensive patients with traumatic brain injury found no difference in neurological outcome [70]. Nevertheless, despite the lack of trial evidence, the use of hypertonic saline is frequently advocated in the management of surgical patients with refractory intra-cranial hypertension [21], requiring the clinician to balance the theoretical advantages against the risk of hypernatremia [71].

Iso-osmolar crystalloid solutions (with an osmolality of ~300 mOsm/L) such as 0.9% saline are generally considered safe for administration in the neurosurgical patient, as they do not alter plasma osmolality and therefore do not increase brain water content. Ringer's lactate, however, has a lower measured osmolality (~254 mOsm/L) and may reduce plasma osmolality when administered in large volumes (greater than 3 L), resulting in increased brain water content and an elevated intracranial pressure [72]; smaller volumes are unlikely to be detrimental.

Colloid solutions appear to confer no benefit over isotonic crystalloids in brain injury. In a prospective animal study, colloid administration did not increase cerebral oxygen delivery or reduce cerebral edema or intra-cranial pressure when compared with Ringer's lactate solution [73].

7.5.4 Summary

The importance of achieving normovolemia (whether administering crystalloid or colloid solutions) is now well established in neuroanesthesia and neurocritical care, and this practice should also be applied to the surgical patient to minimize neurological complications and optimize neurological outcome.

7.6 Patients with liver disease

Liver cirrhosis affects all body systems and results in a reduced life expectancy. Patients with end-stage liver disease are at significant risk of mortality and morbidity after anesthesia and surgery [74], with liver and renal failure, sepsis, and bleeding being common causes of poor perioperative outcome. Liver failure can either be acute or chronic and caused by many different pathologies; however, outcome after surgery and anesthesia are usually dictated by severity of liver impairment rather than the cause [75]. Except for liver transplantation, it is unlikely that a patient with severe decompensated liver disease will present for elective surgery; however, these patients may easily present for emergency surgery. Optimization of perioperative intravenous fluid therapy is essential in reducing the risk of perioperative complications, as these patients have limited physiological reserve.

7.6.1 Changes in physiology

Patients with liver disease tend to have a hyperdynamic circulation with a high cardiac output, low systemic vascular resistance and a high intravascular volume [76]. Tissue perfusion can be poor due to arteriovenous shunting, and often the response to endogenous and exogenous catecholamines is blunted. Consequently, fluid management can be extremely challenging. Patients are also likely to have risk factors for coronary artery disease such as cigarette smoking or hyperlipidemia, but symptoms may be masked by the reduced left ventricular workload. Anesthesia and surgery can unmask this and cardiac ischemia may become apparent.

Intraoperative hypovolemia, hypotension, and hepatorenal syndrome are associated with immediate postoperative kidney dysfunction. Renal failure after liver transplant results in a prolonged hospital stay and increased acute rejection, infection, and overall mortality [77]. Hepatorenal syndrome can develop secondary to ascites or portal hypertension due to reduced renal blood flow, altered hemodynamic responses, or release of hepatic toxins [78]. Maintenance of hepatic blood flow and oxygen delivery is essential, as any relative hypoperfusion may lead to further hepatocellular injury and result in decompensation. Local hepatic autoregulation is impaired, making the cirrhotic liver less tolerant to hemodynamic changes, especially when exposed to general anesthetics [79]. Due to depletion of glycogen stores, one should be vigilant towards the development of hypoglycemia. A background infusion of 5%–10% dextrose can help to avoid hypoglycemia and protect against inadvertent increases in plasma sodium concentration.

7.6.2   Preoperative optimization

Electrolytes can be grossly deranged, and therefore fluid therapy must account for this. Ascites and peripheral edema develop in response to secondary hyperaldosteronism, which causes water retention and hyponatremia. The treatment of ascites includes loop diuretics, which can cause relative hypovolemia and hypokalemia. Conversely, the aldosterone antagonist spironolactone causes hyperkalemia. Prior to surgery, electrolyte disturbance should be corrected. Note that patients with cirrhosis may still have renal impairment with a normal blood creatinine level [80].

7.6.3   Hepatic resection

Although ensuring adequate intravascular volume is important for maintenance of renal perfusion, there has been much work on the relationship between central venous pressure (CVP) and its effect on blood transfusion during liver resection. A previous strategy for reducing blood loss was to keep the patient relatively hypovolemic, as a CVP less than 5 cmH$_2$O has been associated with reduced blood loss [81]. However, a recent Cochrane review showed a low CVP had no significant benefit on mortality or long-term survival. With the importance of avoiding hypovolemia to reduce the risk of renal impairment, a more liberal fluid approach is reasonable.

7.6.4   Types of fluid

Albumin is often the colloid of choice in patients with liver disease. Due to loss of hepatic synthetic function, hypoalbuminemia is often a problem. Although the SAFE study [64] showed no significant differences in mortality, length of stay in the intensive care unit, duration of RRT, or duration of mechanical ventilation between resuscitation with 0.9% saline or albumin, perioperative hypoalbuminemia is associated with a worse prognosis [74]. Previous systematic reviews have shown albumin to be beneficial [82] and, as fluid resuscitation with albumin is well tolerated and similar to 0.9% saline [83], patients with known hypoalbuminemia may benefit from its administration.

As mentioned previously in this chapter in section 7.4.3.2 Crystalloids, liberal chloride-based intravenous fluids have been shown to increase acute kidney injury in general critically ill patients. An observational study of 158 liver transplants showed a similar result [84], suggesting balanced electrolyte solutions are also superior in this setting.

7.6.5   Summary

Patients with liver failure have a high perioperative morbidity and mortality. Renal failure is common and is a predictor of poor outcome. Hypovolemia and hypotension should be avoided to reduce the risk of precipitating renal failure or hepatic hypoperfusion. Previously, maintaining a low CVP was advised, but newer evidence has shown no survival benefit or reduction in blood loss. Often albumin is used as a colloid due to the prevalence of hypoalbuminemia. There is some evidence that high chloride content may increase acute kidney injury and, therefore, a balanced solution is preferable.

7.7   Case study: Perioperative fluid therapy in vascular surgery

A 75-year-old male with a medical history of hypertension, hyperlipidemia, type II diabetes, and renal impairment is scheduled for expedited open repair of an abdominal aortic aneurysm, having presented with a 6 cm infrarenal aortic aneurysm.

Aortic aneurysm surgery is considered high risk due to the acute hemodynamic changes that appear intraoperatively, placing massive physiological demands on patients, who often have limited reserve and extensive preexisting comorbidities (heart disease, hypertension, diabetes, peripheral vascular disease, cerebrovascular disease, and renal insufficiency). These factors together with advanced age (>60 years) contribute to a high probability of severe postoperative morbidity, including myocardial ischemia, cerebrovascular events, respiratory failure, renal and hepatic failure, bleeding, and paraplegia, especially when undertaken in the emergency setting [85].

The primary goals of fluid therapy (and anesthetic management) in this patient is to optimize myocardial, cerebral, and renal perfusion to reduce the associated postoperative complications. Prevailing evidence appears to support a change from traditional liberal replacement of preoperative fluid deficits, insensible losses, and the now-disproved third-space losses to a more judicious demand-based strategy aimed at maintaining intravascular volume and filling pressures and end organ perfusion whilst minimizing overload in the face of extreme intraoperative hemodynamic variation [85]. The application and subsequent release of the aortic cross clamp is a particular challenge. Clamp application causes a sudden increase in cardiac afterload, left ventricular end-diastolic wall stress, and sympathetic stimulation, resulting in a high systemic arterial pressure proximal to the clamp. This sudden increase in afterload can precipitate left ventricular failure in a noncompliant ventricle and myocardial ischemia if the resultant increase in myocardial contractility and oxygen demand is not met by a commensurate increase in coronary blood flow and oxygen supply. Vasodilators and opioids should be used to attenuate this response, which can also be minimized by employing a relatively restrictive fluid strategy prior to cross clamp placement, thus ensuring lower pulmonary artery pressures.

On aortic cross clamp release, there is a dramatic reduction in systemic vascular resistance and arterial blood pressure resulting from the redistribution of blood volume, release of accumulated anaerobic metabolites, ischemia–reperfusion phenomena, and anoxic relaxation of smooth muscle that causes either direct myocardial suppression or profound vasodilatation (relative volume depletion). This hypotensive response can be minimized by slow, partial, or intermittent release of the cross clamp (to enable gradual correction of hemodynamic parameters). Aggressive volume loading is not warranted, as this vasodilatation is self-limiting and will result in hypervolemia when it wears off. Vasopressors such as phenylephrine or metaraminol (neither of these increase heart rate, which is important to avoid in myocardial ischemia) should be used rather than fluid loading [86].

There also remains considerable debate surrounding the best type of fluid for use in open surgical repair, with blood products and/or combinations of crystalloid solutions and colloids all being utilized. A review of 38 randomized trials involving 1,589 patients did not demonstrate significant benefit from any single type of fluid or combination of fluid therapies across a range of outcome measures [87]. Nevertheless, a grossly positive fluid balance during the perioperative period is likely to contribute to the development of left ventricular failure, and with this in mind a handful of relatively recent small studies seem to support the use of either low-volume colloid loading or low-volume hypertonic solutions [88] during the clamping phase. One such trial comparing crystalloid and hyperosmotic–hyperoncotic solutions during aortic clamping demonstrated improved hemodynamic parameters, improved oxygen delivery, and resulted in a less positive fluid balance [89].

7.8   Conclusion

Perioperative fluid therapy is an essential part of anesthesia and perioperative patient care. It poses significant and unique challenges in the high-risk surgical patient. Healthy patients are more able to tolerate injudicious fluid strategies, with less consequence on organ function, but this may still have adverse effects. Preexisting medical disease, major organ dysfunction, and physiological insufficiency combined with biochemical, metabolic, and hemodynamic derangement necessitates particularly meticulous fluid status assessment and targeted administration of the appropriate volume and type of fluids at the right time to optimize patients' physiological parameters, avoid deleterious sequelae, and ultimately improve postoperative outcomes.

Greater knowledge of pathological disease processes and the surgical stress response, the role of the endothelial glycocalyx in vascular permeability, together with an improved understanding of fluid kinetics and the composition of fluid compartments has enabled a paradigm shift, from rather arbitrary uncontrolled intravenous fluid administration to a focused, systematic, and highly monitored approach. Based upon this targeted philosophy, this chapter has taken an organ systems approach to fluid therapy and matched this with the most recent evidence in fluid therapy for the patient at high risk.

Overall, there is a tentative move towards more restrictive fluid strategies for the high-risk surgical patient. Whilst this is an important underlying principle, recipe-based strategies often fail to account for the variation in individual patients and their perioperative status, and therefore one must take an individualized and dynamic approach to perioperative fluid therapy, particularly in high-risk patients where hemodynamic parameters and fluid responsiveness are constantly changing.

References

1. Mak PH, Campbell RC, Irwin MG, American Society of A. The ASA Physical Status Classification: Inter-observer consistency. American Society of Anesthesiologists. *Anaesth Intensive Care.* 2002;30(5):633–40.
2. Gupta PK, Gupta H, Sundaram A, Kaushik M, Fang X, Miller WJ, et al. Development and validation of a risk calculator for prediction of cardiac risk after surgery. *Circulation.* 2011;124(4):381–7.
3. Anderson JL, Antman EM, Harold JG, Jessup M, O'Gara PT, Pinto FJ, et al. Clinical practice guidelines on perioperative cardiovascular evaluation: Collaborative efforts among the ACC, AHA, and ESC. *Circulation.* 2014;130(24):2213–4.
4. Copeland GP, Jones D, Walters M. POSSUM: A scoring system for surgical audit. *Br J Surg.* 1991;78(3):355–60.
5. Knaus WA, Wagner DP, Draper EA, Zimmerman JE, Bergner M, Bastos PG, et al. The APACHE III prognostic system. Risk prediction of hospital mortality for critically ill hospitalized adults. *Chest.* 1991;100(6):1619–36.
6. Chow KY, Liu SE, Irwin MG. New therapy in cardioprotection. *Curr Opin Anaesthesiol.* 2015;28(4):417–23.
7. Goldman L, Caldera DL, Nussbaum SR, Southwick FS, Krogstad D, Murray B, et al. Multifactorial index of cardiac risk in noncardiac surgical procedures. *N Engl J Med.* 1977;297(16):845–50.
8. Botto F, Alonso-Coello P, Chan MT, Villar JC, Xavier D, Srinathan S, et al. Myocardial injury after noncardiac surgery: A large, international, prospective cohort study establishing diagnostic criteria, characteristics, predictors, and 30-day outcomes. *Anesthesiology.* 2014;120(3):564–78.
9. Kheterpal S, O'Reilly M, Englesbe MJ, Rosenberg AL, Shanks AM, Zhang L, et al. Preoperative and intraoperative predictors of cardiac adverse events after general, vascular, and urological surgery. *Anesthesiology.* 2009;110(1):58–66.
10. Mythen MG, Webb AR. Perioperative plasma volume expansion reduces the incidence of gut mucosal hypoperfusion during cardiac surgery. *Arch Surg.* 1995;130(4):423–9.
11. Shoemaker WC, Wo CC, Thangathurai D, Velmahos G, Belzberg H, Asensio JA, et al. Hemodynamic patterns of survivors and nonsurvivors during high risk elective surgical operations. *World J Surg.* 1999;23(12):1264–70; discussion 70–1.
12. Holte K, Sharrock NE, Kehlet H. Pathophysiology and clinical implications of perioperative fluid excess. *Br J Anaesth.* 2002;89(4):622–32.
13. Lobo DN, Bostock KA, Neal KR, Perkins AC, Rowlands BJ, Allison SP. Effect of salt and water balance on recovery of gastrointestinal function after elective colonic resection: A randomised controlled trial. *Lancet.* 2002;359(9320):1812–8.
14. Doherty M, Buggy DJ. Intraoperative fluids: How much is too much? *Br J Anaesth.* 2012;109(1):69–79.
15. Benes J, Giglio M, Brienza N, Michard F. The effects of goal-directed fluid therapy based on dynamic parameters on post-surgical outcome: A meta-analysis of randomized controlled trials. *Crit Care.* 2014;18(5):584.

16. Gu WJ, Wang F, Bakker J, Tang L, Liu JC. The effect of goal-directed therapy on mortality in patients with sepsis - earlier is better: A meta-analysis of randomized controlled trials. *Crit Care.* 2014;18(5):570.
17. Hamilton MA, Cecconi M, Rhodes A. A systematic review and meta-analysis on the use of preemptive hemodynamic intervention to improve postoperative outcomes in moderate and high-risk surgical patients. *Anesth Analg.* 2011;112(6):1392–402.
18. Lopes MR, Oliveira MA, Pereira VO, Lemos IP, Auler JO, Jr., Michard F. Goal-directed fluid management based on pulse pressure variation monitoring during high-risk surgery: A pilot randomized controlled trial. *Crit Care.* 2007;11(5):R100.
19. Reydellet L, Blasco V, Mercier MF, Antonini F, Nafati C, Harti-Souab K, et al. Impact of a goal-directed therapy protocol on postoperative fluid balance in patients undergoing liver transplantation: A retrospective study. *Ann Franc Anesth Reanim.* 2014;33(4):e47–54.
20. Shoemaker WC, Appel PL, Kram HB, Waxman K, Lee TS. Prospective trial of supranormal values of survivors as therapeutic goals in high-risk surgical patients. *Chest.* 1988;94(6):1176–86.
21. Arulkumaran N, Corredor C, Hamilton MA, Ball J, Grounds RM, Rhodes A, et al. Cardiac complications associated with goal-directed therapy in high-risk surgical patients: A meta-analysis. *Br J Anaesth.* 2014;112(4):648–59.
22. Lobo SM, Ronchi LS, Oliveira NE, Brandao PG, Froes A, Cunrath GS, et al. Restrictive strategy of intraoperative fluid maintenance during optimization of oxygen delivery decreases major complications after high-risk surgery. *Crit Care.* 2011;15(5):R226.
23. Silva JM, Jr., de Oliveira AM, Nogueira FA, Vianna PM, Pereira Filho MC, Dias LF, et al. The effect of excess fluid balance on the mortality rate of surgical patients: A multicenter prospective study. *Crit Care.* 2013;17(6):R288.
24. Hillebrecht A, Schulz H, Meyer M, Baisch F, Beck L, Blomqvist CG. Pulmonary responses to lower body negative pressure and fluid loading during head-down tilt bedrest. *Acta Physiol Scand Suppl.* 1992;604:35–42.
25. Collins JV, Cochrane GM, Davis J, Benatar SR, Clark TJ. Some aspects of pulmonary function after rapid saline infusion in healthy subjects. *Clin Sci Mol Med.* 1973;45(3):407–10.
26. Arieff AI. Fatal postoperative pulmonary edema: Pathogenesis and literature review. *Chest.* 1999;115(5):1371–7.
27. Christopherson R, Beattie C, Frank SM, Norris EJ, Meinert CL, Gottlieb SO, et al. Perioperative morbidity in patients randomized to epidural or general anesthesia for lower extremity vascular surgery. Perioperative ischemia randomized anesthesia trial study group. *Anesthesiology.* 1993;79(3):422–34.
28. Holte K, Klarskov B, Christensen DS, Lund C, Nielsen KG, Bie P, et al. Liberal versus restrictive fluid administration to improve recovery after laparoscopic cholecystectomy: A randomized, double-blind study. *Ann Surg.* 2004;240(5):892–9.
29. Jordan S, Mitchell JA, Quinlan GJ, Goldstraw P, Evans TW. The pathogenesis of lung injury following pulmonary resection. *Eur Respir J.* 2000;15(4):790–9.
30. Slinger PD. Perioperative fluid management for thoracic surgery: The puzzle of postpneumonectomy pulmonary edema. *J Cardiothorac Vasc Anesth.* 1995;9(4):442–51.

31. Arslantas M, Batirel H, Bilgili B, Kara H, Yildizeli B, Yuksel M, et al. Effects of the restrictive fluid strategy on postoperative pulmonary and renal function following pulmonary resection surgery. *Crit Care.* 2014;18(Suppl 1):144.
32. Gao T, Li N, Zhang JJ, Xi FC, Chen QY, Zhu WM, et al. Restricted intravenous fluid regimen reduces the rate of postoperative complications and alters immunological activity of elderly patients operated for abdominal cancer: A randomized prospective clinical trial. *World J Surg.* 2012;36(5):993–1002.
33. de Aguilar-Nascimento JE, Diniz BN, do Carmo AV, Silveira EA, Silva RM. Clinical benefits after the implementation of a protocol of restricted perioperative intravenous crystalloid fluids in major abdominal operations. *World J Surg.* 2009;33(5):925–30.
34. Brandstrup B, Tonnesen H, Beier-Holgersen R, Hjortso E, Ording H, Lindorff-Larsen K, et al. Effects of intravenous fluid restriction on postoperative complications: Comparison of two perioperative fluid regimens: A randomized assessor-blinded multicenter trial. *Ann Surg.* 2003;238(5):641–8.
35. Holte K, Foss NB, Andersen J, Valentiner L, Lund C, Bie P, et al. Liberal or restrictive fluid administration in fast-track colonic surgery: A randomized, double-blind study. *Br J Anaesth.* 2007;99(4):500–8.
36. National Heart L, Blood Institute Acute Respiratory Distress Syndrome Clinical Trials N, Wiedemann HP, Wheeler AP, Bernard GR, Thompson BT, et al. Comparison of two fluid-management strategies in acute lung injury. *N Engl J Med.* 2006;354(24):2564–75.
37. Jung B, Pahlman L, Nystrom PO, Nilsson E, Mechanical Bowel Preparation Study G. Multicentre randomized clinical trial of mechanical bowel preparation in elective colonic resection. *Br J Surg.* 2007;94(6):689–95.
38. Payen D, de Pont AC, Sakr Y, Spies C, Reinhart K, Vincent JL, et al. A positive fluid balance is associated with a worse outcome in patients with acute renal failure. *Crit Care.* 2008;12(3):R74.
39. Hand WR, Whiteley JR, Epperson TI, Tam L, Crego H, Wolf B, et al. Hydroxyethyl starch and acute kidney injury in orthotopic liver transplantation: A single-center retrospective review. *Anesth Analg.* 2015;120(3):619–26.
40. Irwin MG, Gan TJ. Volume therapy with hydroxyethyl starches: Are we throwing the anesthesia baby out with the intensive care unit bathwater? *Anesth Analg.* 2014;119(3):737–9.
41. Perner A, Haase N, Guttormsen AB, Tenhunen J, Klemenzson G, Aneman A, et al. Hydroxyethyl starch 130/0.42 versus Ringer's acetate in severe sepsis. *N Engl J Med.* 2012;367(2):124–34.
42. Myburgh JA, Finfer S, Bellomo R, Billot L, Cass A, Gattas D, et al. Hydroxyethyl starch or saline for fluid resuscitation in intensive care. *N Engl J Med.* 2012;367(20):1901–11.
43. Hartog CS, Bauer M, Reinhart K. The efficacy and safety of colloid resuscitation in the critically ill. *Anesth Analg.* 2011;112(1):156–64.
44. Gattas DJ, Dan A, Myburgh J, Billot L, Lo S, Finfer S, et al. Fluid resuscitation with 6% hydroxyethyl starch (130/0.4 and 130/0.42) in acutely ill patients: Systematic review of effects on mortality and treatment with renal replacement therapy. *Intensive Care Med.* 2013;39(4):558–68.
45. Haase N, Perner A, Hennings LI, Siegemund M, Lauridsen B, Wetterslev M, et al. Hydroxyethyl starch 130/0.38-0.45 versus crystalloid or albumin in patients with sepsis: Systematic review with meta-analysis and trial sequential analysis. *BMJ.* 2013;346:f839.

46. Patel A, Waheed U, Brett SJ. Randomised trials of 6% tetrastarch (hydroxy-ethyl starch 130/0.4 or 0.42) for severe sepsis reporting mortality: Systematic review and meta-analysis. *Intensive Care Med.* 2013;39(5):811–22.

47. Perel P, Roberts I, Ker K. Colloids versus crystalloids for fluid resuscitation in critically ill patients. *Cochrane Database Syst Rev.* 2013;2:CD000567.

48. Zarychanski R, Abou-Setta AM, Turgeon AF, Houston BL, McIntyre L, Marshall JC, et al. Association of hydroxyethyl starch administration with mortality and acute kidney injury in critically ill patients requir-ing volume resuscitation: A systematic review and meta-analysis. *JAMA.* 2013;309(7):678–88.

49. Wilcox CS. Regulation of renal blood flow by plasma chloride. *J Clin Investig.* 1983;71(3):726–35.

50. Chowdhury AH, Cox EF, Francis ST, Lobo DN. A randomized, controlled, double-blind crossover study on the effects of 2-L infusions of 0.9% saline and plasma-lyte(R) 148 on renal blood flow velocity and renal cortical tissue perfusion in healthy volunteers. *Ann Surg.* 2012;256(1):18–24.

51. McCluskey SA, Karkouti K, Wijeysundera D, Minkovich L, Tait G, Beattie WS. Hyperchloremia after noncardiac surgery is independently associated with increased morbidity and mortality: A propensity-matched cohort study. *Anesth Analg.* 2013;117(2):412–21.

52. Krajewski ML, Raghunathan K, Paluszkiewicz SM, Schermer CR, Shaw AD. Meta-analysis of high- versus low-chloride content in perioperative and critical care fluid resuscitation. *Br J Surg.* 2015;102(1):24–36.

53. Shenkin HA, Bezier HS, Bouzarth WF. Restricted fluid intake. Rational management of the neurosurgical patient. *J Neurosurg.* 1976;45(4):432–6.

54. Zornow MH, Prough DS. Fluid management in patients with traumatic brain injury. *N Horizons.* 1995;3(3):488–98.

55. Tommasino C. Fluids and the neurosurgical patient. *Anesthesiol Clin North Am.* 2002;20(2):329–46, vi.

56. Hahn RG, Drobin D, Stahle L. Volume kinetics of Ringer's solution in female volunteers. *Br J Anaesth.* 1997;78(2):144–8.

57. Moritz ML, Ayus JC. Hospital-acquired hyponatremia--why are hypotonic parenteral fluids still being used? *Nat Clin Pract Nephrol.* 2007;3(7):374–82.

58. Reasoner DK, Ryu KH, Hindman BJ, Cutkomp J, Smith T. Marked hemodi-lution increases neurologic injury after focal cerebral ischemia in rabbits. *Anesth Analg.* 1996;82(1):61–7.

59. Capampangan DJ, Wellik KE, Aguilar MI, Demaerschalk BM, Wingerchuk DM. Does prophylactic postoperative hypervolemic therapy prevent cerebral vasospasm and improve clinical outcome after aneurysmal subarachnoid hemorrhage? *Neurologist.* 2008;14(6):395–8.

60. Rinkel GJ, Feigin VL, Algra A, van Gijn J. Circulatory volume expansion therapy for aneurysmal subarachnoid haemorrhage. *Cochrane Database Syst Rev.* 2004(4):CD000483.

61. Myers RE, Yamaguchi S. Nervous system effects of cardiac arrest in monkeys. Preservation of vision. *Arch Neurol.* 1977;34(2):65–74.

62. Hahn R. *Clinical Fluid Therapy in the Perioperative Setting.* Robert G. Hahn, editor. New York: Cambridge University Press; 2011.

63. Shapira Y, Artru AA, Qassam N, Navot N, Vald U. Brain edema and neu-rologic status with rapid infusion of 0.9% saline or 5% dextrose after head trauma. *J Neurosurg Anesthesiol.* 1995;7(1):17–25.

64. Finfer S, Bellomo R, Boyce N, French J, Myburgh J, Norton R, et al. A comparison of albumin and saline for fluid resuscitation in the intensive care unit. *N Engl J Med.* 2004;350(22):2247–56.

65. Investigators SS, Australian, New Zealand Intensive Care Society Clinical Trials G, Australian Red Cross Blood S, George Institute for International H, Myburgh J, et al. Saline or albumin for fluid resuscitation in patients with traumatic brain injury. *N Engl J Med.* 2007;357(9):874–84.

66. Wade CE, Grady JJ, Kramer GC, Younes RN, Gehlsen K, Holcroft JW. Individual patient cohort analysis of the efficacy of hypertonic saline/dextran in patients with traumatic brain injury and hypotension. *J Trauma.* 1997;42(5 Suppl):S61–5.

67. Junger WG, Coimbra R, Liu FC, Herdon-Remelius C, Junger W, Junger H, et al. Hypertonic saline resuscitation: A tool to modulate immune function in trauma patients? *Shock.* 1997;8(4):235–41.

68. Doyle JA, Davis DP, Hoyt DB. The use of hypertonic saline in the treatment of traumatic brain injury. *J Trauma.* 2001;50(2):367–83.

69. Shackford SR, Bourguignon PR, Wald SL, Rogers FB, Osler TM, Clark DE. Hypertonic saline resuscitation of patients with head injury: A prospective, randomized clinical trial. *J Trauma.* 1998;44(1):50–8.

70. Cooper DJ, Myles PS, McDermott FT, Murray LJ, Laidlaw J, Cooper G, et al. Prehospital hypertonic saline resuscitation of patients with hypotension and severe traumatic brain injury: A randomized controlled trial. *JAMA.* 2004;291(11):1350–7.

71. Vassar MJ, Perry CA, Holcroft JW. Analysis of potential risks associated with 7.5% sodium chloride resuscitation of traumatic shock. *Arch Surg.* 1990;125(10):1309–15.

72. Prough DS, Johnson JC, Poole GV, Jr., Stullken EH, Johnston WE, Jr., Royster R. Effects on intracranial pressure of resuscitation from hemorrhagic shock with hypertonic saline versus lactated Ringer's solution. *Crit Care Med.* 1985;13(5):407–11.

73. Zhuang J, Shackford SR, Schmoker JD, Pietropaoli JA, Jr. Colloid infusion after brain injury: Effect on intracranial pressure, cerebral blood flow, and oxygen delivery. *Crit Care Med.* 1995;23(1):140–8.

74. Ziser A, Plevak DJ, Wiesner RH, Rakela J, Offord KP, Brown DL. Morbidity and mortality in cirrhotic patients undergoing anesthesia and surgery. *Anesthesiology.* 1999;90(1):42–53.

75. Maze M, Bass N. *Anaesthesia and the Hepatobiliary System.* 5th ed. Miller, editor. Philadelphia, PA: Churchill Livingstone; 2000.

76. Kowalski HJ, Abelmann WH. The cardiac output at rest in Laennec's cirrhosis. *J Clin Investig.* 1953;32(10):1025–33.

77. Gonwa TA, McBride MA, Anderson K, Mai ML, Wadei H, Ahsan N. Continued influence of preoperative renal function on outcome of orthotopic liver transplant (OLTX) in the US: Where will MELD lead us? *Am J Transplant.* 2006;6(11):2651–9.

78. Epstein M, Berk DP, Hollenberg NK, Adams DF, Chalmers TC, Abrams HL, et al. Renal failure in the patient with cirrhosis. The role of active vasoconstriction. *Am J Med.* 1970;49(2):175–85.

79. Gelman S, Dillard E, Bradley EL, Jr. Hepatic circulation during surgical stress and anesthesia with halothane, isoflurane, or fentanyl. *Anesth Analg.* 1987;66(10):936–43.

80. Biancofiore G, Davis CL. Renal dysfunction in the perioperative liver trans-plant period. *Curr Opin Organ Transplant.* 2008;13(3):291–7.
81. Jones RM, Moulton CE, Hardy KJ. Central venous pressure and its effect on blood loss during liver resection. *Br J Surg.* 1998;85(8):1058–60.
82. Haynes GR, Navickis RJ, Wilkes MM. Albumin administration–what is the evidence of clinical benefit? A systematic review of randomized controlled trials. *Eur J Anaesthesiol.* 2003;20(10):771–93.
83. Finfer S. Reappraising the role of albumin for resuscitation. *Curr Opin Crit Care.* 2013;19(4):315–20.
84. Nadeem A, Salahuddin N, El Hazmi A, Joseph M, Bohlega B, Sallam H, et al. Chloride-liberal fluids are associated with acute kidney injury after liver transplantation. *Crit Care.* 2014;18(6):625.
85. Yao F, Malhotra V, Fontes M. *Yao and Artusio's Anaesthesiology: Problem Oriented Patient Management.* 7th ed. Philadelphia, PA: Lippincott Williams & Wilkins; 2012.
86. Reiz S, Peter T, Rais O. Hemodynamic and cardiometabolic effects of infra-renal aortic and common iliac artery declamping in man–an approach to optimal volume loading. *Acta Anaesthesiol Scand.* 1979;23(6):579–86.
87. Toomtong P, Suksompong S. Intravenous fluids for abdominal aortic surgery. *Cochrane Database Syst Rev.* 2010(1):CD000991.
88. Kreimeier U, Messmer K. Small-volume resuscitation: From experimental evidence to clinical routine. Advantages and disadvantages of hypertonic solutions. *Acta Anaesthesiol Scand.* 2002;46(6):625–38.
89. Christ F, Niklas M, Kreimeier U, Lauterjung L, Peter K, Messmer K. Hyperosmotic-hyperoncotic solutions during abdominal aortic aneurysm (AAA) resection. *Acta Anaesthesiol Scand.* 1997;41(1 Pt 1):62–70.

chapter eight

Fluid therapy for the trauma patient

Ronald Chang* and John B. Holcomb
University of Texas Health Science Center at Houston
Houston, TX

Contents

Key points:

- Case presentations
- Coagulopathy
- Damage control
- Minimization and permissive hypotension
- Utilization of blood products
- Resuscitation of patient with traumatic brain injury

* Supported by a T32 fellowship (grant no. 5T32GM008792) from NIGMS.

8.1 Case 1

An 18-year-old male is transported by helicopter after sustaining a gunshot wound to the abdomen. He is transfused one unit of uncrossmatched type AB liquid plasma en route for hypotension and a positive abdominal ultrasound examination. On arrival to the emergency department, he is diaphoretic and confused. Initial vital signs are heart rate 150 breaths/min, blood pressure 90/60 mmHg, respiratory rate 30 breaths/min, and a Glasgow coma scale (GCS) score of 14. On examination, the patient has a single gunshot wound to the left upper quadrant of the abdomen as well as abdominal distension. Chest x-ray demonstrates neither pneumothorax nor hemothorax. Focused assessment with sonography in trauma (FAST) examination is positive. A massive transfusion protocol is initiated. Arterial blood gas demonstrates pH of 7.17 and base deficit of 9; initial hemoglobin is 11 g/dL. The patient is taken urgently to the operating room. Rapid sequence intubation is performed after the patient is prepared and draped. Upon entering the abdomen, 3 L of hemoperitoneum are evacuated as the abdomen is packed with laparotomy sponges. The patient is found to be hemorrhaging from a grade V splenic injury, which is managed by splenectomy. Initial rapid thromboelastography (rTEG) values return, demonstrating activated clotting time (ACT) 156 seconds, angle 58 degrees, maximum amplitude 55 mm, and LY-30 of 6%. After splenectomy, bleeding has been controlled. The patient also undergoes two small bowel resections due to multiple small bowel injuries. After intraoperative transfusion of eight units of packed red blood cells (PRBC), eight units of fresh frozen plasma (FFP), and six units of platelets, as well as bolus and infusion of tranexamic acid (TXA), the patient's acidosis and base deficit are resolving. His heart rate is 90, blood pressure is stable without any vasopressor requirement, and urine output is increasing. The decision is made to proceed with definitive restoration of normal anatomy. The patient undergoes two small bowel reanastomoses and primary abdominal closure. He is transported to the surgical ICU. By this time, the patient has received eight units of PRBC, nine units of plasma, six units of platelets, and 1,500 mL of PlasmaLyte to transfuse the blood products. Massive transfusion protocol is deactivated. Serial laboratory studies including rTEG are continued and guide transfusion of specific blood components. The patient is found to be stable on postoperative Day 1 and is extubated. He has an uncomplicated hospital course and is discharged home on postoperative Day 5.

8.2 Case 2

A 40-year-old female arrives by ambulance after a high-speed head-on motor vehicle collision. On arrival, her vital signs are heart rate

120 breaths/min, blood pressure 108/60 mmHg, respiratory rate 20 breaths/min, and GCS 15. On examination, she has right flank ecchymoses and pelvic instability. Chest x-ray and FAST examination are negative. Pelvic x-ray demonstrates an open book pelvic fracture. As the secondary survey is performed, her blood pressure begins to fall to less than 90 mmHg systolic. She is placed in a pelvic binder and is transfused one unit of uncrossmatched type O⁻ PRBC and one unit of uncrossmatched type AB thawed plasma. After transfusion, her blood pressure rises. She is taken to the CT scanner (with the trauma team closely monitoring for recurrent hypotension), where she is found to have multiple rib fractures, a Grade 2 liver injury, multiple pelvic fractures, and a large pelvic hematoma with questionable active extravasation. At the same time, her admission laboratory studies demonstrate an elevated base deficit and prolonged ACT on rTEG. She is transfused additional units of (crossmatched) FFP and taken to interventional radiology for angiography, where a bleeding vessel is embolized. On repeat labs, her rTEG parameters have corrected, and her base deficit is resolving. She is now normotensive with no suspicion of active bleeding; therefore maintenance fluids with PlasmaLyte are started. She will proceed to the operating room with orthopedics for pelvic fixation within 24 hours of admission.

8.3   Introduction

Advances in the care of the trauma patient have historically been made during times of armed conflict. Treatment of battlefield casualties has not only advanced our knowledge of surgical techniques but also our understanding of physiology and resuscitation strategy. Important milestones in this regard include the resuscitation efforts during World War I, widespread use of dried plasma and whole blood during World War II, and the advent of damage control resuscitation during the wars in Afghanistan and Iraq. Advances such as these, borne out of conflict, were later implemented in civilian trauma systems.

Trauma continues to be a growing problem in the United States and worldwide. Injury is the leading cause of death in those aged 40 years and younger, and it is the fifth leading cause of death overall in the United States [1]. From 2000 to 2010, death rates secondary to trauma increased while death rates secondary to heart disease and cancer actually decreased [2]. Trauma continues to be the number one cause of productive life years lost. The economic burden of trauma not only arises from the initial hospitalization but includes ongoing medical care well after the initial injury as well as missed employment opportunity. With these combined costs, the estimated economic impact of all injuries in the United States occurring in the year 2000 alone was $406 billion [3].

We are discovering more and more that optimal care of the trauma patient includes not only treatment of the specific post-traumatic injuries but also correction of the patient's physiologic derangements that result from the original traumatic insult. Of the trauma patients who survive to presentation to the emergency department, the top two causes of death are exsanguination and traumatic brain injury (TBI). The methodology of resuscitation has obviously a significant impact on the outcomes for the patients with the gravest injuries. However, less than optimal resuscitation can have ramifications in patients with less severe injuries as well. Prolongation of the shock state, increased organ dysfunction, and failure of nonoperative management can all result from a suboptimal resuscitation strategy. Therefore, developing an optimal resuscitation strategy with consideration to the type, timing, and volume of fluids used is of paramount importance to any clinician involved in trauma care.

8.4   The coagulopathy of trauma

The correction of coagulopathy is one of the greatest challenges in the care of the trauma patient, not only because of its prevalence in this patient population but also because of the adverse outcomes associated with its persistence. One-quarter of trauma patients at a civilian trauma center and one-third of combat casualties have been shown to be coagulopathic on initial presentation [4–6]. In a study by May et al. [7], 81% of head-injured patients with GCS less than 7 and all head-injured patients with GCS less than 5 were found to be coagulopathic on admission. Moreover, the degree of coagulopathy has been shown to be an independent predictor of mortality. A study by MacLeod et al. [8] concluded that an abnormal admission prothrombin time (PT) increased the adjusted odds ratio of mortality by 35%, while an abnormal admission partial thromboplastin time (PTT) increased the adjusted odds ratio of mortality by 326%. Exsanguination is clearly the most dramatic result of post-traumatic coagulopathy and has been implicated in 40% of trauma deaths [9]. However, uncorrected coagulopathy may have many other adverse effects, including persistent hypovolemic shock, increasing risk of organ dysfunction [10]; persistent inflammatory state, increasing risk of sepsis [11]; and failure of nonoperative management, leading to increased postoperative morbidity [12].

Previous attempts to explain this problem centered on the "deadly trauma triad" of hypothermia, acidosis, and coagulopathy, but we are beginning to see that this is an overly simplistic model of an exceedingly complex problem. Simmons et al. in 1969 first observed that shock correlated with an acute coagulopathy in combat casualties during the Vietnam War [13]. Recent attention has focused on the relationship between shock, global hypoperfusion, and this so-called acute coagulopathy of trauma.

The mechanism for this coagulopathy is closely associated with injury severity score [4,6,14], independent of traditionally attributed factors (such as fluid administration, hemodilution, or hypothermia) [4], and independent of mechanism of injury [15]. A study by Brohi et al. [16] found that elevated base deficit secondary to global hypoperfusion and shock was associated with coagulopathy and hyperfibrinolysis in trauma patients upon presentation to the emergency department and appears to involve activation of protein C by thrombin–thrombomodulin complexes. A review by Hess et al. [17] proposed six main drivers of post-traumatic coagulopathy: tissue trauma, shock, hemodilution, hypothermia, acidemia, and inflammation. As will be discussed in the next section, the "damage control" paradigm of surgery and resuscitation has evolved to tackle many of these factors in order to rapidly and directly address the problem of post-traumatic coagulopathy.

8.5   Damage control

8.5.1   Surgery

Damage control is a term originating from the US Navy to describe the protocol used to save a ship that has suffered catastrophic structural damage, placing a heavy emphasis on limiting flooding, isolating fires, and thereby maintaining vessel stability [18]. Stone et al. in 1983 published a case series of 31 trauma patients who developed major coagulopathy during initial trauma laparotomy [19]. The first 14 patients underwent definitive surgery with repair of all injuries and "standard" hematologic replacement to treat the coagulopathy—only one patient in this cohort survived. The subsequent 17 patients underwent an abbreviated laparotomy that aimed to terminate the surgery as quickly as possible once major coagulopathy was apparent. Twelve patients survived the initial operation and underwent delayed definitive repair, with eleven patients in this cohort surviving. Rotondo et al. in 1993 published a retrospective review of 46 patients who presented with penetrating abdominal injury and hemorrhagic shock [20]. Overall, there was no difference in survival between patients who underwent an abbreviated initial laparotomy versus initial definitive repair. However, survival was markedly improved in the cohort who had presented with the most severe injuries (major vascular injury and at least two visceral injuries) and underwent abbreviated trauma laparotomy compared to initial definitive repair (77% vs. 11% survival). Rotondo called the abbreviated initial trauma laparotomy "damage control surgery," which is defined by the rapid temporization of life-threatening injuries with deferral of definitive repair until after adequate resuscitation. Patients who benefit from this approach are those with multiple and/or complex injuries presenting with profound

metabolic derangement, most often from hemorrhagic shock (see Case 1).
Goals of a damage control operation include the following:

1. Rapid identification of all injuries.
2. Resection or packing of solid organ injury to achieve hemostasis.
3. Ligation or shunting of vascular injury.
4. Control of gross gastrointestinal spillage with resection and/or drainage, typically leaving the patient in temporary gastrointestinal discontinuity.
5. Temporary wound closure (typically with a negative pressure vacuum system).

However, it should be noted that the surgeon should proceed with definitive repair as soon as the patient is adequately resuscitated, which may occur in the operating room itself [21]. A typical decision tree is shown in Figure 8.1.

8.5.2   Resuscitation

Damage control resuscitation is the resuscitation strategy that has evolved in conjunction with damage control surgery. It is a paradigm shift away from the old days of crystalloid or artificial colloid-based resuscitation and instead uses a blood product–based resuscitation strategy to not only provide hemodynamic support but also correct the patient's coagulopathy and shock state. Major principles of damage control resuscitation include minimization of crystalloid, permissive hypotension, transfusion of a balanced ratio of blood products, and goal-directed correction of coagulopathy.

8.5.3   Minimization of crystalloid

Given the ubiquity of our most commonly used crystalloids, it is easy to forget that normal saline and lactated Ringer's were not designed for the purpose of resuscitation. The exact origin of 0.9% sodium chloride, or normal saline, is unclear. However, it is clear that normal saline is not physiologically normal in any respect. Salt solutions were used by physicians during the European cholera epidemic of the 1830s, but there is no recorded use of any fluid resembling 0.9% sodium chloride from that era. Hartog Jakob Hamburger, a Dutch physiologist, incorrectly concluded the physiologic concentration of sodium chloride in blood to be 0.9% based on red blood cell lysis studies in the 1880s, but it is unclear if he intended for his findings to be the basis for an intravenous salt solution [22].

The origin of lactated Ringer's is better documented. Sydney Ringer was a British physiologist who created a series of electrolyte solutions

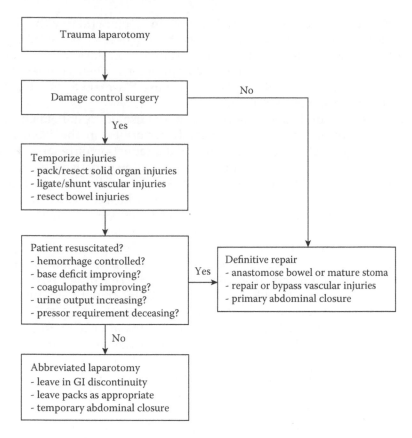

Figure 8.1 A decision tree for the patient requiring a trauma laparotomy. The surgeon should proceed with definitive repair if adequate resuscitation can be achieved in the operating room. Otherwise, the patient's injuries are temporized, and resuscitation is continued in the ICU.

during his studies of explanted frog hearts in the 1880s. He found that the hearts had the strongest ventricular contractions when submerged in a sodium chloride solution that also contained trace bicarbonate, calcium, and potassium [23]. This solution was modified by Alexis Hartmann in 1932, who replaced the bicarbonate with lactate, hence lactated Ringer's or Hartmann's solution.

PlasmaLyte is a relatively new crystalloid solution that gained FDA approval in 1979 for intravenous use in the United States. Unlike normal saline and lactated Ringer's, PlasmaLyte was designed as a physiologic fluid. There are multiple formulations sold to different markets; most formulations contain sodium, potassium, chloride, and magnesium but not calcium. PlasmaLyte has an osmolarity of approximately

294 mOsmol/L and can be safely used in conjunction with blood products [24]. Observational data suggest that the use of a balanced crystalloid like PlasmaLyte may decrease mortality secondary to sepsis and decrease incidence of postoperative complications when compared to normal saline [25,26]. For these reasons, we use PlasmaLyte as the crystalloid of choice at our institution.

Much of our understanding regarding the use of crystalloids in the surgical patient is derived from research performed in the 1950s and 1960s. A study by Shires et al. in 1961 noted a reduction of renal sodium excretion due to a reduction of intravascular volume in patients undergoing major surgery [27]. This fluid was not lost externally and was redistributed into what would later be called the "third space." Observational data from the 1970s and 1980s demonstrated that supranormal values for cardiac index, oxygen demand, and oxygen delivery were associated with increased survival in critically ill surgical patients [28–30]. In 1988, a prospective, randomized trial comparing "supranormalization" of hemodynamic parameters to standard of care in critically ill postoperative patients performed by Shoemaker et al. demonstrated a significantly decreased risk of mortality in the supranormalization arm [31]. Their resuscitation protocol delivered rapid crystalloid boluses to boost cardiac output to supranormal levels and increase oxygen delivery. Fluid and subsequently inotropes continued to be delivered as long as oxygen demand was observed to be increasing. The premise was to repay the oxygen debt that had resulted from the patient's surgery and subsequent critical illness. An increase in oxygen consumption with increased oxygen delivery was seen as evidence that the oxygen debt was not yet adequately repaid. This strategy required monitoring of cardiac index, pulmonary artery wedge pressure, and mixed venous oxygen saturation by pulmonary artery catheterization.

Later studies, however, failed to replicate Shoemaker's earlier success [32]. One criticism of supranormalization was that the increased oxygen consumption seen with continued fluid administration was solely due to increased myocardial oxygen demand from the increased cardiac workload itself. At the same time, investigators began to note increased harm and complications in patients who underwent high-volume resuscitation with crystalloid [33]. A randomized trial in 2003 comparing restricted intravenous versus "standard" fluid resuscitation in patients after elective colorectal surgery found a significantly decreased time of return of gastrointestinal function (4 vs. 6.5 days) [34], as well as a significantly decreased rate of cardiopulmonary (7% vs. 24%) and wound healing (16% vs. 31%) complications [35], in patients who underwent restricted versus standard fluid resuscitation. On a microscopic level, aggressive hydration causes intracellular swelling secondary to osmotic shifts, leading to alterations in multiple cellular biochemical processes, including impaired insulin synthesis and secretion in pancreatic beta islet cells [36], altered glucose metabolism in hepatocytes [37], and altered cardiac myocyte excitability [38].

One of the most dreaded complications of acute volume overload in the trauma patient is perhaps abdominal compartment syndrome, which carries a greater than 50% risk of mortality despite timely diagnosis and decompressive laparotomy [39–41]. A study by Balogh et al. in 2003 demonstrated that the supranormalization resuscitation strategy was associated with increased crystalloid utilization, incidence of abdominal compartment syndrome, and ultimately mortality [42]. A related problem is that of the persistently open abdomen. Failure to achieve fascial closure after damage control laparotomy may be secondary to intestinal and/or retroperitoneal edema, recurrent abdominal compartment syndrome, or persistence of the shock state [43,44]. Hatch et al. [45] demonstrated increasing incidence of multiple complications including intra-abdominal abscess, ventilator-associated pneumonia, and sepsis with delay in fascial closure. Animal studies performed at our institution have shown that hypertonic saline (HTS) reduces bowel edema after fluid resuscitation [46–48], while also reducing bowel reperfusion injury by modulating the inflammatory cascade [49–51]. A retrospective analysis of our experience with the open abdomen after damage control laparotomy found increased rates of early primary fascial closure (100% vs. 76%) in patients who were treated with HTS versus isotonic crystalloid [52]. Our protocol is to start 30 mL/hr of 3% sodium chloride in surgical ICU patients with an open abdomen after hemostasis is obtained. HTS replaces the maintenance fluid for the patient (which would typically be 100–125 mL/hr of isotonic crystalloid), is not titrated, and is continued for 72 hours or until fascial closure, whichever comes first. The use of HTS in this patient population is safe and does not appear to lead to increased renal dysfunction or need for dialysis.

8.5.4 *Permissive hypotension*

The goal of permissive hypotension is to achieve the minimum blood pressure necessary to maintain perfusion with the assumption that an unnecessarily elevated blood pressure will compromise a clot and exacerbate hemorrhage before surgical hemostasis has been achieved, which was first suggested by Cannon [53] during World War I and later by Beecher [54] during World War II. Subsequently, much of this practice is based on animal studies, a meta-analysis of which demonstrated a pooled mortality risk ratio of 0.37 for the animals that underwent hypotensive versus standard fluid resuscitation [55]. Randomized human data in this area is more limited. The most well-known study was performed by Bickell et al. [56] in the 1990s, which compared immediate versus delayed fluid resuscitation for nearly 600 patients who presented with penetrating truncal injuries and hemorrhagic shock. Patients were randomized in the prehospital period to the standard resuscitation arm, where fluids were begun prior to arrival to the emergency department, or to the delayed resuscitation arm, where fluids were not started until the patient was in the operating room. The investigators found a statistically significant relative risk reduction of 11% favoring the delayed resuscitation group. However, subsequent subgroup analysis demonstrated that only patients with penetrating cardiac injuries benefited and that there was no difference in noncardiac injury patients [57]. A subsequent randomized study investigating permissive hypotension versus standard resuscitation did not demonstrate any difference in mortality [58]. Currently, none of the leading trauma organizations offer any specific blood pressure goals or any hard recommendations pertaining to hypotensive resuscitation. The latest edition of the *Advanced Trauma Life Support Student Course Manual* states that the goal of initial resuscitation is "the balance of organ perfusion and hypotension, and not the hypotension itself" [59].

More recently, a pilot study by the Resuscitation Outcomes Consortium (ROC) randomized about 200 hypotensive trauma patients to a standard resuscitation arm (systolic blood pressure [SBP] goal ≥110 mmHg) or a controlled resuscitation arm (SBP goal ≥70). The study found no difference in overall 24-hour mortality but decreased 24-hour mortality in blunt trauma patients who underwent controlled resuscitation [60]. Although further research is warranted, hypotensive resuscitation appears safe and, given what we know about the danger of excess crystalloid in this patient population, likely beneficial in the initial stages of trauma care. However, the clinical picture becomes more complex when the patient has TBI where an increased mean arterial pressure (MAP) may be needed to maintain cerebral perfusion. At our institution, we typically resuscitate to a mean arterial blood pressure goal of 60 mmHg in the absence of central nervous system injury. Additional considerations in the resuscitation of the TBI patient will be discussed later.

8.5.5   Utilization of blood products

The first recorded successful blood transfusion was performed by Richard Lower in England in 1665 when he kept a dog alive by transfusing blood from other dogs. James Blundell performed the first successful blood transfusion in a human subject in 1818 when he successfully treated a patient with postpartum hemorrhage. However, a lack of understanding of blood types continued to make transfusions prohibitively dangerous. It was not until the turn of the twentieth century when human blood groups were discovered that blood transfusions could become routine [61]. Transfusion of whole blood was the norm for the next 80 years.

However, component therapy replaced whole blood therapy by the late 1970s, due to the increasing prevalence of chemotherapy as well as the desire to increase efficiency of resource utilization and decrease transmission of blood-borne pathogens.

Up to 5% of trauma patients at a major trauma center will require a substantial amount of blood products following injury, typically referred to as *massive transfusion* [62,63]. Massive transfusion has historically been defined as transfusion of 10 or more units of red blood cells in the first 24 hours. However, this definition has been challenged because it is prone to survivor bias and does not reflect the critical illness of the hemorrhaging patient in the acute setting [64,65], and there is now general acceptance of defining *massive transfusion* within a shorter time window, such as 2–6 hours [66]. Most trauma centers have developed standing massive transfusion protocols (MTP): delivery of predefined ratios of blood products upon activation, which continue until hemostasis is achieved. Early activation of a predetermined MTP has been shown to decrease blood product waste [67] as well as reduce incidence of organ failure and other complications [68]. However, selection of patients requiring massive transfusion remains difficult [69]. Multiple scoring systems have been developed to predict the likelihood that a trauma patient will require massive transfusion, but early scoring systems including the Trauma-Associated Severe Hemorrhage score and the McLaughlin score relied on laboratory values that may not be available at the time of exsanguinating hemorrhage [70–72], limiting practical implementation. Cotton et al. [73] developed the Assessment of Blood Consumption (ABC) score, which gives one point for each of the following: penetrating mechanism, systolic blood pressure <90 mmHg, heart rate >120 beats per min, and positive FAST exam. A score of 2 or greater predicted need for massive transfusion with 85% accuracy. At our institution, we activate MTP for any trauma patient presenting with shock, hypotension, an ABC score of at least 2, or if an attending physician calls for uncrossmatched blood products from the emergency department refrigerator. Massive transfusion protocol is continued until bleeding is observed to have slowed, which typically occurs after control of "surgical" bleeding in the operating room or interventional radiology suite (see Case 1 above).

The composition of massive transfusion protocol has changed substantially in the last two decades. A typical protocol in the early 2000s consisted of stepwise resuscitation with crystalloid, colloid, and PRBC in the preliminary phase followed by FFP and platelets after 1–2 blood volumes had already been transfused [66]. By the early 2000s, anecdotal reports of increased survival with an increased ratio of FFP to PRBC were surfacing. This culminated in the landmark study by Borgman et al. in 2007, which was a single-center retrospective review of 246 trauma patients who required massive transfusion protocol treated at a US army hospital in Iraq [74]. The patients were split into three cohorts: a low FFP to PRBC ratio (1:8), a medium ratio group (1:2.5), and a high ratio group (1:1.4). Overall mortality was 65%, 34%, and 19% for the low, medium, and high groups, respectively, while mortality secondary to hemorrhage was 92%, 78%, and 37%, respectively. At the same time, Johansson et al. [75] demonstrated that early administration of FFP and platelets in patients with a ruptured abdominal aortic aneurysm reduced postoperative hemorrhage and mortality. The first prospective observational study, PROMMTT, investigated the optimal ratio of blood product components during massive transfusion of trauma patients and demonstrated that early utilization of higher ratios of plasma and platelets to red blood cells was associated with significantly increased survival within the first 6 hours [76]. A subsequent prospective randomized study, PROPPR, demonstrated no difference in 24 hour or 30 day mortality in patients randomized to a 1:1:1 versus 1:1:2 ratio of platelets to FFP to PRBC, although the 1:1:1 group did experience earlier achievement of hemostasis and fewer exsanguination deaths within 24 hours [77]. Our group also recently reviewed the relationship between damage control resuscitation and organ-specific survival, demonstrating increased survival and successful nonoperative management of high-grade blunt liver injury after damage control resuscitation was instituted at our institution in 2008 [12].

Although multiple studies to date have demonstrated improved survival with the use of plasma during trauma resuscitation, very little is known regarding the underlying mechanism. Given that there are tens of thousands of unique proteins in human plasma [78], it is unlikely that the resuscitative effect is due solely to repletion of coagulation factors. Our group has demonstrated *in vitro* [79,80] and in a mouse model of hemorrhagic shock [81,82] that FFP reduces vascular endothelial permeability, which appears to be mediated by restoration of the endothelial glycocalyx. Indeed, recent observational data in trauma patients at our institution demonstrate a relationship between low plasma oncotic pressure, increased shedding of glycocalyx components, and impaired thrombin generation [83]. Thus, the resuscitative effect of plasma appears to be at least threefold: repletion of volume, repletion of clotting factors, and systemic repair of damaged endothelium [84].

Unfortunately, logistical hurdles must be overcome before implementing plasma-based resuscitation. FFP is frozen within hours of donation and stored at −18°C, preventing protein degradation and maintaining maximal clotting factor activity at the time of transfusion. However, FFP takes 20–30 minutes to thaw before it is ready for use, limiting its immediate availability, and can only be stored in a bedside cooler for 6 hours. Alternatives to FFP include thawed plasma and liquid plasma. The most labile clotting factors, factors V and VIII, maintain 65% of their activity 5 days after thawing, giving thawed plasma a shelf life of 5 days when stored at 1°–6°C [85]. The liquid (never frozen) plasma used at our institution has a shelf life of 26 days. Toward the end of this period, we have found that most clotting factors (aside from factors V and VIII) maintain at least 88% of their activity and that liquid plasma has a better coagulation profile than thawed plasma [86]. At our institution, type AB (universal donor) thawed plasma is readily available in the emergency department, while our LifeFlight helicopters carry type AB liquid plasma.

8.5.6   Whole blood

There has recently been increased interest in resurrecting the practice of transfusing whole blood. Military experience with whole blood transfusion in the traumatized patient is extensive, going back to at least World War I, and includes experience in modern conflicts such as the Battle of Mogadishu [87], as well as the first Gulf War and the Kosovo conflict [88]. Thousands of fresh whole blood (FWB) units have been utilized to treat combat casualties in Afghanistan and Iraq, where FWB was used in 13% of all transfused patients in Operation Iraqi Freedom [88].

Due to a dilutional effect when separating whole blood into components, one unit of whole blood has twice the viable platelets, twice the hematocrit, and 50% more clotting factor activity when compared to a 1:1:1 ratio of component therapy (see Table 8.1) [14,87]. Therefore, advantages to FWB include a necessarily balanced ratio of components as well as increased activity of each individual component. Our group recently performed a pilot study demonstrating the feasibility of transfusion of modified whole blood in the trauma setting [89]. The optimal use of blood products, including the potential role of whole blood in the civilian trauma setting, continues to be an exciting area of active research.

8.5.7   Goal-directed resuscitation

Previously, transfusion of platelets and plasma in the trauma patient was predicated on conventional tests such as platelet count, PT, international normalized ratio, and PTT [66]. However, platelet count is not equivalent to platelet function, while the conventional coagulation tests are run *in vitro* on platelet-poor plasma, interrogating only a limited portion of the patient's coagulation profile. The length of time required to

Table 8.1 Whole blood versus 1:1:1 component therapy

	Fresh whole blood	Component therapy
Hematocrit	38%–50%	29%
Platelet count	150–400 K/µL	88 K/µL
Clotting factor activity	100%	65%

Source: Data from Cotton, B.A., et al., *Ann. Surg.*, 258, 530, 2013.

run these tests also makes them suboptimal in managing post-traumatic coagulopathy [90].

To overcome these limitations, multiple devices have been developed that provide a coagulation profile of a whole blood sample. The thromboelastography (TEG) device was developed in 1946 and is utilized at our institution to guide goal-directed resuscitation and correction of coagulopathy when empiric massive transfusion therapy is not indicated. The device consists of a cup containing a whole blood sample and a detector connected to a torsion wire inserted into the blood sample. Tissue factor is added to the blood sample to rapidly initiate the coagulation cascade, which distinguishes a rapid TEG from a standard TEG. The tension transduced by the wire, which increases as the clot forms and decreases as lysis overtakes clot formation, is translated into a real-time tracing. Parameters derived from the tracing include the R-value, ACT, coagulation time (K), maximum amplitude (mA), angle (α), and percent lysis at 30 minutes (LY-30). The ACT is typically available within 5 minutes of running the sample, with most of the other parameters available a few minutes after that. The rTEG software is integrated into our institution's computer network, so tracings are available in real time in our emergency department and in our operating rooms.

An example of an rTEG tracing is provided in Figure 8.2. Interpretation of the rTEG tracing is as follows [91]. The R-value and ACT are a measure

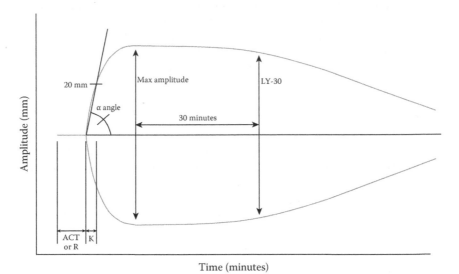

Figure 8.2 Thromboelastography (TEG) provides a coagulation profile of a whole blood sample. The different parameters derived from the TEG tracing are influenced by different components of the coagulation cascade, enabling targeted correction of abnormal TEG parameters.

of the amount of time needed to initiate clot formation, which is dependent on the enzymatic activity of clotting factors. K represents the amount of time needed to form a "preliminary" clot of predefined strength (amplitude of 20 mm) after clot formation has begun, while α measures the rate of initial clot formation. Both K and α are reflective of the cleavage of fibrinogen into fibrin by activated thrombin and the cross-linking of fibrin monomers. Maximum amplitude (mA) reflects the end result of clot formation when maximal binding occurs between platelets and fibrin via glycoprotein IIb/IIIa interactions. After the clot reaches maximal strength, fibrinolysis overtakes coagulation, resulting in decreasing clot strength. The ratio of clot strength lost after 30 minutes compared to the maximum amplitude is the LY-30. Understanding the significance of the rTEG parameters allows targeted therapy to correct abnormal values (see Tables 8.2 and 8.3).

A study by Holcomb et al. investigated the use of rTEG in 1,974 consecutive trauma patients and found that abnormalities in rTEG parameters more reliably predicted fibrinolysis as well as the need for blood products compared to PT and PTT [90]. At our institution, a rapid TEG is sent to the laboratory along with other blood work upon minutes of ED

Table 8.2 Normal rapid thromboelastography values and interpretations

rTEG value (normal range)	Definition	Interpretation
Activated clotting time (86–118 seconds)	Time from start of assay to initiation of clot	Prolonged with factor deficiency or severe hemodilution
R value (0.0–1.0 minutes)	Time between beginning of assay and initial clot formation	Prolonged with factor deficiency or severe hemodilution
K time (1.0–2.0 minutes)	Time needed to reach 20 mm clot strength	Increased with hypofibrinogenemia or platelet dysfunction
Alpha angle (66°–82°)	Rate or acceleration of clot formation	Decreased with hypofibrinogenemia or platelet dysfunction
Maximum amplitude (54–72 mm)	Contribution of platelet function and platelet–fibrin interactions	Decreased with hypofibrinogenemia or platelet dysfunction
LY-30 (0%–7.5%)	Amplitude reduction 30 minutes after achieving mA (degree of fibrinolysis)	Increased with accelerated fibrinolysis

Source: Data from Cotton, B.A., et al., *J. Trauma*, 256, 477, 2012.

Note: rTEG, rapid thromboelastography.

Table 8.3 Goal-directed resuscitation strategy currently used at our institution

rTEG value	Resuscitation strategy
ACT >128 seconds	Transfuse plasma and RBC.
R-value >1.1 minutes	Transfuse plasma and RBC.
K-time >2.5 minutes	Transfuse plasma. Add cryoprecipitate or fibrinogen if angle also abnormal.
Alpha angle <56°	Transfuse cryoprecipitate (or fibrinogen). Add platelets if mA also abnormal.
Max amplitude <55 mm	Transfuse platelets. Add cryoprecipitate or fibrinogen if angle also abnormal.
LY-30 >3%	Administer tranexamic acid if within 3 hours of injury.

Note: ACT, activated clotting time; LY-30, percent lysis at 30 minutes; RBC, red blood cells.

arrival for all highest-level trauma patients. In the absence of an indication for massive transfusion protocol, we will use component blood product therapy to correct abnormal rTEG parameters if ongoing bleeding is known or strongly suspected. We will continue maintenance fluid with crystalloid (typically PlasmaLyte) in the stable patient with no evidence of active bleeding (see Case 2). Resuscitation with crystalloid in the bleeding trauma patient is to be avoided.

Fibrinolysis appears to be an important driver of acute post-traumatic coagulopathy [92], but concrete guidelines on the use of antifibrinolytics in this patient population are lacking. The Clinical Randomisation of an Antifibrinolytic in Significant Haemorrhage (CRASH-2) trial is the largest study to date investigating this topic, enrolling over 20,000 patients in 274 hospitals across 40 countries [93]. Patients were randomized to receive a 1 g bolus followed by a 1 g infusion of TXA over 8 hours or placebo. The study found a small but statistically significant reduction in all-cause mortality and mortality secondary to hemorrhage in the TXA group when the medication was given within 3 hours of injury. Otherwise, mortality increased in the intervention arm after the 3 hour window [94]. One of the criticisms of the study is that TXA was given to all comers without any point of care testing to identify which patients had abnormal fibrinolysis and stood to benefit from this intervention.

At our institution, TXA is given as a 1 g bolus followed by a 1 g infusion over 8 hours if the patient presents within 3 hours of injury with an LY-30 of at least 3% on the admission rTEG. We recently performed a retrospective study in trauma patients with accelerated fibrinolysis (LY-30 ≥3%) and found no difference in mortality in patients who received TXA and those who did not. A retrospective study from the Miami group recently examined their use of TXA. Patients presenting to the ED in hemorrhagic shock who received TXA were compared to matched controls who did not receive the drug. No point-of-care testing was performed to identify accelerated hyperfibrinolysis. The group found that the patients who received TXA had overall increased mortality. However, patients who did not require an operation for hemorrhage control and patients who received fewer than eight units of PRBC tended to have improved outcomes with TXA, but this did not reach statistical significance [95]. The use of TXA in trauma is still highly controversial, and further studies need to be performed to identify those who stand to benefit from this intervention.

8.5.8   Resuscitation of the patient with TBI

TBI is responsible for about 40% of trauma deaths and is a significant cause of morbidity and disability [9] There is currently no practical treatment for primary central nervous system injury except for prevention. Therefore, the goal of the trauma clinician is to prevent secondary cerebral injury, namely from hypoperfusion and hypoxia. It is well known that cerebral perfusion pressure (CPP) is the difference of the MAP and the intracranial pressure (ICP), or CPP = MAP – ICP. Adequate cerebral perfusion is therefore accomplished by maintaining MAP while minimizing ICP.

Due to the limited space of the cranial vault, any cerebral edema will quickly lead to increases in ICP and potential cerebral hypoperfusion. For this reason, hypo-osmolar fluids are avoided in this patient population. The Saline versus Albumin Fluid Evaluation (SAFE) study was a randomized control trial comparing normal saline versus 4% albumin in nearly 7,000 heterogeneous critically ill patients [96]. A *post hoc* analysis of 492 TBI patients was performed, which demonstrated increased mortality in severely brain injured patients (GCS ≤ 8) in the albumin arm (41.8% vs. 22.2% mortality) [97]. Until further evidence is gathered regarding its use in TBI patients, we tend to avoid using albumin or artificial colloid in this patient population at our institution.

An attractive option for the management of TBI patients is HTS. Delivered as a continuous infusion of 3% sodium chloride, HTS should provide both fluid resuscitation and mitigation of cerebral edema. A much more concentrated form (23.4% sodium chloride) can also be delivered as a bolus to increase serum osmolarity as a treatment for intracranial hypertension. Animal data and multiple small human studies suggest that HTS is likely effective in lowering ICP [98–100]. However, a recent study by Bulger et al. from the ROC investigated the prehospital use of HTS in over 2,000 TBI patients not in hemorrhagic shock and found no difference in 6 month neurologic outcome [101]. The role of HTS in this patient population continues to be controversial, and there are no formal recommendations regarding its use from the major trauma and neurotrauma organizations [102].

One of the most difficult treatment conundrums is the polytrauma patient suffering from both hemorrhagic shock and TBI. Use of crystalloid has been shown to exacerbate coagulopathy in the setting of hemorrhagic shock, but use of artificial colloid or albumin in the presence of TBI is controversial because of the previously mentioned *post hoc* analysis from the SAFE trial. HTS should be used cautiously as well, given recent data that prehospital use of HTS actually worsens coagulopathy and hyperfibrinolysis in patients with hemorrhagic shock [103].

Recently, Jin et al. [104] have developed a pig model of TBI, in which a computer-controlled pneumatic device creates reproducible traumatic brain lesions. Using this model, his group compared saline versus artificial colloid versus FFP resuscitation in animals with concurrent TBI and hemorrhagic shock. They found that animals that had been resuscitated with FFP had less cerebral swelling and smaller lesion sizes than animals that had been resuscitated with saline or colloid. Given the aforementioned data demonstrating the ability of plasma-based resuscitation to mitigate endothelial permeability in the setting of shock [81,82], it is plausible that FFP reduced secondary cerebral injury by its actions on the cerebral vasculature that constitute the blood–brain barrier. A recent retrospective study of patients with isolated TBI at our institution demonstrated on subgroup analysis that age and coagulopathy were associated with progression of neurological injury on subsequent head CT for all subtypes of TBI and that intraparenchymal contusion was the subtype most likely to progress [105]. At our institution, we will aggressively correct abnormal rTEG parameters with FFP and platelets as well as perform serial rTEG measurements in any patient with intracranial injury on head CT.

8.6 Conclusion

Although our understanding of trauma resuscitation has increased markedly in the last 20 years, many questions remain. However, it is clear that an optimal resuscitation strategy with correct utilization of crystalloid, blood products, and other adjuncts is just as important as surgical treatment of the specific traumatic injuries. Although progress in the treatment of trauma has historically been made during periods of armed conflict, large scale initiatives such as CRASH-2, PROMMTT, PROPPR, and the ROC trials have allowed a new generation of physician-scientists to gain insight and gather evidence at unprecedented speed and scale outside of the theater of war. With a trend toward increasing collaboration and cooperation across multiple specialties and centers in large consortiums, we will continue to push the boundary of human understanding in this challenging, but exciting, area of medicine.

References

1. U.S. Census Bureau. *The 2012 Statistical Abstract. Table 122: Deaths and Death Rates by Leading Causes of Death and Age: 2007.* 2012. http://www.census.gov/compendia/statab/cats/births_deaths_marriages_divorces/deaths.html (Accessed October 16, 2014).
2. Rhee, Peter, Bellal Joseph, Viraj Pandit, Hassan Aziz, Gary Vercruysse, Narong Kulvatunyou, and Randall S. Friese. Increasing trauma deaths in the United States, *Ann Surg* 260 (2014): 13–21.
3. Finkelstein, Eric A., Phaedra S. Corso, and Ted R. Miller. *The Incidence and Economic Burden of Injuries in the United States.* New York: Oxford University Press, 2006.
4. Brohi, Karim, Jasmin Singh, Mischa Heron, and Timothy Coats. Acute traumatic coagulopathy, *J Trauma* 54 (2003): 1127–1130.
5. Maegele, Marc, Rolf Lefering, Nedim Yucel, Thorsten Tjardes, Dieter Rixen, Thomas Paffrath, Christian Simanski, Edmund Neugebauer, Bertil Bouillon, and The AG Polytrauma of the German Trauma Society (DGU). Early coagulopathy in multiple injury: An analysis from the German Trauma Registry in 8724 patients, *Injury* 38 (2007): 298–304.
6. Niles, Sarah E., Daniel F. McLaughlin, Jeremy G. Perkins, Charles E. Wade, Yuanzhang Li, Philip C. Spinella, and John B. Holcomb. Increased mortality associated with the early coagulopathy of trauma in combat casualties, *J Trauma* 64 (2008): 1459–1465.
7. May, Addison K., Jeffrey S. Young, Kathy Butler, Deeni Bassam, and William Brady. Coagulopathy in severe closed head injury: Is empiric therapy warranted? *Am Surg* 63 (1997): 233–236.
8. MacLeod, Jana B., Mauricio Lynn, Mark G. McKenney, Stephen M. Cohn, Mary Murtha. Early coagulopathy predicts mortality in trauma, *J Trauma* 55 (2003): 39–44.
9. Sauaia, Angela, Frederick A. Moore, Ernest E. Moore, Kathe S. Moser, Regina Brennan, Robert A. Read, and Peter T. Pons. Epidemiology of trauma deaths: A reassessment, *J Trauma* 38 (1995): 185–193.
10. Sauaia, Angela, Frederick A. Moore, Ernest E. Moore, James B. Haenel, Robert A. Read, and Dennis C. Lezotte. Early predictors of postinjury multiple organ failure, *Arch Surg* 129 (1994): 39–45.
11. Esmon, Charles T. The interactions between inflammation and coagulation, *Br J Haemotol* 131 (2005): 417–430.
12. Shrestha, Binod, John B. Holcomb, Elizabeth A. Camp, Deborah J. del Junco, Bryan A. Cotton, Rondel Albarado, Brijesh S. Gill, et al. Damage control resuscitation increases successful nonoperative management rates and survival after severe blunt liver injury, *J Trauma* 78 (2015): 336–341.
13. Simmons, Richard L., John A. Collins, Charles A. Heisterkamp, Douglas E. Mills, Richard Andren, and Louise L. Phillips. Coagulation disorders in combat casualties, *Ann Surg* 169 (1969): 455–482.

14. Duchesne, Juan C., Norman E. McSwain, Jr., Bryan A. Cotton, John P. Hunt, Jeff Dellavolpe, Kelly Lafaro, Alan B. Marr, et al. Damage control resuscitation: The new face of damage control, *J Trauma* 69 (2010): 976–990.
15. Sixta, Sherry L., Quinton M. Hatch, Nena Matijevic, Charles E. Wade, John B. Holcomb, and Bryan A. Cotton. Mechanistic determinates of the acute coagulopathy of trauma (ACoT) in patients requiring emergency surgery, *Int J Burn Trauma* 2 (2012): 158–166.
16. Brohi, Karim, Mitchell J. Cohen, Michael T. Ganter, Marcus J. Schultz, Marcel Levi, Robert C. Mackersie, and Jean-François Pittet. Acute coagulopathy of trauma: Hypoperfusion induces systemic anticoagulation and hyperfibrinolysis, *J Trauma* 64 (2008): 1211–1217.
17. Hess, John R., Karim Brohi, Richard P. Dutton, Carl J. Hauser, John B. Holcomb, Yoram Kluger, Kevin Mackway-Jones, et al. The coagulopathy of trauma: A review of mechanisms, *J Trauma* 65 (2008): 748–754.
18. U.S. Navy. *Surface Ship Survivability*. Naval War, 1996, Washington DC.
19. Stone, H. Harlan, Priscilla R. Strom, and Richard J. Mullins. Management of major coagulopathy with onset during laparotomy, *Ann Surg* 197 (1983): 532–535.
20. Rotondo, Michael F., C. William Schwab, and Michael D. McGonigal. Damage control: An approach for improved survival in exsanguinating penetrating abdominal injury, *J Trauma* 35 (1993): 375–383.
21. Holcomb, John B., Don Jenkins, Peter Rhee, Jay Johannigman, Peter Mahoney, Sumeru Mehta, E. Darrin Cox, et al. Damage control resuscitation: Directly addressing the early coagulopathy of trauma, *J Trauma* 62 (2007): 307–310.
22. Awad, Sherif, Simon P. Allison, and Dileep N. Lobo. The history of 0.9% saline, *Clin Nutr* 27 (2008): 179–188.
23. Ringer, Sydney. Concerning the influence exerted by each of the constituents of the blood on the contraction of the ventricle, *J Physiol* 3 (1882): 380–393.
24. Baxter Healthcare Corporation. *PLASMA-LYTE 148 Injection (Multiple Electrolytes Injection, Type 1, USP)*, 2013. http://www.accessdata.fda.gov/drug-satfda_docs/label/2013/017378s068,017385s059lbl.pdf (Accessed February 5, 2015).
25. Raghunathan, Karthik, Andrew Shaw, Brian Nathanson, Til Stürmer, Alan Brookhart, Mihaela S. Stefan, Soko Setoguchi, Chris Beadles, and Peter K. Lindenauer. Association between the choice of IV crystalloid and in-hospital mortality among critically ill adults with sepsis, *Crit Care Med* 42 (2014): 1585–1591.
26. Shaw, Andrew D., Sean M. Bagshaw, Stuart L. Goldstein, Lynette A. Scherer, Michael Duan, Carol R. Schermer, and John A. Kellum. Major complications, mortality, and resource utilization after open abdominal surgery 0.9% saline compared to plasma-lyte, *Ann Surg* 255 (2012): 821–829.
27. Shires, Tom, Jack Williams, and Frank Brown. Acute change in extracellular fluids associated with major surgical procedures, *Ann Surg* 154 (1961): 804–810.
28. Bland, Richard D., William C. Shoemaker, Edward Abraham, and Juan C. Cobo. Hemodynamic and oxygen transport patterns in surviving and non-surviving patients, *Crit Care Med* 13 (1985): 85–90.
29. Shoemaker, William C., Eileen S. Montgomery, Ellen Kaplan, and David H. Elwyn. Physiologic patterns in surviving and nonsurviving shock patients, *Arch Surg* 106 (1973): 630–636.

30. Shoemaker, William C., Paul Appel, and Richard Bland. Use of physiologic monitoring to predict outcome and to assist in clinical decisions in critically ill postoperative patients, *Am J Surg* 146 (1983): 43–50.
31. Shoemaker, William C., Paul L. Appel, Harry B. Kram, Kenneth Waxman, and Tai-Shion Lee. Prospective trial of supranormal values survivors as therapeutic goals in high risk surgical patients, *Chest* 94 (1988): 1176–1183.
32. Velmahos, George C., Demetrios Demetriades, William C. Shoemaker, Linda S. Chan, Raymond Tatevossian, Charles C.J. Wo, Pantelis Vassiliu, et al. Endpoints of resuscitation of critically injured patients: Normal or supranormal? A prospective randomized trial, *Ann Surg* 232 (2000): 409–418.
33. Cotton, Bryan A., Jeffrey S. Guy, John A. Morris, Jr., and Naji N. Abumrad. The cellular, metabolic, and systemic consequences of aggressive fluid resuscitation strategies, *Shock* 26 (2006): 115–121.
34. Lobo, Dileep N., Kate A. Bostock, Keith R. Neal, Alan C. Perkins, Brain J. Rowlands, and Simon P. Allison. Effect of salt and water balance on recovery of gastrointestinal function after elective colonic resection: A randomised control trial, *Lancet* 359 (2002): 1812–1820.
35. Brandstrup, Birgitte, Hanne Tønnesen, Randi Beier-Holgersen, Else Hjortsø, Helle Ørding, Karen Lindorff-Larsen, Morten S. Rasmussen, et al. Effects of intravenous fluid restriction on postoperative complications: Comparison of two perioperative fluid regimens, *Ann Surg* 238 (2003): 641–648.
36. Lang, Florian, Gillian L. Busch, Markus Ritter, Harald Völkl, Siegfried Waldegger, Erich Gulbins, and Dieter Häussinger. Functional significance of cell volume regulatory mechanisms, *Physiol Rev* 78 (1998): 248–273.
37. Häussinger, Dieter, Freimut Schliess, Ulrich Warskulat, and Stephan vom Dahl. Liver cell hydration, *Cell Biol Toxicol* 13 (1997): 275–287.
38. Tseng, Gea-Ny. Cell swelling increases membrane conductance of canine cardiac cells: Evidence for a volume-sensitive Cl channel, *Am Physiol* 262 (1992): C1056–C1068.
39. Biffl, Walter L., Ernest E. Moore, Jon M. Burch, Patrick J. Offner, Reginald J. Franciose, and Jeffrey L. Johnson. Secondary abdominal compartment syndrome is a highly lethal event, *Am J Surg* 182 (2001): 645–648.
40. Miller, Richard S., John A. Morris, Jr., Jose J. Diaz, Jr., Michael B. Herring, and Addison K. May. Complications after 344 damage control open celiotomies, *J Trauma* 59 (2005): 1365–1371.
41. Raeburn, Christopher D., Ernest E. Moore, Walter L. Biffl, Jeffrey L. Johnson, Daniel R. Meldrum, Patrick J. Offner, Reginald J. Franciose, Jon M. Burch. The abdominal compartment syndrome is a morbid complication of postinjury damage control surgery, *Am J Surg* 182 (2001): 542–546.
42. Balogh, Zsolt, Bruce A. McKinley, Christine S. Cocanour, Rosemary A. Kozar, Alicia Valdivia, R. Matthew Sailors, and Frederick A. Moore. Supranormal trauma resuscitation causes more cases of abdominal compartment syndrome, *Arch Surg* 138 (2003): 637–643.
43. Hatch, Quinton M., Lisa M. Osterhout, Asma Ashraf, Jeanette Podbielski, Rosemary A. Kozar, Charles E. Wade, John B. Holcomb, and Bryan A. Cotton. Current use of damage-control laparotomy, closure rates, and predictors of early fascial closure at the first take-back, *J Trauma* 70 (2011): 1429–1436.
44. Shah, Shinil K., Karen S. Uray, Randolph H. Stewart, Glen A. Laine, and Charles S. Cox Jr. Resuscitation induced intestinal edema and related dysfunction: State of the science, *J Surg Res* 166 (2011): 120–130.

45. Hatch, Quinton M., Lisa M. Osterhout, Jeanette Podbielski, Rosemary A. Kozar, Charles E. Wade, John B. Holcomb, and Bryan A. Cotton. Impact of closure at the first take back: Complication burden and potential overutilization of damage control laparotomy, *J Trauma* 71 (2011): 1503–1511.
46. Cox, Charles S., Jr., Ravi Radhakrishnan, Lindsey Villarrubia, Hasen Xue, Karen Uray, Brijesh S. Gill, Randolph H. Stewart, and Glen A. Laine. Hypertonic saline modulation of intestinal tissue stress and fluid balance, *Shock* 29 (2008): 598–602.
47. Radhakrishnan, Ravi S., Hasan Xue, Stacey D. Moore-Olufemi, Norman W. Weisbrodt, Frederick A. Moore, Steven J. Allen, Glen A. Laine, and Charles S. Cox Jr. Hypertonic saline resuscitation prevents hydrostatically induced intestinal edema and ileus, *Crit Care Med* 34 (2005): 1713–1718.
48. Radhakrishnan, Ravi S., Hari R. Radhakrishnan, Hasen Xue, Stacey D. Moore-Olufemi, Anshu B. Mathur, Norman W. Weisbrodt, Frederick A. Moore, Steven J. Allen, Glen A. Laine, and Charles S. Cox, Jr. Hypertonic saline reverses stiffness in a Sprague-Dawley rat model of acute intestinal edema, leading to improved intestinal function, *Crit Care Med* 35 (2007): 538–543.
49. Attuwaybi, Bashir, Rosemary A. Kozar, Keith S. Gates, Stacey D. Moore-Olufemi, Norio Sato, Norman W. Weisbrodt, and Frederick A. Moore. Hypertonic saline prevents inflammation, injury, and impaired intestinal transit after gut ischemia/reperfusion by inducing heme oxygenase-1 enzyme, *J Trauma* 56 (2004): 749–758.
50. Attuwaybi, Bashir O., Rosemary A. Kozar, Stacey D. Moore-Olufemi, Norio Sato, Heitham T. Hassoun, Norman W. Weisbrodt, and Frederick A. Moore. Hemeoxygenase-1 induction by hemin protects against gut ischemia/reperfusion injury, *J Surg Res* 118 (2004): 53–57.
51. Gonzalez, Ernest A., Rosemary A. Kozar, James W. Suliburk, Norman W. Weisbrodt, David W. Mercer, and Frederick A. Moore. Conventional dose hypertonic saline provides optimal gut protection and limits remote organ injury after gut ischemia reperfusion, *J Trauma* 61 (2006): 66–73.
52. Harvin, John A., Mark M. Mims, Juan C. Duchesne, Charles S. Cox, Jr., Charles E. Wade, John B. Holcomb, and Bryan A. Cotton. Chasing 100%: The use of hypertonic saline to improve early, primary fascial closure after damage control laparotomy, *J Trauma* 74 (2013): 426–432.
53. Cannon, Walter B., John Fraser, and E.M. Cowell. The preventive treatment of wound shock, *JAMA* 70 (1918): 618–621.
54. Beecher, Henry K. Preparation of battle casualties for surgery, *Ann Surg* 121 (1945): 769–792.
55. Mapstone, James, Ian Roberts, and Phillip Evans. Fluid resuscitation strategies: A systematic review of animal trials, *J Trauma* 55 (2003): 571–589.
56. Bickell, William H., Matthew J. Wall, Jr., Paul E. Pepe, R. Russell Martin, Victoria F. Ginger, Mary K. Allen, and Kenneth L. Mattox. Immediate versus delayed fluid resuscitation for hypotensive patients with penetrating torso injuries, *NEJM* 331 (1994): 1105–1109.
57. Wall, Jr., Matthew J., Thomas Granchi, Kathleen Liscum, John Aucar, and Kenneth L. Mattox. Delayed versus immediate fluid resuscitation in patients with penetrating trauma: Subgroup analysis, *J Trauma* 39 (1995): 173.
58. Dutton, Richard P., Colin F. Mackenzie, and Thomas M. Scalea. Hypotensive resuscitation during active hemorrhage: Impact on in-hospital mortality, *J Trauma* 52 (2002): 1141–1146.

59. American College of Surgeons Committee on Trauma. *Advanced Trauma Life Support Student Course Manual,* 9th ed. Chicago, IL: American College of Surgeons, 2012.
60. Schreiber, Martin A., Eric N. Meier, Samuel A. Tisherman, Jeffrey D. Kerby, Craig D. Newgard, Karen Brasel, Debra Egan, et al. A controlled resuscitation strategy is feasible and safe in hypotensive trauma patients: Results of a prospective randomized pilot trial, *J Trauma* 78 (2015): 687–697.
61. American National Red Cross. *History of Blood Transfusion,* 2015. http://www.redcrossblood.org/learn-about-blood/history-blood-transfusion (Accessed December 2, 2014).
62. Huber-Wagner, Stefan, Mike Qvick, Thomas Mussack, Ekkehard Euler, Michael V. Kay, Wolf Mutschler, Karl-Georg Kanz, and The Working Group on Polytrauma of German Trauma Society (DGU). Massive blood transfusion and outcome in 1062 polytrauma patients: A prospective study based on the Trauma Registry of the German Trauma Society, *Vox Sang* 92 (2007): 69–78.
63. Simon J. Stanworth, Timothy P. Morris, Christine Gaarder, J. Carel Goslings, Marc Maegele, Mitchell J. Cohen, Thomas C. König, et al. Reappraising the concept of massive transfusion in trauma, *Crit Care* 14 (2010): R239–R246.
64. Rahbar, Elaheh, Erin E. Fox, Deborah J. del Junco, John A. Harvin, John B. Holcomb, Charles E. Wade, Martin A. Schreiber, et al. Early resuscitation intensity as a surrogate for bleeding severity and early mortality in the PROMMTT study, *J Trauma* 74 (2013): S16–S23.
65. Savage, Stephanie A. Ben L. Zarzaur, Martin A. Croce, and Timothy C. Fabian. Redefining massive transfusion when every second counts, *J Trauma* 74 (2013): 396–402.
66. Johansson, Pär I., Jakob Stensballe, Roberto Oliveri, Charles E. Wade, Sisse R. Ostrowski, and John B. Holcomb. How I treat patients with massive hemorrhage, *Blood* 124 (2014): 3052–3058.
67. Khan, Sirat, Shubha Allard, Anne Weaver, Colin Barber, Ross Davenport, and Karim Brohi. A major haemorrhage protocol improves the delivery of blood component therapy and reduces waste in trauma massive transfusion, *Injury* 44 (2013): 587–592.
68. Cotton, Bryan A., Brigham K. Au, Timothy C. Nunez, Oliver L. Gunter, Amy M. Robertson, and Pampee P. Young. Predefined massive transfusion protocols are associated with a reduction in organ failure and postinjury complications, *J Trauma* 66 (2009): 41–49.
69. Pommerening, Matthew J., Michael D. Goodman, John B. Holcomb, Charles E. Wade, Erin E. Fox, Deborah J. del Junco, Karen J. Brasel, et al. Clinical gestalt and the prediction of massive transfusion after trauma, *Injury* 46 (2015): 807–813.
70. McLaughlin, Daniel F., Sarah E. Niles, Jose Salinas, Jeremy G. Perkins, E. Darrin Cox, Charles E. Wade, and John B. Holcomb. A predictive model for massive transfusion in combat casualty patients, *J Trauma* 64 (2008): S57–S63.
71. Schreiber, Martin A., Jeremy Perkins, Laszlo Kiraly, Samantha Underwood, Charles Wade, John B. Holcomb. Early predictors of massive transfusion in combat casualties, *J Am Coll Surg* 205 (2007): 541–545.
72. Yücel, Nedim, Rolf Lefering, Marc Maegele, Matthias Vorweg, Thorsten Tjardes, Steffen Ruchholtz, Edmund A.M. Neugebauer, et al. Trauma Associated Severe Hemorrhage (TASH)-Score: Probability of mass

transfusion as surrogate for life threatening hemorrhage after multiple trauma, *J Trauma* 60 (2006): 1228–1236.

73. Cotton, Bryan A., Lesly A. Dossett, Elliott R. Haut, Shahid Shafi, Timothy C. Nunez, Brigham K. Au, Victor Zaydfudim, Marla Johnston, Patrick Arbogast, Pampee P. Young. Multicenter validation of a simplified score to predict massive transfusion in trauma, *J Trauma* 69 (2010): S33–S39.

74. Borgman, Matthew A., Philip C. Spinella, Jeremy G. Perkins, Kurt W. Grathwohl, Thomas Repine, Alec C. Beekley, James Sebesta, Donald Jenkins, Charles E. Wade, and John B. Holcomb. The ratio of blood products transfused affects mortality in patients receiving massive transfusions at a combat support hospital, *J Trauma* 63 (2007): 805–813.

75. Johansson, Pär I., Jakob Stensballe, Iben Rosenberg, Tanja L. Hilsløv, Lisbeth Jørgensen, and Niels H. Secher. Proactive administration of platelets and plasma for patients with a ruptured abdominal aortic aneurysm: Evaluating a change in transfusion practice, *Transfusion* 47 (2007): 593–598.

76. Holcomb, John B., Deborah J. del Junco, Erin E. Fox, Charles E. Wade, Mitchell J. Cohen, Martin A. Schreiber, Louis H. Alarcon, et al. The prospective, observational, multicenter, major trauma transfusion (PROMMTT) study, *JAMA* 148 (2013): 127–136.

77. Holcomb, John B., Barbara C. Tilley, Sarah Baraniuk, Erin E. Fox, Charles E. Wade, Jeanette M. Podbielski, et al. Transfusion of plasma, platelets, and red blood cells in a 1:1:1 vs a 1:1:2 ratio and mortality in patients with severe trauma: The PROPPR randomized clinical trial, *JAMA* 313 (2015): 471–482.

78. Anderson, N. Leigh and Norman G. Anderson. The human plasma proteome: History, character, and diagnostic prospects, *Mol Cell Proteomics* 1 (2002): 845–867.

79. Peng, Zhanglong, Shibani Pati, Daniel Potter, Ryan Brown, John B. Holcomb, Raymond Grill, Kathryn Wataha, Pyong Woo Park , Hasen Xue, and Rosemary A. Kozar. Fresh frozen plasma lessens pulmonary endothelial inflammation and hyperpermeability after hemorrhagic shock and is associated with loss of syndecan 1, *Shock* 40 (2013): 195–202.

80. Wataha, Kathryn, Tyler Menge, Xutao Deng, Avani Shah, Ann Bode, John B. Holcomb, Daniel Potter, Rosemary Kozar, Philip C. Spinella, and Shibani Pati. Spray-dried plasma and fresh frozen plasma modulate permeability and inflammation in vitro in vascular endothelial cells, *Transfusion* 53 (2013): 80S–90S.

81. Kozar, Rosemary A., Zhanglong Peng, Rongzhen Zhang, John B. Holcomb, Shibani Pati, Pyong Park, Tien C. Ko, and Angel Paredes. Plasma restoration of endothelial glycocalyx in a rodent model of hemorrhagic shock, *Anesth Analg* 112 (2011): 1289–1295.

82. Potter, Daniel R., Gail Baimukanova, Sheila M. Keating, Xutao Deng, Jeffrey A. Chu, Stuart L. Gibb, Zhanglong Peng, et al. Fresh frozen plasma and spray-dried plasma mitigate pulmonary vascular permeability and inflammation in hemorrhagic shock, *J Trauma* 78 (2015): S7–S17.

83. Rahbar, Elaheh, Jessica C. Cardenas, Gyulnar Baimukanova, Benjamin Usadi, Roberta Bruhn, Shibani Pati, Sisse R. Ostrowski, Pär I. Johansson, John B. Holcomb, and Charles E. Wade. Endothelial glycocalyx shedding and vascular permeability in severely injured trauma patients, *J Transl Med* 13 (2015): 117–123.

84. Holcomb, John B., and Shibani Pati. Optimal trauma resuscitation with plasma as the primary resuscitative fluid: The surgeon's perspective, *Hematology Am Soc Hematol Educ Program* 2013 (2013): 656–659.

85. Downes, Katharine A., Erica Wilson, Roslyn Yomtovian, and Ravindra Sarode. Serial measurement of clotting factors in thawed plasma stored for 5 days, *Transfusion* 41 (2001): 570.

86. Matijevic, Nena, Yao-Wei Wang, Bryan A. Cotton, Elizabeth Hartwell, James M. Barbeau, Charles E. Wade, and John B. Holcomb. Better hemostatic profiles of never-frozen liquid plasma compared with thawed fresh frozen plasma, *J Trauma* 74 (2012): 84–91.

87. Sebesta, James. Special lessons learned from Iraq, *Surg Clin North Am* 86 (2006): 711–726.

88. Kauvar, David S., John B. Holcomb, Gary C. Norris, and John R. Hess. Fresh whole blood transfusion: A controversial military practice, *J Trauma* 61 (2006): 181–184.

89. Cotton, Bryan A., Jeanette Podbielski, Elizabeth Camp, Timothy Welch, Deborah del Junco, Yu Bai, Rhonda Hobbs, et al. A randomized controlled pilot trial of modified whole blood versus component therapy in severely injured patients requiring large volume resuscitations, *Ann Surg* 258 (2013): 527–533.

90. Holcomb, John B., Kristin M. Minei, Michelle L. Scerbo, Zayde A. Radwan, Charles E. Wade, Rosemary A. Kozar, Brijesh S. Gill, et al. Admission rapid thromboelastography can replace conventional coagulation tests in the emergency department, *Ann Surg* 256 (2012): 476–484.

91. Cotton, Bryan A., Gabriel Faz, Quinton M. Hatch, Zayde A. Radwan, Jeanette Podbielski, Charles Wade, Rosemary A. Kozar, and John B. Holcomb. Rapid thrombelastography delivers real-time results that predict transfusion within 1 hour of admission, *J Trauma* 256 (2011): 476–486.

92. Kashuk, Jeffry L., Ernest E. Moore, Michael Sawyer, Max Wohlauer, Michael Pezold, Carlton Barnett Walter L. Biffl, Clay C. Burlew, Jeffrey L. Johnson, and Angela Sauaia. Primary fibrinolysis is integral in the pathogenesis of the acute coagulopathy of trauma, *Ann Surg* 252 (2010): 434–442.

93. CRASH-2 Trial Collaborators, H. Shakur, I. Roberts, R. Bautista, J. Caballero, T. Coats, Y. Dewan, et al. Effects of tranexamic acid on death, vascular occlusive events, and blood transfusion in trauma patients with significant haemorrhage (CRASH-2): A randomised, placebo-controlled trial, *Lancet* 376 (2010): 23–32.

94. CRASH-2 Collaborators, I. Roberts, H. Shakur, A. Afolabi, K. Brohi, T. Coats, Y. Dewan, et al. The importance of early treatment with tranexamic acid in bleeding trauma patients: An exploratory analysis of the CRASH-2 randomised controlled trial, *Lancet* 377 (2011): 1096–1101.

95. Valle, Evan J., Casey J. Allen, Robert M. Van Haren, Jassin M. Jouria, Hua Li, Alan S. Livingstone, Nicholas Namias, Carl I. Schulman, and Kenneth G. Proctor. Do all trauma patients benefit from tranexamic acid? *J Trauma* 76 (2014): 1373–1378.

96. Finfer, Symon, Rinaldo Bellomo, Neil Boyce, Julie French, John Myburgh, Robyn Norton, and The SAFE Study Investigators. A comparison of albumin and saline for fluid resuscitation in the intensive care unit, *NEJM* 350 (2004): 2247–2256.

97. SAFE Study Investigators, Australian and New Zealand Intensive Care Society Clinical Trials Group, Australian Red Cross Blood Service, George Institute for International Health, John Myburgh, D. James Cooper, Symon Finfer, et al. Saline or albumin for fluid resuscitation in patients with traumatic brain injury, *NEJM* 357 (2007): 874–884.

98. Munar, Francisca, Ana M. Ferrer, Miriam de Nadal, Maria A. Poca, Salvador Pedraza, Juan Sahuquillo, and Angel Garnacho. Cerebral hemodynamic effects of 7.2% hypertonic saline in patients with head injury and raised intracranial pressure, *J Neurotrauma* 17 (2000): 41–51.

99. Qureshi, Adnan I., Jose I. Suarez, Alexjandro Castro, and Anish Bhardwaj. Use of hypertonic saline/acetate infusion in treatment of cerebral edema in patients with head trauma: Experience at a single center, *J Trauma* 47 (1999): 659–665.

100. Shackford, Steven R., Paul R. Bourguignon, Steven L. Wald, Frederick B. Rogers, Turner M. Osler, and David E. Clark. Hypertonic saline resuscitation of patients with head injury a prospective, randomized clinical trial, *J Trauma* 44 (1998): 50–58.

101. Bulger, Eileen M., Susanne May, Karen J. Brasel, Martin Schreiber, Jeffrey D. Kerby, Samuel A. Tisherman, Craig Newgard, et al. Out-of-hospital hypertonic resuscitation following severe traumatic brain injury: A randomized controlled trial, *JAMA* 304 (2010): 1455–1464.

102. Brain injury Foundation. Guidelines for the management of severe traumatic brain injury, 3rd edition, *J Neurotrauma* 24 (2007): S1–S20.

103. Delano, Matthew J., Sandro B. Rizoli, Shawn G. Rhind, Joseph Cuschieri, Wolfgang Junger, Andrew J. Baker, Michael A. Dubick, David B. Hoyt, and Eileen M. Bulger. Prehospital resuscitation of traumatic hemorrhagic shock with hypertonic solutions worsens hypocoagulation and hyperfibrinolysis, *Shock* 44 (2015): 25–31.

104. Jin, Guang, Marc A. deMoya, Michael Duggan, Thomas Knightly, Ali Y. Mejaddam, John Hwabejire, Jennifer Lu, et al. Traumatic brain injury and hemorrhagic shock: Evaluation of different resuscitation strategies in a large animal model of combined insults, *Shock* 38 (2012): 49–56.

105. Folkerson, Lindley E., Duncan Sloan, Bryan A. Cotton, John B. Holcomb, Jeffrey S. Tomasek, and Charles E. Wade. Predicting progressive hemorrhagic injury from isolated traumatic brain injury and coagulation, *Surgery* 158 (2015): 655–61. doi: 10.1016/j.surg.2015.02.029.

chapter nine

Fluid management in the ambulatory surgery, gynecologic, and obstetric patient

Ramon Abola and Tong J. Gan
Stony Brook Medicine
Stony Brook, NY

Contents

Key points:

1. **Ambulatory Surgery:**
   - Liberal fluid administration is associated with decreased post-operative nausea/vomiting.
   - Liberal fluid therapy is associated with decreased thirst, dizziness and drowsiness.
   - Patients should be encouraged to drink clear fluids up to 2 hours before surgery.
2. **Gynecology:**
   - Liberal fluid administration for ambulatory gynecological procedures is associated with decreased postoperative nausea/vomiting and thirst.
   - Goal directed and restrictive fluid therapy may improve outcomes after major gynecological surgery.
   - Enhanced recovery programs have improved patients outcomes following major gynecological surgery.
3. **Obstetrics:**
   - For labor epidural placement, there is limited benefit for fluid preloading when using lower concentrations of local anesthetic.
   - Hypotension after spinal anesthesia is less with the use of a fluid co-load versus preload, and less with the use of colloid versus crystalloid.
   - Severe postpartum hemorrhage should be managed with a goal of replacing whole blood, with a 1:1:1 ratio of packed red blood cells, fresh frozen plasma, and platelets.

9.1　Fluid therapy and ambulatory surgery

9.1.1　Introduction

Ambulatory surgery has markedly increased over the past few decades. In 2006, the Centers for Disease Control estimated that there were 34.7 million ambulatory surgery visits in the United States. Of those visits, 19.9 million occurred in hospitals and 14.9 million occurred in free-standing ambulatory surgery centers. The rates of visits to a freestanding ambulatory surgery center increased about 300% from 1996 to 2006 [1]. Advances in surgical and anesthetic techniques have allowed for older and sicker patients to undergo more complex surgeries in the ambulatory setting. Laparoscopic cholecystectomies, shoulder rotator cuff repairs, and tonsillectomies are just some examples of surgeries that are now being performed in ambulatory surgery patients. A recent report in 2013 found that one- or two-level anterior cervical discectomies and fusions could be performed safely in an ambulatory setting with decreasing hospital length of stay and hospital costs [2]. Objectives for safe discharge from ambulatory surgery include rapid recovery focusing on short-acting anesthetics, avoidance of postoperative nausea and vomiting (PONV), and adequate pain control [3]. The question we aim to address is what impact fluid management has on ambulatory surgery.

9.1.2   Fluid management and PONV

Intravenous fluid management appears to have an impact on the incidence of PONV. Gut hypoperfusion has been suggested as a contributing mechanism to developing PONV. Overnight fasting and surgical fluid losses with inadequate fluid replacement can result in decreased blood flow to the gastrointestinal mucosa. Gut ischemia has been associated with the release of serotonin, a potent trigger of nausea and vomiting. Gut mucosal perfusion was improved in cardiac patients who received boluses of hydroxyethyl starch (HES) with an esophageal Doppler system to optimize stroke volume [4]. A gastric tonometer was used to provide noninvasive assessment of gastric mucosal perfusion by calculation of gastric intramucosal pH.

Intravenous fluid administration has been shown to influence PONV in ambulatory patients. Magner et al. randomized 141 patients undergoing elective day-case gynecological laparoscopy to either receive 10 mL/kg or 30 mL/kg of compound sodium lactate [5]. General endotracheal anesthesia with sevoflurane and nitrous oxide was standardized for both groups and prophylactic antiemetics were not administered at any time. In the first 48 hours after anesthesia, the incidence of vomiting was lower (8.6% vs. 25.7%, $P = 0.01$) and the use of antiemetics was lower (2.9% vs. 15.7%, $P = 0.02$) in the group who had received the larger intravenous crystalloid infusion. Maharaj and colleagues randomized 80 patients at high risk for PONV who were undergoing ambulatory gynecologic laparoscopy to receive either a large (2 mL/kg per hour fasting) or small (3 mL/kg) volume infusion of compound sodium lactate solution over 20 minutes preoperatively [6]. The mean amounts for preoperative fluid bolus were 212.5 mL in the control group and 1,799 mL in the large volume group. The incidence (control 87% vs. large volume 59%, $P < 0.05$) and severity of PONV were significantly reduced in the large volume group. Additionally, the group who had received a large volume fluid bolus reported decreased pain scores and required less supplemental analgesia. The reduced opiate requirements did not account for the decrease in PONV. The mechanism of this analgesic effect of intravenous fluids bolus remains to be determined.

Apfel et al. performed a quantitative review evaluating the role of supplemental intravenous crystalloids for the preventions of PONV [7]. Fifteen studies with a total of 1,575 patients were included in their analysis that compared randomized groups to receive supplemental crystalloid versus restricted fluid therapy and the effect on PONV. Several of these studies did not show significance in improving PONV with fluid hydration. However, when the studies were grouped together in a meta-analysis, intravenous crystalloids significantly reduced several PONV outcomes. Supplemental IV crystalloid reduced the need for rescue treatment as effectively as many prophylactic antiemetic drugs.

The use of colloids instead of crystalloid for a preoperative fluid bolus did not alter the incidence of PONV. Haenjens et al. performed a prospective randomized double-blind study on 115 women undergoing gynecological or breast surgery [8]. Women were randomized to either receive a 500 mL bolus of HES (Voluven®) or normal saline to compare the incidence of PONV. There was no difference between the groups in terms of nausea, vomiting, or need for antiemetics.

In summary, supplemental intravenous hydration is an effective strategy for reducing baseline risk for PONV. Several studies have demonstrated this effect in the ambulatory surgery setting associated with minimal fluid shifts. However, there was no difference in the efficacy of fluid hydration between crystalloid and colloids in similar volumes [9].

9.1.3   Fluid management and adverse outcomes

Preoperative fluid bolus has been shown to reduce thirst, drowsiness, and dizziness in the ambulatory surgery patient. Suntheralinham et al. randomized 200 patients, mostly female undergoing dilation and curettage, to either a high infusion or low infusion group [10]. The high infusion group received a 20 mL/kg bolus of PlasmaLyte isotonic solution, and the low infusion group received a 2 mL/kg bolus of PlasmaLyte 30 minutes preoperatively. The average total fluid was 1,215 mL for the high infusion group and 164 mL for the low infusion group. The patients who received the higher fluid bolus were found to have a significantly lower incidence of thirst and drowsiness, at 30 and 60 minutes postoperatively and at discharge. Dizziness was found to be significantly less at 30 and 60 minutes postoperatively but was comparable by the time of discharge.

9.1.4   NPO guidelines—Impact on ambulatory patients

For decades, patients have been ordered or instructed to be "NPO after midnight" (NPO, *nil per os*) before surgery. These orders were intended to minimize the risk of pulmonary aspiration in patients who are to undergo general or regional anesthesia. These fasting guidelines have become more liberal over recent years. The *Practice Guidelines for Preoperative Fasting* published by the American Society of Anesthesiologists recommends a minimum fasting period of 2 hours for clear liquids, 4 hours for breast milk, and 6 hours for a light meal [11]. Examples of clear liquids include water, fruit juices without pulp, carbonated beverages, clear tea, and black coffee. These recommendations were based on meta-analysis of randomized controlled trials that show smaller gastric volumes and increased gastric pH in patients who are given clear fluids 2–4 hours preoperatively versus fluids greater than 4 hours preoperatively. Two questions arise in clinical practice related to our NPO orders and preoperative fasting guidelines. What are the physiological implications of preoperative fasting from midnight? What is the clinical impact of allowing patients to drink clear fluids up to 2 hours preoperatively?

A study by Jacobs on 53 patients undergoing major gynecological surgery found that blood volume was normal after preoperative overnight fasting [12]. After induction of anesthesia, plasma volume was determined by diluting indocyanine green. Red blood cell volume was determined using sodium fluorescein-labeled autologous red cells and using flow cytometry to determine the dilution. The measured blood volume was compared to the calculated expected blood volume for each individual based on her body surface area. A normal blood volume after an overnight fast contradicts the assumption that fasted patients arrive dehydrated and are consequently hypovolemic in the operating room. Thus, these authors question the benefit of preoperative volume loading in patients who are euvolemic.

Preoperative oral intake has been evaluated as a potential mechanism to improve surgical outcomes. A key concept in the enhanced recovery after surgery (ERAS) concept is maintaining homeostasis and reducing the stress response to surgery. Surgery has been associated with insulin resistance secondary to the catabolic state induced by surgical stress [13]. This is potentially made worse in the fasted patient, who is already in a catabolic state. The administration of a carbohydrate-rich drink preoperatively has been associated with decreased rate of insulin resistance postoperatively. This potentially may improve bowel function postoperatively and decrease hospital length of stay [13]. Lidder and colleagues found that colorectal patients who had received a preoperative and postoperative carbohydrate drink demonstrated greater hand strength, pulmonary function as measured by forced expiratory flow rate, and less insulin resistance [14]. Additionally, a carbohydrate-rich drink compared to placebo (flavored water) taken preoperatively relieved thirst, hunger, and anxiety to a greater degree [15]. In the ambulatory surgery setting, in patients undergoing ophthalmological procedures, a carbohydrate load preoperatively was associated with decreased hunger and thirst after surgery, resulting in increased postoperative satisfaction [16]. ERAS will be further covered in Chapter 10.

Oral intake of clear fluids up to 2 hours preoperatively is associated with smaller gastric volumes and higher gastric pH and is not associated with increased incidence of pulmonary aspiration. Allowing intake of clear fluids 2 hours preoperatively increases patient satisfaction and decreases thirst. An oral carbohydrate load preoperatively, which has been shown to improve postoperative bowel function and hospital length of stay, may not be as applicable in the ambulatory setting.

9.1.5   Summary areas for future study/research

The number and complexity of ambulatory surgery cases has steadily increased over the past few decades. Intravenous fluid boluses have been associated with decreased postoperative nausea, vomiting, thirst, hunger, drowsiness, and dizziness. NPO guidelines have become more liberal, and patients should be encouraged to drink clear fluids up to 2 hours preoperatively. Carbohydrate-rich drink preoperatively is associated with decreased insulin resistance and may be associated with improved surgical outcomes. There are no studies that determine the relationship of fluid management to other outcomes measures of ambulatory surgery, such as major complications or readmission rates. Future steps are to define the key aspects of anesthesia and surgical care in the ambulatory setting that could impact patient outcome.

9.2   Fluid therapy and the gynecological surgery patient

Gynecological surgery can be divided into minor procedures (dilation and curettage, operative laparoscopy) and major procedures (hysterectomy, pelvic floor reconstruction). Fluid management strategies have not been well studied in laparoscopic gynecological surgery. Laparoscopic cholecystectomies are a similar intermediate-level surgery. Similar to ambulatory surgery, higher fluid volumes in laparoscopic cholecystectomies have been associated with decreased PONV, thirst, dizziness, and fatigue. Additionally, larger versus smaller intraoperative volume administration (40 mL/kg vs. 15 mL/kg, 997 mL vs. 2,928 mL) was shown to be associated with significant improvement in pulmonary function, exercise capacity, and reduced stress response [17]. Fluid administration in minor and intermediate level surgery appears to improve patient outcome and enhance recovery.

The same may not be true of major gynecological surgery. The extensive tissue trauma related to major abdominal surgery likely creates physiological changes that are very different from minor ambulatory surgery. An extensive amount of research has focused on fluid management and postoperative outcomes in major abdominal surgery [18]. A majority of this research has focused on colorectal surgery. Increasing evidence has suggested that excessive volume replacement can be associated with negative outcomes. Problems that can arise with excessive volume in the perioperative period include pulmonary edema, cardiac dysfunction, renal dysfunction, postoperative ileus, and bowel anastomosis breakdown [19]. There are two major strategies employed to optimize fluid management in major abdominal surgery: goal-directed fluid therapy and restricted fluid therapy [20].

Goal-directed fluid therapy employs the use of a cardiac output monitor to optimize volume status in the perioperative period. The general principal behind this strategy is to move the patients to the top, flat portion of the Frank–Starling curve for maximization of stroke volume. The best-studied modality is the esophageal Doppler in colorectal surgery. Patients are given fluid blouses until an increase in cardiac output is no longer demonstrated, and the patients are presumably on the flat portion of the Frank–Starling curve. Goal-directed fluid therapy has mostly utilized colloid for fluid loading. Studies in colorectal surgery using the esophageal Doppler in this manner have shown improvements in patient outcomes: decreased hospital length of stay and earlier return of bowel function [21,22].

Restricted fluid therapy has also been proposed as a strategy to reduce postoperative complications related to fluid excess. Restricted fluid therapy is accepted as best clinical practice for lung surgery. Avoiding fluid excess minimizes fluid overload and pulmonary edema, which can exacerbate postoperative pulmonary complications. Studies have compared a restricted versus liberal fluid therapy in the operating room. Nisanevich et al. prospectively evaluated 152 patients undergoing elective intraabdominal surgery [23]. Patients were randomly assigned to receive either liberal (10 mL/kg followed by 12 mL/kg/hr) or restrictive (4 mL/kg/hr) amounts of lactated Ringer's solution. The number of patients with complications was significantly lower in the restricted protocol group. Patients in the liberal protocol group had significantly longer times to pass flatus and feces and significantly longer hospital stay.

Application of these fluid protocols has been limited in major gynecological surgery. There are few studies that compared a liberal versus restricted fluid protocol in major gynecologic surgery. McKenny randomized 102 patients undergoing major open gynecological surgery to either a control group or an esophageal Doppler monitor group [24]. In the Doppler group, patients received a 3 mL/kg intravenous bolus of Voluven (6% 130/0.4 HES in 0.9% NaCl). Five minutes later stroke volume was remeasured and if the difference from the previous measurement was <10% a further 3 mL/kg of Voluven was given. This was repeated until there were no further increases in stroke volume. Total volume of intraoperative fluid administered to the Doppler group and control group was 2,020 and 2,881 mL, respectively ($P = 0.22$). The Doppler group received more colloid and less crystalloid than the control group. There was no difference in the length of postoperative stay between the two groups.

The postoperative morbidity survey scores were similar between the two groups. The return of gastrointestinal function postoperatively was also similar. These authors question the assumption that goal-directed fluid therapy is equally beneficial to all patient groups.

ERAS protocols combine multimodal evidence-based interventions aimed at shorter stay and optimizing perioperative care. The principles behind ERAS are covered in detail in the subsequent chapter (Chapter 10), but the key concepts to ERAS are preoperative patient education, reduction of preoperative fasting, omission of bowel preparation, perioperative normovolemia, limited used of nasogastric tubes and drains, early removal of urinary catheters, aggressive multimodal analgesia to minimize opiate consumption, early postoperative mobilization, prokinetics to enhance gastrointestinal motility, and early enteral nutrition [25].

Wijk et al. reported that a structured ERAS protocol reduced hospital length of stay after abdominal hysterectomy. Significantly more patients (73% vs. 56%, $P = 0.012$) in the ERAS group ($n = 85$) compared to the pre-ERAS group ($n = 120$) were discharged within 2 days of surgery and length of stay was significantly reduced (2.35 vs. 2.60 days, $P = 0.011$). There were no significant differences in the rate of complications, reoperations, or readmissions. Better compliance with the ERAS protocol was associated with higher percentage of patients meeting the target length of stay. The fluid management portion of the ERAS used by Wijk and colleagues included the following. Patients were allowed to drink clear fluids until 2 hours before surgery and then received 400 mL of a clear carbohydrate drink containing 200 kcal (Nutricia preOp®). The goal for intravenous fluid during the operation was set to 2–4 mL/kg/hr of crystalloids, and when necessary 500–1,000 mL HES 130/0.4 (Voluven) was given. Postoperative oral fluid intake was encouraged immediately to minimize postoperative fluids to 500–1,000 mL on the day of surgery. Intravenous fluids were to be removed as soon as the patient was able to eat and drink, and on the morning after surgery at the latest. The total intravenous fluid on the day of surgery for the pre-ERAS and ERAS groups was 3,000 mL and 2,000 mL, respectively ($P < 0.001$).

Kalogera et al. reported a similar retrospective study for women undergoing cytoreduction, surgical staging, or pelvic organ prolapse surgery [25]. A total of 241 women managed with an enhanced recovery protocol were compared with consecutive history controls. In the cytoreductive group, patient-controlled analgesia use decreased from 98.7% to 33.3%, and overall opioid use decreased by 80% in the first 48 hours with no change in pain scores. Also in the cytoreduction group, enhanced recovery resulted in a 4-day reduction in hospital stay with stable readmission rates. No difference was seen in complication rate. Similar improvements were noted in the surgical staging and pelvic organ prolapse surgery cohort but to a lesser degree. Yoong et al. reported the effects of an enhanced recovery pathway on outcomes in vaginal hysterectomies [26]. After ERAS implementation, the median length of stay was reduced by 51% (22.0 vs. 45.5 hr, $P < 0.01$) and the percentage of patients discharged within 24 hours was increased by fivefold (87% vs. 15.6%, $P < 0.05$). These three studies each report significant decreases in length of stay after implementation of an ERAS protocol. This data was collected retrospectively, and more randomized controlled trials are needed to further validate the benefit of an ERAS protocol.

9.3   Fluid therapy and the obstetric patient

Hypotension is a common complication associated with neuraxial anesthesia. Much effort has been made in preventing hypotension related to either epidural or spinal anesthesia in the obstetric patient. Uteroplacental blood flow and fetal well-being are dependent on maternal cardiac output and blood pressure. Hypotension associated with neuraxial anesthesia is aggravated in the parturient at term due to the compression of the inferior vena cava by the gravid uterus, decreasing venous return and cardiac preload.

9.3.1   Labor analgesia

Early studies had suggested that a preload of crystalloid prior to epidural placement minimized maternal hypotension. In a trial reported by Collins et al., 49 women received a 1 L preload with Hartmann's solution and 53 women received no preload [27]. Epidural analgesia was initiated with a bolus of 10 mL of 0.375% bupivacaine. This infusion significantly reduced the incidence of abnormalities of fetal heart rate from 34% to 12% and of maternal hypotension from 28% to 2%. On the basis of this and similar studies, it was standard practice to preload pregnant women with crystalloid prior to placement of a labor epidural. Subsequently, obstetric anesthesia practice has evolved and lower doses of bupivacaine were found to provide equally effective analgesia with decreased side effects (less hypotension and motor block).

Further studies using lower concentrations of epidural local anesthesia did not find a benefit with fluid preloading. Cheek et al. randomized women to receive no fluid load, a 500 mL normal saline preload, or a 1,000 mL normal saline preload prior to epidural analgesia with 12 mL of 0.25% bupivacaine [28]. There was no difference in the incidence of severity of hypotension between these three groups. Another group reported similar results with 95 women randomized to either receive 1 L of crystalloid preload or no preload [29]. There were no differences in hypotension after labor analgesia was initiated with 15 mL or 0.1% or 0.2% bupivacaine with fentanyl 50 µg. Additionally, there was no statistically significant difference between the two groups in fetal heart tracing deterioration. Kubli et al. also found a similar result with women randomized to either receive no preload ($n = 85$) or a 7 mL/kg IV crystalloid solution ($n = 83$) before epidural placement. There was no difference in the mean decrease of mean arterial pressure and there were no differences in fetal heart rate abnormalities [30].

There also was no difference in the incidence of hypotension in a small study comparing a no-hydration group ($n = 8$) with a prehydration group ($n = 12$) in patients receiving a combined spinal epidural (CSE) for labor analgesia [31]. Analgesia was initiated with intrathecal doses of bupivacaine 2.5 mg and sufentanil 1.2 µg. A meta-analysis by Hofmeyr et al. concluded that preloading may have some beneficial fetal and maternal effects prior to high-dose local anesthetic blocks. However, low-dose epidural and CSE analgesia techniques may reduce the need for preloading [32].

9.3.2　Spinal anesthesia for cesarean delivery

9.3.2.1　Physiology of spinal anesthesia

Spinal anesthesia is traditionally used for cesarean delivery. Spinal anesthesia causes a sympathetic blockade, which results in hypotension from arterial vasodilation and venodilation and decreased preload. Hypotension following spinal anesthesia has also been associated with decreased cardiac output.

9.3.2.2　Crystalloid preload

Multiple fluid administration strategies have been employed to minimize hypotension associated with spinal anesthesia in the parturient. Preload with crystalloid was found to have limited success in decreasing hypotension after spinal anesthesia. A study by Jackson et al. compared a crystalloid preload of 1 L versus 200 mL and found no difference in the incidence and severity of hypotension between the two groups [33]. The limited success of a crystalloid preload is likely due to the fact that only 28% of crystalloid was measured to be intravascular after 30 minutes [34]. Prevention of hypotension appears to be correlated with a fluid regimen's ability to increase cardiac output and increase blood volume.

9.3.2.3　Crystalloid co-load

Better success in minimizing hypotension was found when crystalloid was rapidly infused after the initiation of spinal anesthesia (co-load) [34]. Dyer et al. randomized 50 women to receive 20 mL/kg of crystalloid solution during 20 minutes prior to induction of spinal anesthesia (preload) or an equivalent volume by rapid infusion immediately after induction (co-load). Clinical outcomes were better in the co-load group.

Fewer patients required vasopressor therapy, and the number of ephed-rine doses for the treatment of maternal hypotension was lower in the co-load group. The co-load was administered over a significantly shorter period of time (20 vs. 9.8 min, P = 0.01). Another study also reported decreased hypotension with a crystalloid co-load versus preload [35]. Despite the improvement in maternal hypotension with crystalloid co-load, the incidence of hypotension was high in both groups (co-load 53% vs. preload 83%, P = 0.026).

9.3.2.4 Colloids

Multiple studies have also evaluated the use of colloids in decreasing spinal hypotension. Colloids given as a preload were found to decrease the incidence of hypotension when compared with a crystalloid preload. Colloids were found to have remained 100% intravascular 30 minutes after administration with associated increase in blood volume and cardiac output [34]. This increase in cardiac output associated with colloid preload was found to eliminate hypotension associated with spinal anesthesia [36]. Co-loading with colloid had a similar efficacy to co-loading with crystal-loid in preventing maternal hypotension. The use of vasopressors was similar between the two groups, as were neonatal outcomes [37].

There are several concerns regarding colloids that have limited their use and acceptance in clinical practice. Colloids are more expensive than crystalloid infusions, and especially albumin, as opposed to HES solu-tions. With colloids, there is an increased risk of allergic reaction compared to crystalloid; however, the risk appears to be less with HES solutions compared with dextrans or gelatins [38]. Additionally, studies have shown effects on the coagulation system with HES solutions. Butwick et al. found that patients prior to a cesarean delivery who had received a preload of 6% HES had longer reaction times and clotting times compared to base-line [39]. These mild coagulation effects were not seen in patients who had received lactated Ringer's preload. Since HES recently has been attributed to cause renal problems in critically ill patients, several medical agencies around the world have put restrictions on the use of HES. Although the evidence for other patient groups is weak, the use of HES has declined.

9.3.2.5 Colloid preload versus crystalloid co-load

A recent study by Tawfik et al. compared colloid preloading with crys-talloid preloading in cesarean section under spinal anesthesia [40]. The authors randomized 210 patients to either 500 mL of 6% HES 130/0.4 before spinal injection (colloid preload), or 1,000 mL of Ringer's ace-tate solution administered rapidly with intrathecal injection (crystal-loid co-load). There was no significant difference in the incidence of hypotension (52.4% vs. 42.2%; P = 0.18) or severe hypotension (15.5% vs. 9.8%; P = 0.31) between colloid preload and crystalloid co-load groups, respectively. These authors concluded that these treatment modalities were equivalent but required the co-administration of vasopressors to minimize maternal hypotension.

9.3.2.6   Vasopressor therapy for spinal hypotension

Vasopressor therapy is a key component to minimizing hypotension secondary to spinal hypotension. Traditionally, ephedrine had been the vasopressor for spinal hypotension due to animal studies in sheep ewes that reported decrease uterine artery blood flow with phenylephrine. More recent studies in humans have disputed these findings and there were no differences in neonatal Apgar scores when phenylephrine or ephedrine was used as a vasopressor. Ephedrine was associated was increased incidence of fetal acidosis when compared with phenylephrine. Therefore, phenylephrine has been increasingly gaining use in the obstetric unit. Ngan Kee et al. reported a marked reduction in hypotension with a phenylephrine infusion with similar umbilical cord gas pH values and neonatal Apgar scores. However, approximately 24% of patients still have spinal hypotension despite a high phenylephrine infusion (100 µg/mL). No crystalloid hydration was given to the patients in this study due to the ineffectiveness of crystalloid preload [41]. A subsequent study by the same group reported a near elimination of maternal hypotension after spinal anesthesia when a high-dose phenylephrine (100 µg/mL) infusion was used in combination with crystalloid co-loading [42]. At the start of intrathecal medication injection, the crystalloid infusion was rapidly administered and the patients received a total of 2 L of lactated Ringer's.

9.3.2.7   Summary

In summary, crystalloid preloading has been found to be ineffective. Administration of crystalloid fluid at the time of spinal anesthetic placement, crystalloid co-loading, reduces the incidence of maternal hypotension. Preloading with colloid solution also reduces maternal hypotension after spinal anesthesia; however, colloid co-loading was not any more effective than colloid preloading. Crystalloid co-loading was found to be as effective as colloid preloading; however, neither could eliminate spinal hypotension. Vasopressor therapy is essential in the management of spinal hypotension. In combination with high-dose phenylephrine infusion (100 µg/min), crystalloid co-loading could essentially eliminate spinal hypotension. Crystalloid co-loading or colloid preloading in combination with vasopressor therapy are likely the most effective regimens to minimize spinal hypotension for cesarean delivery (Table 9.1).

9.3.3   Postpartum hemorrhage

Obstetric hemorrhage is the leading cause of maternal mortality worldwide. A report in 2006 by the World Health Organization stated that hemorrhage

Table 9.1 A comparison of fluid strategies for the management of
spinal hypotension

Fluid modality	Reference	Study design	Conclusions
Crystalloid preload	Jackson [33]	1 L versus 200 mL of crystalloid preload	No difference in the severity of hypotension between the two groups
Crystalloid co-load	Dywer [34] Oh [35]	15–20 mL/kg crystalloid bolus received either prior (preload) or after (co-load) spinal anesthesia	Co-load group: Decreased maternal hypotension and decreased used of ephedrine
Colloid preload	Tawfik [40]	Colloid preload (hydroxyethyl starch) before spinal versus 1,000 mL of crystalloid co-load during spinal placement	No significant difference in hypotension or severe hypotension
Colloid co-load	Teoh [37]	Colloid (hydroxyethyl starch) preload versus co-load (15 mL/kg)	No significant difference in incidence of hypotension, absolute blood pressure values, phenylephrine requirements, or neonatal outcomes

Notes: Crystalloid preload has been found to be ineffective in preventing spinal hypotension. Crystalloid co-load, colloid preload, and colloid co-load have been found to be better fluid strategies, with similar outcomes; however, all three still require vasopressor support to eliminate spinal hypotension.

was the leading cause of death in Africa (33%) and Asia (20%). By comparison, hemorrhage only accounted for 13% of maternal deaths in developed countries. In the United States, a report by the Centers for Disease Control and Prevention reported that hemorrhage was the fifth leading causing of maternal mortality between 2006 and 2010. However, Callaghan et al. reported that from 1994 to 2006 there was an increase in the rate of postpartum hemorrhage in the United States, primarily due to an increase in uterine atony [43]. There are several physiological changes (increased red blood cell mass, increased plasma volume, and hypercoagulability) that prepare a mother for the expected blood loss associated with pregnancy [44]. On average, the estimated blood loss associated with a vaginal delivery is 500 mL and the estimated blood loss associated with a cesarean delivery is 1,000 mL. Postpartum hemorrhage in the obstetric patient is usually due to uterine atony or retained products of conception [45]. Mothers can lose a significant volume of blood rapidly because uterine blood flow can be 700 mL/min to 900 mL/min at term [46].

What is the optimal management for the parturient with severe obstetric hemorrhage? Recent studies that have reviewed data from military trauma in Iraq and Afghanistan have found a correlation between survival and an increased ratio of fresh frozen plasma and platelets in soldiers who received massive transfusions [47]. Hypothermia, coagulopathy, and acidosis are known to be predictive of mortality in adult trauma victims. Damage control resuscitation is a concept that aims to rapidly reverse this "lethal triad" in order to improve outcomes in the trauma patient [48]. Replacement of blood loss with whole blood or blood equivalents has increasing evidence of improving mortality in the trauma patient. The concepts of fluid management in the trauma patient are discussed in more detail in a previous chapter of this book [49] (see Chapter 8). Should this literature from the military and trauma literature guide our clinical practice with obstetric patients who have massive hemorrhage? Pasquier et al. conducted a retrospective review of 12,226 deliveries in a Paris hospital [50]. Of these deliveries, 142 (1.1%) were complicated by severe postpartum hemorrhage. They divided the patients into two groups: hemorrhage that was controlled with medical management with oxytocin and prostaglandin 2E (sulprostone) alone or hemorrhage that required advanced interventional procedures (such as uterine artery ligation, B-lynch suture, arterial angiographic embolization, or hysterectomy). Patients who received a higher ratio of Fresh Frozen Plasma (FFP): Packed Red Blood Cells (PRBC) (1:1.2 vs. 1:1.6) were associated with decreased odds for requiring advanced interventional procedures. Labor and delivery units have adopted transfusion practices with higher ratios of FFP and platelets in massive obstetric hemorrhage [51]. Further studies are required to define which patients will benefit most from these practices.

9.4   Preeclampsia

Preeclampsia is one of the leading causes of maternal mortality and morbidity. Preeclampsia is characterized by maternal hypertension, edema, and proteinuria. In severe forms, preeclampsia can involve multiple organ systems with seizures (eclampsia), renal insufficiency, hepatic dysfunction, and pulmonary edema [52]. These women have decreased oncotic pressures due to low serum albumin levels. This low oncotic pressure can result in peripheral edema, although they may be intravascularly volume depleted because of the hypoalbuminemia. The mechanism of how preeclampsia occurs is not fully understood. Leading theories propose that preeclampsia develops as an immune reaction of the mother to the foreign fetus. Early effects of preeclampsia involve poor placental implantation into the uterus. This can result in intrauterine growth restriction and a fetus that may be less tolerant of labor. Later effects of preeclampsia are suggested to arise from maternal systemic inflammatory response. Preeclampsia is also characterized by increased capillary permeability, which may cause organ system dysfunction [52].

There is significant debate in the literature regarding fluid management in these patients. Due to increased vascular permeability and low oncotic pressure, there is a concern that the preeclampsia patient has intravascular volume depletion [53,54]. This is despite significant peripheral edema, and these patients may in fact be total body volume overloaded. Fluid expansion has been advocated previously to improve the preeclamptic patient's volume status. This improved volume status was proposed to improve uteroplacental blood flow and decrease the risk of renal failure. However, studies that have looked at fluid expansion in the preeclamptic patient have found little improvement in either maternal or fetal outcomes [55]. Other authors advocate fluid loading in these patients during specific interventions—such as initiation of neuraxial anesthesia, administration of antihypertensive medications, or maternal oliguria [53]. Specifically looking at neuraxial anesthesia, fluid loading has been recommended to decrease the incidence of maternal hypotension. However, studies comparing preeclamptic to non-preeclamptic patients have found decreased incidence of hypotension in general in the preeclamptic patients [56]. Specifically, in this study, all patients were given 1,500–2,000 mL of fluid at the time that their spinal anesthetics were administered.

On the other hand, patients with preeclampsia are at risk of developing pulmonary edema. There are multiple factors that contribute to this risk: low oncotic pressure, increased vascular permeability and magnesium administration. Excessive fluid administration can increase the risk of developing pulmonary edema. Currently, there are no specific guidelines from the American College of Obstetrics and Gynecology regarding fluid management in the preeclamptic patient [57]. Avoidance of excessive fluid administration seems reasonable; however, tight fluid restriction seems unnecessary. The exception to this would be patients who have developed pulmonary edema, where fluid administration should be limited.

References

1. Culen KA, Hall MJ, Golosinskiy A. *Ambulatory Surgery in the United States, 2006, Revised.* National Health Statistics Reports, Hyattsville, MD, 2009.
2. Tally WC, Tarabadkar S, Kovalenko BV. Safety and feasibility of outpatient ACDF in an ambulatory setting: A retrospective chart review. *The International Journal of Spine Surgery.* 2013;7(1):e84–7.
3. Brattwall M, Warren-Stomberg M, Jakobsson J. Outcomes, measures and recovery after ambulatory surgery and anaesthesia: A review. *Current Anesthesiology Reports.* 2014;4(4):334–41.

4. Mythen MG, Webb AR. Perioperative plasma volume expansion reduces the incidence of gut mucosal hypoperfusion during cardiac surgery. *Archives of Surgery*. 1995;130:423–9.
5. Magner JJ, McCaul C, Carton E, Gardiner J, Buggy D. Effect of intraoperative intravenous crystalloid infusion on postoperative nausea and vomiting after gynaecological laparoscopy: Comparison of 30 and 10 ml kg(-1). *British Journal of Anaesthesia*. 2004;93(3):381–5.
6. Maharaj CH, Kallam SR, Malik A, Hassett P, Grady D, Laffey JG. Preoperative intravenous fluid therapy decreases postoperative nausea and pain in high risk patients. *Anesthesia Analgesia*. 2005;100(3):675–82.
7. Apfel CC, Meyer A, Orhan-Sungur M, Jalota L, Whelan RP, Jukar-Rao S. Supplemental intravenous crystalloids for the prevention of postoperative nausea and vomiting: Quantitative review. *British Journal of Anesthesia*. 2012;108(6):893–902.
8. Haentjens LL, Ghoundiwal D, Touhiri K, Renard M, Engelman E, Anaf V, et al. Does infusion of colloid influence the occurrence of postoperative nausea and vomiting after elective surgery in women? *Anesthesia and Analgesia*. 2009;108(6):1788–93.
9. Gan TJ, Diemunsch P, Habib AS, Kovac A, Kranke P, Meyer TA, et al. Consensus guidelines for the management of postoperative nausea and vomiting. *Anesthesia and Analgesia*. 2014;118(1):85–113.
10. Suntheralinham Y, Asokumar B, Cheng D, Chung F. A prospective randomized double-blinded study of the effect of intravenous fluid therapy of adverse outcomes on outpatient surgery. *Anesthesia and Analgesia*. 1995;80:682–6.
11. American Society of Anesthesiologists Committee. Practice guidelines for preoperative fasting and the use of pharmacologic agents to reduct the risk of pulmonary aspiration: Application to healthy patients undergoing elective procedures. *Anesthesiology*. 2011;114(3):495–511.
12. Jacob M, Chappell D, Conzen P, Finsterer U, Rehm M. Blood volume is normal after pre-operative overnight fasting. *Acta Anaesthesiologica Scandinavica*. 2008;52(4):522–9.
13. Kratzing C. Pre-operative nutrition and carbohydrate loading. *The Proceedings of the Nutrition Society*. 2011;70(3):311–15.
14. Lidder P, Thomas S, Fleming S, Hosie K, Shaw S, Lewis S. A randomized placebo controlled trial of preoperative carbohydrate drinks and early postoperative nutritional supplement drinks in colorectal surgery. *Colorectal Disease: The Official Journal of the Association of Coloproctology of Great Britain and Ireland*. 2013;15(6):737–45.
15. Hausel J, Nygren J, Lagerkranser M, Hellstrom PM, Hammarqvist F, Almstrom C, et al. A carbohydrate-rich drink reduces preoperative discomfort in elective surgery patients. *Anesthesia and Analgesia*. 2001;93:1344–50.
16. Bopp C, Hofer S, Klein A, Weigand MA, Martin E, Gust R. A liberal preoperative fasting regimen improves patient comfort and satisfaction with anesthesia care in day-stay minor surgery. *Minerva Anestesiologica*. 2011;77:680–6.
17. Holte K, Klarskov B, Christensen DS, Lund C, Nielsen KG, Bie P, et al. Liberal versus restrictive fluid administration to improve recovery after laparoscopic cholecystectomy. *Annals of Surgery*. 2004;240(5):892–9.
18. Holte K. Pathophysiology and clinical implications of perioperative fluid management in elective surgery. *Danish Medical Bulletin*. 2010;57(7):B4156.

19. Holte K, Kehlet H. Fluid therapy and surgical outcomes in elective surgery: A need for reassessment in fast-track surgery. *Journal of the American College of Surgeons.* 2006;202(6):971–89.
20. Della Rocca G, Vetrugno L, Tripi G, Deana C, Barbariol F, Pompei L. Liberal or restricted fluid administration: Are we ready for a proposal of a restricted intraoperative approach? *BMC Anesthesiology.* 2014;14:62.
21. Gan T, Soppitt A, Maroof M, El-Moalem H, Roberston K, Moretti E, et al. Goal-directed intraoperative fluid administration reduced length of hospital stay after major surgery. *Anesthesiology.* 2002;97:820–6.
22. Wakeling HG, McFall MR, Jenkins CS, Woods WG, Miles WF, Barclay GR, et al. Intraoperative oesophageal Doppler guided fluid management shortens postoperative hospital stay after major bowel surgery. *British Journal of Anaesthesia.* 2005;95(5):634–42.
23. Nisanevich V, Felsenstein I, Almogy G, Weissman C, Einav S, Matot I. Effect of intraoperative fluid management on outcome after intraabdominal surgery. *Anesthesiology.* 2005;103:25–32.
24. McKenny M, Conroy P, Wong A, Farren M, Gleeson N, Walsh C, et al. A randomised prospective trial of intra-operative oesophageal Doppler-guided fluid administration in major gynaecological surgery. *Anaesthesia.* 2013;68(12):1224–31.
25. Kalogera E, Bakkum-Gamez JN, Jankowski CJ, Trabuco E, Lovely JK, Dhanorker S, et al. Enhanced recovery in gynecologic surgery. *Obstetrics and Gynecology.* 2013;122(2 Pt 1):319–28.
26. Yoong W, Sivashanmugarajan V, Relph S, Bell A, Fajemirokun E, Davies T, et al. Can enhanced recovery pathways improve outcomes of vaginal hysterectomy? Cohort control study. *Journal of Minimally Invasive Gynecology.* 2014;21(1):83–9.
27. Collins KM, Bevan DR, Beard WR. Fluid loading to reduce abnormalities of fetal heart rate and maternal hypotension during epidural analgeisa in labour. *British Medical Journal.* 1978;2(1978):1460–1.
28. Cheek TG, Samuels P, Miller F, Tobin M, Gutsche BB. Normal saline i.v. fluid load decreases uterine activity in active labour. 1996;77:632–5.
29. Kinsella S, Pirlet M, Mills M, Tuckey J, Thomas T. Randomized study of intravenous fluid preload before epidural analgeisa during labor. *British Journal of Anaesthesia.* 2000;85:311–13.
30. Kubli M, Shennan AH, Seed PT, O'Sullivan G. A randomised controlled trial of fluid pre-loading before low dose epidural analgesia for labour. *International Journal of Obstetric Anesthesia.* 2003;12(4):256–60.
31. Macaulay BD, Barton MD, Norris MC, Bottros L. Prehydration and combined spinal epidural labor analgesia (abstract). *Anesthesiology.* 2000;92(Suppl):A83.
32. Hofmeyr G, Cyna A, Middleton P. Prophylactic intravenous preloading for regional analgesia in labour (review). *Cochrane Database of Systematic Reviews.* 2004;(4):CD000175.
33. Dyer RA, Farina Z, Joubert IA, Du Toit P, Meyer M, Torr G, et al. Crystalloid preload versus rapid crystalloid administration after induction of spinal anaesthesia (coload) for elective caesarean section. *Anesthesia and Intensive Care.* 2004;32(3):351–7.
34. Ueyama H, He Y, Tanigami H, Mashimo T, Yoshiya I. Effects of crystalloid and colloid preload on blood volume in the patient undergoing spinal anesthesia for elective cesarean section. *Anesthesiology.* 1999;91:1571–6.

35. Oh A-Y, Hwang J-W, Song I-A, Kim M-H, Ryu J-H, Park H-P, et al. Influence of the timing of administration of crystalloid on maternal hypotension during spinal anesthesia for cesarean delivery: Preload versus coload. *BMC Anesthesiology*. 2014;14:36.
36. Tamilselvan P, Fernando R, Bray J, Sodhi M, Columb M. The effects of crystalloid and colloid preload on cardiac output in the parturient undergoing planned cesarean delivery under spinal anesthesia: A randomized trial. *Anesthesia and Analgesia*. 2009;109(6):1916–21.
37. Teoh WH, Sia AT. Colloid preload versus coload for spinal anesthesia for cesarean delivery: The effects on maternal cardiac output. *Anesthesia and Analgesia*. 2009;108(5):1592–8.
38. Mercier FJ. Fluid loading for cesarean delivery under spinal anesthesia: Have we studied all the options? *Anesthesia and Analgesia*. 2011;113(4):677–80.
39. Butwick A, Carvalho B. The effect of colloid and crystalloid preloading on thromboelastography prior to cesarean delivery. *Canadian Journal of Anaesthesia = Journal canadien d'anesthesie*. 2007;54(3):190–5.
40. Tawfik MM, Hayes SM, Jacoub FY, Badran BA, Gohar FM, Shabana AM, et al. Comparison between colloid preload and crystalloid co-load in cesarean section under spinal anesthesia: A randomized controlled trial. *International Journal of Obstetric Anesthesia*. 2014;23(4):317–23.
41. Ngan Kee WD, Khaw KS, Ng FF, Lee BB. Prophylactic phenylephrine infusion for preventing hypotension during spinal anesthesia for cesarean delivery. *Anesthesia and Analgesia*. 2004;98(3):815–21.
42. Ngan Kee WD, Khaw KS, Ng FF. Prevention of hypotension during spinal anesthesia for cesarean delivery. *Anesthesiology*. 2005;103:744–50.
43. Callaghan WM, Kuklina EV, Berg CJ. Trends in postpartum hemorrhage: United States, 1994–2006. *American Journal of Obstetrics and Gynecology*. 2010;202(4):353.e1–6.
44. Chandra S, Tripathi AK, Mishra S, Amzarul M, Vaish AK. Physiological changes in hematological parameters during pregnancy. *Indian Journal of Hematology & Blood Transfusion: An Official Journal of Indian Society of Hematology and Blood Transfusion*. 2012;28(3):144–6.
45. American College of Obstetricians and Gynecologists. Postpartum hemorrhage. ACOG Practice Bulletin No 76. *Obstetrics and Gynecology*. 2006;108:1039–47.
46. Konje JC, Kaufmann P, Bell SC, Taylor DJ. A longitudinal study of quantitative uterine blood flow with the use of color power angiography in appropriate for gestational age pregnancies. *American Journal of Obstetrics and Gynecology*. 2001;185(3):608–13.
47. Pidcoke HF, Aden JK, Mora AG, Borgman MA, Spinella PC, Dubick MA, et al. Ten-year analysis of transfusion in operation Iraqi freedom and operation enduring freedom: Increased plasma and platelet use correlates with improved survival. *The Journal of Trauma and Acute Care Surgery*. 2012;73(6 Suppl 5):S445–52.
48. Hess JR, Brohi K, Dutton RP, Hauser CJ, Holcomb JB, Kluger Y, et al. The coagulopathy of trauma: A review of mechanisms. *The Journal of Trauma*. 2008;65(4):748–54.

49. Holcomb JB, del Junco DJ, Fox EE, Wade CE, Cohen MJ, Schreiber MA, et al. The Prospective, Observational, Multicenter, Major Trauma Transfusion (PROMMTT) Study: Comparative effectiveness of a time-varying treatment with competing risks. *JAMA Surgery.* 2013;148(2):127–36.

50. Pasquier P, Gayat E, Rackelboom T, La Rosa J, Tashkandi A, Tesniere A, et al. An observational study of the fresh frozen plasma: Red blood cell ratio in postpartum hemorrhage. *Anesthesia and Analgesia.* 2013;116(1):155–61.

51. Shields LE, Smalarz K, Reffigee L, Mugg S, Burdumy TJ, Propst M. Comprehensive maternal hemorrhage protocols improve patient safety and reduce utilization of blood products. *American Journal of Obstetrics and Gynecology.* 2011;205(4):368.e1–8.

52. Steegers EAP, von Dadelszen P, Duvekot J, Pijnenborg R. Pre-eclampsia. *Lancet.* 2010;376:631–44.

53. Robson SC. Fluid restriction policies in preeclampsia are obsolete. *International Journal of Obstetric Anesthesia.* 1999;8:49–55.

54. Engelhardt T, MacLennan FM. Fluid management in pre-eclampsia. *International Journal of Obstetric Anesthesia.* 1999;8:253–9.

55. Ganzevoort W, Rep A, Bonsel GJ, Fetter WP, van Sonderen L, De Vries JI, et al. A randomised controlled trial comparing two temporising management strategies, one with and one without plasma volume expansion, for severe and early onset pre-eclampsia. *BJOG: An International Journal of Obstetrics and Gynaecology.* 2005;112(10):1358–68.

56. Aya AG, Vialles N, Tanoubi I, Mangin R, Ferrer JM, Robert C, et al. Spinal anesthesia-induced hypotension: A risk comparison between patients with severe preeclampsia and healthy women undergoing preterm cesarean delivery. *Anesthesia and Analgesia.* 2005;101(3):869–75.

57. American College of Obstetricians and Gynecologists, Task Force on Hypertension in Pregnancy. Hypertension in pregnancy, report of the American College of Obstetrician and Gynecologists' Task Force on hypertension in pregnancy. *Obstetrics and Gynecology.* 2013;122(5):1122–31.

chapter ten

Perioperative fluid management in patients undergoing abdominal surgery

Focus on enhanced recovery programs after surgery

Juan C. Gómez-Izquierdo, Gabriele Baldini, and Liane S. Feldman
McGill University
Montreal, QC, Canada

Contents

Key points:
This chapter deals with

- Fluid therapy in enhanced recovery after surgery programs (ERP)
- Preoperative considerations and management of blood transfusion
- Perioperative blood management
- Intraoperative fluid therapy during abdominal surgery with ERP
- Goal-directed fluid therapy
- Postoperative fluid therapy
- Management in the surgical unit

10.1   Introduction

Enhanced recovery programs (ERP) are multidisciplinary care pathways that include standardized perioperative evidence-based interventions aiming at attenuating organ dysfunction induced by surgical stress, reducing morbidity, and supporting rapid functional recovery (Table 10.1) [1–4]. Evidence-based guidelines for best practices in perioperative care are available for different types of abdominal procedures, including colon surgery, rectal and pelvic surgery, gastrectomy, radical cystectomy and pancreaticoduodenectomy [5–9]. In all of these guidelines, perioperative fluid management is considered a key part of ERPs [10], as fluid administration in absence of hypovolemia has been extensively shown to delay the recovery of bowel function, increase overall morbidity, and prolong hospital stay [11–13]. Fluid excess also affects tissue perfusion by increasing intra-abdominal pressure [14], directly reduces absorption of nutrients, and prolongs postoperative ileus [15,16]. On the other hand, hypoperfusion secondary to hypovolemia also increases postoperative complications, especially in patients undergoing gastrointestinal surgery [17–19]. Intravenous fluids should be considered and used as any other medications, administered when indicated, at a predetermined infusion rate, and acknowledging side effects that can negatively affect surgical recovery [10,20].

Perioperative fluid management in patients undergoing abdominal surgery is still controversial. However, over the years the amount of fluids that are commonly infused has been significantly reduced, as common principles supporting the need of infusing large volume of fluids to maintain normovolemia during abdominal surgery have been challenged. In fact, emerging evidence, from clinical and experimental studies, has shown that the volume of fluid needed to maintain adequate organ perfusion is significantly lower than what it is commonly administered. However, large variability in crystalloid administration still exists within and between caregivers [21]. The aim of this chapter is to discuss perioperative fluid management in patients undergoing abdominal surgery,

Table 10.1 Elements included in enhanced recovery programs for abdominal surgery

	Intervention
Preoperative period	Information, education, and counseling
	Preoperative optimization (smoking and alcohol cessation, preoperative nutrition, anemia, physical conditioning)
	Minimization of preoperative fasting
	Carbohydrate loading
Intraoperative period	Anesthetic agents allowing rapid emergence from anesthesia
	Open surgery
	Thoracic epidural blockade
	Laparoscopic surgery
	Spinal analgesia morphine
	Intravenous lidocaine
	Abdominal trunk blocks
	Postoperative nausea and vomiting prophylaxis
	Minimally invasive surgery
	Maintenance of normothermia
	Glycemic control
	Fluid balance
Postoperative period	Avoidance or early removal of tubes and drains
	Early removal of urinary catheter
	Early oral feeding
	Implementation of anti-ileus strategies
	Glycemic control
	Multimodal analgesia
	Early mobilization
	Criteria-based discharge

specifically in the context of an ERP. Fluid management will be influenced by several individual elements of ERPs that differ from traditional care, and these will be discussed to provide an integrated multidisciplinary approach.

10.2   Preoperative considerations and management of blood transfusion

In the preoperative phase, ERPs include interventions that will significantly reduce the intravascular deficit compared to traditional care and therefore will affect the amount of intravenous fluids needed to achieve normovolemia before surgery [22,23]. These include selective use of mechanical bowel preparation (MBP), minimization of preoperative fasting, and use of preoperative carbohydrate drinks.

MBP produces physiological changes that significantly dehydrate patients. Patients receiving MBP lose about 1.2 kg of their weight and experience an increase in their plasma osmolality. Similarly, the plasmatic concentration of urea and phosphate is augmented while the concentration of potassium and calcium decreases [24]. It has been demonstrated that after MBP 1.5–2 L of intravenous fluids are necessary to replace intravascular volume and prevent orthostatic intolerance [25,26]. These physiologic changes are more pronounced in elderly patients [27], and up to 2–3 L of supplemental crystalloids are necessary to maintain them hydrated and normovolemic [22]. While routine MBP prior to gynecologic or urologic surgery should be omitted, its role in bowel surgery, particularly left-sided and rectal resection, remains controversial as emerging evidence suggests that the addition of oral antibiotics may decrease surgical site infections after bowel surgery.

Prolonged preoperative fasting is an unnatural way to prepare for surgery as it induces short-term catabolic changes, magnified by surgical stress, and dehydrates patients. Even though international preoperative fasting guidelines allow clear fluids up to 2 hr before induction of anesthesia and solid food up to 6 hr, it is still common practice to keep patients fasting after midnight the day before an operation [28]. Adherence to international preoperative fasting guidelines improves patients' wellbeing and reduces insulin resistance [29]. Despite early evidence suggesting that preoperative fasting can cause hypovolemia [30], recent studies have shown that even prolonged preoperative fasting (>8 hr) in patients not receiving MBP minimally reduces intravascular volume [31]. Moreover, preoperative intravascular volume in patients following preoperative fasting guidelines and not receiving MBP is on average 200 mL (median 200 mL, interquartile range (IQR) 0–600 mL); and 30% of the patients undergoing surgery under these circumstances are normovolemic before surgery [32]. This implies that replacing intravascular deficit with fixed volumes (e.g., the 4/2/1 rule), instead of individualizing fluid therapy by measuring fluid responsiveness, can significantly increase the risk of fluid overloading.

Preoperative carbohydrate (CHO) drinks are given in attempt to attenuate insulin resistance induced by surgical stress. Although it seems intuitive that administering preoperative CHO drinks 2 hr before induction of anesthesia might also reduce the preoperative intravascular deficit, these benefits have never been proven [33]. Similarly, evidence supporting the use of CHO to improve patients' well-being, reduce postoperative nausea and vomiting, accelerate the recovery of gastrointestinal function, and shorten the length of hospital stay is inconclusive and supported by low-quality trials [33].

Clear preoperative educational material, including institutional preoperative fasting policy and use of CHO drinks, is an essential element of an ERP. Well-designed materials at the appropriate health literacy level that engage patients in their own perioperative care will help patients arrive in a catabolic state to surgery. In addition, they provide information to help reduce the risk of errors in following the guidelines and subsequent cancellation of surgery in case patients do not stop food or fluids at the correct time.

10.3   Perioperative blood management

The goal of administering intravenous fluids is to ensure optimal oxygen delivery by maintaining preload [34]. Oxygen delivery depends on several factors such as cardiac output and arterial oxygen content (determined by hemoglobin levels, oxygen saturation, and less importantly partial arterial oxygen pressure) [35]. As hemoglobin concentration is one of the most important determinants of arterial oxygen content, in patients with adequate perioperative hemoglobin levels, oxygen delivery will mainly depend on preload and myocardial contractility. In patients with chronic anemia, physiological compensatory mechanisms such as increased cardiac output, selective organ vasodilation (brain and heart), and increased oxygen extraction guarantee adequate oxygen delivery [36]. However, this physiological compensation can be inadequate during acute intraoperative anemia secondary to blood losses and hemodilution due to intraoperative fluid administration, resulting in tissue hypoxia [36].

Preoperative anemia is a very common condition, being present in about 75% of the patients undergoing elective surgery and accounting for 90% of postoperative anemia [36]. In colorectal surgical patients, the prevalence of anemia ranges from 22% to 76% depending on the type of diagnosis and on the stage of colorectal cancer [37]. Regardless of its severity (mild, moderate, or severe), preoperative anemia increases the likelihood of adverse clinical outcomes [38,39], and it is associated with increased 30-day mortality and prolonged hospital stays [40]. Similarly, data from large retrospective databases has shown that allogeneic blood transfusions are also associated with increased morbidity, mortality, and increased hospital costs [41,42], suggesting that correcting perioperative anemia by simply transfusing patients does not improve postoperative outcomes. This is also confirmed by studies demonstrating that blood transfusions do not improve survival in nonbleeding patients, likely because of the presence of upregulating prothrombotic mechanisms, damaged red blood cells, and disturbance of the nitric oxide physiology, which may be responsible for some of the perioperative complications related to this intervention [43].

The concept of perioperative blood management (PBM) was recently introduced, with the purpose of implementing perioperative multidisciplinary evidence-based interventions aiming at maintaining perioperative hemoglobin levels within normal values, maintaining homeostasis, and minimizing blood loss [41,44]. Even though inadequate PBM can negatively impact postoperative outcomes [41,44] and significantly affect perioperative fluid management [44,45], it has never been integrated in ERPs.

Perioperative PBM strategies aim at [36,44]

- Optimizing preoperative red cell volume
- Minimizing intraoperative blood loss
- Increasing anemia tolerance and utilizing patient specific hemoglobin thresholds triggering transfusion

Optimizing preoperative red cell volume by prompt detection, evaluation, and correction of preoperative anemia is extremely important [46]. In colorectal patients scheduled for surgery a preoperative hemoglobin level less than 13 g/dL for both genders should require further investigation [47]. Depending on patient's diagnosis and comorbidities, preoperative blood tests such as reticulocyte count, iron levels, folic acid, and when necessary inflammatory markers such as C-reactive protein, depending on the patient context, can provide further useful information to identify the etiology of anemia [47]. Iron replacement therapy to correct iron deficiency anemia has been shown to be effective. Intravenous iron 2–4 weeks before surgery is safe and it has been shown to increase hemoglobin levels. Oral iron replacement is an alternative, but it seems not to be as effective and tolerable as intravenous replacement [48]. Folate and vitamin B12 supplements are useful to correct macrocytic anemia. If anemia is associated to chronic diseases, the concomitant use of intravenous iron and erythropoiesis stimulating agents (ESAs) could also be considered [49]. However, the role of ESAs in correcting perioperative anemia is still debatable and the use of ESAs might increase the risk of thrombotic events [50]. Optimization of preoperative anemia might not be always feasible, as it takes time (up to several weeks). Correction of preoperative hemoglobin levels with red blood cell transfusions and bone marrow stimulating agents might not be sufficient to improve postoperative outcomes [36,41,43].

Several strategies can be used to minimize blood loss during surgery. Promoting preoperative alcohol abstinence in alcohol abusers might also reduce the risk of perioperative bleeding and allogeneic

blood transfusions [51,52]. The results of an observational study performed in chronic alcoholics with more than 10 years of daily alcohol consumption (mean daily ethanol consumption 354 ± 97 grams)
showed an improvement of plasmatic levels of coagulation factors
within 1 week of alcohol abstinence [53]. Although it is a reasonable
hypothesis that alcohol abstinence could decrease perioperative hemorrhagic events, since coagulation factors are synthesized in the liver
and alcoholic liver disease also causes thrombocytopenia [54], stronger evidence is warranted [55]. Minimally invasive surgery (such as
laparoscopy, robotic surgery, or modification of surgical access) [56]
and prevention of intraoperative hypothermia [57] are well-established
ERP elements that decrease intraoperative blood loss. Prophylactic use
of antifibrinolytic agents has also shown to minimize blood loss and
allogeneic blood transfusion [58,59]. Specifically, tranexamic acid has
proven to reduce the risk of transfusions in hepatic (risk ratio [RR] =
0.52, 95% confidence interval [CI] = 0.39–0.68), urological (RR = 0.66, 95%
CI = 0.48–0.91), vascular (RR = 0.58, 95% CI = 0.34–0.99), and gynecological (RR = 0.86, 95% CI = 0.48–1.54) surgery [59]. Acute normovolemic
hemodilution (ANH) has also been proposed as a strategy to minimize
the risk of allogeneic blood transfusions, minimizing the risk of infections and transfusion reactions, mainly in patients undergoing major
urological surgery [60,61]. However, meta-analyses (including 42 and 24
randomized controlled trials [RCTs], respectively) did not confirm these
benefits and the safety of ANH was challenged [62,63], mainly concerning the risk of hypoxic kidney injury [64]. Preoperative autologous
blood donation might constitute a reasonable option in the absence of
preoperative anemia, in patients at high risk (10%–50%) of allogeneic
blood transfusion, with uncommon blood types, or refusing allogeneic transfusions [65]. However, it was demonstrated to be expensive,
time-consuming, and to waste blood products if autologous blood is
not transfused [60]. If indicated, preoperative autologous blood transfusions should be supplemented with iron or erythropoietin to prevent
patients arriving anemic to surgery [65].

Appropriate fluid administration techniques are essential to ensure
adequate oxygen delivery, including prompt use of vasopressor in vaso-
dilated normovolemic patients [66,67]. Based on this principle, oxygen
delivery can be ameliorated even in the presence of reduced levels
of hemoglobin, which might be the case in oncologic patients with
reduced physiological reserve, through the optimization of cardiac output with vasopressors [35,68,69]. If hemoglobin levels cannot be corrected before surgery, judicious use of vasopressors and inotropes can
maintain adequate oxygen delivery to ensure optimal tissue perfusion
and oxygenation [70]. Experimental studies have demonstrated that
norepinephrine increases anemia tolerance by maintaining myocardial

perfusion, and it could represent a short-term therapeutic intervention to bridge acute anemia [35,70,71]. The consensus statement from the Enhanced Recovery Partnership suggests targeting hemoglobin concentration >7 g/dL at the end of the surgery [10]. Even though allogeneic blood transfusions increase the risk of perioperative morbidity, mortality, and potentially the risk of cancer recurrence [72,73], it must be acknowledged that hemoglobin transfusion thresholds might be higher for certain patient populations, particularly patients with coronary artery disease and elderly patients [74,75]. Hemoglobin transfusion threshold should be individualized, taking into account patient comorbidities, markers of tissue hypoxia, surgical risk, and the clinical setting [76,77].

In summary, PBM includes multidisciplinary and multimodal individualized perioperative strategies that aim at attenuating the negative impact of anemia on postoperative outcomes and decrease the perioperative need of allogeneic blood transfusions and its associated risks [47,78].

10.4   Intraoperative fluid therapy during abdominal surgery within an ERP

The main objectives of fluid therapy during abdominal surgery are to:

1. Cover and maintain the needs derived from salt–water homeostasis
2. Maintain normovolemia

10.4.1   Covering and maintaining the needs derived from salt–water homeostasis

Adequate intraoperative fluid management is essential to ensure optimal organ perfusion. This should be achieved by avoiding fluid overload or excessive fluid restriction, which can both significantly impair organ function [10,79]. This is particularly important for patients undergoing abdominal surgery, in whom surgical trauma leads to impairment of gastrointestinal motility, which can be aggravated both by hypovolemia and excessive fluid administration [22]. The former causes splanchnic hypoperfusion [80,81], with perfusion of the bowels a critical determinant of bowel motility [82], while the latter causes edema of the bowel wall and surrounding structures, impairing oxygenation, and affecting bowel peristalsis [18,83]. Furthermore, excessive fluid administration or splanchnic ischemia secondary to hypovolemia can both significantly impair intestinal anastomotic healing and increase the risk of anastomotic dehiscence [84].

Recognizing that the optimal intraoperative fluid regimen in the context of ERP is still a subject of debate [5], the following considerations should be considered when infusing intravenous fluids:

- *Replacement of insensible blood loss*: Traditionally, intravenous fluids up to 7–8 mL/kg/hr have been infused to replace intravascular deficit caused by insensible losses, which include evaporation of fluids caused by surgical wound exposure, respiration, and transpiration. However, insensible blood losses have been measured, and even when the bowel is fully exteriorized from the abdominal cavity insensible blood losses do not exceed 1 mL/kg/hr [85–87]. Moreover, it should be also considered that with the introduction of minimally invasive techniques such as laparoscopic surgery, insensible losses are further reduced [85,87,88].

- *Replacement of third-space losses*: Replacement of third-space losses is a concept described more than 50 years ago [89]. Results from early studies using outdated tracer-dilution techniques showed that surgical trauma induces a reduction of the extracellular volume that was not fully accounted for from external losses (blood, urine, gastrointestinal fluids). To explain this deficit, it was hypothesized that fluids internally redistributed or were sequestrated into another compartment, known as the "third space." This space was hypothesized to be adjacent to the surgical wound, in the splanchnic bed, or in the intracellular compartment, but further research failed to anatomically localize or physiologically characterize this compartment [90–92]. It should be kept in mind that several perioperative factors such as hypotension, fluid overload, and different tracer equilibrium times can affect radiotracer distribution kinetics and might have partially explained these initial results [88,93,94]. In contrast, more recent evidence using advanced tracer-dilution techniques has consistently shown that after surgery extracellular volume is expanded and not decreased [95].

- *Surgical trauma disrupts the endothelial glycocalyx, altering the function of the vascular barrier*: The endothelial glycocalyx is the main determinant of the endothelial permeability. It is a fine layer of proteoglycans and glycoproteins covering the endothelium (see Chapter 1) that maintains the intravascular oncotic pressure by keeping plasma proteins in the intravascular space [96]. There are multiple perioperative factors that disrupt the integrity of the glycocalyx such as inflammation secondary to surgical insult, ischemia/reperfusion, and releasing of atrial natriuretic peptide (ANP) [97–99]. Infusing a large volume of intravenous fluids or rapidly infusing intravenous fluids in normovolemic patients increases intravascular hydrostatic pressure, triggering the release of ANP, which sheds the endothelial glycocalyx. As a result, intravenous fluids shift into the interstitial space and tissue edema occurs. Excessive perioperative fluid administration, aiming to replace third spaces losses into a compartment that has never been identified, further damages the endothelial glycocalyx and augments the amount of intravenous fluids that accumulate in the interstitial space [88,100].

Based on these considerations, an intravenous infusion of 3 ± 2 mL/kg/hr of balanced crystalloid solutions is sufficient to cover the needs derived from salt–water homeostasis during major abdominal surgery, avoiding substantial postoperative weight gain (>2.5 kg per day), which is associated with increased morbidity [11] and mortality [101].

10.4.2   Maintaining normovolemia

Intraoperative blood loss and shift of intravascular fluids into the interstitial space due to an increased endovascular permeability leads to a reduction of intravascular volume. Maintaining normovolemia is challenging since common clinical measures of hypovolemia such as heart rate, blood pressure, urine output, central venous pressure, and pulmonary wedge pressure are inaccurate in measuring preload [102,103] and predicting fluid responsiveness [20]. During laparoscopic abdominal surgery, it is even more complicated, as pneumoperitoneum and frequent changes in position can significantly affect hemodynamic variables, independently from the volume status. These considerations are extremely important in patients undergoing gastrointestinal surgery. Indeed, the gastrointestinal tract is very sensitive to tissue hypoperfusion as it is early affected by reductions of just 10%–15% of the circulating volume, before any clinical sign of hypovolemia is manifested [104,105]. It has been found that gastric perfusion, measured by tonometry, is reduced in healthy subjects exposed to an acute reduction of 25%–30% of their circulating volume without manifesting any change in heart rate or blood pressure [105]. This indicates that the usual variables to guide fluid administration during surgery such as heart rate, blood pressure, urinary output, and central venous pressure are not accurate to early detect splanchnic hypoperfusion [106,107].

10.5   Goal directed fluid therapy

Goal-directed fluid therapy (GDFT) (see also Chapters 3, 4, and 9) aims to optimize intravascular volume based on more objective measures of hypovolemia to ensure optimal cardiac output and organ perfusion. Based on the Frank–Starling curve, the only reason to administer intravenous fluids is to increase preload to the extent that a significant increase in cardiac output ($\geq$10%–15%) is produced. This requires cardiac output measurements before and after volume expansion and, when indicated, the use of inotrope agents to increase myocardial contractility in patients with poor ventricular systolic function. Dynamic indices of preload such as pulse pressure variation, stroke volume variation, and systolic pressure variation are useful hemodynamic indices that can highly predict fluid responsiveness before intravenous fluids are administered. However, it must be acknowledged that the accuracy of these indices to predict fluid responsiveness has been validated in paralyzed, mechanically ventilated patients with a tidal volume of >8 mL/kg, in sinus rhythm and without an open thorax or increased abdominal pressure. These conditions are only present in slightly more than 50% of the patients undergoing general anesthesia for abdominal surgery [108] and probably even less during laparoscopic surgery, limiting the clinical applicability of these indices [109–112]. In these settings a fluid challenge may be a more valuable alternative to predict fluid responsiveness [20,96]. Several GDFT algorithms have been used. However, they can be divided in two categories: GDFT algorithms aiming at preemptively maximizing stroke volume, and GDFT algorithms aiming to optimize stroke volume only when clinically indicated (Figure 10.1).

The beneficial impact of GDFT on postoperative outcomes remains controversial, especially within the context of an ERP [97]. A recent meta-analysis [98], including 31 RCTs of patients undergoing major surgery mainly without an ERAS program, found that GDFT, with or without inotropes, reduced the number of patients with complications, specifically, renal impairment (RR = 0.71, 95% CI = 0.57–0.90), wound infection (RR = 0.65, 95% CI = 0.50–0.84), respiratory failure (RR = 0.51, 95% CI = 0.28–0.93), and shortened the length of hospital stay by approximately 1 day (weighted mean difference = –1.16, 95% CI = –1.89 to –1.43). Table 10.2 summarizes studies assessing the impact of GDFT on postoperative outcomes after abdominal surgery.

However, four consecutive RCTs [99,113–115], mainly conducted in the context of an ERP, and including two large multicenter RCTs (OPTIMISE) [113,114], did not confirm these findings. It might be possible that the benefits observed in patients treated with GDFT and reported in the early studies might be offset by the advancement of perioperative care and more judicious use of intravenous fluids, as represented by the ERP approach. Nevertheless, GDFT might still be beneficial in patients undergoing high-risk surgery (associated with large fluid shifts and with extensive blood loss, >7 mL/kg) or in high-risk patients [5–9,23,116] (Table 10.3; see also Chapter 8). Auditing institutional data (e.g., blood loss, duration of surgery, amount of intraoperative fluid administered, length of hospital stay, morbidity, and mortality) is also important to

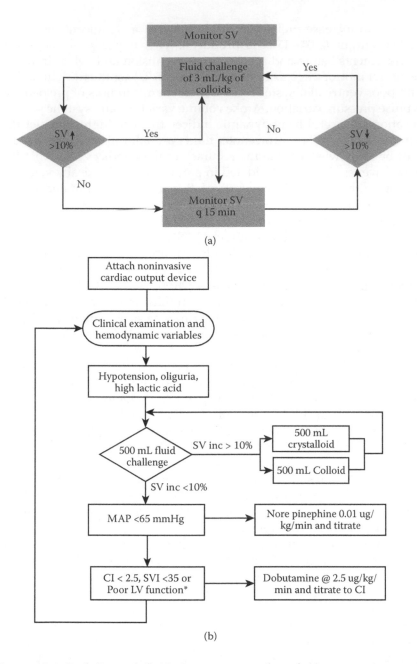

Figure 10.1 Goal-directed fluid therapy: examples of (a) preemptive stroke volume (SV) optimization and (b) SV optimization when clinically indicated. CI, cardiac index; SVI, stroke volume index; LV, left ventricular.

Table 10.2 Articles assessing the impact of GDFT on postoperative outcomes after abdominal surgery

Study/population	ERP	GDFT (Monitor/type of fluids, inotropes/volume/ hemodynamic parameters followed to guide fluid administration)	Control group (Type of fluids, inotropes/ clinical and hemodynamic parameters followed to guide fluid administration)	Outcomes
Benes, 2010 $n = 120$, high-risk Major abdominal surgery (open)	No	Vigileo/FloTrac®. 6% HES (130/0.4), 3 ml⁻¹ kg⁻¹. Dobutamine. CVP and cardiac index, stroke volume variation.	Basal PlasmaLyte® infusion 8 ml⁻¹ kg⁻¹ h⁻¹. Additional intravenous fluids if needed. MAP, HR, CVP, urine output.	• GDFT decreased incidence of organ and infectious complications in the 30-day POP ($P = 0.0033$). • GDFT decreased the incidence and number of total ($P = 0.0132$) and severe complications ($P = 0.0028$). • No significant difference in mortality, ICU and hospital LOS.* • No significant difference in GI tract paresis.*

(*Continued*)

Table 10.2 (Continued) Articles assessing the impact of GDFT on postoperative outcomes after abdominal surgery

Study/population	ERP	GDFT (Monitor/type of fluids, inotropes/volume/ hemodynamic parameters followed to guide fluid administration)	Control group (Type of fluids, inotropes/ clinical and hemodynamic parameters followed to guide fluid administration)	Outcomes
Bisgaard, 2013 $n = 70$ Open abdominal aortic surgery	No	LiDCOplus. Dobutamine (postoperative). 6% HES (130/0.4), 250 ml. Stroke volume index. Intervention extended to POP.	6% HES (130/0.4). Fluid losses, hemodynamic parameters, arterial blood gas.	• No significant difference in the overall number or incidence of complications.* • No significant difference in ICU length of stay or LOS.* • No significant difference in the incidence of "gastrointestinal paralysis."*
Brandstrup, 2012 $n = 150$ Open and laparoscopic colorectal surgery	Yes	Esophageal Doppler. 6% HES, 200 ml. Stroke volume.	Normal saline infusion if preoperative oral intake <500 ml. 6% HES (130/0.4), 200 ml if needed. BP, HR, CVP.	• No significant difference in LOS nor in readiness for discharge.* • No significant difference in mortality nor in the incidence of complications.* • No significant difference in "ileus paralysis."*

(Continued)

Table 10.2 (Continued) Articles assessing the impact of GDFT on postoperative outcomes after abdominal surgery

Study/population	ERP	GDFT (Monitor/type of fluids, inotropes/volume/hemodynamic parameters followed to guide fluid administration)	Control group (Type of fluids, inotropes/clinical and hemodynamic parameters followed to guide fluid administration)	Outcomes
Bundgaard-Nielsen, 2013 *n* = 42 Open radical prostatectomy	No	Esophageal Doppler. 6% HES (130/0.4), 3 ml^{-1} kg^{-1}. Stroke volume. GDFT extended to POP.	Basal infusion of crystalloids associated to replacements of blood losses 1:1 with 6% HES (130/0.4) to a maximum of 50 ml^{-1} kg^{-1}.	• No difference in orthostatic intolerance or hypotension.* • No difference in LOS.* • GDFT improved muscle tissue oxygenation at standing position during an orthostatic tolerance test ($P < 0.05$).

(Continued)

Table 10.2 (Continued) Articles assessing the impact of GDFT on postoperative outcomes after abdominal surgery

Study/population	ERP	GDFT (Monitor/type of fluids, inotropes/volume/ hemodynamic parameters followed to guide fluid administration)	Control group (Type of fluids, inotropes/ clinical and hemodynamic parameters followed to guide fluid administration)	Outcomes
Challand, 2012 $n = 179$ (High-risk, $n = 56$) Major open and laparoscopic colorectal surgery	Yes	Esophageal Doppler. 6% HES (130/0.4), 200 ml. Stroke volume.	Crystalloid, colloid, blood products, and/or inotropes. Fluid losses, hemodynamic parameters.	• No significant difference in LOS nor in readiness for discharge.* • No significant difference in mortality or incidence of complications.* • No significant difference in readmissions.* • No significant difference in time to pass flatus, tolerate diet, and first bowel motion.* • In fit patients, GDFT: readiness for discharge ($P = 0.01$) and LOS ($P = 0.01$) were longer and there was a higher rate of critical care admissions ($P = 0.03$).

(Continued)

Table 10.2 (Continued) Articles assessing the impact of GDFT on postoperative outcomes after abdominal surgery

Study/population	ERP	GDFT (Monitor/type of fluids, inotropes/volume/ hemodynamic parameters followed to guide fluid administration)	Control group (Type of fluids, inotropes/ clinical and hemodynamic parameters followed to guide fluid administration)	Outcomes
Colantonio, 2015 *n* = 80 Cytoreductive surgery with peritonectomy and hyperthermic intraperitoneal chemotherapy High risk (due to the magnitude of the surgical trauma)	No	Vigileo/FloTrac. 6% HES (130/0.4), 250 ml. Dopamine. Cardiac index, stroke volume index, and stroke volume variation.	Basal infusion of crystalloid between 4 and 10 ml^{-1} kg^{-1} h. Boluses of 250 ml of 6% HES (130/0.4). CVP, diuresis, and MAP. Dopamine.	• GDFT decreased the incidence of major abdominal ($P = 0.005$), hepatic ($P < 0.0001$), and cardiac complications ($P = 0.006$). • GDFT decreased the length of hospital stay ($P < 0.0001$). • No difference in the incidence of readmissions to the ICU.* • No significant difference in mortality.*

(Continued)

Table 10.2 (Continued) Articles assessing the impact of GDFT on postoperative outcomes after abdominal surgery

Study/population	ERP	GDFT (Monitor/type of fluids, inotropes/volume/ hemodynamic parameters followed to guide fluid administration)	Control group (Type of fluids, inotropes/ clinical and hemodynamic parameters followed to guide fluid administration)	Outcomes
Forget, 2010 $n = 86$ Major abdominal surgery	No	Datex Ohmeda® S/5. 6% HES (130/0.4), 250 ml. Pleth variability index.	Baseline infusion of crystalloid 4–8 ml $^{-1}$ kg $^{-1}$ h $^{-1}$. Colloid if needed. Acute blood loss, MAP, CVP.	• No significant difference in the incidence of complications nor in mortality.* • No significant difference in LOS in ICU and overall LOS.* • No significant difference in the incidence of postoperative nausea and vomiting.*
Gan, 2002 $n = 100$, high-risk Major open elective general, urologic, gynecologic surgery	No	Esophageal Doppler. 6% HES (130/0.4), 200 ml. Flow time corrected, stroke volume.	Baseline infusion of lactated Ringer's solution 5 ml $^{-1}$ kg $^{-1}$ h $^{-1}$. Intravenous fluids, 200 ml if needed. Urine output, HR, CVP, systolic blood pressure.	• GDFT decreased LOS ($P = 0.03$). • GDFT shortened the time to tolerate solid diet ($P = 0.01$) and the incidence of postoperative nausea and vomiting ($P < 0.05$). • No significant difference in incidence of complications.*

(Continued)

Table 10.2 (Continued) Articles assessing the impact of GDFT on postoperative outcomes after abdominal surgery

Study/population	ERP	GDFT (Monitor/type of fluids, inotropes/volume/ hemodynamic parameters followed to guide fluid administration)	Control group (Type of fluids, inotropes/ clinical and hemodynamic parameters followed to guide fluid administration)	Outcomes
Jammer, 2010 *n* = 241 Open colorectal surgery	No	Central venous catheter. 6% HES (130/0.4), 3 ml^{-1} kg^{-1}. Central venous oxygen saturation. Intervention extended to POP.	Basal infusion of lactated Ringer's solution 10–12 ml^{-1} kg^{-1} h^{-1}. Lactated Ringer's solution or 6% HES (130/0.4) if needed. Blood loss, BP, urine output.	• No significant difference in number of patients with complications.* • GDFT decreased the POP weight gain (*P* = 0.001) • No significant difference in the incidence of renal impairment.* • GDFT decreased the incidence of paralytic postoperative ileus (OR = 0.25, 95% CI 0.09–0.73)

(Continued)

Table 10.2 (Continued) Articles assessing the impact of GDFT on postoperative outcomes after abdominal surgery

Study/population	ERP	GDFT (Monitor/type of fluids, inotropes/volume/ hemodynamic parameters followed to guide fluid administration)	Control group (Type of fluids, inotropes/ clinical and hemodynamic parameters followed to guide fluid administration)	Outcomes
Noblett, 2006 $n = 103$ Elective open and laparoscopic colorectal surgery	No	Esophageal Doppler. 4% succinylated gelatin, 3 and 7 ml^{-1} kg^{-1}. Flow time corrected, stroke volume.	Crystalloids and/or colloids. Fluid losses, hemodynamic parameters.	• GDFT decreased LOS ($P = 0.005$). • GDFT reduced time to fitness for discharge ($P = 0.003$). • GDFT reduction in number of intermediate and major complications ($P = 0.043$). • GDFT decreased number of ICU admissions ($P = 0.012$). • GDFT improved the time to tolerate diet ($P = 0.029$). • GDFT decreased the incidence of ileus nausea and vomiting ($P = 0.012$). • No significant difference in time to first flatus.*

(Continued)

Table 10.2 (Continued) Articles assessing the impact of GDFT on postoperative outcomes after abdominal surgery

Study/population	ERP	GDFT (Monitor/type of fluids, inotropes/volume/ hemodynamic parameters followed to guide fluid administration)	Control group (Type of fluids, inotropes/ clinical and hemodynamic parameters followed to guide fluid administration)	Outcomes
Pearse, 2014 $n = 730$ High-risk GI surgery	No	LiDCO rapid. Colloid (type of colloid was not standardized), 250 cc. Dopexamine. Stroke volume, heart rate, arterial pressure, urine output, core–peripheral temperature gradient, serum lactate, and base excess. Extended to POP.	Maintenance with 5% dextrose at 1 ml⁻¹ kg⁻¹ h⁻¹. Additional fluids at the discretion of the treating anesthesiologist. Heart rate, arterial pressure, urine output, core–peripheral temperature gradient, serum lactate, base excess, and CVP.	• No significant difference in 30-day postoperative morbidity and mortality.* • No significant difference in POMS-defined morbidity on day 7, infectious complications, critical care free days and all-cause mortality at 30 days.* • No significant difference in LOS.* • No significant difference in incidence of paralytic ileus.*

(Continued)

Table 10.2 (Continued) Articles assessing the impact of GDFT on postoperative outcomes after abdominal surgery

Study/population	ERP	GDFT (Monitor/type of fluids, inotropes/volume/hemodynamic parameters followed to guide fluid administration)	Control group (Type of fluids, inotropes/clinical and hemodynamic parameters followed to guide fluid administration)	Outcomes
Pestaña, 2014 *n* = 142 Open GI surgery (colorectal small bowel, gastrectomy) with high risk	No	Noninvasive cardiac output monitor. Colloids (starch or gelatin), 250 ml. Norepinephrine or dobutamine. MAP, cardiac index.	Use of fluids and vasopressors at the discretion of the anesthesiologist.	• No significant difference in overall complications.* • No significant difference in mortality.* • No significant difference in overall LOS or LOS in ICU.* • No significant difference in time to first flatus or the incidence of paralytic ileus.* • GDFT decreased the number of reoperations ($P = 0.049$).

(Continued)

Table 10.2 (Continued) Articles assessing the impact of GDFT on postoperative outcomes after abdominal surgery

Study/population	ERP	GDFT (Monitor/type of fluids, inotropes/volume/hemodynamic parameters followed to guide fluid administration)	Control group (Type of fluids, inotropes/clinical and hemodynamic parameters followed to guide fluid administration)	Outcomes
Phan, 2014 $n = 100$ Open and laparoscopic elective colorectal surgery	Yes	Esophageal Doppler. Starch colloid (type of colloid at the discretion of the anesthesiologist), 250 ml. Blood pressure, the stroke volume index, and corrected flow time.	Postinduction bolus of 5 ml^{-1} kg^{-1} of Hartmann's solution. Maintenance 5 ml^{-1} kg^{-1} h^{-1} of Hartmann's solution. Boluses to replace blood losses or hypotension not responsive to vasopressors.	• No significant difference in LOS.* • No significant difference in readiness to be discharged.* • No significant difference in the overall incidence of complications.* • No difference in the number of readmissions or deaths.* • GDFT reduced the number of total major complications ($P = 0.007$).
Ramsingh, 2013 $n = 38$, high-risk Major open abdominal, nonvascular surgery	No	FloTrac/Vigileo. 5% albumin, 250 ml. Stroke volume variation.	Intravenous fluids. Hemodynamic parameters.	• GDFT decreased LOS ($P = 0.04$). • GDFT: higher quality of recovery score on Day 4 ($P = 0.03$). • GDFT decreased the time to first bowel motion and time to tolerate diet ($P = 0.004$).

(Continued)

Table 10.2 (Continued) Articles assessing the impact of GDFT on postoperative outcomes after abdominal surgery

Study/population	ERP	GDFT (Monitor/type of fluids, inotropes/volume/ hemodynamic parameters followed to guide fluid administration)	Control group (Type of fluids, inotropes/ clinical and hemodynamic parameters followed to guide fluid administration)	Outcomes
Srinivasa, 2013 $n = 74$ Elective open or laparoscopic colectomy	Yes	Esophageal Doppler. 4% succinylated gelatin, 3 and 7 ml⁻¹ kg⁻¹. Flow time corrected, stroke volume.	PlasmaLyte, maximum 1,500 ml. Gelofusine®, maximum 500 ml. Blood loss, BP, HR, and urine output.	• No significant difference in surgical recovery score at any point after surgery.* • No significant difference in LOS.* • No significant difference in number of patients with complications.* • No significant differences in readmissions.* • No significant difference in the incidence of ileus.*

(Continued)

Table 10.2 (Continued) Articles assessing the impact of GDFT on postoperative outcomes after abdominal surgery

Study/population	ERP	GDFT (Monitor/type of fluids, inotropes/volume/ hemodynamic parameters followed to guide fluid administration)	Control group (Type of fluids, inotropes/ clinical and hemodynamic parameters followed to guide fluid administration)	Outcomes
Wakeling, 2005 $n = 128$ Large bowel surgery	No	Esophageal Doppler. 3.5% gelatin polypeptides. 4% succinylated gelatin, 250 ml. Stroke volume, CVP.	Intravenous fluids. CVP.	• GDFT decreased LOS ($P = 0.031$) and fitness to be discharged ($P = 0.012$). • GDFT decreased the incidence of GI complications (GI morbidity) ($P < 0.001$). • GDFT decreased overall number of complications ($P = 0.013$). • GDFT improved quality of recovery score at Days 5 ($P < 0.001$) and 7 ($P = 0.007$). • GDFT decreased time to bowel recovery: flatus ($P = 0.085$), bowel opening ($P = 0.014$), and tolerance of full diet ($P < 0.001$).

(Continued)

Table 10.2 (Continued) Articles assessing the impact of GDFT on postoperative outcomes after abdominal surgery

Study/population	ERP	GDFT (Monitor/type of fluids, inotropes/volume/ hemodynamic parameters followed to guide fluid administration)	Control group (Type of fluids, inotropes/ clinical and hemodynamic parameters followed to guide fluid administration)	Outcomes
Zhang, 2012 $n = 60$ Elective open GI surgery	No	Datex Ohmeda® S/5 First group LR 250 ml based on pulse pressure variation. Second group HES 250 ml based on pulse pressure variation. Both groups received 6% HES (130/0.4) 1:1 to replace blood loss.	Baseline infusion of LR 5 ml^{-1} kg^{-1} h^{-1}. Lactated Ringer's solution, 250 ml. 6% HES (130/0.4). Blood loss, CVP, urine output.	• GDFT with colloids: decreased LOS compared to the other two strategies ($P < 0.01$). • GDFT with colloids: shortened the time to first flatus compared to the other two regimens ($P < 0.05$). • No significant differences among the groups in incidence of complications.*

(Continued)

Table 10.2 (Continued) Articles assessing the impact of GDFT on postoperative outcomes after abdominal surgery

Study/population	ERP	GDFT (Monitor/type of fluids, inotropes/volume/hemodynamic parameters followed to guide fluid administration)	Control group (Type of fluids, inotropes/clinical and hemodynamic parameters followed to guide fluid administration)	Outcomes
Zheng, 2013 $n = 65$ Coronary patients undergoing high-risk open GI surgery	No	Vigileo/FloTrac. Crystalloid, 500 ml. Cardiac index, stroke volume index, stroke volume variation, stroke volume. Intervention extended to POP.	Crystalloid and 6% HES (130/0.4). "4/2/1 rule," insensible loss, blood loss.	• GDFT decreased LOS in ICU ($P < 0.001$) and overall LOS ($P = 0.001$). • GDFT decreased time to extubation ($P = 0.009$). • No significant difference in the incidence of adverse cardiac events.* • GDFT shortened the time to first flatulence ($P < 0.001$), defecation ($P < 0.001$), and resumption of diet ($P = 0.007$). • GDFT decreased the incidence of severe postoperative nausea and vomiting ($P = 0.015$).

Note: ERP, enhanced recovery program; BP, blood pressure; CVP, central venous pressure; HES, hydroxyethyl starch; HR, heart rate; MAP, mean arterial pressure; n, number of patients; GDFT, goal-directed fluid therapy; POP, postoperative period; POMS, Postoperative Morbidity Survey; ICU, intensive care unit; LOS, length of hospital stay; GI, gastrointestinal; ml, milliliters; kg, kilogram; h, hour; OR, odds ratio.

*P-value ≥ 0.05.

Table 10.3 Common clinical and surgical features used in characterizing
high-risk patients and surgery

Surgical risk factors

Major surgery with a 30-day mortality rate >1%.

Major surgery with an anticipated blood loss >500 milliliters (>7 milliliters^{-1}
kilogram^{-1}).

Major intra-abdominal surgery: any laparotomy, bowel resection, gastric
resection, and cholecystectomy with choledochotomy. Complex major also
includes any aortic procedure, abdominoperineal resection,
duodenopancreatectomy, pancreatic or liver resection, and
esophagogastrectomy [94,100].

Intermediate surgery (30-day mortality >0.5%) in high-risk patients: older than
80 years, history of left ventricular failure, myocardial infarction,
cerebrovascular accident, or peripheral arterial disease [65].

Unexpected blood loss and/or fluid loss requiring >2 liters of fluid replacement.

Patient risk factors

Anaerobic threshold <11 milliliters O_2^{-1} kilogram^{-1} minute^{-1} [85,101].

Patients with ongoing evidence of hypovolemia and/or tissue hypoperfusion,
e.g., persistent lactic acidosis.

Source: Vassallo, R., et al., *Transfus. Med. Rev.*, 29(4), 268–275, 2015.

Note: Goal-directed fluid therapy is commonly recommended for use in this population
of patients undergoing major abdominal surgery.

establish if implementing GDFT as a standard of care in patients undergoing major abdominal surgery might add further advantages.

Studies extending intraoperative GDFT to the early postoperative period
(6–24 hr after surgery) have shown a beneficial impact on the recovery of the
bowel function [117–119]. Reduced length of hospital stay and decreased ICU
admissions were also reported [117]. Continuing GDFT in the early postoperative period does not reduce the incidence of postoperative orthostatic
intolerance or hypotension [120]. Several noninvasive cardiac output monitors have been used to guide GDFT [121], but most of the evidence available is based on the use of the esophageal Doppler and on the analysis of
the arterial pressure waveform [98,122]. It has been shown that in high-risk
patients the benefit of GDFT is independent on the type of hemodynamic
monitor used [116].

Colloids have been mainly used to optimize intravascular volume during GDFT. Despite experimental studies showing that colloids are superior
to crystalloids in improving macro- and microcirculatory splanchnic perfusion [123], clinical studies comparing GDFT with colloid versus GDFT with
crystalloid have failed to reproduce these findings [124]. Patients treated
with GDFT with crystalloids receive more vasopressors [125] and intravenous fluids resulting in a greater postoperative weight gain [124–126].
Nevertheless, large volumes of colloids (2,605 ± 612 mL) can impair coagulation and increase blood loss [126].

10.6   Zero weight balance

Zero weight balance fluid regimens aim at minimizing weight gain (or loss) after surgery by avoiding hypervolemia and organ hypoperfusion and protecting the vascular barrier to prevent fluid shifting into the intestinal space [99]. In part this goal is achieved by avoiding replacing the third space and insensible losses with unnecessary intravenous fluids [90] and limiting the amount of intravenous fluids to replace only intravascular losses due to blood loss and interstitial accumulation, the latter caused by a deteriorated endothelial barrier. It must be acknowledged that while blood loss can be estimated during surgery, intravascular losses due to interstitial accumulation are not easy to quantify without objective measures of hypovolemia.

Colloid 1:1 (and blood transfusions when indicated) are commonly infused to replace blood loss. Although data from ICUs have shown that colloid use can increase mortality and risk of acute kidney injury [127,128], colloids appears to be safe in surgical patients [129]. However, the restrictions put on starch-based solutions for critically ill patients have caused the use of colloids even in the surgical settings to decline. Alternatively, crystalloids can be used 1:2 to replace blood loss when colloids are contraindicated, considering that the intravascular effect of crystalloids is prolonged during general anesthesia [130,131].

Vasopressors should be used to treat hypotension induced by general and neuroaxial anesthesia, after ensuring that the patients are normovolemic [99,132], as intravascular volume is not reduced by anesthetic agents [67]. The use of low-dose vasopressors has not shown to negatively affect mesenteric perfusion, microcirculatory flow, and oxygenation of the small bowel or colon [133,134]. On the contrary, vasopressors are more efficient than intravenous fluids to improve splanchnic circulation [134].

The results of two RCTs aiming at maintaining postoperative weight gain <2.5 kg indicated that zero weight balance regimens, in comparison with GDFT, provide adequate organ perfusion in low-risk patients treated with an ERP [99,132]. It was also found that patients in the zero weight balance group received less intravenous fluids and colloids than patients in the GDFT group [99,132].

10.7   Postoperative fluid therapy

10.7.1   Postoperative anesthesia care unit

Oral fluid intake should be restarted as soon as the patient is fully awake and without postoperative nausea and vomiting. With this goal, prevention of postoperative nausea and vomiting is essential to tolerate early feeding [135]. In the meantime, administration of 1.5 mL/kg/hr of crystalloids is appropriate to keep patients well hydrated. Additional crystalloids are used to replace (1:1) gastrointestinal losses. Hypotension induced by epidural analgesia should be treated with vasopressors after ensuring the patient is normovolemic [67]. Perioperative low urine output should be expected as a physiologic response to surgical stress [22,136]. This includes the release of vasopressin, the activation of the axis renin–angiotensin aldosterone, and liberation of other antidiuretic hormones such as cortisol and norepinephrine that overall lead to retain salt and water and reduce urine output [136–138]. In this context, attempts to replace urine output by administering intravenous fluids in the absence of any other signs of hypovolemia can further damage the endothelial glycocalyx, facilitating fluid shifting into the interstitial space, and increase the risk of complications without improving renal function [23,101]. Based on the recent Risk, Injury, Failure, and End-stage kidney disease (RIFLE) criteria a urine output of <0.5 mL/kg/hr for less than 6 hr should not even be considered a risk factor for the development of acute kidney injury [139].

10.7.2   Surgical unit

Avoidance of nasogastric tubes, early resumption of oral intake soon after surgery, and subsequent early discontinuation of intravenous fluids are important ERP interventions [5–9,140–142]. Patients should be encouraged to drink at least 1.5 L (25–35 mL/kg) of water per day to cover the physiologic needs derived from water and salt hemostasis [143]. If oral intake is tolerated, intravenous fluids can be discontinued right after the surgery and restarted only if clinically indicated [5] (Table 10.4). Oral nutritional

Table 10.4 Most common indications for restarting intravenous fluids in the postoperative period

Intolerance of oral intake
Parenteral nutrition
Anastomotic dehiscence
Postoperative ileus
High stoma output
High output by fistulas or drains
Sepsis
Postoperative bleeding
Hypotension secondary to hypovolemia not corrected with oral intake
  (e.g., diarrhea or vomiting)
Patients with nasogastric tube
Electrolyte imbalances not susceptible to oral correction
Medical complications requiring intravenous fluids (e.g., diabetes
  decompensation and pulmonary emboli)

Table 10.5 Perioperative fluid management in two patients undergoing
colorectal surgery with an ERP

	Case 1	Case 2
Patient presentation	68-year-old male. ASA 2. *Weight*: 75 kg. *Comorbidities*: anemia, arterial hypertension on ACE inhibitors. *Diagnosis*: colon cancer. *Scheduled surgery*: right laparoscopic hemicolectomy. The surgery is planned for 10:30 a.m. *Anesthesia and analgesia*: general anesthesia. A bilateral TAP block plus PCA morphine is provided to control postoperative pain. *Duration of surgery*: 2 h. *EBL*: 200 ml. Uncomplicated surgery, discharged on postoperative Day 2.	76-year-old female. ASA 3. Weight: 60 kg. *Comorbidities*: hypertension, coronary artery disease, diabetes mellitus type 2 on insulin. *Diagnosis*: Rectal cancer. *Scheduled surgery*: open rectal anterior resection. The surgery is planned for 7:30 a.m. *Anesthesia and analgesia*: general anesthesia plus TEA (T9–T10). *Duration of surgery*: 3 h. *EBL*: 500 ml. Uncomplicated surgery, discharged on postoperative Day 3.
Preoperative	*Last solid meal*: 9 h before surgery. *Clear fluids*: 2 h before surgery. No MBP. Carbohydrate drink (400 ml) at 8:30 a.m.	*Last solid meal*: 35 h before surgery. *Clear fluids*: 2 h before surgery. MBP plus fluid diet the day before surgery. Carbohydrate drink (400 ml) at 5:30 a.m. 1.5 L of balanced crystalloid solution to replace.
Intraoperative	Standard hemodynamic monitoring.[a] Hypotension following induction of anesthesia is restored using ephedrine. Balanced crystalloid solution: 2 ml^{-1} kg^{-1} h^{-1}. *Colloid*: 200 ml. No blood transfusion.	Standard hemodynamic monitoring[a] + SV optimization (GDFT). Hypotension following induction of anesthesia and following epidural boluses is restored using ephedrine. Balanced crystalloid solution: 3 ml^{-1} kg^{-1} h^{-1}. *Colloid*: 600 ml. No blood transfusion.

(Continued)

Table 10.5 (Continued) Perioperative fluid management in two patients
undergoing colorectal surgery with an ERAS program

	Case 1	Case 2
Postoperative PACU Unit	Infusion rate of 1.5 ml^{-1} kg^{-1} h^{-1} for the duration of stay (1.5 h). Clear fluids are allowed. Intravenous fluids kvo (15 ml^{-1} h^{-1}). Full fluid diet the day of surgery and full diet the morning after. Water oral intake: ~1.5 L^{-1}day^{-1}. Daily weight balance. Additional IV crystalloids to replace GI loss (e.g., vomiting).	Infusion rate of 1.5 ml^{-1} kg^{-1} h^{-1} for the duration of stay (1.5 h). Clear fluids are allowed. Hypotension following induction of epidural boluses is restored using ephedrine. IV-lock. Full fluid diet the day of surgery and full diet the morning after. Water oral intake: ~1.5 L^{-1}day^{-1}. Daily weight balance. Adjust epidural infusion rate in case of hypotension. Additional IV crystalloids to replace GI loss (e.g., vomiting).
Total IV fluids (ml)[b]	~1,000 ml	~2,800 ml

Notes: ERAS, enhanced recovery after surgery; ACE, angiotensin-converting enzyme; kvo, keep vein open; SV, stroke volume; TEA, thoracic epidural analgesia; TAP block, transversus abdominis plane; PCA, patient-controlled analgesia; MBP, mechanical bowel preparation; ml, milliliter; L, liters; kg, kilogram; h, hour; IV, intravenous; EBL, estimated blood loss; ASA, American Society of Anesthesia physical status classification system; GI, gastrointestinal; PACU, postoperative anesthesia care unit.

[a] Standard hemodynamic monitoring includes heart rate, invasive blood pressure, and pulse oximetry.
[b] First 24 h.

supplements for the first 4 postoperative days can be added to ensure adequate caloric intake [144]. Decisions to administer intravenous fluids should also take into consideration postoperative weight gain, since excessive postoperative fluid administration resulting in postoperative weight gain >2.5 kg increases overall morbidity [11] and prolongs the recovery of bowel function [18]. Diuretics can be useful to eliminate fluid excess [86].

10.8   Summary

Inadequate perioperative fluid management increases morbidity and delays immediate surgical recovery. Even though perioperative fluid management for patients undergoing abdominal surgery remains controversial, principles supporting the infusion of large amounts of intravenous fluids to maintain that patients are euvolemic and well hydrated during abdominal surgery have been challenged over the years. Moreover, ERPs include multiple interventions, such as minimization of preoperative fasting, selective use of MBP, and early recovery of oral intake, that further minimize the amount of intravenous fluids needed. The adjunct of GDFT algorithms to optimize cardiac output with the aim of ensuring optimal tissue perfusion and avoiding fluid overloading could be considered in high-risk patients or in patients undergoing major surgery associated with extensive blood loss and large fluid shifts. However, the beneficial impact of GDFT on postoperative outcomes still remains to be proven, especially in the context of an ERP. Table 10.5 summarizes perioperative fluid management in two patients undergoing colorectal surgery with an ERAS program.

References

1. Basse L, Hjort Jakobsen D, Billesbolle P, Werner M, Kehlet H. A clinical pathway to accelerate recovery after colonic resection. *Annals of Surgery.* 2000 Jul;232(1):51–7.
2. Basse L, Raskov HH, Hjort Jakobsen D, Sonne E, Billesbolle P, Hendel HW, et al. Accelerated postoperative recovery programme after colonic resection improves physical performance, pulmonary function and body composition. *The British Journal of Surgery.* 2002 Apr;89(4):446–53.
3. Wind J, Hofland J, Preckel B, Hollmann MW, Bossuyt PM, Gouma DJ, et al. Perioperative strategy in colonic surgery; laparoscopy and/or fast track multimodal management versus standard care (LAFA trial). *BMC Surgery.* 2006;6:16.
4. Nicholson A, Lowe MC, Parker J, Lewis SR, Alderson P, Smith AF. Systematic review and meta-analysis of enhanced recovery programmes in surgical patients. *The British Journal of Surgery.* 2014 Feb;101(3):172–88.
5. Gustafsson UO, Scott MJ, Schwenk W, Demartines N, Roulin D, Francis N, et al. Guidelines for perioperative care in elective colonic surgery: Enhanced recovery after surgery (ERAS((R))) Society recommendations. *World Journal of Surgery.* 2013 Feb;37(2):259–84.
6. Mortensen K, Nilsson M, Slim K, Schafer M, Mariette C, Braga M, et al. Consensus guidelines for enhanced recovery after gastrectomy: Enhanced Recovery After Surgery (ERAS(R)) Society recommendations. *The British Journal of Surgery.* 2014 Sep;101(10):1209–29.
7. Cerantola Y, Valerio M, Persson B, Jichlinski P, Ljungqvist O, Hubner M, et al. Guidelines for perioperative care after radical cystectomy for bladder cancer: Enhanced Recovery After Surgery (ERAS(R)) Society recommendations. *Clinical Nutrition.* 2013 Dec;32(6):879–87.
8. Lassen K, Coolsen MM, Slim K, Carli F, de Aguilar-Nascimento JE, Schafer M, et al. Guidelines for perioperative care for pancreaticoduodenectomy: Enhanced Recovery After Surgery (ERAS(R)) Society recommendations. *World Journal of Surgery.* 2013 Feb;37(2):240–58.
9. Nygren J, Thacker J, Carli F, Fearon KC, Norderval S, Lobo DN, et al. Guidelines for perioperative care in elective rectal/pelvic surgery: Enhanced Recovery After Surgery (ERAS(R)) Society recommendations. *World Journal of Surgery.* 2013 Feb;37(2):285–305.

10. Mythen MG, Swart M, Acheson N, Crawford R, Jones K, Kuper M, et al. Perioperative fluid management: Consensus statement from the enhanced recovery partnership. *Perioperative Medicine.* 2012;1:2.

11. Brandstrup B, Tonnesen H, Beier-Holgersen R, Hjortso E, Ording H, Lindorff-Larsen K, et al. Effects of intravenous fluid restriction on post-operative complications: Comparison of two perioperative fluid regimens: A randomized assessor-blinded multicenter trial. *Annals of Surgery.* 2003 Nov;238(5):641–8.

12. Donati A, Loggi S, Preiser JC, Orsetti G, Munch C, Gabbanelli V, et al. Goal-directed intraoperative therapy reduces morbidity and length of hospital stay in high-risk surgical patients. *Chest.* 2007 Dec;132(6):1817–24.

13. Chowdhury AH, Lobo DN. Fluids and gastrointestinal function. *Current Opinion in Clinical Nutrition and Metabolic Care.* 2011 Sep;14(5):469–76.

14. Burch JM, Moore EE, Moore FA, Franciose R. The abdominal compartment syndrome. *The Surgical Clinics of North America.* 1996 Aug;76(4):833–42.

15. Wilmore DW, Smith RJ, O'Dwyer ST, Jacobs DO, Ziegler TR, Wang XD. The gut: A central organ after surgical stress. *Surgery.* 1988 Nov;104(5):917–23.

16. Ratner LE, Smith GW. Intraoperative fluid management. *The Surgical Clinics of North America.* 1993 Apr;73(2):229–41.

17. Bundgaard-Nielsen M, Secher NH, Kehlet H. "Liberal" vs. "restrictive" perioperative fluid therapy—A critical assessment of the evidence. *Acta Anaesthesiologica Scandinavica.* 2009 Aug;53(7):843–51.

18. Lobo DN, Bostock KA, Neal KR, Perkins AC, Rowlands BJ, Allison SP. Effect of salt and water balance on recovery of gastrointestinal function after elective colonic resection: A randomised controlled trial. *Lancet.* 2002 May 25;359(9320):1812–18.

19. Bellamy MC. Wet, dry or something else? *British Journal of Anaesthesia.* 2006 Dec;97(6):755–7.

20. Marik PE, Lemson J. Fluid responsiveness: An evolution of our understanding. *British Journal of Anaesthesia.* 2014 Apr;112(4):617–20.

21. Lilot M, Ehrenfeld JM, Lee C, Harrington B, Cannesson M, Rinehart J. Variability in practice and factors predictive of total crystalloid administration during abdominal surgery: Retrospective two-centre analysis dagger. *British Journal of Anaesthesia.* 2015 May;114(5):767–76.

22. Holte K. Pathophysiology and clinical implications of perioperative fluid management in elective surgery. *Danish Medical Bulletin.* 2010 Jul;57(7):B4156.

23. Miller TE, Roche AM, Mythen M. Fluid management and goal-directed therapy as an adjunct to Enhanced Recovery After Surgery (ERAS). *Canadian Journal of Anaesthesia = Journal canadien d'anesthesie.* 2015 Feb;62(2):158–68.

24. Holte K, Nielsen KG, Madsen JL, Kehlet H. Physiologic effects of bowel preparation. *Diseases of the Colon and Rectum.* 2004 Aug;47(8):1397–402.

25. Sanders G, Mercer SJ, Saeb-Parsey K, Akhavani MA, Hosie KB, Lambert AW. Randomized clinical trial of intravenous fluid replacement during bowel preparation for surgery. *The British Journal of Surgery.* 2001 Oct;88(10):1363–5.

26. Junghans T, Neuss H, Strohauer M, Raue W, Haase O, Schink T, et al. Hypovolemia after traditional preoperative care in patients undergoing colonic surgery is underrepresented in conventional hemodynamic monitoring. *International Journal of Colorectal Disease.* 2006 Oct;21(7):693–7.

27. Phillips PA, Rolls BJ, Ledingham JG, Forsling ML, Morton JJ, Crowe MJ, et al. Reduced thirst after water deprivation in healthy elderly men. *The New England Journal of Medicine.* 1984 Sep 20;311(12):753–9.
28. de Aguilar-Nascimento JE, de Almeida Dias AL, Dock-Nascimento DB, Correia MI, Campos AC, Portari-Filho PE, et al. Actual preoperative fasting time in Brazilian hospitals: The BIGFAST multicenter study. *Therapeutics and Clinical Risk Management.* 2014;10:107–12.
29. Brady M, Kinn S, Stuart P. Preoperative fasting for adults to prevent perioperative complications. *Cochrane Database of Systematics Reviews.* 2003;(4):CD004423.
30. Ackland GL, Singh-Ranger D, Fox S, McClaskey B, Down JF, Farrar D, et al. Assessment of preoperative fluid depletion using bioimpedance analysis. *British Journal of Anaesthesia.* 2004 Jan;92(1):134–6.
31. Muller L, Briere M, Bastide S, Roger C, Zoric L, Seni G, et al. Preoperative fasting does not affect haemodynamic status: A prospective, non-inferiority, echocardiography study. *British Journal of Anaesthesia.* 2014 May;112(5):835–41.
32. Bundgaard-Nielsen M, Jorgensen CC, Secher NH, Kehlet H. Functional intravascular volume deficit in patients before surgery. *Acta Anesthesiologica Scandinavica.* 2010 Apr;54(4):464–9.
33. Smith MD, McCall J, Plank L, Herbison GP, Soop M, Nygren J. Preoperative carbohydrate treatment for enhancing recovery after elective surgery. *The Cochrane Database of Systematic Reviews.* 2014;8:CD009161.
34. Navarro LH, Bloomstone JA, Auler JO, Jr., Cannesson M, Rocca GD, Gan TJ, et al. Perioperative fluid therapy: A statement from the international fluid optimization group. *Perioperative Medicine.* 2015;4:3.
35. Boyd O. Optimisation of oxygenation and tissue perfusion in surgical patients. *Intensive and Critical Care Nursing: The Official Journal of the British Association of Critical Care Nurses.* 2003 Jun;19(3):171–81.
36. Hare GM, Tsui AK, Ozawa S, Shander A. Anaemia: Can we define haemoglobin thresholds for impaired oxygen homeostasis and suggest new strategies for treatment? *Best Practice and Research Clinical Anesthesiology.* 2013 Mar;27(1):85–98.
37. Shander A, Knight K, Thurer R, Adamson J, Spence R. Prevalence and outcomes of anemia in surgery: A systematic review of the literature. *The American Journal of Medicine.* 2004 Apr 5;116(Suppl 7A):58S–69S.
38. Musallam KM, Tamim HM, Richards T, Spahn DR, Rosendaal FR, Habbal A, et al. Preoperative anaemia and postoperative outcomes in non-cardiac surgery: A retrospective cohort study. *Lancet.* 2011 Oct 15;378(9800):1396–407.
39. Saager L, Turan A, Reynolds LF, Dalton JE, Mascha EJ, Kurz A. The association between preoperative anemia and 30-day mortality and morbidity in noncardiac surgical patients. *Anesthesia and Analgesia.* 2013 Oct;117(4):909–15.
40. Leichtle SW, Mouawad NJ, Lampman R, Singal B, Cleary RK. Does preoperative anemia adversely affect colon and rectal surgery outcomes? *Journal of the American College of Surgeons.* 2011 Feb;212(2):187–94.
41. Shander A, Hofmann A, Isbister J, Van Aken H. Patient blood management— The new frontier. *Best Practice and Research Clinical Anesthesiology.* 2013 Mar;27(1):5–10.
42. Shander A, Javidroozi M, Ozawa S, Hare GM. What is really dangerous: Anaemia or transfusion? *British Journal of Anaesthesia.* 2011 Dec;107 Suppl 1:i41–59.

43. Hare GM, Freedman J, David Mazer C. Review article: Risks of anemia and related management strategies: Can perioperative blood management improve patient safety? *Canadian Journal of Anaesthesia = Journal canadien d'anesthesie.* 2013 Feb;60(2):168–75.
44. Goodnough LT, Shander A. Patient blood management. *Anesthesiology.* 2012 Jun;116(6):1367–76.
45. Casans Frances R, Ripolles Melchor J, Calvo Vecino JM, Grupo Espanol de Rehabilitacion Multimodal GE-S. [Is it time to integrate patient blood management in ERAS guidelines?] *Revista Espanola de Anestesiologia y Reanimacion.* 2015 Feb;62(2):61–3.
46. Goodnough LT, Maniatis A, Earnshaw P, Benoni G, Beris P, Bisbe E, et al. Detection, evaluation, and management of preoperative anaemia in the elective orthopaedic surgical patient: NATA guidelines. *British Journal of Anaesthesia.* 2011 Jan;106(1):13–22.
47. Munoz M, Gomez-Ramirez S, Martin-Montanez E, Auerbach M. Perioperative anemia management in colorectal cancer patients: A pragmatic approach. *World Journal of Gastroenterology: WJG.* 2014 Feb 28;20(8):1972–85.
48. Auerbach M, Ballard H. Clinical use of intravenous iron: Administration, efficacy, and safety. *Hematology/The Education Program of the American Society of Hematology American Society of Hematology Education Program.* 2010;2010:338–47.
49. Norager CB, Jensen MB, Madsen MR, Qvist N, Laurberg S. Effect of darbepoetin alfa on physical function in patients undergoing surgery for colorectal cancer. A randomized, double-blind, placebo-controlled study. *Oncology.* 2006;71(3–4):212–20.
50. Devon KM, McLeod RS. Pre and peri-operative erythropoietin for reducing allogeneic blood transfusions in colorectal cancer surgery. *The Cochrane Database of Systematic Reviews.* 2009;(1):CD007148.
51. Tonnesen H, Kehlet H. Preoperative alcoholism and postoperative morbidity. *The British Journal of Surgery.* 1999 Jul;86(7):869–74.
52. Tonnesen H, Rosenberg J, Nielsen HJ, Rasmussen V, Hauge C, Pedersen IK, et al. Effect of preoperative abstinence on poor postoperative outcome in alcohol misusers: Randomised controlled trial. *BMJ.* 1999 May 15;318(7194):1311–16.
53. Wallerstedt S, Cederblad G, Korsan-Bengtsen K, Olsson R. Coagulation factors and other plasma proteins during abstinence after heavy alcohol consumption in chronic alcoholics. *Scandinavian Journal of Gastroenterology.* 1977;12(6):649–55.
54. Murali AR, Attar BM, Katz A, Kotwal V, Clarke PM. Utility of platelet count for predicting cirrhosis in alcoholic liver disease: Model for identifying cirrhosis in a US population. *Journal of General Internal Medicine.* 2015 Feb 21;30(8):1112–17.
55. Oppedal K, Moller AM, Pedersen B, Tonnesen H. Preoperative alcohol cessation prior to elective surgery. *Cochrane Database of Systematic Reviews.* 2012;7:CD008343.
56. Tjandra JJ, Chan MK. Systematic review on the short-term outcome of laparoscopic resection for colon and rectosigmoid cancer. *Colorectal Disease: The Official Journal of the Association of Coloproctology of Great Britain and Ireland.* 2006 Jun;8(5):375–88.

57. Schmied H, Kurz A, Sessler DI, Kozek S, Reiter A. Mild hypothermia increases blood loss and transfusion requirements during total hip arthroplasty. *Lancet*. 1996 Feb 3;347(8997):289–92.
58. Royston D. The current place of aprotinin in the management of bleeding. *Anaesthesia*. 2015 Jan;70(Suppl 1):46–9, e17.
59. Ker K, Edwards P, Perel P, Shakur H, Roberts I. Effect of tranexamic acid on surgical bleeding: Systematic review and cumulative meta-analysis. *BMJ*. 2012;344:e3054.
60. Terai A, Terada N, Yoshimura K, Ichioka K, Ueda N, Utsunomiya N, et al. Use of acute normovolemic hemodilution in patients undergoing radical prostatectomy. *Urology*. 2005 Jun;65(6):1152–6.
61. Furuya R, Oda T, Tachiki H, Miyao N. [Acute normovolemic hemodilution in urologic surgery]. *Nihon Hinyokika Gakkai zasshi. The Japanese Journal of Urology*. 2003 Jan;94(1):25–8.
62. Segal JB, Blasco-Colmenares E, Norris EJ, Guallar E. Preoperative acute normovolemic hemodilution: A meta-analysis. *Transfusion*. 2004 May;44(5):632–44.
63. Bryson GL, Laupacis A, Wells GA. Does acute normovolemic hemodilution reduce perioperative allogeneic transfusion? A meta-analysis. *The International Study of Perioperative Transfusion. Anesthesia and Analgesia*. 1998 Jan;86(1):9–15.
64. Crystal GJ. Regional tolerance to acute normovolemic hemodilution: Evidence that the kidney may be at greatest risk. *Journal of Cardiothoracic and Vascular Anesthesia*. 2015 Apr;29(2):320–7.
65. Vassallo R, Goldman M, Germain M, Lozano M, Collaborative B. Preoperative autologous blood donation: Waning indications in an era of improved blood safety. *Transfusion Medicine Reviews*. 2015 May 6;29(4):268–75.
66. Soni N. British Consensus Guidelines on Intravenous Fluid Therapy for Adult Surgical Patients (GIFTASUP): Cassandra's view. *Anaesthesia*. 2009 Mar;64(3):235–8.
67. Holte K, Foss NB, Svensen C, Lund C, Madsen JL, Kehlet H. Epidural anesthesia, hypotension, and changes in intravascular volume. *Anesthesiology*. 2004 Feb;100(2):281–6.
68. Chawla LS, Ince C, Chappell D, Gan TJ, Kellum JA, Mythen M, et al. Vascular content, tone, integrity, and haemodynamics for guiding fluid therapy: A conceptual approach. *British Journal of Anaesthesia*. 2014 Nov;113(5):748–55.
69. Gurgel ST, do Nascimento P, Jr. Maintaining tissue perfusion in high-risk surgical patients: A systematic review of randomized clinical trials. *Anesthesia and Analgesia*. 2011 Jun;112(6):1384–91.
70. Meier J, Pape A, Loniewska D, Lauscher P, Kertscho H, Zwissler B, et al. Norepinephrine increases tolerance to acute anemia. *Critical Care Medicine*. 2007 Jun;35(6):1484–92.
71. Cocchi MN, Kimlin E, Walsh M, Donnino MW. Identification and resuscitation of the trauma patient in shock. *Emergency Medicine Clinics of North America*. 2007 Aug;25(3):623–42, vii.
72. Obi AT, Park YJ, Bove P, Cuff R, Kazmers A, Gurm HS, et al. The association of perioperative transfusion with 30-day morbidity and mortality in patients undergoing major vascular surgery. *Journal of Vascular Surgery*. 2015 Apr;61(4):1000–9.e1.

73. Schiergens TS, Rentsch M, Kasparek MS, Frenes K, Jauch KW, Thasler WE. Impact of perioperative allogeneic red blood cell transfusion on recurrence and overall survival after resection of colorectal liver metastases. *Diseases of the Colon and Rectum.* 2015 Jan;58(1):74–82.
74. Carson JL, Grossman BJ, Kleinman S, Tinmouth AT, Marques MB, Fung MK, et al. Red blood cell transfusion: A clinical practice guideline from the AABB. *Annals of Internal Medicine.* 2012 Jul 3;157(1):49–58.
75. Sakr Y, Lobo S, Knuepfer S, Esser E, Bauer M, Settmacher U, et al. Anemia and blood transfusion in a surgical intensive care unit. *Critical Care.* 2010;14(3):R92.
76. Vincent JL. Indications for blood transfusions: Too complex to base on a single number? *Annals of Internal Medicine.* 2012 Jul 3;157(1):71–2.
77. Carson JL, Duff A, Poses RM, Berlin JA, Spence RK, Trout R, et al. Effect of anaemia and cardiovascular disease on surgical mortality and morbidity. *Lancet.* 1996 Oct 19;348(9034):1055–60.
78. Acheson AG, Brookes MJ, Spahn DR. Effects of allogeneic red blood cell transfusions on clinical outcomes in patients undergoing colorectal cancer surgery: A systematic review and meta-analysis. *Annals of Surgery.* 2012 Aug;256(2):235–44.
79. Prowle JR, Echeverri JE, Ligabo EV, Ronco C, Bellomo R. Fluid balance and acute kidney injury. *Nature Reviews Nephrology.* 2010 Feb;6(2):107–15.
80. Bennett-Guerrero E, Panah MH, Bodian CA, Methikalam BJ, Alfarone JR, DePerio M, et al. Automated detection of gastric luminal partial pressure of carbon dioxide during cardiovascular surgery using the Tonocap. *Anesthesiology.* 2000 Jan;92(1):38–45.
81. Hamilton MA, Mythen MG. Gastric tonometry: Where do we stand? *Current Opinion in Critical Care.* 2001 Apr;7(2):122–7.
82. Kapral S, Gollmann G, Bachmann D, Prohaska B, Likar R, Jandrasits O, et al. The effects of thoracic epidural anesthesia on intraoperative visceral perfusion and metabolism. *Anesthesia and Analgesia.* 1999 Feb;88(2):402–6.
83. Holte K, Sharrock NE, Kehlet H. Pathophysiology and clinical implications of perioperative fluid excess. *British Journal of Anaesthesia.* 2002 Oct;89(4):622–32.
84. Marjanovic G, Villain C, Juettner E, zur Hausen A, Hoeppner J, Hopt UT, et al. Impact of different crystalloid volume regimes on intestinal anastomotic stability. *Annals of Surgery.* 2009 Feb;249(2):181–5.
85. Chappell D, Jacob M, Hofmann-Kiefer K, Conzen P, Rehm M. A rational approach to perioperative fluid management. *Anesthesiology.* 2008 Oct;109(4):723–40.
86. Jacob M, Chappell D, Hofmann-Kiefer K, Conzen P, Peter K, Rehm M. [Determinants of insensible fluid loss. Perspiration, protein shift and endothelial glycocalyx]. *Der Anaesthesist.* 2007 Aug;56(8):747–58, 60–4.
87. Lamke LO, Nilsson GE, Reithner HL. Water loss by evaporation from the abdominal cavity during surgery. *Acta chirurgica Scandinavica.* 1977;143(5):279–84.
88. Jacob M, Chappell D, Rehm M. The "third space"—Fact or fiction? *Best Practice & Research Clinical Anaesthesiology.* 2009 Jun;23(2):145–57.
89. Shires T, Williams J, Brown F. Acute change in extracellular fluids associated with major surgical procedures. *Annals of Surgery.* 1961 Nov;154:803–10.
90. Brandstrup B. Fluid therapy for the surgical patient. *Best Practice & Research Clinical Anaesthesiology.* 2006 Jun;20(2):265–83.

91. Nielsen OM. Extracellular fluid and colloid osmotic pressure in abdominal vascular surgery. A study of volume changes. *Danish Medical Bulletin.* 1991 Feb;38(1):9–21.
92. Doty DB, Hufnagel HV, Moseley RV. The distribution of body fluids following hemorrhage and resuscitation in combat casualties. *Surgery, Gynecology & Obstetrics.* 1970 Mar;130(3):453–8.
93. Roberts JP, Roberts JD, Skinner C, Shires GT, 3rd, Illner H, Canizaro PC, et al. Extracellular fluid deficit following operation and its correction with Ringer's lactate. A reassessment. *Annals of Surgery.* 1985 Jul;202(1):1–8.
94. Fukuda Y, Fujita T, Shibuya J, Albert SN. The distribution between the intra-vascular and interstitial compartments of commonly utilized replacement fluids. *Anesthesia and Analgesia.* 1969 Sep–Oct;48(5):831–8.
95. Brandstrup B, Svensen C, Engquist A. Hemorrhage and operation cause a contraction of the extracellular space needing replacement—Evidence and implications? A systematic review. *Surgery.* 2006 Mar;139(3):419–32.
96. Cecconi M, Parsons AK, Rhodes A. What is a fluid challenge? *Current Opinion in Critical Care.* 2011 Jun;17(3):290–5.
97. Gomez-Izquierdo JC, Feldman LS, Carli F, Baldini G. Meta-analysis of the effect of goal-directed therapy on bowel function after abdominal surgery. *The British Journal of Surgery.* 2015 May;102(6):577–89.
98. Grocott MP, Dushianthan A, Hamilton MA, Mythen MG, Harrison D, Rowan K, et al. Perioperative increase in global blood flow to explicit defined goals and outcomes after surgery: A Cochrane systematic review. *British Journal of Anaesthesia.* 2013 Oct;111(4):535–48.
99. Brandstrup B, Svendsen PE, Rasmussen M, Belhage B, Rodt SA, Hansen B, et al. Which goal for fluid therapy during colorectal surgery is followed by the best outcome: Near-maximal stroke volume or zero fluid balance? *British Journal of Anaesthesia.* 2012 Aug;109(2):191–9.
100. Pries AR, Secomb TW, Gaehtgens P. The endothelial surface layer. *Pflugers Archiv: European Journal of Physiology.* 2000 Sep;440(5):653–66.
101. Lowell JA, Schifferdecker C, Driscoll DF, Benotti PN, Bistrian BR. Postoperative fluid overload: Not a benign problem. *Critical Care Medicine.* 1990 Jul;18(7):728–33.
102. Marik PE, Baram M, Vahid B. Does central venous pressure predict fluid responsiveness? A systematic review of the literature and the tale of seven mares. *Chest.* 2008 Jul;134(1):172–8.
103. Kumar A, Anel R, Bunnell E, Habet K, Zanotti S, Marshall S, et al. Pulmonary artery occlusion pressure and central venous pressure fail to predict ventricular filling volume, cardiac performance, or the response to volume infusion in normal subjects. *Critical Care Medicine.* 2004 Mar;32(3):691–9.
104. Mythen MG. Postoperative gastrointestinal tract dysfunction. *Anesthesia and Analgesia.* 2005 Jan;100(1):196–204.
105. Hamilton-Davies C, Mythen MG, Salmon JB, Jacobson D, Shukla A, Webb AR. Comparison of commonly used clinical indicators of hypo-volemia with gastrointestinal tonometry. *Intensive Care Medicine.* 1997 Mar;23(3):276–81.
106. Osman D, Ridel C, Ray P, Monnet X, Anguel N, Richard C, et al. Cardiac filling pressures are not appropriate to predict hemodynamic response to volume challenge. *Critical Care Medicine.* 2007 Jan;35(1):64–8.

107. Bundgaard-Nielsen M, Holte K, Secher NH, Kehlet H. Monitoring of perioperative fluid administration by individualized goal-directed therapy. *Acta Anaesthesiologica Scandinavica*. 2007 Mar;51(3):331–40.
108. Maguire S, Rinehart J, Vakharia S, Cannesson M. Technical communication: Respiratory variation in pulse pressure and plethysmographic waveforms: Intraoperative applicability in a North American academic center. *Anesthesia and Analgesia*. 2011 Jan;112(1):94–6.
109. Renner J, Gruenewald M, Quaden R, Hanss R, Meybohm P, Steinfath M, et al. Influence of increased intra-abdominal pressure on fluid responsiveness predicted by pulse pressure variation and stroke volume variation in a porcine model. *Critical Care Medicine*. 2009 Feb;37(2):650–8.
110. Lansdorp B, Lemson J, van Putten MJ, de Keijzer A, van der Hoeven JG, Pickkers P. Dynamic indices do not predict volume responsiveness in routine clinical practice. *British Journal of Anaesthesia*. 2012 Mar;108(3):395–401.
111. Biais M, Ouattara A, Janvier G, Sztark F. Case scenario: Respiratory variations in arterial pressure for guiding fluid management in mechanically ventilated patients. *Anesthesiology*. 2012 Jun;116(6):1354–61.
112. Liu F, Zhu S, Ji Q, Li W, Liu J. The impact of intra-abdominal pressure on the stroke volume variation and plethysmographic variability index in patients undergoing laparoscopic cholecystectomy. *Bioscience Trends*. 2015;9(2):129–33.
113. Pearse RM, Harrison DA, MacDonald N, Gillies MA, Blunt M, Ackland G, et al. Effect of a perioperative, cardiac output-guided hemodynamic therapy algorithm on outcomes following major gastrointestinal surgery: A randomized clinical trial and systematic review. *JAMA*. 2014 Jun 4;311(21):2181–90.
114. Pestana D, Espinosa E, Eden A, Najera D, Collar L, Aldecoa C, et al. Perioperative goal-directed hemodynamic optimization using noninvasive cardiac output monitoring in major abdominal surgery: A prospective, randomized, multicenter, pragmatic trial: POEMAS study (PeriOperative goal-directed thErapy in Major Abdominal Surgery). *Anesthesia and Analgesia*. 2014 Sep;119(3):579–87.
115. Srinivasa S, Taylor MH, Singh PP, Lemanu DP, MacCormick AD, Hill AG. Goal-directed fluid therapy in major elective rectal surgery. *International Journal of Surgery*. 2014 Nov 15;12(12):1467–72.
116. Hamilton MA, Cecconi M, Rhodes A. A systematic review and meta-analysis on the use of preemptive hemodynamic intervention to improve postoperative outcomes in moderate and high-risk surgical patients. *Anesthesia and Analgesia*. 2011 Jun;112(6):1392–402.
117. Zheng H, Guo H, Ye J-R, Chen L, Ma H-P. Goal-directed fluid therapy in gastrointestinal surgery in older coronary heart disease patients: Randomized trial. *World Journal of Surgery*. 2013;37(12):2820–9.
118. Bisgaard J, Gilsaa T, Ronholm E, Toft P. Optimising stroke volume and oxygen delivery in abdominal aortic surgery: A randomised controlled trial. *Acta Anaesthesiologica Scandinavica*. 2013;57(2):178–88.
119. Jammer I, Ulvik A, Erichsen C, Lodemel O, Ostgaard G. Does central venous oxygen saturation-directed fluid therapy affect postoperative morbidity after colorectal surgery? A randomized assessor-blinded controlled trial. *Anesthesiology*. 2010;113(5):1072–80.

120. Bundgaard-Nielsen M, Jans O, Muller RG, Korshin A, Ruhnau B, Bie P, et al. Does goal-directed fluid therapy affect postoperative orthostatic intolerance? A randomized trial. *Anesthesiology.* 2013 Oct;119(4):813–23.

121. Thiele RH, Bartels K, Gan TJ. Inter-device differences in monitoring for goal-directed fluid therapy. *Canadian Journal of Anaesthesia.* 2015 Feb;62(2):169–81.

122. Roche AM, Miller TE, Gan TJ. Goal-directed fluid management with trans-oesophageal Doppler. *Best Practice & Research Clinical Anaesthesiology.* 2009 Sep;23(3):327–34.

123. Hiltebrand LB, Kimberger O, Arnberger M, Brandt S, Kurz A, Sigurdsson GH. Crystalloids versus colloids for goal-directed fluid therapy in major surgery. *Critical Care.* 2009;13(2):R40.

124. Yates DR, Davies SJ, Milner HE, Wilson RJ. Crystalloid or colloid for goal-directed fluid therapy in colorectal surgery. *British Journal of Anaesthesia.* 2014 Feb;112(2):281–9.

125. Zhang J, Qiao H, He Z, Wang Y, Che X, Liang W. Intraoperative fluid management in open gastrointestinal surgery: Goal-directed versus restrictive. *Clinics (Sao Paulo).* 2012 Oct;67(10):1149–55.

126. Rasmussen KC, Johansson PI, Hojskov M, Kridina I, Kistorp T, Thind P, et al. Hydroxyethyl starch reduces coagulation competence and increases blood loss during major surgery: Results from a randomized controlled trial. *Annals of Surgery.* 2014 Feb;259(2):249–54.

127. Myburgh JA, Finfer S, Bellomo R, Billot L, Cass A, Gattas D, et al. Hydroxyethyl starch or saline for fluid resuscitation in intensive care. *The New England Journal of Medicine.* 2012 Nov 15;367(20):1901–11.

128. Perner A, Haase N, Guttormsen AB, Tenhunen J, Klemenzson G, Aneman A, et al. Hydroxyethyl starch 130/0.42 versus Ringer's acetate in severe sepsis. *The New England Journal of Medicine.* 2012 Jul 12;367(2):124–34.

129. Gillies MA, Habicher M, Jhanji S, Sander M, Mythen M, Hamilton M, et al. Incidence of postoperative death and acute kidney injury associated with i.v. 6% hydroxyethyl starch use: Systematic review and meta-analysis. *British Journal of Anaesthesia.* 2014 Jan;112(1):25–34.

130. Hahn RG. Volume kinetics for infusion fluids. *Anesthesiology.* 2010 Aug;113(2):470–81.

131. Woodcock TE, Woodcock TM. Revised starling equation and the glycocalyx model of transvascular fluid exchange: An improved paradigm for prescribing intravenous fluid therapy. *British Journal of Anaesthesia.* 2012 Mar;108(3):384–94.

132. Srinivasa S, Taylor MH, Singh PP, Singh PP, Yu TC, Soop M, Hill AG. Randomized clinical trial of goal-directed fluid therapy within an enhanced recovery protocol for elective colectomy. *British Journal of Surgery.* 2013 Jan;100(1):66–74.

133. Hiltebrand LB, Koepfli E, Kimberger O, Sigurdsson GH, Brandt S. Hypotension during fluid-restricted abdominal surgery: Effects of norepinephrine treatment on regional and microcirculatory blood flow in the intestinal tract. *Anesthesiology.* 2011 Mar;114(3):557–64.

134. Gould TH, Grace K, Thorne G, Thomas M. Effect of thoracic epidural anaesthesia on colonic blood flow. *British Journal of Anaesthesia.* 2002 Sep;89(3):446–51.

135. Gan TJ, Diemunsch P, Habib AS, Kovac A, Kranke P, Meyer TA, et al. Consensus guidelines for the management of postoperative nausea and vomiting. *Anesthesia and Analgesia.* 2014 Jan;118(1):85–113.

136. Desborough JP. The stress response to trauma and surgery. *British Journal of Anaesthesia*. 2000 Jul;85(1):109–17.
137. Wilmore DW. Metabolic response to severe surgical illness: Overview. *World Journal of Surgery*. 2000 Jun;24(6):705–11.
138. Bessey PQ, Watters JM, Aoki TT, Wilmore DW. Combined hormonal infusion simulates the metabolic response to injury. *Annals of Surgery*. 1984 Sep;200(3):264–81.
139. Bellomo R, Ronco C, Kellum JA, Mehta RL, Palevsky P. Acute dialysis quality initiative w. Acute renal failure—Definition, outcome measures, animal models, fluid therapy and information technology needs: The Second International Consensus Conference of the Acute Dialysis Quality Initiative (ADQI) Group. *Critical Care*. 2004 Aug;8(4):R204–12.
140. Nygren J, Soop M, Thorell A, Hausel J, Ljungqvist O, Group E. An enhanced-recovery protocol improves outcome after colorectal resection already during the first year: A single-center experience in 168 consecutive patients. *Diseases of the Colon and Rectum*. 2009 May;52(5):978–85.
141. Henriksen MG, Hansen HV, Hessov I. Early oral nutrition after elective colorectal surgery: Influence of balanced analgesia and enforced mobilization. *Nutrition*. 2002 Mar;18(3):263–7.
142. Soop M, Carlson GL, Hopkinson J, Clarke S, Thorell A, Nygren J, et al. Randomized clinical trial of the effects of immediate enteral nutrition on metabolic responses to major colorectal surgery in an enhanced recovery protocol. *The British Journal of Surgery*. 2004 Sep;91(9):1138–45.
143. Varadhan KK, Lobo DN. A meta-analysis of randomised controlled trials of intravenous fluid therapy in major elective open abdominal surgery: Getting the balance right. *The Proceedings of the Nutrition Society*. 2010 Nov;69(4):488–98.
144. Fearon KC, Luff R. The nutritional management of surgical patients: Enhanced recovery after surgery. *The Proceedings of the Nutrition Society*. 2003 Nov;62(4):807–11.

chapter eleven

Pediatric fluid therapy

Andreas Andersson and Per-Arne Lönnqvist
Karolinska University Hospital
Karolinska Institutet
Stockholm, Sweden

Contents

Key points:

- Pediatric physiology
- Renal maturation
- Dehydration and hypovolemia
- Fasting guidelines
- Considerations in choice of fluid and the problem with *hyponatremia*
- Hypoglycemia
- Hyperglycemia
- Postoperative fluid therapy
- Monitoring aspects

11.1   Body water distribution and blood volume

In adults, 60% of body weight is water. Two-thirds of total body water (TBW) is intracellular fluid, and the remaining one-third is extracellular fluid. In neonates, TBW is considerably higher than in adults, representing 75%–80% of body weight. In the first years of life, the distribution of body fluid undergoes significant changes (Figure 11.1). The weight loss seen in the first week of life is due to a rapid decrease in TBW, and after approximately 12 months TBW has decreased to 60% of body weight, thereby reaching adult levels. The initial decrease in TBW is mainly due to a decrease in extracellular

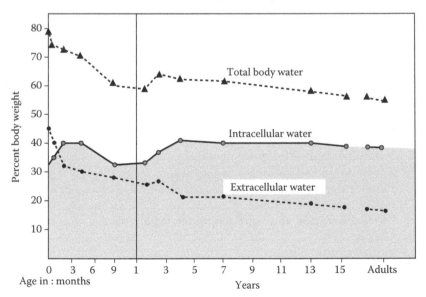

Figure 11.1 Changes in the amount and distribution of total body water according to age. (Reprinted from Friis-Hansen, B., *Pediatrics*, 28, 169–181, 1961. With permission.)

fluid volume (ECV). In the full-term newborn, ECV represents 45% of body weight and intracellular fluid volume (ICV) 30% of body weight. During the first year ECV decreases to 25% of body weight and reaches adult levels of 20% at 5–6 years of age. ICV increases slightly and reaches adults levels, 40% of body weight, after 12 months [1].

The blood volume in children also constitutes a greater proportion of body weight compared to adults. In premature infants blood volume is approximately 100 mL/kg, in the full-term neonate 80–90 mL/kg, in infants 80 mL/kg, and in older children 70–80 mL/kg [2]. Body habitus also influences blood volume, and obese children will have a relatively lower blood volume.

Hemoglobin levels are high at birth, usually 140–200 g/L in the full-term neonate. After the neonatal period, infants develop a physiological anemia reaching a nadir in hemoglobin level of 90–130 g/L at 2–3 months of age. This is due to decreased erythropoietin levels and a shorter red blood cell half-life. At birth, 70% of the full-term neonate's hemoglobin is fetal hemoglobin (HbF), resulting in a leftward displacement of the oxygen–hemoglobin dissociation curve and decreased oxygen delivery to tissues. Over the first 6 months HbF is gradually replaced by adult hemoglobin.

11.2 Renal maturation

In the newborn, urine output is low during the first 24–48 h due to high levels of antidiuretic hormone (ADH), but in the first few days after birth the level of atrial natriuretic peptide increases, resulting in a brisk diuresis. This postnatal diuresis results in isotonic fluid losses from the ECV and an initial weight loss of 5%–10% of body weight in the first week.

In the neonate, both glomerular and tubular function are immature. By 35–36 weeks of gestation, the number of nephrons has reached adult levels; after this glomeruli and nephrons continue to grow and mature in function.

At birth, glomerular filtration rate (GFR) is low, reaching approximately 20% of adult levels. After birth, renal vascular resistance decreases, leading to an increase in renal blood flow and GFR. After 2 weeks GFR has doubled, and adults levels are reached at approximately 18 months of age [3]. The rapid postnatal increase in GRF means that the infant's capability to excrete a water load develops early in life.

The immature tubular function of neonates makes sodium reabsorption and excretion less effective. Urine concentrating ability at birth is only about half that of adults (600–800 mmol/L vs. 1,200–1,400 mmol/L) while adult levels are reached at 1–2 years of age. The inability to concentrate urine increases the risk of dehydration in conditions of water depletion such as diarrhea. Tubular immaturity also lowers the renal threshold for glucose, making infants prone to glucosuria.

The immature glomerular and tubular function makes the neonate and small infant vulnerable to fluctuations in water and solute loads. Consequently, careful control of fluid management and sodium balance is important in the perioperative setting.

11.3   Energy expenditure and maintenance fluids

The basal energy requirements are considerably larger in a neonate than in an adult. This is partly because children need more energy to maintain body homeostasis and partly because energy is needed for growth.

Under normal conditions, the metabolism of 1 kcal requires 1 mL of water, including water lost as insensible loss and urine. This means that maintenance fluid requirements are closely correlated to the child's metabolic rate. Holliday and Segar measured the metabolic needs of children at rest and used these data to produce a widely used formula for estimating the required daily maintenance fluid [4]:

- For infants with body weight <10 kg: daily fluid requirements are estimated to 100 mL/kg.
- For children with body weight 10–20 kg: 1,000 mL + 50 mL/kg for every kg body weight above 10 kg.
- For children with body weight above 20 kg: 1,500 mL + 20 mL/kg for every kg bodyweight above 20 kg.

The corresponding rule for hourly fluid requirements is the 4-2-1 rule (Table 11.1).

One must keep in mind that this formula provides a rough estimate of the maintenance fluid required and that individual factors can have significant impact on fluid requirements. Energy expenditure and fluid requirements increase in situations such as surgery, sepsis, and sweating. Fever will increase water requirements by 12% per degree Celsius above 37°C, and hypothermia will decrease fluid needs correspondingly.

Holliday and Segar also determined electrolyte requirements in healthy children. A child normally needs 2–3 mmol/kg/day of sodium

Table 11.1 Maintenance fluid requirements in children

Weight	Daily fluid requirements	Hourly fluid requirements
First 10 kg	100 ml/kg/d	4 ml/kg/h
10–20 kg	50 ml/kg/d	2 ml/kg/h
every kg >20 kg	20 ml/kg/d	1 ml/kg/h

Source: Holliday, M.A. and Segar, W.E., *Pediatrics*, 19(5), 823–32, 1957.

and 1–2 mmol/kg/day of potassium to replace urinary electrolyte losses and to provide electrolytes needed for growth. However, in acutely ill children the need for electrolyte substitution can differ substantially, making monitoring of sodium and potassium levels essential. This is especially true for children at risk of increased secretion of ADH.

11.4 Dehydration and hypovolemia

It is not uncommon for the child admitted to acute surgery to be dehydrated to some degree. Before the start of surgery, the degree of dehydration needs to be assessed, and adequate intravascular volume status needs to be restored. The acute weight loss of the child can be used to estimate the severity of dehydration, if a recent and reliable pre-illness body weight is available. If this is not the case, clinical signs can give an estimate of the degree of dehydration. Based on clinical signs, dehydration is normally divided into three categories expressed in percent of body weight (Table 11.2).

- <5% (<50 mL/kg) is considered mild dehydration.
- 5%–10% (50–100 mL/kg) is considered moderate dehydration.
- >10% (>100 mL/kg) is considered severe dehydration.

Normal values for vital signs are presented in Table 11.3.

The estimated degree of dehydration based on clinical signs should be considered an initial approximation, and it is important to monitor the clinical response to the prescribed fluid therapy. Besides replacing the

Table 11.2 Clinical signs of dehydration in children

Clinical sign	Mild dehydration	Moderate dehydration	Severe dehydration
Weight loss (% of body weight)	3–5	5–10	>10
Appearance	Normal	Irritable	Lethargic
Blood pressure	Normal	Normal to low	Low
Pulse rate	Normal	Increased	Tachycardia, weak pulse
Respiration	Normal	Tachypnea	Tachypnea, deep breathing
Mucous membranes	Normal/dry	Dry	Very dry
Capillary refill time	≤2 sec	2–4 sec	>4 sec
Urine output	Decreased	Oliguria	Oliguria/anuria
Anterior fontanelle	Normal	Sunken	Sunken

Table 11.3 Normal vital signs for age

Age	Heart rate (bpm)	Systolic blood pressure (mmHg)	Respiratory rate	Diuresis (mL/kg/hr)
Term newborn	100–160	60–90	30–60	1–2
<1 year	90–140	70–100	25–40	1–2
1–3 years	80–130	80–110	20–35	0.5–1
3–5 years	80–120	80–110	20–30	0.5–1
6–12 years	70–110	80–120	20–30	0.5–1
>12 years	60–90	90–120	15–20	0.5–1

fluid deficit, fluid must also be prescribed for normal maintenance needs and ongoing losses.

11.5   Fasting guidelines

Preoperative fasting is routine in elective surgery to minimize the risk of regurgitation of gastric contents and subsequent pulmonary aspiration. However, although measures to prevent aspiration are of great importance, there are also potential adverse effects of prolonged fasting, and children should not be fasted longer than recommended in current guidelines [5,6] (Table 11.4).

Although a recent paper by Schmidt and colleagues indicates that a 1-hour fast is sufficient after drinking clear fluids [7], current guidelines recommends that clear fluids (water, pulp-free juice, carbonated beverages, tea or coffee without milk) can be given up to 2 hours before surgery without affecting gastric pH or volume at induction of anesthesia. Children should be encouraged to drink up to this time point, since this will reduce dehydration, hypoglycemia, and thirst and increase the comfort and cooperability of the child.

Human breast milk can be safely ingested up to 4 hours before surgery. Concerning infant formula, fasting time is somewhat more controversial. ASA guidelines recommend a 6-hour fasting interval for infant formula [5], whilst European guidelines recommends stopping infant formula 4–6 hours prior to anesthesia, depending on the age of the child and local considerations [6]. For solid food and cow's milk, a 6-hour fasting interval is recommended.

If current guidelines are followed and the child can drink clear fluids until 2 hours before surgery, fluid status can be expected to be normal. However, often children are fasted for longer periods than clinically motivated [8]. If the child still is fasted for a prolonged time, IV fluid substitution corresponding to maintenance needs must be prescribed.

Table 11.4 Preoperative fasting guidelines for children

Ingested substance	Fasting time
Clear fluids	2 h
Breast feeds	4 h
Infant formula	4–6 h
Solids	6 h

Source: Anesthesiology, 114(3), 495–511, 2011; and Smith, I., et al., *Eur. J. Anaesthesiol.*, 28(8), 556–569, 2011.

It should be kept in mind that these guidelines apply to healthy children having planned, elective surgery. Several factors can reduce gastric emptying, including diabetes mellitus, obesity, trauma, pain, and acute abdominal conditions, and individual risk factors must be taken into consideration when deciding whether a child can be regarded as adequately fasted or not.

11.6   Important considerations in the choice of perioperative IV fluid

11.6.1   Hyponatremia

Based on the daily requirements of fluid and electrolytes published by Holliday and Segar, traditionally hypotonic maintenance fluids with low sodium levels (0.18%–0.45%) and 5%–10% glucose have been used [9]. However, in recent years it has become evident that this strategy in many cases leads to hyponatremia and hyperglycemia, with potentially severe consequences.

11.6.2   Pediatric fluid therapy and hyponatremia

When prescribing IV fluids for children, the risk of *iatrogenic hyponatremia* must be considered. Hyponatremia will result in free water passing into brain cells, with resultant cerebral edema. Children have a relatively larger brain compared to intracranial volume, and this makes them more vulnerable to hyponatremia. Over 50% of children will show signs of hyponatremic encephalopathy when plasma sodium levels fall below 125 mmol/L [10]. Hyponatremia in children is a severe complication and can result in encephalopathy, seizures, permanent neurologic damage, and even death [11].

The two main factors contributing to the development of hyponatremia in sick children in general, and surgical children in particular, is ADH secretion and the administration of hypotonic fluids [12].

11.6.3 Antidiuretic hormone

ADH is a posterior pituitary gland hormone, and it has an important role in regulating renal water excretion. Normally, ADH is secreted in response to increasing plasma osmolality. However, ADH secretion also increases in response to several non-osmotic stimuli, such as hypovolemia, stress, pain, nausea, and vomiting. Many of these factors are common in the perioperative period and contribute to increased levels of ADH in children undergoing surgery [13]. The increase in ADH levels leads to retention of free water in the body and subsequently to decreased sodium levels.

11.6.4 Hypotonic or isotonic fluids in the perioperative setting?

In situations with increased levels of ADH, the impaired ability to excrete the free water content of hypotonic solutions will increase the risk of perioperative hyponatremia. Several studies and meta-analyses have shown that the risk for hyponatremia in hospitalized children is significantly lower when using isotonic solutions compared to hypotonic solutions [14–17]. In the surgical setting, Choong and colleagues randomized 258 children to postoperative fluid therapy with isotonic saline or 0.45% saline [18]. In this study, hypotonic saline increased the risk of hyponatremia, whilst isotonic saline did not increase the risk of hypernatremia. Similar results have been found in other studies including pediatric surgical patients.

Modern recommendations encourage the use of isotonic solutions in the perioperative setting. A European consensus document from 2011 recommended the use of isotonic solutions in children intra-operatively [19], and the 2007 guidelines from the Association of Paediatric Anaesthetists of Great Britain and Ireland recommended against the use of hypotonic solutions as maintenance fluid in postoperative children [20].

With the risks of hyponatremia in mind, fluids used in pre-, peri-, and postoperative care should preferentially have a sodium concentration near the physiological range. In the postoperative period, fluids should be given at a lower rate than normal maintenance fluid, since the postoperative increase in ADH will diminish free water excretion. Also, it is important to bear in mind that the use of isotonic fluids will decrease but not abolish the risk of hyponatremia in the perioperative period.

Concerns have been raised about the development of hypernatremia with the use of isotonic solutions. However, in a recent study McNab and colleagues randomized 690 children to either isotonic (sodium 140 mmol/L) or hypotonic (sodium 77 mmol/mL) solution as maintenance fluid and found that patients receiving the isotonic solution were less likely to develop hyponatremia, without any increased risk of hypernatremia or any other adverse event [17].

The use of large volumes of 0.9% saline carries the risk of concomitant hyperchloremic acidosis [21]. Hyperchloremia can be avoided by instead using balanced solutions with an electrolyte composition more similar to extracellular fluid, such as acetated or lactated Ringer's.

Regardless of which type of fluid is chosen, fluid therapy needs to be monitored regularly to ensure the adequacy of therapy. Fluid input/output should be carefully monitored. A baseline weight should be obtained before the start of therapy and followed daily if possible. Many authors recommend following serum electrolytes daily in all children receiving IV fluids.

11.6.5   Pediatric fluid therapy and glucose

Previous concerns about intraoperative hypoglycemia has been balanced by a growing awareness of the potentially negative effects of hyperglycemia. Many pediatric anesthetists have changed their practice, moving away from the use of solutions containing 5%–10% glucose to instead prescribing solutions containing 1%–2.5% glucose.

11.6.6   Hypoglycemia

With its potential for causing irreversible damage to the central nervous system [22], unrecognized hypoglycemia is a feared complication of anesthesia. The described incidence of hypoglycemia at induction of anesthesia varies depending on the fasting time applied and the definition used. However, when using modern fasting guidelines that avoid prolonged fasting periods and allow children to drink clear fluids until 2 hours before surgery, hypoglycemia is very rare [23]. During surgery, the release of cortisol and epinephrine in response to the surgical trauma will normally increase the intraoperative blood glucose level. Even small infants are capable of coping with this stress response, and most pediatric patients will not be at risk of hypoglycemia even if glucose-free solutions are administered during surgery. Although most patients will not need glucose-containing solutions during surgery, some patients will still be at risk of hypoglycemia. Risk factors for intraoperative hypoglycemia include premature babies (and neonates ≤48 hours of age), children receiving total parental nutrition or already on IV glucose solutions, beta-blocker therapy, prolonged surgery, liver disease, metabolic disease, and the use of combined regional and general anesthesia (thereby reducing the surgical stress response). These groups of patients should be given solutions containing at least 2.5% glucose perioperatively, and blood glucose should be monitored during surgery.

11.6.7   Hyperglycemia

The use of intravenous solutions containing 5%–10% glucose in the peri-operative period has repeatedly been shown to induce hyperglycemia in pediatric patients [24].

Although a causal relationship between hyperglycemia and adverse outcome has not yet been proven, hyperglycemia has several potentially negative effects in both adults and children. An important concern is the potential for hyperglycemia to worsen cerebral cell damage and enhance structural alterations after brain ischemia/hypoxia. This is supposedly due to anaerobic metabolism of glucose, leading to an accumulation of lactate and intracellular acidosis, subsequently compromising cellu-lar function and increasing cell death. In children with traumatic brain injury, hyperglycemia has been shown to be an independent risk factor for poor outcome [25].

Furthermore, hyperglycemia negatively affects fluid balance through glucosuria and osmotic diuresis, possibly resulting in dehydra-tion and hypovolemia. Infants have a lower renal threshold for glucose, making them especially vulnerable in this respect. Moreover, hyper-glycemia is associated with an increased rate of postoperative wound infections.

11.6.8   Which type of fluid should be used
in the perioperative setting?

In the perioperative period, an intravenous solution that minimizes the above described risks of deranged sodium and glucose homeostasis should be used. The fluid should have a sodium level close to the physi-ological range to avoid perioperative hyponatremia, the most common complication of perioperative fluid therapy. The glucose content should be 1%–2.5%, thereby avoiding hypoglycemia as well as hyperglycemia. The small amount of glucose in the solution will also prevent lipolysis and the release of ketone bodies and free fatty acids [26]. Moreover, the solution should preferably have a balanced pH to avoid the hyperchlore-mic acidosis seen when larger amounts of saline are given.

In recent years, several studies have confirmed the safety of using IV solutions with physiological sodium levels and 1% glucose as the pre-ferred perioperative fluid [17,18,27,28], and a European consensus state-ment from 2011 recommended the intraoperative use of balanced IV fluids with sodium concentrations close to the physiological range and glucose content of 1%–2.5% [19]. Such a solution was recently registered in Sweden for pediatric use (Benelyte®, newborn up to 14 years of age, treatment of isotonic dehydration, contains glucose 10 mg/mL, balanced and isotonic). Although fluids of this type will be adequate for most pediatric patients, individual patient characteristics must, as always, be considered when choosing what type of fluid to use.

11.7 Intraoperative fluid therapy

Intraoperative fluid therapy can be divided into three different parts:

1. Substitution of existing fluid deficit
2. Maintenance fluid requirements
3. Replacement of ongoing losses

11.8 Substitution of existing fluid deficit

Preoperative fluid deficit can be related to prolonged fasting or the underlying surgical condition.

In elective surgery where modern fasting guidelines are applied, the fluid deficit will be minimal and does not need to be replaced. However, if the child has been fasted for a prolonged period without receiving IV fluids, a significant fluid deficit can develop. Multiplying the hourly maintenance fluid requirement by the number of hours the child has been fasted can, in combination with clinical signs of dehydration, give an estimate of the size of the deficit. A 10–20 mL/kg bolus of Ringer's acetate or lactate before induction of anesthesia is often sufficient, and the remaining fluid deficit can be replaced over the first 2–3 hours of surgery.

Preoperative dehydration is common in many conditions requiring acute surgery. This can be due to fever, vomiting, diarrhea, ileus, or reduced oral intake. Children presenting with acute abdominal conditions can be assumed to have at least a mild degree of dehydration. For the patient presenting for emergency surgery with mild to moderate dehydration, rehydration can be achieved by administering 50 mL/kg over 4 hr, and for patients with moderate to severe dehydration 100 mL/kg can be given over 4–8 hr. However, if the need for surgery is imminent, fluid resuscitation may have to be administered in a considerably shorter time. When fluid losses are mainly due to vomiting, normal saline should be used to avoid the development of hypochloremic, hypokalemic alkalosis.

In moderate and severe cases of dehydration, intravascular volume will be reduced and the child will also be hypovolemic, in severe cases even in shock. In the case of hypovolemia, fluid boluses should be used to restore intravascular volume and organ perfusion. This is usually achieved with 10–20 mL/kg boluses of isotonic crystalloids; the amount and speed of fluid administered should be guided by the degree of hypovolemia and the clinical response to therapy. A child with severe dehydration and shock may need 60–80 mL/kg of IV fluid during the first hour.

11.9   Maintenance fluid requirements

Crystalloid solutions with sodium 130–140 mmol/L and 1% glucose are preferred as maintenance fluids perioperatively. However, these solutions are not yet readily available in many countries. Balanced crystalloids, such as acetated or lactated Ringer's, can be used as an alternative. However, if the patient is at risk of hypoglycemia, solutions containing 2.5% glucose should be used, and extra sodium added to achieve sodium levels of 130–140 mmol/L.

During surgery, extracellular fluid losses generally rise, leading to an increase in maintenance fluid requirements. The surgical wound will increase intraoperative evaporative losses, and the surgical trauma will induce local and systemic inflammation, which results in fluid extravasation and edema.

The required rate of intraoperative maintenance fluid will depend on the size of the surgical trauma. In children, data are lacking regarding the optimal strategy for perioperative fluid therapy, but the following guidelines have traditionally been used for intraoperative maintenance fluid:

- For minor surgery, 3–5 mL/kg/hr
- For moderate surgical trauma, 7–8 mL/kg/hr
- For major surgical trauma, 10 mL/kg/hr

However, in adults a more restrictive approach to the need for maintenance fluid has been adopted in recent years. Also, recent pediatric studies have shown the deleterious effects of fluid overload [29,30]. More data is needed on the effects of restrictive perioperative fluid therapy in children, but unnecessary fluid administration should be avoided. Ideally, fluid administration should be individualized and not only prescribed according to predetermined standards. At least for children >1 year, traditionally used rates of maintenance fluids can likely be reduced, given that the patient is closely monitored and clear hemodynamic goals are used to determine the need for additional fluid. The history of the patient as well as the type of surgery also need to be considered. For instance, up to 50 mL/kg/hr may be needed for necrotizing enterocolitis surgery in premature infants [31]. On the other hand, children with bronchopulmonary dysplasia are very vulnerable to fluid overload, and maintenance fluid may have to be kept to a minimum [32]. For children over 12 years of age, adult rates of fluid replacement can be used during surgery.

Substantial amounts of fluids can be administered as carrier solutions for drugs or saline flush injections, and when calculating the need for maintenance fluid all sources of IV fluid should be considered.

11.10   Crystalloids and colloids

During surgery, additional fluid administration may be necessary to compensate for hypovolemia and/or blood loss. The question of whether to use crystalloids or colloids for this purpose remains a subject of debate, as does the choice of colloid [33]. Currently, evidence regarding the choice of colloid is weak.

The natural colloid albumin has been used extensively in pediatric patients to increase colloid osmotic pressure and minimize edema formation, the main drawback being the relatively high cost. Data from premature infants indicate that a 4.5% albumin solution is more effective as volume replacement than 20% albumin [34].

Synthetic colloids are less expensive, and third-generation hydroxyethyl starch (HES) products have been used as an alternative plasma expander in children. However, recent randomized controlled trials in critically ill adult patients have shown an increased mortality and incidence of renal failure in patients given HES as fluid resuscitation [35,36], and this has dramatically decreased the use of HES. Data from the pediatric population is more limited, but a recent meta-analysis of available data concluded that HES significantly decreased platelet count and increased the length of ICU stay in pediatric patients [37]. A trend towards adverse effects on renal function was also found in the HES group. Given the potential side effects (increased bleeding, renal failure, pruritus) and the lack of proof regarding clinically relevant positive effects of HES compared to alternative fluids, the use of HES in children cannot be recommended. There are also safety concerns regarding the use of gelatin solutions [38], and until robust safety data exist the use of gelatins in children is best avoided. Considering the safety concerns with synthetic colloids, albumin remains the colloid of choice in pediatric patients.

Plasma has previously been used in children for volume expansion, but this practice cannot be recommended. The main indications for plasma transfusion are to compensate for blood loss and/or correct coagulation abnormalities [39].

11.11   Replacement of ongoing losses

The relative plasma volume expanding effect of colloids is better than that of crystalloids, but probably less than previously believed. This can in part be explained by newer theories on capillary fluid exchange, described as the *revised Starling theory* or the *glycocalyx model* [40].

If intraoperative signs of hypovolemia arise, a 10–20 mL/kg bolus dose of isotonic crystalloid is often used as initial volume replacement. This bolus could be given over 10–60 minutes depending on the urgency of the situation but should not be given faster than motivated by the clinical picture, since capillary extravasation is likely to increase with increasing speed of delivery. Colloids, preferably albumin, are usually added after 40–60 mL/kg of isotonic crystalloids have been given.

For substitution of blood loss, initial replacement with two to three times the volume in isotonic crystalloids is still common practice. Another option is replacement by albumin 5% with a volume equal to the estimated blood loss. Normally blood loss up to 20%–30% of blood volume can be replaced using this strategy. When transfusing red blood cells in stable patients, 10 mL/kg are often given over 4 hours, which will increase hemoglobin (Hb) level by approximately 25 g/L. In 2007, the Transfusion Requirements in Pediatric Intensive Care Units trial [41] found that in stable, critically ill children a restrictive transfusion strategy aiming at level of 70 g/L Hb was safe compared to a more liberal strategy targeting 95 g/L. These results are in line with studies in the adult population [42,43]. In combination with data indicating a higher rate of transfusion-related adverse events in children [44], this has resulted in recommendations favoring a transfusion trigger of 70 g/L in stable children [45,46]. However, for certain groups higher transfusion triggers may be necessary, for instance children <3 months and children with cyanotic heart failure, congestive heart failure, or in need of mechanical ventilation. Anemia increases the risk of postoperative apnea in premature children before 60 weeks of postconceptual age. However, whether preoperative transfusion reduces the risk of postoperative apnea or not is still unclear [47].

In the child with an ongoing bleeding, transfusion triggers need to be higher, and a target of 90 g/L is often used. There is little evidence to guide the use of blood products during major hemorrhage in infants and children. A transfusion protocol where blood, plasma, and platelets are administered in the ratio 20:20:10 mL/kg can be used in pediatric massive bleeding [48]. In patients with body weight >50 kg, adult massive bleeding protocols should be used, administering blood, plasma, and platelets in a 4:4:1 ratio.

Infants and children are sensitive to hypothermia, and blood products need to be administered through a blood warming system. Transfusion-related hypocalcemia is commonly encountered in children, and the administration of IV bolus doses of 10% calcium gluconate 0.5 mL/kg should be considered early in the course when transfusing larger amounts of blood products. Indications for platelet transfusion in children do not significantly differ from adults. Often 10 mL/kg is given, which can be expected to raise platelet count by approximately 50,000/μL.

11.12   Postoperative fluid therapy

Children are often allowed and able to tolerate oral intake shortly after surgery, and IV fluid therapy can then be discontinued. In more complex cases that need prolonged fluid substitution, careful planning of postoperative fluid therapy is essential.

As previously discussed, children are at risk of postoperative hyponatremia due to ADH secretion and diminished free water excretion. Besides the perioperative stress response, pain, postoperative nausea and vomiting, drugs, and anxiety contribute to the release of ADH. Postoperative fluids should preferably be isotonic and given at a lower rate than normal maintenance fluid. Several authors recommend using 50%–70% of a normal maintenance volume postoperatively. Obviously, postoperative fluid restriction should only be applied if the child is considered normovolemic.

11.13   Monitoring fluid status in the pediatric patient

The adequacy of fluid therapy in pediatric patients is usually estimated from clinical signs. However, individual clinical signs can be inaccurate, and it is important to consider the entire clinical situation before deciding upon a strategy. For instance, tachycardia can imply hypovolemia but may also be the result of untreated pain or anxiety.

Heart rate, blood pressure, capillary refill time, and core–peripheral temperature difference are often used as markers of fluid status in the child. Monitoring urine output is of great help, but it should be kept in mind that excessive ADH release can cause oliguria even in a well-hydrated child. A perioperative fluid balance recording fluid input and loss should be calculated, and, if available, the pre- and postoperative difference in patient body weight can give a god estimate of changes in volume status. Laboratory measurements of Hb, hematocrit, base excess, and lactate are useful and can often be obtained from a blood gas (arterial, venous, or capillary) analysis. If a central venous catheter is in place, measuring central venous oxygen saturation can be of help. Central venous pressure (CVP) has been shown to be a poor predictor of fluid responsiveness in both children [49] and adults [50], and the use of CVP in this context cannot be recommended.

In adult practice, noninvasive cardiac output monitoring, such as pulse-contour analysis and esophageal Doppler, is often used to assess fluid responsiveness in goal-directed therapy protocols for high-risk surgery [51]. Noninvasive cardiac output monitoring devices can also be used to assess fluid responsiveness in pediatric anesthesia. Esophageal Doppler analysis has been found to be useful in predicting volume responsiveness in anesthetized infants and neonates [52]. However, there are relevant cardiopulmonary differences between adults and children, and there is a need for further validation of methods and protocols in small children and infants undergoing surgery [49,53].

Near-infrared spectroscopy (NIRS) is a noninvasive technique that monitors regional tissue oxygenation in cerebral or splanchnic tissue [54]. NIRS has gained increasing popularity as a monitor of cerebral perfusion and as a substitute for cardiac output monitoring in neonates and small infants during and after cardiac surgery. The drawbacks of NIRS include the lack of defined normal values and that NIRS values differ significantly both interindividually and between devices from different manufacturers [55,56]. If NIRS has a role in predicting volume responsiveness in children, it remains to be shown.

11.14   Conclusion

The management of perioperative fluid therapy in infants and children requires an understanding of pediatric physiology and knowledge of reference values for age-related physiologic parameters. ADH secretion is often increased in pediatric surgical patients, leading to retention of free water and risk for symptomatic hyponatremia. Current guidelines for pediatric fluid therapy support the use of isotonic solutions in the perioperative period to avoid hyponatremia. Further, postoperative maintenance fluid should be reduced to 50%–70% of normal maintenance fluid. For most patients, it is not necessary to add glucose to the intraoperative fluid. Although adequate guidelines for maintenance fluid and intraoperative replacement fluid exist, fluid therapy needs to be adapted to the individual patient, and the clinical response to the prescribed therapy needs to be monitored.

11.15   Pediatric fluid case

A 3-year-old boy weighing 15 kg is scheduled for surgery due to acute appendicitis. His past medical record is unremarkable. He has had bowel pain and loss of appetite for 2 days, with minimal oral intake. During the last 24 hours he has had a temperature of 39 degrees centigrade, and over the last 12 hours he has had only minimal urine output.

When admitted he is found to be tired but responds adequately to verbal and tactile stimulation. Unfortunately, no recent preadmission weight is known. The boy is thirsty, with dry oral mucous membranes. His heart rate is 135 beats/min, blood pressure is 90/65, and capillary refill time is 3 seconds. A blood gas is taken in the emergency department; the hemoglobin value is 145 g/L, base excess –4 mEq/L, lactate 1.8, serum sodium is 138, and serum potassium 3.8.

Based on clinical and laboratory findings the boy is estimated to be dehydrated to a moderate (5%–10% of bodyweight) degree. Initial fluid resuscitation is started with a 10 mL/kg bolus of Ringer's acetate given over 20 minutes. Capillary refill time is now 2 seconds, and heart rate has decreased to 115 beats/min.

The child is further rehydrated with Ringer's acetate 50 mL/kg given over 4 hr. After rehydration he is taken to the operating theatre for surgery. He now has a heart rate of 100 beats/min, while blood pressure and capillary refill time are unchanged, and he has produced some urine in the ward.

During surgery a balanced isotonic crystalloid containing sodium 140 mmol/L and 1% glucose at a rate of 5 mL/kg/hr is used as maintenance fluid. After induction of anesthesia, the boy's blood pressure drops significantly and heart rate again increases to 130 beats/min. Hypovolemia is suspected, and a fluid bolus of 10 mL/kg of albumin 5% is administered, with prompt effect on blood pressure and heart rate. The surgical procedure is uneventful and the boy is hemodynamically stable throughout the operation.

For postoperative fluid therapy, a balanced isotonic crystalloid solution with 5% glucose is used. Normal hourly maintenance fluid need is estimated at 50 mL/hr according to the Holliday and Segar method (4 mL/kg/hr for the first 10 kg + 2 mL/kg/hr per kg >10 kg = 50 mL/hr). To avoid water retention and hyponatremia due to ADH secretion, postoperative fluid therapy is prescribed at a rate of 2/3 of normal maintenance needs, corresponding to 33.5 mL/hr for the first postoperative 24 hr.

References

1. Friis-Hansen B. Body water compartments in children: Changes during growth and related changes in body composition. *Pediatrics.* 1961;28:169–81.
2. Linderkamp O, Versmold HT, Riegel KP, Betke K. Estimation and prediction of blood volume in infants and children. *European Journal of Pediatrics.* 1977;125(4):227–34.
3. Arant BS, Jr. Postnatal development of renal function during the first year of life. *Pediatric Nephrology* (Berlin, Germany). 1987;1(3):308–13.
4. Holliday MA, Segar WE. The maintenance need for water in parenteral fluid therapy. *Pediatrics.* 1957;19(5):823–32.
5. Apfelbaum JL, Caplan RA, Connis RT, Epstein BS, Nickinovich DG, Warner MA. Practice guidelines for preoperative fasting and the use of pharmacologic agents to reduce the risk of pulmonary aspiration: Application to healthy patients undergoing elective procedures: An updated report by the American Society of Anesthesiologists Committee on Standards and Practice Parameters. *Anesthesiology.* 2011;114(3):495–511.
6. Smith I, Kranke P, Murat I, Smith A, O'Sullivan G, Soreide E, et al. Perioperative fasting in adults and children: Guidelines from the European society of anaesthesiology. *European Journal of Anaesthesiology.* 2011;28(8):556–69.
7. Schmidt AR, Buehler P, Seglias L, Stark T, Brotschi B, Renner T, et al. Gastric pH and residual volume after 1 and 2 h fasting time for clear fluids in childrendagger. *British Journal of Anaesthesia.* 2015;114(3):477–82.
8. Engelhardt T, Wilson G, Horne L, Weiss M, Schmitz A. Are you hungry? Are you thirsty?–Fasting times in elective outpatient pediatric patients. *Paediatric Anaesthesia.* 2011;21(9):964–8.

9. Way C, Dhamrait R, Wade A, Walker I. Perioperative fluid therapy in children: A survey of current prescribing practice. *British Journal of Anaesthesia.* 2006;97(3):371–9.
10. Moritz ML, Ayus JC. Preventing neurological complications from dysnatremias in children. *Pediatric Nephrology* (Berlin, Germany). 2005;20(12):1687–700.
11. Arieff AI, Ayus JC, Fraser CL. Hyponatraemia and death or permanent brain damage in healthy children. *BMJ* (Clinical research ed). 1992;304(6836):1218–22.
12. Oh GJ, Sutherland SM. Perioperative fluid management and postoperative hyponatremia in children. *Pediatric Nephrology* (Berlin, Germany). 2015;31(1):53–60.
13. Moritz ML, Ayus JC. New aspects in the pathogenesis, prevention, and treatment of hyponatremic encephalopathy in children. *Pediatric Nephrology* (Berlin, Germany). 2010;25(7):1225–38.
14. Montanana PA, Modesto I, Alapont V, Ocon AP, Lopez PO, Lopez Prats JL, Toledo Parreno JD. The use of isotonic fluid as maintenance therapy prevents iatrogenic hyponatremia in pediatrics: A randomized, controlled open study. *Pediatric Critical Care Medicine.* 2008;9(6):589–97.
15. Yung M, Keeley S. Randomised controlled trial of intravenous maintenance fluids. *Journal of Paediatrics and Child Health.* 2009;45(1–2):9–14.
16. Neville KA, Sandeman DJ, Rubinstein A, Henry GM, McGlynn M, Walker JL. Prevention of hyponatremia during maintenance intravenous fluid administration: A prospective randomized study of fluid type versus fluid rate. *The Journal of Pediatrics.* 2010;156(2):313–9.e1–2.
17. McNab S, Duke T, South M, Babl FE, Lee KJ, Arnup SJ, et al. 140 mmol/L of sodium versus 77 mmol/L of sodium in maintenance intravenous fluid therapy for children in hospital (PIMS): A randomised controlled double-blind trial. *Lancet.* 2015;385(9974):1190–7.
18. Choong K, Arora S, Cheng J, Farrokhyar F, Reddy D, Thabane L, et al. Hypotonic versus isotonic maintenance fluids after surgery for children: A randomized controlled trial. *Pediatrics.* 2011;128(5):857–66.
19. Sumpelmann R, Becke K, Crean P, Johr M, Lonnqvist PA, Strauss JM, et al. European consensus statement for intraoperative fluid therapy in children. *European Journal of Anaesthesiology.* 2011;28(9):637–9.
20. APA. Consensus guideline on perioperative fluid management in children 2007.
21. O'Dell E, Tibby SM, Durward A, Murdoch IA. Hyperchloremia is the dominant cause of metabolic acidosis in the postresuscitation phase of pediatric meningococcal sepsis. *Critical Care Medicine.* 2007;35(10):2390–4.
22. Inder T. How low can I go? The impact of hypoglycemia on the immature brain. *Pediatrics.* 2008;122(2):440–1.
23. Paut O, Lacroix F. Recent developments in the perioperative fluid management for the paediatric patient. *Current Opinion in Anaesthesiology.* 2006;19(3):268–77.
24. Leelanukrom R, Cunliffe M. Intraoperative fluid and glucose management in children. *Paediatric Anaesthesia.* 2000;10(4):353–9.
25. Elkon B, Cambrin JR, Hirshberg E, Bratton SL. Hyperglycemia: An independent risk factor for poor outcome in children with traumatic brain injury. *Pediatric Critical Care Medicine.* 2014;15(7):623–31.
26. Nishina K, Mikawa K, Maekawa N, Asano M, Obara H. Effects of exogenous intravenous glucose on plasma glucose and lipid homeostasis in anesthetized infants. *Anesthesiology.* 1995;83(2):258–63.

27. Sumpelmann R, Mader T, Dennhardt N, Witt L, Eich C, Osthaus WA. A novel isotonic balanced electrolyte solution with 1% glucose for intra-operative fluid therapy in neonates: Results of a prospective multicentre observational Postauthorisation Safety Study (PASS). *Paediatric Anaesthesia.* 2011;21(11):1114–8.

28. Sumpelmann R, Mader T, Eich C, Witt L, Osthaus WA. A novel isotonic-balanced electrolyte solution with 1% glucose for intraoperative fluid therapy in children: Results of a prospective multicentre observational Post-Authorization Safety Study (PASS). *Paediatric Anaesthesia.* 2010;20(11):977–81.

29. Bhaskar P, Dhar AV, Thompson M, Quigley R, Modem V. Early fluid accu-mulation in children with shock and ICU mortality: A matched case-control study. *Intensive Care Medicine.* 2015;41(8):1445–53.

30. Lex DJ, Toth R, Czobor NR, Alexander SI, Breuer T, Sapi E, et al. Fluid overload is associated with higher mortality and morbidity in pediat-ric patients undergoing cardiac surgery. *Pediatric Critical Care Medicine.* 2016;17(4):307–14.

31. Murat I, Dubois MC. Perioperative fluid therapy in pediatrics. *Paediatric Anaesthesia.* 2008;18(5):363–70.

32. Bancalari E, Wilson-Costello D, Iben SC. Management of infants with bron-chopulmonary dysplasia in North America. *Early Human Development.* 2005;81(2):171–9.

33. Bailey AG, McNaull PP, Jooste E, Tuchman JB. Perioperative crystalloid and colloid fluid management in children: Where are we and how did we get here? *Anesthesia and Analgesia.* 2010;110(2):375–90.

34. Emery EF, Greenough A, Gamsu HR. Randomised controlled trial of colloid infusions in hypotensive preterm infants. *Archives of Disease in Childhood.* 1992;67(10 Spec No):1185–8.

35. Perner A, Haase N, Guttormsen AB, Tenhunen J, Klemenzson G, Aneman A, et al. Hydroxyethyl starch 130/0.42 versus Ringer's acetate in severe sepsis. *The New England Journal of Medicine.* 2012;367(2):124–34.

36. Myburgh JA, Finfer S, Bellomo R, Billot L, Cass A, Gattas D, et al. Hydroxyethyl starch or saline for fluid resuscitation in intensive care. *The New England Journal of Medicine.* 2012;367(20):1901–11.

37. Li L, Li Y, Xu X, Xu B, Ren R, Liu Y, et al. Safety evaluation on low-molecular-weight hydroxyethyl starch for volume expansion therapy in pediatric patients: A meta-analysis of randomized controlled trials. *Critical Care* (London, England). 2015;19(1):79.

38. Thomas-Rueddel DO, Vlasakov V, Reinhart K, Jaeschke R, Rueddel H, Hutagalung R, et al. Safety of gelatin for volume resuscitation–a systematic review and meta-analysis. *Intensive Care Medicine.* 2012;38(7):1134–42.

39. Roback JD, Caldwell S, Carson J, Davenport R, Drew MJ, Eder A, et al. Evidence-based practice guidelines for plasma transfusion. *Transfusion.* 2010;50(6):1227–39.

40. Woodcock TE, Woodcock TM. Revised Starling equation and the glyco-calyx model of transvascular fluid exchange: An improved paradigm for prescribing intravenous fluid therapy. *British Journal of Anaesthesia.* 2012;108(3):384–94.

41. Lacroix J, Hebert PC, Hutchison JS, Hume HA, Tucci M, Ducruet T, et al. Transfusion strategies for patients in pediatric intensive care units. *The New England Journal of Medicine.* 2007;356(16):1609–19.

42. Holst LB, Haase N, Wetterslev J, Wernerman J, Guttormsen AB, Karlsson S, et al. Lower versus higher hemoglobin threshold for transfusion in septic shock. *The New England Journal of Medicine*. 2014;371(15):1381–91.
43. Hebert PC, Wells G, Blajchman MA, Marshall J, Martin C, Pagliarello G, et al. A multicenter, randomized, controlled clinical trial of transfusion requirements in critical care. Transfusion requirements in critical care investigators, Canadian critical care trials group. *The New England Journal of Medicine*. 1999;340(6):409–17.
44. Harrison E, Bolton P. Serious hazards of transfusion in children (SHOT). *Paediatric Anaesthesia*. 2011;21(1):10–3.
45. Lacroix J, Tucci M, Pont-Thibodeau GD. Red blood cell transfusion decision making in critically ill children. *Current Opinion in Pediatrics*. 2015;27(3):286–91.
46. Secher EL, Stensballe J, Afshari A. Transfusion in critically ill children: An ongoing dilemma. *Acta Anaesthesiologica Scandinavica*. 2013;57(6):684–91.
47. Sale SM. Neonatal apnoea. *Best Practice & Research Clinical Anaesthesiology*. 2010;24(3):323–36.
48. Nystrup KB, Stensballe J, Bottger M, Johansson PI, Ostrowski SR. Transfusion therapy in paediatric trauma patients: A review of the literature. *Scandinavian Journal of Trauma, Resuscitation and Emergency Medicine*. 2015;23:21.
49. Gan H, Cannesson M, Chandler JR, Ansermino JM. Predicting fluid responsiveness in children: A systematic review. *Anesthesia and Analgesia*. 2013;117(6):1380–92.
50. Marik PE, Cavallazzi R. Does the central venous pressure predict fluid responsiveness? An updated meta-analysis and a plea for some common sense. *Critical Care Medicine*. 2013;41(7):1774–81.
51. Perel A, Habicher M, Sander M. Bench-to-bedside review: Functional hemodynamics during surgery—should it be used for all high-risk cases? *Critical Care* (London, England). 2013;17(1):203.
52. Raux O, Spencer A, Fesseau R, Mercier G, Rochette A, Bringuier S, et al. Intraoperative use of transoesophageal Doppler to predict response to volume expansion in infants and neonates. *British Journal of Anaesthesia*. 2012;108(1):100–7.
53. Gueli SL, Lerman J. Controversies in pediatric anesthesia: Sevoflurane and fluid management. *Current Opinion in Anaesthesiology*. 2013;26(3):310–7.
54. Mittnacht AJ. Near infrared spectroscopy in children at high risk of low perfusion. *Current Opinion in Anaesthesiology*. 2010;23(3):342–7.
55. Dullenkopf A, Frey B, Baenziger O, Gerber A, Weiss M. Measurement of cerebral oxygenation state in anaesthetized children using the INVOS 5100 cerebral oximeter. *Paediatric Anaesthesia*. 2003;13(5):384–91.
56. Schneider A, Minnich B, Hofstatter E, Weisser C, Hattinger-Jurgenssen E, Wald M. Comparison of four near-infrared spectroscopy devices shows that they are only suitable for monitoring cerebral oxygenation trends in preterm infants. *Acta Paediatrica* (Oslo, Norway : 1992). 2014;103(9):934–8.

chapter twelve

Burn resuscitation

**Fredrick J. Bohanon, Paul Wurzer, Charles Mitchell,
David N. Herndon, and George Kramer**
University of Texas Medical Branch
Galveston, TX

Contents

Key points:

- Case presentations
- Burn resuscitation history and formulae
- Choice of fluids
- Route of administration
- Lung injury
- Fluid creep
- Emerging new approaches

12.1   Clinical scenario 1: A resuscitation without significant complications

A previously healthy 52-year-old male patient sustained a burn injury to his face, anterior torso, bilateral upper extremities/hands, bilateral thighs, and penis. The patient was starting an outdoor fire with a gasoline accelerant and suffered a 36% total body surface area (TBSA) burn. He arrived at the burn unit approximately 2 hours post-injury and underwent resuscitation with a computerized decision support system (CDSS). Figure 12.1a shows the total volume of lactated Ringer's (LR) infused over time and for comparison, volumes calculated from the Parkland and modified Brooke formulae through 23 hours post-burn when the patient went to surgery. During the first 23 hours of resuscitation, the patient received a total volume of 10.7 L (LR) or 3.1 mL/kg/% TBSA burned.

Hourly inputs and outputs are shown in Figure 12.1b. After the first 8 hours post-burn, infused volumes and rates were virtually identical to the Parkland rate, with urinary output (UOP) improving to slightly above target levels. At Hour 11, the LR infusion rates were rapidly reduced per CDSS recommendations to maintenance levels; after this time, the patient continued to receive LR infusion at maintenance levels in addition to the volume from intravenous drugs and oral intake. Lactate had returned to a normal concentration of 1.4 mEq/L at Hour 26, down from 3.0 mEq/L at admission. At post-burn Hour 18, albumin and Lasix were co-administered to accelerate removal of sequestered fluid. Subsequent hospital course was uneventful; the patient did not develop organ failure, sepsis, acute lung injury, or acute respiratory distress syndrome. Patient had a length of stay of 23 days and had a follow-up period of 18 months.

12.2   Clinical scenario 2: A resuscitation of an older patient with multiple comorbidities

An 81-year-old male patient sustained a 55% TBSA burn caused by an outdoor fire. The patient had several preexisting conditions including coronary artery disease with multiple stent placements, diabetes mellitus, endovascular repair of an abdominal aortic aneurysm, obesity, and hypertension. Upon arrival at 2 hours post-burn, the patient was pulseless but had successful return of rhythm and blood pressure with epinephrine.

The patient was placed on a ventilator to secure airway and maintain Peripheral capillary oxygen saturation (SpO$_2$) > 90. Fluid resuscitation was started using the CDSS. During the first 24 hours of resuscitation, the patient received a total volume of 27.5 L or 3.9 mL/kg/% TBSA burned. Figure 12.2a shows a comparison of the actual volume to the volumes estimated using the Parkland or modified Brooke formulae.

Figure 12.1 Initial fluid resuscitation of the 52-year-old-patient using a computerized decision support system (CDSS). (a) Total volume of lactated Ringer's infused over time and compared to volumes calculated from the Parkland and modified Brooke formulae through 23 hours post-burn when the patient went to surgery. (b) Hourly inputs and outputs during the first 24 hours post-injury. HPB, hours post-burn; IV ABX, intravenous antibiotics.

Figure 12.2 Initial fluid resuscitation the 81-year-old-patient using a CDSS. (a) Comparison of the actual volume to the volumes estimated using the Parkland or modified Brooke formulae. (b) Hourly inputs and outputs. HPB, hours post-burn; Epi, epinephrine; IV ABX, intravenous antibiotics.

Hourly inputs and outputs are shown in Figure 12.2b. With this resuscitation strategy, the patient achieved the target hourly UOP only 28% of the time. The patient continued to decline and required high levels of vasoactive agents to maintain blood pressure. After consultation with the family, supportive measures were discontinued, and patient status was changed to DNR with comfort measures. The patient expired on hospital Day 2.

12.3   Introduction

The severely burned patient presents in a state of cardiogenic, hypovolemic, and distributive shock [1,2]. The hypovolemia is largely due to loss of fluid and plasma protein extravasation from the burn wounds and other soft tissues of the body. There is a direct increase in microvascular permeability in the burn wound [3,4]. In addition, circulating mediators in other soft tissues, particularly the skin, intestines, and muscle, also contribute to microvascular permeability at these sites. Fluid resuscitation is the treatment for these profound states, but fluid resuscitation often cannot adequately treat burn shock and poor hemodynamics.

The goal of fluid resuscitation, which should be instituted promptly, is to ameliorate and ideally to prevent the development of burn shock at the lowest physiologic cost and volume administered [5,6]. If burn shock develops, the patient's body undergoes a massive adaption in which all components and regulators of fluid balance are altered. This results in volume depletion, cardiac depression, decreased pulmonary artery occlusion pressures, elevated systemic and pulmonary vascular resistance, and activation of catecholamine and cytokine cascades [6,7]. Therefore, timely and effective fluid resuscitation must be universal. If fluid therapy is delayed by more than 2 hours after injury, complications and mortality are increased [2,8]. On the other hand, care must be taken to not over-resuscitate patients, which can result in as severe morbidity and mortality as under-resuscitation. Over-resuscitation appears to occur more often than under-resuscitation.

12.4   Burn resuscitation—where it started

One of the earliest accounts of fluid therapy for burns was in the 1700s by Herman Boerhaave and his apprentice Gerard van Swieten, who wrote, "there is but one remedy that can be used universally recommended in all the species of burns, namely, the use of a thin anti-phlogistic or 'cooling drink'" [8]. He further describes Boerhaave's self-treatment following a scald burn, stating, "by the use of a thin diet, and plentiful drinking of cool liquors at the same time" he appeared in public in 8 days [8].

In 1831, the second cholera pandemic swept across Europe from India and reached North America, leaving tens of thousands dead [9]. Cholera causes massive hypovolemic shock characterized by decreased circulating blood volume, metabolic acidosis, decreased cardiac output (CO), and tachycardia [10]. W. B. O'Shaughnessy, an Irish physician, analyzed the blood of cholera patients in 1831 and found electrolyte depletion, acidosis, and nitrogen retention. He stated that there was "universal stagnation of the venous system and rapid cessation of the arterialization of the blood" [11]. Following these findings, O'Shaughnessy carried out a series of animal experiments and proposed that treatment must be based on intravenous replacement of the salt and water [11]. Thomas Latta, a physician not given acclaim for his work at the time, took the theory of O'Shaughnessy and put it into practice. He initially attempted rectal rehydration with mixed results, but in a paper presented in *The Lancet*, he reported successful fluid replacement via the basilic vein [11]. Further studies on cholera continued to provide insight into fluid replacement for burn injuries. In 1854, Ludwig von Buhl reported that hemoconcentration occurred in both burn victims and victims of cholera, and he suggested that all patients receive fluid replacement [12].

In 1905, the American surgeon Haldor Sneve published research on skin grafting and burn treatment in a large series of patients, and he recommended fluid replacement with a saline solution either via hypodermoclysis or intravenous routes [13]. Unfortunately, his recommendations and work on goal-focused resuscitation were overlooked and not built upon for many years [12].

Mass casualty events and war have been one of the largest contributors to advancements of burn care. On November 27, 1921, the Rialto Theatre in New Haven, Connecticut, caught fire, killing 6 and injuring 80 [14]. During this time, Dr. Frank Underhill laid the foundation for the management of fluid and electrolytes [15,16]. Underhill examined 21 patients who were admitted following the theatre fire. He reported that the more severe the burn, the more severe the hemoconcentration and that fluid replacement must be rapid and is of paramount importance in survival [15,16]. Additionally, he reported that blister fluid was similar in composition to plasma and that the fluid lost could be replaced with a salt solution [16]. On November 28, 1942, the Cocoanut Grove nightclub caught fire, killing 492 people and injuring hundreds more, making it the deadliest nightclub fire in US history. The patients were sent to Boston City Hospital and Massachusetts General Hospital (MGH). Dr. Charles Lund led the team at Boston City Hospital, while Dr. Oliver Cope led the team at MGH. Both institutions began resuscitation with IV fluid containing equal parts saline and plasma [12]. Cope used a resuscitation formula that provided 500 mL plasma plus 500 mL saline for every 10% TBSA burned in the first 24 hours, followed by adjustments based on hemoconcentration [17]. Dr. Lund did not use a formula to guide resuscitation, but he did use clinical parameters such as heart rate, blood pressure, and hematocrit [18]. Later, Cope and Francis Moore reported the first burn formula based on burn surface area for fluid therapy, recommending that 75 mL plasma and 75 mL noncolloid isotonic fluid be administered for every 1% TBSA burned in the first 24 hours, with one-half being given in the first 8 hours and the remainder being given in the next 16 hours. This practice of providing half of the fluid needs within the first 8 hours remains a feature of nearly all modern burn resuscitation formulae. Additionally, 2,000 mL fluid was to be given on each day for insensible losses [19]. These formulae were based on a "normal" sized adult and could be unfavorable for some patient cohorts. Thus, more accurate formulae based on weight and TBSA burned were needed.

12.5   Burn resuscitation formulae

Following the contributions of Cope and Moore, Dr. Everett Evans developed a formula based on TBSA burned and weight. This formula sets infusion at 1 mL/kg/% TBSA burned of normal saline and an equal part colloid plus 2,000 mL D5W in the first 24 hours, followed by 0.5 mL/kg/% TBSA burned of saline and an equal part colloid plus an equal amount of D5W in the second 24 hours [20,21]. In 1968, Baxter and Shires, using an animal model, described the ongoing fluid shifts into the interstitial space and cellular space following thermal injury and showed that most of the edema fluid in burn wounds is isotonic [22]. In studies performed on dogs and primates, they found that, in burn-injured and unresuscitated animals, the greatest volume loss occurred throughout the extracellular fluid compartment due to cellular edema. Further, the decreased vascular volume reduced CO by 25% within 4 hours post-burn. In clinical trials, mortality rates were comparable, whether sodium fluids or colloid-containing resuscitation formulae were used for resuscitation, and both led to the same plasma volume at 24 hours post-burn, although more crystalloid was used than albumin. They suggested not using colloid until after the first 24 hours post-burn because of transient capillary leak. These findings were the basis for the Baxter or Parkland formulae, 4 mL/kg/% TBSA burned of crystalloid (most often LR) [23]. This remains the most commonly used formula today.

Soon after Baxter's work, Pruitt and colleagues reviewed burn resuscitation records at the Brooke Army Medical Center and reported that the average amount of fluid collectively received in their patients approximated half the needs of the Parkland formula [24]. They also concluded that colloids given within the first 24 hours do not affect protein plasma content, prompting them to propose infusion of 2 mL/kg/% TBSA burned of crystalloids during the first 24 hours (i.e., Pruitt-modified Brooke formula).

Table 12.1 Common burn resuscitation formulae

Formula	First 24 hours post-burn	Next 24 hours post-burn
Evans Formula	NS: 1 mL/kg/% TBSA burn Colloid: 1 mL/kg/% TBSA burn D5W: 2,000 mL	NS: 0.5 mL/kg/% TBSA burn Colloid: 0.5 mL/kg/% TBSA burn D5W: 2,000mL
Brooke Formula	LR: 1.5 mL/kg/% TBSA burn Colloid: 0.5 mL/kg/% TBSA burn D5W: 2,000 mL	LR: 0.5 mL/kg/% TBSA burn Colloid: 0.25 mL/kg/% TBSA burn D5W: 2,000 mL
Modified Brooke Formula	LR: 2 mL/kg/% TBSA burn Colloid: None	LR: None Colloid: 0.3–0.5 mL/kg/% TBSA burn D5W: Volume needed to maintain UOP
Parkland Formula	LR: 4 mL/kg/% TBSA burn Colloid: None	LR: None Colloid: given as 20–60% of calculated plasma volume D5W: Volume needed to maintain UOP
Modified Parkland Formula	LR: 4 mL/kg/% TBSA burn Colloid: None	LR: None Colloid: 5% albumin given at 0.3–1 mL/kg/% TBSA burn/16 per hour
Shriner's Cincinnati (For Children)	LR: 4 mL/kg/% TBSA burn + 1,500 mL/m², ½ given over 1st 8 h and the remaining over the next 16 h (older children) LR: 4 mL/kg/% TBSA burn + 1,500 mL/m² + 50 mEq sodium bicarbonate for the 1st 8 h, followed by LR alone in 2nd 8 h, followed by 5% albumin in LR in 3rd 8 h (younger children)	
Galveston Formula (For Children)	LR: 5,000 mL/m² burn + 2,000 mL/m² total. ½ volume in 1st 8 h, followed by rest in 16 h	

Source: Adapted from Hansen, S.L., *Wounds*, 20(7), 206–213, 2008.

Note: NS, normal saline; D5W, 5% dextrose in water; TBSA, total body surface area; LR, lactated Ringer's solution; UOP, urinary output; h, hours.

Pruitt, as Baxter before him, emphasized that formulae were to be used as an estimated guide and the actual amount given needs to be based on clinical response.

Both the Parkland and Brooke formulae use crystalloids for the first 24 hours, with the first calculated half being given within the first 8 hours and the next half within the following 16 hours; administration of colloids should be considered after the first 24 hours [25]. Two additional formulae, the Shriner's Cincinnati and Galveston formulae, have been developed specifically for children. Both account for the larger body surface area-to-weight ratio and provide for relatively greater insensible losses per body weight [1,26]. These burn resuscitation formulae are provided in Table 12.1.

12.6 Transition from colloid to crystalloid and back

Despite the earlier findings and strong positions that both Baxter and Pruitt took against early colloid use, stating that "colloids are expensive salt water" [27], the debate concerning if, when, and how much colloid is needed is ongoing. Prior to the 1960s, burn resuscitation formulae relied on the use of colloid, mainly in the form of plasma, early in the resuscitation phase.

Resuscitation with colloids, almost always albumin, is attractive to burn physicians because of its potential advantage over crystalloids in more efficiently replenishing the intravascular volume with less volume infused and reduced tissue edema. The argument against early colloid is the increased macromolecular capillary permeability that allows more protein to leak into tissue spaces, which may actually hold water in the interstitial spaces of the burn wound and soft tissues. The infused colloidal macromolecules increase colloid osmotic or "oncotic" pressure and typically are predominately distributed in the vascular compartment, with sustained expansion, which can reduce the formation of tissue edema. Goodwin et al. undertook a randomized trial comparing the effects of colloid and crystalloid on lung water and hemodynamics in thermally injured patients. The colloid group received 2.5% albumin in LR from the start of resuscitation, while the crystalloid group received LR alone. In both groups, the rate of infusion was titrated to achieve a UOP of 30 to 50 mL/hr. The colloid group received a significantly smaller total volume than the crystalloid group. However, the albumin group did develop significantly more lung water [28]. In a more recent prospective randomized trial, O'Mara and colleagues compared fresh frozen plasma (FFP) resuscitation and crystalloid resuscitation [29]. In this trial, the FFP group received a mixture of 75 mL/kg FFP (titrated to maintain a UOP of 0.5 to 1.0 mL/kg/hr) plus 2,000 mL LR (83 mL/hr), while the crystalloid group received LR according to the Parkland formula (titrated to maintain a UOP of 0.5 to 1.0 mL/kg/hr). The crystalloid group required significantly more fluid volume than the FFP group (0.26 vs. 0.14 L/kg). Additionally, FFP resuscitation was associated with a significantly lower peak intra-abdominal pressure (16 vs. 32 mmHg). Further, the crystalloid group developed significantly elevated creatinine, blood urea nitrogen, and peak airway pressure from the time of admission to peak values, while the FFP group developed only significantly elevated peak airway pressure.

There are several systematic approaches to colloid use: (1) use colloids during all hours of burn resuscitation, (2) use of colloids starting around 12 hours post-injury, and (3) no use of colloids for resuscitation during the first 24 hours [30]. A specific approach taken at the University of Utah burn center involves use of "albumin rescue" when the fluid infused-to-UOP ratio increases above expected levels [31,32].

Crystalloid resuscitation solution, mainly in the form of LR solution, is predominately used in the United States, with most burn centers using some colloid per physician discretion [30]. The Parkland and modified Brooke formulae are the two most commonly used formulae to start fluid infusion rates, but it cannot be emphasized enough to adjust infusion rates to a target UOP, usually 0.5 to 1.0 mL/kg/hr, sometimes approximated as 30–50 mL/hr. Recent updates to these formulae dictate the use of LR du ing the first 24 hours and minimal use of colloids during this time frame [33]. As mentioned above, the reliance on crystalloid alone for resuscitation is associated with significantly greater volume infused, and the possible complications from this are discussed below. Selecting the optimal fluid to use and time to institute it is not a simple matter. The American Burn Association committee on fluid therapy concluded that evidence is lacking to standardize any single protocol [33]. Optimizing fluid therapy always depends upon many factors such as percent TBSA burned, depth of injury, and age; however, two challenging factors are significant comorbidities (e.g., heart failure, obesity, and renal dysfunction) and presence of inhalation injury (discussed below) [34].

12.7   Route of administration

A survey of burn specialists performed by Greenhalgh revealed that the peripheral intravenous route (70%) is preferred for burn shock fluid resuscitation. However, central venous access is often established and used (48%) [35]. In cases of severe injury with widespread deep burns and edema, use of peripheral veins is sometimes impossible. As a temporary option, intraosseous access can be obtained, but flow rates are limited due to hydraulic resistance of the bone marrow. Later, central venous access can be established in the intensive care setting and provides the best means for the administration of large amount of fluids.

Early fluid resuscitation (within the first hours of burn trauma) is essential for the prevention of organ failure but often cannot be performed due to delayed access to care providers [36,37]. This is particularly true in austere environments, combat casualty care, and mass casualties where patients outnumber caregivers. One approach may be the reintroduction of an enteral or oral route of burn shock resuscitation, which evidence suggests is effective for burns between 10% and 40% TBSA [21,38]. Clinical use of enteral resuscitation of burns was first described by Fox in 1944 [39]. However, its use might be limited by paralytic ileus and reduced gastric function. The effectiveness and safety of enteral resuscitation in prehospital settings and in early burn resuscitation certainly merit further investigation.

12.8 Lung injury necessitates more fluid

In 1981, Baxter and Shires showed that patients with inhalation injuries and large burns have the greatest fluid requirements in the burn population; however, they did not describe how much additional fluid is needed [40]. Most studies have reported increased fluid requirements of 20%–30% when compared to equal size burns without inhalation injury [41,42].

12.9 Monitoring resuscitation

Optimizing resuscitation—i.e., ensuring administration of sufficient volume to obtain organ and tissue perfusion at the lowest physiologic cost—requires hourly monitoring (UOP, hemodynamics, and clinical signs of adequate perfusion) and titration of fluid based on these end points. Several factors can influence monitoring, including time from burn to admission, extent and mechanism of injury, concurrent injuries (e.g., blast, electrical, polytrauma), preexisting diseases, age, sex, and inhalation injury. The most commonly used assessments rely on vital signs, laboratory-based parameters, and UOP. The primary endpoint is often UOP, with the rationale that it is a surrogate metric for glomerular filtration rate, renal blood flow, end organ perfusion, and CO. However, UOP is only one metric for adequate perfusion and requires careful attention. Heart rate, blood pressure, and electrocardiography can serve as indices of cardiovascular status. These can be obtained non-invasively or invasively, depending upon the clinical detail needed for assessment. Large burns with complex comorbidities can benefit from monitoring of CO, central venous pressure, and lung water. Beyond UOP, mean arterial pressure (MAP) is considered one of the most reliable indicators of resuscitation [43]. MAP should be maintained at greater than 60 mmHg to safeguard against cerebral perfusion. Recommended UOP is 0.5–1.0 mL/kg/hr in adults and 1.0–2.0 mL/kg/hr in children, although recent trends have many burn caregivers targeting the lower values of these ranges. UOP is usually monitored and recorded hourly; however, studies verifying this frequency are lacking.

Laboratory values are an important assessment tool. Complete blood count, electrolytes, glucose, albumin, and acid–base status should be monitored frequently, although evidence regarding the optimal frequency of analysis is lacking. Large volumes of fluid can cause large changes in these parameters. Therefore, they should be monitored and abnormalities corrected. Lactate and base deficit (BD) are often used as indices of adequacy of global perfusion and an end point for increased fluids and other supportive therapy (e.g., transfusion and vasoactive drugs). Elevated BD and serum lactate correlate with larger burn size, inhalation injury, greater fluid requirements, and mortality [37,44]. In a prospective study of BD and outcomes in burn patients, Cartotto et al. reported that patients with severe BD had greater fluid requirements as well as higher rates of sepsis, acute respiratory distress syndrome, and multiple organ dysfunction syndrome [45]. Kamolz et al. showed that lactate levels and the rate of lactate clearance are useful markers of shock and resuscitation status [46]. Additionally, they demonstrated that if the lactate levels were normalized within 24 hours the survival rate was 68%, compared to 32% if lactate normalization did not occur within 24 hours.

Invasive cardiac monitoring provides a means of directly assessing patients' physiologic status [1]. Using these invasive techniques, one can determine central venous pressure, pulmonary capillary wedge pressure, systemic and pulmonary vascular resistances, CO, and oxygen consumption. The pulmonary artery catheter (PAC) has been used for decades to assess these parameters. Literature describing the routine and effective use of PAC in burns is lacking, and there are no clear indications for PAC use in burn patients [43].

In addition to standard vital signs and hourly UOP monitoring, transpulmonary thermodilution (TPTD) guided fluid resuscitation is a minimally invasive option for hemodynamic observation in patients with severe burns. In comparison to PAC, TPTD requires one access point via a central venous line as well as one access point via a peripheral artery (femoral artery or brachial artery) to allow beta-to-beat measurements of MAP, CO, and cardiac index. In addition, one can measure global end-diastolic volume, a marker for cardiac preload as well as extravascular lung water, a marker for pulmonary edema. Sanchez et al. showed that TPTD accurately detected hypovolemia during acute resuscitation (within 24 hours of burn), while hypovolemia was not reflected by MAP or hourly UOP [47]. A recent study in burned children by Kraft et al. confirmed these findings [48]. Thus, TPTD is an additional tool for monitoring ongoing hemodynamic changes during acute burn fluid resuscitation. End points and target values must be adjusted precisely to provide reliable hemodynamic measurements [47–49].

Medical imaging, including transesophageal echocardiography (TEE) and transthoracic echocardiography (TTE), has evolved to be one of the most common procedures for cardiac evaluation of burn patients [50]. TTE provides real-time assessment of volume status and cardiac function, allowing for critical decision support for fluid and vasoactive drug management. In contrast to the more invasive TEE, TTE can be performed easily without the need for pre-assessment sedation. Nevertheless, TTE needs to be performed by well-trained and certified clinicians to minimize and prevent user-dependent errors [51]. A further advantage of echocardiography, in comparison to PAC and TPTD, is that it can help physicians by diagnosing cardiac failure caused by the hyperdynamic response to burns. In a recent systematic review, Maybauer et al. showed that TEE is beneficial for a better understanding of the actual fluid status of burn patients; however, further prospective randomized controlled trials comparing different echocardiography techniques are warranted [50].

12.10   Fluid creep

In the acute phase of burns, the need to maintain adequate blood perfusion in internal organs during ongoing intercompartmental fluid shifts (arising from increased vascular permeability) and the failure to titrate fluid needs appropriately can lead to over-resuscitation of the burn patient [32]. Fluid creep was first described by Pruitt as the trend toward infusing greater volumes of fluid than those calculated using burn formulas and increased reports of fluid overload and associated organ dysfunction during the acute phase of hospitalization [52]. Delivery of fluid volumes in excess of needs causes life-threatening consequences. Over-resuscitation may lead to an abdominal compartment syndrome [53], pulmonary edema [54], and vast general edema on uninjured extremities [55]. In addition, there is greater morbidity and mortality due to additional fasciotomies in uninjured extremities and tracheostomies to save the upper airways [53–55]. Fluid creep also prolongs hospital stays and increases the care needed.

We performed a meta-analysis of studies comparing actual 24-hour volume requirements and found large volumes of fluid continue to be administered, with most studies showing that infused volumes exceed Parkland estimations (Figure 12.3). While the data suggest a trend towards increased fluid volumes, more striking are the wide variations reported for mean values and the large standard deviations reported for most individual studies. These data stand in sharp contrast to Baxter's original

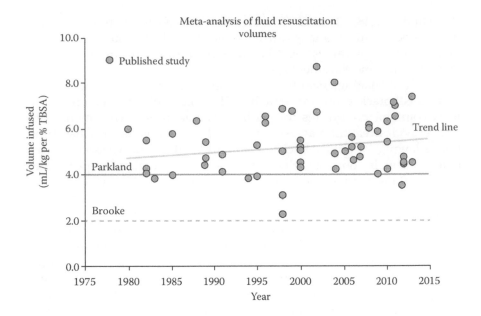

Figure 12.3 Meta-analysis of published studies showing actual fluid infused over 24 hours compared to fluid requirements estimated using the Parkland and Brooke formulae. Studies of computerized decision support have revealed that total fluid infused is less than Parkland volumes. On the other hand, studies have shown that, from 1980 to 2014, the mean fluid infused was 5.3 ± 1.2 (SD) mL/kg per % total body surface area burned.

publications, which suggested that most patients can be resuscitated with 4 mL/kg/% TBSA burned.

The ultimate goal during burn shock is to resuscitate the patient adequately and to titrate the fluid according to individual patient needs. In a recent study, Faraklas et al. suggested that clinicians could be lax in hourly adjustments of infusion rates, especially in decreasing them. Further, they concluded from their retrospective analysis that seriously injured patients, pediatric patients, and patients with the combination of burns and inhalation injuries are more prone to fluid creep [56]. Greater fluid volumes were associated with significantly more escharotomies and complications as well as longer hospital stays. Reasons for the increased fluid needs might be that the amount of fluid received before admission was unknown and/or that clinicians overly responded to inadequate hourly UOP with greater infusion rates [56].

In 2004, Sullivan et al. suggested that fluid creep might be associated with an increased administration of opioids during burn shock resuscitation [57]. They compared fluid requirements in a cohort of burn patients who received low doses of opioids (treated in 1975) to those in a group of patients (treated in 2000) that received four times higher doses of opioids. A significant correlation was noted between opioid dose and fluid requirements within the first 24 hours of acute hospitalization. Nevertheless, opioids remain a crucial part of pain management in severely burned patients and parts of care protocols [58]. The cardiovascular effects of opioids and benzodiazepines need to be considered, and the amount given must be strictly monitored. As of yet, no other studies in the burn population have confirmed these findings, but trials are warranted to clarify the interaction between the amount of opioids and fluids given during burn shock resuscitation.

In 2010, Lawrence et al. described a "colloid rescue" in which they included 5% human albumin in resuscitation fluid for patients who required excess amounts of fluids; this approach reduced the subsequent infusion rates during resuscitation [31]. In a study performed by Chung et al. during Operation Iraqi Freedom, fluid creep was prevented by incorporating large-molecular-weight colloids (i.e., hydroxyethyl starch) instead of crystalloids into their resuscitation protocol [59]. It should be pointed out that the safety of starch-based colloids has been recently challenged and should not be used during burn resuscitation in the absence of new data supporting specific benefits over albumin [60].

In summary, fluid creep can be reduced by close monitoring of UOP (0.5 mL/kg/hr in adults and 1.0 mL/kg/hr in children) and subtle adjustments to patients' individual fluid requirements based on CO and peripheral perfusion. The use of colloids should be considered in patients heading towards fluid needs in excess of Parkland volume estimates.

12.11   Emerging new approaches

Burn surgeons and critical care teams continue to pursue promising new approaches to burn care. Advances such as the use of vitamin C (ascorbic acid), nurse-driven protocols, decision support systems, and closed-loop computerized resuscitation are making great inroads into the care of patients. In a prospective randomized controlled trial, Tanaka and colleagues showed that high-dose vitamin C significantly reduced 24-hr fluid requirements (from 5.5 to 3.0 mL/kg), weight gain, and edema. Additionally, vitamin C-receiving patients had fewer mechanical ventilation days, less lung water, and lower rates of acute lung injury [61]. The vitamin C group, although given significantly less fluid than the control group, had comparable hemodynamics and hourly UOP. The authors proposed that vitamin C achieves these beneficial effects owing to the fact that it is a free radical scavenger capable of reducing post-burn lipid peroxidation, microvascular leakage, and wound edema [61]. Dubick and coworkers reported that, in an ovine model of burns, high-dose isotonic vitamin C reduced total volume infused over the 48-hour study. Further, the vitamin C group had markedly elevated plasma antioxidant potential and reduced lipid peroxidation [62]. A small retrospective review of high-dose vitamin C yielded similar findings [63]. Specifically, vitamin C-treated patients had significantly lower resuscitation volumes and reduced vaso-pressor use. These above studies suggest that high-dose vitamin C holds promise in resuscitation; however, the optimal dose, potential side effects, and mechanism of action all require further investigation.

Nurse-driven burn resuscitation using hourly flow charts is another approach to providing greater diligence and tighter control of fluid therapy. Nurse-implemented protocols allow nurses to make timely and effective changes to the resuscitation rates without having to wait for physicians' orders, which can delay needed adjustments in therapy. Additionally, these protocols diminish the effects that experience and/or comfort level have on titration (a new nurse or intern may be reluc-tant to make significant changes). Faraklas and colleagues instituted a nurse-driven resuscitation protocol (Figure 12.4) as a quality control project and showed excellent protocol adherence. However, fluid creep remained in patients with the largest burns or inhalation injury [56]. An additional study from another group with a different nurse-driven pro-tocol revealed that total volume infused was reduced at 24 and 48 hours. Although underpowered, this study also showed that patients treated according to the protocol had a lower incidence of abdominal compart-ment syndrome [64]. Nurse-driven protocols offer a standardized proto-col that may provide a better solution to burn resuscitation than current means of team communication. More importantly, it ameliorates fluid creep and reduces morbidity.

A logical next step to paper decision trees (nurse-driven protocols) is a CDSS. CDSS is an open-loop system that provides recommendations to the clinical care team using UOP data obtained from the patient [65]. Salinas et al. developed an algorithm for hourly infused volumes most likely to return UOP of burn patients to a target range. The algorithm was implemented in CDSS software and was shown to decrease total volume delivered, while increasing UOP rates in the target range. Data also showed a shortening of ventilator time and length of ICU stay [65]. However, the study was small and awaits validation in large trials.

Adjusting fluid therapy each hour is an arbitrary time interval, and the kidneys respond to increased fluids by increasing urine production in real time. Thus, there may be value in developing a closed-loop sys-tem that automatically measures UOP in real time and automatically makes corrections to the infusion rate in a timely manner. Closed-loop fluid resuscitation systems have been evaluated and shown to be effec-tive (maintaining resuscitation targets) and efficient (reducing volume

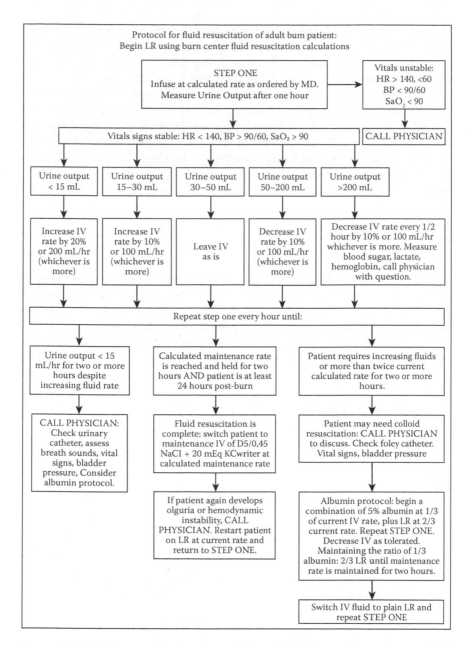

Figure 12.4 Fluid resuscitation protocol for adults. The pediatric protocol differs from the adult protocol in that urine output is targeted to 1.0–1.9 mL/kg/hr and patients younger than 2 years receive 25 mL/hr of 5% dextrose in lactated Ringer's (LR) throughout resuscitation. (Reprinted from Faraklas, I., et al., *J. Burn. Care Res.*, 33(1), 74–83, 2012. With permission.)

requirements) in models of burn injury and hemorrhage [66,67]. Further, closed-loop systems could reduce much of the bedside caregiver's time and effort in measuring and transcribing UOP and making manual adjustments in infusion rates, allowing them more time for other needed tasks. However, a closed-loop system should not replace careful patient monitoring, and such systems must allow the immediate caregiver to override the automation and regain manual control. A closed-loop system may be particularly valuable in non-burn center settings or mass casualty scenarios where burn expertise is lacking or diluted. Closed-loop systems are a promising avenue for the care of injured patients, although further research is needed to develop and validate these systems.

12.12   Summary

Burn injury is one of the most severe and prolonged forms of trauma with optimal care requiring a specialized clinical team. Fluid resuscitation is the important first step in the critical care of burn patients. Despite the many years that these injuries have been treated, there is still great controversy surrounding optimal resuscitation of patients. Indeed, there are a multitude of strategies designed to improve resuscitation, with no single approach having universal acceptance. More important than any formula or technology is a diligent burn team of physicians and nurses assessing the overall adequacy of hemodynamics, end organ perfusion, and oxygen delivery and making adjustments as needed.

References

1. Herndon, D. N. 2012. *Total Burn Care: Expert Consult-Online*. Elsevier Health Sciences: New York, NY.
2. Snell, J. A., N. H. Loh, T. Mahambrey, and K. Shokrollahi. 2013. Clinical Review: The Critical Care Management of the Burn Patient, *Crit Care* 17: 241.
3. Cancio LC, Bohanon FJ, Kramer GC. Burn Resuscitation. In: Herndon DN, ed. *Total Burn Care*. 5th ed. New York, NY: Elsevier; 2017:77–86.
4. Wurzer P, Culnan D, Cancio LC, Kramer GC. Pathophysiology of burn shock and burn edema. In: Herndon DN, ed. *Total Burn Care*. 5th ed. New York, NY: Elsevier; 2017:66–76.
5. Bacomo, F. K., and K. K. Chung. 2011. A Primer on Burn Resuscitation, *J Emerg Trauma Shock* 4: 109–113.
6. Latenser, B. A. 2009. Critical Care of the Burn Patient: The First 48 Hours, *Crit Care Med* 37: 2819–2826.
7. Jeschke, M. G., D. L. Chinkes, C. C. Finnerty, G. Kulp, O. E. Suman, W. B. Norbury, L. K. Branski, G. G. Gauglitz, R. P. Mlcak, and D. N. Herndon. 2008. Pathophysiologic Response to Severe Burn Injury, *Ann Surg* 248: 387–401.

8. Kentish, E. *An Essay on Burns in Two Parts.* London: Longman, 1817, 1797 (1st part) & 1800 (2nd part).
9. Chan, C. H., A. R. Tuite, and D. N. Fisman. 2013. Historical Epidemiology of the Second Cholera Pandemic: Relevance to Present Day Disease Dynamics, *PLoS One* 8: e72498.
10. Harvey, R. M., Y. Enson, M. L. Lewis, W. B. Greenough, K. M. Ally, and R. A. Panno. 1968. Hemodynamic Studies on Cholera. Effects of Hypovolemia and Acidosis, *Circulation* 37: 709–728.
11. O'Shaughnessy, W. B. 1831. Proposal of a New Method of Treating the Blue Epidemic Cholera by the Injection of Highly-Oxygenised Salts into the Venous System, *Lancet* 17: 366–371.
12. Hansen, S. L. 2008. From Cholera to "Fluid Creep": A Historical Review of Fluid Resuscitation of the Burn Trauma Patient, *Wounds* 20: 206–213.
13. Sneve, H. 1905. The Treatment of Burns and Skin Grafting, *JAMA* XLV: 1–8.
14. Yale Students in Theatre Fire, *The Cornell Daily Sun*, November 28, 1921. Accessed October 13, 2015. http://cdsun.library.cornell.edu/cgi-bin/cornell?a=d&d=CDS19211128.2.7
15. Underhill, F. P., G. L. Carrington, R. Kapsinow, and G. T. Pack. 1923. Blood Concentration Changes in Extensive Superficial Burns, and Their Significance for Systemic Treatment, *Arch Intern Med (Chic)* 32: 31–49.
16. Underhill, F. P. 1927. Changes in Blood Concentration with Special Reference to the Treatment of Extensive Superficial Burns, *Annals of Surgery* 86: 840–849.
17. Cope, O., and F. W. Rhinelander. 1943. The Problem of Burn Shock Complicated by Pulmonary Damage, *Ann Surg* 117: 915–928.
18. Stewart, C. L. 2015. The Fire at Cocoanut Grove, *J Burn Care Res* 36: 232–235.
19. Cope, O., and F. D. Moore. 1947. The Redistribution of Body Water and the Fluid Therapy of the Burned Patient, *Ann Surg* 126: 1010–1045.
20. Evans, E. I., O. J. Purnell, P. W. Robinett, A. Batchelor, and M. Martin. 1952. Fluid and Electrolyte Requirements in Severe Burns, *Ann Surg* 135: 804–817.
21. Kramer, G. C., M. W. Michell, H. Oliveira, T. L. Brown, D. Herndon, R. D. Baker, and M. Muller. 2010. Oral and Enteral Resuscitation of Burn Shock the Historical Record and Implications for Mass Casualty Care, *Eplasty* 10: e56.
22. Baxter, C. R., and T. Shires. 1968. Physiological Response to Crystalloid Resuscitation of Severe Burns, *Ann N Y Acad Sci* 150: 874–894.
23. Baxter, C. R. 1974. Fluid Volume and Electrolyte Changes of the Early Postburn Period, *Clin Plast Surg* 1: 693–703.
24. Pruitt, B. A., Jr., A. D. Mason, Jr., and J. A. Moncrief. 1971. Hemodynamic Changes in the Early Postburn Patient: The Influence of Fluid Administration and of a Vasodilator (Hydralazine), *J Trauma* 11: 36–46.
25. Alvarado, R., K. K. Chung, L. C. Cancio, and S. E. Wolf. 2009. Burn Resuscitation, *Burns* 35: 4–14.
26. Haberal, M., A. E. Sakallioglu Abali, and H. Karakayali. 2010. Fluid Management in Major Burn Injuries, *Indian J Plast Surg* 43: S29–S36.
27. Pruitt, B. A. 1979. The Burn Patient: I. Initial Care, *Curr Probl Surg* 16: 1–55.
28. Goodwin, C. W., J. Dorethy, V. Lam, and B. A. Pruitt, Jr. 1983. Randomized Trial of Efficacy of Crystalloid and Colloid Resuscitation on Hemodynamic Response and Lung Water Following Thermal Injury, *Ann Surg* 197: 520–531.

29. O'Mara, M. S., H. Slater, I. W. Goldfarb, and P. F. Caushaj. 2005. A Prospective, Randomized Evaluation of Intra-Abdominal Pressures with Crystalloid and Colloid Resuscitation in Burn Patients, *J Trauma* 58: 1011–1018.

30. Cartotto, R. 2009. Fluid Resuscitation of the Thermally Injured Patient, *Clin Plast Surg* 36: 569–581.

31. Lawrence, A., I. Faraklas, H. Watkins, A. Allen, A. Cochran, S. Morris, and J. Saffle. 2010. Colloid Administration Normalizes Resuscitation Ratio and Ameliorates "Fluid Creep", *J Burn Care Res* 31: 40–47.

32. Saffle, J. I. 2007. The Phenomenon of "Fluid Creep" in Acute Burn Resuscitation, *J Burn Care Res* 28: 382–395.

33. Gibran, N. S., S. Wiechman, W. Meyer, L. Edelman, J. Fauerbach, L. Gibbons, R. Holavanahalli, C. et al. 2013. American Burn Association Consensus Statements, *J Burn Care Res* 34: 361–385.

34. Pham, T. N., L. C. Cancio, and N. S. Gibran. 2008. American Burn Association Practice Guidelines Burn Shock Resuscitation, *J Burn Care Res* 29: 257–266.

35. Greenhalgh, D. G. 2010. Burn Resuscitation: The Results of the ISBI/ABA Survey, *Burns* 36: 176–182.

36. Barrow, R. E., M. G. Jeschke, and D. N. Herndon. 2000. Early Fluid Resuscitation Improves Outcomes in Severely Burned Children, *Resuscitation* 45: 91–96.

37. Wolf, S. E., J. K. Rose, M. H. Desai, J. P. Mileski, R. E. Barrow, and D. N. Herndon. 1997. Mortality Determinants in Massive Pediatric Burns. An Analysis of 103 Children with > or = 80% TBSA Burns (> or = 70% Full-Thickness), *Ann Surg* 225: 554–565; discussion 565–559.

38. Michell, M. W., H. M. Oliveira, M. P. Kinsky, S. U. Vaid, D. N. Herndon, and G. C. Kramer. 2006. Enteral Resuscitation of Burn Shock Using World Health Organization Oral Rehydration Solution: A Potential Solution for Mass Casualty Care, *J Burn Care Res* 27: 819–825.

39. Fox, C. L. J. 1944. Oral Sodium Lactate in the Treatment of Burns and Shock, *JAMA* 124: 207–212.

40. Baxter, C. R., and G. T. Shires. 1981. Guidelines for Fluid Resuscitation In: Proceedings of the Second Consensus Development Conference on Supportive Therapy in Burn Care, *J Trauma* 21 (suppl): 687–689.

41. Herndon, D. N., R. E. Barrow, H. A. Linares, R. L. Rutan, T. Prien, L. D. Traber, and D. L. Traber. 1988. Inhalation Injury in Burned Patients: Effects and Treatment, *Burns Incl Therm Inj* 14: 349–356.

42. Navar, P. D., J. R. Saffle, and G. D. Warden. 1985. Effect of Inhalation Injury on Fluid Resuscitation Requirements after Thermal Injury, *Am J Surg* 150: 716–720.

43. Mosier, M. J., and N. S. Gibran. 2014. Management of the patient with thermal injuries, In *Acs Surgery: Principles and Practice*, edited by Mosier, M. J., and N. S. Gibran. New York: B C Decker Inc., 2099–2113.

44. Kaups, K. L., J. W. Davis, and W. J. Dominic. 1998. Base Deficit as an Indicator or Resuscitation Needs in Patients with Burn Injuries, *J Burn Care Rehabil* 19: 346–348.

45. Cartotto, R., J. Choi, M. Gomez, and A. Cooper. 2003. A Prospective Study on the Implications of a Base Deficit During Fluid Resuscitation, *J Burn Care Rehabil* 24: 75–84.

46. Kamolz, L. P., H. Andel, W. Schramm, G. Meissl, D. N. Herndon, and M. Frey. 2005. Lactate: Early Predictor of Morbidity and Mortality in Patients with Severe Burns, *Burns* 31: 986–990.

47. Sanchez, M., A. Garcia-de-Lorenzo, E. Herrero, T. Lopez, B. Galvan, M. Asensio, L. Cachafeiro, and C. Casado. 2013. A Protocol for Resuscitation of Severe Burn Patients Guided by Transpulmonary Thermodilution and Lactate Levels: A 3-Year Prospective Cohort Study, *Crit Care* 17: R176.
48. Kraft, R., D. N. Herndon, L. K. Branski, C. C. Finnerty, K. R. Leonard, and M. G. Jeschke. 2013. Optimized Fluid Management Improves Outcomes of Pediatric Burn Patients, *J Surg Res* 181: 121–128.
49. Aboelatta, Y., and A. Abdelsalam. 2013. Volume Overload of Fluid Resuscitation in Acutely Burned Patients Using Transpulmonary Thermodilution Technique, *J Burn Care Res* 34: 349–354.
50. Maybauer, M. O., S. Asmussen, D. G. Platts, J. F. Fraser, F. Sanfilippo, and D. M. Maybauer. 2014. Transesophageal Echocardiography in the Management of Burn Patients, *Burns* 40: 630–635.
51. Howard, T. S., D. G. Hermann, A. L. McQuitty, L. C. Woodson, G. C. Kramer, D. N. Herndon, P. M. Ford, and M. P. Kinsky. 2013. Burn-Induced Cardiac Dysfunction Increases Length of Stay in Pediatric Burn Patients, *J Burn Care Res* 34: 413–419.
52. Pruitt, B. A., Jr. 2000. Protection from Excessive Resuscitation: "Pushing the Pendulum Back", *J Trauma* 49: 567–568.
53. Ivy, M. E., N. A. Atweh, J. Palmer, P. P. Possenti, M. Pineau, and M. D'Aiuto. 2000. Intra-Abdominal Hypertension and Abdominal Compartment Syndrome in Burn Patients, *J Trauma* 49: 387–391.
54. Zak, A. L., D. T. Harrington, D. J. Barillo, D. F. Lawlor, K. Z. Shirani, and C. W. Goodwin. 1999. Acute Respiratory Failure That Complicates the Resuscitation of Pediatric Patients with Scald Injuries, *J Burn Care Rehabil* 20: 391–399.
55. Sheridan, R. L., R. G. Tompkins, W. F. McManus, and B. A. Pruitt, Jr. 1994. Intracompartmental Sepsis in Burn Patients, *J Trauma* 36: 301–305.
56. Faraklas, I., A. Cochran, and J. Saffle. 2012. Review of a Fluid Resuscitation Protocol: "Fluid Creep" Is Not Due to Nursing Error, *J Burn Care Res* 33: 74–83.
57. Sullivan, S. R., J. B. Friedrich, L. H. Engrav, K. A. Round, D. M. Heimbach, S. R. Heckbert, G. J. Carrougher, et al. 2004. "Opioid Creep" Is Real and May Be the Cause of "Fluid Creep", *Burns* 30: 583–590.
58. MacLennan, N., D. M. Heimbach, and B. F. Cullen. 1998. Anesthesia for Major Thermal Injury, *Anesthesiology* 89: 749–770.
59. Chung, K. K., L. H. Blackbourne, S. E. Wolf, C. E. White, E. M. Renz, L. C. Cancio, J. B. Holcomb, and D. J. Barillo. 2006. Evolution of Burn Resuscitation in Operation Iraqi Freedom, *J Burn Care Res* 27: 606–611.
60. European Medicines Agency – Science, Medicines, Health. 2013. *Hydroxyethyl-Starch Solutions (Hes) Should No Longer Be Used in Patients with Sepsis or Burn Injuries or in Critically Ill Patients—CMDh Endorses Prac Recommendations*, European Medicines Agency, London, UK.
61. Tanaka, H., T. Matsuda, Y. Miyagantani, T. Yukioka, H. Matsuda, and S. Shimazaki. 2000. Reduction of Resuscitation Fluid Volumes in Severely Burned Patients Using Ascorbic Acid Administration: A Randomized, Prospective Study, *Arch Surg* 135: 326–331.
62. Dubick, M. A., C. Williams, G. I. Elgjo, and G. C. Kramer. 2005. High-Dose Vitamin C Infusion Reduces Fluid Requirements in the Resuscitation of Burn-Injured Sheep, *Shock* 24: 139–144.

63. Kahn, S. A., R. J. Beers, and C. W. Lentz. 2011. Resuscitation after Severe Burn Injury Using High-Dose Ascorbic Acid: A Retrospective Review, *J Burn Care Res* 32: 110–117.
64. Yang, Q., M. A. Orman, F. Berthiaume, M. G. Ierapetritou, and I. P. Androulakis. 2012. Dynamics of Short-Term Gene Expression Profiling in Liver Following Thermal Injury, *J Surg Res* 176: 549–558.
65. Salinas, J., K. K. Chung, E. A. Mann, L. C. Cancio, G. C. Kramer, M. L. Serio-Melvin, E. M. Renz, C. E. Wade, and S. E. Wolf. 2011. Computerized Decision Support System Improves Fluid Resuscitation Following Severe Burns: An Original Study, *Crit Care Med* 39: 2031–2038.
66. Kramer, G. C., M. P. Kinsky, D. S. Prough, J. Salinas, J. L. Sondeen, M. L. Hazel-Scerbo, and C. E. Mitchell. 2008. Closed-Loop Control of Fluid Therapy for Treatment of Hypovolemia, *J Trauma* 64: S333–S341.
67. Salinas, J., G. Drew, J. Gallagher, L. C. Cancio, S. E. Wolf, C. E. Wade, J. B. Holcomb, D. N. Herndon, and G. C. Kramer. 2008. Closed-Loop and Decision-Assist Resuscitation of Burn Patients, *J Trauma* 64: S321–S332.

chapter thirteen

Fluid therapy in the intensive care unit, with a special focus on sepsis

Jean-Louis Vincent and Diego Orbegozo
Erasme Hospital, Université Libre de Bruxelles
Brussels, Belgium

Christer H. Svensen
Karolinska Institutet, Stockholm South General Hospital
Stockholm, Sweden

Contents

Key points:
    This chapter deals with fluid therapy in the ICU with particular focus on septic patients.

- SOSD mnemonic
- Optimization of fluids

- Echocardiography
- Central venous pressure
- Dynamic signs of fluid responsiveness, fluid challenge, and passive leg raising test
- Blood lactate and $S_{cv}O_2$
- Colloids and crystalloids

13.1   Introduction: Optimal fluid balance

Many critically ill patients have some degree of *hypo*volemia, whether absolute, due to external (bleeding, sweating, vomiting, diarrhea) or internal (edema formation, intraperitoneal reaction) losses; relative due to vasodilation; or, frequently, a mixture of both. Hypovolemia is associated with reduced tissue perfusion, potentially leading to reduced tissue oxygenation with organ dysfunction and failure. Adequate fluid administration is therefore a key concern in the management of these patients. However, *hyper*volemia can be associated with edema formation, especially in the presence of altered capillary permeability due to an inflammatory response, such as sepsis. There is then a direct relationship between the increase in intravascular pressure and the degree of edema. Edema formation is important because edema can have multiple deleterious effects on organ function. Lung edema is often a primary concern, but this is in part because it is easily recognized relatively early in its development: lung infiltrates are rapidly visible on the chest x-ray and the consequences are immediately apparent in terms of altered gas exchange (hypoxemia). However, edema in other parts of the body, although often less apparent, can also be harmful. For example, edema in the brain may contribute to the development of delirium; edema in the heart may contribute to the development of systolic and diastolic dysfunction; edema in the abdominal wall can contribute to abdominal compartment syndrome; edema in the gut may limit tolerance to feeding; edema in the kidneys is likely to contribute to altered renal function; edema in the muscle may contribute to general weakness and can impair mobilization; edema in the subcutaneous tissues can impair wound healing.

In the Sepsis Occurrence in Acutely Ill Patients study, one of the most important independent prognostic factors for mortality in patients with acute renal failure (assessed by multivariable analysis considering several other variables) was a positive fluid balance [1]. In patients admitted to the intensive care unit (ICU) after major surgery, Silva et al. [2] reported that fluid balance was an independent risk factor for death (odds ratio per 100 mL 1.024, 95% confidence interval [CI] 1.007–1.041, $P = 0.006$). More recently, Acheampong and Vincent showed that a positive fluid balance in patients with septic shock was independently associated with worse outcomes (adjusted hazard ratio for mortality 1.014, 95% CI 1.007–1.022,

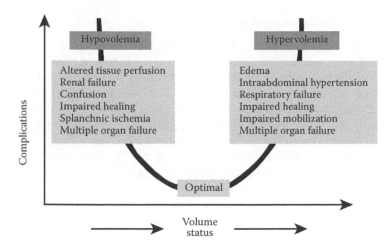

Figure 13.1 The U-shaped curve of fluid balance. Hypovolemia and hypervolemia are both associated with worse outcomes.

per mL/kg increase, $P < 0.001$) [3]. In an analysis of more than 1,800 patients with sepsis, a higher cumulative fluid balance at Day 3 following ICU admission was independently associated with an increase in the hazard of death [4]. Other studies in various groups of critically ill patients have similarly reported worse outcomes in patients with positive fluid balances [5–7].

The relationship between volume status and complications can therefore be considered as a U-shaped curve with both ends of inadequate volume status—*hyper-* and *hypo*volemia—being associated with worse outcomes (see Figure 13.1). Fluid therapy must therefore be considered carefully in all critically ill patients, to ensure the balance is optimal.

13.2   Fluid management

Fluid administration in the hemodynamically unstable patient must take the time factor into account as suggested by the SOSD mnemonic [8,9]:

- *S* stands for *salvage*: In this initial phase, there is no time for monitoring and the patient should receive fluid boluses until proper monitoring can be placed.
- *O* stands for *optimization*: During this phase the need for fluid should be guided primarily by repeated fluid challenges (see section 13.2.1).
- *S* stands for *stabilization*: Here the patient is stable and fluids are administered just for maintenance.
- *D* stands for *de-escalation*: In this stage, the aim is to remove excess fluid.

13.2.1   Optimization of fluids

All too often, fluid is given to oliguric patients without sufficient monitoring or without careful attention to whether the patient is a fluid responder. Concerns about excess fluid administration, as mentioned earlier, may encourage the use of diuretics, but this may not be a good idea if the patient's hemodynamic status is not stable. The major risk with using diuretics is that the patient will be forced into a hypovolemic state unless they are hypervolemic, and it is difficult to judge how much diuretic to give and when to stop. In the oliguric patient, diuretics often increase urine output regardless of the volume status and may therefore aggravate the volume deficit. Indeed, sometimes too much attention is placed on urine output. For example, imagine a patient with oliguria who is given 1 L of crystalloid fluid, which has a small effect on urine output, for example, 15 mL in 1 hr. This encouraging effect prompts the administration of another liter of fluid and the urine output again seems to increase somewhat, from 15 to 25 mL/hr. This fluid administration could, therefore, be considered a success. However, the patient has now received 2 L of fluid and eliminated only 40 mL in the urine! It is unlikely that all the remaining fluid will stay in the circulation, and the patient will almost certainly develop edema.

Assessing the fluid status of a patient is thus of paramount importance, but it can be difficult, particularly in the critically ill patient with sepsis or other inflammatory conditions associated with capillary leak, because large fluid shifts can occur into the interstitial space, resulting in edema, despite ongoing intravascular hypovolemia. Static indices of fluid status are not very helpful: signs such as tachycardia or hypotension are not specific for hypovolemia, and measurements of cardiac filling pressures are relatively easy to obtain but have considerable restrictions, for example, low cardiac filling pressures do not necessarily mean the patient will respond to fluid administration and high filling pressures do not necessarily mean that the fluid status has been optimized. Measurements of ventricular end-diastolic or intrathoracic volumes reflect fluid status no better than do filling pressures.

13.2.1.1   Echocardiography

In the presence of any uncertainty regarding fluid status, one of the first hemodynamic tools should be echocardiography. It is not necessary to be a specialist in this area to conduct and interpret echocardiographic imaging for this purpose. All intensivists should now be able to perform basic echocardiography, not for complicated diagnoses, but to be able to evaluate the size of the ventricles (and the presence of pericardial fluid, which is common in septic shock).

13.2.1.2   Central venous pressure

Measurement of the central venous pressure (CVP) can be useful to assess fluid status. Although single values correlate poorly with blood volume [10], changes in CVP over time can still provide some guidance to ongoing fluid requirements. An increase in CVP can result in a decrease in venous return (which is determined by the pressure gradient between the peripheral veins and the right atrium and, at the same time, the degree of stretch of the right atrium). Thus, an increase in CVP can increase cardiac output by the Frank–Starling mechanism but could potentially decrease cardiac output by reducing venous return. This phenomenon is seldom, if ever, predominant because the Frank–Starling relationship typically shows a horizontal part (i.e., a stable cardiac output) at high degrees of filling. Nevertheless, organ blood flow is determined by the difference between mean arterial pressure (MAP) and CVP, and this gradient should be monitored, as recommended in the most recent pediatric guidelines [11]. An increase in CVP greater than the increase in MAP (i.e., a reduced MAP–CVP gradient) suggests that too much fluid has been given.

A central venous catheter also enables fluid administration of high osmolality and is preferred over peripheral catheters for concomitant vasopressor infusion. Although the evidence is weak, it is noteworthy that norepinephrine may safely be given through a well-functioning peripheral venous catheter, precluding the need for immediate central venous catheterization in ICU patients [12]. A central line also allows measurement of the central venous oxygen saturation ($S_{cv}O_2$), which provides some indication of the balance between oxygen consumption (VO_2) and oxygen delivery (DO_2). Hypovolemia is associated with a low cardiac output and thus oxygen delivery (DO_2) and this is therefore associated with a low $S_{cv}O_2$. Septic patients usually have a normal or increased $S_{cv}O_2$. A routine strategy aimed at achieving an $S_{cv}O_2 > 70\%$ in all patients with septic shock has not been associated with lower mortality rates in large randomized controlled studies [13], but measurements of $S_{cv}O_2$ are still of value in complex cases [14].

13.2.1.3   Dynamic signs of fluid responsiveness

Studies in heterogeneous groups of critically ill and injured patients and those undergoing surgery have shown that only about 50% of hemodynamically unstable patients are fluid responders [15]. In the mechanically ventilated, profoundly sedated patient, dynamic signs of fluid responsiveness can be determined, including observation of pulse pressure variation from arterial pressure tracings (if the patient has an arterial catheter) or stroke volume variation (if the patient has a cardiac output monitor allowing stroke volume calculations from a beat-by-beat analysis of the arterial

Figure 13.2 Performance of a passive leg raising test.

pressure tracing). A stroke volume variation of at least 10%–13% strongly suggests fluid responsiveness [16]. However, these measures are only reliable in patients who are receiving mechanical ventilation with relatively high tidal volumes and without any spontaneous respiratory effort, which generally requires heavy sedation, and we are increasingly avoiding use of sedation in critically ill patients.

An alternative technique that can be used in all critically ill patients, even when not receiving mechanical ventilation, is passive leg raising (PLR; see Figure 13.2), which effectively is an "internal fluid challenge" and thus makes physiological sense. However, PLR is not as easy to perform as it may seem at first glance [17] and requires a cardiac output monitor that can measure stroke volume beat by beat, because the changes in stoke volume are very short lived.

13.2.1.4 *Fluid challenge*

Given the limitations and difficulties assessing fluid status in critically ill patients, in most patients fluids are primarily guided by repeated fluid challenges [18] in a "trial and error" approach. However, the fluid challenge must be done correctly and carefully. An amount of fluid, typically 100–200 mL, is given as a bolus over a relatively short time while the response, generally in terms of change in cardiac output or stroke volume, is assessed. If the patient responds and a predefined safety limit, for example, a CVP value, is not reached, further fluids can be given until there is no further increase in the target variable. The idea is that in the presence of hypovolemia there will be a greater increase in cardiac output and a limited minimal increase in CVP. In contrast, if well-filled, there will be no increase in cardiac output, but filling pressures will increase sharply. Hence, patients must be closely monitored during administration of the fluid and no other interventions performed during the fluid challenge (not even touching the patient!). And fluid administration must be interrupted immediately if there is no benefit. This is what the Surviving Sepsis Campaign (SSC) guidelines currently recommend. Also, the most recent pediatric guidelines state that the observation of little change in the CVP in response to a fluid bolus suggests that the venous capacitance system is not overfilled and that more fluid is indicated [11].

13.2.1.5   Blood lactate levels

We do not yet have reliable methods of directly monitoring tissue perfusion and we must rely on surrogates, such as $S_{cv}O_2$ and blood lactate levels. Single blood lactate levels are less useful than changes over time. However, changes in blood lactate levels (the balance between lactate elimination and production) occur relatively slowly, so they cannot be used alone to guide therapy; rather changes in levels over time, perhaps every hour, can provide an indication that the patient is (or is not) responding to treatment. One study reported that targeting treatment of ICU patients with hyperlactatemia to reduce blood lactate levels by at least 20% over 2 hours was associated with improved organ function, reduced need for mechanical ventilation and vasopressors, and improved survival [19]. Nevertheless, the changes in lactate concentrations are too slow to be the only guide to resuscitation, and measurement every hour during resuscitation is usually sufficient. This topic has been reviewed recently elsewhere [20].

13.2.2   Types of intravenous fluid

Each fluid type has its own advantages and disadvantages, and optimal fluid choices are important to maximize the chances of survival and limiting organ dysfunction. The type of fluid to use is still a major topic of discussion and debate, although reference to physiology can provide answers to many of the remaining questions. Clearly, colloid solutions, with their larger molecules that escape less into the interstitium, can result in less edema formation. In a systematic study of 48 studies comparing (any) crystalloid with (any) colloid (usually combined with crystalloids) in acutely ill patients, we recently showed that greater crystalloid than colloid fluid volumes are required to meet the same targets, with an estimated ratio of 1.5 (1.36–1.65) [21]. If maintenance of blood volume is of paramount importance, colloids may be beneficial; however, excessive use of colloids may result in hyperoncocity, which may induce renal failure. Hence, colloid solutions are never administered alone. Indeed, discussing the use of colloids versus crystalloids is a misnomer, as in practice the comparison is colloids and crystalloids versus crystalloids alone.

13.2.2.1   Colloids

In recent years, several large studies have been conducted comparing different colloid solutions, making these choices somewhat clearer than in the past. Dextrans are now rarely used because they may induce allergic reactions, alter hemostasis, and complicate blood type and crossmatch. Gelatin solutions are generally considered to be fairly safe (although this has never been well studied). They can induce anaphylactic reactions that are usually transient and of limited severity. Moreover, with their relatively small molecular weight, gelatin solutions have a limited effect on volume expansion and relatively short (2–3 hr) intravascular persistence, making them less effective colloids than the available alternatives. In addition, gelatin solutions are not available in all countries. Hydroxyethyl starch (HES) solutions were first used in humans in the 1960s and by 2007 had become the most widely used colloid solution in critically ill adults [22]. However, HES may persist in the organism for long periods of time after infusion, and concerns about harmful renal effects in critically ill patients [23,24] and increased mortality rates in one study [25] led to the recommendation from the US Food and Drug Administration that they should not be used in critically ill patients, including those with sepsis [26]. The European Medicines Agency has ruled that HES-containing products should be contraindicated in patients with sepsis, in the critically ill, and in burn patients [27].

Albumin solution, the only natural colloid, has often been considered as a more expensive option, but the costs are not so high in relative terms today, and artificial colloids are used less, making albumin a more interesting alternative. In addition to its effects on regulation of colloid osmotic pressure, albumin has multiple other physiological activities, including transportation of various substances (e.g., drugs, hormones) within the blood, antioxidant effects, and positive effects on vascular barrier integrity and function [28]. Albumin administration may be of interest in specific groups of patients, notably those with septic shock and hypoalbuminemia [29–31]. As long as hyperoncocity is avoided, albumin may offer renal protective effects in critically ill patients [32]. Use of albumin compared to no albumin is also associated with reduced renal failure and improved survival in patients with cirrhosis and spontaneous bacterial peritonitis [33].

13.2.2.2   Crystalloids

Although there has been a focus in the literature on differences between colloid solutions, there are also important differences among the available crystalloid solutions. So-called normal (0.9%) saline solution is not the "physiological serum" it was termed in the past. Indeed, with 154 mEq/L of sodium ion and 154 mEq/L of chloride ion, excessive saline administration can result in hyperchloremic acidosis [34]. This can alter intrarenal hemodynamics and thereby contribute to the development of renal failure [35]. So-called balanced solutions, which have been developed to more closely resemble the composition of plasma, may therefore be preferable. Since Ringer's lactate (RL) has an osmolarity of less than 280 mOsm/L, it is slightly hypotonic and should be avoided in hypotonic states or in cases of cerebral edema (including brain trauma). The hyperlactatemia that may result with administration of large amounts of RL does not seem to be harmful, and lactate may even serve as a cellular nutrient. Nevertheless, a massive lactate load in the presence of liver dysfunction may complicate the interpretation of serial blood lactate levels. In other balanced solutions, the lactate is replaced by gluconate and acetate, but the fate of gluconate is not very well defined and acetate can have vasodilating and myocardial depressant effects [36].

13.2.3   Personalized fluid prescription

Instead of continuing to conduct studies that compare one type of fluid to another [37], it is better to individualize fluid choices to the type of patient, the electrolyte concentration, and the type of fluid that the patient has recently received, remembering that any fluid in excessive amount can have adverse effects. Intravenous fluids should in fact be treated in a similar manner to other drugs and prescribed for individual patients rather than using a protocolized, standard, "one size fits all" approach.

13.3   Blood transfusions

When to give blood transfusions in critically ill patients has been hotly debated since the early study by Hebert et al. [38] that suggested that a restrictive approach (transfusing at a lower hemoglobin threshold) may be as good as, or better than in certain patients, the more widely used liberal approach. A more recent study also suggested similar outcomes with restrictive (transfuse when hemoglobin decreases to less than 7 g/dL) and liberal (transfuse when hemoglobin decreases to less than 9 g/dL) approaches in septic patients [39], but perhaps the main message of this study was that patients should not be overtransfused, as 64% of patients in the restrictive group and 99% of patients in the liberal group received a blood transfusion. Although a transfusion threshold of 7 g/dL can be recommended for septic patients in general, somewhat higher thresholds are reasonable in patients with cardiovascular disease [40]. As with fluids in general, blood transfusions should be administered according to individual patient characteristics, taking into account age, comorbid conditions, and disease severity [41].

13.4   Combination with vasoactive agents

Although fluid administration is widely used as the first-line treatment to restore a minimal tissue perfusion pressure in critically ill patients with shock, this should be individualized. Hence, norepinephrine, considered as the first vasopressor of choice to restore tissue perfusion pressure, can be added even before full fluid resuscitation is obtained. Recent data have indicated that any period of hypotension should be prevented and that early norepinephrine administration is associated with better outcomes than when it is delayed [42,43]. Vasopressors should be stopped if the response to fluids is still positive. If fluid administration is poorly tolerated primarily based on an excessive increase in cardiac filling pressure without an increase in cardiac output, the inotrope, dobutamine, can be added; small doses of 5 mcg/kg/min are usually sufficient.

The addition of vasopressin or its selective V1a receptor, selepressin, may decrease the degree of capillary leak in patients with sepsis [44], but there are still too few clinical data for this approach to be recommended and we must await the results of ongoing clinical studies (ClinicalTrials. gov identifier: NCT02508649).

13.5   Conclusion

Fluid therapy in the ICU patient must be individualized and adjusted to the patient's condition. The amount of saline solution should be restricted and replaced by balanced crystalloid solutions in case of hyperchloremia. Albumin may be added if large fluid volumes are expected to be necessary. Fluids should be given according to the SOSD mnemonic, with an initial bolus followed by careful fluid administration guided by repeated fluid challenges and hemodynamic monitoring, and finally excess fluid removed to avoid a harmful positive fluid balance.

References

1. Payen D, de Pont AC, Sakr Y, Spies C, Reinhart K, Vincent JL. A positive fluid balance is associated with a worse outcome in patients with acute renal failure. *Crit Care*. 2008;12:R74.

2. Silva JM, Jr., de Oliveira AM, Nogueira FA, Vianna PM, Pereira Filho MC, Dias LF et al. The effect of excess fluid balance on the mortality rate of surgical patients: A multicenter prospective study. *Crit Care*. 2013;17:R288.
3. Acheampong A, Vincent JL. A positive fluid balance is an independent prognostic factor in patients with sepsis. *Crit Care*. 2015;19:251.
4. Sakr Y, Rubatto Birri PN, Kotfis K, Nanchal R, Shah B, Kluge S et al. Higher fluid balance increases the risk of death from sepsis: Results from a large international audit. *Crit Care Med*. 2017;45:386–94.
5. Lee J, de Louw E, Niemi M, Nelson R, Mark RG, Celi LA et al. Association between fluid balance and survival in critically ill patients. *J Intern Med*. 2014;277:477.
6. de Oliveira FS, Freitas FG, Ferreira EM, de Castro I, Bafi AT, de Azevedo LC et al. Positive fluid balance as a prognostic factor for mortality and acute kidney injury in severe sepsis and septic shock. *J Crit Care*. 2015;30:97–101.
7. Micek ST, McEvoy C, McKenzie M, Hampton N, Doherty JA, Kollef MH. Fluid balance and cardiac function in septic shock as predictors of hospital mortality. *Crit Care*. 2013;17:R246.
8. Vincent JL, De Backer D. Circulatory shock. *N Engl J Med*. 2013;369:1726–34.
9. Hoste EA, Maitland K, Brudney CS, Mehta R, Vincent JL, Yates D et al. Four phases of intravenous fluid therapy: A conceptual model. *Br J Anaesth*. 2014;113:740–7.
10. Marik PE, Baram M, Vahid B. Does central venous pressure predict fluid responsiveness? A systematic review of the literature and the tale of seven mares. *Chest*. 2008;134:172–8.
11. Davis AL, Carcillo JA, Aneja RK, Deymann AJ, Lin JC, Nguyen TC et al. American college of critical care medicine clinical practice parameters for hemodynamic support of pediatric and neonatal septic shock. *Crit Care Med*. 2017;45:1061–93.
12. Cardenas-Garcia J, Schaub KF, Belchikov YG, Narasimhan M, Koenig SJ, Mayo PH. Safety of peripheral intravenous administration of vasoactive medication. *J Hosp Med*. 2015;10:581–5.
13. Rowan KM, Angus DC, Bailey M, Barnato AE, Bellomo R, Canter RR et al. Early, goal-directed therapy for septic shock—A patient-level meta-analysis. *N Engl J Med*. 2017;376:2223–34.
14. De Backer D, Vincent JL. Early goal-directed therapy: Do we have a definitive answer? *Intensive Care Med*. 2016;42:1048–50.
15. Marik PE, Monnet X, Teboul JL. Hemodynamic parameters to guide fluid therapy. *Ann Intensive Care*. 2011;1:1.
16. Marik PE, Cavallazzi R, Vasu T, Hirani A. Dynamic changes in arterial waveform derived variables and fluid responsiveness in mechanically ventilated patients: A systematic review of the literature. *Crit Care Med*. 2009;37:2642–7.
17. Monnet X, Teboul JL. Passive leg raising: Five rules, not a drop of fluid! *Crit Care*. 2015;19:18.
18. Vincent JL, Weil MH. Fluid challenge revisited. *Crit Care Med*. 2006;34:1333–7.
19. Jansen TC, van Bommel J, Schoonderbeek FJ, Sleeswijk Visser SJ, van der Klooster JM, Lima AP et al. Early lactate-guided therapy in intensive care unit patients: A multicenter, open-label, randomized controlled trial. *Am J Respir Crit Care Med*. 2010;182:752–61.
20. Vincent JL, Quintairos ES, Couto L, Jr., Taccone FS. The value of blood lactate kinetics in critically ill patients: A systematic review. *Crit Care*. 2016;20:257.

21. Orbegozo CD, Gamarano BT, Njimi H, Vincent JL. Crystalloids versus colloids: Exploring differences in fluid requirements by systematic review and meta-regression. *Anesth Analg*. 2015;120:389–402.
22. Finfer S, Liu B, Taylor C, Bellomo R, Billot L, Cook D et al. Resuscitation fluid use in critically ill adults: An international cross-sectional study in 391 intensive care units. *Crit Care*. 2010;14:R185.
23. Brunkhorst FM, Engel C, Bloos F, Meier-Hellmann A, Ragaller M, Weiler N et al. Intensive insulin therapy and pentastarch resuscitation in severe sepsis. *N Engl J Med*. 2008;358:125–39.
24. Myburgh JA, Finfer S, Bellomo R, Billot L, Cass A, Gattas D et al. Hydroxyethyl starch or saline for fluid resuscitation in intensive care. *N Engl J Med*. 2012;367:1901–11.
25. Perner A, Haase N, Guttormsen AB, Tenhunen J, Klemenzson G, Aneman A et al. Hydroxyethyl starch 130/0.42 versus Ringer's acetate in severe sepsis. *N Engl J Med*. 2012;367:124–34.
26. FDA Safety Communication: Boxed Warning on increased mortality and severe renal injury, and additional warning on risk of bleeding, for use of hydroxyethyl starch solutions in some settings. Available at: http://www.fffenterprises.com/assets/downloads/Article-FDASafetyCommunicationBoxedWarning6-13.pdf (Accessed 20 November, 2017).
27. European Medicine's Agency. Assessment report for solutions for infusion containing hydroxyethyl starch. Available at: http://www.ema.europa.eu/docs/en_GB/document_library/Referrals_document/Hydroxyethyl_starch-containing_medicines_107/Recommendation_provided_by_Pharmacovigilance_Risk_Assessment_Committee/WC500154254.pdf (Accessed 20 November, 2017).
28. Vincent JL, Russell JA, Jacob M, Martin G, Guidet B, Wernerman J et al. Albumin administration in the acutely ill: What is new and where next? *Crit Care*. 2014;18:231.
29. Finfer S, McEvoy S, Bellomo R, McArthur C, Myburgh J, Norton R. Impact of albumin compared to saline on organ function and mortality of patients with severe sepsis. *Intensive Care Med*. 2011;37:86–96.
30. Caironi P, Tognoni G, Masson S, Fumagalli R, Pesenti A, Romero M et al. Albumin replacement in patients with severe sepsis or septic shock. *N Engl J Med*. 2014;370:1412–21.
31. Rochwerg B, Alhazzani W, Sindi A, Heels-Ansdell D, Thabane L, Fox-Robichaud A et al. Fluid resuscitation in sepsis: A systematic review and network meta-analysis. *Ann Intern Med*. 2014;161:347–55.
32. Wiedermann CJ, Dunzendorfer S, Gaioni LU, Zaraca F, Joannidis M. Hyperoncotic colloids and acute kidney injury: A meta-analysis of randomized trials. *Crit Care*. 2010;14:R191.
33. Sort P, Navasa M, Arroyo V, Aldeguer X, Planas R, Ruiz-del-Arbol L et al. Effect of intravenous albumin on renal impairment and mortality in patients with cirrhosis and spontaneous bacterial peritonitis. *N Engl J Med*. 1999;341:403–9.
34. Orbegozo Cortes D, Rayo Bonor A, Vincent JL. Isotonic crystalloid solutions: A structured review of the literature. *Br J Anaesth*. 2014;112:968–81.
35. Chowdhury AH, Cox EF, Francis ST, Lobo DN. A randomized, controlled, double-blind crossover study on the effects of 2-L infusions of 0.9% saline and plasma-lyte(R) 148 on renal blood flow velocity and renal cortical tissue perfusion in healthy volunteers. *Ann Surg*. 2012;256:18–24.

36. Vincent JL, Vanherweghem JL, Degaute JP, Berre J, Dufaye P, Kahn RJ. Acetate-induced myocardial depression during hemodialysis for acute renal failure. *Kidney Int.* 1982;22:653–7.
37. Young P, Bailey M, Beasley R, Henderson S, Mackle D, McArthur C et al. Effect of a buffered crystalloid solution vs. saline on acute kidney injury among patients in the intensive care unit: The SPLIT randomized clinical trial. *JAMA.* 2015;314:1701–10.
38. Hebert PC, Wells G, Blajchman MA, Marshall J, Martin C, Pagliarello G et al. A multicenter, randomized, controlled clinical trial of transfusion requirements in critical care. Transfusion requirements in critical care investigators, Canadian Critical Care Trials Group. *N Engl J Med.* 1999;340:409–17.
39. Holst LB, Haase N, Wetterslev J, Wernerman J, Guttormsen AB, Karlsson S et al. Lower versus higher hemoglobin threshold for transfusion in septic shock. *N Engl J Med.* 2014;371:1381–91.
40. Docherty AB, O'Donnell R, Brunskill S, Trivella M, Doree C, Holst L et al. Effect of restrictive versus liberal transfusion strategies on outcomes in patients with cardiovascular disease in a non-cardiac surgery setting: Systematic review and meta-analysis. *BMJ.* 2016;352:i1351.
41. Sakr Y, Vincent JL. Should red cell transfusion be individualized? Yes. *Intensive Care Med.* 2015;41:1973–6.
42. Bai X, Yu W, Ji W, Lin Z, Tan S, Duan K et al. Early versus delayed administration of norepinephrine in patients with septic shock. *Crit Care.* 2014;18:532.
43. Beck V, Chateau D, Bryson GL, Pisipati A, Zanotti S, Parrillo JE et al. Timing of vasopressor initiation and mortality in septic shock: A cohort study. *Crit Care.* 2014;18:R97.
44. He X, Su F, Taccone FS, Laporte R, Kjolbye AL, Zhang J et al. A selective V1A receptor agonist, selepressin, is superior to arginine vasopressin and to norepinephrine in ovine septic shock. *Crit Care Med.* 2016;44:23–31.

chapter fourteen

Fluid therapy for the cardiothoracic patient

Thuan M. Ho and Ronald G. Pearl
Stanford University School of Medicine
Stanford, CA

Contents

Key points:

- Fluid management related to cardiopulmonary bypass
- Fluid therapy for cardiac surgery
- Fluid therapy for thoracic surgery

14.1   Introduction

Cardiothoracic surgery is an evolving field with multiple recent innovations. Although fluid management in cardiothoracic surgery shares many concepts with fluid management in other settings, there are unique aspects of cardiothoracic surgery that affect both the choice of fluid and the volume of fluid administration. The majority of cardiac surgery procedures involve cardiopulmonary bypass (CPB), either to allow surgery inside the heart or to provide the surgeon with an optimal operating environment. Fluid management in cardiac surgery cases using CPB requires understanding the physiologic effects of CPB and the options for priming the CPB circuit. The first section of this chapter will therefore focus on fluid issues specific to CPB, the second section on fluid therapy for different cardiac surgery procedures (both those using CPB and off-pump procedures), and the third section on fluid issues for thoracic surgery.

As general comments, all fluids can produce complications, especially when used in excess amounts in cardiothoracic surgery. Crystalloids are the most widely used fluids but are associated with pulmonary and cardiac edema due to the larger volumes needed to attain adequate intravascular volume for tissue perfusion [1]. Saline may produce a non-anion gap hyperchloremic metabolic acidosis, which can depress cardiac function in the intraoperative and postoperative period [1,2]. Albumin increases colloid oncotic pressure (COP) and can increase the risk of acute kidney injury (AKI) and the need for renal replacement therapy in both cardiac and thoracic surgery [2,3]. Hydroxyethyl starches and gelatin can affect coagulation and impair clot strength after cardiac surgery [4]. Dextran negatively affects coagulation and increases bleeding risk in cardiac surgery patients [5]. Fluid increases the risk of specific complications and must be used judiciously.

Although studies are conflicting, many recommend albumin for cardiac surgery and crystalloid for thoracic surgery [5,6]. In cardiac surgery, albumin causes the least increase in interstitial fluid and decreases pulmonary and myocardial edema [1]. In thoracic surgery, crystalloid used as part of a defined protocol decreases postoperative pulmonary edema [7]. Colloids such as hydroxyethyl starch, gelatin, and dextran may produce less edema than crystalloids but are associated with significant complications [4,5]. Hypertonic saline increases the cardiac index and decreases pulmonary edema in cardiac surgery patients, but improved outcomes have not yet been demonstrated [8].

Patients undergoing cardiac or thoracic surgery require careful titration of fluid administration to optimize systemic hemodynamics and avoid pulmonary edema. As discussed in this chapter and elsewhere in this book, the trend for monitoring is away from static measurements such as central venous pressure (CVP) for fluid administration and towards continuous and less invasive monitoring devices. Noninvasive monitors such as the PiCCO and FloTrac, described elsewhere in this book, can provide real-time hemodynamic and cardiac parameters to guide fluid management in cardiothoracic surgery. Esophageal Doppler is a minimally invasive device that measures stroke volume variation (SVV), which correlates with whether a patient will respond to fluid administration. These and similar devices can be used in goal-directed therapy (GDT), which has been demonstrated to improve outcomes across a spectrum of surgical procedures [9]. In cardiac surgery, pulmonary artery catheters are frequently used to guide fluid therapy [10] but have not been demonstrated to improve outcome [11]. However, transesophageal echocardiography is frequently used to assess both filling volumes and ventricular function and therefore is a valuable tool for guiding fluid therapy [12].

14.2   Fluid management related to CPB

CPB produces hemodilution, tissue edema, and increased extravascular lung water [13]. The CPB circuit constitutes a new external vascular compartment, and its size depends on the perfusionist, the fluid used to prime the circuit, and how blood is processed [2]. CPB may decrease effective intravascular volume due to vasodilation as well as extravascular leakage from damage to the endothelial glycocalyx [6]. Shaw and Raghunathan describe two phases of CPB (ebb and flow) with different physiologic effects [2]. During the ebb phase, CPB produces a stress or shock-like response, which includes peripheral vasoconstriction and centralization of blood. In the subsequent flow phase, increased catecholamines result in increased cardiac output, capillary permeability, temperature, and vasodilation with peripheral accumulation of fluid [2,14]. The volume of fluid that accumulates in the extravascular space will depend on the type and amount of fluid used during CPB priming and surgery.

Prior to initiation of CPB, the bypass circuit (tubing, oxygenator, and reservoir) must be primed with fluid. The optimal fluid for priming and the associated costs and impact on patient outcomes remain a topic of research and debate, with strong preferences among individual institutions. The three main approaches are the use of balanced crystalloid solutions, the use of albumin or other colloids, and retrograde autologous priming (RAP) using the patient's intravascular blood volume. Each approach affects COP, platelet function, net fluid balance, probability of blood transfusion, inflammatory response, and postoperative pulmonary, cardiac, peripheral, and organ edema [15–18]. For adults, traditional priming volumes are 1.5–2.5 L, but newer circuits can be primed with volumes as low as 450 mL [19]. The larger priming volumes produce significant hemodilution and physiologic derangements, so the concentration and composition of the fluid used have important clinical implications.

Crystalloid solutions are inexpensive and have been the main priming fluid since the development of CPB. However, crystalloid solutions cause hemodilution, platelet aggregation in the CPB circuit, and increased risk of bleeding in the immediate postoperative period. Furthermore, crystalloid solutions increase fluid shifts into the interstitial space by disrupting the endothelial glycocalyx (thereby increasing capillary permeability) and decreasing COP. Thus, when compared to albumin at volumes required for hemodynamic stability and adequate organ perfusion, crystalloid solutions result in a higher net-positive fluid balance. Yeoman et al. reported that crystalloid priming causes a 45% decrease in COP within 5 minutes of priming.

Crystalloid priming increases pulmonary and cardiac edema, resulting in decreased ventricular compliance, contractility, and cardiac output [13]. In a randomized clinical trial, Rex et al. [20] demonstrated that crystalloids resulted in a decreased stroke volume index (SVI) and an increase in CVP, indicating decreased myocardial compliance consistent with cardiac edema. The adverse effects of crystalloids may result in delayed postoperative extubation and increased ICU and hospital length of stay.

Albumin priming has been studied extensively. Albumin priming results in less hemodilution compared to crystalloid priming [15–17]. Albumin, a normal blood protein, may result in better preservation of the vascular barrier due to less disruption of the glycocalyx [17]. Isotonic albumin maintains normal COP, which, in combination with the preserved vascular permeability, may decrease fluid shifts into the interstitial space. Albumin (compared to crystalloid) may produce less pulmonary and cardiac edema, with better preservation of cardiac output and function [13,18]. Albumin priming may improve hemodynamic stability and decrease vasopressor requirements. In addition, perioperative blood transfusion and albumin use may decrease [16]. Multiple studies suggest that albumin priming results in a lower net-positive fluid balance. Albumin coats the CPB circuit and prevents fibrinogen from binding, thereby preventing platelet aggregation, activation, adhesion, and platelet consumption [16,20]. Albumin priming may also decrease oxygenator thrombosis. Preservation of fluid balance and normal coagulation and decreased inflammation may decrease perioperative blood loss. Some studies suggest that albumin priming can decrease hospital morbidity and ICU and hospital length of stay. However, albumin priming is expensive and does not decrease mortality, so its use remains controversial. Synthetic colloids such as hydroxyethyl starches and dextrans have also been studied, but concerns about increased coagulation abnormalities, anaphylactic reactions, and adverse effects on renal function have limited their use [21].

RAP initially primes the CPB circuit with crystalloid but then uses the patient's blood to remove most of the crystalloid from the circuit. The process takes 5–8 minutes and uses approximately 1 L of autologous blood. After cannulation, a 1-L transfer bag is connected to the circuit's venous line. Using a gravity or vacuum assisted pressure gradient, blood flows retrograde from the arterial cannula into the circuit and displaces the crystalloid from the arterial line and filter into the transfer bag. Next, the crystalloid in the venous reservoir and oxygenator is displaced. Lastly, the rest of the crystalloid in the venous line is displaced into the transfer bag with autologous blood. This entire process may cause hemodynamic instability, requiring use of vasopressor or even termination of the procedure. In addition, air embolism can occur if vacuum assisted venous drainage is used. Because RAP primes the circuit with the patient's blood, it maintains COP and normal capillary permeability, thereby decreasing vascular leakage. RAP decreases overall fluid administration and blood transfusion in the majority of studies, but studies have not yet demonstrated improvement in patient outcome [22].

In summary, despite multiple studies that suggest potential physiological benefits, there is no consensus regarding the optimal approach to priming the CPB circuit other than the use of circuits that require smaller priming volumes. Adequately sized randomized controlled trials to determine the risks and benefits of different approaches are needed. In infants and neonates, the priming volume represents a larger proportion of blood volume than in adults, so that many institutions use albumin, allogeneic blood, and blood products such as fresh frozen plasma for priming [23].

During CPB, hyperkalemia frequently occurs as a result of the high concentration of potassium used in cardioplegia solution combined with hemolysis, tissue damage, blood transfusion, acidosis, and renal insufficiency [24]. In addition to the usual treatment options such as insulin-glucose, bicarbonate, and beta agonist administration to shift potassium intracellularly, adding hemodialysis or ultrafiltration to the CPB circuit can effectively remove potassium and treat hyperkalemia [25].

14.3 Fluid therapy for cardiac surgery

Fluid management in cardiac surgery involves decisions regarding the choice of fluid and the amount of fluid to administer. Although the goal of fluid management is to prevent both hypovolemia (which results in tissue hypoperfusion) and hypervolemia (which results in tissue edema and heart failure), the optimal approach to determining fluid administration remains a topic of research and debate. Cardiac surgery patients may respond differently to fluid administration at different times in their hospital course [2]. In a randomized controlled trial of patients undergoing coronary artery bypass graft (CABG) or valve surgery, Kalus et al. [26] found that patients with a higher net fluid balance (1,032 vs. 400 mL) had a higher risk of atrial fibrillation in the postoperative period. Pradeep et al. [27] reported increased 90-day mortality when patients received more than 3.5 L of intraoperative fluid, and ICU and hospital length of stay and rates of hospital readmission also increased. However, the same study also demonstrated that intraoperative hypotension was an independent predictor of death, emphasizing the need to administer enough fluid to maintain normovolemia and adequate tissue perfusion.

There are marked differences among institutions in the use of a liberal versus restrictive fluid management strategy, reflecting the lack of any definitive national or international standards [1]. Several small randomized controlled trials have suggested that a restrictive fluid strategy can paradoxically result in increased ventricular filling (preload), as well as increased contractility and cardiac index [28,29]. The likely explanation is that restrictive fluid administration may decrease myocardial edema, thereby preventing an increase in left ventricular stiffness (i.e., a decrease in ventricular compliance) and a decrease in contractility [27]. Fluid-restricted patients have higher global end-diastolic volume index (GEDVI) and lower intrathoracic blood volume index. In contrast, liberal fluid approaches often produce hypervolemia instead of normovolemia, which may overdistend the ventricle and markedly impair ventricular function. In addition, liberal fluid approaches can increase the risks for blood transfusion and postoperative hypoxemia [27,29].

Multiple studies have demonstrated that traditional parameters of assessing volume status such as blood pressure, heart rate (HR), CVP, and pulmonary arterial occlusion pressure are unreliable estimates for predicting whether patients will improve with additional volume administration [30]. These variables also correlate poorly with other measurements of preload, left ventricular function, and oxygen delivery [31,32]. In addition to intravascular volume, factors such as cardiac function, airway pressure, intra-abdominal pressure, and pulmonary vascular resistance alter these traditional parameters [33].

Fluid management in both cardiac and noncardiac surgery has increasingly focused on the concept of GDT, which attempts to optimize fluid administration and cardiac function to achieve adequate tissue perfusion while avoiding excessive fluid administration. GDT may use nontraditional parameters such as pulse pressure variation (PPV) with respiration, aortic velocity flow patterns measured with esophageal Doppler, or derived indices from transesophageal echocardiography. In some studies, GDT to guide both fluid management and inotropic support decreased ICU and hospital length of stay and improved overall outcomes in cardiac surgery [1,2,33,34]. When used early in the perioperative period, GDT increased colloid administration but decreased vasopressor support, duration of mechanical ventilation, and hospital length of stay [2,32]. A meta-analysis by Aya et al. [33] of five cardiac studies reported that GDT decreased the odds ratio for postoperative complications to 0.33.

Although GDT has been effective in some cardiac surgery studies, there are disagreements regarding which hemodynamic parameters should be used to correlate with volume status and tissue perfusion. CO, mixed venous oxygen saturation (S_vO_2), SVV, PPV, SVI, systemic vascular resistance index (SVRI), GEDVI, and intrathoracic volume index have been used for GDT with similar results [31–33,35]. The goal of fluid therapy in cardiac surgery is to achieve adequate tissue oxygen delivery index (DO_2I), which is cardiac index (CI) times arterial oxygen content. Kapoor et al. [34] showed that titration of CI, SV, SVRI, S_vO_2, and SVV to keep DO_2I between 450 and 600 mL/min/m^2 improved oxygen delivery and outcome. In addition, increased central venous oxygen saturation decreased length of stay (LOS) and mortality. Decreased DO_2I is an independent predictor of altered preload, afterload, contractility, and prolonged ICU stay after cardiac surgery [34]. Some studies have also shown correlations between GEDVI, SVV, and PPV with cardiac index [1,32]. In general, the most reliable parameters for GDT appear to be SVV, PPV, and GEDVI in cardiac surgery patients. However, not all studies have agreed upon a specific parameter or set of parameters to guide GDT. Figure 14.1 is a proposal for an approach for GDT based on five studies of GDT in cardiac surgery [34,36–39]. However, GDT based on dynamic variables such as SVV, PPV, and SVI may have decreased applicability in cardiac surgery since it is not reliable with low tidal volume ventilation, in the absence of sinus rhythm, in patients with right heart failure, or when the chest is open.

Fluid therapy in cardiac surgery may depend upon the specific cardiac disease and the surgical procedure. In patients undergoing CABG surgery, a GDT approach to avoid hyper- and hypovolemia while maintaining adequate tissue perfusion is appropriate. Patients undergoing off-pump CABG do not experience hemodilution or the coagulopathies associated with CPB, but capillary permeability may still be increased due to surgical stress. Early implementation of GDT using S_vO_2, CI, and DO_2I as goals decreased hospital LOS and ICU stay and improved outcomes [39]. Other studies have shown that GDT results in increased use of colloid and inotropic support and improves outcomes [4,31,33].

GDT in cardiac surgery may need to be modified if patients have left ventricular dysfunction, right ventricular dysfunction, or valvular disease. In the setting of pulmonary hypertension and right ventricular hypertrophy (RVH), excess fluid administration can produce right ventricular (RV) distention, RV failure, decreased hypotension, and RV ischemia due to decreased RV coronary perfusion [40]. Crystalloid is often avoided, as it increases CVP but decreases SVI, and the need for four times as much total fluid can depress cardiac function [20,41]. A GDT approach can be used to guide fluid therapy in these patients.

Fluid management in patients with valvular disease should be based upon the specific pathophysiology in terms of the effects of the valvular disease on preload, afterload, contractility, and right heart function. Patients with mitral valve disease, particularly mitral stenosis, commonly

Parameters	Intervention	Goals

Figure 14.1 One approach to the use of goal-directed therapy for the cardiac surgery patient.

have pulmonary hypertension and RVH. These patients may require increased fluid administration to achieve adequate left ventricular filling across the stenotic mitral valve. However, they are also sensitive to fluid overload, which can lead to myocardia edema, cardiac dysfunction and worsened outcome [20].

Aortic stenosis is the most common valvular disorder worldwide and is associated with left ventricular hypertrophy (LVH) and diastolic dysfunction. These patients require increased preload (especially when measured by pulmonary artery pressures rather than by ventricular filling) to achieve adequate cardiac output. A GDT approach based on SVV and PPV has been effective in patients with aortic stenosis [42]. Patients with aortic regurgitation may require increased preload to achieve adequate forward flow [43]. Similar to mitral disease, fluid overload can lead to myocardial edema, which worsens diastolic dysfunction.

Heart failure patients are often maintained on diuretics and may present on the day of surgery with hypovolemia, resulting in increased afterload to maintain blood pressure and coronary perfusion [44]. However, the combination of hypovolemia and increased systemic vascular resistance (SVR) will further depress cardiac output. Many anesthesiologists are concerned that fluid administration to patients with chronic heart failure will result in decompensated heart failure and pulmonary edema. However, Stone and colleagues found that fluid loading prior to CPB resulted in decreased HR and SVR, increased CI and SV, and a smoother transition to CPB compared to patients without fluid loading. In patients with severe heart failure, such as those undergoing heart transplantation, GDT may help in determining the best balance between hypovolemia with organ hypoperfusion and fluid overload with pulmonary and cardiac edema.

Aortic dissection continues to result in high morbidity and mortality [45]. The 30-day mortality is around 10%–35% for patients with ascending aortic dissection requiring emergent surgical intervention. Blood pressure should be maintained as low as possible, consistent with adequate tissue perfusion, and impulse control should prevent rapid rises in aortic pressure during left ventricular ejection [44,46,47]. Although patients with aortic dissection may be hypovolemic from bleeding or vasodilation, the rate of fluid administration should be titrated to avoid rapid increases in blood pressure as hypovolemia is corrected.

14.4   Fluid therapy for thoracic surgery

Currently, the trend in thoracic surgery is towards less invasive procedures, with wedge resection or lobectomy with video-assisted thoracoscopic surgery rather than open thoracotomy [7]. Although postoperative pulmonary complications are highest with pneumonectomy, other thoracic surgeries have similar complications. Pulmonary complications after thoracic surgery remain the main cause of mortality, and the acute respiratory distress syndrome (ARDS) is associated with mortality as high as 40% [48]. Excessive intravenous fluid has been associated with increased pulmonary complications and ARDS, but fluid restriction has been linked to postoperative AKI [7,48].

Thoracic surgery produces surgical stress, inflammatory reaction, alterations to the endothelial glycocalyx, increased capillary permeability, and hormonal responses similar to cardiac surgery [48–51]. Since both hypovolemia and hypervolemia increase morbidity, finding the optimal fluid management strategy is challenging. Inappropriate fluid management can result in major complications, particularly in patients who receive one-lung ventilation (OLV), since adaptive mechanisms can be overwhelmed [7]. OLV alters both endothelial and alveolar epithelial permeability and decreases fluid clearance, thereby increasing the risk of pulmonary edema [49]. Therefore, careful titration of fluid during thoracic surgery is critical to prevent postoperative complications.

Fluid therapy in thoracic surgery requires understanding the risks and benefits of both restrictive and liberal fluid strategies. A restrictive strategy decreases postoperative systemic and pulmonary edema but is associated with an AKI rate of 5.9%, which decreases long-term survival [7,52]. A liberal strategy may also increase AKI and is associated with increased pulmonary complications [50]. A liberal fluid approach has an odds ratio of 2.91 for ARDS after lung resection [50]. An increased net fluid balance increases extravascular lung water and worsens outcome [48]. Cardiac complications are increased in thoracic surgery patients who receive more than 2 L of fluid [53]. Overall, studies suggest that the optimum fluid approach in thoracic surgery is a compromise between restrictive and liberal strategies, with normovolemia being maintained with intraoperative fluid administration between 1 and 2 mL/kg/hr [48–50].

Three main fluid types have been studied in thoracic surgery: crystalloids, albumin, and hydroxyethyl starch. In general, crystalloid administration is safe, although a larger amount of fluid is required to achieve and maintain the same intravascular volume expansion as with colloid, so crystalloids may produce more tissue and pulmonary edema [7,48]. Albumin produces intravascular volume expansion with lower administration volumes, but in patients undergoing lung resection albumin is associated with kidney dysfunction and does not improve survival [7]. Hydroxyethyl starch solutions can increase the incidence of AKI and the need for renal replacement therapy [7,54,55]. Overall, a reasonable approach is to use limited volumes of crystalloid solutions with GDT to maintain tissue perfusion and avoid pulmonary edema.

Although the potential benefits of a GDT approach to fluid administration in thoracic surgery are straightforward, many of the parameters (such as PPV and SVV) used in GDT may be misleading due to OLV, an open thoracic cavity, or overall pulmonary dysfunction and right heart dysfunction. PPV may be more reliable than SVV during OLV with tidal volumes less than 6 mL/kg [7].

Pneumonectomy patients have a 10.5% incidence of lung injury and an even higher risk of postoperative pulmonary edema secondary to increased capillary permeability [56–58]. Patients with postoperative pulmonary edema had a mortality as high as 100% in one retrospective analysis. Waller and colleagues demonstrated increased pulmonary capillary permeability after pneumonectomy versus lobectomy using a radioactive tracer. Therefore, meticulous fluid management is critical in these patients. The increased risk of postoperative pulmonary edema in patients undergoing pneumonectomy may be due to the fact that after pneumonectomy the full cardiac output flows through only half the vascular bed. This results in increased pulmonary artery pressure and increased shear stress, which further increases capillary permeability and edema formation. Therefore, it is critical to use the least amount of fluid compatible with adequate tissue perfusion. Colloid administration does not appear to decrease edema formation after thoracic surgery, and studies demonstrate increased colloid leak after pneumonectomy. However, liberal crystalloid administration increases the risk of postoperative pulmonary edema [59]. Suehiro and colleagues observed that higher fluid balance, higher urine output, increased blood loss, blood transfusion, and vasopressor therapy were significant risk factors for development of acute right heart failure. Parquin concluded that intraoperative fluid administration greater than 2 L is associated with pulmonary edema. Overall, a GDT approach using limited amounts of crystalloid to ensure adequate tissue perfusion appears to be effective in prevention of postoperative pulmonary edema.

Wedge resection and lobectomy cause less hemodynamic derangement than pneumonectomy and are associated with a mortality risk of 1%–7%, a major complication rate of 7.9%, an ARDS rate of 2%–5%, and a postoperative pulmonary edema rate of 4%. Again, the goal of fluid therapy in lung resection is to avoid both hypervolemia and hypovolemia. In addition to the usual pulmonary complications (ARDS, reintubation, pneumonia, and air leak), patients with higher intraoperative and postoperative fluid balances are at higher risk for AKI. Increased intraoperative fluid administration causes lung injury and decreases lung function in patients undergoing lung resection [49,60]. Arslantas and colleagues concluded that intraoperative fluid administration of greater than 6 mL/kg/hr is a risk factor for pulmonary complications, which increase mortality and LOS. Similar to pneumonectomy, GDT with an intraoperative fluid rate between 1 and 2 mL/kg/hr seems to provide the best outcome.

Although data are limited on optimal fluid management during lung transplantation, the goal remains to provide these patients with adequate organ perfusion while avoiding postoperative morbidity. Since the transplanted lung does not have normal lymphatic drainage and is at risk of ischemia–reperfusion injury, many centers limit fluid administration and use low doses of vasopressors to maintain blood pressure. GDT monitoring, possibly with tools such as the PiCCO, FloTrac, or esophageal Doppler, may be beneficial [48].

Thoracic surgery involving the esophagus or gastroesophageal junction has a high complication rate with morbidity of 38%–50% and mortality of 7%–10% [51]. Patients with higher intraoperative and postoperative fluid balance have a higher rate of pulmonary complications [51,61]. Wei and colleagues reported higher rates of cardiac and pulmonary complications in patients with a net fluid balance of 598 mL compared to those with a net fluid balance of 208 mL. Patients undergoing esophageal surgery frequently are malnourished and have low serum albumin levels, increasing edema formation. Therefore, these patients may benefit from an albumin-based fluid administration approach.

14.5 Conclusion and recommendations

Cardiothoracic surgery procedures have high morbidity and mortality, often related to hypovolemia, which produces tissue hypoperfusion and organ dysfunction, and hypervolemia, which produces pulmonary and systemic edema and corresponding organ dysfunction. Despite an extensive number of studies, there remains a lack of consensus on the choice of fluid and the rate and volume for administration. In addition, the choice and volume of fluid may depend upon the specific cardiothoracic procedure. However, new approaches to monitoring fluid administration and outcome studies with different fluids have resulted in some overall themes. In contrast to other surgical and medical patients, albumin appears to be beneficial in most cardiac surgery patients and in some selected thoracic surgery patients. Standard static parameters such as CVP are not useful in determining fluid administration, especially in cardiothoracic surgery patients. Increased fluid administration is frequently associated with worse patient outcome, suggesting a restrictive fluid approach when organ perfusion and cardiac function are acceptable. GDT is a valuable approach to fluid administration in cardiac and thoracic surgery, especially in the context of cardiac dysfunction and altered systemic vascular tone. However, many of the parameters used in GDT often are not valid in cardiothoracic surgery patients, who may have abnormal cardiac rhythms, right ventricular dysfunction, and open chests. In the future, advances in GDT and in additional monitors of tissue perfusion will allow further improvements in patient outcome.

References

1. Habicher M, Perrino A, Jr., Spies CD, von HC, Wittkowski U, Sander M. Contemporary fluid management in cardiac anesthesia. *J Cardiothorac Vasc Anesth.* 2011;25:1141–1153.
2. Shaw A, Raghunathan K. Fluid management in cardiac surgery: Colloid or crystalloid? *Anesthesiol Clin.* 2013;31:269–280.
3. Licker M, Cartier V, Robert J, Diaper J, Villiger Y, Tschopp JM, Inan C. Risk factors of acute kidney injury according to RIFLE criteria after lung cancer surgery. *Ann Thorac Surg.* 2011;91:844–851.
4. Young R. Perioperative fluid and electrolyte management in cardiac surgery: A review. *J Extra Corpor Technol.* 2015;44:P20–P26.
5. Schumacher J, Klotz KF. Fluid therapy in cardiac surgery patients. *Appl Cardiopulm Pathophysiol.* 2009;13:138 142.
6. Nussbaum C, Haberer A, Tiefenthaller A, Januszewska K, Chappell D, Brettner F, et al. Perturbation of the microvascular glycocalyx and perfusion in infants after cardiopulmonary bypass. *J Thorac Cardiovasc Surg.* 2015;150:1474–1781.
7. Assaad S, Popescu W, Perrino A. Fluid management in thoracic surgery. *Curr Opin Anaesthesiol.* 2013;26:31–39.
8. Lomivorotov VV, Fominskiy EV, Efremov SM, Nepomniashchikh VA, Lomivorotov VN, Chernyavskiy AM, et al. J Hypertonic solution decreases extravascular lung water in cardiac patients undergoing cardiopulmonary bypass surgery. *Cardiothorac Vasc Anesth.* 2013;27:273–282.
9. Corcoran T, Rhodes JE, Clarke S, Myles PS, Ho KM. Perioperative fluid management strategies in major surgery: A stratified meta-analysis. *Anesth Analg.* 2012;114:640–651.
10. Brovman EY, Gabriel RA, Dutton RP, Urman RD. Pulmonary artery catheter use during cardiac surgery in the United States, 2010 to 2014. *J Cardiothorac Vasc Anesth.* 2016;30:579–584.
11. Chiang Y, Hosseinian L, Rhee A, Itagaki S, Cavallaro P, Chikwe J. Questionable benefit of the pulmonary artery catheter after cardiac surgery in high-risk patients. *J Cardiothorac Vasc Anesth.* 2015;29:76–81.
12. Gouveia V, Marcelino P, Reuter DA. The role of transesophageal echocardiography in the intraoperative period. *Curr Cardiol Rev.* 2011;7:184–196.
13. Toraman F, Evrenkaya S, Yuce M, Turek O, Aksoy N, Karabulut H, et al. Highly positive intraoperative fluid balance during cardiac surgery is associated with adverse outcome. *Perfusion.* 2004;19:85–91.
14. Jacob M, Chappell D, Rehm M. The "third space"–fact or fiction? *Best Pract Res Clin Anaesthesiol.* 2009;23:145–157.
15. Moret E, Jacob MW, Ranucci M, Schramko AA. Albumin-beyond fluid replacement in cardiopulmonary bypass surgery: Why, how, and when? *Semin Cardiothorac Vasc Anesth.* 2014;18:252–259.
16. Riegger LQ, Voepel-Lewis T, Kulik TJ, Malviya S, Tait AR, Mosca RS, et al. Albumin versus crystalloid prime solution for cardiopulmonary bypass in young children. *Crit Care Med.* 2002;30:2649–2654.
17. Russell JA, Navickis RJ, and Wilkes MM. Albumin versus crystalloid for pump priming in cardiac surgery: Meta-analysis of controlled trials. *J Cardiothorac Vasc Anesth.* 2004;18:429–437.

18. Yeoman PM, Vence-Pastor DE, Rithalia SV. Changes in colloid osmotic pressure in patients undergoing cardiothoracic surgery. *Resuscitation.* 1981;9:307–313.

19. Mak MA, Smołka A, Kowalski J, Kuc A, Klausa F, Kremens K, et al. Can cardiopulmonary bypass system with blood priming become a new standard in coronary surgery? *Kardio Pol.* 2016. doi: 10.5603/KP.a2016.0018

20. Rex S, Scholz M, Weyland A, Busch T, Schorn B, Buhre W. Intra- and extravascular volume status in patients undergoing mitral valve replacement: Crystalloid vs. colloid priming of cardiopulmonary bypass. *Eur J Anaesthesiol.* 2006;23:1–9.

21. Appelman MH, van Barneveld LJ, Romijn JW, Vonk AB, Boer C. The impact of balanced hydroxyethyl starch cardiopulmonary bypass priming solution on the fibrin part of clot formation: Ex vivo rotation thromboelastometry. *Perfusion.* 2011;26:175–180.

22. Sun P, Ji B, Sun Y, Zhu X, Liu J, Long C, Zheng Z. Effects of retrograde autologous priming on blood transfusion and clinical outcomes in adults: A meta-analysis. *Perfusion* 2013;28:238–243.

23. Pouard P, Bojan M. Neonatal cardiopulmonary bypass. *Semin Thorac Cardiovasc Surg Pediatr Card Surg Annu.* 2013;16:59–61.

24. Khoo MS, Braden GL, Deaton D, Owen S, Germain M, O'Shea M, et al. Outcome and complications of intraoperative hemodialysis during cardiopulmonary bypass with potassium-rich cardioplegia. *Am J Kidney Dis.* 2003;41;1247–1256.

25. Heath M, Raghunathan K, Welsby I, Maxwell C. Using zero balance ultrafiltration with dialysate as a replacement fluid for hyperkalemia during cardiopulmonary bypass. *J Extra Corpor Technol.* 2014;46:262–266.

26. Kalus JS, Caron MF, White CM, Mather JF, Gallagher R, Boden WE, et al. Impact of fluid balance on incidence of atrial fibrillation after cardiothoracic surgery. *Am J Cardiol.* 2004;94:1423–1425.

27. Pradeep A, Rajagopalam A, Kolli HK, Patel N, Venuto R, Lohr J, et al. High volumes of intravenous fluid during cardiac surgery are associated with increased mortality. *HSR Proc Intensive Care Cardiovasc Anesth.* 2010;2:287–296.

28. Kvalheim VL, Farstad M, Steien E, Mongstad A, Borge BA, Kvitting PM, et al. Infusion of hypertonic saline/starch during cardiopulmonary bypass reduces fluid overload and may impact cardiac function. *Acta Anaesthesiol Scand.* 2010;54:485–493.

29. Vretzakis G, Kleitsaki A, Stamoulis K, Bareka M, Georgopoulou S, Karanikolas M, et al. Intra-operative intravenous fluid restriction reduces perioperative red blood cell transfusion in elective cardiac surgery, especially in transfusion-prone patients: A prospective, randomized controlled trial. *J Cardiothorac Surg.* 2010;5:7.

30. Marik PE, Lemson J. Fluid responsiveness: An evolution of our understanding. *Br J Anaesth.* 2014;112:617–620.

31. Fergerson BD, Manecke GR Jr. Goal-directed therapy in cardiac surgery: Are we there yet? *J Cardiothorac Vasc Anesth.* 2013;27:1075–1078.

32. Goepfert MS, Reuter DA, Akyol D, Lamm P, Kilger E, Goetz AE. Goal-directed fluid management reduces vasopressor and catecholamine use in cardiac surgery patients. *Intensive Care Med.* 2007;33:6–103.

33. Aya HD, Cecconi M, Hamilton M, Rhodes A. Goal-directed therapy in cardiac surgery: A systematic review and meta-analysis. *Br J Anaesth.* 2013;110:510–517.
34. Kapoor PM, Kakani M, Chowdhury U, Choudhury M, Lakshmy, Kiran U. Early goal-directed therapy in moderate to high-risk cardiac surgery patients. *Ann Card Anaesth.* 2008;11:27–34.
35. Scheeren TW, Wiesenack C, Gerlach H, Marx G. Goal-directed intraoperative fluid therapy guided by stroke volume and its variation in high-risk surgical patients: A prospective randomized multicenter study. *J Clin Monit Comput.* 2013;27:225–233.
36. McKendry M, McGloin H, Saberi D, Caudwell L, Brady AR, Singer M. Randomised controlled trial assessing the impact of a nurse delivered, flow monitored protocol for optimization of circulatory status after cardiac surgery. *BMJ.* 2004;329(7460):258.
37. Mythen MG, Webb AR. Perioperative plasma volume expansion reduces the incidence of gut mucosal hypoperfusion during cardiac surgery. *Arch Surg.* 1995; 130:423–429.
38. Pölönen P, Ruokonen E, Hippeläinen M, Pöyhönen M, Takala J. A prospective, randomized study of goal-oriented hemodynamic therapy in cardiac surgical patients. *Anesth Analg.* 2000;90:1052–1059.
39. Smetkin AA, Kirov MY, Kuzkov VV, Lenkin AI, Eremeev AV, Slastilin VY, et al. Single transpulmonary thermodilution and continuous monitoring of central venous oxygen saturation during off-pump coronary surgery. *Acta Anaesthesiol Scand.* 2009;53: 505–514.
40. Bayya PR, Varma PK, Raman SP, Neema PK. Emergency mitral valve replacement for acute severe mitral regurgitation following balloon mitral valvotomy: Pathophysiology of hemodynamic collapse and peri-operative management issues. *Ann Card Anaesth.* 2014;17:52–55.
41. Lee S, Lee SH, Chang BC, Shim JK. Efficacy of goal-directed therapy using bioreactance cardiac output monitoring after valvular heart surgery. *Yonsei Med J.* 2015;56:913–920.
42. Høiseth LØ, Hoff IE, Hagen OA, Landsverk SA, Kirkeboen KA. Dynamic variables and fluid responsiveness in patients for aortic stenosis surgery. *Acta Anaesthesiol Scand.* 2014;58:826–834.
43. Stone JG, Hoar PF, Calabro JR, DePetrillo MA, Bendixen HH. Afterload reduction and preload augmentation improve the anesthetic management of patients with cardiac failure and valvular regurgitation. *Anesth Analg.* 1980;59:737–742.
44. De Vecchis R, Baldi C, Cioppa C, Giasi A, Fusco A. Effects of limiting fluid intake on clinical and laboratory outcomes in patients with heart failure. Results of a meta-analysis of randomized controlled trials. *Herz.* 2016;41:63–75.
45. Cook C, Gleason T. Great vessel and cardiac trauma. *Surg Clin North Am.* 2009; 89:797–820.
46. Goldfinger JZ, Halperin JL, Marin ML, Stewart AS, Eagle KA, Fuster V. Thoracic aortic aneurysm and dissection. *J Am Coll Cardiol.* 2014;64:1725–1739.
47. Nienaber CA, Clough RE. Management of acute aortic dissection. *Lancet.* 2015;385:800–811.
48. Searl CP, Perrino A. Fluid management in thoracic surgery. *Anesthesiol Clin.* 2012;30:641–655.

49. Arslantas MK, Kara HV, Tuncer BB, Yildizeli B, Yuksel M, Bostanci K, et al. Effect of the amount of intraoperative fluid administration on postoperative pulmonary complications following anatomic lung resections. *J Thorac Cardiovasc Surg.* 2015;149:314–320.

50. Evan RG, Naidu B. Does a conservative fluid management strategy in the perioperative management of lung resection patients reduce the risk of acute lung injury? *Interact Cardiovasc Thorac Surg.* 2012;15:498–504.

51. Wei S, Tian J, Song X, Chen Y. Association of perioperative fluid balance and adverse surgical outcomes in esophageal cancer and esophagogastric junction cancer. *Ann Thorac Surg.* 2008;86:266–272.

52. Ishikawa S, Griesdale DE, Lohser J. Acute kidney injury after lung resection surgery: Incidence and perioperative risk factors. *Anesth Analg.* 2012;114: 1256–1262.

53. Pipanmekaporn T, Punjasawadwong Y, Charuluxananan S, Lapisatepun W, Bunburaphong P, Patumanond J, et al. Incidence of and risk factors for cardiovascular complications after thoracic surgery for noncancerous lesions. *J Cardiothorac Vasc Anesth.* 2014;28:948–953.

54. Schortgen F, Girou E, Deye N, Brochard L.; CRYCO Study Group. The risk associated with hyperoncotic colloids in patients with shock. *Intensive Care Med.* 2008;34:2157–2168.

55. Searl et al. 2015.

56. Alam N, Park BJ, Wilton A, Seshan VE, Bains MS, Downey RJ, et al. Incidence and risk factors for lung injury after lung cancer resection. *Ann Thorac Surg.* 2007;84:1085–1091.

57. Suehiro K, Okutani R, Ogawa S. Anesthetic considerations in 65 patients undergoing unilateral pneumonectomy: Problems related to fluid therapy and hemodynamic control. *J Clin Anesth.* 2010;22:41–44.

58. Waller DA, Gebitekin C, Saungers NR, Walker DR. Noncardiogenic pulmonary edema complicating lung resection. *Ann Thorac Surg.* 1993;55:140–143.

59. Parquin F, Marchal M, Mehiri S, Herve P, Lescot B. Post-pneumonectomy pulmonary edema analysis and risk factors. *Eur J Cardiothorac Surg.* 1996;10:929–933.

60. Matot I, Dery E, Bulgov Y, Cohen B, Paz J, Nesher N. Fluid management during video-assisted thoracoscopic surgery for lung resection: A randomized, controlled trial of effects on urinary output and postoperative renal function. *J Thorac Cardiovasc Surg.* 2013;146:461–466.

61. Eng OS, Arlow RL, Moore D, Chen C, Langenfeld JE, August DA, et al. Fluid administration and morbidity in transhiatal esophagectomy. *J Surg Res.* 2016;200:91–97.

62. Winsor G, Thomas SH, Biddinger PD, Wedel SK. Inadequate hemodynamic management in patients undergoing interfacility transfer for suspected aortic dissection. *Am J Emerg Med.* 2005;23:24–29.

chapter fifteen

Fluid management in neurosurgical patients

Stefanie Fischer and Donald S. Prough
University of Texas Medical Branch at Galveston
Galveston, TX

Contents

Key points:

- Influence of fluid composition and volume on intracranial volume
- Influence of composition and volume on outcome in traumatic brain injury
- Influence of fluid composition and volume in specific neurological situations

15.1   Introduction

As a therapeutic goal, keeping neurosurgical patients "dry" is a venerable concept. For many years, dating to the often-cited publication by Shenkin [1], *dry* has meant strict restriction of intravenous fluids. Shenkin [2] studied 10 perioperative neurosurgical patients with then-current techniques for measuring body weight, electrolytes, total body water, extracellular water, and plasma volume. The patients had received

5% dextrose in water (D5W) intraoperatively plus replacement of blood loss; postoperatively they received D5W until they tolerated oral liquids. For the first several days, patients tended to lose weight, lose both total body water and extracellular water, excrete low urinary volumes and minimal urinary sodium, and to maintain sodium and potassium concentrations (Na^+ and K^+) within normal ranges, although Na^+ decreased slightly. These data were interpreted as consistent with postoperative sodium and water retention, in response to which fluid restriction, especially sodium restriction, was considered reasonable. Subsequently, Shenkin [1] published clinical data suggesting that fluid restriction to ~1,000 mL per day was associated with stable Na^+, slightly increased blood urea nitrogen (BUN) (although still within the normal range) and greater weight loss. This approach, literally keeping patients dry, influenced perioperative neurosurgical fluid management for at least the ensuing quarter century.

However, in the context of neurosurgical fluid management, the meaning of *dry* has changed. Current management is based on the concept that *dry* means avoidance of unnecessary administration of free water but does not imply hypovolemia. Relative fluid restriction has been associated with worse outcomes in head-injured patients. Clifton [3] analyzed data on patients entered prospectively into the National Acute Brain Injury Study: Hypothermia and reported that net fluid balance in the lowest quartile (more negative than 594 mL) was associated with a greater proportion of poor outcomes and, along with admission Glasgow Coma Scale score, age, mean arterial pressure (MAP) <70 mmHg, intracranial pressure (ICP) >25 mmHg, and cerebral perfusion pressure (CPP) <60 mmHg, independently predicted poor outcome.

The concept that hypovolemia may worsen outcome requires attention to the composition of administered fluids. Fluids that lead to reductions in serum osmolality may increase cerebral edema, so iso-osmolar (normonatremic) normovolemia represents an appropriate goal, perhaps occasionally replaced by hypernatremic normovolemia. Changing concepts regarding appropriate fluid management of neurosurgical patients have developed in parallel with rapidly changing concepts regarding appropriate fluid management of non-neurosurgical patients. Unfortunately, to date, prospective, randomized controlled trials of perioperative fluid therapy have been conducted in non-neurosurgical patients.

This review will focus on three key topics:

1. The influence of fluid composition and volume on intracranial volume
2. The influence of fluid composition and volume on outcome in traumatic brain injury (TBI)
3. The influence of fluid composition and volume in specific neurosurgical situations

15.2 Influence of fluid composition and volume on ICP

Management of intracranial volume is important in any patient who is at risk for intracranial hypertension and, in patients undergoing craniotomy, in achieving adequate brain relaxation. Intracranial volume is a function of brain tissue volume, cerebrospinal fluid volume, and cerebral blood volume, which is the sum of intracranial arterial and venous blood volume. Perioperative fluid management potentially can increase or decrease brain tissue volume and intracranial venous blood volume.

Compensatory mechanisms can adjust for substantial increases in intracranial volume, particularly if increases occur slowly; however, larger or more rapid increases will result in increased ICP. Preservation of CPP (CPP = MAP – ICP) necessitates maintenance of normovolemia without adversely influencing ICP. Several physiologic principles underlie the relationship between fluid management, volume status, and ICP.

First, cerebral venous volume is a function of cerebral venous capacitance and cerebral venous pressure. Cerebral venous pressure is equal to central venous pressure in the supine position but is reduced as the head is elevated above the chest. Although it is reasonable to assume that hypervolemia could increase central venous pressure and consequently increase cerebral venous pressure and intracranial volume, few clinical data support that assumption. It is likely that the magnitude of differences in central venous pressure that are associated with moderate differences in fluid administration are too small to significantly influence ICP. In comparison, considerable clinical evidence demonstrates that changes of head elevation (Trendelenburg and reverse Trendelenburg positions) alter ICP, dural tension, and CPP (Table 15.1) [4–6].

However, overly exuberant fluid administration in neurosurgical patients may exert adverse effects on organ systems other than the brain.

Table 15.1 Pressures during craniotomy in supine and 5°, 10°, and 15° reverse Trendelenburg positions

Variable	0° rTP	5° rTp	10° rTp	15° rTp
ICP	7.6 ± 5.1	5.1 ± 5.3	3.2 ± 5.1	1.8 ± 5.0
MABP	82.9 ± 15.8	79.9 ± 15.6	76.9 ± 15.2	73.6 ± 15.4
CPP	75.3 ± 15.5	74.7 ± 15.3	73.7 ± 14.8	71.8 ± 15.2
JVBP	2.5 ± 3.1	0.6 ± 2.8	−1.3 ± 2.7	−2.9 ± 2.7

Source: From Tankisi, A., et al., *J. Neurosurg.*, 106, 239, 2007. With permission.

Note: In 53 patients undergoing craniotomy for supratentorial tumors, ICP, intracranial pressure; MABP, mean arterial blood pressure; CPP, cerebral perfusion pressure; and JVBP, jugular venous bulb pressure were measured in the supine and 5°, 10°, and 15° reverse Trendelenburg positions (rTP).

In patients with severe TBI, greater net cumulative fluid balance was associated with greater severity of pulmonary infiltrates, although not with a higher incidence of refractory intracranial hypertension (Figure 15.1) [7].

Second, brain tissue volume is a function of the integrity of the blood–brain barrier (BBB), which describes the characteristics of the capillaries that separate blood from surrounding tissue. In nonbrain tissues, the distribution of fluid between plasma volume and extracellular volume is determined by capillary membrane permeability, transcapillary hydrostatic pressure gradients, transcapillary colloid osmotic (oncotic) pressure gradients, and the status of the glycocalyx. Systemic capillary membranes are highly permeable to water, ions, and other low molecular weight (MW) compounds but limit the movement of high MW substances, including albumin. Oncotic pressure is generated by solutes larger than approximately 30,000 MW (albumin has an average MW of 69,000).

In contrast to systemic capillary membranes, the cerebral capillary membranes that constitute the BBB are impermeable to most hydrophobic solutes, including sodium. Osmotic pressure = osmolality × 19.3 mmHg/mOsm/kg. A gradient of 1 mEq/L of Na^+ across the intact BBB generates an osmolality difference of 2.0 mOsm/kg because each sodium ion is

Pulmonary edema–cardiogenic or ARDS
(Uncensored)

Figure 15.1 In a retrospective cohort study of 41 patients with severe traumatic brain injury (TBI), there was no association between cumulative net fluid balance and refractory intracranial hypertension. However, cumulative fluid balance was significantly greater in patients who developed pulmonary edema. (From Fletcher, J.J., et al., *Neurocrit Care*, 13, 47, 2010. With permission.)

accompanied by an anion. Therefore, a gradient of 1 mEq/L of Na$^+$ across the intact BBB generates an osmotic pressure difference of 38.6 mmHg, much higher than total colloid osmotic pressure (~24 mmHg). A rapid increase in plasma osmotic pressure will tend to pull water from the brain; in contrast, a rapid decrease in plasma osmotic pressure will tend to result in movement of water into the brain. In patients with disruption of the BBB, regionally or globally, all solutes may pass more freely, making prediction of responses difficult. In addition, patients with apparently similar clinical presentations after apparently similar injuries may have markedly different intracranial pathology, presumably associated with substantial variability in responses to changes in solute gradients across the BBB (Figure 15.2) [8].

Third, the terms *hypotonic*, *isotonic*, and *hypertonic* refer to intravenous fluids in which the total osmolality is, respectively, less than, roughly equal to, or greater than serum osmolality. The sodium concentration (Na$^+$) in intravenous fluids is the most important component of osmolality and must be considered in relation to plasma Na$^+$ and osmolality. Normal plasma osmolality averages 290 mOsm/kg, of which 280 mOsm/kg is attributable to sodium and its associated anions.

Figure 15.2 Patients with similar clinical presentations, including Glasgow Coma Scale scores, may have markedly different intracranial pathologies and consequently markedly different amounts of brain in which the blood–brain barrier is compromised. (From Marshall, L.F., et al., *J. Neurotrauma.*, 9(Suppl 1), S287, 1992. With permission.)

The calculated osmolalities of lactated Ringer's solution and 0.9% NaCl are 270 mOsm/kg and 308 mOsm/kg, respectively. However, the measured osmolalities are considerably lower (Table 15.2) [9].

As an example of changes in Na$^+$ produced by rapid fluid infusion, in gynecological patients receiving rapid infusions (60 mL/kg over 2 hr) of lactated Ringer's solution (Na$^+$ 130 mEq/L), plasma Na$^+$ decreased approximately 2.0 mEq/L, while in patients receiving 0.9% saline (Na$^+$ 154 mEq/L), plasma Na$^+$ increased nearly 2.0 mEq/L (Figure 15.3) [10]. These changes are equivalent to decreases and increases in osmolality of ~4.0 mOsm/kg and in plasma osmotic pressure of ~75 mmHg, with a total difference in osmolality and osmotic pressure between the two acute infusions of ~8.0 mOsm/kg and 150 mmHg, respectively.

Although not conducted in neurosurgical patients, the study by Sheingraber et al. [10] suggests that rapid administration of lactated Ringer's solution to patients at risk for intracranial hypertension (e.g., hypotensive patients with TBI) could substantially increase brain water and worsen ICP; conversely, rapid administration of 0.9% saline could exert opposite effects. However, there are few clinical data to support that contention, and considerable clinical data address adverse effects, including mortality, of hyperchloremia and metabolic acidosis associated with rapid administration of 0.9% saline [11]. In practice, the choice between lactated Ringer's solution and 0.9% saline could be avoided by choosing a commercially available balanced salt solution that is not hyponatremic.

However, therapeutic induction of hyperosmolality is routine practice in neurosurgery. Acute induction of hyperosmolality to reduce brain water and ICP is routinely accomplished with mannitol, but hypertonic saline solutions are preferred by some clinicians [12,13]. Hypertonic saline solutions and mannitol solutions of similar osmolality have similar effects on brain water and ICP. However, infusion of hypertonic saline,

Table 15.2 Calculated osmolarity and measured osmolality of fluid preparations

Product	Theoretical vs. measured *in vitro* osmolality of common colloid and crystalloid solutions		
	Albumex 4% (human albumin 4%)	0.9% saline	LRS
Theoretical osmolality (mOsm/kg H$_2$O)	274.4	308	276
Measured osmolality (mOsm/kg H$_2$O)	266 [266–267]	285 [282–286]	257 [257–258]

Source: Modified from Van Aken, H.K., et al., *Curr. Opin. Anaesthesiol.*, 25, 563, 2012. With permission.

Note: The measured osmolality of intravenous fluid solutions are lower than the theoretical (calculated) osmolalities. LRS, lactated Ringer's solution.

Figure 15.3 Acute changes in serum Na$^+$ produced by infusion of 60 mL/kg of 0.9% saline or lactated Ringer's solution over 120 minutes in patients undergoing gynecologic surgery. (Modified from Scheingraber, S., et al., *Anesthesiology*, 90, 1265, 1999. With permission.)

unlike mannitol, increases intravascular volume [14]. While few complications relate specifically to osmotic therapy, acute severe hyperosmolality could theoretically precipitate BBB opening. Clinical use of hypertonic saline is associated, as is 0.9% saline, with hyperchloremic acidosis, which usually requires no treatment but must be differentiated from other causes of metabolic acidosis.

In contrast to sodium ions, colloids contribute minimally to osmolality and osmotic pressure and therefore to gradients for water movement across the intact BBB. While some clinicians infer that increasing colloid osmotic pressure will decrease cerebral edema in neurosurgical patients, most experimental evidence suggests that, if the BBB is intact, the small portion of total osmotic pressure contributed by colloid exerts little effect.

15.3   Influence of fluid composition and volume on outcome in TBI

Hypotension in TBI patients should prompt the suspicion of hemorrhagic hypovolemia due to associated injuries or other treatable causes (e.g., tension pneumothorax, tamponade, myocardial contusion). Post-TBI hypotension is strongly associated with worse outcome [15]. Although few data specifically address the influence of intraoperative hypotension on long-term outcome after TBI, the frequency of intraoperative hypotension is high in both adults [16] and children [17]. Physicians caring for these patients should target adequate volume resuscitation while avoiding increases in ICP. Isotonic crystalloid solutions (excluding conventional, slightly hypotonic, lactated Ringer's solution) are often the first solutions to be infused in hypotensive trauma patients because they are readily available and inexpensive. As an initial resuscitation fluid, 0.9% saline is acceptable, perhaps even defensible based on slight hyperosmolality, but more prolonged use will inevitably produce hyperchloremia and metabolic acidosis and potentially worsen outcome. In septic patients, increasing serum Cl⁻ over the first 3 days of hospitalization was associated with statistically worse hospital mortality, although the association was stronger in patients who were hypernatremic on admission (Table 15.3) [11]. In TBI patients, if the initial clinical evaluation suggests intracranial hypertension, empirical mannitol (0.5 g/kg) may also be appropriate, although the ensuing osmotic diuresis may aggravate existing volume deficits. Infusion of packed red blood cells suspended in 0.9% saline or thawed fresh frozen plasma is a suitable alternative if severe dilutional anemia is present or suspected.

The role of colloids in management of TBI patients continues to be debated. In anesthetized rats subjected to fluid-percussion TBI followed by hemorrhage of 20 mL/kg, resuscitation with 90 mL/kg of isotonic lactated Ringer's solution was associated with equivalent blood volume expansion to 20 mL/kg of 5% albumin, but at the expense of higher brain water. Resuscitation with only 50 mL/kg of isotonic lactated Ringer's solution did not increase brain water but also failed to restore blood volume [18]. In contrast, a randomized trial that compared 4% albumin to 0.9% saline for fluid management of critically ill patients after admission to intensive care units, suggested that the subset of trauma patients with TBI had substantially worse long-term outcomes in the albumin group [19]. One possible explanation for the superiority of albumin in experimental TBI may be disruption of the BBB by fluid-percussion TBI, perhaps causing the cerebral capillary bed to function more like systemic capillary beds. In contrast, the adverse influence on clinical outcome is potentially attributable to suspension of 4% albumin in a hypotonic solution [9]. Although changes in Na⁺ were not reported, a reduction in Na⁺ could potentially explain the greater frequency of refractory intracranial hypertension seen in the first week after TBI in those patients receiving 4% albumin 20].

Hypertonic saline solutions, which tend to reduce ICP and increase blood volume, are used by some clinicians for rapid volume resuscitation of hypovolemic trauma victims with TBI and intracranial hypertension. However, Cooper et al. [21] found no differences in mortality or neurologic outcome when they randomized 219 patients with TBI to prehospital resuscitation beginning with 250 mL of either 7.5% saline or lactated Ringer's solution. Subsequently, Bulger et al. [22] randomized 1,331 patients with severe TBI but without shock to initial infusion of 250 mL of 0.9% saline, 7.5% saline, or 7.5% saline containing 6% dextran and found no difference in outcome.

Table 15.3 Hospital mortality, serum chloride at ICU admission and 72 hours, and hyperchloremia

Variable	All patients' odds ratio	P	No hyperchloremia on admission ($Cl_0 < 110$) Odds ratio	P	Hyperchloremia on admission ($Cl_0 > 110$) Odds ratio	P
Cl_0 (per 5 mEq/L)	1.04 (0.97–1.12)	0.25	0.95 (0.84–1.08)	0.43	1.18 (0.99–1.40)	0.07
Cl_{72} (per 5 mEq/L)	1.12 (1.01–1.24)	0.03*	1.05 (0.92–1.20)	0.46	1.38 (1.13–1.68)	0.002*
ΔCl (per 5 mEq/L)	1.15 (1.05–1.29)	0.003*	1.13 (0.99–1.28)	0.07	1.35 (1.11–1.64)	0.003*

Source: Neyra, J.A., et al., *Crit. Care Med.*, 43, 1938, 2015. With permission.

Notes: Univariate association of hospital mortality with (1) serum chloride and the time of ICU admission, (2) serum chloride at 72 hours of ICU stay, and (3) within-subject time-related change in serum chloride from ICU admission to 72 hours (ΔCl) in all patients and stratified by the presence of hyperchloremia at the time of ICU admission; Cl_0 serum chloride at the time of ICU admission; $Q72$, serum chloride at 72 hr of ICU stay; $\Delta Cl = Cl_{72} - Cl_0$.

*Statistically significant, $P < 0.05$.

15.4 The influence of fluid composition and volume in specific neurosurgical situations

15.4.1 Craniotomy

Generally, isotonic crystalloid solutions should be used to replace preexisting deficits and blood loss. Because of the potential for aggravation of ischemic or TBI, solutions containing dextrose are best avoided unless there is a specific indication for use (e.g., hypoglycemia). Transfusion may be indicated at a hemoglobin concentration (Hgb) of 8 g/dL, with a higher threshold being appropriate if there is evidence of tissue hypoxia or ongoing uncontrolled hemorrhage. Fresh frozen plasma may be infused if there is persistent hemorrhage despite adequate surgical hemostasis. There are few clear indications for the administration of albumin; increasing colloid osmotic pressure does not prevent the formation of brain edema. To reduce brain volume and improve operating conditions, hypertonic mannitol is frequently given, with hypertonic saline representing an alternative. In 238 neurosurgical patients randomized to receive either 160 mL of 3% saline or 150 mL of 20% mannitol to induce brain relaxation during neurosurgery, brain relaxation was superior in the group receiving 3% saline, although there were no differences in major outcomes (Table 15.4) [23].

Table 15.4 Randomized trial of hypertonic saline or hypertonic mannitol for brain relaxation during surgery

	HTS Group (n = 122)	M Group (n = 116)	P
Brain condition (soft/adequate/ tight)	**58/43/21**	**39/42/35**	**0.02**
Operation time (min)	268 (150–656)	257 (149–520)	0.29
Total urinary output (mL)	596 (350–980)	150 (150–300)	<0.0001
Number of patients requiring additional doses	**21**	**35**	**0.02**
Number of patients requiring additional hyperventilation	8	15	0.13

Source: Wu, C., et al., *Anesth. Analg.*, 110, 903, 2010. With permission.

Notes: Patients undergoing supratentorial brain tumor surgery (n = 238) were randomized to receive either 3% saline or 20% mannitol for brain relaxation. Surgical conditions were statistically significantly better in those receiving 3% saline, although major outcomes were not different; HTS, hypertonic saline; M, hypertonic mannitol.

Are there implications for perioperative neurosurgical fluid management in the multiple clinical trials of liberal versus restrictive fluid therapy that have been conducted in other patient populations? The concepts *restrictive* and *liberal* have been debated per se since it is obvious that restrictive therapy in one study can mean more liberal in another. However, *restrictive* means more judicious and less. Restrictive fluid therapy appears to most strongly improve clinically important outcomes, such as cardiopulmonary complications and tissue healing, in patients undergoing intra-abdominal surgery, especially colectomy [24]. However, after less complication-prone procedures, such as laparoscopic cholecystectomy and arthroscopic surgery, more liberal fluid administration has been associated with fewer, less severe complications, such as nausea and vomiting [25,26].

15.4.2   Disorders of antidiuretic hormone

After TBI, a surprisingly high proportion of patients develop pituitary dysfunction. Acutely, after TBI approximately 30% of patients have anterior pituitary dysfunction, an incidence that gradually declines to around 20%; approximately 5% of patients have posterior pituitary dysfunction [27]. In a subset of neurosurgical patients, a relative excess of antidiuretic hormone (ADH) is associated with hyponatremia [28], although the syndrome of inappropriate antidiuretic hormone must be distinguished from other, more common causes of mild hyponatremia [29]. Recent publications have demonstrated that conivaptan is useful in hyponatremic neurosurgical patients in which fluid restriction is not sufficient to resolve hyponatremia [30].

Less commonly, neurogenic diabetes insipidus (DI), characterized by the production of large volumes of dilute urine in the face of a normal or elevated plasma osmolality, may occur in association with hypothalamic lesions or after pituitary surgery or TBI. After TBI or pituitary surgery, polyuria may be present for only a few days within the first week, may be permanent, or may demonstrate a triphasic sequence: early DI, return of urinary concentrating ability, then recurrent DI. In severe cases, urinary output can exceed 1 L/hr. The diagnosis of DI requires a high index of suspicion when dealing with patients at risk. Confirmatory evidence consists of low urinary osmolality despite hyperosmolality and hypernatremia.

Left untreated or unrecognized in patients who cannot ingest sufficient water to balance urinary output, DI can quickly result in severe hypernatremia, hypovolemia, and hypotension. Hypernatremia may produce secondary neurologic symptoms, including stupor, coma, and seizures. The clinical consequences of hypernatremia are most serious at the extremes of age and when hypernatremia develops abruptly. Brain shrinkage may damage delicate cerebral vessels, leading to subdural

hematoma, subcortical parenchymal hemorrhage, subarachnoid hemorrhage (SAH), and venous thrombosis. Polyuria may cause bladder distention, hydronephrosis, and permanent renal damage.

Although after transphenoidal pituitary surgery patients may drink
sufficient fluids to prevent dehydration, treatment will often require volume
expansion in hypovolemic patients and replacement of endogenous ADH.
In hypovolemia, secondary to DI, hypernatremia will virtually always
accompany volume deficits. Hypovolemia should be corrected promptly
with 0.9% saline, after which the TBW deficit can be replaced. The TBW
deficit can be estimated from the plasma Na$^+$ using the following equation:

$$\text{TBW deficit} = 0.6 \left[(\text{weight in kg}) (\text{actual Na}^+ - 140)/140\right]$$

Hypernatremia must be corrected slowly because of the risk of neurologic sequelae such as seizures or cerebral edema [31]. The water deficit should be replaced over 24–48 hr, and the plasma Na$^+$ should not be
reduced by more than 1–2 mEq•L-1•hr-1. Once hypovolemia has been corrected, water can be replaced orally (if the patient can drink fluids), enter-
ally, or with intravenous hypotonic fluids.

Replacement of exogenous ADH can be accomplished with either
aqueous vasopressin (5–10 units intravenously or intramuscularly) or
desmopressin (DDAVP), 1–4 mcg subcutaneously or 5–20 mcg intrana-
sally every 12–24 hr. Incomplete ADH deficits (partial DI) may respond
to agents such as chlorpropamide and clofibrate, or a thiazide diuretic, to
stimulate ADH release or enhance the renal response to ADH.

15.5   Cerebral aneurysms and vasospasm

Patients who present for surgery after rupture of a cerebral aneurysm
require careful consideration of fluid management. Cerebral vasospasm
is a leading cause of morbidity in these patients, producing death or
severe disability in approximately 14% of patients who survive rupture of
their aneurysm; angiographic evidence of vasospasm occurs in approximately 50% of patients after SAH; symptomatic vasospasm occurs in
approximately half as many, with some variability based on aneurysm
location [32]. Arteriography in patients who have vasospasm demonstrates luminal irregularities in large conducting vessels, although these
are not the major site of precapillary resistance. CBF is not reduced until
the angiographic diameter of the cerebral arteries is decreased by 50%
or more compared to normal. The intraparenchymal cerebral resistance
vessels tend to dilate after the onset of spasm of the larger vessels, thus
partially compensating for increased upstream resistance.

The incidence of vasospasm peaks between the fourth and tenth days
after SAH. Symptomatic vasospasm is often heralded by disorientation

and drowsiness, developing over a period of hours. Focal deficits may follow. Vasospasm is presumed to be the cause if recurrent hemorrhage, mass lesions, intracranial hypertension, meningitis, or metabolic encephalopathy can be excluded. The diagnosis may be confirmed by angiography or documentation of high-velocity flow patterns by Doppler examination of the cerebral vessels.

Two currently accepted therapeutic interventions—calcium entry blockers and hypervolemic–hyperdynamic therapy—address the incidence or severity of vasospasm. In patients suffering from neurologic impairment secondary to vasospasm, volume loading in conjunction with inotropic support and vasopressors can reverse or reduce neurologic morbidity [33]. Pressor-induced hypertension, which can only be used after a ruptured aneurysm is clipped or coiled, improved cerebral blood flow and brain tissue oxygenation more effectively than volume loading [34]. Normovolemic hypertension may well be the most appropriate goal for patients with vasospasm after definitive therapy for a ruptured intracranial aneurysm [35]. Therapeutic expansion of blood volume or elevation of systemic blood pressure may also provide diagnostic information; of 95 patients with symptomatic vasospasm in whom symptoms improved in response to volume expansion or pressure elevation, death and disability were much less likely (Table 15.5) [36]. A well-designed clinical trial is necessary to distinguish between the influence of hypervolemia and increased arterial blood pressure on outcome after SAH [37].

Table 15.5 Hypertensive hypervolemic therapy and outcome after SAH/vasospasm

| Outcome | Clinical response to intravenous pressors | | | |
	Number (%) responders	Number (%) nonresponders	aOR (95% CI)	*P*-value
mRs 6	4 (21)	14 (74)	0.1 (0.01–0.3)	0.001
mRs 4–6	10 (37)	15 (56)	0.2 (0.1–0.8)	0.016
Lawton IADL Scale >8	33 (69)	14 (29)	1.5 (0.4–5.0)	0.546
TICS < 30	16 (65)	8 (35)	0.5 (0.1–4.6)	0.556

Source: Frontera, J.A., et al., *Neurosurgery*, 66, 35, 2010. With permission.

Notes: Patients with symptomatic vasospasm (*N* = 95) after subarachnoid hemorrhage received volume expansion followed by intravenous pressors to increase systolic blood pressure to 180–220 mmHg. More patients responded to pressors than to volume expansion. Of those who responded to pressors, a significantly lower percentage had low mRs (modified Rankin scale; 0 = full recovery, 6 = death), high Lawton IADL scale scores (Instrumental Activities of Daily Living scale; 8 = fully independent, 30 = completely dependent, dichotomized to 8 vs. >8) and low TICS (Telephone Interview of Cognitive Status; 51 = best, 0 = worst); SAH, subarachnoid hemorrhage; aOR, adjusted odds ratio.

15.6   Summary

Appropriate fluid therapy for patients with neurologic disorders requires an understanding of the basic physical principles that govern the distribution of water between the intracellular, interstitial, and plasma compartments. In the intact CNS, unlike peripheral tissues, osmolar gradients are major determinants of the movement of water. In addition to management of intravascular volume, fluid therapy often must be modified to account for disturbances of Na^+, which are common in patients with neurologic disease. Because of the limited amount of data to guide perioperative fluid therapy, current management is often empirical and based on inferences from basic research or clinical trials in related populations.

References

1. Shenkin HA, Bezier HS, Bouzarth WF. Restricted fluid intake: Rational management of the neurosurgical patient. *J Neurosurg* 1976; 45: 432–6.
2. Shenkin HA, Bouzarth WF, Tatsumi T. The analysis of body water compartments in postoperative craniotomy patients. 1. The effects of major brain surgery alone. 2. The effects of mannitol administered preoperatively. *J Neurosurg* 1968; 28: 417–28.
3. Clifton GL, Miller ER, Choi SC, Levin HS. Fluid thresholds and outcome from severe brain injury. *Crit Care Med* 2002; 30: 739–45.
4. Tankisi A, Cold GE. Optimal reverse trendelenburg position in patients undergoing craniotomy for cerebral tumors. *J Neurosurg* 2007; 106: 239–44.
5. Tankisi A, Rasmussen M, Juul N, Cold GE. The effects of 10 degrees reverse Trendelenburg position on subdural intracranial pressure and cerebral perfusion pressure in patients subjected to craniotomy for cerebral aneurysm. *J Neurosurg Anesthesiol* 2006; 18: 11–7.
6. Agbeko RS, Pearson S, Peters MJ, McNames J, Goldstein B. Intracranial pressure and cerebral perfusion pressure responses to head elevation changes in pediatric traumatic brain injury. *Pediatr Crit Care Med* 2012; 13: e39–47.
7. Fletcher JJ, Bergman K, Blostein PA, Kramer AH. Fluid balance, complications, and brain tissue oxygen tension monitoring following severe traumatic brain injury. *Neurocrit Care* 2010; 13: 47–56.
8. Marshall LF, Marshall SB, Klauber MR, Clark MV-B, Eisenberg HM, Jane JA, Luerssen TG, Marmarou A, Foulkes MA. A new classification of head injury based on computerized tomography. *J Neurosurg* 1991; 75: S14–20.
9. Van Aken HK, Kampmeier TG, Ertmer C, Westphal M. Fluid resuscitation in patients with traumatic brain injury: What is a SAFE approach? *Curr Opin Anaesthesiol* 2012; 25: 563–5.
10. Scheingraber S, Rehm M, Sehmisch C, Finsterer U: Rapid saline infusion produces hyperchloremic acidosis in patients undergoing gynecologic surgery. *Anesthesiology* 1999; 90: 1265–70.
11. Neyra JA, Canepa-Escaro F, Li X, Manllo J, Adams-Huet B, Yee J, Yessayan L. Association of hyperchloremia with hospital mortality in critically ill septic patients. *Crit Care Med* 2015.

12. Bentsen G, Breivik H, Lundar T, Stubhaug A. Predictable reduction of intracranial hypertension with hypertonic saline hydroxyethyl starch: A prospective clinical trial in critically ill patients with subarachnoid haemorrhage. *Acta Anaesthesiol Scand* 2004; 48: 1089–95.
13. Thongrong C, Kong N, Govindarajan B, Allen D, Mendel E, Bergese SD. Current purpose and practice of hypertonic saline in neurosurgery: A review of the literature. *World Neurosurg* 2014; 82: 1307–18.
14. Forsyth LL, Liu-Deryke X, Parker D, Jr., Rhoney DH. Role of hypertonic saline for the management of intracranial hypertension after stroke and traumatic brain injury. *Pharmacotherapy* 2008; 28: 469–84.
15. Chesnut RM, Marshall LF, Klauber MR, Blunt BA, Baldwin N, Eisenberg HM, Jane JA, Marmarou A, Foulkes MA. The role of secondary brain injury in determining outcome from severe head injury. *J Trauma* 1993; 34: 216–22.
16. Algarra NN, Lele AV, Prathep S, Souter MJ, Vavilala MS, Qiu Q, Sharma D. Intraoperative secondary insults during orthopedic surgery in traumatic brain injury. *J Neurosurg Anesthesiol* 2016; 29(3): 228–35.
17. Fujita Y, Algarra NN, Vavilala MS, Prathep S, Prapruettham S, Sharma D. Intraoperative secondary insults during extracranial surgery in children with traumatic brain injury. *Childs Nerv Syst* 2014; 30: 1201–8.
18. Jungner M, Grande PO, Mattiasson G, Bentzer P. Effects on brain edema of crystalloid and albumin fluid resuscitation after brain trauma and hemorrhage in the rat. *Anesthesiology* 2010; 112: 1194–203.
19. Myburgh J, Cooper DJ, Finfer S, Bellomo R, Norton R, Bishop N, Kai LS, Vallance S. Saline or albumin for fluid resuscitation in patients with traumatic brain injury. *N Engl J Med* 2007; 357: 874–84.
20. Cooper DJ, Myburgh J, Heritier S, Finfer S, Bellomo R, Billot L, Murray L, Vallance S. Albumin resuscitation for traumatic brain injury: Is intracranial hypertension the cause of increased mortality? *J Neurotrauma* 2013; 30: 512–8.
21. Cooper DJ, Myles PS, McDermott FT, Murray LJ, Laidlaw J, Cooper G, Tremayne AB, Bernard SS, Ponsford J. Prehospital hypertonic saline resuscitation of patients with hypotension and severe traumatic brain injury: A randomized controlled trial. *J Am Med Assoc* 2004; 291: 1350–7.
22. Bulger EM, May S, Brasel KJ, Schreiber M, Kerby JD, Tisherman SA, Newgard C, Slutsky A, Coimbra R, Emerson S, et al. Out-of-hospital hypertonic resuscitation following severe traumatic brain injury: A randomized controlled trial. *J Am Med Assoc* 2010; 304: 1455–64.
23. Wu CT, Chen LC, Kuo CP, Ju DT, Borel CO, Cherng CH, Wong CS. A comparison of 3% hypertonic saline and mannitol for brain relaxation during elective supratentorial brain tumor surgery. *Anesth Analg* 2010; 110: 903–7.
24. Brandstrup B, Tonnesen H, Beier-Holgersen R, Hjortso E, Ording H, Lindorff-Larsen K, Rasmussen MS, Lanng C, Wallin L, Iversen LH, et al. Effects of intravenous fluid restriction on postoperative complications: Comparison of two perioperative fluid regimens: A randomized assessor-blinded multicenter trial. *Ann Surg* 2003; 238: 641–8.
25. Holte K, Kristensen BB, Valentiner L, Foss NB, Husted H, Kehlet H. Liberal versus restrictive fluid management in knee arthroplasty: A randomized, double-blind study. *Anesth Analg* 2007; 105: 465–74.

26. Holte K, Klarskov B, Christensen DS, Lund C, Nielsen KG, Bie P, Kehlet H. Liberal versus restrictive fluid administration to improve recovery after laparoscopic cholecystectomy: A randomized, double-blind study. *Ann Surg* 2004; 240: 892–9.
27. Scranton RA, Baskin DS. Impaired pituitary axes following traumatic brain injury. *J Clin Med* 2015; 4: 1463–79.
28. Rahman M, Friedman WA. Hyponatremia in neurosurgical patients: Clinical guidelines development. *Neurosurgery* 2009; 65: 925–35.
29. Prough DS, Wolf SW, Funston JS, Svensen CH. *Acid-Base, Fluids, and Electrolytes, Clinical Anesthesia*, Fifth edition. Edited by Barash PG, Cullen BF, Stoerker J. Lippincott Williams & Wilkins, 2006, pp. 175–207.
30. Potts MB, DeGiacomo AF, Deragopian L, Blevins LS, Jr. Use of intravenous conivaptan in neurosurgical patients with hyponatremia from syndrome of inappropriate antidiuretic hormone secretion. *Neurosurgery* 2011; 69: 268–73.
31. Griffin KA, Bidani AK. How to manage disorders of sodium and water balance. Five-step approach to evaluating appropriateness of renal response. *J Crit Ill* 1990; 5: 1054–70.
32. Abla AA, Wilson DA, Williamson RW, Nakaji P, McDougall CG, Zabramski JM, Albuquerque FC, Spetzler RF. The relationship between ruptured aneurysm location, subarachnoid hemorrhage clot thickness, and incidence of radiographic or symptomatic vasospasm in patients enrolled in a prospective randomized controlled trial. *J Neurosurg* 2014; 120: 391–7.
33. Diringer MN, Axelrod Y. Hemodynamic manipulation in the neuro-intensive care unit: Cerebral perfusion pressure therapy in head injury and hemodynamic augmentation for cerebral vasospasm. *Curr Opin Crit Care* 2007; 13: 156–62.
34. Muench E, Horn P, Bauhuf C, Roth H, Philipps M, Hermann P, Quintel M, Schmiedek P, Vajkoczy P. Effects of hypervolemia and hypertension on regional cerebral blood flow, intracranial pressure, and brain tissue oxygenation after subarachnoid hemorrhage. *Crit Care Med* 2007; 35: 1844–51.
35. Treggiari MM, Deem S: Which H is the most important in triple-H therapy for cerebral vasospasm? *Curr Opin Crit Care* 2009; 15: 83–6.
36. Frontera JA, Fernandez A, Schmidt JM, Claassen J, Wartenberg KE, Badjatia N, Connolly ES, Mayer SA. Clinical response to hypertensive hypervolemic therapy and outcome after subarachnoid hemorrhage. *Neurosurgery* 2010; 66: 35–41.
37. Togashi K, Joffe AM, Sekhar L, Kim L, Lam A, Yanez D, Broeckel-Elrod JA, Moore A, Deem S, Khandelwal N, et al. Randomized pilot trial of intensive management of blood pressure or volume expansion in subarachnoid hemorrhage (IMPROVES). *Neurosurgery* 2015; 76: 125–34.

Index